D1392050

Martin Millar was born in Scotland and now lives in London. He is the author of such novels as *Lonely Werewolf Girl* and *The Good Fairies of New York*. Under the pseudonym of Martin Scott, he, as the *Guardian* put it, 'invented a new genre: pulp fantasy noir'. *Thraxas*, the first book in his Thraxas series, won the World Fantasy Award in 2000. As Martin Millar and as Martin Scott, he has been widely translated.

To find out more about Martin Millar, visit his website at www.martinmillar.com

Also by Martin Millar, published by Piatkus:

Lonely Werewolf Girl

Curse of the Wolf Girl

MARTIN MILLAR

piatkus

PIATKUS

First published in Great Britain as a paperback original in 2010 by Piatkus

Copyright © 2010 Martin Millar

A CIP catalogue record for this book
is available from the British Library.

ISBN 978-0-7499-4288-5

Typeset in Sabon by M Rules
Printed in the UK by CPI Mackays, Chatham ME5 8TD

Papers used by Piatkus are natural, renewable and
recyclable products sourced from well-managed forests and certified
in accordance with the rules of the Forest Stewardship Council.

Mixed Sources
Product group from well-managed
forests and other controlled sources
www.fsc.org Cert no. SGS-COC-004081
© 1996 Forest Stewardship Council

Piatkus
An imprint of
Little, Brown Book Group
100 Victoria Embankment
London EC4Y 0DY

An Hachette UK Company
www.hachette.co.uk

www.piatkus.co.uk

Prologue

Not all werewolves are unhappy. Most of the MacRinnalch werewolf clan live quite contentedly at Castle MacRinnalch, hidden away safely in the Scottish Highlands. They've lived there for centuries, largely untroubled by the outside world.

But some werewolves are unhappy. Kalix, for instance. Her father was head of the clan, but after his violent death she was forced to flee the castle. She headed south to London, and there she existed for several years as a lonely teenage werewolf. Kalix pined for her lover Gawain, and wondered if she'd ever see him again.

Life did improve when she met a pair of friendly students, Daniel and Moonglow, but Kalix still had problems. Her own clan were pursuing her, and the werewolf hunters were after her too. It all led to a terrible confrontation. Kalix survived, though many werewolves didn't.

Afterwards she couldn't go home, so she stayed on in London. Kalix MacRinnalch still wasn't a happy werewolf, but she hoped her life might become more peaceful for a while.

1

'I think I might cry,' said Moonglow.

'Why?'

'Kalix is going to school.'

Daniel looked puzzled. 'Why would that make you cry?'

'First day at school can be very traumatic. What if her teachers are horrible? What if someone bullies her?'

'Kalix is a werewolf with super-strength and a history of violence. If anyone picks on her, she'll rip their head off.'

'Well, that wouldn't be a very good thing to happen, would it?' said Moonglow, alarmed at the prospect. She poured tea from her delicate black china teapot into her favourite black mug.

'Maybe it wasn't a good idea to encourage her to go to college. We shouldn't have pushed her into it. She's too young to manage on her own.'

'Kalix is seventeen! That's only two years younger than us. And again, as you said, she's a werewolf with savage strength. Even in human form she can throw people around. I really don't think there's any need to worry. Anyway, Vex will be with her.'

'That's not very reassuring.'

'I think it is. I mean, one teenage werewolf and one teenage fire elemental, on their way to remedial college to learn how to read and write . . . what can go wrong?'

'Everything, if people discover they aren't human. Kalix is very sensitive about her poor reading skills. What if she gets upset and starts tearing the place to pieces? What if Vex bursts into flames?'

'Kalix can't change into a werewolf in daylight.' Daniel remained unconcerned. 'And I don't think Vex even knows how to burst into flames. Maybe a little orange glow when she gets excited, nothing more.'

They were interrupted by the noisy arrival of Kalix and Vex, who clattered down the stairs into the living room, each clutching a bag of books. Vex was in a state of particularly high excitement. Since her aunt, Queen Malveria, ruler of the Hiyasta fire elementals, had agreed to let her move into the attic of the small house in South London so that she might attend a human college and learn something – anything – she had been beside herself with anticipation. Vex had become increasingly bored in Malveria's Imperial Palace, and was now exhilarated at the prospect of spending time in the human dimension, in London, with continual access to clothes, gigs, clubs and enjoyment.

The same couldn't be said of Kalix MacRinnalch. She stood forlornly with her bag of books, and looked very young, and rather small and nervous. Though the MacRinnalch werewolf clan took care to educate its children in Scotland, the peculiar circumstances of Kalix's life meant that she had received almost no schooling. She was close to being both illiterate and innumerate, and was keenly aware of it. Though renowned for her savagery in battle, the prospect of displaying her ignorance in a class full of strangers filled Kalix with dread.

Moonglow had tried to reassure her, in her kindly way. Despite her rather foreboding black attire and heavy dark make-up, Moonglow could be reassuring. She'd told Kalix it wasn't all that unusual for a person to reach the age of seventeen and still be unable to read or write. It happened to a lot of people.

'You'll fit in perfectly well. There will be plenty of others there who missed school. You know, with family problems. Or they might have been ill.'

'Or they might have been in prison,' added Daniel, cheerfully.

Moonglow glared at him.

'It's no disgrace catching up on your education. You'll have fun at college.'

Kalix was unconvinced. She would never have agreed to go were it not for the offer of money from her mother. Verasa MacRinnalch, the Mistress of the Werewolves, cared enough about her youngest daughter to support her, even though, like the rest of the family, she was estranged from Kalix. Kalix could not return to Castle MacRinnalch in Scotland. Through the intermediary of Thrix, Kalix's older sister, Verasa had offered Kalix an allowance if she remained where she was in London, and went to college. It was better than having her wander off again, to live on the streets and sleep in warehouses.

Kalix sat at the table, head bowed, her hair hung down to her hips. She was still the skinniest girl Moonglow had ever seen. When they'd first encountered her, Kalix had been achingly thin, filthy and ragged. Now, several months later, she was clean, better fed, and reasonably healthy. Though she still refused to look after herself properly, her inner werewolf vitality was starting to show.

Kalix sighed. If only she could have refused her mother's offer. Unfortunately, she needed money. Moonglow and Daniel had looked after her for the past few months, providing her with plenty of raw meat and buying her what second-hand clothes they could afford, but she knew this couldn't go on. The two young students weren't wealthy and she couldn't live off them for ever. London was an expensive city and there were bills to pay.

Then there was the matter of laudanum. Kalix still needed money for her addiction, shameful though it was. Really, the offer of an allowance from her mother solved many of her problems. If only she didn't have to go to college and let everyone know how stupid she was.

Vex bounded over to the table.

'Isn't it fantastic? I never thought Aunt Malvie would allow it, but here I am, all ready to learn stuff! I have new coloured pencils!' She glanced at her feet. 'I could have done with new boots, though. You might have thought she'd stump up for a new pair. It's a scandal, really, sending me to college in old boots.'

There was a violent flash of orange light in the small living room. Queen Malveria had arrived.

'The only scandal, dismal niece, is that you will soon inflict your dreadful self on an unsuspecting group of tutors who will probably be driven to despair trying to force knowledge into your head. A task made harder, no doubt, by the preposterous jumble you call a hairstyle.'

Vex grinned. She was dark-skinned, like all the Hiyasta, which made the severe bleaching of her hair all the more noticeable. It stood out from her head in great peroxide spikes, each one welded in place with assorted hair products. In Queen Malveria's elegant palace it made the young elemental stand out like a beacon, and it was the sight of Vex strolling into her last elegant banquet with her hair in flaming spikes which had finally made the Fire Queen decide that it might not be such a bad idea to send her niece away for a while. Her loyal subjects deserved some respite from Vex's sartorial outrages, which were starting to reflect badly on the Queen. Malveria was renowned for her elegance. She was dressed by Thrix MacRinnalch, and Thrix MacRinnalch was second to no one as a fashion adviser.

Malveria glared at Vex with displeasure.

'What on Earth is that T-shirt made of?'

'Plastic,' said Vex.

'Where did you obtain such a garment?'

'I made it from a bin liner.'

'You amaze me,' replied the Queen, acidly. 'Even young Daniel here, well known for the scruffiness of his attire, would know better than to wear such a thing.'

'Thanks,' muttered Daniel, and let his hair flop over his face, slightly embarrassed to be called scruffy by the elegant Malveria.

'Now, Agrivex,' continued the Queen, 'attend my words carefully. For me to let you live in this world, even for a few days, costs me a great deal of power. So I trust you will make better efforts to behave properly than you have done up till now. The most brilliant of my Hiyasta scholars were driven to despair by your unparalleled stupidity. Do not let it be the same at this human college. If you let me down I will personally throw you into the Great Volcano, a fate which you have deserved for many years.'

Malveria turned her eyes on Daniel and Moonglow.

'Once more, young humans, you have my thanks for accommodating Agrivex. Though she can only live with you for three days each week—'

'Maybe four,' interrupted Vex, eagerly.

'—Possibly four, though I would rather not expand such power – I regard it as a great favour that you have let her live here.'

Malveria paused, then turned her eyes back on Vex and Kalix. 'So,' she declared, imperiously, 'are the pupils ready to begin learning?'

'I am *so* ready!' screamed Vex, and began jumping around the room.

All eyes turned towards Kalix, but the young werewolf made no reply. She looked down at her feet, and wished she were anywhere else but on her way to college.

2

Princess Kabachetka was not happy. Though her status as most popular princess in the Hainusta nation was secure, her hair a shade of golden blonde unmatched by any other fire elemental, and her clothes quite splendid, she had recently suffered several disappointments. At the Sorceress Livia's 500th-birthday celebration, the Princess had been eclipsed by Queen Malveria, ruler of the Hiyasta. In the fierce rivalry for the position of fashion leader, Queen Malveria had come out on top.

'And all,' mused the Princess, with some bitterness, 'because that dreadful werewolf Thrix MacRinnalch designed her clothes. Without her, Queen Malveria would be exposed as the style-less fraud she really is.'

Thrix MacRinnalch wasn't the only werewolf to arouse the Princess's ire. Perhaps unwisely, she'd recently taken an interest in the affairs of the MacRinnalch werewolf clan. The Princess had found herself deeply involved in the feud over their leadership, supporting the great werewolf Sarapen and developing something of a passion for him. But Sarapen had been defeated, thanks to an assortment of werewolves who'd opposed him; notably Kalix MacRinnalch, her cousin Dominil, and, once more, Thrix, the Werewolf Enchantress. Not that this motley collection could have defeated Sarapen and the Princess had it not been for the aid they'd received from Queen Malveria. Ever since, the Princess had burned with anger against Malveria and her shabby assortment of werewolf companions.

The Empress Asaratanti, ruler of the realm, was surprised to receive an early-evening visit from her eldest daughter. At this hour Princess Kabachetka would normally be busy in her chambers, dressing for her evening engagement. As far as the Empress could recall, this process had never been interrupted. Asaratanti eyed her with some suspicion. If she had come to borrow money again, the Empress would want a good reason. The Princess did suffer from an unfortunate tendency to profligacy.

'Greetings, daughter.'

The Empress's throne room was bright and splendid, as befitted the ruler of the Hainusta fire elementals, and the deep red jewels on the Empress's throne reflected the bright, flickering light from the torches on the walls. Hainusta torches were particularly splendid, and they never went out.

'Empress Mother,' said the Princess. 'I've come to you for advice.'

The Empress waited. If her daughter wasn't here to borrow money, it could only be that she found herself involved in some fashion crisis. Possibly she was looking for a new designer.

'It concerns the werewolves,' said the Princess, surprising her mother.

'Werewolves? What werewolves?'

'The MacRinnalchs.'

The Empress was puzzled. The Hainusta had little contact with the Earth these days, and almost none with the MacRinnalchs or any other werewolves.

'I need to punish them,' continued the Princess.

'Punish them? For what?'

'For illegally attacking Sarapen, and placing Markus MacRinnalch at the head of their clan.'

Empress Asaratanti could make nothing of this. The MacRinnalchs lived in Scotland, a small country on the planet Earth, a whole dimension away from the fire elementals. Why the Princess should pay them the slightest attention was beyond the Empress. 'Why should I involve myself with a small subspecies of the race of humans? I have affairs of state to occupy my mind, and no time to waste on obscure groups of ill-bred creatures in different dimensions.'

'These werewolves' actions have affected our dimension. They should be punished.'

'The only effect I'm aware of, dearest daughter, is that Queen Malveria now seems to be better dressed than you. Which is regrettable, as it reflects poorly on our people, but hardly enough reason for me to start breaching the dimensional walls.'

'I have suffered!' cried the Princess, her voice rising in anguish, 'and I want revenge! I appeal to you, Mother Empress, for help in taking this revenge.'

3

Queen Malveria transported herself to the apartment of Thrix MacRinnalch, Scottish werewolf and Enchantress, currently residing in London. She composed herself before knocking.

'My dearest Thrix!'

'Malveria. Is there something wrong?'

'Nothing is wrong, Enchantress. Why do you ask?'

'You've got flames coming out your fingers.' Thrix ushered Malveria inside before anyone appeared in the corridor. The Fire Queen knew how to blend in with the human realm but there were times when her emotions got the better of her. Malveria had been known to destroy a new pair of shoes, scorching them with the force of her excitement. Not that Thrix could blame Malveria too much. She felt as much excitement over new shoes as the Fire Queen.

Malveria quickly extinguished the flames.

'I'm sorry. I've just seen Agrivex. One tries not to become upset, but really, she is an immense trial. Do you know she was actually wearing a plastic T-shirt?'

Thrix winced. It did sound bad.

'And then she proceeded to call me Aunt Malvie, which I particularly hate. It shows such disrespect. Also, it makes me feel old. Do you have a glass of wine?'

Thrix snapped her fingers, bringing a bottle and two glasses from the drinks cabinet.

'At least she'll be out of your way for a while.'

Malveria nodded in agreement. 'Her three days a week at this human college will be a blessed relief. One only wishes it could be longer. But much sorcery is required to allow a fire elemental to remain in this world, particularly one with so little natural power as my appalling niece. The foolish girl would wither and die without the spells of protection I've placed around her.'

The Queen sipped her wine with some relish. 'No doubt she

7

will never study, but will instead spend her time swarming around boys, musicians and dubious market stalls. Disaster will ensue, I am certain.'

'Wasn't the whole thing your idea?' asked Thrix.

'Yes,' admitted Malveria, 'but I had to get her out of the palace somehow. I was driven to desperation by the hedgehog affair.'

'Hedgehogs?'

'Agrivex had been wearing a T-shirt featuring a picture of a hedgehog, though I had forbidden her to do so, naturally.'

'Why?'

'Hedgehogs are foul and dangerous creatures, filthy and taboo in the land of the Hiyasta. Is it not the same here? No? Very strange. I would have thought that hatred of hedgehogs was universal. Agrivex's T-shirt was a clear act of rebellion. What goes on in that girl's mind is a mystery to me.'

'Perhaps what was going on was a desire for you to send her to college in London.'

'Quite possibly. While lacking intelligence, Agrivex is not without her share of devious cunning.'

Thrix had been the one responsible for finding a suitable college for Kalix and Vex. It wasn't a task the Enchantress had relished, given her aversion to her younger sister, but she'd felt obliged after the request from her mother, the Mistress of the Werewolves. Thrix had turned the task over to her assistant Ann, who'd come up with a range of likely establishments. There were plenty of places willing to teach remedial skills to slow learners, for a price. It had been only a matter of making sure that Kalix and Agrivex ended up somewhere reputable. The small college they'd settled on was associated with the university which Daniel and Moonglow attended, and that was reassuring. Thrix didn't much care for Daniel or Moonglow, but she did admit they'd had a beneficial effect on Kalix.

Malveria picked up a copy of French *Vogue*. She couldn't read French, but was very attracted by the shoes on the cover. 'A pleasing shade of lilac. But I am already well equipped with lilac shoes for the coming season, am I not?'

'You are,' replied Thrix, who had successfully kept Malveria ahead of the trends for some time now.

Malveria looked pleased, though even the knowledge that she was well supplied with fashionable shoes could not entirely drive Agrivex from her mind. 'It is strange. The Hiyasta used to persecute mankind. When men lived in caves we would make war on them over the use of fire. Now I'm spending my gold sending my niece to a human college.' The Fire Queen frowned, and shook her head. 'My Advisory Council found it hard to understand. Though they did appreciate that desperate measures were permissible in getting rid of Agrivex. Her hedgehog garments had already caused widespread offence. As had her mittens.'

'Mittens?'

Malveria shuddered. 'She must be the only Hiyasta ever to wear them. One would think that no matter how hopeless a fire elemental she is, she would at least be able to keep her hands warm. Do you think Daniel and Moonglow will be able to cope with her?'

Thrix shrugged. 'You probably know them as well as I do. Since Markus became Thane I've hardly seen them.'

'You are not monitoring Kalix, as your mother wished?'

'No, I'm not,' stated Thrix, forcibly.

'You still resent that her lover Gawain toyed with your affections before cruelly discarding you?'

Thrix's lips tightened and she swallowed an angry retort. 'It's not about Gawain. You know how I hate getting dragged into clan affairs.'

'One might almost think you regret being a werewolf,' said Malveria, archly.

'I'm fine being a werewolf,' replied Thrix. 'It's all the other werewolves that bother me.'

'I would like to remain longer, Enchantress, so that we may watch the Japanese fashion show together on your excellent cable television. But now I must away to play whist.'

'Whist?' Thrix was surprised. 'I didn't know you played.'

'Since the Duchess Gargamond initiated a whist evening at her castle it has become popular with the ladies of my court. I don't love the playing of cards but it will give me a splendid opportunity to show off the fabulous pale blue dress you provided me with last week.'

Malveria dematerialised in an aroma of jasmine. Thrix wasn't sure it was a good idea for Agrivex to move into the same household as her young sister Kalix. A household consisting of two young students, one young werewolf and one young fire elemental was a troubling mix. As long as it didn't engulf Thrix in some sort of family crisis, she didn't much care. Thrix and Kalix's friendship had never been strong, and it had ended the day her younger sister discovered that Thrix had been sleeping with Gawain, the great love of Kalix's young life. Since then they'd taken care to avoid each other, and Thrix wouldn't have minded if she were never to encounter her sister again.

4

Decembrius MacRinnalch remained in London after the great battle. He had no desire to return to the castle in Scotland. Decembrius had been a loyal supporter of Sarapen's. Now that Sarapen was dead, the young red-haired werewolf didn't know what to do with himself.

He could have gone home, had he wanted. Markus, the new Thane, had extended a pardon to everyone who'd fought against him. The werewolf barons – MacGregor, MacAllister and MacPhee – had all made their peace with the MacRinnalch Clan. Some more sincerely than others, no doubt, but now Sarapen was gone there was nothing more to fight about. Markus might not be to everyone's taste as Thane, but it was done now.

Decembrius sat in a small Italian cafe in Camden, as he often did in the afternoons. He drank coffee, read a newspaper, and felt dissatisfied with life. Really, he should go back to Scotland. Due to the deaths in the recent feud he'd found himself elevated to the Great Council of the MacRinnalchs. That was an honour which his mother Lucia had trumpeted all round the clan, but Decembrius couldn't share her enthusiasm. He'd looked up to Sarapen. He'd been sure that the huge, forceful werewolf, eldest son of the late Thane, would emerge victorious in the struggle over the Thaneship. His death had left Decembrius shaken and disillusioned. He couldn't raise any enthusiasm for clan affairs.

He stared over the top of his newspaper, focusing his eyes on a spot just above the da Vinci print of the Last Supper that adorned the cafe wall. He let his gaze float over the wall, then tried to focus on nothing. After a few moments he frowned, and shook his head. From a young age, Decembrius had had an ability to glimpse the future and observe things that were hidden to others. Though he'd never been able to control the power well, in the past year he'd been making some progress. Since the battle in which Sarapen had fallen, his powers of prescience had disappeared. Whatever was in his future, Decembrius couldn't see it.

His mother, Verasa's sister Lucia, couldn't wait to see him in the council chamber. But the thought of sitting round a table with Thrix and Dominil horrified Decembrius. Both had fought against Sarapen. Thrix had protected Kalix, and Dominil had killed Andris, Sarapen's bodyguard, another werewolf whom Decembrius had held in high regard.

His anger subsided back into depression. Decembrius had always had a tendency towards depression and he was worried that he might be heading for a serious episode. While he'd been busy working for Sarapen, he hadn't noticed it. Now that Sarapen was dead it had come back, and the loss of his powers made it worse. It was another reason not to return to Scotland. The MacRinnalch werewolf clan tended to lack sympathy for depressed werewolves.

Decembrius tried to distract himself from his gloomy thoughts by looking round the cafe, and staring openly at two girls who'd just sat down at one of the small tables. Decembrius was young and good-looking in an angular sort of way. As a werewolf of the MacRinnalch Clan, his vigour shone through. Here in London he wasn't short of female company. Decembrius preferred to keep these affairs hidden from prying eyes at Castle MacRinnalch, particularly his mother's. Like many of the traditional werewolves in Scotland, Lucia didn't really approve of the philandering of the younger generation.

Decembrius brushed his fingers through his thick dark red hair; he'd grown it longer in recent months, and swept it back. He had another gold stud in his left ear. Since encountering Beauty and Delicious, the notorious cousins of whom the family did not use to speak, Decembrius had made an effort to make himself more stylish. The twins' wild appearance and lifestyle had made him feel older than his twenty-six years.

The twins had fought against Sarapen too, of course, albeit not very effectively. Beauty and Delicious weren't fierce, by werewolf standards. Not like Kalix. There was a werewolf you wouldn't want to encounter in battle. Even Sarapen had been unable to subdue her. Of course, Kalix was mad. She probably didn't feel pain like a normal werewolf. Her father, the Thane, had died of injuries she'd inflicted, resulting in her being banished, and setting off the whole chain of events that led to the vicious feud. His wife Verasa had nominated her second son Markus as Thane, instead of Sarapen, her eldest. It led to war, and many deaths. Kalix had started it all and she'd finished it. Kalix had delivered the fatal blow. She'd killed Sarapen. There were many in the Clan who would never forgive her.

Outside an ambulance went by, its siren wailing as it edged its way through the heavy traffic. The bustle of London was very different to the peaceful Scottish Highlands where Decembrius had been raised. These days, he preferred the noise of the city. He stared into his empty coffee cup, and realised he'd been thinking about his young cousin Kalix a lot recently. He could still picture her, fighting with an unquenchable fury. Decembrius almost smiled. Kalix was insane in battle. Insane in other ways too, depending on which member of the family you listened to.

She was beautiful as well, in a waiflike way. What had she been doing since Sarapen's death? he wondered. But Kalix's location was a secret. Technically she was still a fugitive from the clan, and the Mistress of the Werewolves was not about to risk having her youngest daughter dragged back to Castle MacRinnalch to face punishment. Thrix and Dominil probably knew where she lived, but they wouldn't pass on any information to a recent enemy like himself. Kalix was hidden, by secrecy and sorcery, and couldn't be found.

Decembrius pursed his lips. Was she still seeing Gawain? She had taken up with him at a young age, in an affair which had scandalised the Clan. Gawain had been banished, though they'd got back together eventually. Whether their renewed relationship had survived the trauma of the MacRinnalch feud, Decembrius

12

didn't know. He hoped it hadn't. Decembrius had never much liked Gawain.

Decembrius scowled as he ordered more coffee. He glanced at the clock on the wall. He still had some time to kill before meeting the Douglas-MacPhees. It wasn't an encounter he was looking forward to. Duncan, Rhona and Fergus were a vicious, criminal trio of wolves who had no regard for the Clan or anyone else. Or rather, they had been a vicious trio until Kalix had killed the huge werewolf Fergus. Remembering this, Decembrius almost smiled. Fergus had also been fighting for Sarapen but Decembrius couldn't pretend he was sorry about his death. Kalix had destroyed him, ripped him apart in the full fury of her battle madness. Fergus's superior size and strength had counted for nothing.

'Duncan and Rhona won't be quite so sanguine about it,' mused Decembrius, and wondered if they might be seeking Kalix, looking for revenge. The thought troubled him, and he resolved to find out from them if they had any clue as to her whereabouts.

5

Moonglow's anxiety over Kalix's debut at college persisted throughout the day. No amount of entreaties from Daniel could ease her concern.

'Should we pick her up after class?' Kalix's college wasn't far from their university building, just south of the river.

Daniel was against the idea. 'If we meet her at the gate she might think we're treating her like a kid. It'll just annoy her. Stop worrying, everything will be fine.'

Moonglow was unconvinced. As she travelled home with Daniel she was too preoccupied to listen to anything he had to say. His eternal campaign to persuade Moonglow to go out with him was proving even less successful than usual. He'd tried to explain to her how he'd powered his way through level nine of *Grimcat*, his current favourite game, but she hardly seemed to listen, even though Daniel was sure the story reflected well on him. Level nine was notably difficult.

13

When they arrived home Moonglow hurried up the stairs to their small flat above the empty shop.

'I'll make tea for them. It'll be welcoming. And maybe I should light a scented candle. Something soothing.'

A few minutes later, the downstairs front door banged heavily and there was the sound of two pairs of booted feet ascending the stairs. The living-room door opened and Kalix trudged into the room. As Moonglow greeted her brightly, she kept on trudging, an obviously unhappy werewolf.

'Stupid college,' she muttered, and disappeared upstairs to her room. Vex bounded into the living room behind her.

'I got a gold star!' she shrieked, and leapt around, brandishing a notebook which, Moonglow noted, she had already decorated with luminous coloured inks.

'I got a gold star for my poem!'

Daniel and Moonglow were puzzled. They knew that the college Vex was attending did cater for people with poor reading skills, but it was for adults, not children. They hadn't expected it would be handing out gold stars.

'Look!' yelled Vex, happily. Moonglow looked. On the first page there was a very short poem, and beneath it Vex had written 'goldd starr.'

'Eh . . . did the teacher give you that?'

'Yes! She told the whole class how great it was! So obviously it was worth a gold star. Do you want to read it?'

Moonglow smiled at the young fire elemental's enthusiasm and took the proffered book.

I wish I had a hedgehog.
I'd take it for walks up the great volcano
which is close to the palace.
I live in a golden palace.

'The teacher said it was really imaginative!' explained Vex, still very excited. 'Isn't it great? I got a gold star on my first day at college!'

'It is imaginative,' agreed Moonglow, sincerely. Almost every word was misspelled but English, after all, was not Vex's first language. She noticed that Vex had taken the notion of decorating

14

each letter to great extremes. Having started out by putting little hearts over each 'i', she'd decided that the idea could be expanded. Now every letter seemed to have some colourful decoration. It made for a bright and confusing page.

'Do you want to read my poem too?'

'I already – eh, yes, of course,' said Daniel, looking at her eager face.

'How did Kalix get on?' asked Moonglow.

Vex stopped smiling. 'I don't think she liked it so much.'

'I better go and see,' said Moonglow, and departed the living room to the sound of Vex reciting her poem.

Upstairs in her tiny room Kalix lay on her bed, mildly intoxicated from laudanum. Recently she'd been taking less of the opiate but she still used it regularly. While laudanum was rarely found in the world these days, as humans had moved on to other drugs, a few werewolves still preferred it. Every week Kalix would make the long journey over to Merchant MacDoig's premises in East London to replenish her supply. The Merchant had introduced her to the opium derivative at a young age. Now the young werewolf was dependent on it. It was expensive, which was a continual problem for Kalix.

The young werewolf hadn't enjoyed her first day at college at all. She'd been surrounded by people she didn't know. Kalix was never comfortable with strangers. While Vex had talked cheerfully to anyone who came within range, Kalix had resisted all efforts to engage her in conversation, maintaining a hostile silence all day. Unlike Vex, who was eager to throw herself into college life, Kalix had no such ambitions. Though it frustrated and embarrassed her that she was practically illiterate, she had no desire to sit in a classroom and display her ignorance to everyone.

She had been horrified when the teacher had announced that everyone was going to compose a poem. Though Kalix made an effort to record her own life, and wrote every day in her private journal, she'd never written a poem. She had no idea how to do it, or even where to start. The teacher's instructions that each student should just use their own imagination had seemed to her completely inadequate. While other students, some of them

15

foreign, with hardly any grasp of the language at all, had grappled with the task, Kalix had sat quite still, head bowed, staring forlornly at her exercise book. She'd written nothing at all and found the whole experience very embarrassing, bordering on the traumatic. College was even worse than she'd expected. Vex, naturally, had been thrilled by the whole thing. On the Tube home she wouldn't shut up about her poem; a poem which, as far as Kalix could see, was the most stupid thing ever written. By that time all Kalix wanted to do was get home and fill herself with laudanum, which she'd now accomplished. She felt a brief nausea, then some welcome drowsiness. She pulled her quilt over her, and wished she never had to go back to college.

6

Dulled by laudanum, Kalix drifted into an ugly dream. Misshapen trees loomed above her as she crept through a darkened wood, and though she thought she knew her way she suddenly found her route blocked by bushes, bushes that crackled with a fierce array of thorns.

'I'm lost,' she whispered.

'Lost? You've been to the Forests of the Werewolf Dead before.'

Kalix cried out in alarm and tried to see who spoke, but the figure was hidden behind a huge tree, an ash that moved towards her, branches reaching out like long fingers. Kalix lashed out with her claws and as she did so she woke quite violently. Her body was covered with sweat. She'd fallen asleep fully dressed, and overheated beneath her quilt. Kalix threw off the cover and sat upright, shaking her head to clear it. It was the second time this week she'd dreamed of the Forests of the Werewolf Dead.

I went there once already, thought the young werewolf. I'm not ready to go back.

She stood up, and was momentarily disorientated because she imagined herself to be in werewolf shape, as she had been in the dream. But she was human at the moment; seventeen and a half years old, attending college and living in London. Much the same as thousands of others, except that she'd been born into the ruling family of the MacRinnalchs, the largest clan of were-wolves in the country. For the first part of her life, she'd lived at Castle MacRinnalch in the Scottish Highlands. For much of the past two years, she'd been on the run; hiding from her family, hiding from werewolf hunters, living in alleyways and abandoned warehouses. Now she was no longer running, her life should be better. Kalix wasn't sure that it was.

Her new domestic setting was more comfortable than sleeping rough, but she hadn't yet become used to sharing her life with other people. It annoyed her that she had to moderate her behaviour. When she'd lived on the streets, she had begged for money, or stolen it. Now she couldn't do that. Moonglow wouldn't like her to beg or steal, particularly to buy laudanum. Kalix frowned, and felt angry. What did she care what Moonglow thought? She was Kalix MacRinnalch. Only three months ago she'd slain her brother Sarapen in combat, and he'd been the most ferocious werewolf in the land. Kalix MacRinnalch shouldn't have to worry about what Moonglow thought. And yet, it wasn't really that simple. Moonglow had been kind. She'd given Kalix a place to live when she'd had nowhere else to go. She'd bathed her wounds and provided her with food. Moonglow had saved her life. Kalix's frown deepened. It was a strange feeling, being obligated to someone. She didn't like it.

Kalix wondered, as she often did, whether she should leave. She didn't have anywhere else to go. She had no other friends apart from Daniel and Moonglow and she couldn't return to the family home at Castle MacRinnalch. If she did she'd be liable to punishment for her past crimes. The family still held her responsible for the death of her father.

Today's experiences at college hadn't brightened her mood. Kalix sighed, and sipped from her bottle of laudanum. Though the opiate dulled the anxiety to which she was prone, it exacerbated her depression.

Far above, the moon appeared, a small crescent. Kalix felt it. She considered changing into her werewolf shape, for comfort. Like all the purest-blooded MacRinnalchs, Kalix didn't need the full moon in order to change. She could do it under any moon, on any night. On the three nights around the full moon the change came on automatically: other nights the MacRinnalchs were free to choose. On their remote Scottish estates the werewolves would change very frequently. Though they were discreet about their true nature, they weren't ashamed of it. Nor was Kalix. She was proud to be a werewolf. But here in London, she had to take more care to keep it secret. Daniel and Moonglow had accepted her as she was. That didn't mean others would. Besides, there were the hunters to think about.

Kalix shook her head, still not completely over her nightmare. She felt the moon above her. It would be comforting to change but she still hesitated. Being werewolf dulled her anxiety and depression, but it affected her in other ways she didn't like. When she was in her werewolf shape she'd gorge herself on almost anything. In her days of living on the streets she'd killed and eaten dogs, and wolfed down the contents of supermarket skips. Now she was well provided for by Daniel and Moonglow. The fridge was full of meat, bought to satisfy her eager werewolf appetite. The werewolf feasting was good for her health, but next day, when Kalix reverted to human, she'd remember how much she'd eaten, and how much she disliked eating, and then she'd feel bad again. Sometimes she'd be sick, quite violently.

Moonglow knocked on the door.

'Go away,' said Kalix.

'Don't you want to talk about your first day at college?'

'No.'

'Why not?'

'College is stupid.'

Kalix felt an urge to add 'and so is poetry,' but refrained, not wanting to engage in conversation.

'There's a letter here for you.'

Kalix blinked. In her semi-stupor, she wondered if she'd heard correctly. A letter? No one ever wrote to her. Hardly anyone knew where she lived. Her location was well hidden by spells provided by her sister Thrix.

'Who's it from?'

'I don't know,' called Moonglow, through the door. 'Should I bring it in?'

'No,' said Kalix, but it was too late. Moonglow came in anyway, and smiled as she handed Kalix the letter. Kalix scowled at her. She took the envelope in her hand, then buried it under her duvet as if pointedly telling Moonglow that whoever the letter came from, she wasn't going to discuss it with her.

The air was thick with the smell of laudanum. Kalix remained silent, daring Moonglow to lecture her about it. Moonglow didn't mention it, however, instead asking her brightly about her first day at college. Kalix, who quite clearly remembered telling Moonglow she'd hated it only a few moments ago, refused to discuss it.

Realising that Kalix was intent on resisting all attempts at friendly communication, Moonglow began to withdraw, having satisfied herself that at least Kalix wasn't cutting herself – which she was also prone to – or descending into the grip of an anxiety attack, or dying of a laudanum overdose.

As Moonglow reached the door, Kalix, despite herself, suddenly burst out: 'Wasn't Vex's poem the most stupid thing ever? How could the teacher like it?'

Moonglow paused. 'Well, it was imaginative, I guess,' she answered.

'No, it wasn't! It was awful. I hate her poem.'

'Did you write one as well?' asked Moonglow, brightly.

'No. And I hate college,' said Kalix, and pulled her duvet over her head.

7

The Empress Asaratanti, a fire elemental of regal aspect and, since her recent trip to the cosmetic surgeon in Los Angeles, a very good figure, still couldn't understand why her daughter was so keen to punish a group of werewolves who lived in the human dimension. It was true that since the mania for high fashion had swept through the courts of both the Empress Asaratanti and her neighbour Queen Malveria, there had been rather more contact with the world of humans. The great ladies of their courts had hurried to make use of their fashion designers. They did have a way with clothes. But werewolves?

'Werewolves are low creatures, Princess. Beneath our notice. Why trouble yourself?'

'They assisted Queen Malveria!' exclaimed the Princess. 'Without the MacRinnalchs' help I would have overshadowed her. Does it please you that your daughter now suffers mockery and derision from the ladies of Malveria's court?'

The Empress considered this. Though they were at peace these days, the Hainusta and the Hiyasta had never got along well. There was no denying that Malveria was very full of herself. Asaratanti couldn't blame her daughter for disliking her.

Around the Empress's throne, her ministers and courtiers stood at a respectful distance, careful not to let any flames emerge from their bodies, something which was frowned on at court as rather common.

'So what, dearest daughter, do you want me to do?'

'Provide help to the enemies of the werewolves.'

'You already helped their enemies by giving them sorcery. Without asking my permission.'

The Princess shifted uncomfortably. It was true that she'd provided Thrix and Malveria's enemies with powerful spells without consulting her mother, something Asaratanti had not been slow to point out afterwards. The Empress's own sorcery was of great importance for the defence of her realm, and its secrets were not to be transmitted to all and sundry at the whim of her irresponsible daughter.

'And when you did this,' continued the Empress, 'you failed. Which made it all the more lamentable. I don't intend to allow any more of my private sorcery to be shipped to Earth, where it may be examined and copied.'

'Then we could send someone to assist the Avenaris Guild instead,' suggested the Princess.

'The Avenaris Guild? The werewolf hunters? According to your report of that sorry affair, they were soundly defeated.'

'That's why we should help them now. With our help they'd soon put an end to the Werewolf Enchantress. Once the Enchantress is defeated, she won't be making any more clothes for Queen Malveria. Without a new outfit every day the woman is nothing.'

The Empress mused on her daughter's words. Dealing Malveria a blow wouldn't go amiss. Particularly now, with the border dispute over the Western Desert still dragging on.

'What I require,' continued the Princess, 'is a Hainusta who can go to Earth. A strong warrior to defeat the werewolves.'

'No fire elemental can survive for long on Earth. You know our visits to that dimension are limited. And incidentally, that blue dress does not flatter you.'

'My designer is not up to the task!' exploded the Princess, 'which is another reason to destroy Thrix MacRinnalch!' The Princess was indeed enraged by the deficiencies of her outfit, but calmed herself by glancing at her feet. She wore a new pair of high-heeled sandals fresh from Italy, a beautiful shade of grey with a delicate strap, which were beyond reproach. Even if her dress was deficient, her shoes were excellent, which was something at least. 'As for the matter of how we might send a warrior to Earth, I was hoping you might think of something.'

'I'll ponder the matter,' replied the Empress.

'Might you ponder it quickly?'

The Empress yawned. 'I'm two thousand years old, dearest daughter. I don't like doing much quickly, these days. But I'll consider it.'

As the Princess withdrew from the jewelled throne room, passing under the great burning arch of state, she was reasonably satisfied. If she could elicit her mother's support, she was sure she could defeat the hated Werewolf Enchantress. Thrix MacRinnalch, however, was not uppermost in the Princess's mind as she made her way back to her chambers. There was another werewolf the Princess was much keener to destroy: Kalix MacRinnalch. Princess Kabachetka hated the young werewolf because it was she who'd plunged the knife deep into Sarapen's heart. Princess Kabachetka had fallen in love with Sarapen and now she intended to take revenge for his downfall. The Princess had sworn to herself that Kalix MacRinnalch was going to die.

8

Dominil MacRinnalch examined the living room with distaste. As ever, the twins' house was extremely messy. Dominil found the untidiness offensive. On occasion, when the mess had reached crisis proportions, she had been obliged to call in professional help. A team of domestic cleaners had put the house back in some sort of order. Unfortunately, Beauty and Delicious were incapable of keeping it that way. The floor was littered with guitars, clothes, CDs, DVDs, magazines, plates, cups, glasses, food cartons and several empty bottles of the MacRinnalch whisky.

Dominil knew she shouldn't let it bother her. After all, she didn't live here. She had a comfortable flat of her own in London, lent to her by the Mistress of the Werewolves, who seemed quite happy that Dominil was again helping Butix and Delix. Beauty and Delicious, as they preferred to call themselves, were also notoriously incapable of helping themselves.

If the werewolf twins were incapable of keeping their house in Camden in any sort of order, they did at least have talent in other directions. Several months ago Dominil had helped them re-form their band. They'd played a gig which had gone surprisingly well. The sisters wanted success above anything else and they might even be able to achieve it if they could only focus their attention.

Which, of course, they can't, thought Dominil, picking up a CD from the floor and placing it on a nearby shelf. She wondered if it had been wise to agree to help the twins again. She'd done it first as a favour to Verasa, the Mistress of the Werewolves. Dominil had succeeded in that task to everyone's satisfaction. The sisters had been so grateful to Dominil that they'd actually gone back to Castle MacRinnalch and voted for Markus as Thane. That had been the point of the whole exercise from Verasa and Dominil's point of view. Markus had needed their votes to be elected. Now that was done, there was really nothing else that the family needed from the twins. Yet here Dominil was in London again, with the declared intention of helping them. Yum Yum Sugary Snacks, the twins' band, needed more rehearsals, more gigs, and more publicity. Dominil could make that happen. Though only a few months ago Dominil had had no knowledge of the music business, she was both competent and determined, and could generally do whatever she set her mind to.

'It wouldn't be so bad,' mused Dominil, 'if the twins weren't so fond of drinking. And continually surrounded by a drunken rabble of admirers and hangers-on.'

Dominil stared at her reflection in the glass of a cabinet. Her snow-white hair was long and in fine condition. While not particularly vain, Dominil nonetheless liked to take good care of her hair. She was the only living MacRinnalch to have white fur when she transformed into her werewolf shape. If she changed into her full-wolf form, as many of the MacRinnalchs could do, she appeared as a great arctic wolf. It was commonly held that the icy-white coat reflected her character, and Dominil did nothing to dispel the notion.

Dominil sensed Kalix's approach before the doorbell rang. Dominil's sense of smell was extremely acute, allowing her to identify potential threats, even in the city where the competing odours could be overpowering. Heightened senses were not the only characteristic that differentiated the MacRinnalchs from humans. As werewolves under the moon they were abnormally strong, but even in daylight, in human shape, the MacRinnalchs were unusually powerful creatures.

Kalix arrived at exactly the agreed time, which pleased Dominil. People tended not to be late for appointments with her. The young werewolf looked better than she had when Dominil had first encountered her in London. She was still extremely thin, and rather pale, but her unusually long hair was well cared for, rather than knotted and tangled. Her eyes had lost the haggard look they'd had while she'd been on the run. She wore a long dark coat, a style that seemed to be favoured by the MacRinnalchs. Kalix was now almost eighteen but since she'd regained her health, she looked younger.

Kalix stood hesitantly on the doorstep, looking up at Dominil, who was tall for a MacRinnalch woman. Though she liked Dominil, Kalix was a little nervous of her. Besides, Kalix was not the sort of person to stride confidently into anyone's house. She'd faced too much rejection and hostility in her life to feel confident about her welcome. They looked at each other without expression. Kalix was too shy to smile and Dominil rarely did. The awkwardness continued as they walked through to the twins' living room.

'You'll notice that the twins' liking for mess hasn't changed,' said Dominil.

Kalix nodded. She knew that the untidiness offended Dominil.

No doubt it was partly for this reason that the white-haired werewolf had chosen to stay at the apartment provided for her by Verasa, rather than with the twins. Kalix didn't know where Dominil's apartment was. Possibly no one did, apart from Verasa. Dominil wasn't forthcoming on personal details.

'Have you organised any more gigs?' asked Kalix, in an attempt to make conversation before coming to the real point of her visit.

'Not yet. I could, but first I'd like to introduce some order into their chaotic lives. I've put their website up, with some music for people to listen to. I've got an agent interested in them, which will help us get more gigs.'

As always, Kalix was impressed by Dominil's endeavours. When Dominil had first arrived in London she'd been displeased to find the sisters even more degenerate and disorganised than their reputation suggested. Despite this, Dominil had swiftly managed to galvanise their careers. She'd managed to reunite their band and get them onstage in the space of a few weeks, something that none of their many acquaintances in Camden would have thought possible. The gig had been a success. Unfortunately it had been followed by a ferocious battle during which many werewolves had died. Still, the twins had played well.

Dominil fetched a bottle of whisky from a cabinet. The MacRinnalch Malt, distilled on the clan estates in Scotland, was an exclusive drink, available only to the clan. The MacRinnalchs used it as a traditional token of hospitality towards guests. Kalix accepted a glass of whisky gratefully. She'd been drinking the MacRinnalch whisky from a young age. Too young an age, even by the standards of the MacRinnalch werewolves, which were not quite the same as those of their human neighbours.

'Sit down,' said Dominil.

Kalix sat down.

'What did you want to talk to me about?'

Kalix looked at her feet, and felt uncomfortable. She noticed that her boots were in a poor state. She supposed she could buy a new pair, if she kept on accepting the allowance from her mother, though her mother would stop sending her money if she left college.

After a pause of only a few seconds, Dominil spoke again.

'Please get to the point quickly. I have things to do.'

Kalix flushed. Rather unwillingly, she dragged an envelope from the pocket of her long overcoat.

'I got a letter,' she said. 'It's from Gawain.'

Kalix fell silent.

'And?' said Dominil.

Kalix's face went bright red with embarrassment. She stared down at the floor.

'I take it you are unable to read the letter?' said Dominil. She rose and plucked the letter from Kalix's hand. Kalix continued to stare at her feet, intensely ashamed that her reading skills were so poor. Though she'd made some progress in recent months, the close handwritten script of Gawain's letter had completely defeated her. Kalix was unwilling to take this problem to either of her flatmates. It was too personal. She'd much rather not have shown it to anyone, but after agonising over it for days she'd realised that she had no choice. Either she asked someone to read it to her or she'd never know what was in it. At least Dominil was trustworthy. Kalix was certain she wouldn't repeat any of the letter's contents to anyone.

'Would you like me to read it all out to you, or simply summarise it?'

'Just tell me what's in it,' muttered Kalix, who didn't think she could bear to hear Dominil read out every word. Dominil scanned the letter quickly.

'Gawain professes his love for you. He apologises profusely for forming a relationship with your sister Thrix. He also apologises for disappearing so abruptly after the battle at the gig, but says he was unable to face you after you learned of the affair. He suggests that you may be able to make another attempt at forming a relationship.' Dominil paused. 'His language is rather more romantic than my summary.'

'Is it?' Kalix looked up eagerly. 'Is it romantic?'

'I would say so. Though I may not be the best judge. It's certainly heartfelt.'

'Read it all out to me!' said Kalix, who was now feeling better about this shameful experience.

9

'There is no need, dearest Enchantress,' said Queen Malveria, 'to tell me how splendid I look. This dress you provided for me is of such fine design as to render compliments superfluous. One does not need reassurance when one is attired in such a superb garment.' The Queen examined herself in Thrix's huge wall mirror. 'It does look splendid, does it not?'

'It does,' agreed Thrix.

'I apologise for my minor impatience after the third fitting.'

'Don't mention it,' said Thrix.

'And my hair is coiffured to perfection?'

'It is.'

'Thank you. You are looking splendid yourself, Enchantress, and are a credit to werewolves everywhere, and to blondes, and to blonde werewolves.'

Tonight Thrix and Malveria were going to the Opera House at Covent Garden. While Thrix was not a great fan of the opera, it was an excellent opportunity for some fine evening wear. The opera house was an expensive and fashionable place and no one was going to turn up more expensively or fashionably dressed than the Werewolf Enchantress and the Fire Queen.

'Tell me again – what is this musical event?'

Thrix almost laughed. She'd already explained to Malveria several times what an opera was, but the Fire Queen found it difficult to understand. In Malveria's realm, there was music and there was singing, but there was no theatre. Malveria could just about imagine what a spoken dramatic performance might be like, but the idea of a story being told through song seemed very strange.

'This is not normal, surely? People do not sing songs as they go about their business?'

'It's an artistic convention,' explained Thrix, which only added to the Queen's puzzlement. In reality, Thrix herself was unsure about operatic conventions. She'd only been a few times, each of these for reasons of fashion rather than art. She was looking forward to showing off her excellent outfit but she wasn't particularly excited by the prospect of the performance.

'It all seems most baffling,' said the Fire Queen, for the twentieth time, 'but if as you say it is a fashionable place I am satisfied to attend. Explain to me again why we're going?'

'My mother wants me to impress a singer. Felicori, the tenor. He's the star of the show. She's planning on asking him to sing at some charitable event she's sponsoring. I'm part of the advance party to weaken his resistance.'

'Ah.' Malveria nodded. 'You are to seduce him with your golden beauty?'

The Enchantress looked alarmed.

'I hope not. I'm just meant to impress on him how worthwhile the MacRinnalchs are. Without revealing we're werewolves, of course. That would probably put him off.'

Thrix finished the last of her wine and waved her hand, causing the glass to float through to the kitchen.

'It'll be quite a coup for Mother if she pulls it off. Felicori's a big star.'

'He is big indeed!' cried Malveria, and laughed quite raucously. When Thrix had shown her a picture of Mr Felicori, the Queen had marvelled at his girth, and wondered how it was possible that such a large man could be an object of adoration. Malveria had very strict views on all matters pertaining to weight, views which were completely unmitigated by human standards of charity or tact. She was apt to shudder and shift uncomfortably in the presence of overly large people. Thrix had not yet informed her that some of the women on view at the opera might not be quite sylphlike either, and was rather looking forward to Malveria's reaction when she first set eyes on them.

Malveria checked her lipstick. 'So, we attend the opera, we dazzle the crowd with our fabulous frocks, and afterwards, you enthral this Mr Felicori so that he follows you to Scotland and sings at your mother's important event. I have the whole programme memorised, and will do my utmost to help.' Malveria paused, and looked troubled. 'This lipstick. Now it is perfect, but in a few hours I know it will have faded. Why cannot a lipstick be manufactured that does not rub off? Sometimes my evenings have been quite ruined by this dreadful phenomenon.'

'It's a trial,' agreed Thrix. 'But we just have to carry on the best we can.'

Malveria adorned herself in her wrap and accompanied Thrix downstairs to the waiting taxi. Though it was a short journey to the opera house, the evening traffic was heavy and progress was slow.

'Though I remain dubious about this large man telling us his problems through song, I welcome the diversion,' Malveria said. 'Life at court has been stressful of late. First Minister Xakthan has once more been dropping hints about the succession. Much as I don't wish to discuss this, it is a problem. Were I to die, with no one in line to succeed me, the nation would descend into chaos. It is a poor prospect for everyone. So poor that there have even been hints that it may be time for me to formally adopt Agrivex.'

The Enchantress raised her eyebrows. 'Surely you can't really be considering Vex as the next Queen?'

Malveria shuddered.

'Indeed not. Having built up my realm, one would not like to see it destroyed by the foolishness of my almost-adopted niece. But if I were to adopt Agrivex she would at least be a figurehead behind whom my First Minister Xakthan could rally support. With Agrivex as figurehead and Xakthan in control, the nation might be spared a great deal of strife. It would placate those ministers who are becoming anxious, until I think of some better plan.'

'Have you thought of actually producing a successor?' asked Thrix.

Malveria sighed. 'Again, very difficult. I really don't know of any suitable fire elemental with whom I would wish to raise children.'

The Queen fretted at the memory of the last meeting of her Advisory Council. 'My councillors are intensely annoying. Really, Distikka is the only one I trust.'

'Distikka?' Though the Enchantress was familiar with the Queen's court, she hadn't heard the name before.

'A new member of my council, and our only female. Though the history of the Hiyasta is littered with Queens and Princesses, our females do not make politicians, as a rule. Distikka, however, has recently come to prominence. She talks good sense, even if she does have an unfortunate habit of being badly dressed.'

The taxi slowed to a crawl as the narrow streets around the opera house became crowded with pedestrians, pushing their way between the traffic. Many of them were formally dressed, having parked nearby to walk the last few yards to the opera.

'And yourself, Thrix? Do you have any romantic dalliances in prospect?'

'Definitely not,' Thrix answered, firmly.

'You cannot give up. Though your recent affairs all ended in disaster, your next may not necessarily do so.'

Thrix wasn't flattered to hear her affairs described as disasters, but she didn't protest. It was true. 'I think I'll just manage without male company for a while.'

The Queen was about to lecture Thrix on the necessity of finding a suitable lover when she halted, and peered closely at her friend.

Thrix shifted uncomfortably. 'Would you mind studying me a little less closely?'

'I apologise, dearest Enchantress. But I thought I saw in your aura some longing for Gawain?'

'Absolutely not!' cried Thrix.

'It would not be so strange. After all, it was a passionate affair, and he was a handsome wolf.'

'I'm not longing for anyone,' declared Thrix. 'I'm concentrating on business.'

'Sometimes you terrify me with your business obsessions. Surely you deserve some enjoyment?'

'If I can't persuade some buyers to start stocking my clothes soon, I won't have any business,' muttered Thrix, but the Queen didn't hear her. She was too preoccupied with observing the fashionable crowd that was assembling.

Malveria became excited. 'It's time to dazzle the public. Let us proceed inside where we may make the men in the audience regret that they are not in our company. There will be sadness tonight as they return home with their frankly unsatisfactory wives, still yearning hopelessly for Queen Malveria and Thrix MacRinnalch.'

Dominil drove from Camden through East London with Kalix beside her. They sat in silence as Dominil carefully negotiated the heavy traffic, edging her way past temporary traffic lights that bordered a long stretch of roadworks. Kalix was occupied with thoughts of Gawain. Occasionally she'd glance at Dominil, and make as if to ask her a question, but she held back. It took some nerve to broach any sensitive subject with Dominil, who could be alarmingly unsympathetic.

'So do you think I should go and visit Gawain?' she asked eventually, trying not to sound too emotional.

Dominil remained silent for a few moments, then looked round as they halted in traffic. 'Do you want to see him?'

'I think so.'

'Then visit,' said Dominil.

'But what if it turns out badly?' said Kalix, anxiously.

Dominil frowned. 'Well, you will just have to take the risk.'

'Do you think it's a bad idea?'

Dominil's frown turned into a scowl. 'Do we really have to continue discussing this endlessly?'

Kalix sank back into her seat, feeling young and stupid, and the conversation, like the car, ground to a halt.

They were on their way to Merchant MacDoig's shop to buy laudanum. Kalix's shameful addiction to the opiate was widely known throughout the MacRinnalch Clan, but Dominil had managed to keep her own dependency a secret. Only Kalix knew of it. Were it to become widely known, Dominil would be disgraced. However, though Dominil took pains to be discreet, she hadn't been that displeased when Kalix had learned her secret. The white-haired werewolf guarded her personal affairs very closely, but having a sympathetic fellow addict made the whole thing a little more bearable, for some reason. The shared addiction had occasionally caused Dominil to confide in Kalix. Not much, but more than with anyone else.

Merchant MacDoig plied his trade mainly in Scotland. He'd done a great deal of business with the werewolf clan in the course of his unnaturally long life. Quite how the Merchant had managed to extend his lifespan, no one knew, but as he was fond of saying, when a man had travelled as far and wide as he had, he picked up a thing or two. The small shop in East London was normally staffed by his son the Young MacDoig, who, like his father, was a curious figure; large, florid, and dressed in a peculiarly old-fashioned manner. An encounter with Merchant MacDoig and his son, with their black hats, silver-topped canes, stiff collars and embroidered waistcoats, was like stepping back into the nineteenth century and the world of Dickens.

Dominil was a precise driver. Near the River Thames she parked, very carefully. The two werewolves emerged from the car into an area that had once been part of the old docks but was now completely renovated, and strode past an array of high glass-fronted business blocks. Businessmen and businesswomen who passed between offices glanced curiously at the pair as they walked by; two unusual young women, both with exceedingly long hair and long coats, both wearing rather sturdy boots, though Dominil's were new and Kalix's were shabby. Dominil ignored the attention. Kalix felt uncomfortable.

As they turned into the small alleyway that was their destination, the modern world abruptly disappeared. Here in the narrow darkness there was a smell of dampness and antiquity, with green mould on the walls and cracked cobblestones underfoot. Huge rats looked up in alarm and quickly scuttled away, sensing that Dominil and Kalix were not creatures to be interfered with. The pair made their way silently down the alley in the fading early-evening light. As darkness fell, Dominil suddenly took on her werewolf shape, changing in an instant into a creature that remained on two legs but was covered in shaggy fur, with a wolf's face, claws, talons, and very sharp fangs. Kalix was puzzled. In the alleyway they were unlikely to be observed, but, even so, it was unusual for any of the MacRinnalch werewolves to make the change while there was a possibility of being observed.

Dominil turned and scanned the alleyway suspiciously. Kalix followed her lead, and changed into her own werewolf shape. As she did, she too sensed danger – danger she hadn't noticed earlier due to her preoccupation with Gawain.

Suddenly Dominil sprinted towards the mouth of the alley and, as she approached, a man with a gun appeared out of the gloom. He seemed untroubled as the werewolf raced towards him, perhaps confident of his ability to put a silver bullet through her heart. It was a serious mistake. Whatever training he'd received had not prepared him sufficiently to meet the fury and athleticism of a MacRinnalch werewolf. Dominil leapt high in the air, launching herself off the wall and pouncing on her attacker even as a bullet whistled harmlessly past her shoulder. She slashed out with a great talon, catching the man hard. He spun backwards. Before he could fall to the ground he was caught in Kalix's jaws. She'd followed Dominil, at great speed, and arrived in time to finish off the affair. The werewolf hunter fell dead at her feet, blood gushing from the teeth marks in his throat.

Dominil gazed down the long dark alleyway, sniffing the air. 'He's on his own,' she muttered eventually. 'Let's go.'

Dominil changed back into her human form, a change that was as smooth and instantaneous as before. But Kalix remained as werewolf, and snarled. Fighting always brought on Kalix's battle madness and she paced around expectantly, hoping for more hunters to kill.

'Come on,' said Dominil, but Kalix refused to move. She kept turning this way and that, still snarling and growling.

Though Kalix could still think rationally while in werewolf shape, any form of violence propelled her into a state of extreme aggression that she couldn't easily control. It could be hard to bring her back to normal.

Dominil laid her hand on Kalix's shoulder. Kalix angrily shook it off. The white-haired werewolf stared into her eyes. 'Kalix. Calm down. Return to human.'

Kalix only growled more, and bent down toward the hunter's body, thinking perhaps to savage it again. Dominil drew a small antique bottle from within her long leather coat. She unscrewed the top. The bottle was empty but still smelled strongly of laudanum. It was strong enough to capture Kalix's attention.

'We need laudanum,' said Dominil calmly.

Kalix shuddered, then changed back to human, the change being less smooth than Dominil's. Laudanum was a powerful factor in the young werewolf's life; powerful enough even to penetrate her agitated state of mind. She shook her head to clear it, then followed Dominil along the alleyway. Neither of them spared a thought for the dead hunter. Dead hunters were a way of life to the MacRinnalchs. Neither side showed any mercy in their endless war.

At the far end of the long alley there was a small black door. Dominil knocked, quite heavily.

'Who's there?' came a voice with a familiar Scottish accent.

'Dominil MacRinnalch.'

'Come in,' came the reply, friendly enough, and there was the sound of bolts being drawn. The Young MacDoig appeared at the door, red-haired and red-faced, wearing an old black hat, shiny with age. Dominil stepped swiftly inside, followed by Kalix.

'Did you know there were hunters in the alleyway?'

The Young MacDoig shook his head, looking concerned. When a man traded with werewolves, it was bad news to learn that hunters were close. Dominil regarded him with suspicion. The MacDoigs were dealers in all things esoteric. It wouldn't have surprised her to learn that they'd traded with werewolf hunters in their time. Merchant MacDoig was notorious as a man who liked a profit from any source. But whether the MacDoigs would actually betray a werewolf to the hunters, she doubted. They did too much trade with Castle MacRinnalch to risk it. She told the Merchant's son briefly about what had happened.

'You should get rid of the body.'

'We'll take care of it,' said the Young MacDoig, 'and I'll tell Father what's happened. He's due in London any day now. You'll be here for your laudanum, I expect? Would you like a dram while you wait?'

Neither Dominil nor Kalix was keen to remain in the Merchant's shop any longer than necessary but they accepted the whisky anyway, drinking it back quickly while the Young MacDoig fetched the laudanum for them. The faintest expression of distaste flickered across Dominil's face. The whisky that the MacDoigs provided for their customers was far below the quality of the private supply the MacRinnalchs distilled for themselves. Kalix gulped hers down eagerly, hardly noticing the difference.

'It's fine to see the pair of you, anyway,' said the Young

MacDoig in the jovial manner he'd learned from his father. 'The MacRinnalchs are always welcome in our shop.'

The two werewolves chose not to respond. The high price the Merchant charged them for laudanum had never endeared him to them. Dominil settled the bill, and they left the shop, carefully sniffing the air for any sign of more hunters. Halfway along the alley they paused to look down at the corpse.

'I recognise him,' said Dominil. 'He was one of the hunters who attacked us at the rehearsal studio. That means he's from the Avenaris Guild.' She narrowed her eyes. 'I've had enough of the Guild harassing us.'

Kalix nodded in agreement. She herself had been pursued by their agents many times.

'Perhaps it's time the Clan did something about it,' said Dominil.

They walked on quickly, out of the alley, back into the modern world of tower blocks where office workers were now spilling out of their buildings, heading for home.

11

Decembrius walked through the centre of London, pausing on Charing Cross Road in front of St Martin's College of Art. The building itself was of grey stone, almost indistinguishable from the buildings around it save for a small window exhibiting some work by their students, but Decembrius stood there a while anyway. The Sex Pistols had played their first gig here, which interested him. He'd watched a programme last week about famous gigs in London, and that had been one of them. Several students walked past him on their way into the building. The girls examined him with interest. With his swept-back red hair, leather jacket and multiple earrings, Decembrius was quite a noticeable figure these days.

He walked on down Charing Cross Road, and turned the corner into Oxford Street, crossing the road swiftly to avoid the constant stream of taxis and large red buses. He paused again in front of the 100 Club, an unprepossessing entrance. Outside there was a small board advertising tonight's gig, featuring some jazz musicians he'd never heard of. But here at the 100 Club,

Decembrius now knew, the Sex Pistols had played at a famous punk festival in 1976, with other very early punk-rock innovators. That had been an influential gig too, according to the programme he'd watched.

Decembrius was on his way to meet the Douglas-MacPhees, not an encounter he was looking forward to. He wondered why they'd contacted him. If they were hoping that he might use his powers of seeing to find something, they were going to be disappointed.

Though his prescience had vanished, and his moods were tending towards depression, Decembrius at least felt physically well. Last night, in his apartment, he'd slept as a werewolf. He usually did. The transformation was a revitalising experience for any MacRinnalch, though changing into werewolf form in the city could be awkward. A MacRinnalch werewolf didn't lose control but did feel rather differently about life. The urge to prowl through the night and hunt could be very strong. Decembrius was experienced enough to control his urges. He had no intention of being discovered, particularly as the Avenaris Guild had their headquarters in London. The Guild had killed many werewolves, and Decembrius was acutely aware that since the death of Sarapen he was on his own. He had no allies to turn to for assistance.

He walked on for a while, then hesitated, unsure of his direction. He scowled, and cursed silently. I'm not supposed to get lost. I'm a werewolf, he thought.

But lost he was. There had been a time when Decembrius could have tracked anyone anywhere, always knowing by instinct where he was. Now he found himself wandering around looking for any street or building that looked familiar. Eventually he was obliged to go into a small tourist shop and buy a street map of London, an experience that he found rather embarrassing. He opened it as discreetly as he could, huddling in a doorway, checking his directions, and trying not to look like a tourist.

12

In the lair of Baron MacPhee, Marwanis MacRinnalch was courted by both Wallace MacGregor, the Baron's son, and

Lachlan MacGregor, the Baron's chief adviser. Marwanis had no interest in her suitors. She wanted revenge for the death of Sarapen, whom she had loved.

'Sarapen was murdered. He was the eldest son of the Thane. The Clan should take revenge but it won't, because the Clan is run by accomplices to his murder. His family should take revenge but it won't, because his family were the killers. The Great Council should take revenge but it won't, because the council is dominated by his murderers. There's no one to take revenge for Sarapen's death.'

Marwanis raged against the injustice of it.

'The Thane, the Mistress of the Werewolves, and their lackeys on the council might think they can forget that Kalix killed Sarapen. I'll show them they can't. I'll see Kalix dead for it if it's the last thing I do.'

Lachlan MacGregor was troubled. He'd hoped that here, in the house Baron MacGregor had provided for Marwanis on his estates in the Rinnalch hills, far to the north of Castle MacRinnalch, Marwanis might start to forget. Like many of the MacGregor werewolves, Lachlan had supported Sarapen. But he was dead now, and the feud was over.

'There's no point in more bloodshed,' Lachlan declared.

'No point if you're a coward in a clan of cowards who'll lie down and roll over for Markus and his mother,' said Marwanis. 'You make me sick, all of you. And if none of you are prepared to do what should be done, I'll find some werewolves who are.'

Lachlan had the uncomfortable feeling that there might be plenty of werewolves prepared to do what Marwanis wanted. Marwanis wasn't a warrior, or even particularly strong by the standards of the werewolf clan, but she was much admired, and persuasive. Marwanis had long been the most popular of the younger werewolves who made up what could be termed the MacRinnalch ruling family. In contrast to Thrix, who'd abandoned the clan to seek fame in London, Butix and Delix, who'd departed to bring shame on the clan with their degenerate lifestyle, and Dominil, with her notoriously hostile demeanour, Marwanis was a symbol of MacRinnalch tradition. Respected, respectful, elegant, and almost everything that a proper werewolf should be.

The older werewolves, and many of the younger ones too, didn't approve of those who left home in search of excitement. It was a danger to the clan, and shouldn't be encouraged. It was something of a blemish on the reputation of even such a renowned werewolf as Verasa MacRinnalch that her children had not turned out as respectably as Marwanis.

There was no need to make comparisons with Kalix, of course. Kalix was universally regarded as mad, and beyond redemption.

Marwanis, for all her respectability, had refused to declare peace after the feud was over. She'd stopped attending meetings of the Great Council. She asked Lachlan if he could put her in touch with the Douglas-MacPhees, and though Lachlan was troubled at the thought he nonetheless did as she asked. Marwanis made contact with them, and arranged to meet, and then wondered who else she might recruit in her quest for revenge against Kalix.

13

Dominil drove Kalix back to Tottenham Court Road Tube station where she caught a late train to Kennington. She had a fresh bottle of laudanum in her pocket and kept her hand on it. As Kalix journeyed south she was deep in thought, oblivious to the passengers around her. The attack by the werewolf hunter hadn't troubled her unduly, but Gawain's letter had. Kalix wished she'd been able to formulate some sort of question about Gawain which Dominil might have been willing to answer, but Dominil had been characteristically unforthcoming. Dominil was focused on helping the twins' band and had no time for Kalix's problems.

As always, Kalix's recent change into werewolf shape had invigorated her. She drew strength from it, and it showed. These days she was quite a striking figure. The current generation of female MacRinnalchs were noted for their beauty. Dominil, Marwanis, Beauty and Delicious, all caused heads to turn. The seventeen-year-old Kalix was perhaps the most beautiful of them. She was skinny, waiflike, with thick, dark hair flowing down to her waist. Her eyes were large and very dark, and she had an unusually wide mouth, characteristic of the MacRinnalch women. Now that she was looking after herself better her complexion was clear and the dark shadows under her eyes had disappeared. As some of the passengers eyed her surreptitiously, they wondered about her. Why, for instance, was such a beautiful young girl dressed so shabbily, in an old coat, an oversized shirt, and boots that were falling apart? Was she too poor to buy clothes? Or just following some trend for ragged garments? A fashion student making a statement, perhaps? It was difficult to say.

Kalix stared at her feet, unaware of the attention. The news that Gawain wanted to see her was monumental. Her mind raced in all directions. In the past few months she'd felt every possible emotion towards Gawain, from the deepest, most painful yearnings to a savage, murderous fury. Gawain, the son of a very respectable werewolf family, had once been her lover. Her lover at far too young an age for the family's liking. Kalix's father, the Thane, had banished him from the castle, exiling him from the clan. It was this which had finally tipped the troubled young Kalix over the edge, leading to her madness, her attack on the Thane, and her own exile. In the three years they'd been apart Kalix had never stopped thinking of Gawain. When they'd finally met, thrown together by the chaotic events that followed the Thane's death, it had not gone the way either of them would have planned. Gawain, believing himself to be rejected by Kalix, had become involved in an affair with Thrix, Kalix's older sister. To Kalix, this had been a staggering act of betrayal. She'd probably have attacked them both had she not simultaneously been plunged into battle with her elder brother Sarapen and his supporters. By the time the ferocious combat was over, Sarapen was dead at Kalix's hands. Sarapen, the strongest and fiercest werewolf in the country, had been unable to overcome her.

Afterwards Kalix had been too drained to think of anything. Gawain had survived, badly wounded. He'd limped off without speaking to anyone. Though Kalix had seen her sister Thrix since, she'd never raised the matter of the affair with her ex-lover. It was too painful. She'd been miserable in a way she thought would never end. Though the raw wound had lessened a little over the past few months, it hadn't gone away. Kalix still yearned for Gawain but now it was more hurtful, with the image of Thrix mixed in with it. Sometimes she still felt like killing them both. Other times she wished she could just be back with Gawain, forgetting all their troubles. Occasionally she wished she'd never met him in the first place.

Now Gawain wanted to meet her. Kalix didn't know what to think. She felt a familiar anxiety creeping up on her, and wished she could drink some laudanum, here in the Underground. Kalix was frequently plagued by anxiety. Any unusual event could trigger it. She felt her palms go moist and began to fear that she might have a panic attack right now. She clenched her fists, and tried to ward it off.

When the train eventually pulled into Kennington station, Kalix rushed off, barging her way past people and running up the escalator, desperate to be above ground. As she reached the outside world and sensed the night and the moon above her, she felt a little better. She had an urge to take on her werewolf shape, for comfort, but there were still too many people around. So the young werewolf hurried on towards the flat she shared with Daniel and Moonglow, where she could retire to the privacy of her own room, drink laudanum, and curl up on her bed in her werewolf shape, and perhaps stop feeling anxious about the letter from Gawain.

14

In Daniel and Moonglow's small flat above an empty shop in Kennington, an unfashionable part of South London, Daniel was stressed. Exams were not far away. Having turned in some fairly acceptable coursework, he was approaching them in better shape, academically, than he might have been if he hadn't had extensive help from Moonglow. Without her he'd have been sunk already, which he freely acknowledged. Nonetheless, he railed against his fate. Surely this system of exams was antiquated, and out of place in the modern world?

'Don't they want us to be fully developed, capable of tackling problems in a non-conventional way?' he complained.

'Possibly,' replied Moonglow. 'But you still have to pass your exams.'

'It's ridiculously old-fashioned. You'd think we were stuck in the eighteenth century or something.'

Moonglow looked up from her book. 'Study,' she said, 'and stop complaining.'

Daniel made a face, and tried to reapply himself, meanwhile thinking harsh thoughts about the novels of George Eliot, which he'd never particularly taken to. Both young students sat at the table in the living room, studying, but the silence lasted only for a few minutes.

'It's not a fair system. Look at all these other students with nothing to do except study. Then think of the problems we've faced. We have a werewolf to look after.'

Moonglow smiled. It was a reasonable point. They *did* have a werewolf to look after. Since meeting Kalix they'd had a lot of distractions. They'd found themselves pitched into the middle of a ferocious war, an affair that involved not only Scottish were-wolves but also strange beings from another dimension. The Queen of the fire elementals had actually stored clothes in their attic. Surely no other students had encountered such difficulties.

'We haven't had that many werewolf distractions recently,' Moonglow pointed out. 'The feud's over and Kalix has been fairly quiet.'

Daniel was unconvinced. It still seemed unjust.

'Anyone that has to look after a werewolf should get extra marks in the exam. It's the only fair thing to do.'

Daniel's tirade against the iniquities of the education system was interrupted as they heard the door slam downstairs.

Moonglow smiled as Kalix entered the room. 'Hello, Kalix. You're just in time for a tea break. We've been studying and Daniel keeps complaining about everything.'

'I was just pointing out—'

Daniel halted. Kalix was gone. She'd barely acknowledged them before disappearing to her own room. 'You still couldn't say her social skills were great, could you?'

Moonglow shrugged. 'Oh well. They're better than they used to be.'

'Do you think she's still upset about college?'

While Vex had professed to having a wonderful time at the remedial institution, they were both aware that Kalix had still not shown any enthusiasm.

'I'm sure she'll like it when she gets used to it.'

'I'm sure she won't,' said Daniel. 'I still expect her to eat her teachers. We'd better use the Mistress of the Werewolves's money to pay the rent quickly before Kalix gets expelled. Verasa won't send us any more after that.' He rose from the table. 'Time for tea. I'll put the kettle on.'

He wandered through to the kitchen. Though it had been rude of Kalix to barely acknowledge them, Daniel had already forgotten about it. Kalix's emotions could be so extreme that a little rudeness was hardly noticeable. Mainly, he was preoccupied by Moonglow. It was time she started going out with him. It should have happened by now, and it could only be wilful unreasonableness on her part that prevented it.

Suddenly moody, Daniel deliberately made a lot of noise washing cups, as if banging some crockery around might repay Moonglow for her lack of reasonableness. When he took the teapot back into the living room, he thumped it down quite violently on the table. Moonglow was immersed in a book and didn't notice. Daniel glared at her, then took a cup of tea towards Kalix's room. He found Kalix sitting on the bed in her small, bare room.

'Cup of tea?' he asked, pleasantly. 'Very refreshing for werewolves.'

Kalix smiled. Only a few months ago Daniel had found Kalix's werewolf nature terrifying. Now he could be light-hearted about it. Neither he nor Moonglow regarded it as very strange any more.

Kalix had never regarded it as strange. She'd been born a werewolf and was proud of it.

'Moonglow is being completely unreasonable,' said Daniel, sitting down.

'Why?'

'She won't be my girlfriend. Isn't that the most unreasonable thing you've ever heard? I mean, we're obviously well suited. I'm a far better alternative than the string of useless boyfriends she's had. And you know, it was close to happening. Did you notice that? I definitely noticed it. There was a moment when Moonglow was right on the verge of being my girlfriend. And then something happened. I can't understand it. It was like . . .'

Daniel stopped. He couldn't describe what had happened, but something had. After the MacRinnalch werewolf feud ended, Moonglow had become very close to him. It seemed like any moment she would take Daniel in her arms and tell him he was the boyfriend she'd always yearned for. Perhaps not yearned, admitted Daniel. But they'd definitely been getting there. Then, abruptly, she'd backed away. Since then, Daniel had been unable to rectify the situation.

Daniel flicked his hair back from his face. At nineteen, he was finding life and romance increasingly frustrating.

'Seriously, how am I meant to study for exams when Moonglow just refuses to acknowledge that I'm the boyfriend she needs?' he said, warming to the theme.

Kalix, not really interested in any of this, sat on the bed, staring at the letter in her hand.

'You'd think Moonglow would show a little human sympathy, and—'

Daniel stopped abruptly. Kalix had changed into her werewolf shape. Kalix didn't have to transform – the change only came on automatically on the three nights around the full moon – but as a full-blooded MacRinnalch she was able to take on her werewolf form any night she chose. Having changed earlier in the evening when confronting the hunter, she had a lingering werewolf appetite, which now needed to be satisfied. Kalix, who was never concerned with food when she was human, became very concerned with it when she was a werewolf.

'Need meat,' she said. In her transformed state Kalix was half-wolf, half-girl, walking on two legs, but with a covering of shaggy fur, a wolf's face, quite alarming jaws and sharp-taloned paws. She brushed past Daniel, heading for the kitchen, where Moonglow had thoughtfully provided several joints of beef for her, all of which Kalix would now devour with enthusiasm, along with anything else she came across.

Daniel watched her go, and felt hard done by. He was sharing a flat with a girl he loved who wouldn't go out with him, and an unsympathetic werewolf. He wished that Vex was around to listen to his problems. She wasn't the best listener but she was better than no one. Vex, however, had been whisked back to the Imperial Palace by Malveria for interrogation about her first days at college. Suddenly depressed, Daniel retreated upstairs to his room to lie on his bed, play music loudly, and stare at the ceiling. He put on his new We Slaughtered Them and Laughed CD, in which he found some consolation.

Downstairs in the living room, Moonglow smiled as the young werewolf trotted by on her way to the kitchen. Kalix had such a poor appetite that it was a relief for Moonglow when she made the change into werewolf form and gorged herself on meat. As a vegetarian, Moonglow didn't relish the sight of Kalix chomping her way enthusiastically through a side of raw beef, and licking the blood off her fangs, but it was certainly good for her health.

Kalix arrived back in the living room, still moving gracefully despite her cargo of meat. She was as agile as a cat, and capable of extremely swift movement. 'Meat,' she said, sitting down at the table and licking her lips, before taking a huge bite out of the joint.

'Is it good?' asked Moonglow.

'Mmm . . . good meat,' muttered Kalix, devouring it eagerly.

There had been a time when Kalix, on regaining her human form after the werewolf change, had been so upset at the thought of the food she'd consumed that she'd fall ill, vomit, and dissolve in waves of anxiety. After some months with Moonglow and Daniel, she seemed to have calmed down.

'Is there pizza?' said Kalix, finishing the beef. Moonglow smiled again. When they'd first met Kalix they'd had some trouble understanding her while she was a werewolf. Her strong Scottish accent, transmitted via her wolf jaws, could be difficult to comprehend. They were used to it now.

'I was just about to phone them,' replied Moonglow. 'I'll ask Daniel what he wants.'

'He wants you,' said Kalix.

Moonglow blushed, and suddenly regretted Kalix's less complicated werewolf emotions.

'That's why he's sulking in his room. Because you won't go out with him. Why won't you go out with him?'

Moonglow was flustered and didn't know how to reply. Even if she'd wanted to be Daniel's girlfriend, something of which she wasn't sure, she couldn't. It would be complicated to explain, though, particularly to Kalix.

'How was Dominil?' she asked, to change the subject.

'OK,' said Kalix. Her face fell. She pawed at the string that had encircled her joint of beef.

'Gawain sent me a letter,' she said, suddenly, then looked down at her plate.

Moonglow nodded. It wasn't a surprise that the letter had come from Gawain. Kalix had loved him dearly. He'd loved her too, apparently. Enough to be banished from the clan. Though not enough to stop himself having an affair with her sister, something of which Moonglow heartily disapproved. It had driven Kalix mad when she'd learned of it; later she'd settled into a dull depression, and refused to speak about it.

'He wants to see me,' said Kalix quietly. 'Dominil thinks I should go.'

'Do you want to?'

Kalix didn't know if she wanted to or not. She'd been separated from Gawain for three years. When they'd been reunited they'd had one day of happiness. Then everything had gone drastically wrong. It had all been too painful to bear. She didn't know if she could stand opening the wound again.

'Do you still love him?' asked Moonglow.

'I'll call Daniel and tell him it's pizza time,' said Kalix, and hurried from the room.

15

The Douglas-MacPhees, Duncan and his sister Rhona, were waiting in the pub when Decembrius arrived. They were with a man Decembrius didn't recognise and, although the bar was full with a lunchtime crowd, there was space around them. Even as humans, the Douglas-MacPhees looked tough; people who should be avoided. Douglas's long hair was held in place by a black bandanna. He wore a leather waistcoat that showed the wolf tattoo on his shoulder, and he hadn't shaved for several days. Rhona wore a battered leather jacket. Neither smiled as Decembrius approached. He glanced at their companion.

'Our cousin William.'

'He's almost as big as Fergus,' said Decembrius.

Rhona scowled at the mention of her late brother's name. It was a touchy subject. Decembrius had once fired a silver bullet into Fergus's shoulder. Though it had been accidental, it was a taboo action which might have got him expelled from the clan had other, weightier matters not been occupying them at the time.

'Poor Fergus,' said Duncan. 'Never seen a werewolf in such pain.' He laughed, and didn't seem particularly annoyed at the memory. He leaned forward. 'At least you didn't kill him.'

There was an intense silence.

Rhona was the first to break it. 'We're looking for Kalix.'

'We thought you might know where she was,' added Duncan.

Decembrius eyed each of them in turn, and sipped at the beer William brought to the table. William, he noted, was cast from the same mould as his cousins. No doubt he was just as vicious and unlawful as they were.

'Why do you want to find her?'

'She killed Fergus,' said Rhona.

'There were a lot of werewolves killed that day,' said Decembrius. 'But the clan's at peace now.'

Rhona leaned forward. Her hair, spilling from her bandanna, was thick and black. When she spoke her Scottish accent was very strong, like her brother's.

'I thought you'd be keen to help us. She killed Sarapen too.'

'They've all made peace in Scotland,' repeated Decembrius.

The Douglas-MacPhees laughed. Their newest associate, cousin William, had a deep bellowing voice, matching his frame, and his laughter made the table vibrate.

'You think so?' growled Duncan. 'Marwanis MacRinnalch hasn't made peace. Nor Red Ruraich MacAndris and his clan.'

'And the new Baron MacPhee isn't a peaceful sort of were-wolf,' added Rhona. 'There's quite a lot of people who don't like Markus as Thane.'

'I don't like him myself,' countered Decembrius. 'That doesn't mean there's anything to be done about it. The Great Council support him. No one's going to start another war over it.'

'Who said anything about starting a war?' growled Duncan. 'We don't care who leads the MacRinnalchs. A plague on the Thane, whoever he is. We're talking about revenge on Kalix. No one can find her since the Enchantress gave her the pendant that hides her. She has no scent to track. But that doesn't mean she can't be found. We could use Gawain to lead us to her.'

The Douglas-MacPhees stared at Decembrius.

'So what about it?'

Decembrius took a while to reply. He'd been thinking much the same himself. Gawain might well lead an enquiring werewolf to Kalix.

'I don't know where Gawain is,' he said, finally.

'But you've got powers of seeing, have you not?'

Decembrius gave a slight nod. Though his powers had all but disappeared he didn't intend to let the Douglas-MacPhees know about it.

There was a burst of raucous laughter from the table by their side, where a group of office workers were having some refreshment before heading back to work. Duncan scowled in their direction. The last time he'd been in this bar it had been an old establishment, dilapidated and comfortable. Now it had been modernised, smartened up, and he didn't feel at ease.

'I don't know why they can't just leave these pubs the way they were,' he muttered.

'So can you find Gawain or not?' demanded Rhona, impatiently.

'Maybe,' replied Decembrius. 'If I wanted to. But I don't know that I want to.'

'Why not?'

'I'm a member of the Great Council now. I'm not going to be the one who starts trouble again.'

'He's a member of the Great Council,' said Rhona, mockingly. 'He's important.'

Duncan and William laughed, though their laughter was drowned out by the increasing hilarity at the next table, where the office workers seemed to be celebrating someone's birthday. Duncan pulled out a wallet and opened it to reveal a thick wad of banknotes.

'I don't imagine you're so well off these days, what with not being on Sarapen's payroll any longer.'

Decembrius didn't care one way or the other about Gawain, but he had no intention of doing anything that might lead the Douglas-MacPhees to Kalix. He'd once witnessed the Douglas-MacPhees trying to kill the young werewolf and it wasn't something he wanted to see again.

'I can't help you,' he said abruptly.

William glared at him scornfully. 'I don't believe he's got any seeing powers at all,' he said to the others.

The atmosphere soured. Decembrius prepared himself in case there was violence. Intimidating as the Douglas-MacPhees were, he didn't intend to back down.

'Never mind,' said Duncan, and grinned, showing a set of teeth that were very white, and rather large and sharp. 'We'll find Gawain ourselves. He's probably still wandering around south of the river.'

Duncan picked up his wallet again. 'There's something else you could do for us, if you're not too scared of offending the Great Council. We need someone to visit the Merchant.'

'MacDoig?' Decembrius knew Merchant MacDoig. All the MacRinnalchs did.

'We've got some goods the Merchant might like to buy. Unfortunately . . .' Duncan paused for a second. 'It's a little awkward for us to visit him these days.'

'A small misunderstanding,' added Rhona, 'when he got the impression we were trying to make off with some of his belongings.'

The Douglas-MacPhees laughed.

Decembrius could imagine that they'd have been interested in the Merchant's belongings. He tended to have valuable items around. The Merchant was well protected, however. He'd lived long enough and dealt with powerful entities in his time, and was generally believed to own various spells or talismans which kept him safe, even from the likes of the Douglas-MacPhees.

'So, if you could see your way to visiting the Merchant's shop in Limehouse, and offering him certain items, we'd cut you in,' offered Duncan.

Decembrius leaned forward. He was short of money. Acting as

go-between in a transaction with the Merchant didn't sound like such a bad thing to do.

'What are these items?' he asked.

'Books. Old books. Old enough to be valuable, we reckon. From one of London's many institutes of learning. It wasn't what we were looking for, but we don't like to pass up an opportunity.'

Decembrius nodded his understanding. No doubt the Douglas-MacPhees could easily have got rid of the stolen electrical goods or drugs in which they normally traded, but antiquarian books were a different matter.

'I'll do it,' he said, partly because he needed the money, and partly because he felt like he should keep in contact with the Douglas-MacPhees, in case they did manage to find Gawain, who might then lead them to Kalix.

Decembrius walked home, deep in thought. Though he had no real intention of helping the Douglas-MacPhees, he was already wondering how he might find Gawain. It irritated him that Gawain had access to Kalix and he didn't. He wondered if he could discover where Gawain lived, and force him to divulge information. Perhaps, if he really turned his mind to it, his old powers of seeing might reveal something about Gawain's location.

When he arrived home there was a message on his answering machine from his mother Lucia, urging him to come to Scotland for the next meeting of the Great Council. Decembrius ignored it. He poured himself a small glass of the clan whisky and drank it quickly, then sat down to think some more about how to find Gawain.

16

As Daniel, Moonglow and Kalix waited for their pizzas there was a sudden flash of light. Queen Malveria appeared, bringing with her the aroma of jasmine. It was another potentially start-ling event to which they'd now become accustomed. The Queen of the Hiyasta fire elementals had been a frequent visitor to their house a few months ago.

'Greetings, young humans! How splendid to see you again. Excuse me for not ringing the bell, as is the polite custom, but I noticed a young man on a motorbike, carrying boxes, and suspected he was about to visit you with food. I did not wish to distress him by materialising suddenly. I have been interrogating Agrivex.'

Moonglow was alarmed at the thought of an interrogation. 'She really hasn't been doing anything wrong,'

'So she insists,' agreed the Queen, 'but I needed to satisfy myself as to her behaviour. One does not wish to learn that she has caused any of her tutors to fling themselves out of windows in despair.'

'She seems to get on well at college,' said Moonglow.

The Queen nodded. 'So she tells me. Indeed she claims to have obtained a gold star for a poem. I understand that this is a good sign?'

'Eh . . . yes,' agreed Moonglow.

'Has she committed any outrages in your house? Destroyed items of value?'

Daniel and Moonglow assured the Queen that Vex hadn't destroyed anything.

'That is a surprise,' said the Queen, 'but perhaps the abominable niece will astonish us all, and not create chaos. Very well.' She snapped her fingers, summoning Agrivex back from her dimension.

'Agrivex. The young humans inform me that you have behaved yourself. So you may continue with your programme.'

'Fantastic!' yelled Vex. 'Can I have—'

'You cannot have new boots. It will take more than a few days of good behaviour to earn such a reward.'

Just then the doorbell rang, and Daniel went downstairs to collect their pizza. Moonglow offered Malveria a cup of tea, which she accepted. The Queen appreciated the care that Moonglow took over her tea, making it in a pot, then serving it in delicate cups, with a small jug of milk and a bowl of sugar on a tray.

'How have you been?' enquired the Queen. 'And have you noticed my most fabulous mid-evening ensemble?'

'It's lovely,' said Moonglow. Despite her own preference for black clothes and dark make-up, Moonglow did appreciate the fashionable garments that Thrix created for Malveria. The Queen could tell that Moonglow was sincere, and it pleased her.

'It was something of a triumph. The frock, shoes, hat and matching bag were noted by all to be a remarkable achievement. But this is not the whole reason for my excellent mood. I have been to the opera!'

With that the Queen began humming an air, something neither Daniel nor Moonglow could remember happening before.

'It was such a splendid experience! I am amazed I have never been before! Such music and costume! Such glorious scenes!' The Fire Queen broke off to hum a little more. Moonglow had pulled out a seat at their small table but Malveria showed no inclination to sit down.

'So great was my enthusiasm that I found myself in sympathy with a rather oversized man,' continued Malveria. 'He is called Falstaff, I believe. Are you familiar with him?'

'Yes,' said Moonglow, who knew Falstaff from Shakespeare, though not from the opera.

'How I laughed at his antics! The scoundrel attempted most basely to seduce respectable women in a scandalous fashion, but I could not be completely out of sympathy with his efforts, as he had such a beautiful voice. And he was handsomely dressed, in a manner which made the best of a bad job, as it were. One wishes that he had been less generously proportioned, but even so I was prepared to support his endeavours.' The Fire Queen paused, and looked thoughtful. 'It has to be said that the women he was attempting to seduce were not of the most slender figures either, and would have benefited from the strict regime of diet and exercise with which Malveria continues to gladden the hearts of her subjects, by remaining the slenderest of queens. Nonetheless, they also had most beautiful voices. After the performance I went with Thrix to a place called "backstage" and I met the large singer who was Falstaff! He has a wonderful voice, that Mr Felicori!'

'Felicori?'

'An Italian. Thrix's mother is staging a singing event in Scotland, for charity, and wishes Mr Felicori to appear there.'

Malveria sat down gracefully at their table, not displeased to rest her feet. The heels she was wearing, while extremely stylish, were far from comfortable, though that was something she would never have admitted. Daniel meanwhile was distributing pizza. Next to him Kalix, in her werewolf form, ate hungrily. At the mention of her sister, a scowl had appeared on her face, but she remained silent.

'My dear friend the Enchantress was supposed to impress and seduce Mr Felicori. But impressing and seducing is not her strongest point. When a bold advance is called for, she has a tendency to hang back.'

'Did she really want to seduce him?' asked Moonglow, who, knowing Thrix, couldn't quite imagine it.

'In the sense of forming a sexual relationship with him, no,' admitted the Fire Queen. 'But in the sense of persuading him to oblige the Mistress of the Werewolves, yes. As I understand it, Mr Felicori has many calls on his time and it is not easy to make him agree to such an engagement. Fortunately for all, I took matters in hand, brushed his admirers out of the way, confronted the great singer, and made a strong case to him that he should agree to appear in Scotland.' The Queen smiled at the memory. 'Mr Felicori was favourably impressed, I assure you. It was a service I was pleased to do for my good friend Thrix, even though –' Malveria's expression clouded slightly '– even though I, of course, will not be welcome at the event.'

Moonglow nodded. She remembered that the Hiyastas and the MacRinnalch werewolves were historical enemies, and had fought each other in the past. No Hiyasta would be welcome at a MacRinnalch event.

'Would you like a Pop-Tart?' asked Moonglow, to cover Malveria's disappointment.

'I would love a Pop-Tart,' replied Malveria. 'Though only one, as I am on a strict health regime. I must look fabulous for next month's important sacrifice on the Great Volcano. One cannot disappoint one's adoring subjects by turning up with unwanted extra poundage. Word would reach Princess Kabachetka and she would spread it round all the realms in no time.'

'Are you still rivals with Princess Kabachetka?' asked Moonglow.

'I am indeed. The ladies – I use the term loosely – of the Hainusta court are due to visit my realm shortly, and while I have no fears of being overwhelmed by Kabachetka's shoddy attempts at fashion, my intelligence services tell me that she has been studying whist most assiduously. No doubt she hopes to embarrass me at the card table.' The Queen looked troubled. 'Embarrassment is a possibility. My partner, the Duchess Gargamond, has a tendency to reckless play, thereby leading us into ruin and catastrophe.'

The Queen nibbled on her Pop-Tart, and suddenly noticed Moonglow's fingernails, which had been varnished matt black, overlaid with silver stars. 'How very original!' she exclaimed. 'Who is your nail-varnish assistant?'

Moonglow didn't have a nail-varnish assistant. She'd done it herself. The Queen was impressed at the girl's talent. Really, it all seemed like a trial, living in this small apartment without even a servant to make life easier, but the girl seemed to manage. The Fire Queen admired her for it. Moonglow was attractive, enterprising, and sympathetic. It was no wonder that young Daniel was so besotted with her. With her skill in reading auras, Malveria could tell quite easily that Daniel's romantic hopes had been disappointed. His romance with Moonglow, which had once, unexpectedly, threatened to flare into life, was now dead. Malveria was satisfied. Though Daniel didn't know it, Malveria herself had been instrumental in thwarting his hopes. The Queen liked Daniel, but she didn't see friendship in quite the same way that people did, and the fire elementals had never entirely lost their appetite for tormenting humans.

Malveria took a small mirror from her handbag and studied her lips. She sighed loudly. 'Once more my lip gloss lets me down. Though this product absolutely swore that it would not fade, it is now wearing off. The bold crimson has dimmed to an unalluring pink. Do you have a solution to this, Moonglow?'

Moonglow didn't. She'd suffered with fading lipstick herself, and entered into a prolonged discussion with the Queen about the iniquities of make-up manufacturers who falsely promised that their lipstick would last all night.

17

Princess Kabachetka didn't enjoy the state banquet given in honour of her brother, Prince Esarax, on his promotion from colonel to general. She was bored by the series of long speeches about her brother's many fine qualities. As applause for Prince Esarax rang out around the stateroom she turned to her lady-in-waiting, Alchet, and complained about the night's events.

'It's not like he's just won a war or anything. All he did was get promoted. Hardly that difficult when your mother is the Empress.'

'He's very popular with the army,' said Alchet.

'Who cares about the army?'

'The people love him too.'

Princess Kabachetka frowned at her lady-in-waiting. 'Must you keep praising my wretched brother?'

'I apologise, Princess.'

The Princess had never liked her elder brother. They'd never got along well, and had nothing in common. She counted it a blessing that he spent most of his time with his regiment. It amazed her that her mother, a woman who did understand the value of clothes, could value him so. Esarax had never been well dressed. Yet here he was, having banquets thrown in his honour just because he'd received another promotion.

The Princess's evening wasn't improved by having to be polite to Lady Krimsich, her brother's consort.

'What a dreadful woman she is, with her cheap shoes and arrogant laughter. Quite what the woman has to be arrogant about I can't imagine. She's the sixth daughter of an impoverished Earl! If she hadn't got her hooks into my brother she'd have been thrown in the volcano long ago.'

The evening worsened after the Princess finally succeeded in gaining her mother's attention.

'About my request for help with the werewolves,' began the Princess. 'I wondered if—'

'The answer is no,' said the Empress.

'What?'

'No.'

'But I require your help.'

'And I'm not going to give it,' said the Empress, sharply. 'The whole notion is ridiculous. Leave these low creatures alone and concentrate on being a proper Princess for a change. You could learn some things from your elder brother.'

'Like how to dress poorly and drink too much at banquets?'

The Empress glowered at her daughter. 'Prince Esarax does not drink too much. He knows how to relate to our citizens. I'd like to see you making more of an effort to please the population instead of spending their taxes on endless new outfits.'

'But I don't want to please the population,' protested the Princess. 'They are all such dreadful people.'

The Princess was forced to break off while some tedious ambassadors offered the Empress their congratulations on Esarax's promotion. As they departed she made a final attempt to win her mother over.

'Think of how pleased the population will be if I outshine Queen Malveria! Which I will do if you lend me several powerful sorcerers to defeat Thrix MacRinnalch.'

'I will do no such thing. The imperial sorcerers are for the defence of the realm, not your foolish whims. If you hate this Thrix MacRinnalch so much, go down to Earth and hire some werewolf hunters.'

The Princess felt momentarily faint.

'Hire werewolf hunters? Where will it end? Soon you will be asking me to sweep the streets.'

The Empress glared at her daughter, broke off the conversation, and swept across the room, taking Prince Esarax's arm on the way. Princess Kabachetka stared after them with loathing.

'The way everyone fawns on my brother is just appalling. You'd think he was Emperor.'

'Well, I expect he will be one day,' said Alchet, her lady-in-waiting.

The Princess's blood froze. 'What did you say?'

'I said I expect he will be Emperor one day, Princess.'

'Why? The succession has not been decided.'

Alchet looked at the Princess with something that might have been pity. 'Everyone expects it will be Esarax. He would have the military on his side.'

Kabachetka gaped at her lady-in-waiting. As she paid little

54

attention to politics herself, she was surprised to discover that Alchet seemed to know something about the subject.

'I expect it will not happen for a long time, however,' said Alchet.

Princess Kabachetka wasn't so sure. The Empress Asaratanti showed no signs of infirmity, but one could never be sure. She was very old. She had to go some time. What if Esarax decided to encourage the process? It wouldn't be the first time a Hainusta monarch had been tactfully disposed of. The Empress had given the Hainusta nation a very long period of stability, but before her reign there had been a time where one ruler had followed another in rapid succession.

The Princess pursed her lips. Could her overwhelming obsession with fashion have blinded her to other realities? Now she was facing the worrying possibility of her hated elder brother taking power, perhaps not that far in the future. Her brother disliked her quite as much as she disliked him. If he ever succeeded to the throne, he'd get rid of her as quickly as he could.

'I'd be lucky to survive till the day after his coronation,' muttered the Princess, and clenched her fists in annoyance as she wondered what she could possibly do about it.

18

Daniel and Kalix were watching cartoons when Vex appeared in the room wearing an unusually large scarf and holding a comic.

'Hey, look what I just found in Daniel's room!'

Daniel looked up sharply, though it meant missing the denouement of the cartoon. 'Have you been in my room?'

'That's what I just said.'

'Why?'

'I was looking through your stuff.'

'Why were you doing that?'

'I wanted to see what sort of stuff you had,' replied Vex, logically.

'You're not meant to look through other people's stuff!'

Vex looked puzzled. 'But then how would I know what stuff you had?'

Moonglow emerged from the kitchen with a tray containing a teapot, several cups, and her copy of the Sumerian translation she was working on.

'Moonglow, Vex has been looking through my things!'

Vex couldn't understand why Daniel was making a fuss. 'Moonglow doesn't mind me looking through her things.'

'Yes, I do!' cried Moonglow.

'See? She's fine with it. Moonglow, could you take me shopping for some nice underwear like yours?'

Moonglow put the tray down on the table, rather more roughly than she'd intended, causing a drop of water to emerge from the spout of the teapot.

'Vex, I know you're not used to living with humans but—'

'Look at Daniel's funny scarf,' said Vex cheerily, and wound the long woolly item round her face, making Kalix laugh. Daniel scowled, not keen on seeing the odd garment, a present from his grandmother, displayed in public. Vex made a small slit in the scarf so she could peer through it at them.

'And look! You've got a comic about Kalix.'

It was Kalix's turn to look up sharply. 'What?'

'*Curse of the Wolf Girl!*' Agrivex waved the comic around. Daniel attempted to snatch it but was beaten by the swifter fingers of Kalix. She stared at the cover, a luridly coloured depiction of some sort of werewolf creature apparently about to bite a man's head off.

'It's just an old comic,' explained Daniel. 'It's not any good.'

Kalix frowned, and strained to read the words on the cover. 'Why's it called *Curse of the Wolf Girl*? What's the curse?'

'She turns into a werewolf.'

Kalix was immediately offended. 'That's not a curse.'

'I know. It's just a comic.'

Daniel glared at Vex. 'See, this is why you shouldn't go through other people's stuff. Now you've offended Kalix. And me. And Moonglow.'

Vex peered over Kalix's shoulder. Her reading skills were much better than the young werewolf's.

'"Arabella Wolf was a normal girl until she was bitten by a

56

mysterious wolflike creature in New York City! Now at the full moon she prowls the streets in *Curse of the Wolf Girl!*" It sounds great!'

'It doesn't sound great at all.' Kalix brushed Vex aside before settling down to make an effort to read the comic.

'Is Wolf her real name?' asked Moonglow. 'Or does she just get called that because she's a werewolf?'

'It's her real name! Isn't that ridiculous?' cried Kalix. 'Her name is Arabella Wolf and then she just happens to become a werewolf! What are the chances of that? Who writes this rubbish? I want to complain.'

19

The Avenaris Guild had dedicated itself to hunting and killing werewolves for many hundreds of years. There were numerous successes recorded in the Guild's archives, but they'd suffered a serious defeat in their last campaign against the MacRinnalchs. Their attack had gone disastrously wrong and many of their operatives had been killed. It occurred to Mr Carmichael, the head of the Guild, that if the MacRinnalchs had decided to take the offensive while the Guild was weakened, it could have caused serious problems. With so many hunters dead or injured, an onslaught by the werewolf clan would have been hard to resist. Thankfully the MacRinnalchs had not taken the offensive. Most of their strength lay in Scotland, and they had never mounted a major campaign as far south as London.

'If they tried it now they'd be too late,' he mused. In the past few weeks a stream of new recruits had arrived from central and eastern Europe. The Guild was almost back up to strength. He looked up as his secretary came into the office.

'Captain Easterly is here,' she announced.

Mr Carmichael nodded. Captain Easterly was one of the Guild's most senior hunters. He'd just returned from a fortnight of training new recruits from Poland.

'How are they?' he asked Easterly after they had exchanged greetings.

'Good, mostly. They've all had some experience. Though none of them have encountered as many beasts as they're likely to meet here in Britain.'

There had been a time when it had been difficult to bring in hunters from abroad. Now, with the European Union and the free movement of labour around the Continent, it was much easier. Workers could travel easily from one country to another. Not that anyone actually had 'werewolf hunter' written on their passport as a job description. The four Polish recruits had arrived in the guise of electricians.

'What's this I hear about Albermarle going into the field?' Easterly asked.

'We've approved his application.'

Captain Easterly was incredulous. 'Albermarle isn't a werewolf hunter. He's a computer man.'

'He passed our training course for active hunters.'

'But he's an idiot.'

'Albermarle was the Guild's most valuable information technology specialist,' said Mr Carmichael.

'He's still an idiot. You should keep him behind a computer where he belongs.'

Mr Carmichael smiled. He was aware that Easterly and Albermarle didn't get along. They were distant cousins, and had disliked each other from a young age.

'Albermarle's a strong man these days. Good performances on the training course and shooting range.'

Easterly scoffed at this. 'That's not the same as hunting a werewolf in real life. Albermarle will be ripped apart. Why are you letting him do it?'

'He requested the transfer to active duties. We've been short of men, remember. And I repeat, he performed well in training.'

'And I repeat, if that overweight *Star Trek* fan ever comes up against a real werewolf he'll wish he was back with his computers and comic books.'

Captain Easterly was fair-haired, almost blond, with blue eyes and a weather-beaten complexion. He had good features, roughened by long service in the army. Though he was no longer in the military, the other hunters in the Guild tended to still use his old rank of captain as a mark of respect. As a hunter, he was worthy of it. He was skilful, efficient, and he hated werewolves quite passionately.

'Would you really trust Albermarle to put a silver bullet through a werewolf's heart? The way he blunders around he'd be lucky to get a shot off before he was killed.'

Mr Carmichael was unmoved. Albermarle had been with the organisation for several years and had earned their trust. It wasn't unheard of for a member of the back-room staff to request a move into an active unit. Having passed the relevant tests, Albermarle was ready to hunt werewolves.

'I'm sure he'll be fine. You should be more supportive. He is a relative of yours, after all.'

Easterly laughed, quite good-naturedly. 'I'm still trying to live that down. All right, I'll try. But really, the thought of Albermarle lumbering around the streets looking for werewolves isn't going to fill anyone with confidence.'

'He weighs a lot less than he used to. Took his training very seriously.'

Easterly couldn't imagine why his ungainly, obese cousin had suddenly decided to transform himself from computer specialist into an active hunter, but he assured the chairman of the board that he'd do his best to help him. 'Or at least keep him alive for a few months, which is about the most we can expect.'

20

Castle MacRinnalch stood in a remote part of the Scottish Highlands. The MacRinnalch estates, sweeping over mountains, woodlands and glens, were little disturbed by the outside world. It was an ideal place for werewolves to flourish. Displacement of the human population during the Highland Clearances of the eighteenth century, followed by a general movement of the remaining rural community towards the cities in the south, had left the area one of the most sparsely populated in Europe.

When times had been hardest, some of the MacRinnalchs had also departed, ending up in Australia, New Zealand, America and Canada, but most had remained on the ancestral lands. Mainly they'd avoided human contact, but in recent years the Mistress of the Werewolves had brought them closer to the outside world, while taking good care to preserve the secret of their true nature.

An immense black stone building, constructed in the thirteenth century and added to since then, Castle MacRinnalch had been the home of the werewolf clan for many hundreds of years. During that time the castle had seen treachery, bloodshed and warfare, and only recently had been besieged in the course of the violent feud over the Thaneship. The three werewolf Barons – MacPhee, MacAllister and MacPherson – had not supported Markus, but now that he was in power they were content to live in peace.

Inside the castle life had almost returned to normal, although the relationship between the new Thane and the Mistress of the Werewolves was still a little uneasy. Markus attempted to exercise his authority, and his mother Verasa strove to maintain hers. It had led to some awkwardness, though not as much as might have been expected. Verasa and Markus MacRinnalch had always been close, and knew that they'd reach an accommodation eventually.

At this moment, all arguments had been put to one side. Verasa and Markus were both great opera enthusiasts, and were collaborating on the plan to stage a performance in aid of one of Verasa's charities. She was fast becoming an influential figure among the ranks of Scotland's charitable fundraisers. As she often said, 'We may be werewolves but that doesn't mean we shouldn't contribute to society.'

It was because of Verasa's desire to integrate the clan more fully with the modern world that she'd supported her younger son Markus as Thane. To her mind, he'd been a far more suitable choice than her elder son, the warlike Sarapen. Had Sarapen become head of the clan, trouble would surely have followed. Verasa would not now be talking with pleasure of her plan to stage her event at Andamair House. The MacRinnalchs were very wealthy, and Andamair House, situated a long way south, on the outskirts of Edinburgh, was one of the many properties they owned throughout Britain. Verasa had flirted briefly with the idea of actually holding the event at the castle. It would have been a beautiful location. She'd swiftly rejected the notion. It was not unknown for tourists to go missing on the MacRinnalch lands. The clan discouraged its members from actually eating people, but during the physical transition to werewolf, temptation remained strong.

'Nothing would draw unwelcome attention onto us more than the unexpected devouring of important civic dignitaries,' reasoned Verasa. 'Not that I would expect any MacRinnalch to do such a thing, of course. But some of the MacPhees are hardly civilised. And you really can't trust the MacAndrises at all. Andamair House will solve our problems.'

Andamair House was an imposing Georgian country mansion, surrounded by landscaped grounds, close enough to Edinburgh for people to travel there easily. Markus agreed that it was the ideal location, and plans were laid for the event.

The moon had only just risen as Markus appeared in his mother's chambers in the west of the castle. He'd changed into his werewolf shape, though his mother remained human. She had some calls to make and modern phones were so small as to be almost impossible to manipulate with werewolf talons.

'How did Thrix get on with Felicori?' asked Markus.

Verasa smiled, pleased to see her son. He was such a handsome boy, with his thick curly chestnut hair and fine features.

'Quite well, she tells me. Though I wish she hadn't taken that Hiyasta with her.'

'Queen Malveria is not so bad,' said Markus. 'She fought on our side.'

'That doesn't mean I have to like her. She is a Hiyasta after all, and they've been enemies of the MacRinnalchs for a very long time. I'll always regret that Thrix became friends with her.'

'You regret most things about Thrix,' pointed out Markus.

'That's not true. I admire her ambition.'

Markus was sceptical. His mother might claim to admire Thrix's drive, and her success in the fashion world, but he knew Verasa resented her eldest daughter's distancing herself from the Clan.

'Perhaps Malveria would appeal to the opera crowd. She's dramatic enough.'

'Perhaps. Though if she has any notion of attending my event, she can abandon it,' said Verasa, sternly. 'Anyway, Thrix has an appointment with Felicori's agent, and if that goes well I'll go down to London next week to meet them both.'

The Mistress of the Werewolves sipped some wine, and lit a last cigarette before changing. She glanced out the window at the darkening sky. The windows had been greatly extended recently, providing her chambers with more light than anywhere else in the rather gloomy castle. It was an improvement that her late husband, the old Thane, would never have approved of. He'd never really approved of anything Verasa did. Since he'd died, Verasa couldn't honestly have said she'd missed him, though she had continued to pay his memory the proper respect in public.

Verasa took another sip of wine, put the glass down on a small oak table, then changed instantly into her werewolf form. 'Has anyone heard from Decembrius?' she asked.

Markus shook his head. 'He doesn't seem to want to get in touch.'

Verasa frowned, though her frown was mostly hidden by her shaggy fur. 'Lucia isn't pleased.'

Markus almost laughed. Verasa's sister Lucia had been so proud when Decembrius was elevated to the Great Council. Her pride had quickly evaporated when her son showed no desire to come back to the castle.

'Why is he staying in London? Now that Sarapen's gone, what is there to keep him there?'

Markus didn't know. Unless it was just the desire to distance himself from Lucia, something which Markus could understand. Markus had always been very close to his own mother, but he knew the feeling of being suffocated by his family. 'Maybe he likes the pretty girls,' he suggested.

The Mistress of the Werewolves was not amused. 'There are plenty of pretty girls in the clan. The castle is full of them. Please try to contact him again. He really should make an appearance at the next council meeting.'

21

Between the impressive edifice that was Waterloo Station, and the dull concrete blocks that formed the National Theatre, sat several streets of dark old tenements, constructed of huge blocks of grey stone. They emanated a certain seediness, home to some of the city's less important companies, and smaller banks from far-flung corners of the globe, too insignificant to occupy any of the capital's main commercial areas. Here lay Kalix's college, occupying a building which had seen better days. From the window of Kalix's classroom she could see the grey concrete roof of the Hayward Gallery. Across the river, though just out of sight, was King's College, where Moonglow and Daniel were studying. Though Kalix had never been inside King's College she was sure it must be a grander place than this. The walls were a faded cream, undecorated for many years. The language charts on the walls were faded, and the computers on the desks bulky and old-fashioned. The drab classroom didn't encourage Kalix to learn anything. Perhaps nothing could. She was too preoccupied with thoughts of Gawain and the letter he'd written her.

A Chinese teenager who'd said hello to her yesterday greeted her in a friendly manner. Kalix stared at him. She didn't intend to make friends with any of her fellow students. She paid little attention to anything the teacher said, and was surprised when, on hearing Vex's voice, she looked up to find the young fire elemental once more reciting a poem. Kalix was puzzled. As far as she knew, they weren't studying poetry today. Possibly Vex had just stood up and started reciting anyway. Kalix looked expectantly at the teacher, hoping she might tell Agrivex to sit down and be quiet, but she didn't. Apparently, just getting up and reading a poem was something to be encouraged.

I am sure I will one day have a hedgehog
And we will be great friends.
Perhaps my hedgehog will help overthrow the evil Queen
    Malveria
Whose subjects hated her for her persecution of Princess
    Agrivex.
She would never buy her anything
Not even new boots she really needed.

Kalix was bewildered. It was even worse than the last poem. She hoped the class might rise up in rebellion and ridicule Vex for her dreadful poetry. Failing that, the teacher could at least expel her. Unfortunately, neither of these things happened. The teacher seemed impressed, and once more complimented Vex on her imagination. Several Japanese students at the front of the class were busy copying it down. Kalix sighed. She really wasn't enjoying being here.

'Would you like to pick some verbs out of Agrivex's poem?' said the teacher, and looked at Kalix. Kalix quailed. She couldn't remember the poem and wasn't entirely sure what a verb was anyway. She glanced round at Vex, but Vex was preoccupied in writing 'gold star' under her poem. The teacher looked encouragingly at Kalix. Kalix looked down at the blank paper in front of her, and wished desperately that she was somewhere else. She couldn't bear it that the whole class was looking at her. Eventually, after what seemed like a very long time, the teacher moved on to another student.

At lunchtime Kalix made her way to the refectory. She wasn't hungry and intended to simply sit on her own and think about Gawain. He wanted to see her. Kalix didn't know whether she should go or not. Perhaps she should reply to the letter? But, of course, she couldn't write well enough to manage a whole letter, and she couldn't ask anyone to do it for her.

The young werewolf slumped into a chair with the air of a person who did not want company. Ignoring this, Vex arrived immediately with a tray of food, followed by several more students, all of whom Vex appeared to have made friends with already. Kalix hadn't made any friends. She was irritated to be surrounded by a group of teenagers all talking excitedly about things she knew nothing about.

'Hey Kalix, aren't you going to eat anything? This soup looks good.' Vex tasted her soup, and winced. 'OK, I was wrong. Maybe they have some raw steak? You'd like that.'

Kalix glared at Vex. They were meant to be keeping their true natures secret. No one was supposed to know that Kalix was a werewolf and Vex a fire elemental. Kalix was experienced in hiding her true nature and could do it easily enough, but Agrivex seemed almost oblivious to the necessity of being discreet. Kalix wouldn't be surprised to hear herself described as a Scottish werewolf in Vex's next poem.

'You should eat,' said Vex. 'Build up your strength for the house meeting.'

Kalix was immediately alarmed. 'House meeting? What house meeting?'

Vex didn't seem to know much about it. 'Moonglow just said to tell you we were having a house meeting tonight.'

Kalix's alarm grew, and her heart began to race. 'Is it about me?'

'Probably,' said Vex, cheerfully. 'But don't worry, I keep telling them we have to make allowances for you.'

Before Kalix could pursue the matter further a small, pale girl sat down next to them. Vex greeted her enthusiastically, having befriended her earlier in the day.

'I like your hair,' the girl said, turning towards Kalix. 'I wish mine would grow like that.'

Kalix was disturbed to find her hair being complimented by a girl she didn't know, and shrank away, unsure how to respond. She wished again that Vex hadn't brought all these strangers to their table. The whole experience of being at college was proving even more painful than she'd anticipated. She wondered if she should just leave. But then everyone would be annoyed at her – her mother, Daniel, Moonglow, Vex. Kalix bridled. Why was she bothered if these people were annoyed at her? She was Kalix MacRinnalch, daughter of the Thane of the MacRinnalchs. She shouldn't have to care what anyone thought of her.

'What conditioner do you use?'

Kalix sighed, shrank further down in her chair, and worried again about the house meeting.

22

Kalix arrived home to find Daniel in the kitchen, making tea.

'What's the house meeting for?' she asked.

Daniel didn't know. 'Just some whim of Moonglow's.'

'I don't want to come. Have the meeting without me.'

'Moonglow insists,' said Daniel. He didn't want to attend a house meeting either but had resigned himself to his fate.

'But I didn't do anything wrong.'

Daniel attempted to calm the young werewolf's agitation.

'No one's accusing you of doing anything wrong. We just have to talk about, eh . . . whatever Moonglow wants to talk about.'

'I need to go to my room.'

Daniel smiled. 'If you fill yourself up with laudanum and pass out, Moonglow will know.'

The young werewolf sighed. She didn't like the sound of this at all, and imagined she was about to be blamed for something. During her upbringing at Castle MacRinnalch, any time she'd been summoned to a meeting it had been to receive some serious telling-off from her parents. Her shoulders drooped as she followed Daniel into the living room. Moonglow and Vex were already sitting at the dining table, which Daniel had recently stopped from tilting by folding up a music magazine and putting it under one of the legs, a home improvement of which he was rather proud.

'It's a bit cold in here,' said Daniel, and went to turn on the gas fire.

'Leave the fire alone!' exclaimed Moonglow.

'But it's cold.'

Moonglow held up a bill on which there was an alarming amount of red ink. 'We can't afford to pay the gas bill.' She swept her hand through a pile of paper in front of her. 'We can't afford any of these bills. That's why we have to talk.'

'What's a bill?' asked Vex.

'It's the money we have to pay for gas. And electricity. And council tax. And rent. And the water bill. And the TV licence. And our broadband connection and cable TV. And the phone.'

Daniel felt himself weakening and hastily sat down. 'Are we behind with everything?'

Moonglow held up a series of bills, all of them final demands. Several of them threatened swift action by collection agencies.

'Why do we have to pay so much council tax?' asked Daniel, mystified. 'The place is a dump. What does the council do for us?'

'Collects the rubbish. Maintains the sewers. Provides schools for our children if we had any. It does seem like a lot but we have to pay it, and quickly, or they'll send round the bailiffs. As will the electricity company.'

Vex looked disappointed. 'This house meeting isn't as much fun as I thought it was going to be.'

Moonglow had organised the bills in order of the most urgent. 'We shouldn't have let ourselves get into this position. We'll need to see what money we have now and pay the most important bills. Then I'll phone the others and work out some sort of payment schedule. But we'll all have to start budgeting better, and we'll have to start saving money around the house. Kalix, why have you just turned into a werewolf?'

'No reason.'

'Being a werewolf doesn't mean you don't have to pay bills.'

'Oh.' Kalix changed back into human.

'I thought it might.'

'Hey, I'm a fire elemental and I pay bills,' proclaimed Vex.

'No, you don't.'

'Don't I?'

'No.'

'I thought Aunt Malvie took care of things like that?'

'Malveria gives you a set amount each month. You're meant to pay the bills out of that. She explained it to you very clearly when you moved in.'

'Are you sure about that?'

'Quite sure. Next day you went off and bought twelve T-shirts.'

'I like T-shirts,' said Vex, brightly. She noticed everyone was staring at her. 'Maybe I could manage with less.'

'We'll all just have to economise,' said Daniel, diplomatically. 'No point blaming anyone.'

'Really?' said Moonglow. 'I was thinking of blaming you for buying so much music and video games that you can't pay the phone bill.'

'Well, Kalix eats a lot of meat! Think how expensive that is!'

'Hey!' protested Kalix. 'I don't use as much heating as Daniel. He's always got the fire on.'

'I don't have a comfy werewolf coat. I need the fire on. Who is it spends hours in hot showers?'

'I need to keep my coat clean. At least I don't use the hair dryer for an hour at a time.'

'My hair takes a lot of careful drying!' protested Moonglow.

'And I'm the only one who's budgeted properly to pay these bills! You've all just spent your money on everything else!'

'Well, to be fair . . .' began Daniel, but dried up.

'Yes?' demanded Moonglow.

'Nothing.'

'Were you going to say I have more money than you?'

'No. Maybe.'

'Yes you were. Fine, my parents give me a little more money than yours do. I still have to budget. You don't see me walking around in new shoes all the time.'

'You bought new shoes last week.'

Moonglow flushed. 'They were my first pair for ages. And who helped pay for your car tax last month?'

Kalix and Vex shrank in their chairs at the mention of Daniel's car. They were meant to give him money for a share of the petrol, but neither of them had done so.

Daniel sighed, but tried to remain diplomatic. It was unlike Moonglow to voice such annoyance but he realised she'd been driven to it by the rest of the household's reluctance to heed her warnings.

'OK, we're in a mess. Moonglow, if you tell us all what we owe, we'll just have to raise the money as best we can.'

'So am I forbidden to buy clothes and stuff?' asked Vex, who for the first time seemed to be appreciating the seriousness of the situation.

'You're not forbidden to buy anything. You just have to make sure you pay your share of the bills.'

'Is that before or after I buy clothes?'

'Before.'

Vex looked miserable. 'House meetings really suck,' she muttered.

After the meeting was over Kalix escaped to her own room as quickly as possible. She was relieved not to have been directly blamed for their problems, but now she was worried about money. The allowance her mother gave her wasn't overly generous, but it should have been enough to pay for her rent, bills and upkeep. Unfortunately Kalix spent a large proportion of it on laudanum, and that wasn't something she could do without. She sipped a little from her bottle, and wondered if she could cut down on her intake. The thought made her anxious.

As she lay on the bed, she had the troubling feeling that she was spending her life pretending to be a normal person, making a budget and paying bills, when really she wasn't normal at all. She was a werewolf. She'd never felt strange about being a werewolf before. But now, trying to fit in with the rest of the household, she found herself troubled by the differences between them all, and it made her unhappy.

She took Daniel's werewolf comic from her table to distract her attention, and struggled to read more of it. As far as Kalix could make out, Arabella Wolf had been bitten by a werewolf, changing into a werewolf herself, and now terrorised New York every full moon. Kalix looked disapprovingly at a picture of Arabella growling at a pair of young lovers in an alleyway.

'She looks ridiculous. Werewolves don't look like that.'

Later Arabella woke up in Central Park. She couldn't remember anything that had happened. Outside the park, newspaper vendors were selling papers with headlines about more grisly murders. Arabella was worried as she made her way back to her boyfriend's apartment. Her boyfriend worked for the FBI.

'I've been assigned to solve these terrible killings,' he told Arabella. 'There's an insane beast on the rampage and the city is terrified.'

'I hate this comic,' muttered Kalix. 'It's completely anti-werewolf from start to finish.'

23

Thrix arrived later than she intended at Castle MacRinnalch. Her mother was displeased.

'Markus needs your support, Thrix.'

Thrix scowled. She and her brother Markus heartily disliked each other, as her mother knew very well.

'Support? What for? The war's ended.'

'There are plenty of other affairs the MacRinnalchs need to attend to.'

'I have more important things to worry about.'

The Mistress of the Werewolves was shocked. The Enchantress cared more for her business than she did for the clan but there was no need to be so rude about it. Verasa looked at her daughter curiously. Thrix was as glamorous as ever, golden-haired and beautifully attired, but there was something unusual about her manner.

'Is anything wrong?' she asked Thrix.

'I told you, I'd rather not be here.'

'You'd always rather not be here, but you're not normally this hostile. Has something upset you?'

Thrix felt uncomfortable. Though she was a skilled sorceress who'd studied with the renowned Minerva MacRinnalch, it was difficult to fool her mother. The Mistress of the Werewolves was a very shrewd wolf. Not much escaped her notice, particularly in family matters.

'Nothing's wrong. I'm just stressed from work.'

'I thought business was good? Didn't *Tatler* print that nice piece about your last show?'

Thrix made a face. 'They did. But it's not enough. Buyers are not necessarily impressed by catwalk reviews. I've spent the last three months trying to persuade London stores to sell my clothes and I don't seem to be getting anywhere.'

It was a problem which was much on Thrix's mind at the moment. Her standing in the fashion world had risen recently. Her clothes were generally liked. Unfortunately, she needed to sell them to keep her business going, and fashionable outlets had a remarkable ability to delay making decisions.

'They keep you waiting for months and then tell you they've decided to go with someone else. It's infuriating.' Thrix poured herself some whisky from the crystal decanter on the table. In common with virtually every other member of the family, the Enchantress was fond of the MacRinnalch malt.

'Have you seen Kalix?' asked Verasa.

If this was an attempt to change the subject, it was a poor choice. Thrix bristled at the mention of her young sister's name.

'No, I have not. And please don't say you need me to look after her. I've done enough of that.'

'I wouldn't say you ever took to the task that well.'

'I helped her to hide,' said Thrix, 'which was more than anyone else in the family did for her.'

Verasa nodded. It was true. Thrix had helped to hide Kalix and she was grateful for that. The Mistress of the Werewolves was an elegant woman who always looked her best for council meetings. If her clothes were conservative by Thrix's standards, she couldn't fault them. Her mother was never less than immaculate. The MacRinnalch children had inherited her good looks. At least Thrix, Kalix and Markus had. Sarapen had been much more like their late father. Sarapen was on Verasa's mind at the moment. Her eldest son had died in battle but there had been no burial. At the moment of death his body had been spirited away by Princess Kabachetka. It was not fitting that his body should be missing. It should be buried respectably on the estate. Verasa had asked Thrix to make enquiries through Queen Malveria about its return, but that was awkward, with Verasa's aversion to the Hiyasta Queen, and the Queen's aversion to the Hainusta Princess.

'Malveria's doing her best,' Thrix told her mother, 'but Princess Kabachetka is more than a rival, she's an enemy. I don't know if we can get the body back. It's possible.'

Verasa nodded, and asked her daughter to keep on trying.

The Enchantress was keen to return to her rooms to check her business email but her mother wasn't finished.

'Do you think Kalix is back in contact with Gawain?'

Thrix gritted her teeth.

'Who knows?'

'You should be more concerned,' said Verasa. 'He's still banished from the clan, you know—'

'I don't want to talk about Gawain!' yelled the Enchantress.

'You're surely not still concerned about him?'

Thrix didn't reply, but she looked uncomfortable.

'Have you seen him?' demanded Verasa.

'No,' replied Thrix.

Verasa wasn't convinced. 'Gawain is still exiled. I really can't understand why you would—'

The Mistress of the Werewolves broke off. Thrix had picked up her handbag and stormed out, her high heels making a rapid clicking sound as she departed swiftly along the stone corridor.

Verasa was puzzled. Minor arguments with her daughter were not uncommon, but it was unusual for Thrix to storm from the room. What was the matter with her?

24

The Empress Asaratanti's palace sat on the northern edge of the Eternal Volcano, the huge natural feature that dominated the central plain of the Hainusta. Despite the violent nature of the volcano, the palace was unthreatened. Empress Asaratanti controlled the volcano – or rather, she existed in harmony with it. The Empress claimed to be the most powerful fire elemental in existence, and though Queen Malveria might dispute this, the Hainusta believed it. The harnessing of the power of the Eternal Volcano was a visible sign of the Empress's strength. Her subjects looked to her in awe, as they had done for more than a thousand years. She was ageless and immutable.

'Or so we are led to believe,' muttered the Empress's daughter, Princess Kabachetka, alone in her secret cavern. 'But is it really so?'

North of the palace lay the simmering Pools of Chelios, a huge expanse of lava pools and melting rock. Beneath them lay a small network of caves and tunnels, and there Princess Kabachetka had her secret cavern. Recently the Princess had found herself spending more of her time there. She was pondering the future, and not liking what she saw. For instance, there was the disputed territory in the western desert. The Empress had been content to let her army handle it. There was a time when she would have gone there herself and taken control.

'Perhaps,' mused Kabachetka, 'she's growing old and careless. Careless enough to allow some treacherous snake to usurp her power. And there's only one snake treacherous enough to make the attempt. My brother.'

The Princess pursed her lips. Really, she couldn't believe she hadn't seen this before. All it would take would be a swift, decisive move by Prince Esarax, and the Empress would be gone. He'd take her place unopposed, with the full support of the army. The government, the aristocracy and the rest of the population would all fall into line. And where would that leave the Princess?

'It would leave me making a swift trip to the Eternal Volcano,' bridled the Princess, and clenched her fists angrily. 'My brother would like nothing better than to throw me into the volcano.'

Princess Kabachetka paced anxiously around her secret cavern. It made it worse that there was no one she could confide in. In the gossip-ridden environs of the palace, any such talk would soon reach unwelcome ears. The Empress had spies everywhere. Probably her brother did too. The Princess felt alone and powerless, and shook her head in frustration. Though she would never admit it to the outside world, Kabachetka was aware of some of her own failings. She knew, for instance, that she was not a great strategist. She'd seen her plans fail before.

'My brother will defeat me. I'm not cunning enough. I'm doomed to end up in the volcano.'

She strode to the furthest edge of her cavern, to the place where the realm of the fire elementals merged with that of the ice creatures and the beings of the Earth. A place in between realms, where time never passed. There lay the body of Sarapen, greatest of the MacRinnalch werewolves. Not alive, but not quite dead. He'd been struck down by the Begravar knife, a weapon so deadly to werewolves that there was no recovering from its wound. Princess Kabachetka had brought his body here, placing it in a state of suspended animation just before he expired. Having done that, she could do no more. Were she to attempt to revive him he would certainly die. No one could prevent it.

Apart from, possibly, the Empress Asaratanti. With her mastery over the Eternal Volcano she had a fantastic amount of power at her disposal. Enough, perhaps, to save Sarapen's life. But the Empress would never expend that power to save a werewolf. The Empress regarded werewolves as low creatures. As did Princess Kabachetka, normally. It was the Princess's misfortune that she'd fallen in love with Sarapen.

'A partner not suitable for your fire,' muttered the Princess, quoting a line from a well-known Hainusta poet whose name she couldn't remember.

'Of course, if I were Empress I'd be in control of the volcano.

I'd have enough power to revive Sarapen, suitable partner or not.'

She had a happy vision of herself as ruler of the nation, fabulously dressed, with Sarapen at her side, sweeping all before them, disposing of her annoying brother, and then crossing the border to conquer Malveria's realm.

That would teach the Queen of the Hiyasta not to give herself such airs just because she happens to have a few nice frocks, thought the Princess crossly. She desperately wanted to defeat and humiliate Malveria, and Thrix, and Kalix, and her brother – everyone who'd conspired against her, and harmed her. Unfortunately for the Princess, she couldn't think of any way to do it.

25

It was the night of the full moon. When darkness fell every werewolf in Castle MacRinnalch would make the change. Verasa could feel it tingling in her bones already. Every werewolf could. Apart, possibly, from Dominil. Verasa wouldn't have been surprised to learn that the white-haired werewolf underwent the change without feeling anything at all. It was hard to warm towards Dominil. That didn't mean the Mistress of the Werewolves didn't appreciate her.

'We were all amazed that you managed to discipline the twins into actually playing a concert. Have they stuck with it, or reverted back to their old ways?'

'Somewhere in between. Though they still drink too much I've managed to make them keep rehearsing. They sound reasonably good, by the standards of their contemporaries.'

Dominil had a strange, formal manner of speaking, and she had discarded her Scottish accent at Oxford. Here in Castle MacRinnalch, her neutral tones stood out.

Verasa was grateful for Dominil's help. Though the Mistress of the Werewolves had never previously imagined that she'd find herself willing a rock band to success, particularly one containing Butix and Delix, it was better that the twins did something positive rather than roll around in drunken degeneracy.

'I still worry about them giving themselves away.'

'With good reason,' said Dominil. 'It's something of a miracle they've concealed their werewolf nature for so long. It's fortunate that they find it difficult to make the change most nights.'

Though the pure-blooded MacRinnalch werewolves could transform on any night they chose, Beauty and Delicious were so degenerate and intoxicated they'd forgotten how to do it. They only became werewolves on the three wolf nights around the full moon.

Verasa shook her head. 'They'll bring the hunters down on their heads.'

'Perhaps. The Avenaris Guild has regrouped more quickly than I anticipated.' Dominil had informed the clan that a new group of experienced hunters had arrived in the country from Poland and Croatia. 'The MacRinnalchs are famous, in certain circles. It seems there is no shortage of humans eager to kill us.' She paused, and stared at the wall for a while. 'I've been wondering if we should start taking the fight to them.'

'How do you mean?' asked Verasa.

'Up till now we've merely reacted to their attacks. I know you want the clan to move forward but I'm not certain we can while this carries on. Perhaps it's time we took some offensive action.'

'What sort of action?'

'Attack the Guild's headquarters, if we could find it.'

The Mistress of the Werewolves was alarmed. She hadn't expected to hear such a suggestion from Dominil.

'I was offended to be attacked in London last week,' continued the white-haired werewolf. 'I've a right to go about my business the same as anyone else without someone trying to kill me.'

'You'd all be safer if you came back to Scotland,' pointed out Verasa, which was true. Castle MacRinnalch was a stronghold which the Guild could never attack.

'Perhaps. But you know the twins won't come back. Nor will Thrix, nor Kalix.'

Verasa wasn't pleased to hear her two daughters named among the werewolves who had no desire to return home, though she knew it was true.

'I'm not in favour of initiating violence,' she said. 'We've had more than enough recently. I don't believe the Guild can seriously hurt us. There aren't that many werewolves who are vulnerable.'

'The twins are.'

'Are Yum Yum Sugary Snacks playing again soon?' Verasa stumbled over the band's name.

'Not yet. I'd like them to be a little more competent before they set foot on stage again.'

'Would it be a good thing to appear in some less fashionable location, for practice? Like a play touring the suburbs before reaching the capital?'

'Perhaps,' said Dominil, unsure of where this was going.

'Doctor Angus's grandson visited the castle only last week, and apparently he's involved in putting on concerts. Or gigs, as you'd call them. At small venues in Edinburgh.'

Doctor Angus was a venerable werewolf, respected throughout the clan. Dominil hadn't been aware that he had any family.

'Cameron is a medical student. He heard about Yum Yum Sugary Snacks from some of the younger werewolves in the castle – Beauty and Delicious did make quite an impression – and he asked me if they'd like to play in Edinburgh.' The Mistress of the Werewolves stopped, and looked unsure of herself. 'Of course, this might be no use to you.'

'It might be,' said Dominil. 'Do you know any more about his promotions?'

Verasa admitted she didn't, but told Dominil that Cameron would be arriving at the castle tomorrow and she'd introduce them.

'It might be a good idea. I'll talk to Cameron.'

Verasa was pleased to have done Dominil a favour. A moment later she looked troubled again. 'I just can't understand why Decembrius won't come to council meetings. Lucia is mortified. What can he possibly be doing in London?'

'Perhaps he's hoping to bump into Kalix,' suggested Dominil.

'Why?'

'He's attracted to her.'

'Attracted to Kalix?' Verasa looked puzzled. It seemed strange to her that anyone could be attracted to her waiflike, troubled daughter. 'Are you sure?'

'Quite sure.'

The Mistress of the Werewolves said no more about it, but later, reflecting on Dominil's words, she wasn't pleased. It was bad enough that the outlaw Gawain had formed a relationship with her daughter. Decembrius was hardly any better. He'd supported Sarapen against the wishes of the Great Council. He was neither respectable nor trustworthy. She didn't mind him being on the Great Council where she could keep an eye on him, but she didn't like him sniffing round Kalix.

Verasa had a brief yearning for Kalix to settle down and live out her life peacefully on the family estates. It was very brief. The Mistress of the Werewolves always wished the best for her family but really, she couldn't see Kalix coming to a peaceful end.

26

Kalix sat upstairs on the bus feeling small, lonely and hopeless. She didn't know what she was going to say to Gawain. She didn't even know if she should be going to meet him. In the days since she'd received his letter she seemed to have gone through every possible emotion: joy at hearing from him, rage at the memory of his betrayal, and misery at the knowledge that she might be about to experience it all again. Unable to sort out her feelings Kalix became depressed. As often happened, this led to serious anxiety, so that by the time she set out for Camberwell she hadn't eaten for days, hadn't slept properly, and was existing mainly on laudanum and Daniel's beer.

She shuddered in her seat. If only Gawain hadn't slept with her sister. She could have forgiven him anything else. But not Thrix. It was too much to take. Since then, Kalix's feelings towards Thrix had vacillated between hatred and a dull, hopeless antagonism. As for her feelings towards Gawain . . . They had begun their relationship when Kalix was just fourteen. That wasn't quite as taboo amongst werewolves as it would have been amongst humans, but it was still too young for the liking of the Thane. Gawain had been banished from the castle.

Kalix stared at her boots as the bus trundled through South London. Camberwell wasn't far from her home in Kennington.

She'd be there soon. What was Gawain going to say? Was he going to tell her he still loved her, and ask her back? What would she say then?

Kalix remembered how Gawain had put his life at risk by returning to the castle to look for her. She also remembered how he'd secretly made the journey to Kennington to watch over her while the clan was trying to capture her. Even when Gawain knew that Kalix hated him, he'd carried on the silent task of protecting her. He'd fought at her side during the great battle with Sarapen. He'd told her how much he loved her. But then he'd also started an affair with her sister.

Kalix just didn't know what to make of it all. She felt herself trembling, even though she'd dosed herself liberally with laudanum. She gnawed at her lip. To divert herself from her anxiety she turned to look out the window. The pane was heavily graffitied, not with ink or paint but with scratches. There were names deeply embedded in the glass. Kalix couldn't read them. The jagged letters were too stylised for her to make out.

When the bus arrived in Camberwell, Kalix crept off with her head bowed. A few passengers downstairs looked curiously at her as she passed. Though spring was near, it was a chilly day, with grey skies and a cold wind which tugged at Kalix's hair as she crossed the open expanse of Camberwell Green. The streets were lined with small shops, bars, and cheap letting agencies, and the pavements were busy. Outside a sports supplies shop Kalix had to pause as another bus pulled up and a great crowd of passengers surged towards it. She found herself jostled by a group of youths, young boys and their girlfriends in tracksuits and sportswear who shot Kalix contemptuous glances, not liking the look of her shabby clothes, or her mass of hair, or the ring through her nose.

Kalix ignored them, and hurried on round the corner As she trudged on, she felt like a great weight was crushing her into the ground. She turned the final corner, and halted abruptly. It struck her that, no matter what, she was still in love with Gawain. She experienced a moment of confusion and panic, then her anxiety lessened. At least she had some idea of what she felt. She was still in love with him. She remembered again that before Gawain had taken up with Thrix, he'd thought that Kalix herself had formed a new relationship. It didn't excuse his behaviour but it made it not quite so bad.

Kalix found the house. It was an old building, subdivided into small apartments and bedsits. Inside the porch there were a lot of doorbells, one for each apartment. Beside each was a small name tag, most of them illegible. Kalix didn't know which one to press so she tried pushing the front door. It swung open. As she made her way up the dark staircase, she put her hand in her pocket and clutched Gawain's letter for comfort. She could smell Gawain's werewolf scent and followed it up the stairs.

At the top of the building, she paused. This was it. She raised her hand to knock on the dark, stained door, then halted. Something was wrong. The smell wasn't right. Kalix knocked on the door. And then, without waiting for an answer, she smashed her hand into the wood, just above the lock. The door gave way, buckling under her tremendous strength. Kalix leapt inside, scared of what she might find.

She didn't have far to look. Gawain was lying in the hallway, face down. A great pool of dark blood had congealed around his body. Kalix threw herself at him, taking him by the shoulder and turning him over. Then she was forced to acknowledge what really she'd known before she broke down the door. She'd scented too much dried blood for it to be otherwise. Gawain had a terrible wound in his heart. He was dead, and he'd been dead for some time.

27

Kalix sat down beside the body, took hold of Gawain's cold hand, and started to cry. She didn't think about what might have happened, or what she should be doing; she just sat and cried.

She was still sitting by his dead body when a werewolf hunter kicked open the front door and rushed into the small flat. Kalix leapt to her feet and flew at him, kicking him so savagely in the midriff that he doubled over and crashed to the floor. She raised her foot to stamp on him. Even as human, she was strong enough to kill him. At that moment another hunter appeared at the door with a gun in his hand. He reacted quickly, aiming his pistol, but Kalix was too fast. Before he could squeeze the trigger she'd tackled him and they crashed back into the hall outside the flat, with Kalix using her fists to beat him to the ground. The hallway was dark but it lit up suddenly as someone threw the switch downstairs, and there was the sound of many heavily booted feet running up the stairs. Kalix hesitated for a second. Though always ready to fight, she was not quite as reckless in combat as a human as she was as a werewolf. She knew she was at a serious disadvantage in the open against so many armed hunters.

She turned and ran, arriving back in the apartment just as the first hunter was rising to his feet. Kalix struck him with her forearm and he slumped again to the floor. She slammed the door shut in the face of a group of hunters who'd appeared at the top of the stairs, and managed to bolt it. She sniffed the air. Winter was passing but the days were still short. The moon was already visible, a tiny sliver in the sky. Soon night would fall and she could transform. Then she would kill them all. Kalix had no thought of fleeing. She was going to kill every one of the hunters who'd killed Gawain.

The hunters started beating on the door, shouting out to their companion who lay at Kalix's feet. The door shook as they tried to force it open and Kalix desperately used her strength to hold it shut. She had to survive till night fell. She held the door shut with all her might but, though she was strong, her stamina was limited. As a werewolf Kalix was imbued with ferocious power, but as a girl she wasn't. She didn't take enough care of herself. She ate too little, and took too much laudanum. Her human muscles quickly began to tire, and the door began to splinter under the weight of blows.

'Shoot through the door!' someone shouted. Seconds later there was a loud explosion and a bullet tore through the woodwork, zipping past Kalix's ear. The young werewolf gasped in fear and anger. It was unusual for werewolf hunters to use silver bullets against a werewolf in human form. Kalix let go of the door and leapt backwards, but not before another bullet had ripped through the panel. It went straight through Kalix's left hand. She screamed in pain. The silver, so deadly to werewolves, burned as it penetrated her flesh. As the front door burst open,

Kalix hurdled Gawain's body and sprinted for the back of the small flat, ending up in a tiny kitchen with a small window so dark that whatever was outside couldn't be seen. Kalix heard another gunshot and carried on running. She leapt straight for the window. The glass and wood disintegrated, tearing her flesh as she went through. Next moment she found herself in mid-air, descending rapidly towards a small concrete yard, three floors below.

That instant, the sun dipped below the horizon and night fell. Kalix instantly changed into her werewolf form and landed on all fours, shaken, but undamaged. There were shouts from above as the hunters leaned out of the small broken window, looking for her.

'She's escaped!'

Kalix flattened herself against the wall, then jumped a long way into the air, grabbing hold of the roof of what appeared to be a garage. From there she leapt onto a drainpipe, then again towards another pipe. Now out of sight of the hunters, she made her way up to the roof. Kalix could no longer feel the pain in her damaged hand, nor the bruises from her fall. She'd entered her state of battle madness, and could feel only the overwhelming desire to destroy her enemies.

She ran across the roof, with the vague notion that there might be some sort of skylight. Finding none, she hurried to the edge of the roof and leaned over. She could smell the hunters downstairs, and hear their excited voices behind the broken window. Further off there was a hubbub of more voices, but Kalix ignored that, focusing on her prey. The werewolf swung herself off the roof, took one leap towards the drainpipe and another towards the shattered window. She crashed back into the tiny kitchen where she was confronted by a startled-looking hunter, a very tall man who looked down at her with dismay. Kalix could still smell Gawain's blood from along the hallway. It maddened her even more. She swung her claw at the hunter and her brutal strike almost decapitated him. As he fell his blood spurted over Kalix, covering her face as she rushed past him to find more victims.

As she arrived in the hallway the two remaining werewolf hunters were still taking their guns from their holsters. The first one never got any further. Kalix leapt on him, put her teeth round his throat, shook him like a doll, then threw his body at the remaining hunter. Both crashed backwards. The second hunter had by this time got his gun out and fired but it discharged harmlessly into the ceiling. Kalix leapt on her prey, first biting the wrist that held the gun then stamping with her taloned foot on the man's chest with such power that his ribs caved in and blood rushed from his mouth. Kalix took the other hunter in her jaws, tossed him against the wall then slashed his throat with her claws. Satisfied that he was dead, she turned to deal with the remaining hunter and was disappointed to find that he was dead as well. She growled, and ripped her talons through his throat anyway, just in case.

The dull hubbub of voices she'd heard earlier intensified, and there were footsteps on the stairs outside. Kalix looked up, an insane light in her eyes, hoping that more hunters were going to arrive so she could kill them. They all deserved to die for what they'd done to Gawain. The thought of Gawain pulled her back a little from her battle madness. His body still lay in the hallway. Kalix crossed again to his side, and stared down at his corpse. Surely she couldn't just leave him here.

There was a violent knocking from the end of the hallway.

'Police! Open the door.'

Had the police arrived a few seconds earlier Kalix would have killed them too, unable to differentiate between them and the werewolf hunters. But the sight of Gawain lying dead in the hallway had helped bring her back to reality. She looked around despairingly at the carnage everywhere, at the bodies, and the blood over all the walls and carpet, and felt the blood dripping from her own talons and jaws. She couldn't let herself be found like this. The repercussions of confronting the police as a werewolf would be endless. The trouble would never go away. She'd never be able to avenge Gawain. Kalix already intended to exact a terrible revenge for his death.

The door had been bolted again by the hunters as they chased Kalix inside, but, weakened as it was, it wouldn't keep out the police for more than a few seconds. Kalix took one last agonised look at her dead lover, then ran back to the kitchen. For the second time she exited via the window. Her werewolf agility allowed her to twist in mid-air and catch hold of the drainpipe.

She slid safely down to the ground, then vaulted onto a garage roof. From there she hurried across to the next rooftop. With her acute senses Kalix could still hear raised voices in the flat below as the police swarmed in. She leapt towards the next slate-grey roof, but even as she travelled in mid-air she sensed something that immediately caught her attention. In the street below, almost concealed behind a parked van, stood Duncan Douglas-MacPhee. Or so it seemed to Kalix, though she only saw his face for a fraction of a second. When Kalix landed she looked again, but there was no sign of him. The young werewolf longed to run back and find out what the Douglas-MacPhee was doing there, but at that moment another two police vans arrived in the street below. She had to leave. By the time police officers climbed out onto the roof, Kalix MacRinnalch was far away, hidden in the darkness, still covered in the blood of her victims.

28

Queen Malveria, First Minister Xakthan and Councillor Distikka walked through the gloriously illuminated Corridor of Splendour that connected the council chambers to the Queen's own reception rooms at the palace. The Corridor of Splendour was encrusted with diamonds. The fire elementals had a great many diamonds, of white, blue and yellow. Though valuable, they were not rare enough for the Queen to wear them in her realm, and she saved her diamond jewellery for visits to Earth. If she wanted to impress her fellow elementals, the Queen wore her Santorini necklace.

The Queen's heels clacked on the hard floor, in contrast to the soft tread of Xakthan, dressed as always in the restrained court attire of the Queen's councillors. The small figure of Distikka tramped along behind them. She wore boots that were more suited to warfare than palace meetings. That was unusual, but Distikka was an unusual woman. She was clad in a shirt of dark chain mail. An empty scabbard hung by her side. It was forbidden to carry weapons in the palace, and Distikka occasionally gave the impression that she resented it. She had, after all, been promoted to the council by the Queen after her efficient handling of the dissatisfied citizens of Cho, a village in the western desert. This had left most of the citizens dead, but, as the Queen said, it had certainly ended the problem. Distikka was now the only female elemental on the Queen's council, and Malveria had given her the title of Personal Adviser. She was not a popular figure among the other councillors, but was acknowledged to be efficient.

First Minister Xakthan was very popular. He'd always been a loyal ally of the Queen. It made it all the more galling that Xakthan now seemed reluctant to let drop a matter that she would much rather have avoided.

'First Minister,' said Malveria. 'Did I not make it clear that I didn't want to discuss the succession again?'

'I intended not to raise the matter. Our agenda was to discuss the site for our new armaments foundry, but . . .' He tailed off.

The Queen frowned, as she had done for much of the meeting. While discussing the factory, it had been mentioned by some councillor or other that the Sword-Makers' Guild, loyal supporters of the Queen, had expressed concerns in private as to whether she was ever going to produce an heir. That had started the whole discussion off again, much to the Queen's annoyance. She didn't enjoy hearing her Advisory Council discussing possible suitors.

'One is not a prize heifer from which to breed,' the Queen said with displeasure.

It quietened the council, but the problem wasn't going away. For some reason the entire Hiyasta nation, from the First Minister to the lowest serf, seemed to have developed an obsession with the heir to the throne.

It might have been better, reflected the Queen, if she hadn't slaughtered every one of her surviving relatives after the war. There might have been an heir in place by now. But it had been such a bloody affair, with all her relatives leading armies and factions against her, that slaughtering them all had seemed the natural thing to do. If she had left any of them alive, you could be sure they'd have led a rebellion by now, or tried to seize control of the Great Volcano, something that only a member of the Royal Family could do. Having left no members of her family alive, Malveria was very secure in her power over the volcano.

'If the Queen doesn't want to discuss the succession then the council should be quiet about it,' declared Distikka.

The Queen smiled. It was an opinion Distikka had voiced strongly several times in recent council meetings, in the face of far more experienced and senior councillors. The Queen appreciated her support. Distikka might be an odd character, with her small stature, chain mail and reputation for military violence, but she was proving to be a powerful supporter. She didn't take any nonsense from these elderly council members who seemed to want the Queen to breed with the first half-suitable aristocrat who came along. The Fire Queen was about to bid a gracious farewell to her advisers when she noticed her First Minister raising his eyebrows.

'Why are you raising your eyebrows in that pointed manner?'

'I believed we had concluded the meeting early in order for the Queen to deliver an opinion on the timing of the next Fire Festival.'

The Queen pursed her lips. It was true. She'd brought the meeting to an early close on the pretext that she had to perform these important calculations. The Fire Festival, or Vulcanalia, was an important event, but its precise timing was shrouded in mystery, requiring a combination of mathematics and divination that only the Queen could perform. Malveria, however, was far keener to get on with the business of importing her new evening attire. Bringing clothes from Thrix's fashion house into the realm of the fire elementals also required expertise and sorcerous skill. A few ill-chosen words in the summoning spell and one could easily end up with scorched fabric and missing buttons.

'Eh . . . other matters are pressing,' said the Queen. 'Kindly remove that stern look from your face, First Minister. The calculations will be done in good time, I assure you.'

'Time is pressing, and they can't be done by anyone else.'

The Queen tapped her foot on the diamond floor. She really should get on with making the calculations for the Vulcanalia, but she yearned to see her new evening gown. Thrix's drawings had been really fabulous.

'I can perform the necessary calculations,' said Distikka.

Xakthan looked at her dubiously. 'You can?'

Distikka nodded. She had short dark hair, rather boyishly cut.

It was a style the Queen herself had worn a long time ago, during the war, though for many years now her hair had been long and perfectly styled.

'Splendid,' cried Malveria. 'Well, Xakthan, no need to worry. Distikka will make the required calculations, while I attend to other, more pressing business. Good day.'

With that the Queen turned on her heel and departed swiftly, leaving behind her a rather discontented First Minister.

'It's all very irregular,' complained Xakthan, and sighed. 'The Queen has always calculated the date of the Fire Festival before.'

The First Minister was troubled. He wasn't the only councillor who'd noticed that the Queen seemed to be paying less and less attention to matters of state.

Malveria was already in her dressing room, pulling a dress from Thrix's warehouse through the dimensions. Her ladies-in-waiting gasped with pleasure as it appeared. The Queen was gratified. It was just what she needed for her upcoming evening of whist. She'd suffered some uncomfortable moments at the card tables recently, but the dress revived her spirits. She felt she was capable of anything while wearing such a beautiful garment.

Adding to the Queen's pleasure, today was one of the three days each week that Agrivex was absent from the palace.

'It is such a relief to be able to dress with the certain knowledge that my idiot niece will not barge in at some inappropriate moment,' said Malveria, to her nine dressers. They nodded in agreement, though none of them spoke. Preparing the Queen for an evening engagement was a serious matter, and there was no time for idle talk.

29

It hadn't been a good day for Moonglow. Believing that the weather was improving, she'd worn a thin black jacket to college. It was new – or rather, new from a charity shop – and she'd wanted to show it off. Unfortunately, after the early-morning sun, the day had turned very cold with some drizzle. Moonglow had shivered through her journey to college. Once there she realised she'd forgotten to update the file on the Sumerian poetry she was translating, and she'd left her handwritten notes at home. Moonglow's tutor held her in high regard and didn't think for a moment that she hadn't done the work, but Moonglow still felt bad.

Making things worse, Daniel had apparently decided to be in a bad mood all day. Though this mood seemed to be directed mainly at Moonglow, he perversely chose to spend every available minute with her, rather than leaving her alone. When Moonglow met her friend Alicia for lunch, Daniel stood resolutely beside her as she queued in the canteen, muttering about what a poor choice of food she'd made. Then he sat with them but spent the entire time in angry silence. It was a trying performance, one of Daniel's worst.

Moonglow knew why Daniel was in a bad mood. He was frustrated by her refusal to countenance having a relationship. She'd been tempted to inform him that hanging around a girl and being grumpy all the time wasn't the best way to encourage a romance, but she refrained. Really, Moonglow felt very sorry about the whole thing. She knew she'd been close to going out with Daniel. She'd given him some quite obvious signals. Then she'd abruptly ceased all contact, as it were, without explanation. She could understand why he felt frustrated.

She wondered if she should just tell Daniel about her bargain with the Fire Queen, but she hesitated. If she did tell him, she could imagine Daniel making things worse by doing something foolish like insulting Malveria. That could be a disaster.

Though King's College was a prestigious university there were parts of it that were surprisingly dilapidated. As Moonglow made her way into one of the older buildings she found herself walking through a large puddle. Round the next corridor she came across several workmen standing outside her tutor's room, struggling to contain the overflow from a leaking pipe in the ceiling. Her tutor was standing beside them, a resigned expression on his face.

'I told the Dean these pipes were about to go,' he said to the workmen. 'Tutorial's cancelled,' he added, to Moonglow.

Moonglow decided to go home. It hadn't been a very good day and it was probably wise to give up, particularly as it would allow her to sneak away from college without Daniel catching up. As she made her way through the rain to the Tube station, she wondered if they'd now be a couple had it not been for the Fire Queen's bargain. It was possible.

Moonglow's last relationship had been with Markus MacRinnalch. Markus was now Thane but there had been a time when he was in such a poor state of mental and physical health that he'd been fit for nothing. Moonglow's love and attention had helped him recover. As Markus was a charismatic figure, and beautiful, and a werewolf – which was quite thrilling – Moonglow had quickly fallen in love with him. Unfortunately, Markus had discarded her as soon as his health returned. It had been a shattering experience. Perhaps, after such an emotional disaster, it would be best not to have a boyfriend for a while. Or perhaps it would be best to have a nice stable boyfriend like Daniel who wouldn't do anything crazy. Moonglow wasn't sure. However, the bargain with Malveria had ended the possibility so there was no point even thinking about it.

The days were still short and darkness had fallen by the time Moonglow climbed out of the Tube station at Kennington. She shivered as she walked home through the backstreets of terraced houses. When she entered the living room, she put her bag down with a weary sigh and felt automatically for the light switch. As the light went on she froze in shock. Kalix was lying on the floor, unconscious. This wasn't a total surprise. Kalix had done it before, usually as a result of too much laudanum. But something worse had obviously happened, because there was an ugly wound on her hand, and blood was congealing around it on the carpet.

30

The werewolves of the Great Council of the MacRinnalch Clan sat in the long stone chamber at the heart of Castle MacRinnalch that had hosted their meetings for centuries. A huge log fire burned at one end of the chamber. Torches flickered on the walls and the stonework was draped with banners in the dark green

MacRinnalch tartan, some of them very ancient. The councillors sat round a huge circular oaken table, the heavy varnish of which could not disguise the damage caused by werewolf claws at past meetings. Over the centuries there had been many an angry scene in the chamber, and many powerful fists banged on the table in anger. Only a few months had passed since the ill-tempered encounter when Sarapen had left the chamber in a fury after failing to secure enough votes to make him Thane.

Since then, meetings had been more peaceful. The bad feelings had begun to dissipate. Though the three Barons had all come out against Markus as Thane, Verasa had welcomed them back at the end of the affair. The Mistress of the Werewolves had many years' experience in soothing angry werewolf barons. While she regretted the loss of life that the feud had caused, she didn't really resent their rebellion. A little dissension in the ranks of the clan and its allies wasn't such a terrible thing, on occasion. It helped to clear the air. Now Barons MacPhee and MacGregor had almost returned to their normal state of conviviality. Only Baron MacAllister still displayed any hostility, and he was very young. He'd soon learn to reconcile himself to the realities of life.

There were twelve werewolves in the great chamber, five short of the council's full complement. Butix and Delix were not expected to attend. Though Dominil had miraculously succeeded in dragging them to a meeting some months ago, they had no intention of returning. Kalix could not attend, still being outlawed. Marwanis was still furious about Sarapen's death and hadn't been to a meeting since the feud. The other missing council member was Decembrius, for whom there was no excuse.

The meeting began peacefully. There seemed to be no business of great importance to discuss, which made Thrix even more annoyed than usual to be there. As Baron MacPhee related a dull account of some drainage problems he'd been having on his estate, her thoughts turned to her business, and the problem of getting shops to stock her clothes. The public couldn't buy her clothes if shops didn't stock them, and Thrix had had very little success so far in persuading stores that they should.

The chief buyers for these stores are idiots, thought Thrix. They've got no taste. And you can't get through to them anyway.

Persuading the people who ordered the stock for the main

retailers was extremely difficult. Only recently, Thrix had seemed to be on the verge of a breakthrough. Kirsten Merkel, chief buyer for Eldrige's, one of the capital's most important outlets, had expressed an interest. If they decided to start stocking Thrix's clothes, it would be an enormous step forward. Unfortunately Merkel had gone quiet of late and wasn't returning Thrix's calls.

If only that damned journalist had written the piece she said she was going to write, thought Thrix, bitterly, and broadened her anger at clothes buyers to include fashion journalists as well. She stifled a sigh and waited for the meeting to end. She swept back the golden hair that hung in long tresses from her werewolf head and shoulders, and was surprised to find her mother asking her a question. Thrix looked at her mother quite blankly.

'Pardon?'

Verasa clamped her jaws together, the werewolf equivalent of pursing her lips. 'I was asking you what you felt about Dominil's comments.'

'What comments?'

Thrix felt the eyes of the council boring into her.

'Eh . . .'

'Do you feel in increased danger?' prompted the Mistress of the Werewolves.

Thrix still had no idea what they were talking about.

'From the Guild,' interjected Dominil coolly. 'I've been telling the council that the activity of the Avenaris Guild has not decreased as we anticipated.'

'I'm not in any danger. No werewolf hunter can trouble me.'

Dominil nodded. 'Probably not. Your powers of sorcery are a considerable defence. Although Princess Kabachetka did manage to overwhelm your defensive sorcery not long ago. But regardless of that, Butix, Delix, Kalix and any other werewolves travelling through London are in danger. Not only that, I believe I may be being targeted.'

'Have you been reading their private files again?'

Dominil nodded a second time. 'So perhaps we should do something about it.'

'I agree with Dominil,' said Markus, sounding keen.

His mother was less eager. 'There would be no danger if you all moved back to Scotland.'

'Butix and Delix will never return willingly. Kalix is forbidden to return.'

'I don't see why the twins can't come back to Scotland,' said Kurian, brother of the old Thane, and there were murmurs of agreement from the Barons. They tended to agree with Verasa's view that the MacRinnalch werewolves should stick to their homelands where they were safe, instead of moving to faraway cities where the Guild could trouble them.

'Would it be such a bad idea to take action against the Guild?' said Markus. Verasa looked with displeasure at her son but the young Thane met her gaze. 'We've been running from them for a long time. Always reacting to their attacks instead of initiating our own. Dominil's right. We should do something instead of waiting till they pick us off.'

But though the council took the Thane's opinion with due seriousness, they were more inclined to follow his mother's lead. Most of them were safe in their castles and keeps in Scotland. Why start a potentially damaging war with the Avenaris Guild?

'We lost enough werewolves in the feud,' growled old Baron MacPhee. 'I don't want to send more of my wolves to London to fight for Butix and Delix.'

Markus was frustrated. Even though he was Thane, the Barons inevitably favoured his mother's opinion over his own. He opened his great jaws to speak again but was interrupted by Thrix's mobile phone. The Enchantress jumped in her seat as it rang. It was a dreadful breach of etiquette and the Enchantress found herself confronted by eleven sets of angry werewolf eyes. Never before had anyone been careless enough to allow their phone to ring during a meeting. Barons MacPhee and MacAllister, both grown to adulthood long before mobile phones were invented, looked particularly outraged.

'Sorry,' mumbled Thrix. She groped on her chair for her phone, which was concealed beneath the werewolf fur of her thighs.

Markus looked at his sister with particular disdain. It was so like her to disrupt the affairs of the MacRinnalchs with her own outside concerns. As the respected members of the Great Council looked on in disgust, Thrix finally managed to locate her phone, picking up the tiny object in her paw with some difficulty.

'Sorry,' she muttered again, as the ring tone thundered out

with surprising volume, its electronic notes reverberating off the stone walls of the chamber. Finding it impossible to switch it off with her werewolf talons, the Enchantress did the next-best thing and fled from the chamber. The corridor outside was better lit and, free from the intimidating stares of her fellow werewolves, the Enchantress finally succeeded in answering the phone.

'Who is it?' she snapped angrily.

'Moonglow,' came the reply, which made her angrier.

'What's the idea of phoning me here?'

'Kalix is in trouble.'

'Sort it out yourself,' snarled the Enchantress.

'She's been shot,' said Moonglow. 'And I think she killed some hunters. And that's not all.'

The Enchantress gritted her fangs. Would the trouble surrounding Kalix never go away? She listened as Moonglow related the recent events. When she was finished, Thrix grunted in frustration and annoyance.

'I'll have to tell the council,' she said. 'I'll call you back.'

She snapped her phone shut and muttered a curse under her breath, before striding back into the council chamber. Thrix didn't bother to conceal her phone and she paid no attention to the hostile glares of her fellow council members. She sat down quite heavily, then looked directly at the Mistress of the Werewolves.

'Kalix has been shot. A silver bullet through the hand. As far as her flatmates can gather, she was involved in a fight with some hunters and killed them. Unfortunately the police arrived, so God knows what's going on there now.'

There were alarmed expressions all round the table. Kalix's reputation in battle was well known. If some scene of carnage had been discovered by the police, it was already a major incident, and exactly the sort of thing the clan tried to avoid.

'Is Kalix safe?' asked Verasa.

'I think so. But if it really was a silver bullet she'll need attention anyway. There's more. Gawain MacRinnalch is dead.'

There was a ripple of shock in the chamber. Gawain MacRinnalch was a notable werewolf. Though he'd been banished from the clan, he came from an ancient and well-respected family.

'Gawain is dead? Who killed him?' asked Tupan, eldest brother of the late Thane, and Dominil's father.

'The hunters, I suppose.'

'Are you sure it wasn't Kalix?' asked Tupan, voicing a thought that had already occurred to everyone. Given Kalix's instability, it wasn't an unreasonable assumption. Gawain had been a fierce warrior himself. He wasn't the sort of werewolf to fall easy prey to the Guild.

'My daughter does not murder her fellow werewolves,' growled Verasa, and looked menacing. 'You should return to London, Thrix. They'll need you there.'

The Enchantress nodded. Normally she'd have been pleased at the opportunity to return early, but only if it involved getting back to her fashion business. Hurrying back to deal with another Kalix-related incident was not what she had in mind, and she silently cursed her young sister for yet again plunging them all into crisis.

31

In the early afternoon Decembrius called into one of the book-maker's shops on Camden High Street. Betting on horse racing was a habit he'd developed recently. He staked only small amounts but found that the temporary excitement distracted him from his depression. The shop was small and clean, though the ten or so customers had a slightly shabby air about them. Decembrius looked out of place, though no one paid him much attention. Everyone was too preoccupied with the racing results that were displayed on the screens on the wall.

Decembrius took one of the tiny pens and scribbled a few words on a small betting slip, then queued at the counter to place his bet. The assistant took it swiftly and gave Decembrius a friendly smile. As he left the betting shop, Decembrius paused, musing on what he might do with his winnings if he was fortunate, before walking along to the Tube station and disappearing underground.

*

In East London he was warmly welcomed by Merchant MacDoig.

'Decembrius MacRinnalch! Come in, lad. I've hardly heard a word of you since the sad affair of Sarapen.' The Merchant shook his head. 'I've not long since come from the castle, doing some business for the Mistress of the Werewolves. It's not the same place these days, what with Markus as Thane. Not the same at all. Sarapen would have been much the better choice in my opinion.'

Merchant MacDoig would have undoubtedly said the opposite to the Mistress of the Werewolves. The Merchant's opinions were famously malleable, depending on which customer he wanted to please. There was something about his wholehearted manner that made this less objectionable than it might have been.

'I believe your mother was asking after you,' the Merchant added.

Decembrius didn't reply. Merchant MacDoig always liked to be abreast of the latest gossip but Decembrius wasn't going to provide him with any if he could help it. Sensing his reluctance to speak of clan affairs, the Merchant smiled affably, tapped his silver-headed cane on the wooden floorboards of his ancient shop, and asked the red-haired werewolf how he could help him.

'I have some books to sell. Old books. Valuable, I'd say.' Decembrius fished for the list he'd been given by the Douglas-MacPhees. It was very neatly handwritten. Even a degenerate gang of werewolves like the Douglas-MacPhees had been well educated in their youth. The Mistress of the Werewolves insisted on it, and Baron MacPhee made sure that all the wolves in his clan went to school.

The Merchant took a seat on an old leather couch, put on his reading glasses, and studied the list. After a few minutes he looked up, and told Decembrius that while books weren't his specialist subject, he imagined there were a few items on the list that might be of some value.

'More than a few, I'd say,' Decembrius responded. 'The sellers will want a reasonable price.'

'The sellers might have difficulty obtaining *any* price. I imagine they came by them under dubious circumstances?'

'I imagine they did,' agreed Decembrius.

Merchant MacDoig felt for his tobacco in the pouch of his embroidered waistcoat. In keeping with the rest of his attire, it belonged to a bygone era. He lit his pipe, and smiled. 'Would you care to tell me who's selling them?'

'No. But they're not the sort of werewolves you'd want to take advantage of.'

The Merchant chuckled. He had no fear of werewolves. 'I'm not a man that takes advantage, young Decembrius, as many a MacRinnalch can tell you. You wouldn't be working for the Douglas-MacPhees, would you?'

'I can't say.'

The Merchant chuckled louder. 'Last time they were here they tried to take a few things that didn't belong to them. I had to chase them off.'

Decembrius remained impassive, though inside he was wondering exactly what sort of protection, sorcerous or otherwise, the Merchant had, which could allow him to speak casually of chasing off the Douglas-MacPhees.

Merchant MacDoig took another glance at the list. 'Well, I'm sure we could come to some arrangement. If you'll give me a moment to consult a few books of my own, I'll see about offering a price.'

With that Merchant MacDoig rose rather stiffly to his feet and left the room, leaving Decembrius to gaze at the incredible clutter in the small shop: a mixture of ancient artefacts, jewellery, works of art, and items that didn't seem to fall into any specific category. Decembrius wasn't enjoying his mission as a go-between for the Douglas-MacPhees. He dreaded to think what his mother would say. Or Kalix. Decembrius knew that Kalix was a regular visitor to the Merchant's shop. He wondered if MacDoig might give him any information as to her whereabouts. He decided against asking. If he did, word would probably get back to the castle, somehow or other.

MacDoig returned, wearing the expression of a man who'd just received very bad news. He puffed seriously on his pipe and shook his head.

'Not so valuable after all, I'm afraid.'

'Have you seen Kalix recently?' blurted Decembrius, and regretted it immediately.

The Merchant eyed him with interest. 'Young Kalix MacRinnalch? Why do you ask?'

'No reason,' said Decembrius. To get over the embarrassment he proceeded to haggle as hard as he could over the value of the ancient books. But as he left the shop, having obtained a price that was barely satisfactory, he was still regretting the impulsiveness that had made him mention Kalix's name.

When he arrived home he put on the TV to check the racing results. The horse he'd backed had finished fifth. Decembrius immediately felt depressed, and spent the next hour or so thinking gloomily about Kalix, who, he admitted to himself, he wanted to see very much.

When night fell and the moon rose, he changed into his werewolf form, alone in his flat. It helped his mood a little, though he still felt depressed about losing his bet, and he still wanted Kalix.

32

Queen Malveria strolled through the Garden of Small Blue Flames in the company of her old friend and ally Duchess Gargamond. The garden was one of her favourite spots in the palace grounds. The tiny burning flowers were restful, and she'd had taken to walking there after her council meetings.

'You would not believe how my ministers of state badger me about producing an heir. One would think they might show more respect.'

'You do need an heir,' said the Duchess, rather mischievously.

The Fire Queen shuddered. 'Really, Gargamond, you would be astonished by some of the suggestions they've put forward for marriage. One simply can't help but wince. But enough of these tedious matters. Tell me, Duchess, are you really convinced by these slippers?'

The Duchess smiled. She was well aware of Malveria's penchant for clothes. She complimented Malveria's new shoes, pink court slippers with a delicate three-inch heel and the imperial motif picked out in silver thread. The Queen accepted the compliment graciously. It was wonderful the way Thrix MacRinnalch could breathe new life into even a relatively mundane item of clothing like court slippers. Once more she found herself profoundly grateful to the Enchantress's powers of fashion design. As for the Duchess, it was a mark of her loyal friendship that she could be relied on to offer a compliment when required.

Unfortunately, the Duchess's status as loyal friend was proving to be a problem. Her whist playing had not improved, and the Queen desperately wanted a new partner. It was a delicate matter. Duchess Gargamond would be mortally offended if the Queen were to discard her. Badly handled, it might even lead to a scandal in court circles, with gossip, whispering, and angry reports of the affair being transmitted from one end of the realm to the other. The great ladies of Malveria's court were very prone to gossip, whispering, and angry reports.

Malveria was the absolute ruler of the Hiyasta Nation. In theory, she could do whatever she liked. However, in reality there were many social constraints. The Duchess could not be treated badly. It was still remembered by the population that on one famous occasion the Duchess had ridden to the Queen's assistance at the head of a troop of cavalry, bringing much-needed relief when the Queen's forces were in danger of being outflanked. She remained a popular figure among the mass of ordinary fire elementals. Were the Queen to treat her unfairly, the population wouldn't like it.

The Queen smiled at the Duchess, opened her mouth, then closed it again. She really didn't know how to broach the subject. She turned away, ostensibly to look at a small flower of blue flame. The depressing thought struck her that she might be stuck with the Duchess as her card partner for ever, no matter how many foolish plays Gargamond made. She would find herself always on the losing side, forever having to accept the sympathies of her victorious opponents. Eventually Beau DeMortalis would make some comment. DeMortalis, the Duke of the Black Castle, was an infamous dandy and an equally infamous wit. Though he hadn't yet said anything cruel about the Queen's card playing, it was surely only a matter of time. And when he did, his comment was bound to be repeated endlessly. Malveria felt herself flushing with annoyance. She refused to let her card playing be a topic of mirth among her subjects.

The Queen was gathering her energies for another assault on the tricky subject when there was a sudden interruption. There was the sound of the swift patter of feet, and a few plants being trampled, then Agrivex rushed into view, breathing heavily.

'Aunt Malvie!' she called.

Queen Malveria drew herself up to her full height and cast her most ferocious stare at her niece. She had told her a thousand times not to call her Aunt Malvie, particularly in company.

'What do you mean by interrupting my pleasant walk, dismal niece?'

'Kalix has been shot by a silver bullet! You have to come and help her!'

'I beg your pardon?'

'Kalix!' yelled Vex, obviously agitated. 'I just went to her house and she was lying there all shot and groaning and stuff. Moonglow's really worried and the Enchantress is in Scotland so she needs some help right away!'

The Fire Queen blanched. She could feel the Duchess and the Duchess's handmaiden staring at them with interest. Though it had apparently escaped Vex's notice, werewolves were regarded as inferior creatures by the elementals. Not only that, the MacRinnalchs were historical enemies. The idea that the Fire Queen should drop everything and rush to their assistance was quite bizarre. Attempting to draw herself up further, and finding that she was already at full height, Malveria levitated a few inches off the ground.

'If Kalix MacRinnalch is in distress I'm quite sure her clan can assist her. Why you imagine I would trouble myself is beyond me, foolish girl.'

The Queen turned to the Duchess and smiled pleasantly. 'Agrivex is prone to these ridiculous fancies.'

Vex started to jump up and down, not an easy feat given the size and weight of her boots. 'But you healed her before, Aunty! You're great at healing werewolves! You have to come quickly!'

The tiniest flicker of flame appeared at the Queen's fingertips. 'Should you not be in class, learning something?'

'How can I learn anything when Kalix has been shot? We need to hurry!'

Duchess Gargamond coughed tactfully. 'Perhaps I should withdraw, to allow you time to talk to your niece?'

'Niece is an honorary title,' growled Malveria. 'I have not yet adopted her.'

She was about to abuse Vex further, but halted. By now the damage was done. Like all Hiyasta nobility, Duchess Gargamond was a skilful reader of auras. The Queen could successfully mask her own aura but Vex couldn't. To an experienced observer it was quite obvious that Vex was telling the truth when she claimed that the Queen had already healed werewolves. There was no point in pretending otherwise. Malveria nodded apologetically to the Duchess, glanced rather ruefully at the Duchess's handmaiden – a gossipy young elemental if ever she saw one – and apologised for cutting their meeting short. Gargamond and her attendant withdrew from the garden.

'Will I see you at the card table tonight?' called the Duchess.

'Most certainly,' replied the Queen, and smiled frigidly. 'I look forward to it.'

As she turned away the flames that played around Malveria's fingers grew longer. She glared at Vex with loathing. 'Why, you vile, irritating, annoying—'

'Can we go now?' cried Vex. 'I really think we should get there quickly.'

The Queen attempted to speak, but abandoned the attempt, something she seemed to be doing a lot recently. She snapped her fingers angrily, transporting both herself and her tactless niece from the burning land of the Hiyasta to the dampness of South London where they materialised abruptly in Moonglow's living room. There they found Kalix unconscious on the floor, Moonglow kneeling over her anxiously, and Daniel hovering around with a pot of tea in his hand.

'Would you like some tea?' asked Daniel.

'A cup of tea will not compensate for the dreadful indignity,' snapped the Queen.

Moonglow looked up, relieved to see Malveria. Moonglow had great faith in her healing powers.

'A werewolf hunter shot her through the hand.'

'Through the hand? That does not sound so serious.' Malveria glowered at Vex. 'You brought me here for this, you foolish girl? Have you any idea how much embarrassment you've caused me? What possessed you to run into the garden and blurt out such a thing in front of Gargamond and her handmaiden?'

'Kalix needs help!' protested Vex.

'She needs to stop filling herself with cheap wine and laudanum,' retorted the Fire Queen, 'which, I perceive, is more the cause of her current state of collapse than the minor wound.'

Moonglow rose to her feet, a bewildered look on her face. She couldn't understand the Queen's hostility. 'She probably needed some laudanum to dull the pain,' suggested Moonglow. 'I think a silver bullet would be agony for her, even a minor wound.'

'Pah,' snapped Malveria. 'As a young warrior I suffered worse on countless occasions. I may have given assistance to this degenerate young werewolf in the past but that does not mean you can send my niece rushing hither and thither to seek me out any time she has a minor scratch. I have a Kingdom to run. Now if you will excuse me—' Malveria raised her hand to snap her fingers, and dematerialise.

'I really think you should help,' said Moonglow forcefully. 'After all, we're helping your niece go to college.'

The Fire Queen's lips compressed in anger. 'Are you implying that you may stop helping her?'

She took a step towards Moonglow. In her high heels she towered over the student. 'You would be very unwise to think you can blackmail the Queen of the Hiyasta,' she snarled, sounding angrier than Moonglow or Daniel had ever heard her.

'Wooaahh,' said Daniel, stepping between Malveria and Moonglow. 'Queen Malveria, we're sorry if this is inconvenient. We didn't send Vex to find you; she just shot off on her own. But now you're here, could you take a look at the wound? Please? Everyone says silver is really bad for werewolves.'

Malveria glared at Daniel, though her expression softened a few degrees. She'd liked Daniel from the moment they'd met, because he'd called her beautiful and then blushed, which had amused her.

'Oh . . . very well,' she said.

Kalix's skinny frame lay raglike on the floor. Queen Malveria examined her wound. There was a lot of dried blood on the werewolf's hand and the flesh was torn where the bullet had passed through.

'The damage is not great,' said Malveria, 'though it will have been painful. The silver will indeed have burned her inside.'

She spoke a short sentence in an unknown language, then pressed her lips to Kalix's palm. Kalix's hand glowed faintly orange for a second or two.

The Queen rose gracefully. 'I have repaired the damage. The bones will heal in a few days. I've removed what traces of silver remained and the pain should be less. Now I must return to my palace and repair the terrible damage that Agrivex has done to my reputation.'

The Fire Queen pointed at Vex. 'You will return to class and when that is finished you will report to the throne room for whatever substantial punishment I decide on. Never bring such embarrassment on me again if you wish to remain alive.'

With barely a nod to Daniel, and without acknowledging Moonglow at all, Queen Malveria dematerialised, leaving the two students uncomfortable. They'd never seen Malveria quite so unfriendly before.

'Help me get Kalix into bed,' said Moonglow. 'Her hand's looking better. I suppose we should be grateful for that, anyway.'

33

Marwanis MacRinnalch didn't attend the council meeting but after it was over she visited Morag MacAllister, the Baron's young sister. Morag had received a full report of the proceedings, which she repeated to Marwanis.

Marwanis allowed herself a moment of sadness at the news of Gawain's death. At one time they'd been close.

'So Kalix was shot by a hunter? A shame she wasn't killed.' Marwanis's hatred for Kalix was uncompromising, and had grown rather than faded in the few months since she'd killed Sarapen.

Morag clicked a button on her computer.

'You really expect this to work with the Douglas MacPhees?' Marwanis asked.

'Video conferencing isn't hard,' said Morag.

Marwanis was sceptical. Werewolf children these days might be learning about the internet at school but the Douglas-MacPhees belonged to an earlier generation. She doubted whether any of them had any technical expertise. She was surprised when Duncan's face appeared in a small window on the screen.

Duncan grinned, and called over his shoulder, 'Well done, William. Got the wi-fi working.'

'Any sign of Kalix?'

Duncan scowled. 'No. And we're fed up with looking for her.'

'The reward's still on offer.'

Duncan nodded. Before his death Sarapen had offered the fantastic prize of four gold nobles for Kalix's head. A gold noble was an ancient Scottish coin, rare and extremely valuable, taken from the deepest vaults of the MacRinnalchs' wealth. It was a reward rich enough to tempt many werewolves.

'Have you met Ruraich?' asked Morag. Red Ruraich MacAndris was chieftain of the MacAndrises. He liked to think of himself as equal to the barons, though he wasn't.

'He's playing tonight.'

'Didn't you tell him I wanted to talk to him?'

'Ruraich's keen on his fiddle music. He wanted to go.'

Red Ruraich was a noted fiddler. While in London he'd find a pub with an open session and join in with the other musicians.

'Don't worry, he took his phone.'

'What?'

There was a bleeping sound from the computer. Morag clicked the mouse and Red Ruraich's face appeared on-screen. He was a large man, and his thick red hair hung down past his shoulders, giving him the unkempt look of a travelling musician. He greeted Morag and Marwanis, raising his voice to make himself heard over the noise in the background. Ruraich was apparently still at the music session in the pub and had withdrawn to one side of the room to call them.

'Shouldn't you go somewhere private to talk about werewolf affairs?'

Ruraich shrugged. 'If anyone overhears me they'll just think I'm crazy. So, has anyone found Kalix?'

'No,' said Duncan.

'Is anyone likely to?'

'I'm coming down to London with Morag,' said Marwanis. 'Between us we ought to be able to find her.'

Duncan Douglas-MacPhee was doubtful. 'The Enchantress hid her too well.'

An annoyed and confused conversation ensued, about the iniquity of the Enchantress hiding Kalix when she was an outlaw from the clan, and the Mistress of the Werewolves covering up for her. If clan law had been followed properly, Kalix would have been dragged back to the castle, not hidden by her relatives.

'It sickens me,' added Red Ruraich MacAndris. 'I saw her kill Sarapen with my own eyes. For even using a weapon like the Begravar knife she should be punished.'

The other werewolves nodded in agreement. The Begravar knife, an heirloom of the MacRinnalchs, had uniquely destructive powers. Its use was utterly forbidden.

'But she'll never be punished as long as Markus and Verasa protect her.'

Rhona's face appeared on-screen, over her brother's shoulder. 'We're not giving up. She killed our brother Fergus.'

Ruraich looked over his shoulder. 'The music's starting again. I have to go.'

'We'll be down in London soon,' said Morag.

Ruraich disconnected, followed swiftly by the Douglas-MacPhees.

'That went better than I expected,' observed Marwanis. 'Who says werewolves can't adapt to technology?'

'When are we going to London?' Morag asked.

'As soon as possible.'

'If the council finds out there will be trouble.'

'They won't find out,' said Marwanis firmly. 'Who's going to report anything to Markus or Verasa? Everyone despises them.'

34

Kalix woke up in her small bedroom and couldn't remember where she was. Though her eyes adjusted instantly to the darkness she felt disorientated. Not until she moved and her hand burned with pain did she remember what had happened. Gawain had been murdered. Immediately she was swamped with feelings of rage and despair. She leapt from her bed and transformed into her werewolf shape, ready to rush out and kill whoever had murdered Gawain. She halted. She didn't know who had killed him.

Kalix stood for a few moments in darkness, then put on the light, changed back to human, and sat on the bed. She looked at her hand. It hurt but the wound seemed to be healing rapidly. She remembered the dreadful pain as the silver bullet had penetrated her skin, a burning sensation the like of which she'd never experienced before. The memory made her shudder, and she reached out for the bottle of laudanum hidden in her small cabinet beside the bed. She took a sip and then, because she was feeling anxious, took another.

The young werewolf tried to piece together her thoughts. If she was to take revenge for Gawain's murder, she had to know who was responsible for his death. It could only have been the hunters. They must have come from the Guild. Kalix stood up. All she had to do was visit the Guild's headquarters, and then kill everyone there. Kalix realised that she didn't know where their headquarters were. She sat down again. Abruptly, a tidal wave of misery engulfed her as she realised that Gawain was really dead and she'd never see him again. Tears formed in her eyes. Kalix hated crying and would normally strive not to, but this time she let the tears flow. Full of misery, she took another sip of laudanum to dull the pain. She hung her head so that her huge mane of hair hung down like a curtain in front of her face. She closed her eyes but immediately the image of Gawain lying dead in the hallway began to haunt her and she opened them again in a panic. What would happen to Gawain now? Where was his body? Who would take it? She remembered the police flooding up the stairs and thought of Gawain lying in some police morgue, which made her feel even worse. She should have stayed where she was, killed them all and taken Gawain's body away to safety.

Then she remembered that as she'd fled she'd seen one of the Douglas-MacPhees. What had he been doing there? Had he killed Gawain? Kalix felt confused. The young werewolf sipped more laudanum, and felt scared of everything. Any strong emotion tended to bring on anxiety and when she felt herself in its clutches she would panic, which made it worse. The anxiety and the panic fed off each other. She clenched her fists, and tried to pull herself together. Kalix slammed her bottle of laudanum down on the cabinet and rose to her feet.

'I'm not going to panic,' she said to herself. 'I refuse to panic. Gawain is dead and I'm going to take revenge and nothing is going to stop me.'

But even as she thought this she was aware that she was lying to herself. The walls were starting to close in and a disturbing darkness was visible at the periphery of her vision. Her palms began to sweat.

'I'm not going to panic,' she repeated, this time out loud, 'and I don't need laudanum. I'm going to take revenge.'

She sat down again and drank some more laudanum. It made her feel sick. She had a sudden memory of the huge pool of dried blood under Gawain's body, a sight so horrifying that she wished she could somehow go back in time and make it never happen. The anxiety grew worse. Kalix screwed up her face and changed back into her werewolf shape. It helped a little and she felt fierce again but it didn't last. Kalix clumsily manipulated her bottle of laudanum into her werewolf paw, drank some more, then lay down. Exhausted by her exertions and her wound, worn out with anxiety and dosed with a great deal of laudanum, Kalix abandoned her thoughts of immediate revenge. She curled up on her bed, drew the quilt over her head to protect her from the world, and fell into a stupor.

35

Markus had enjoyed his first few months as Thane. Since being elected as head of the clan he'd reorganised business affairs to his liking. At one time the Mistress of the Werewolves had expected him to look after much of the clan's property. Markus always found this tedious and had now delegated the task to others. He was an enthusiastic supporter of the planned fundraising event. Like his mother, Markus was a great opera fan, excited at the prospect of Felicori coming to perform.

He was listening to a recording of Felicori when Dominil appeared at his door. He greeted her with a show of conviviality, which was rather forced. Markus often felt uncomfortable in Dominil's presence. Many people did. Her frozen demeanour didn't help to put a person at ease. Even the werewolves in the castle who'd known her for a long time rarely felt much warmth towards her, nor did they receive any warmth back. She preferred to keep her own company and was reputed to spend her time working on her computer skills and translating Latin poetry. That was odd in itself. The Latin poetry and computer skills didn't seem to sit easily together as interests, though both might be seen as indications of her intellect. Dominil's intelligence was commonly acknowledged: it didn't make her any more popular.

'We should do something about the Avenaris Guild,' said Dominil, coming straight to the point.

'The council didn't think so.'

Markus smiled, which made him look young. He had soft, thick chestnut hair, curling round his shoulders. He was rather pretty for a werewolf, which wasn't really a good attribute for the Thane.

'They didn't,' agreed Dominil, 'but the council members are safe in their castles and keeps. It's different in London. I'm offended that I should be attacked. Furthermore, it's making my work with Yum Yum Sugary Snacks difficult. We should move against the hunters.'

'The council has never agreed to pre-emptive action. You know how much my mother wants us all to fit in with the world. She'll never consent to any sort of offensive.'

Dominil waited till Markus offered her a glass of whisky. She sipped from it before speaking again.

'Last week four new hunters flew in from Croatia. They're being trained specifically to search for Butix, Delix and me.'

'How do you know that?'

106

'I still have access to the Guild's computers.'

Markus nodded. It was said that Dominil's prodigious computer skills extended to hacking, which was a mysterious art to Markus and quite troubling in its way. He wondered if Dominil might have reason to examine any of his own private files. There were many things on his computer he wouldn't want her to see. Pictures of him in women's clothing, for instance, for which he had a liking. Suddenly uncomfortable, Markus paced around the room.

'My mother would really rather you all returned to Scotland.'

'I know. But I don't intend to be chased out of London.'

'Attacking werewolf hunters doesn't sit well with integrating into society.'

'Perhaps not. Although I don't see why werewolves killing hunters is any more likely to expose us to society than hunters killing us. We just need to do it discreetly.'

'We could raise the matter again at the next meeting,' Markus suggested.

'I have something else in mind. The Guild pays its hunters a bonus each time they kill a werewolf. I suggest we turn that around.' Dominil sipped her whisky. For a second there was an expression on her face that could almost have been described as a smile. 'I'll kill the hunters and you pay me for it.'

Markus laughed. 'That's not a bad idea but no one's going to agree to it.'

'No one has to agree. As Thane you have access to the clan's money. You can pay me in secret.'

Markus stared at the white-haired werewolf, realising that she was serious. 'Just how offended are you that you were attacked?'

'Very offended,' replied Dominil. 'But that's not my main reason. It's the logical thing to do. There's no point waiting for the Avenaris Guild to attack Beauty, Delicious and me. I'm certain it's going to happen so I'd be better simply preventing it.'

Markus didn't know how to reply. He was in favour of killing werewolf hunters but dreaded to think what his mother would say if she learned of the scheme. Besides, he wasn't entirely convinced by Dominil's reasoning. Was she really in such danger that she needed to embark on a campaign of assassination? Perhaps she just wanted to earn money. It was whispered around the castle that Dominil's father, Tupan, wasn't liberal with his wealth. Though Dominil was now twenty-six he hadn't turned over any substantial portion to her.

There was a long silence.

'So are you prepared to pay me for killing werewolf hunters?'

'I'll need to think about it.'

'Kindly think about it quickly,' said Dominil.

36

Captain Easterly was no longer in the army but the title of captain still lingered. Partly this was because the staff at the magazine regarded it as strange that an ex-soldier was now deputy editor in charge of fashion. When he first arrived there was suspicion; it was widely reported that he'd only got the job because of his father's connections. The term 'captain' had been used about him in a rather derogatory way. But he'd won them over by proving to be good at his job. His connections helped rather than hindered his work. He seemed to have no problems procuring samples, tickets, invitations and anything else that his staff needed to make their work run smoothly. At thirty-five he was young enough to fit in with his readership and old enough not to be carried away by ridiculous fads, and he brought to the men's fashion pages a solid style that they'd previously lacked. He was now well liked, and though the title of captain had stuck, it was no longer used in a derogatory manner.

As for his simultaneous career as a werewolf hunter, his fellow employees were completely in the dark. Easterly was far too discreet to let anything about his other life slip through into his life at the magazine. The need for discretion was one of several reasons he regretted living in the same apartment block as Albermarle. His distant cousin was a fellow member of the Avenaris Guild who, in Easterly's eyes, was everything a werewolf hunter shouldn't be: indiscreet, foolish, juvenile and, as far as could be ascertained, mainly interested in watching science fiction on TV. Albermarle had done good service for the Guild in intelligence gathering but Easterly still found it difficult to believe that his cousin was actually going into active service. He didn't like Albermarle at all, but would still be sorry to hear that he'd had his neck broken by a werewolf.

Easterly took the unusual step of visiting his cousin. They both lived in a large block by the river in the London borough of Chelsea. It was an expensive area to live in, which made Easterly regret that the same family money that had supported him throughout his career was also available to Albermarle, albeit not quite so much. Albermarle had inherited enough money to let him overeat, buy endless computers and a host of paraphernalia, which Easterly found almost inexplicable. His three-bedroom apartment was crammed with an incredible array of comics, figurines, DVDs and so on, more suitable for a fifteen-year-old boy than a grown man. Albermarle had been to Oxford, and done well there. There was no disputing his intellect. But, as Easterly thought when Albermarle opened the door with a slice of pizza in one hand and a comic in the other, raw intellect didn't count for everything in the real world.

'What do you want?' asked Albermarle, suspiciously.

'You not to get yourself killed,' replied Easterly. 'Or at least, not while I'm meant to be looking after you.'

37

Thrix's assistant Ann wasn't surprised to receive a phone call from her employer informing her that the Enchantress would be returning home earlier than expected. She knew Thrix resented the time she was obliged to spend away from work. She also knew that Thrix was a werewolf; Ann was the only person to whom Thrix had volunteered this information. Thrix was almost ninety years old, which was still young in werewolf terms. She had the appearance of a thirty-year-old woman, and a glamorous one at that. Her mother Verasa was over 300 years old, and she hadn't lost her style either.

Ann was surprised at Thrix's poor temper. An early departure from Castle MacRinnalch should have put her in a good mood.

'I've been dragged back into clan affairs,' explained Thrix

testily, on the phone, while driving into London from the airport. 'No matter how I try and distance myself, Kalix always drags me back in.'

Thrix lowered her voice. 'And Gawain's dead.'

Ann wasn't sure what to say. She knew Thrix didn't remember her affair with Gawain as a particularly glorious experience. It had involved deceiving her sister and her mother, and cavorting with a banished werewolf. A werewolf to whom, Ann suspected, Thrix had become much more attached than she'd ever admitted. A werewolf who'd abandoned her for Kalix at the earliest opportunity. No wonder Thrix didn't remember the affair fondly. Ann wouldn't have been too surprised to learn that Thrix had killed him herself.

She made arrangements to postpone Thrix's business engagements while her employer went about the difficult business of smoothing over the difficulties in which the MacRinnalch Clan now found itself. The police were in possession of a werewolf body, and that in itself was troubling. A werewolf body looked much the same as a human one, even on the inside, but there were certain organic and chemical differences which a careful autopsy might discover. Even if that didn't happen, Gawain's body had been discovered in the midst of a scene of carnage. His identity, and his death, were now the subject of a police inquiry. Gawain had one living relative in Scotland: his werewolf sister, who was attending St Andrew's University. Neither she nor the clan would welcome close investigation.

'There's no telling where this might end,' Thrix told Ann. She cursed her sister again, and Gawain for good measure.

Thrix had agreed to visit the crime scene, after she was urged to by her mother. With her sorcerous powers, she might learn more about the affair. She arrived home, checked her email, and showered. Then, knowing that she couldn't put it off any longer, she headed for Camberwell.

The Enchantress could transport herself through space for short distances. It wasn't something she enjoyed. When Malveria teleported the journey was swift and painless, but the Enchantress's powers of dimensional travel were not equal to those of the Fire Queen. She had to drag herself through a cold, hostile vacuum, full of unfriendly shapes and disturbing whispers. The short journey drained her and when she materialised in Gawain's flat her mood worsened. The bodies were gone but the blood remained, and the overwhelming scent of death was everywhere.

Thrix, perfectly attired in a blue dress with matching heels, looked and felt out of place in the tiny apartment, with grime on the woodwork and blood on the walls. She could still smell Kalix's presence, Gawain's death, and the hunters' blood. And there was something else. More werewolves. Whose scent was that? She sniffed again, but couldn't make it out. Though it was daylight, Thrix transformed into her werewolf shape. No other MacRinnalch could transform during daylight, but Thrix had learned how to from Minerva MacRinnalch a long time ago. It increased her sense of smell by a magnitude. Now the various scents were clearer. The Douglas-MacPhees had been here. So had Decembrius MacRinnalch. Thrix prowled the flat, absorbing it all. There were so many scents that it was difficult to distinguish them all. Thrix's werewolf brow furrowed, and she got down on all fours, padding around, her nose to the floor. As a werewolf Thrix was still blonde, and her long hair, which had once captivated her lover Gawain, trailed along the floor as she investigated the scene of his recent violent death.

38

Kalix woke in the afternoon. The weak sunlight made her blink. It was some days since she'd seen daylight. How many days? She wasn't sure. She couldn't remember exactly how long it was since she'd found Gawain. She climbed quickly to her feet. At least her mind had cleared. She intended to find out who killed Gawain, and then take her revenge.

Kalix snarled, thinking of revenge, and even in her human form there was something disturbing about her expression. Like all the MacRinnalch women, Kalix had a very wide mouth, red lips, and a lot of white teeth. Enough to give a powerful bite, even before transforming.

Kalix crossed to the middle of her room and stood there uncertainly. Despite her determination, she was unsure how to proceed. How could she find the killer? Had Gawain been murdered by the Avenaris Guild? It seemed most likely, but Kalix wasn't sure. The men who'd arrived while she'd been there had certainly been professional werewolf hunters, which meant they were probably from the Guild, but had they been the killers? Gawain had already been dead when they arrived. Why would the killers come back? To look for more werewolves? Kalix wasn't sure. They might have been hunting for Gawain, not knowing he was already dead. Someone else might have killed him. Like the Douglas-MacPhees, she thought, remembering that she'd seen Duncan skulking in the shadows as she'd fled. He was definitely a possible candidate.

Kalix felt baffled, then had a sudden bolt of inspiration. She crossed over to the small table, one of the few pieces of furniture in her bare room, and took her journal from the drawer. She turned to the back of the book, and on a fresh page wrote 'list of suspects for killing gawain'. It took her a long time to form each letter and complete each word, but she stuck to her task, determined to make progress. She sipped some laudanum, from habit, and drew a line under her title. Then she wrote 'the guild', and under that 'duncan douglas-macphee'. After some consideration, she wrote 'other douglas-macphees'.

Kalix shivered. The room was cold. She slipped her old coat round her shoulders and looked at her page. She was quite pleased at her progress. Then, in her shaky script, she wrote 'Thrix'. Because it seemed to Kalix that her sister might have been involved somehow. She wasn't sure why. She just felt suspicious of her. Thrix might have been trying to win Gawain back and killed him when he spurned her. Kalix wouldn't put it past her sister. She'd proved her treacherous nature in the past.

It occurred to Kalix that Gawain had still been banished and her mother, the Mistress of the Werewolves, hadn't approved of Kalix having a relationship with a banished werewolf. She'd never approved of Gawain. Markus had never liked him either. Kalix immediately felt suspicious. What if the clan had killed Gawain? They might have been trying to kidnap him and take him back to Scotland to punish him for having a relationship with her. But that wasn't very likely. Or was it? Kalix began to feel confused. She'd started the list to help clear her thoughts but now it was becoming more complicated. Suddenly she felt angry, and wished that the murderer was right in front of her, because then she would rip him apart, no matter who it was. That was something she could certainly do. When Kalix found Gawain's murderer she'd tear their head from their shoulders, and nothing would stop her.

Kalix looked at her list again. She took another sip of laudanum, more this time. She hadn't eaten for several days and the opiate coursed quickly through her thin frame, instantly affecting her concentration. She shook her head, and felt angry at herself for not being intelligent enough to know what to do. She thought of Gawain's body again, and the smell of death in his apartment. All of a sudden the creeping anxiety that had been playing around the edge of her consciousness since she woke expanded in a fearful manner and threatened to overwhelm her. Kalix gritted her teeth. She couldn't let herself give in to the anxiety. She dropped the pen, then fingered the ring that pierced her nose, turning it round sharply, a nervous habit she'd picked up recently.

Suddenly it was all too much. Kalix stood up as if to flee, then realised she had nowhere to go. Her breathing became irregular, and it sounded like she couldn't quite catch her breath. Her palms became damp with sweat and her limbs went very cold. Her chest beat furiously as her heart pounded. Kalix was now in the grip of anxiety. When it came on, it fed on itself, and she became more and more anxious about being anxious. Now trembling quite violently, she thrust her hand into the drawer and grabbed the small knife hidden there. Then, naked save for the coat that was draped round her shoulders, she made a short deep cut on her thigh. The skin opened and blood flowed out. Kalix watched it flow down her leg. Immediately she felt a little better. Not well, but better. Her anxiety receded a little. She crossed to the bed, not caring about the blood that stained the sheet, dragged the quilt over her, drank some more laudanum, and sat back against the wall. The warm blood on her leg soothed her. It was a relief to feel better. She opened her eyes and tried to rise, to get back to her list of suspects. But it was too difficult. She was too full of laudanum. The young werewolf closed her eyes and drifted off into an intoxicated slumber, blood still seeping from the cut in her thigh.

39

Beauty and Delicious were bored and dissatisfied. They sat in their living room in Camden, on furniture which, while expensive, had been badly worn by their continual partying.

'We could watch some TV,' suggested Beauty.

'I'm too bored to watch TV,' replied Delicious.

There was a long pause.

'We could go and have our hair done.'

'We did that yesterday.'

'Oh.' Beauty took a strand of hair in her fingers and examined it. It was very long, and a violent blue colour. Delicious's hair was also long, and a very shocking pink. Despite intensive colouring their hair remained in good condition. The stylist they frequented was more used to taking care of models, actresses and young society women than two inebriates from Camden, but the twins were very wealthy and quite prepared to pay any amount of money to have their hair looked after well. Other clients were now used to the sight of Beauty and Delicious slumped almost unconscious in their chairs while a team of experts surrounded them: washing, styling, colouring and conditioning with infinite care. Their hairdresser was fond of them. As well as being wealthy, they brought some exotic colour to his establishment.

'We could try finishing the new song.'

'I hate the new song.'

Beauty sighed. 'So do I.'

The twins lapsed into silence again, and sipped idly from a bottle of the MacRinnalch malt whisky. It was sent to them from Castle MacRinnalch, though not as frequently as they'd have liked.

'It's all Dominil's fault,' exclaimed Delicious. 'We should be playing more gigs. Then we wouldn't be bored.'

'She's useless as a manager.'

'Worst manager ever.'

A key sounded in the lock. Dominil strode into the house, placed her suitcase carefully on the floor, and regarded the sisters with distaste. The sisters glared back at her.

'You're the worst manager ever,' said Delicious.

Dominil didn't reply.

'And we're bored,' added Beauty, 'because you won't let us play more gigs.'

'You have plenty to do,' said Dominil. 'I left you with clear instructions on rehearsal and musical composition.'

The twins sniggered. Only Dominil would use a phrase like 'musical composition'.

Beauty dragged herself upright in her chair. 'We want to play. You were keen enough for us to play earlier. You practically forced us onstage before we were ready. Now you won't get us more gigs. Why not?'

'She just got us one gig so we'd vote for Markus as Thane,' said Delicious, accusingly.

Dominil pressed her lips together with annoyance. 'We have been over this many times. Your first gig was necessary to resurrect your careers. It gave you focus for getting your band back together. Now I'd like you to improve. Various music journalists have expressed an interest in seeing you play and I don't want you to disappoint them.'

Beauty and Delicious looked blank.

Dominil sighed. 'I've got you a gig in Edinburgh.'

'Edinburgh? Who wants to play there?'

'Many people. It's a vibrant city.'

Beauty and Delicious were unenthusiastic. Travelling to Edinburgh seemed like a lot of trouble.

'I hate Scotland. It's too far away.'

'It's less than an hour by air. And how can you hate Scotland? You're Scottish.'

'There's too much heather,' said Beauty. 'And kilts.'

'It's full of castles and stuff,' said Delicious. 'I hate castles.'

'You're talking nonsense,' replied Dominil, calmly. 'Edinburgh is a modern city, the same as cities everywhere.' She paused. 'I admit it does have a large castle right in the middle. Which may be surrounded by men in kilts. And some heather. But apart from that it's a modern city. I thought you'd be pleased to play at a gig promoted by a fellow MacRinnalch werewolf.'

'Who is he?'

'Cameron MacRinnalch. Doctor Angus's grandson. He's a student at the medical faculty at Edinburgh University. He puts on gigs in his spare time.' Dominil paused, reflecting that she didn't really approve of a student putting on gigs in his spare time. It seemed to imply a lack of application to his studies. Nonetheless, it suited her purpose.

'You'll be less in danger of giving away your werewolf nature and it will be an excellent opportunity to hone your onstage skills. Now—' Dominil bent down to pick up a CD from the floor, placing it safely on the cabinet beside her. 'I suggest we work out an intensified schedule of rehearsal. We have no time to waste.'

Beauty and Delicious sighed. Anything that involved Dominil also involved a seemingly endless amount of work, and they suddenly felt less enthusiastic about playing than they had before.

Dominil left them to their dissatisfaction, retreating upstairs to the room she used as an office. She was hoping there'd be a message from a woman in Singapore whom she'd first met on a Perl forum some years ago and had stayed in touch with since. The woman was particularly skilful at cracking passwords, and ran a small private on-line business providing these passwords to people who were prepared to pay. The message was there. Dominil copied it with satisfaction. The Avenaris Guild kept upgrading their on-line security but, with help from her acquaintance in Singapore, Dominil remained one step ahead.

Dominil was interrupted several times by her phone ringing. Each time she looked at the screen it said the caller was Pete. Pete was the guitarist in Yum Yum Sugary Snacks. The first few times she ignored it. Finally she answered in frustration.

'Stop ringing me. I'm busy.' Dominil switched off her phone and returned to her work. After another twenty minutes she allowed herself the tiniest flicker of a smile, satisfied with her accomplishments. Having read more of the private files of the Guild, she now had the address of a werewolf hunter she'd like to meet.

'I'll be seeing you soon,' muttered Dominil.

She was interrupted by Beauty and Delicious stomping noisily into the room.

'Hey, we just heard from Pete!' cried Beauty. 'He says he can't play guitar any more!'

'What?'

'He's too depressed to play!' yelled Delicious. 'Did you ever hear anything like it?'

'How can he be too depressed to play?' demanded Beauty. 'Why is he depressed?'

They stared at Dominil expectantly.

'Why would you expect me to know?'

'You're our manager. You should know stuff like that. Why is our guitarist too depressed to play?'

'I've no idea,' said Dominil defensively.

'It's probably some woman,' said Beauty. 'Has he been seeing some woman?'

'I bet it's that barmaid at the Red Lion,' declared Delicious. 'Dominil, has the barmaid from the Red Lion broken Pete's heart?'

'I really don't know.'

'Well, you should find out. You can't just let our guitarist go around being broken-hearted and depressed. You have to sort it out.'

'I will,' said Dominil, menacingly.

40

Thrix was trying to design a cocktail dress. Though the Enchantress hated any interruption to her work, she had to admit that inspiration had deserted her. She sat back and drummed her fingers on the desk. Dealing with the mess surrounding Gawain's death was exceptionally troublesome, and it wasn't over yet. There was no sorcery that would easily make everything better once the police had taken away the body of a murder victim. The Mistress of the Werewolves wanted Gawain's body sent back to Scotland for a decent werewolf burial. Thrix could, conceivably, transport herself into the police mortuary and send the body back. But what then? The police were already in the middle of their investigation. What was going to happen if one of the bodies mysteriously disappeared?

Thrix wondered how their investigation was progressing. Was Kalix involved? If the police had a description of her from the crime scene, then that was another serious problem.

There was a sudden flash of light in the office, accompanied

117

by the faint aroma of jasmine, and there stood the Fire Queen. She wore a white evening dress under a stylish white coat and her dark features were set off beautifully by a tiny white hat.

'Thrix, my esteemed friend!' cried Malveria. 'You have returned from Scotland just in time!'

'Just in time for what?'

'To admire the splendid opera ensemble I am wearing. When you provided me with this beauteous white dress I was unsure of the correct occasion on which to wear it but now the occasion has presented itself admirably. I am off to see *The Marriage of Figaro* in the company of Lady Flamina, Beau DeMortalis and his companion Prince Garamlock.'

'Do they know what they're in for?'

'No. But I have inflamed their curiosity with tales of operatic splendour and I will impress them even more with this magnificent outfit! You are aware that Mr Felicori is singing once more?'

Thrix wasn't. Since Gawain's death she hadn't given any thought to her mother's project, or to Felicori.

'You do not seem remarkably happy.' The Queen perched elegantly on the edge of Thrix's table, and examined herself with satisfaction in the large mirror on the opposite wall. 'Fortunately I have some time to spare so you may unburden yourself of your unhappiness. Is it connected to the shooting of Kalix and the death of Gawain?'

'Partly. Incidentally, thanks for healing her hand.'

'A minor healing only. Hardly worth mentioning, had it not humiliated me in front of the entire Hiyasta nation.'

According to the Queen, since Vex's intervention in the garden of small blue flames, word had spread like wildfire around the Hiyasta nation that the Queen was in the habit of healing MacRinnalch werewolves.

'I shall never recover from the disgrace. It is partially for this reason that I have fled to the opera. That, and to avoid my Advisory Council.'

'Why?'

'Because they want me to marry and reproduce. I have left the very capable Distikka to hold the fort, as it were. So what is happening in the sad affair of Gawain?'

'I went to the scene of the crime.'

The Queen leaned forward with interest. 'Did you discern who did the killing?'

'No. All I discerned was a lot of stale blood. Gawain must have been dead for days when Kalix found him. With the number of people who'd been there since, I couldn't make out much. I don't know who killed Gawain or how he died. I won't know unless I examine the body. I'm not keen to do that.'

The Enchantress tried to explain about the potential difficulties involved in infiltrating the police morgue but the Queen found this quite hard to follow.

'It all sounds very trying. And of course, it is Gawain. Who, not so long ago, you were very involved with.'

'I was not very involved with him. We had a brief affair.'

'Before he went off with Kalix.'

'Thanks for reminding me. Again.'

The Queen decided it was time to change the subject. 'It's such a shame you cannot come to the opera tonight. I am expecting another sensational performance from Mr Felicori. Such a wonderful singer! After the performance I will again urge him to attend your mother's event in Edinburgh. I'm wearing his resistance down, I am quite certain of it.'

This made Thrix smile. She could believe it. She thanked the Queen quite sincerely for her efforts to recruit Felicori, because Thrix herself didn't feel up to the task.

'And perhaps, at the opera,' continued the Fire Queen, 'I may meet a suitable man to take your mind off your current problems?' She beamed at her own suggestion, which was met by a cold stare from the Enchantress.

'I don't need you to set me up with anyone, Malveria.'

'Of course you do not. A successful woman of your golden beauty needs no assistance. Given enough time, I am quite certain a suitable man will come along who may erase the sad memory of your long string of romantic failures.'

'Thanks.'

'But perhaps the process could be hurried along a little. After all, you will have much to celebrate very soon, when the huge department store buys all your clothes. Why does that make you frown, Enchantress?'

'The deal seems to be off. They're not returning my calls.'

Malveria was mystified. 'But your clothes are so beautiful, Enchantress. Surely this buyer from the department store must purchase them?'

'There's a lot of competition. I'm not the only one trying to get them to stock my designs.'

'They should bow down before your superior styles.'

'They won't.'

'Could we attack them?' suggested Malveria brightly. 'I can have a warehouseful of enemy clothes in flames in seconds.'

Thrix smiled. Malveria's term 'enemy clothes' wasn't far off the way she'd come to think of her fellow designers' efforts.

'I thought the deal was done. Eldridge's would have bought my summer line if Susi Surmata had just written her article.'

'Now I am baffled again. Who is this Susi Surmata?'

'A fashion journalist. She started off as an anonymous blogger and now she's the most influential style-writer in the country. She's so successful it's annoying. If she enthuses about something, buyers just line up to stock it. And she did say she'd review my new collection.' Thrix sighed. 'I actually told the buyer at Eldridge's that Susi Surmata was going to write about me, and she said "Fine, when that happens I'll buy your collection." Which would have been great if Susi hadn't then failed to write the article. Now the buyer thinks I was making the whole thing up.'

Queen Malveria looked stern. 'We cannot let this go unpunished. Take me to this wretched Surmata woman and I will cause burning needles to pierce her flesh.'

'I was thinking more of buying her lunch.'

Malveria was disappointed. 'I feel she deserves the burning needles.'

'Well, I'd like to try some persuasion before moving on to medieval torture. If I could just talk to her I'm sure I could sort it out. Unfortunately Susi Surmata is hard to pin down. No one knows who she really is. She's managed to remain completely anonymous.'

It was a puzzling phenomenon.

'One would have thought she would relish publicity,' said Malveria. 'She does work in fashion, after all. What secret is she trying to protect?'

'I've no idea.'

'Could she have an abnormally large nose? Very bad skin? No, I have it – she is hideously overweight. Laid low by the shame of her enormous extra poundage, she flits silently from one fashion show to another, looks longingly at the models, gazes in wonder at the slender grace of Queen Malveria in the front row, then goes home unhappily to write her bitter articles full of venom and hatred towards the world.'

Thrix gaped at Malveria's speech. 'I see the opera is improving your creative imagination.'

'Do not worry, Enchantress. I am sure we can find this Susi Surmata. And then you must assure her that she is not as hideously fat as she imagines herself to be. If that fails, we will move on swiftly to the burning needles. One way or another, she must write about your clothes.'

The Queen broke off, suddenly distracted by her make-up. She examined herself in the mirror. 'Is this lipstick perfect?'

'Yes.'

Malveria regarded it suspiciously. 'It will not remain so. Really, my lipstick problems are quite wearing me out. One yearns for the perfect long-lasting solution.'

The Queen applied a little more colouring. 'If only the fairies were not so secretive about these things.'

'The fairies?' Thrix was confused.

'Queen Dithean has the most perfect lip-colouring, which never wears off. Have you not noticed? She is famous for it. The fairies produce their own exquisite lipstick from the juice of wild cherries – cunningly mixed, no doubt, with other fabulous ingredients. Unfortunately, the fairies do not give up their secrets easily. But do not despair, Enchantress. I am working on the problem, and may yet wrest the secret from her.'

'Well, that'll be one less thing to worry about,' said Thrix.

41

Decembrius stood in front of a small electrical goods shop in South London, admiring his reflection. He'd grown his dark red hair longer and swept it back. It accentuated his cheekbones, which were rather finer than those of the standard MacRinnalch male. He had a second gold stud in his left ear and a new pair of boots, quite expensive, with thin metal rims on the soles which gave them a gothic look. His long black leather coat had been inflexible when he bought it but had now moulded itself to his frame. He let his coat hang open even though it was a cold day. Decembrius didn't feel the cold. Though lean, he was strong, and always had been. He was a handsome young man, which he knew, and a handsome young werewolf.

After admiring himself for some moments, he frowned. There was no point in looking good if he couldn't find Kalix. He'd travelled south of the river in the hope that his extra sense of perception might somehow reappear, leading him to her. It hadn't. Decembrius could stand on this cold pavement for the rest of his life and not find her. There was no chance of simply picking up her scent. Thanks to the sorcerous pendant provided for her by the Enchantress and Malveria, Kalix's scent was hidden.

Decembrius shook his head. He was feeling worse and worse about the loss of his powers. Until now he'd reassured himself that they were bound to return sometime. Surely a werewolf born with the second sight couldn't just lose it. Yet there was no sign of his powers reappearing. He was gripped by a sudden feeling of loneliness, and wished he had someone to discuss it with. That was impossible, of course. He didn't want to admit his loss to anyone. Besides, who was there to talk to? The only werewolves he knew in London were the Douglas-MacPhees and he wasn't about to discuss anything personal with them. Even in Scotland there was no one he felt close to. When Sarapen died, Decembrius had lost his place in werewolf society and was now effectively an outcast. He sagged a little, and felt depressed, and wished he knew where Kalix was.

He tried to distract himself by studying the goods in the shop window. TVs, DVD players, kettles, most of them cheap, all of them obscure brands not normally seen in larger stores. Suddenly he became alert. Though his powers of far-seeing had vanished, his normal werewolf senses were still sharp, and there was a scent in the air he was familiar with: the girl who lived in the same flat as Kalix. He'd only encountered her briefly but he remembered her quite distinctly. Decembrius felt excited but remained where he was, looking in the window. Moonglow went by on the pavement behind him. The werewolf waited till she'd travelled some way before setting off in pursuit. This was fortunate. If he couldn't find Kalix with his powers then perhaps her flatmate would lead him to her.

Moonglow was returning early from university, having had only two classes in the morning. Sumerian history had gone well, but the day had taken a turn for the worse when she'd met Daniel at lunchtime and he'd started acting weirdly again. These days it was rare for the atmosphere between them to be completely normal. Moonglow regretted this. For a time Daniel had been the ideal flatmate. Though perhaps, she reflected, it hadn't been so ideal for him. He'd always been attracted to her and she'd always known it. He hadn't enjoyed hearing tales of her relationships, particularly her brief affair with Markus MacRinnalch, or as Daniel referred to him, 'that crazy werewolf'.

Markus wasn't really crazy. Daniel just objected to his liking for cross-dressing. Moonglow hadn't objected at all. He had been quite beautiful no matter what he wore. When he'd discarded her, Moonglow had been totally devastated. Daniel had undoubtedly planned to step in to repair the damage. Moonglow would probably have gone along with it. She had found herself increasingly attracted to him. Unfortunately there was the matter of Malveria's curse, which couldn't be ignored. Daniel didn't know about the curse and probably thought that Moonglow had just been toying with his emotions.

Leading to his weird and hostile behaviour, thought Moonglow morosely, and shook her head, not knowing how to make things better. She shivered, and hurried through the narrow side street that led to her small flat above the old row of shops, her clumpy heels thudding dully on the pavement. She let herself in, manoeuvred her way up the permanently dark stairs, and entered the living room. Forcing some cheer into her voice she shouted a greeting to Kalix. There was no reply.

Moonglow went upstairs and knocked on Kalix's door. Again there was no reply. Moonglow, who'd learned not to be tactful in this situation, opened the door and stepped inside. She halted abruptly, appalled at the sight that greeted her. Kalix was sitting on her bed, slumped unconscious against the wall, naked except for the duvet round her shoulders. Her bottle of laudanum was beside her and the whole room stank of the opiate. There was a gash in Kalix's thigh and blood had congealed over her leg and the sheets.

Moonglow felt angry. Kalix couldn't go on like this. It was ridiculous. Moonglow wasn't going to just stand around and do nothing while Kalix starved and bled herself to death. No doubt Gawain's death had been a terrible shock but this wasn't the way to deal with it. Moonglow stalked over the threadbare rug, prepared to wake Kalix and give her a piece of her mind. As she reached the side of the bed she halted, and noticed that Kalix's journal was beside her. It was open at the back page, which was unusual. Kalix was quite organised in the way she wrote, starting at the front and using a new page every time. Moonglow suppressed her feelings of guilt as she picked up the journal. She knew she shouldn't read it but her anger at Kalix's behaviour overcame her inhibitions and she looked at the latest entry, hoping it might contain something that might help her get Kalix into a better frame of mind.

As always, it was very hard to decipher. Ill-formed letters, misspelled words, shaky handwriting made even worse by Kalix's intoxication. 'list of suspects for killing gawain.' She read the list. 'the avenaris guild. duncan douglas-macphee. other douglas-macphees. thrix. markus and the clan.'

Moonglow's anger melted away. The thought of Kalix sitting in her room trying to write out a list of suspects for the murder of Gawain seemed unbearably sad. It was such a pathetic image that Moonglow felt overwhelmed with guilt for feeling angry at Kalix. She blinked away a tear, put the notebook down, covered Kalix with the quilt, and resolved that when she emerged from her stupor she would do something to help.

42

Princess Kabachetka sat on her own in her private caves and wept fiery tears. Their brilliance illuminated the cavern, turning even her bright blonde hair an angry shade of red.

'My life has plumbed new depths of humiliation from which I can never recover,' she groaned, and hung her head.

Two days ago the Princess had attended a small get-together organised by Apthalia the Grim at her desert mansion. Thanks to a garbled invitation, for which she would never forgive her chief lady-in-waiting, the Princess and her retinue had turned up at the event too early and found themselves forced to wait in private rooms.

'Which are really not up to the required standard,' complained the Princess. 'Has she modernised them at all since the days she used to kill lonely travellers?'

Worse was to follow. The Princess found that the gathering was not the daytime soirée she had imagined, but a late dance for which evening dress was the only correct attire. When Queen Malveria arrived majestically in full evening dress, the incorrectly attired Princess had been utterly mortified. To be wrongly dressed for the occasion had been the most shameful thing imaginable. Princess Kabachetka had burned with humiliation throughout the entire evening. She left as quickly as she decently could, but not before suffering the indignity of the mocking stares of Malveria's handmaidens who, while undoubtedly slatterns of the lowest order, had at least been properly attired.

The succeeding two days had not lessened the Princess's humiliation. She knew that people were gossiping about her. The Princess who couldn't dress properly. The humiliation would never end. Kabachetka hung her head even lower, and wailed.

'It's useless. I admit defeat. I tried to wage warfare on the dreadful Thrix and I failed. I tried to battle Malveria and I have also failed. Now I'm reduced to turning up at formal events in daytime attire and the disgrace will never end. My attempts to gain revenge on Kalix MacRinnalch for her assault on Sarapen have also failed. Perhaps it will be a blessing when my brother seizes power and throws me into the Eternal Volcano.'

Suddenly, to the Princess's surprise, there was a polite cough from the shadows. This was impossible. No one was permitted to enter the Princess's private cavern under *any* circumstances.

'Prepare to die,' she hissed, and summoned up a powerful spell.

'I can help you defeat your enemies,' said the intruder.

The Princess put her spell on hold. 'Which enemies in particular?'

'The werewolf fashion designer. And Queen Malveria.'

The Princess stared at her visitor. She was a dark-skinned Hiyasta, below average height, with rounded features and an old-fashioned shirt of black chain mail. No one wore chain mail like that any more. It was most peculiar.

'What is your name and how did you penetrate my private cavern?'

'Distikka,' replied the stranger, but left the second part of the question unanswered.

'And?'

'I am Queen Malveria's adviser.'

Princess Kabachetka wondered briefly if she might have become deranged due to a surfeit of guilt and shame. This certainly didn't seem to be making much sense. 'The Fire Queen's adviser? In those clothes? Not very likely. You are a wanderer from the desert, driven mad by the sun. As I'm late for an important moisturising, I may spare your life if you depart immediately.'

Distikka showed no inclination to depart. The Princess noticed that her visitor's black eyes burned with a peculiar intensity.

'The defeat of the werewolf clothes designer and the Fire Queen may also lead to the defeat of your brother Prince Esarax. He's a great threat to you.'

Princess Kabachetka stared at her visitor, who seemed to know far too much about her private thoughts. No one was supposed to know that Kabachetka feared and hated her brother. She looked over Distikka from head to toe and tried to study her aura, but the Hiyasta elemental had it well masked and the Princess could discern little.

'Do you always wear that elderly collection of chain mail which hangs so unflatteringly?'

'I do.'

'Do you plan to suddenly take up with high fashion and set yourself up as a style icon among the fire elementals?'

'Certainly not.'

'In that case,' said Kabachetka, 'I may be prepared to listen to what you have to say.'

43

Captain Easterly remembered why he never visited his cousin Albermarle. The clutter was intolerable. As an adult, Albermarle hadn't given up on his teenage enthusiasms, he'd indulged them. His spacious apartment was packed full of books, comics, games, toys and models. It was beyond Easterly's comprehension why a grown man would devote an entire row of shelves to replica spaceships, but Albermarle did. Running out of shelf space, his spaceships had overflowed onto the floor, and Easterly had to tread carefully to avoid splintering some of the small silver models.

'Don't go hunting werewolves, Albermarle. It's not like in a comic. It involves violence, blood and death. You'll be very bad at it. Stay in the office where you belong.'

'I've completed the training course.'

'That's not the same. It doesn't prepare you.'

'Mr Carmichael obviously thinks I'm ready. He's assigned me a team.'

Quite why Mr Carmichael had done that, Easterly couldn't fathom. Surely Easterly wasn't the only one who could see that Albermarle was unfit for duties as a hunter?

'You're just worried I'll eclipse you,' said Albermarle.

Captain Easterly shook his head. He knew his cousin was jealous of his own reputation within the Guild, but he hadn't imagined his jealousy would make him volunteer to actually face werewolves, and, inevitably, die.

Albermarle, moving quite rapidly, rescued a spaceship from under Easterly's feet.

'You've never treated me like a grown-up.'

'That's true.'

Albermarle glared at him. 'And I'm not overweight any more.'

'I didn't say you were.'

'You were thinking it.'

There had been a period in Albermarle's life when he'd been very overweight. In his last year at university he'd ballooned to an incredible size. When he'd started working for the Guild he could hardly fit behind a desk. He'd lost most of that weight over the years and recently become rather fit. Though Easterly might not have acknowledged it, his cousin had been working hard in the gym beneath their apartments. He was now a large, strong man, with only a hint of surplus flesh.

'You should just stay behind the scenes at the Guild. You do good work, locating werewolves for us.'

'Now I'm going to hunt them,' said Albermarle, stubbornly.

'My father was killed by a werewolf.' Easterly tried to adopt a conciliatory tone. 'I've got a good reason for risking my life. You don't. Just stay out of the front line.'

Albermarle drew himself up, and put down his spaceship with some dignity. Though he was large, his rounded face had never lost its boyish features, and his pink skin, thick curly hair and small wispy beard didn't make him look any older.

'I have my reasons.'

'What did werewolves ever do to you?'

'That's a curious thing for a werewolf hunter to say,' countered Albermarle. 'Aren't we meant to hate them anyway, no matter what they've done?'

'Yes. We are. But most people won't take the risk of hunting them unless they've been personally affected in some way.'

'My life was ruined by a werewolf at Oxford,' said Albermarle, rather dramatically.

'What did he do? Break one of your spaceships?'

'It wasn't a *he*. It was a she. But I didn't know she was a werewolf then. Now I do, and I'm going to hunt her down.'

Captain Easterly looked enquiringly at his younger cousin. 'Is this something to do with the time you became depressed in your final year and put on all that weight?'

'Stop calling me fat.'

'What happened? Did some female werewolf break your heart?'

'It's none of your business,' shouted Albermarle, suddenly flaring up. 'Just look after your own werewolf hunting. Which isn't really all that great, when you look at the numbers.' Easterly had indeed been going through a lean spell. These things happened. He was still one of the leading hunters in the organisation.

Albermarle ushered him out of his flat. 'Excuse me. I need to go to the gym and then the firing range.'

'Suit yourself,' said Easterly. 'But if I was you, I'd just forget whatever happened at Oxford. You're no match for a werewolf. She'll kill you.'

'No, she won't.' Albermarle closed the door emphatically on the Captain.

44

Thrix's mood had deteriorated. She complained to her designers, shouted at models and abused Ann for failing to set up an interview with German *Vogue*. Her assistant pointed out that Thrix had refused to do the interview.

'I didn't refuse. Why would I refuse?'

'You said you were too busy.'

'I said no such thing!' yelled Thrix.

'You did. What's the matter? Why are you in such a terrible mood?'

'I'm not in a terrible mood.'

'Yes, you are.'

'Fine. I'm in a terrible mood.'

'Why?'

'Because I had to move Gawain's body from a police morgue and send it to Scotland for burial!'

The whole operation – to remove the body and cover her tracks – had been extremely difficult, requiring all of the Enchantress's skill. Whether it would extricate the MacRinnalch Clan from the potential problems of a police investigation remained to be seen.

'I suppose that explains it,' said Ann. 'I thought you were just annoyed about business being bad.'

'I'm annoyed about that too. You know that woman Markoza? She only left fashion college last year and now she's selling clothes all over America just because Susi Surmata liked her last collection. And will Surmata write about me?'

'No?'

'No!' Thrix clenched her fists and swore under her breath. There was a long pause.

'Were you very sad about Gawain?'

Thrix prepared to lie, but stopped herself. She trusted Ann, and might as well be honest with her.

'Yes.'

Ann knew that Thrix had felt a powerful attraction for Gawain, even if she'd professed not to like him very much. Thrix growled, sounding very wolflike. It was a trait shared by all the MacRinnalchs, as if their werewolf voices never entirely left them, even when they were human.

'So is it all right to just remove the body? Won't they notice?'

'Of course they'll notice!' roared Thrix, her temper flaring up again. She attempted to calm herself. 'I did what I could. Spells of forgetfulness, some altering of records. If we're lucky it might blow over. If not . . .'

At that moment there was a flash of pink light and Agrivex tumbled into the room, ending up on Thrix's desk, her heavy boots sending a pile of papers onto the floor.

'Hi!' she cried, and struggled to her feet. 'I'm OK, don't worry, I just bumped my elbow a little bit.' The young fire elemental looked ruefully at her elbow, and rubbed the injured limb.

Ann was used to the Fire Queen teleporting in but had never encountered Vex before. She took a step back in case this was some enemy, which was always possible, given Thrix's connections.

'Agrivex!' exclaimed Thrix. 'What are you doing here?'

'I've come about college! It's so great that me and Kalix are going to college! Thanks for organising it!'

The Enchantress was surprised. While it was true that she had made enquiries about a suitable institute, she hadn't expected the young fire elemental to come and thank her for it. Vex leapt from the desk, sending more papers flying everywhere.

'The teacher gave me another gold star for my new poem! Do you want to hear it?'

'Eh . . .'

At that moment there was a brighter flash and the Fire Queen stood in their midst, looking at Vex with some displeasure.

'Foul niece! Are you attempting to hide from me?'

'Absolutely not.'

'She was thanking Thrix for finding a college,' said Ann.

'An unlikely story. Agrivex has been attempting to avoid me since I informed her it was time for the pre-adoption ceremony. Prepare yourself, vile niece.'

Vex looked pained. 'I don't want to.'

'What you want is of no importance.'

'They'll make me wear a fire wrap.'

'The fire wrap is the traditional garb of the well-bred young Hiyasta. And, in this instance, you.'

'It's ugly. And the ceremony sounds boring.'

'Boring?' Malveria was outraged. 'The opportunity is presented to move towards adoption by the Queen of the Hiyasta and you dismiss this as boring?'

Vex looked towards Thrix. 'Have you ever seen a fire wrap? It's the most stupid piece of clothing ever. And the ceremony takes hours.'

'The ceremony will take ten minutes,' said the Fire Queen. 'This is necessary for affairs of state, Agrivex.'

'I won't do it. Maybe I don't want to be your niece. Did you ever think of that?'

'Then perhaps I should withhold your allowance and stop granting you the power to live in the human dimension.'

'You see how she treats me?' said Vex. 'It's scandalous. No real relation would treat me as meanly as Aunt Malvie. If that's even her real name.'

'It is not my real name, you imbecile.'

'Aha!' cried Vex. 'I knew it. You've been lying to me all along.'

A flicker of flame appeared from the Queen's eyes. She controlled it swiftly. 'Cease this stupidity, dismal niece. I have not yet forgiven you for the dreadful humiliation you heaped on my head in the Garden of Small Blue Flames. What induced you to ask me to heal werewolves in front of the Duchess Gargamond?'

'Kalix needed help. She'd been shot.'

'So? That does not mean that the Queen of the Fire Elementals has to rush to her assistance. Has it escaped your attention, witless one, that the MacRinnalchs are historical enemies of our people, with the exception of Thrix, of course, who has won over everyone with her immense grace and beauty, including Beau DeMortalis, Duke of the Black Castle?' The Queen turned towards Thrix. 'He sends his fond regards.'

131

By this time Ann had left the room and returned with wine for the Queen, which Malveria accepted with thanks.

'Thank you, Ann. My life has been most trying recently.'

'I'm sorry about the humiliation,' said Thrix. 'Mother said to thank you for healing Kalix's hand anyway. Any wound by silver can go bad in a werewolf, even a minor one.'

'Will Kalix still come to college? I don't want her to stop going.' Vex suddenly looked very glum. 'Someone killed Gawain. She'll want revenge. She won't want to go to college.' The young fire elemental turned towards Thrix. 'Can you make her go? She has lots of friends there and all the teachers like her. And she's learning a lot.'

Thrix almost laughed. Vex was a poor liar. Thrix doubted very much if Kalix had made any friends, or was popular with the teachers. The Enchantress had always found Vex oddly amusing and she appreciated her coming to thank her, even if she was really hiding from her aunt.

'I don't know if Kalix will keep going or not.'

'Can you make her?'

'No one can make Kalix do anything.'

'I really think she might leave,' said Vex, and looked gloomy again. 'But I've got a plan to cheer her up.'

She fumbled around in her large Hello Kitty bag, and produced an aged-looking comic.

'Look! *Curse of the Wolf Girl!*'

Malveria regarded the garish comic with some distaste.

'What is this shabby item?'

'It's Kalix's favourite comic!'

'Really?'

'She loves it. If you give me some money I'll buy more copies for her. Then she'll cheer up and won't leave college.'

Vex looked at them expectantly. Malveria, always suspicious of ulterior motives when her niece asked for money, regarded her coolly.

Thrix seemed surprised that Kalix would enjoy reading a werewolf comic. But who knew what Kalix might like?

'The adoption ceremony awaits,' said Malveria.

'I'll come if you give me money to buy comics for Kalix and also new boots.'

'How did boots make an appearance? There will be no new boots. You may have the money for comics, if you actually believe it will encourage Kalix's education. Now depart, wretched girl, to the palace, and prepare yourself for the ceremony.'

The Fire Queen snapped her fingers, sending Vex back to her own dimension. 'The girl will be the death of me,' she sighed. 'I may not make it through the pre-adoption ceremony.'

'Are you actually making her your heir?'

'Not quite, though she will be close. It will pacify my council for a while.'

'At least she's showing some enthusiasm about college,' said Ann.

'True. Apparently she has received many gold stars, which she assures me is a good sign. Is it a good sign, Enchantress?'

'Eh . . . yes, I'm sure it is.'

'Excellent. Perhaps my niece will surprise us all, and actually learn something.'

45

Alone in her frugal apartment, Dominil tucked her long white hair into the black woolly hat she'd bought for the occasion, put on an anonymous brown jacket, and placed a pair of glasses with plain lenses on her face. She studied herself in the mirror. It wasn't an impenetrable disguise but it was good enough for her purposes. At least with her distinctive white hair covered she wouldn't be instantly recognisable.

She paused at the door, wondering if she should take a book with her. She wasn't likely to find herself in a situation where she needed something to read, but long habit made her feel uncomfortable leaving the house without a book. She tucked a copy of Xenophon's *Expedition to Persia* in her pocket before setting off.

Dominil was now ready to kill the hunters who were pursuing her. The first of them, anyway, a Mr Krakow. From her last glimpses of the Guild's files Dominil had learned that Krakow had not only seen her in Camden, he'd seen the twins too. He'd now been assigned to hunt them down.

Dominil drove smoothly from the car park beneath her block of flats into the streets which were becoming quieter after midnight. She headed north, towards King's Cross, where the Guild had housed Krakow. Travelling through the city at night was far quicker than during the day and she arrived sooner than she'd expected. The white-haired werewolf parked in the darkest side street she could find, then slipped silently out of the car. She walked swiftly and very quietly into the main road, then back along another side street till she found the small semi-detached house she was looking for.

Checking first to see that no one observed her, she walked over the tiny front garden to the passage at the side of the house which led to another small garden at the back, blocked by a tall gate. Dominil vaulted the gate with ease, again making not the slightest sound. She peered in the back window. There, watching TV, was Krakow. A large man, Dominil judged, though he was sitting down.

Dominil tried the back door. It wasn't locked. Apparently the werewolf hunter was not very security-conscious while at home. Perhaps he had no reason to be. Until now, werewolves had never hunted them. Dominil crept inside. Then, in the kitchen, she transformed into her werewolf shape so that she was covered in her perfect white coat, with long hair over her whole body, and longer strands of hair hanging down from her head and shoulders. Slightly hunched, she crept through the kitchen, the small hall, and up to the living room. The hunter was still watching television. Dominil could leap on him now and kill him before he knew what had happened. Break his neck from behind. It would be easy.

Dominil couldn't quite do it. She'd killed hunters before and never regretted it for a second. But there was something about just killing this man from behind that didn't quite feel right. She mused for a second or two, then spoke, in her harsh werewolf voice.

'Mr Krakow?'

The hunter leapt from the couch and spun round, startled but not afraid. He reached inside his jacket for a weapon and Dominil saw the glint of a revolver. The werewolf leapt into the living room. She was too fast for Krakow, fastening her jaws round his neck before he could reach the trigger. She killed him in an instant, and let his body drop to the floor. She looked at the corpse.

'You won't be hunting me any more,' she muttered, and returned calmly to the kitchen where she changed back into her human shape and left the house as swiftly and silently as she'd arrived.

When she got home she found three messages from Pete on the phone, asking if he'd like to join her for a late-night drink, and another message from the twins, demanding to know what was wrong with their guitarist, who was still refusing to rehearse.

Dominil shook her head in disgust at all of them, and went to change her clothes. Then she sat on the couch in silence, reading Xenophon's *Expedition to Persia*.

46

Decembrius knew he was unlikely to receive a warm welcome. He shrugged, and pressed the doorbell. If he wanted to see Kalix there was no point wasting time. He'd been fortunate to run into Moonglow, enabling him to follow her home. He probably wouldn't get the chance again.

Decembrius noted that the small shop below the flat was boarded up, and the paving stones beneath his feet were cracked and worn. The street had an air of decay about it. He wasn't surprised when the door opened on a similarly shabby hallway. He'd have been more surprised to find Kalix living anywhere comfortable. Decembrius himself now lived in modest surroundings, though in his youth, at the castle, he'd been used to a degree of comfort. Few werewolves left the clan to move up in the world, he thought. If you abandoned the castle it was generally a sign that your fortunes were on the wane.

He found himself confronted by a young man he didn't remember meeting before, wearing a T-shirt with some unfamiliar band's name on it, and long hair that fell over his eyes.

'I've come to see Kalix.'

The young man looked at him suspiciously. 'She doesn't like visitors.'

'I've brought her some good news from home. From the castle.' Decembrius improvised as best he could, wishing he'd prepared a better story. The young man pondered for a moment or two, then invited him inside. Decembrius followed him up a dark stairway that had bare plaster on the wall, cracked and flaking.

The small flat at the top of the stairs was as cheap as its surroundings but Decembrius noticed immediately the warm atmosphere. There were posters on the walls, a few small arte-facts strewn around, a glowing gas fire and a rug. None of it was expensive but it seemed welcoming.

'Kalix!' yelled Daniel. 'Someone's here to see you.'

A door opened upstairs and Moonglow emerged. 'Who is it?'

'Someone with good news from the castle.'

Moonglow's eyes widened in alarm. 'From the werewolf castle? And you just let them in? Are you crazy?'

'He said he had good news,' said Daniel, defensively.

Moonglow hurried downstairs, cast an angry glance at Daniel, then confronted Decembrius.

'Who are you and what's the good news?' she demanded.

'I'm Decembrius MacRinnalch. I'm afraid I don't really have any good news.'

'Hey!' cried Daniel. 'He tricked me.'

'I take it you're a werewolf?'

'I am.'

'Werewolves looking for Kalix is always bad news,' said the girl, 'so you'd better leave.'

Decembrius was surprised. He hadn't expected the friendliest of receptions but, even so, the girl seemed unusually hostile. And also quite familiar with werewolves, to the extent of not showing the slightest fear or distress at meeting another one.

'I came to see how Kalix was,' he said, a little lamely. He scanned Moonglow's expression, hoping it might soften a little. It didn't.

'Decembrius,' she muttered. 'I remember that name. Weren't you one of Sarapen's supporters?'

'I see you're familiar with the clan.'

'Of course I'm familiar with them. We've been trying to pro-tect Kalix from all of you. You have to leave.'

Decembrius felt a twinge of anger. He didn't enjoy being

ordered about by anyone, particularly a human girl he'd never met before. He had an urge to simply brush her out of the way and march upstairs to see Kalix. He was picking up the aroma of laudanum. She obviously hadn't changed her ways. But he couldn't start any trouble. Kalix would just hate him more than she probably already did.

'How did you get here, anyway?' demanded Moonglow. 'We're supposed to be hidden.'

'I followed you,' replied Decembrius. 'I'm good at that. I really want to see Kalix. Perhaps you could tell her I'm here?'

'No,' said Moonglow. 'Go away.'

Daniel stood at her side, facing Decembrius, and attempted to look resolute.

Decembrius found himself at a loss. Though he had a reputation as quite a cunning werewolf he couldn't think of anything to say to make these people less suspicious of him. There was a faint noise from the top of the stairs, and a few soft footsteps. It was Kalix, wrapped in an old blue dressing gown. Her face contorted with anger.

'What are you doing here?' she growled.

'I came to see how you were.'

'I'm fine and I don't want to see you,' said Kalix, still growling. She took a few steps down the stairs, then abruptly lost consciousness. She fell, and bumped her way quite slowly down the stairs. There was a brief, surprised pause while the three looked at her, then Moonglow rushed to her side.

'Does she do that often?' asked Decembrius.

'Quite often,' admitted Daniel.

'I take it she's not very well?'

'Not in the best of health, no.'

Moonglow attempted to help Kalix towards the couch. Decembrius went to lend assistance but was crowded out by Daniel.

'What is this?' asked Decembrius. 'Too much laudanum?'

Moonglow looked uncomfortable. 'Partly. But she won't eat. She hasn't eaten since—'

'Since Gawain died?' guessed Decembrius.

Moonglow nodded, and looked glum. Anxiety over Kalix made her forget for a moment how much she wanted Decembrius to leave. 'I think she's trying to starve herself to death again.'

'A werewolf can't starve herself to death,' stated Decembrius.

'You'd be surprised,' replied Moonglow.

'Haven't any of the family tried to help?' asked Decembrius. 'Her sister?'

'They don't get on. You should leave. We'll look after her.'

'You don't seem to be doing that well.'

'We've been doing fine,' said Daniel, supporting Moonglow. 'Or we would be if there weren't so many crazy werewolves trying to kill Kalix all the time. Didn't Moonglow say you should leave?'

Decembrius stared at them both. He didn't like either of these two hostile young humans but knew that if he wanted to talk to Kalix, he couldn't afford to offend them.

'I think I can help,' he said. 'I'll be back in a little while.'

Without another word the red-haired werewolf left the room, leaving Daniel and Moonglow puzzled as to why he'd arrived, and how.

'I thought we were hidden from other werewolves. Doesn't Kalix's pendant keep them away?'

'He said he followed me home.'

'Doesn't it stop that from happening?' Daniel asked.

Neither of them knew.

'I hope we don't get flooded out with werewolves.' Daniel looked concerned, then perked up. 'Do you think I could get some sort of exemption from exams?'

The appearance of a potentially hostile werewolf had made Daniel and Moonglow temporarily forget their strained relationship.

'Poor Kalix,' continued Daniel. 'She gets her life in order, then Gawain goes and gets killed. No wonder she's upset. Of course, you never know when something like that's going to happen. What if I got killed in a road accident?'

'Then I'd miss you,' said Moonglow.

'How much?' demanded Daniel. 'Really badly, or just a little?'

Moonglow was spared from answering by the doorbell. Decembrius had returned, bearing a carrier bag from the small shop on the far corner.

'Their selection of meat isn't that good,' he said.

'It doesn't matter,' said Daniel. 'She won't eat it anyway.'

Decembrius dumped the bag on the floor, then went to the

couch and prodded Kalix. At first she didn't respond but as he prodded her again she stirred, and her nose twitched. Abruptly she opened her eyes and the moment she saw Decembrius standing over her she became alert and sat up.

'What are you doing here?' she demanded again.

Decembrius grinned. 'I've come for you,' he said, and then, to the surprise of everyone, he changed into his werewolf shape and growled.

Kalix leapt to her feet and started growling back, ready to defend herself. Her tiredness and intoxication slipped away as her wolf nature took over. Decembrius snarled at her fiercely. Kalix snarled back, even more fiercely. For a period there was snuffling and snarling in the room as the two werewolves faced each other, eyes blazing. Just as it seemed that Kalix was about to attack, Decembrius withdrew. Still in werewolf form, he picked up his carrier bag, emptied the raw meat on the floor, and began to eat. Moonglow and Daniel looked on dumbfounded as Decembrius buried his snout in a great pile of supermarket cuts of chops, sausages and burgers.

'Well, really,' said Moonglow. 'Couldn't you use the table?'

There was a sudden blur of movement as Kalix flew across the room. As she reached Decembrius she crouched down and buried her own nose in the pile of raw meat. There was a moment of snarling as they fought over a lamb chop, then each busied themselves in eating.

'Well . . .' said Daniel to Moonglow. 'I suppose that wasn't a bad idea.'

'I suppose not.'

More snarling broke out as the pile of food grew smaller. Decembrius withdrew, letting Kalix finish it off. He changed back into human form. Kalix remained as she was, still snuffling round on the carpet, looking for scraps.

'Can't starve yourself when you're a werewolf.' Decembrius looked pleased with himself. Moonglow was impressed, though Daniel still resented how Decembrius had tricked his way into the house.

'You should go now,' said Moonglow.

'I thought I might stay a while . . .'

Kalix looked up from the floor. 'Go away.'

Confronted by two students and a young werewolf, none of whom seemed as friendly as they ought to be, Decembrius decided against arguing. He rose quite gracefully.

'I'll call back and see if you're feeling better,' he said, and nodded to them all as he left.

47

Queen Malveria balanced comfortably on a large mushroom, and sipped from a buttercup full of whisky. Far above, a bitter wind shook the treetops, but the Queen was protected from the weather by the soft golden glow surrounding the woman sitting on the next mushroom. Malveria felt unusually relaxed. It was always a pleasant excursion, visiting the Fairy Queen of Colburn Woods. Since entering into a business relationship, Queen Dithean and Queen Malveria had become friends. Only recently Dithean had been Malveria's guest at a chariot race, agreed by all to have been a thrilling event.

Malveria took care to nurture her friendship. Queen Dithean Wallace Cloud-of-Heather NicRinnalch had control over a very important resource. The water that flowed through the wood was exceptionally pure. Malveria declared it the purest to be found in the known realms, and used it in her potions of rejuvenation. The Fire Queen believed it did wonders for her skin. For her part, Dithean NicRinnalch was pleased with the thimblefuls of gold that were proffered in exchange for the water. It was a satisfactory arrangement all round.

Though Queen Malveria now spent most of her time flitting between her luxurious palace and the fashion showrooms of Europe, the outdoor environment was not as alien to her as might have been supposed. Malveria had spent many long years in her youth as a fugitive, hiding in the harsh wastelands of the Hiyasta nation, sleeping in caves, tramping over fields of molten lava and living off the land. The guerrilla campaign that took her from renegade princess to absolute ruler had been long and harsh. The Fire Queen could do without luxury if she needed to. Not that the mushroom was uncomfortable, given her present small size. Queen Dithean could change the stature of visitors to her realm, and Malveria had politely agreed to be shrunk down so that they could converse more easily.

'The pre-adoption ceremony was not as dreadful as I feared. Agrivex mumbled her way through without too much complaint.'

A badger passed by. The Fairy Queen waved, and it nodded its striped head in salute before disappearing into the undergrowth.

'But with the adoption ceremony, and my Council of Ministers afterwards, and then a small soirée with the Duchess Gargamond, I've had little time to attend to my own affairs,' continued Malveria. 'And little time to put on make-up. I really despair, the way the colour fades from my lips.'

Malveria looked hopefully at the Fairy Queen, but she didn't take the hint.

'One longs for a lip-colouring that would never fade, in any circumstances.'

Queen Dithean remained silent.

This Fairy Queen is not about to hand over her secrets, thought Malveria disconsolately.

'How is Thrix?' asked Queen Dithean.

'Excellent. In general terms. Though her business is in a little trouble. And she can't find a man. Apart from that, splendid.'

'She used to visit, when she was younger,' said the Fairy Queen. 'But rarely these days.'

Malveria nodded. She had the impression that Queen Dithean didn't think the MacRinnalch werewolves paid her enough respect.

'Perhaps if the MacRinnalch women were to visit more often, they might not be so cursed in love.'

Malveria sat up, alerted by the word 'curse'. 'Curse, dearest Dithean? What is this curse?'

'Nothing really. The MacDonald Elves say they once cursed the Thane's family so that no son, daughter or niece would ever be happy in love. But it's an old story, and probably not true. The MacDonald Elves don't have the power to make such a curse, and they're liars anyway.'

'But what was the reason, true or not?' enquired Malveria,

who loved a good gossip, particularly about cursed love lives.

'It was said that a Princess of the MacDonald Elves had the power to turn into a beautiful white deer. Which she often did, being keen on roaming through the glens in deer shape. Unfortunately she roamed rather too far on the night of the full moon, and encountered a son and daughter of the MacRinnalch werewolves.'

'What happened?'

'The werewolves ate her.'

'Oh dear.'

'It is a sad tale.'

'One can see why the Elves would be upset.'

'Indeed.' The Fairy Queen nodded. 'But unlikely to be true, I'd say. I hold the MacDonald Elves in low regard, and they're full of half-truths and jumbled legends.'

Queen Malveria pondered for a while.

In the bushes there was a rustling sound as a pine marten scurried towards its den.

'It's true that none of them seem to have much luck in romance,' Malveria observed. 'Thrix's love life is simply a disaster. Kalix, of course, has fared no better, and as for Dominil, can one imagine her ever engaging in a satisfying love affair?'

The Fairy Queen laughed. 'I know. The Thane's family is always like this, and has been for generations. Markus himself will never settle down happily. But it's not because of a curse. It's because the daughters and nieces in the Thane's family are so self-centred they never think of anyone else.'

Malveria was surprised at the Fairy Queen's unsympathetic judgement. 'Surely that is a little severe?'

'I've known them all a very long time, Malveria. It's a family trait. None of them will ever be happy in love, I'm certain. They're too selfish, and concerned only with their own affairs. Thrix is the worst example of all, I'm afraid.'

Queen Malveria was interested, but troubled. She didn't like to think of her good friend Thrix never having a successful romance, and wondered if the Fairy Queen's judgement was sound, or perhaps coloured by her feeling that the MacRinnalchs had forgotten how to pay her proper respect these days.

48

'That was strange,' said Moonglow. 'Are you friends with Decembrius?'

Kalix shook her werewolf head and licked some fragments of food from her long sharp teeth. 'I don't like him. He supported Sarapen.'

'Why did he come here? Was he spying on you?'

Kalix shrugged. She was in a better mood now she'd eaten, and didn't seem to hold it against Decembrius that he'd tricked her into becoming a werewolf, which always gave her an appetite.

They were interrupted by a loud crashing from the kitchen. Fearing that they were being invaded, Daniel, Moonglow and Kalix hurried to investigate. There they found Vex, stuck in the sink.

'A few problems teleporting.' The young fire elemental grinned. 'Haven't quite mastered it yet.' She tumbled out of the sink and stood beaming at them. 'I had to do a stupid pre-adoption cere-mony. And now I'm back! We have college tomorrow. Isn't it great?' She smiled broadly at Daniel, and then at Kalix. 'Having a little werewolf practice? Good idea. Ready for school tomorrow?'

Kalix sagged. She transformed back from her werewolf shape into human and her shoulders slumped. 'I'm not going to school.'

'Yes, you are. We have classes. It'll be great!'

'I'm not going,' repeated Kalix, and left the kitchen.

Vex hurried after her. 'But you have to come!'

'I don't care.'

Vex looked round at Daniel and Moonglow, puzzled. 'What's the matter? Why won't Kalix come to college?'

'I'm too busy hunting down Gawain's killer!' declared Kalix, and sounded fierce.

'Oh,' said Vex, and pondered for a moment. 'Wouldn't that be easier if you knew how to read?'

'What?!'

'Detectives are always reading stuff. I saw it on TV.' Vex looked worried, and ran her fingers through her spiky bleached hair. 'Aunt Malvie might stop me going if you don't come. She doesn't trust me.'

'Can't you look for the killer and go to college as well?' suggested Daniel.

'Of course you can,' said Vex enthusiastically. 'Like a crime fighter. You know, college student by day, superhero by night. And werewolf by night as well.'

'I'm not going to college!' yelled Kalix, flaring up. 'And you can't make me.'

'But if you don't go to college you won't have any money,' protested Vex.

'What do you mean, I won't have any money?'

'Your mother won't pay you your allowance if you don't go. And you need money for rent. Isn't that right?' Vex looked hopefully at Moonglow for support. Moonglow shifted uncomfortably.

'She won't know I'm not going,' said Kalix.

'Yes, she will!' said Vex. 'Moonglow will tell her.'

'You wouldn't tell her, would you?' Kalix asked Moonglow.

'Well . . .'

'Of course she would,' said Vex, sensing victory. 'Moonglow has to tell your mother if you leave college, it's part of the agreement. I heard it from Aunt Malvie.'

'What!' exploded Kalix. 'Is this true?' Kalix's only source of income was her allowance from the Mistress of the Werewolves. Life would be impossible without it. She had rent to pay, and bills, and, most importantly, laudanum to purchase.

Moonglow seemed close to actually wringing her hands. She looked towards Daniel for support but Daniel was apparently preoccupied with a speck of dust on his sleeve.

'Well . . . eh . . . yes. I am meant to tell your mother how you're getting on. It was part of our agreement about her paying your rent.'

'I can't believe you've all been making agreements behind my back! What's the idea of speaking to my mother anyway?'

'I didn't speak to your mother,' said Moonglow. 'It was sort of negotiated through your sister.'

'Thrix! You've been talking about me with Thrix! How dare you!'

'Well, I'm glad that's all sorted out!' exclaimed Vex, blithely ignoring the general antagonism all around. 'And I brought you something to set you up for learning more. Look! Two more issues of your favourite comic!' Vex triumphantly produced two copies of *Curse of the Werewolf* from her Hello Kitty bag. 'Now you can learn more about her werewolf adventures and practise your reading at the same time.' She grinned.

Kalix looked at her in astonishment, then exploded in anger. 'That's not my favourite comic! I hate it! I'm never reading it again!'

'It's not so hard,' protested Vex. 'Look, I'll help you with the first page. You see this picture? That's Bella the werewolf just about to attack someone. She's growling. See, I'll help you spell it. G-R-O-W-L—'

Kalix clenched her fists, turned rapidly and marched out of the room, slamming the door behind her.

'Hey, it's really not that hard,' insisted Vex, and ran in pursuit.

Moonglow sighed. 'I wish Kalix hadn't found out I'm meant to report to her mother. Now I feel like I'm a spy.'

'She was bound to find out eventually,' said Daniel. 'But I can see why she isn't happy.'

'I didn't have any choice. Her mother wasn't going to hand over money if I didn't give some account of how Kalix was managing.'

'I expect she'll get used to—' began Daniel, but was interrupted as Agrivex ran shrieking into the room.

'Help! Kalix is being savaged by an animal!'

'What now?' said Daniel, jumping to his feet. He ran after Vex to Kalix's room, ready to confront whatever beast had appeared to torment them now. He burst into the room to find Kalix looking suspiciously at a small cat which was pawing at her leg. They halted, surprised.

'Is it dangerous?' said Vex.

'It's not dangerous at all,' sighed Daniel. 'It's a cat.'

'What?'

'You're wearing pictures of cats,' said Moonglow.

Vex stared down at her T-shirt, trying to reconcile the pictures of Hello Kitty with the small creature that was now playing with Kalix's bootlaces.

'Go away, you stupid cat,' said Kalix.

'Where did it come from?'

'It jumped in the window.'

'It's hardly more than a kitten,' said Moonglow. 'Maybe it's homeless.' She advanced towards it but the kitten didn't take kindly to Moonglow. It hissed at her, and rushed behind Kalix's legs for protection.

'Stop hiding behind me, you stupid cat,' demanded Kalix.

'It likes you,' said Daniel.

'I hate it,' replied Kalix. 'I'm going to throw it out.' She bent down to pick the cat up. It leapt into her arms and began pawing at her chest.

'Is it savaging her now?' asked Vex.

'I don't think so. It's friendly.'

'Stupid cat,' said Kalix, and stood holding it very awkwardly, not looking pleased at this new development.

49

'You've made many mistakes,' said Distikka, in the depths of Princess Kabachetka's private caves.

'I am aware of that,' replied the Princess.

'You should never have confronted the Fire Queen and the Enchantress. They're too strong. Add in your brother Esarax and the position becomes hopeless. You can't fight against so many powerful opponents.'

'If I wished to hear about my deficiencies I could spend time with my mother,' said the Princess, angrily. 'Do you have anything useful to say before I propel you through the floor into the lava pool below?'

'I'm simply pointing out where you've gone wrong.'

'Then what would you suggest, you who hold the not-very-mighty position of adviser to Queen Malveria?' Princess Kabachetka stared intently at her visitor.

'It's no use trying to interpret my aura,' said Distikka. 'I grew up in a monastery with fire monks where I learned the art of mental control. My aura can't be read, even by Queen Malveria.'

'Which means you may be an even bigger liar than I assume you are already,' said the Princess.

146

Distikka sat down on a small outcrop of rock in the cave, far too comfortably for the Princess's liking. 'My advice is to avoid confrontation. You should make new allies, and work against your enemies by stealth.'

'Brilliant,' sneered the Princess. 'You have read the beginner's book of military tactics.'

'If you'd paid any attention to your brother you might have realised how powerful he was becoming, and done something to prevent it. If you'd paid attention to Malveria's actions, you might have stopped her from forming her alliance with Thrix. But you didn't.'

Once more the Princess strained and failed to interpret Distikka's aura. She had the alarming thought that this might all be a plot by Malveria.

'And now you have a powerful enemy in the Earthly dimension. Too powerful to attack with any safety.'

'I managed before,' countered the Princess. 'I removed Thrix's power.'

Distikka nodded. 'True. You took her by surprise, and you used the Empress's sorcery against her. Can you do that again?'

The Princess looked pained. The lecture that her mother had given her for illicitly transporting her secret spells to the Earth still stung. She couldn't risk it again.

'So you have no power against the Enchantress, and having once attacked her, you can no longer take her by surprise.'

The Princess flared up in anger, causing a spout of yellow flame to shoot from one end of the cavern to the other. 'I am aware of this already!'

'Then find a new weakness in the Enchantress,' continued Distikka, calmly.

'What weakness does she have? Do you mean her hair? I checked carefully, and she seems to be a natural blonde.'

Distikka's face twitched. 'I was not referring to her hair. Did you know that she's notoriously unfortunate in affairs of the heart?'

'Really?' The Princess was pleased. 'She's a failure in love?'

'A string of unsatisfactory romances. Malveria has often mentioned it. You could exploit this.'

'How?'

'Find her a suitable lover. One who will also be your spy and agent.'

For the first time since their meeting, a smile passed over the Princess's face. 'I like this notion! Send a lover to Thrix MacRinnalch who will destroy her.' Her face fell. 'If I were to send anyone to woo the Enchantress she would sense immediately that he was a Hainusta elemental.'

'Find someone on Earth. A human. Give Thrix the lover she wants and you can attack her. And Malveria too.' Distikka stood up. 'Where is Sarapen's body?

Princess Kabachetka glowed an angry crimson. 'That's not your concern.'

'You've already wasted time by leaving his body in a state of suspended animation. It's a potent bargaining tool. It gives you access to the MacRinnalchs.'

Princess Kabachetka felt confused, not understanding Distikka's meaning. She had a brief desire to escape from the conversation and relax by trying on some new shoes and dresses. With an effort of will, she persevered. Distikka, though poorly dressed, did seem like a woman who was worth listening to.

50

Kalix had never rung a doorbell without hesitating. She always feared that she might be an unwelcome visitor. She stood nervously on the doorstep of the twins' house in Camden for several minutes, wondering whether she should ring the bell or just go away. Finally she plucked up the courage.

'Kalix! Come in!' Beauty and Delicious welcomed their young cousin inside. Though the twins' lives revolved around their band, they hadn't completely forgotten the way Kalix had helped them. When Sarapen attacked their gig, they'd have been hard pressed to survive without Kalix's savage fighting skills.

It was midday and the sisters were still sober. Perhaps feeling that something should be done about this, Beauty poured three glasses of the MacRinnalch malt. It was customary for any

MacRinnalch to offer a fellow clan member a small glass of the MacRinnalch whisky as a token of friendship; Beauty and Delicious were glad of the excuse.

'Have you come to hear our new songs?' asked Delicious. The twins had been at their hairdresser yesterday and Delicious's hair was now a particularly gaudy shade of pink. Aided by skilfully inserted extensions, it poured over her head and shoulders in an enormous wave. Kalix shook her head. Her own hair, a natural dark brown, had never been cut and was even longer than that of the twins. Beauty pointed out to her sister that they hadn't finished any new songs.

'Oh. Do you want to hear some old ones?'

Kalix struggled to answer. The twins always seemed to be so active, so in control of their lives, and having such a good time, that Kalix ended up feeling young and stupid. She'd sometimes wished that she could have fun like them, instead of having everything go wrong all the time. 'I was looking for Dominil,' she mumbled.

The twins shuddered in an exaggerated fashion.

'Dominil? You know she wants us to play a gig in Edinburgh? Why would anyone want to play in Edinburgh? It's the end of the world.'

Kalix couldn't quite see how this could be true, but she didn't comment.

'And she's moaning about how we should be rehearsing more. The woman gets no enjoyment out of life.'

'Doesn't like us getting drunk or going out, wants us to practise all the time. What kind of manager is that?' asked Delicious indignantly.

'Is she your manager now?' asked Kalix.

'Sort of,' said Beauty. 'She does all the manager stuff. She's good at it except she's an unbearable pain.'

'How can we rehearse, anyway,' demanded Delicious, 'when our guitarist doesn't show up?'

'We think he's upset over some woman but he won't tell us about it.'

'I still think it's that barmaid,' said Delicious. 'What's he upset for anyway? Just because someone's breaking his heart it's no reason not to show up for rehearsal.'

'I thought Dominil would kill him for that,' said Beauty, 'but she didn't.'

'She hasn't been tough enough on him. She should sort him out.'

Beauty studied herself in the wall mirror that was squeezed into a gap in the shelves housing part of their huge music collection. Many more CDs and DVDs were strewn around the floor and there were instruments left carelessly around. The twins didn't take care of anything. They were wealthy enough not to have to. Their parents had invested their share of the clan wealth wisely, and then died early, leaving Beauty and Delicious to enjoy their inheritance.

'Do you think I need more extensions?' Beauty's hair, as violently blue as her sister's was pink, was equally thick and long.

'You'd fall over,' said Delicious, and they both laughed quite raucously at the thought of falling over because they had too much hair.

A key sounded in the lock, there were light footsteps in the hall, and Dominil appeared.

'Dominil! Have some whisky.'

'The token of friendship does not have to be offered to a fellow werewolf who visits every day,' said Dominil calmly.

'Well, have some anyway.'

Dominil declined. The sisters filled up their own glasses again.

'Kalix, what brings you here?' Dominil asked.

'I want to talk about . . . things,' replied Kalix, not wanting to mention Gawain's death in front of the twins.

'Come upstairs,' said Dominil.

'Did you talk to Pete?' asked Beauty.

'Not yet.'

'You said you were going to.'

'I'll get round to it.'

'What's the matter?' demanded Delicious. 'When we do something wrong you're always shouting and screaming about it, but now Pete's not even playing guitar and you're letting him get away with it!'

'I do not shout and scream,' said Dominil.

'It's just not good enough. Our guitarist is depressed because some slutty barmaid has hooked him with a few free pints of lager.'

'And cleavage,' added Delicious. 'She really bends over when she serves drinks.'

'True. Pete was probably powerless to resist. No wonder he fell for her.'

Beauty looked puzzled. 'Hang on. If she's been luring him with free beer and cleavage, why's he depressed? That should be enough to keep him happy.'

'Maybe she rejected him?'

'She never rejected anybody. Pete must be in love with someone else. Who could it be?'

The twins thought for a few moments, and then turned to each other in surprise.

'Could it be one of us?' Beauty asked.

'That would be a disaster!' exclaimed Delicious. 'You can't have the guitarist going around moping about the singer. It's really bad for the band. Dominil, is Pete in love with one of us?'

'I really wouldn't know,' said Dominil. 'And I don't want to—'

'He should show more self-control,' cried Beauty. 'Though I have noticed him looking at me. I expect he tried to hold out for a while, then just abandoned the attempt.'

'It's sad he's fallen for me in such a big way,' said Delicious, 'but I'm not going out with him.'

The twins looked at each other.

'What do you mean, fallen for *you*? He's fallen for *me*.'

'No, he hasn't, he's fallen for *me*.'

The twins paused, and then laughed. They'd never argued over a boy before and weren't about to start now.

'We'll just have to let him down without crushing him too much.'

'Dominil should do it, she's the manager.'

'Dominil, could you try and make him fall in love with someone else?'

Dominil regarded them with icy dislike. 'I'm not a dating agency.'

'How about giving him a whirl yourself? He's not bad-looking in a sort of hollow-cheeked-guitarist way.'

The twins exploded with laughter at the thought of Dominil being a groupie for their guitarist. Beauty choked on her drink, and needed assistance from her sister.

Dominil turned her back on them. 'Kalix. I don't imagine you came here to listen to this pair of idiots. Come upstairs to my office and we'll talk.'

51

At the top of the house Dominil had cleared out a small room and installed some shelves for files, and a computer, making a small haven of efficiency in the chaotic household. She sat at her desk, directed Kalix to a wooden chair, and looked directly at her. 'What do you want to see me about?'

Kalix gazed at the ceiling.

'I have a lot of work to do,' said Dominil, 'so please get to the point.'

Kalix shrank back a little. Even though she'd experienced Dominil's abrupt manner in the past, it could still be alarming. 'Gawain,' she whispered.

'What about him?'

'I want to find out who killed him.' Kalix shrank a little more, half expecting Dominil to throw her out for wasting her time.

Instead the white-haired werewolf nodded. 'That sounds reasonable. You did have a close relationship. I don't imagine the police are going to solve the case, especially as Thrix has removed the body and sent it back to the castle.'

Kalix's heart lurched. 'What?'

'Weren't you aware of that?'

Kalix shook her head. No one had told her. Tears formed in her eyes at the thought of Gawain's body being transported across the country. She wiped them away angrily, not wanting to cry in front of Dominil.

'You found his body,' said Dominil, ignoring Kalix's tears. 'Was there anything there to suggest who killed him? Or even how he died?'

Kalix managed to control her tears but her voice was small as she spoke. 'I don't know. It all happened so quickly. I'd just found him and then the hunters arrived and then I was fighting them and the police came.'

'Was he freshly killed?'

Kalix shook her head, and felt quite miserable. 'He'd been dead for days. I could smell it.'

'With a wound in his heart?'

'A bad one. It had bled a lot.'

'A silver bullet?'

Kalix was uncertain. She'd gone over it in her mind since, trying to remember all the details, but she wasn't certain about the wound. 'I think the wound in his chest was too big for a bullet.'

'If he was shot from behind, the bullet would have torn a large hole in his chest when it exited the body,' said Dominil.

Kalix broke down completely. She thought she might have cried enough about Gawain already, but apparently she hadn't. She sat in the small wooden chair and sobbed. Her thin frame shook and she panted for breath as she cried miserably, once more picturing Gawain lying dead. It took a long time for her to compose herself. She wiped her face with her sleeve. 'Gawain was strong and fast. It wouldn't have been easy for a hunter to even fire a shot at him. Gawain would have killed him first.' Kalix paused, gathering her thoughts. 'I wondered if it might have been a Begravar knife.'

The fabled Begravar knife was a weapon deadly to werewolves. Once activated, it disorientated and confused them, and its blade could pierce their hide.

'It's possible. You killed Sarapen with a Begravar knife. Though Thrix returned it to the castle.'

'There was another. Mikulanec had one.' Kalix had killed the hunter Mikulanec but she didn't know what had happened to his knife.

'So that's one weapon, deadly to werewolves, not accounted for,' continued Kalix, 'and there are other ways he could have died. Another werewolf with a silver-coated knife could do it. It could have been the Douglas-MacPhees.' Kalix looked down at her list of suspects. 'And there's sorcery.'

'Who would use sorcery against Gawain?'

'My sister,' said Kalix.

'She seems an unlikely suspect.'

'I don't think she's unlikely. She could have killed him through

153

jealousy.' Kalix growled, a long, low sound. 'I don't trust the clan either. Plenty of people at the castle hated Gawain.' She looked directly at Dominil. 'So will you help me?'

'Help you? With what?'

'Finding the killer.'

'No,' said Dominil, immediately.

Kalix was shocked. She'd been expecting her cousin to agree. 'I can't. I have too much to do.'

'But I need your help,' pleaded Kalix.

'Sorry,' said Dominil. 'I can't.'

Kalix was bewildered. She'd been certain that Dominil would help her. 'But I need to find out. I'm going to kill whoever murdered Gawain.'

'I don't blame you for that. But I have too much to do.'

'What?'

'Private matters,' said Dominil. 'Important to me.'

Kalix felt on the verge of tears again. She knew she couldn't really count Dominil as a friend, but the white-haired werewolf had helped her in the past. She'd thought she would again.

'I suggest you talk to Thrix about it,' said Dominil.

'I don't want to talk to my sister!'

'You should. She examined the scene of death. She might have picked up useful information.'

'But Thrix slept with Gawain!' yelled Kalix, and stood up in agitation. 'I'm not going to talk to her. She probably killed him herself!'

'I don't think that's likely.'

Kalix tried to think of something else to say, something persuasive. She couldn't come up with anything. 'Why won't you help?' she said, for want of anything better.

Dominil remained impassive. 'I have too many things to do.'

'You don't care about Gawain!' screamed Kalix, losing her temper completely. 'You're glad he's dead! Everyone's glad he's dead! The MacRinnalchs probably killed him! You all did it!'

Kalix smashed her fist into the shelf beside her and broke it, sending folders tumbling to the floor. Once more her eyes flooded with tears. She wrenched open the door and stormed downstairs and out of the house. The young werewolf rushed along the quiet side street in Camden, back to the busy area around the Tube station. Then she stepped into a shop doorway, took her bottle of laudanum from her bag, and sipped from it, something she would not normally have done in public.

As she replaced the cap she noticed the bottle was almost empty. She'd have to replenish her supply soon. For that she'd need money. The only money she had was the allowance from her mother. Kalix scowled quite ferociously, hating Moonglow for her treacherous behaviour in threatening to tell Verasa if she didn't go to college. Kalix wondered how she'd managed to get herself into the position where she was forced to go to college when she had other things she should be doing. She raged against her fate, and by the time she arrived back in Kennington, she'd added Moonglow, Daniel and Vex to the list of people she hated.

52

Captain Easterly didn't need to arrive at work at the magazine early, and had time to deliver a case of wine to the warehouse. He was something of a wine connoisseur and paid for a specialised storage space. He drove from the warehouse into town, trying not to think about Albermarle. If his cousin wanted to get himself killed over some girl he'd known at Oxford, that was his problem. Negotiating the large roundabout at the foot of Hyde Park, he glanced in his rear-view mirror and discovered, rather shockingly, that he wasn't alone in the car. There was a woman sitting in the back seat. Easterly was quite certain she hadn't been there a moment ago. He jammed on the brakes and thrust his hand beneath his jacket to draw his gun, assuming that a werewolf had somehow tracked him down. Before he could produce the gun, the woman vanished. The Captain was stunned, wondered briefly why he'd started hallucinating, and was still wondering a second later when she appeared in the front seat alongside him.

The woman glanced in the mirror and adjusted a strand of long blonde hair. 'You seem to have no protection at all,' she said, in an accent that was both exotic and difficult to identify.

'Did you just travel through space?' demanded Easterly.

The woman shrugged. 'In your terms, perhaps.' She studied Easterly. She didn't find him the most imposing hunter she'd ever encountered, but at least he hadn't panicked when she'd materialised. That would have been a bad sign.

Easterly pulled over to the side of the road, demonstrating impressive driving skills in the heavy traffic. 'Who are you?'

'Princess Kabachetka of the Hainusta.'

'The Hainusta?'

'The mightiest of fire elementals.'

The Captain stared at her. He'd read about the Hainusta and the Hiyasta in the files of the Avenaris Guild, but had never really believed in them before. The Guild had a great store of esoteric knowledge, gathered over hundreds of years, but he'd never expected to meet any sort of otherworldly being. Apart from werewolves, of course.

'What are you doing here?' he asked.

'I want you to kill a werewolf.'

'How do you know I know anything about werewolves?'

'I just know. And I know you have a good reputation within your organisation, though you've had little success recently. But please don't question me on matters of no consequence. I have many demands on my time. You need a new werewolf target. I'll show you one who's more powerful than any other werewolf in London.'

'How can you travel through space?'

The Princess frowned. That didn't seem like a relevant question. She held up her hand, and briefly caused one of her fingers to ignite.

'I can do many things you would find strange. But they are not of great importance at this moment. What is important is that you must kill Thrix.'

Easterly's brow furrowed. Thrix was an unusual name, and he seemed to know it from somewhere.

'She owns a small fashion house. Thrix fashions.'

He almost laughed. He'd met Thrix briefly at a fashion show. Quite a well-regarded designer, he recalled. 'I know her. She's not a werewolf.'

'She's the most powerful werewolf in London.'

'She certainly isn't.'

The Princess compressed her lips.

'I did fear that this would be a tedious conversation. Captain Easterly, believe me when I tell you that Thrix MacRinnalch—'

'MacRinnalch? You're saying that Thrix, the fashion designer, is a member of the MacRinnalch clan?'

'Of course.'

'That's ridiculous.'

'It only sounds ridiculous because she's a powerful sorcerer and has spells of bafflement that hide her from hunters. Anyone who wishes evil on Thrix cannot hold on to his thoughts. The memory of her werewolf nature is made to fade.'

Easterly looked at her very sceptically. 'So now she's a werewolf and a sorcerer? This isn't sounding very convincing.'

Princess Kabachetka help up one hand, beautifully manicured. 'Enough. It's beneath my dignity to try and persuade a human that I'm telling the truth. You should be honoured I'm talking to you at all. Fortunately, I am prepared.'

With that the Princess touched her fingertips to Captain Easterly's forehead. Easterly looked concerned, then interested, then amazed.

'Thrix MacRinnalch is a werewolf,' he said, very surprised.

'As I just said. I have removed her spells of bafflement from you. And though your memory will fade again, I can replenish the energy, and keep it in your mind that she is a werewolf. You can hunt and kill her.'

'I can't believe that Thrix is a werewolf. I really admired her last collection.'

'I don't believe her clothes are really so fine. It's irrelevant, in any case. Now that you know what she is, I'll help you defeat her.'

'Why are you so keen to see her dead?' asked Easterly, who felt he had good reason to be suspicious of this so-called Princess.

'Because I don't like her. Not that, once again, it is of any relevance.'

'Are you really sure you've got the right woman?' he asked.

The Princess touched her fingertips to his forehead again and transmitted some clear knowledge of Thrix's past, knowledge that didn't fade immediately. Easterly shook his head, and felt angry that a powerful werewolf like Thrix MacRinnalch could have passed herself off as human for so long.

'The first thing to do is secure you an introduction,' said the Princess. 'Do you like opera, Captain Easterly?'

53

'I sense some sadness in you,' said Dithean NicRinnalch.

'You do? How?' asked the Fire Queen.

'The trees tell me that you're not happy.'

'Hmm . . . Perhaps the trees should mind their own business. But I admit that I'm not entirely happy. Despite my brilliant success in securing the services of Mr Felicori for the Mistress of the Werewolves, I myself will not be able to attend the event. Really, it's intolerable. One almost wishes there was no feud between the Hiyasta and the MacRinnalchs.'

'Could you end the feud?' asked Queen Dithean, reasonably.

'Not without a heartfelt apology from the MacRinnalchs, who were the prime instigators of the whole affair. The Queen of the Hiyasta cannot go cap in hand to a bunch of werewolves.'

'Then you must take pleasure in doing your friend Thrix MacRinnalch a good favour, without any benefit to yourself,' said Queen Dithean.

'I suppose so. But I'd like it better if there was some benefit to myself. I have never claimed to be a philanthropist. Beau DeMortalis sends his best regards, by the way.'

The Fairy Queen laughed. At the chariot races he had shamelessly flattered her. 'Perhaps you should take DeMortalis as a consort?'

'Impossible. He was an enemy in the war. I like him, but he has too many detractors among my loyal supporters. How lucky you are, Queen Dithean, to have many children already fluttering around. Had I not the estimable Distikka to protect me from the constant complaints of my government, I would have despaired. A little more whisky in my buttercup? Thank you, Dithean, that would be very acceptable.' Queen Malveria sipped her drink, but though she was comfortable in Colburn Woods she couldn't shake the feeling of dissatisfaction that clouded her mind. 'Thrix will be at the operatic event. I can't help feeling that she could have applied more pressure on her mother to enable me to attend. But she seems unwilling.'

'Did I not say that the MacRinnalch women think mainly of themselves?'

'Really, Dithean, that was not my meaning at all. You are far too severe in your judgements. Thrix has many warm and selfless emotions, and has often helped me out.'

'For payment, in the main.'

'Perhaps, but she is a businesswoman.' Malveria felt slightly annoyed by Queen Dithean's criticism of her good friend Thrix. When the Fairy Queen again mentioned the Enchantress's notable lack of romantic success, Malveria refused to let it pass unchallenged. 'Once more, you are being unfair. True, she may have scared off men all over London, but these were unsuitable men. It's not her fault.'

The Fairy Queen smiled sweetly. 'I've known her longer than you, Malveria. Like her siblings, she's too self-obsessed to enter into a fulfilling relationship.'

'I am certain you are wrong, dearest Fairy Queen.'

'And I'm certain I'm not, dearest Fire Queen.'

Malveria smiled sweetly herself. The Fire Queen's agile mind had spotted an opportunity. 'Would you care for a wager on the matter?'

'A wager? What sort of wager?'

'A small bet, for our entertainment. I understand the fairies are not averse to betting?'

The fairies weren't. Queen Dithean looked interested.

'I really feel that Thrix is capable of a happy romance. You may look cynical, Dithean – far more cynical than I would have guessed for a fairy queen – but I have faith it will happen. I'm prepared to bet on it.'

Dithean chuckled. 'What do you want to bet?'

'Your fairy lipstick,' said Malveria, a little too quickly.

The Fairy Queen raised her eyebrows. 'That is a fairy secret.'

'Well, obviously, dearest friend. If it were not, I wouldn't have to make the wager.'

A very delicate frown played over the Fairy Queen's brow as

she considered Malveria's offer. The secret of her lip colouring was an ancient one, not to be dispensed lightly. She would be loath to give it up. On the other hand, she did enjoy a good wager. And Malveria had something she rather craved.

'What will you stake?'

'Gold?' suggested Malveria.

'How about your necklace?'

Malveria's hand went involuntarily to her neck. She immediately regretted that she was wearing the Santorini necklace. It was one of the Hiyasta Royal Family's most valuable heirlooms. First Minister Xakthan would be appalled at the thought of it being gambled away.

But I am Queen, thought Malveria. And it's my necklace. Besides, no one will ever know providing I win the bet.

'You appreciate the value of this necklace? It dates back more than three and a half thousand years,' Malveria told the Fairy Queen. 'It was made from the flaming elements of the volcanic eruption at Santorini, captured in mid-flight by my ancestor Queen Malmardi. Who had rather encouraged the explosion, so the family legend goes. It contains the living fire of a previous era and is quite priceless.'

'I admire the way it glitters. I always have.'

The Fire Queen grappled with emotion. She really shouldn't be betting her Santorini necklace. But she really wanted the Fairy Queen's lipstick.

'Very well,' said Malveria at last. 'It's a bet. Provided you extend our parameters somewhat. Shall we say that if any of the MacRinnalch women engage in a happy romance in the next four months, I shall be the winner?'

'Three months.'

'Dithean, you drive a hard bargain, as fairies often do. Very well, three months.'

54

Vex's enthusiasm for college had not dimmed. She infuriated Kalix by rushing into her room, demanding to know why she wasn't ready yet. Kalix regarded the morning with bleary eyes. She wished it was still dark, so she might turn into a werewolf and kill Vex on the spot. Instead, she rose slowly from her bed, pulled on some old clothes, and trooped miserably downstairs. Moonglow was up already, making tea, and yawning. Moonglow wasn't at her best in the early morning, which was some relief to Kalix. At least it spared her the annoyance of having to listen to an encouraging lecture.

Daniel and Moonglow both had classes at university and Daniel drove them all into the centre of town. As they moved slowly through the morning traffic, hemmed in by buses and a great fleet of parental vehicles carrying children to school, the mood in the car settled into a familiar pattern. Daniel was morose, Moonglow was thoughtful, Kalix was in a bad mood, and Vex was agog with excitement.

'Isn't this great! We're going to college again! We're going to learn maths today!'

Vex's long-suffering tutors in her own dimension would have been amazed at the enthusiasm she now displayed for studying mathematics. Vex had proved herself resistant to their best efforts. Now, liberated from the constraints of the Imperial Palace, she showed almost as much enthusiasm for college as she did for Camden Market.

'Good luck,' said Moonglow, sincerely. Moonglow had been impressed by Vex's enthusiasm, though she knew that Vex and Kalix's maths class was nothing more than a simple entry-level affair, designed to bring them up to the level of numeracy shown by eight- or nine-year-olds.

'Do you think we should be cheerleaders?' screamed Vex, and began to make up a cheer.

'There aren't any cheerleaders,' said Kalix angrily.

'There must be.'

'We're not going to school in California, you idiot,' said Kalix. 'It's just some small college for stupid people. There aren't any cheerleaders.'

'Are you sure about that?' asked Vex. 'I've never seen any college on TV where they don't have cheerleaders.'

Agrivex's entire experience of education had been formed from television, most of it American. The fact that the shabby old building they now attended bore no relation to anything ever shown on television hadn't disturbed her illusions.

'Do you have cheerleaders at your university?' she asked Moonglow.

'No. I don't even know if there's any sport.'

Daniel didn't know either. Neither he nor Moonglow had ever paid any attention to sports, whether at school or university. It had never been an important subject at any institute they'd attended.

'Look, I've got new paper and a pencil and a marker pen!'

Vex brandished her college supplies enthusiastically. Kalix sank down in the back seat and wished that she were somewhere else. It was bad enough having to display her ignorance in front of strangers without Agrivex making the whole thing intolerable. When Daniel dropped them off just south of the river, Vex leapt from the car.

'I am so ready to learn things!'

Catching sight of Kalix's unhappy face Moonglow was again moved to pity. 'Poor Kalix,' she said, as they drove off. 'If the lessons don't kill her, Vex might.'

Daniel didn't reply. In recent days his conversation had dropped to a series of grunts. His demeanour was now so hostile that Moonglow felt they couldn't go on like this. It was too much of a strain. Moonglow regretted that she couldn't go out with him, but there was nothing to be done about it. Although, thought Moonglow, even if it wasn't for the curse, he's not exactly showing himself in an attractive light anyway.

At the remedial college Vex was rushing into class, exchanging greetings with everyone. She was already a well-known figure, both for her extravagant appearance and her outgoing personality. She exchanged friendly smiles with two young Chinese students, here to improve their English skills, and a rather sinister-looking middle-aged man with dark tattoos on his arms. He was a prisoner nearing the end of his sentence, now on day release to improve his education. Their teacher for the day stood in front of the class. A prematurely aged fellow in a grey suit that had seen better days, he had the air of a man who was disappointed with his lot.

'We're about to learn the basics of long division,' he began.

'I have a new marker pen!' came a voice from the middle of the class. The teacher looked up in surprise. 'Pardon?'

'Bright yellow!' said Vex, waving the pen. 'I can really highlight things now.'

'Very good,' said the teacher, dryly. 'Now, if you'll look at the example on—'

'Will there be a lot of stuff to highlight?'

'I'm sure you'll find plenty of opportunities.'

'I like highlighting,' said Vex, and beamed at the teacher. A few people in the class giggled. The teacher seemed to shrink a little. Attempting to gather himself, he directed the attention of his students towards the blackboard and continued to speak. 'As you can see—'

'Kalix, do you need to borrow a highlighter?' cried Vex, loudly. 'I have some spare ones – green and pink and yellow. I like yellow best.'

'Please pay attention,' said the teacher firmly. The young fire elemental smiled at him broadly, to show she was paying attention.

The two Chinese students next to her frowned at her, wanting to get on with the lesson. Vex beamed at them too. Kalix slumped in her chair and wondered if this would ever end.

55

The Enchantress relaxed on her couch. There was a bottle of wine on the table next to her, and two glasses hovering in the air. She made the wine bottle float too, filled both glasses, and snapped her fingers to bring one towards her.

The Fire Queen materialised beside her on the couch. 'Am I on time?'

'Just about to begin.'

'Excellent. I do so love the Japanese fashion cable network.' Malveria drew the other glass of wine towards her and then sat contentedly beside the Enchantress, watching their favourite programme.

'These shoes are not good at all,' said the Fire Queen, after ten minutes or so. 'I have many better pairs. Nor do I like her handbag. Though I have some liking for the cocktail dress.'

Thrix agreed with Malveria. 'It's nice. Not too much like the one I'll show you tomorrow, though.'

The Queen smiled in anticipation of the new range of cocktail dresses that the Enchantress had prepared for her. 'I am expecting many triumphs at my upcoming social events. My subjects may ever after speak with awe of the fabulous age of Malveria's splendid cocktail dresses.' She smiled warmly, and picked her bag off the floor to cradle it in her lap. 'Ever since I obtained this bag, life has felt good.'

The Enchantress nodded. Her own bag, a match for the Fire Queen's, rested on the floor beside the couch. Since the Enchantress had secured two advance copies of the Abukenti handbag, a bag which had rapidly become the number one item that the fashionable woman must have, both Malveria and Thrix had felt themselves enveloped in the warm glow that only having the most wanted handbag on the planet could produce. There were important people in the fashion world – editors, billionaires' wives, princesses – who would have done anything to get hold of an Abukenti bag, but couldn't. The range had sold out immediately. It was a great triumph for Thrix that she'd secured them, and one that had brought both herself and the Fire Queen much happiness.

'There's nothing like a really good handbag,' sighed Malveria, during the advert break. 'It gets one through all sorts of crisis.' She sipped her wine. 'Have you located Susi Surmata, the reluctant fashion writer?'

Thrix frowned, and brought her own bag from the floor onto her lap for comfort. 'No. I've emailed the woman five more times and she still hasn't got back to me. She obviously hated my clothes and decided not to write about them. Leaving me looking foolish in the eyes of the fashion buyer at Eldridge's, who will now never buy any clothes from me. Leading to debt, failure and bankruptcy.'

'Perhaps you exaggerate a little?'

'Not much. Damn Susi Surmata.'

'We must find her. Bring forth all the information you have on her, and we will work great sorcery. Did I tell you that I recently tricked the vile Princess Kabachetka? My intelligence services managed to convince her that she was turning up merely for some daytime event when it was in fact an evening soirée and the poor woman had to remain for hours, incorrectly dressed! Such hilarity has not been seen in my realm for years.' The Fire Queen paused, and looked puzzled. 'What were we talking about?'

'Susi Surmata not writing about me.'

'Ah yes. And indeed, I've learned that this Susi woman does have great power. Every magazine I read seems to quote her, and fashion editors hang on her words. It is most strange that she has let you down.'

The two friends drank more wine, and watched the next segment of the programme together.

'Were we speaking of your love life?' asked Malveria after a while.

'No.'

'I'm sure it was mentioned somewhere.'

'It definitely wasn't,' declared Thrix.

'Ah,' mused Malveria, 'a sure sign that it's going badly. The terrifying lack of romance in your life may have destructive consequences, Enchantress. Something has to be done.'

'No it doesn't.'

'Yes it does. Now I know, Enchantress, that you do not enjoy outsiders meddling and I would never dream of doing such a thing. However, I have been searching for a suitable partner for you.'

'How is that not meddling?'

'A little help hardly counts as meddling. Anyway, I have met the perfect man, at the opera. I've arranged for you to have dinner with him tomorrow night.'

'What?' Thrix's blue eyes widened in alarm. 'You've set me up on a blind date? For tomorrow night?'

'Is it not splendid?'

'No! I'm busy. And besides, blind dates are always a disaster.'

'But *all* your dates are disasters, dearest friend. You may at least try this one. Really, he is a most suitable man, employed in the fashion industry and with a keen eye for a good frock. I found him charming and attractive.'

Thrix felt an urgent need to fill up her wine glass. 'How am I meant to make conversation with a man I don't know?'

'Enchantress, a woman who masterminded the defeat of the terrible Three-headed Dragon of Despair does not just send her friend out on a date without planning in advance. I will be there to move things along. I've arranged for you, your date, myself, and Mr Felicori to eat together in that splendid restaurant near the opera house. Do not worry about piling on surplus pounds, Mr Felicori is a large man with a hearty appetite and can no doubt eat for both of us.'

Thrix was by this time staring at the Queen open-mouthed.

'You're having dinner with Felicori? The opera singer?'

'Is it not excellent? I have separated him from the herd of women who pursued him, and now we will have dinner. Your mother's opera venture is secure. Mr Felicori will sing for her, not wishing to fail to do me a favour.'

Thrix, while not liking the sound of the plan at all, was forced to admit that the Queen had done well if she'd persuaded Felicori to sing in Edinburgh. 'Thanks, Malveria. Mother will be pleased. But did you really have to include me in your plans? I don't want to go on a date.'

'Nonsense, Enchantress. Your body is screaming for sex.'

'No it isn't.'

'Then it should be. I am so looking forward to our dinner together.'

Thrix sighed. There seemed no way out of it. 'What's this man's name?'

'James. Or, if you wish to refer to him by his old military title – which some women do find thrilling – Captain Easterly.'

56

Verasa MacRinnalch, wife of the late Thane, mother of the new Thane, and still Mistress of the Werewolves, sat in her airy chamber in the castle and contemplated her forthcoming fundraising event with pleasure. Markus had proved to be a very able organiser and she was delighted with the way he'd helped. Now it seemed almost certain that Felicori would sing at her event, so it was bound to garner a lot of attention. Verasa felt unusually warm towards Thrix. Verasa didn't quite know how she'd done it, but Thrix had persuaded the notoriously difficult Felicori to sing for them. It was splendid news. Even more satisfying than the letter she'd received recently from the Moderator of the Church of Scotland, thanking her for her generous contribution to the restoration of the old church in Cromarty.

She took a few sips from her glass of red wine, savouring the drink and feeling more relaxed than she had for a long time. Her event was going to be successful. Markus was a good Thane. Life was satisfactory.

A servant knocked discreetly and entered her chambers.

'There's a woman at the castle gates asking to see you, Mistress.'

'At the gates? Someone we know?' Castle MacRinnalch was located in a very remote part of the Highlands. Strangers didn't just appear at the gates.

'Apparently not. The guard would have dismissed her but she introduced herself as Princess Kabachetka. Not wishing to offend a member of the Royal Family, he asks for advice.'

Verasa stared. Princess Kabachetka was indeed a member of a Royal Family, but not of this world. She rose from her chair and spoke rather urgently. 'Kabachetka? She was an ally of Sarapen and an enemy of Thrix.' Verasa stubbed out her cigarette and finished her wine with a quick gulp. 'Tell the guard to escort her to my reception room. Make that several guards. And make sure they don't let her out of their sight.'

Minutes later there was a hasty conference in Verasa's chambers as Clan Secretary Rainal arrived in a hurry, as troubled and perplexed as Verasa. Fire elementals were not welcome visitors at Castle MacRinnalch.

'Has Markus returned from Edinburgh?' Rainal asked.

The Mistress of the Werewolves shook her head. The Thane was away on business and wasn't expected back till the next day.

'Perhaps you should delay the interview till night falls,' suggested Rainal.

'So I can transform? Rainal, I hardly think it's going to come to open combat.'

'She fought for Sarapen.'

'The war's over. I can't see why she'd carry it on. It's not like the MacRinnalchs have ever been enemies of the Hainusta.'

It was true. The Hiyasta and the MacRinnalchs had been enemies for a very long time, due to some unfortunate incidents in the past, but the antagonism had never extended to the neighbouring realm of the Hainusta. Indeed, it was hard to remember any contact between the two races.

'It's like stepping back in time,' mused Verasa. 'The fire elementals hardly trouble the Earth these days. Or at least they didn't till Thrix started making clothes for them.'

'Princess Kabachetka was the last person to see Sarapen alive. She took his body away.' The disappearance of Sarapen's body was a lingering cause of discomfort.

'I suppose I should find out what she wants,' said Verasa briskly. She made her way down the short stone corridor that led to her reception room. Like the rest of her chambers, it was more comfortably furnished than the rest of the castle. Outside the reception room, Verasa greeted the guard, opened the door and strode inside.

The Princess, sitting on a red chaise longue, rose gracefully to meet her.

Verasa's first reaction was one of surprise. In her limited experience of fire elementals, she'd never encountered one with blonde hair before. She hadn't imagined they existed.

'Verasa MacRinnalch, Mistress of the Werewolves? I am Princess Kabachetka, eldest daughter of the Empress Asaratanti, ruler of the realm of the Hainusta.' If the Princess was at all uncomfortable to find herself in the midst of a clan of werewolves, she didn't show it. Her voice was relaxed, each syllable rolling off her tongue in what seemed like an exaggeratedly exotic manner.

The Mistress of the Werewolves eyed her curiously, taking in her expensive clothes, her perfectly coiffured hair, her elegant high heels. She could see why she was a rival to Malveria.

'I apologise for turning up unannounced, in breach of all protocols. But I felt a swift visit in person was best. I have come about Sarapen.'

'What about him?' said Verasa, stiffly.

'I am sorry to tell you that he is dead.'

'I believe we knew that already. The Begravar knife to the heart was a killing blow.'

'Not quite,' said the Princess. 'I withdrew the knife and removed his still-living body in an attempt to save him. I placed him in a state of suspended animation at the root of the great Eternal Volcano of the Hainusta. There, the energies kept him alive. It was my intention to try and revive him. To that end, I utilised all the power of the Hainusta – our fire, our volcano, and our sorcery. For months I struggled to save his life.' The Princess paused, and her brow wrinkled delicately. 'I am most sorry to report that I failed.' Her brow wrinkled further and she passed her hand across her forehead. She pursed her lips, as if struggling to control some deep emotion.

'Do you mind if I sit? The teleportation from my dimension to your castle was long and cold.' She took her seat on the chaise longue, and stared at the floor.

When she looked up again, a tear was glistening on her cheek. 'I held your son in very high regard. I'm so sorry I could not save him.'

The Mistress of the Werewolves was quite startled by the Princess's tale. She'd believed that Sarapen had died months ago, victim to the mortal wound of the Begravar knife. Apparently this wasn't the case. She sat down beside the Princess.

'Did he regain consciousness?'

Princess Kabachetka shook her head. 'No, we could not bring him back to consciousness. But he rested peacefully in these last months, sustained by the volcano.'

The Mistress of the Werewolves found herself unsure of what to say, and touched by more emotion that she'd expected to feel. At the end of his life Sarapen had been her bitter enemy. In truth, they had never really been friends. Sarapen had been the Thane's favourite. Verasa much preferred Markus. But now, hearing of his last days, and Princess Kabachetka's efforts to save his life, she found herself almost sharing in the Princess's tears. Verasa held out her hand and placed it on the Princess's shoulder to comfort her.

Kabachetka cried for a minute or so, then shook her head, and brought herself under control. 'So now I must return the body to you for proper burial, which is the fitting thing to do.'

169

'I appreciate you coming here,' said Verasa. She felt genuinely grateful to the Princess. It couldn't have been easy to walk alone into a stronghold of werewolves bearing such news. It spoke well of Kabachetka's character.

57

When her lessons ended for the day Kalix felt as if there was a wide-open space where her thoughts would normally be. Several hours of studying English and maths had led her through anxiety, anger, unhappiness and depression; at the end of it all she just felt blank.

I hate going to college, she thought, making her way wearily from the building. I'm never coming back.

She quickened her pace, hoping to make it to the bus stop before Vex appeared. She turned a corner, speeded up, and then abruptly collided with the youthful fire elemental, who'd suddenly materialised in front of her.

'Whoa!' cried Vex as they tumbled to the ground. 'Watch where you're going!'

'What do you mean, watch where I'm going? You materialised right in front of me! You're not meant to teleport around here!'

'Is there a rule against it?' asked Vex.

'You're meant to be human!' said Kalix, lowering her voice as other students appeared. 'Humans don't teleport.'

Vex nodded as she rose to her feet. 'I forgot. Wasn't that another good day?'

Kalix glared at her, and marched on, hoping that Vex might leave her alone. She was wasting her time. The concept that someone might want to be on their own seemed completely alien to Vex and she skipped after the werewolf, still chattering away brightly.

'Did you understand that long division?'

'Not really,' grunted Kalix.

'Me neither. But I did highlight everything and I think that was the main point.'

The street outside the college was surprisingly dilapidated.

Though they were just south of the river, the area around the college had not been renovated. Even at the main junction, close to the railway station, there were shabby hoardings and the pavement was cracked and broken. At the bus stop they met Decembrius. Kalix's heart sank further.

'It's the funny red-haired werewolf,' said Vex, cheerfully.

'What do you want?' demanded Kalix.

'I've come to carry your schoolbooks,' said Decembrius.

Kalix scowled. 'Is that meant to be funny?'

Decembrius shrugged.

Kalix had had enough strain for one day and felt herself losing her temper. 'You better hope the bus comes before the darkness does,' she said, quite loudly, 'because if it gets dark I'm going to transform and then I'm going to kill you.'

'Right here in this busy street?'

'Yes.'

Kalix looked fierce enough to mean it. Decembrius realised that he wasn't going to impress Kalix with small talk at the bus stop. 'I thought you could do with some help finding out who killed Gawain,' he said.

'Why would I want your help?'

'I don't see anyone else volunteering. The rest of the clan don't care.'

A bus arrived at the stop, a bright red double-decker. Kalix and Vex pressed their bus passes against the scanner beside the driver. Neither would have managed such a feat had Moonglow not taken them to the local shop and organised their bus passes for them. Behind them Decembrius was forced to scrabble in his pockets for change, while passengers behind him grumbled at the delay.

Kalix climbed the stairs, sitting upstairs at the front. Vex planted herself firmly beside her.

Decembrius came up the stairs a minute later, having finally sorted out his ticket, and sat behind them. He leaned forward to speak in Kalix's ear. 'Have you talked to Thrix yet?'

Kalix shook her head.

'You should. She examined the crime scene. She could probably tell you a lot about what happened.'

'I don't want to see Thrix.'

171

'No doubt. But you need to. I'll come with you.'

Kalix twisted her head round and looked fierce. 'I don't need your help,' she hissed.

'Suppose it was the Guild that killed him? How are you going to take revenge? Do you even know where the Guild's head-quarters is?'

Kalix looked blank. She didn't know. No one knew.

'I could find it, if I put my mind to it,' said Decembrius. 'I'm good at finding things.' He grinned, and showed his very white teeth under his angular features. He knew he was presenting quite a strong argument. No matter how determined Kalix might be to hunt down Gawain's killer there didn't seem much she could do on her own. The trail was too cold for her to follow. It would take some serious detective work to warm it up again.

'Why do you want to help?' said Kalix.

Decembrius shrugged. 'I liked Gawain. He deserves some jus-tice.'

Kalix sat in silence for a while, considering Decembrius's offer. 'Can you really see things?'

'I can,' replied Decembrius blithely, though in reality his powers of seeing hadn't shown any signs of returning.

58

Dominil stood in front of the gigantic statue of Ramesses the Great, pondering both its smooth lines and the damage inflicted by age. A large crack ran across the left shoulder, but neither the injury nor the 3,000 years that had passed since its creation had lessened its majesty. Dominil stood as motionless as the statue while visitors to the museum flowed slowly around her. She remained there for a long time. As others arrived to admire the statue, many of them discreetly studied Dominil herself. Dominil didn't react. With her snow-white hair and frozen beauty, she had grown used to being stared at. Finally she gave way to the pressure of a stream of small children, and moved on through the gallery, pausing at the Rosetta Stone, the huge slab of carved letters and ideograms from which Egypt's ancient pictographic writing had first been deciphered.

Since arriving in London, Dominil had made numerous trips to the British Museum. Though not specifically a student of ancient history, she had a keen interest in the subject. She knew much about the history of the ancient world and always took a quiet pleasure in studying the mass of artefacts gathered in the galleries. The British Museum always relaxed her. Even when her phone vibrated in her pocket and she guessed, correctly, that it was a text message from Pete, she didn't feel too annoyed.

Why Pete the guitarist had decided to start obsessing about her was a mystery. They'd slept together once, on the night before the confrontation with Sarapen. Dominil had initiated the brief affair. It had seemed quite likely she was going to die the next day. Spending the night in company had seemed like a good idea. It had proved reasonably enjoyable. Pete was quite a pleas-ant-looking young man, and not too foolish, by the standards of Beauty and Delicious's friends. Next morning Dominil had asked him to keep quiet about their rendezvous and then dismissed it from her mind. Or she would have, had Pete not later decided that he felt passionate about her. Now he was missing rehearsals, calling her constantly, and generally interfering with the smooth running of Yum Yum Sugary Snacks. Dominil felt rather irritated about it.

And it will be worse if the twins find out, thought Dominil, pausing again in front of another huge statue, this one of Amenhotep III, ruler of Egypt a hundred years before Ramesses. Dominil wasn't looking forward to the glee with which Beauty and Delicious would greet the news that the reason for their gui-tarist's current misery was that he'd fallen hopelessly in love with her. Dominil spent much of her time lecturing the pair on acting responsibly. The twins would doubtless spare no efforts in mock-ing her were they to get the chance.

How can the idiot be broken-hearted, anyway? fumed Dominil. I made it quite clear that we should sleep together only on that one occasion. There was never any question of our association continuing.

Dominil returned her attention to the Rosetta Stone. As she compared the lettering and ideograms she could see the reflection of her long white hair in the glass that shielded the artefact. She noticed another reflection, quickly followed by the thought that the person it belonged to seemed to be very close to her. She turned round swiftly. No more than a foot away from her stood a man she recognised.

'Albermarle.'

'Dominil.'

He grinned at her. Dominil regarded him impassively. Albermarle shifted uncomfortably and took a step back. Dominil noticed that though he was still large, he'd lost weight. His wavy brown hair was unkempt; a little shorter than when she'd known him at Oxford, but still tumbling over his collar.

'How have you been?'

'Very well,' said Dominil. 'Excuse me, I'm heading for the Roman galleries.'

Dominil made to leave but Albermarle moved sharply to intercept her.

'Hey, we should catch up. You know . . . tell each other what we've been up to since university.'

Dominil stared at him blankly. She had had no interest in finding out what he'd been up to. A further stream of schoolchildren jostled past them, foreign students on a trip, very noisy, shepherded through the galleries by two harassed-looking teachers.

'Let's go to the cafe,' suggested Albermarle.

Dominil shook her head. 'I'm busy.'

'You're always busy,' said Albermarle, his voice rising.

Dominil's eyebrows went up a fraction. While she had no feelings at all for Albermarle, she was aware that he'd shown signs of being attracted to her at university. He'd had a habit of appearing at her door in the Halls of Residence on some pretext or other, or sitting close to her when they were attending the same lecture. But Dominil had had many admirers at Oxford, and rarely cared for any of them. Albermarle was too far down the list to raise even a flicker of interest.

'Goodbye,' she said curtly, and moved away, leaving Albermarle staring after her while some children, attempting to force their way past, found themselves bouncing off his large, solid frame.

174

59

Princess Kabachetka appeared distracted. Her fellow aristocrats were puzzled. Her outfit had been widely admired. At the card table she'd scored a notable success against her cousins, the Letaka sisters. It should have been enough to put her in a good humour. Yet as soon as was possible, without being dreadfully rude, the Princess called for her coat, her servants and her carriage, and left the soirée with the briefest of thanks to her hostess, the Countess of the Greenest Flame.

The young Countess felt rather insulted by the whole thing. 'The Princess barely touched her dinner.'

'Perhaps she's worrying about her weight,' suggested one of the Letaka sisters.

'I've heard she struggles with it,' agreed the other.

Difficult as it would have been for her friends to believe, Princess Kabachetka had more important matters on her mind than the social calendar.

She urged the carriage on as it made its way through the sheet of flame that swept up from the third level of the Eternal Volcano, finally depositing her at the small ravine that led into her private lair. Distikka, with her customary punctuality, was already waiting for her. The Princess greeted her in a friendlier manner than she had previously.

'Your plan is proceeding well, Distikka. For a Hiyasta, you have an effective cunning.'

Distikka barely acknowledged the compliment; she wasn't given to displays of emotion. Small, methodical, intelligent; not an elemental who would ever pour out flames of excitement. Of course, pouring out flames of excitement was rather a low-class thing to do.

'How did the Mistress of the Werewolves react to your visit?' enquired Distikka.

'Rather well. For a werewolf she's not as uncivilised as I'd feared. Though the castle is a dank and unlovely place. No wonder Thrix left to go to London.'

'And your proposal?' continued Distikka.

The Princess peered at something in the far corner. 'Before we discuss that, there's something else I want to talk about.'

'What?'

'Your motives,' said the Princess. 'You arrive here full of trai-torous intentions towards Queen Malveria, although she seems to have treated you well, given your humble origins. You suggest plans for my advancement. And for this you claim to want noth-ing more than a large sum of money.' The Princess paused, and took a few steps up and down the cavern, as if gathering her thoughts. 'Of course, money is a powerful incentive, particularly to someone who was born poor. But it seems strange that you're prepared to risk so much. If Queen Malveria were to learn of your treachery, you would die, very swiftly.'

Distikka rose. Though small in stature, when she confronted the Princess she seemed equally strong. 'Is there a point to this?'

'Of course. At first I thought it likely that you were a spy sent here by Malveria. It would be quite in keeping with her despica-ble behaviour. But no matter. I have discovered your true intentions.'

They stared at each other for a few moments. Distikka seemed interested, but not intimidated. 'I doubt you could discover much about me,' she said.

'And that is where you are wrong,' replied the Princess, tri-umphantly. 'Because, like Malveria, you do not realise the full extent of Hainusta sorcery. The power of our volcano is greater than yours. The Empress Asaratanti uses spells of which you have no knowledge. For instance . . .' She paused, as if to savour her next sentence. 'The Empress's Spell of Reverse Inheritance. Are you familiar with that? No? Of course not. Few people are. My mother Asaratanti developed it to deal with a troublesome case where a young man appeared at court claiming to be the long-lost son of a Duke who had died intestate. As the inheri-tance involved was considerable, and my mother did not wish to hand it over without good reason, she set her sorcerers to work. They created a spell for checking the heritage and parentage of a fire elemental which was far more powerful than anything that had been used before.'

'Was he the son of the Duke?'

'No. Simply an adventurer, who was swiftly executed. I've used the Spell of Reverse Inheritance to examine you, Distikka.' Though Distikka controlled her aura so effectively that it was virtually impossible to read, now, for the first time, the Princess could discern the tiniest flicker of discomfort. 'You are the last living relative of Queen Malveria. A granddaughter of a long-forgotten brother who died before Queen Malveria came to power in the great war. Though she slaughtered all her remaining relatives soon afterwards, it was not known that this long-dead brother had produced any offspring. I assume you are the result of some casual dalliance with the temple prostitutes of the western desert. Am I correct?'

Distikka had regained control of her aura, and remained impassive.

'That makes you her heir,' concluded the Princess, with satisfaction. 'Her only heir. Virtually the equivalent of a death sentence, given how fond Malveria is of executing her relatives. It was clever of you to work your way into a position of confidence, given your origins. It speaks highly of your abilities. And yet, you're not satisfied, are you?'

Distikka was unabashed. She smiled, a small smile that failed to light up her face. 'No, I'm not.'

'You'd much rather be Queen of the Hiyasta yourself. That does go a long way towards explaining your treachery.' The Princess looked pleased with herself. 'So now we understand each other much better. Shall we examine the corpse?'

They crossed the cavern together and stood over a body which lay on the bare stone floor.

'Similar build, and not a bad resemblance,' said the Princess. 'The Mistress of the Werewolves will be seeking a quick and private burial for her son. With some sorcerous help, we should be able to pass this off as Sarapen.'

60

Albermarle had taken two hunters with him to the museum, both junior members of the Guild. He met them, as arranged, in the Roman gallery. It was their first mission and their excitement showed.

'Did you make contact with the white-haired werewolf?'

'I did.'

'So now what do we do?'

'We set out to demoralise and confuse her.'

Albermarle's companions looked concerned.

'Shouldn't we just kill her?' one of them asked.

'Of course we shouldn't just kill her!' exclaimed Albermarle. Noticing that he was attracting attention from other museum visitors, he lowered his voice and ushered his companions towards the far side of a large display cabinet. 'Didn't I tell you this was a special mission? Dominil isn't your standard werewolf. She needs careful handling. And some demoralising.'

'I don't remember anything about demoralising werewolves in training.'

'I thought we were just meant to kill them.'

'Who's in charge of this mission, you or me?' snapped Albermarle. 'I say she has to be demoralised and that's what we're going to do. By the time we're finished with her, Dominil will be baffled, defeated, and forced to admit that she's not as smart as she thinks she is. And she's not that attractive either.'

Albermarle led his companions round to the other side of the huge display cabinet. There he almost bumped straight into Dominil, who was studying the coins in the cabinet. He leapt back in alarm.

'From the reign of Vespasian. I always thought he was one of the better Emperors. He certainly stabilised Rome after the civil wars of AD 69. I don't think you'll make a very good werewolf hunter, Albermarle.'

'She heard us!' croaked one of Albermarle's companions.

Albermarle shushed him. 'No matter. Yes, Dominil, your time has come. I know you're a werewolf.'

'How fascinating.'

'You think you're smart just because you were top of the year at Oxford? Well, you're not so smart. You can't get into the Guild's computers now, can you? That's because I stopped you! Me, Albermarle. I've always been a better programmer than you.'

Though the news that Albermarle was a werewolf hunter had come as a great surprise, Dominil took it calmly. It was five years or so since she'd last seen him. He'd been a post-graduate student at Oxford while she was in the final year of her degree. Though Dominil had never held him in any regard as a person, she was aware of his intellect.

It was taxing, confronting hunters in daylight when she couldn't transform. Her own natural strength was such that she didn't fear anyone, but there was always the possibility of a hunter using his gun, even though shooting a werewolf in human form was against the Guild's normal policy.

'I don't suppose you thought you'd ever have to pay for your crimes at Oxford.'

'Refusing to attend a dance with you is not a crime,' said Dominil dryly.

'That's not what I was referring to,' yelped Albermarle. 'I mean the mysterious deaths on campus.'

'Nothing to do with me,' said Dominil.

'I know you were behind them.'

Dominil raised an eyebrow. 'Are you still upset I took your place on the quiz team?'

'No! But that was my place! You stole it.'

Dominil almost smiled. 'Hunting doesn't seem like an ideal profession for you, Albermarle.'

Albermarle stared into Dominil's dark eyes. 'I found out about you and tracked you down, didn't I?'

Dominil stared back, looking up at him though she was a tall woman herself.

'I hate werewolves.'

'We're a dangerous breed,' said Dominil, evenly. The display cabinet backed up against the wall, making it impossible for her to retreat. Deciding that it was time to leave, she stepped forward to pass by the hunters.

'Look out!' cried the youngest. With that he pulled a gun from under his jacket.

'Put that away,' said Albermarle, but the young hunter was panicking. He knew that even in human form Dominil had the strength to break his neck. He levelled his gun. Dominil reacted instantaneously, grabbing his wrist, yanking him forward and striking his throat all in one swift action. The other hunter leapt backwards and reached for his own weapon. Dominil knocked him over, then ran from the room. As she exited the gallery there was a loud explosion and a bullet whistled over her head.

Dominil sprinted for her life. She hated fleeing, but three guns wielded by nervous hunters was too risky. A silver bullet would kill her just as surely in her human form as in her werewolf shape. She ran through the next two galleries, the tails of her long leather coat flying out behind her. She wove her way through the crowd of visitors, barging past them so that a trail of shouted protests followed her as she ran. As she burst into the corridor another shot rang out. The young hunter had apparently lost all control and was intent of killing her right here, witnesses or not.

Dominil had already formulated a plan of escape. Remembering the layout of the vast museum from her previous visits, she knew there was a small exit at the back of the building. To get there she'd have to circle round through some of the galleries and corridors. Once outside she could outdistance her pursuers.

Dominil ran through two galleries of Greek artefacts. A uniformed attendant shouted at her but stepped back sharply as two hunters burst into view, one of them with a gun in his hand. There were screams from a family of tourists. The werewolf sprinted into the next gallery which she remembered had a door leading back to the Egyptian section. From there she could make for the exit.

Unfortunately, the door was locked.

Dominil skidded to a halt, almost crashing into the woodwork in her haste. A sign on the wall informed visitors that the gallery was undergoing alterations. There was no exit other than the door she'd come in by.

Dominil spun round in time to see the two young hunters racing into the room, followed by Albermarle. She didn't hesitate for a second. As they raised their guns she grabbed hold of an enormous cabinet of Greek vases. She wrenched it free of its fastenings and hurled the glass case straight at the hunters. It crashed into them, showering them with broken glass and pottery. Alarms sounded as the exhibit was destroyed. Attendants flooded in, and stared in surprise at the sight of three men lying on the floor under the shattered cabinet.

Dominil brushed the attendants aside as she headed for the

exit. She hurtled into the huge marble hall at the front of the museum, then out the door and through the great stone pillars in the courtyard. Sprinting towards Museum Street she knocked students out of the way as they studied their visitors' maps. Alarms were still going off behind her. Dominil kept running till she reached Gower Street where she paused briefly to sniff the air, searching for Albermarle's scent. As far as she could tell, he wasn't close.

Dominil disappeared into the nearby warren of buildings that made up the university campus. The flight hadn't fatigued her. She maintained a brisk pace till she was a long way north of the museum, then stepped onto a bus that took her towards Euston station. Sitting on the lower deck, she appeared quite calm. Inside, she seethed with anger. Dominil didn't like to be pursued.

When she finally arrived home Dominil spent some time carefully checking that she hadn't been followed. As she opened the door and slipped inside, the sun dipped below the horizon. Dominil felt a strong desire to take on her werewolf shape, to replenish her strength, but resisted the urge for the few moments necessary to take the carefully measured dose of laudanum she required each day. That done, she transformed, then sat on the couch in her sparsely furnished living room, pondering the surprising news that her old acquaintance Albermarle was now a werewolf hunter. It was bad enough that the Avenaris Guild was seeking to destroy Yum Yum Sugary Snacks. Now they were chasing her out of museums as well. Dominil bared her fangs. She was fond of her trips to the museum, and wasn't about to give them up for anybody.

61

Vex, having received her allowance from her aunt, skipped down Tottenham Court Road quite cheerfully, a large plastic bag in each hand. The day had started off well when she put on her new *Tokyo Top Pop Boom Boom Girl* T-shirt, and improved even further when she found a great new pair of boots in Camden Market. They were of the huge gothic variety she favoured and

Vex, wise to the potential skin-chafing problems that new boots could bring, had also purchased some new Hello Kitty ankle socks to wear underneath them. Life, she thought, could hardly be better.

She paused in front of a large computer store to check her reflection. Completely oblivious to passers-by, she adjusted several of her blonde spikes, forcing them back into the golden sphere which now encompassed her features.

As Vex turned the corner onto Oxford Street her thoughts turned to Kalix. It was unfortunate that her werewolf friend seemed so unhappy. Suddenly she spied a comic shop.

Ah, thought Vex. The very thing. Nothing will cheer Kalix up like some new werewolf comics.

The young fire elemental rushed enthusiastically into the shop but was momentarily confused to find it packed with everything except comics. Vex looked round with wonder at the huge array of models, T-shirts, figurines, posters and DVDs. It all looked like it was worth investigating, but she stuck to her task, and approached the counter.

'I'm looking for comics.'

'Downstairs,' said the assistant, a rather surly-looking young woman in an X-Men T-shirt.

Vex hurried downstairs but once there she looked in bewilderment at the huge array of comics in boxes and on racks on the walls. At the counter there was another gloomy-looking assistant.

'I'm looking for *Curse of the Wolf Girl*,' she said to him.

'What for?'

'I want to buy it.'

The assistant looked at her with contempt. 'Waste of money. Terrible comic. Try under C.'

Vex looked again at the boxes of comics. 'Could you show me?'

The assistant frowned. 'In a minute. I'm busy.'

Vex was puzzled. When she went to buy T-shirts and boots, the assistants were usually friendlier. She wandered over to the comics, where a large man was flicking through a box with a determined air. Vex wasn't sure if he was an assistant or a customer.

'Is there any *Curse of the Wolf Girl*?' she asked hopefully. The man looked at Agrivex with interest, taking in her dark complexion, odd make-up, spiky blonde hair and cheerful grin. He smiled down at her.

'*Curse of the Wolf Girl*? That was a good comic.'

'The assistant said it was terrible.'

'He knows nothing. He's an idiot. He has no taste in comics whatsoever.'

Vex was slightly alarmed at the large man's apparent vehement dislike of the assistant. '*Curse of the Wolf Girl*?' she repeated, still hopefully.

'Yes, that was a good comic. Early artwork by Nathaniel Smith-Morris, as you probably remember. Of course, *Curse* only ran for twelve issues before it was cancelled, back in the 70s, so there's not that many of them around these days.'

Vex looked on expectantly as the large man riffled through another box.

'Here we are!' he said triumphantly. 'Issues 3, 7 and 8. Not bad condition.'

Vex's face lit up. She thanked him sincerely. She liked this helpful stranger, even though he wore a rather shabby grey shirt, draped loosely over a Batman T-shirt, and his hair hung over his podgy face in quite an odd manner. To her surprise, he took the comics to the counter, went behind the cash register, and rang them up himself. Apparently he worked here too, despite his contempt for his fellow assistant.

'Are there any more?'

'Not right now. We get a few old issues in every now and then. If you come in again, ask for me, and not any other dim-witted assistant who might work here. I'm Albermarle.'

Vex thanked him, and left the shop feeling happy. Now she had new boots, new socks, new make-up, and three comics that were bound to cheer Kalix up. It really had been a good day's shopping.

62

'Is that red hair natural? Does it stay red when he's a werewolf?'

Thrix frowned at her assistant. Decembrius was sitting in her waiting room and she didn't feel like discussing his hair.

'He was very insistent about seeing you,' Ann explained.

'Of course,' muttered Thrix. 'Every MacRinnalch is insistent about seeing me. It never occurs to them I might not want to see them.'

Despite her persistent attempts to separate herself from the clan, the past few months had brought visits to her London office by Markus, her mother, Dominil, Kalix, Gawain, and now Decembrius.

'Why don't they just organise their damned council meetings here and have done with it?' she grunted, putting her computer to sleep. 'You might as well show him in and get it over with.'

The last time Thrix had seen Decembrius he'd been slinking out of the wreckage after the great battle in which Sarapen had died. Though the feud was supposedly over now, Thrix readied herself with a defensive spell, just in case.

Decembrius walked into her office with a self-assured air.

'What do you want?' asked Thrix, making no attempt to sound friendly.

'The normal token of MacRinnalch hospitality?' said Decembrius, and grinned.

Thrix wasn't amused, but took her bottle of whisky from the cabinet and poured two glasses. There were times when she found the need to offer this token of hospitality intensely annoying. 'Here. Now, what do you want?'

'Kalix wants to know who killed Gawain.'

'So?'

'We thought you might have some ideas.'

'Why isn't she asking me herself?'

Decembrius shrugged. 'I suppose she doesn't feel like visiting.'

'So you thought you'd come instead?'

Decembrius smoothly ignored her irritation. 'Do you have any idea who killed Gawain?'

'Why should I? Does Kalix think I killed him?' The Enchantress shook her head. 'It wouldn't surprise me if she did. I still don't see what it's got to do with you.'

'What's so strange about me wondering about the murder of a fellow werewolf?' said Decembrius.

'The fact that you don't care whether Gawain is alive or dead, for one thing. Is this your way of trying to win Kalix over?' Dominil had once told Thrix that she believed Decembrius was very attracted to Kalix. 'Try taking her a bottle of laudanum. She'll like that better.'

'You studied the crime scene, Thrix. You sent the body back to Scotland. You might have picked up some clues.'

The Enchantress stared at Decembrius with dislike, taking in his longer and brighter hair, and his new piercings. 'When did you turn into Ziggy Stardust anyway? It's a bit late for your teenage rebellion.'

Decembrius hadn't expected the Enchantress to be pleased to see him but he was surprised by the level of her hostility. He endeavoured to remain calm, though that was never the easiest thing for a MacRinnalch to do while being insulted by a fellow member of the clan.

'What about your famous second-sight? Learned anything with that?' asked Thrix, witheringly. She had a feeling that Decembrius's much-vaunted powers of extrasensory perception might not be working so well these days. Not that she had ever held them in high regard, anyway.

The intercom buzzed. 'You've got a meeting in ten minutes,' said Ann.

'I'll tell you what I know if it will get you out of my office quickly. I work for my living, unlike certain other MacRinnalchs. Gawain was killed by a huge wound in his heart. I'm not certain what caused the wound because when I visited his bedsit he'd been dead for days and the body had gone. When I saw it later at the morgue it had already been touched by a lot of people. I couldn't learn that much. It's possible the wound was caused by a Begravar knife but I can't be certain.'

'I thought the knife was back at the castle?'

'There were two Begravar knives. One is at the castle but we don't know where the other one is. It's possible it was picked up by a hunter. Or the wound might have been caused by a silver knife. A human wouldn't have been able to drive it through Gawain's chest but a werewolf might. As for a silver bullet, it didn't seem like a bullet wound to me but I'm not an expert on ballistics. It might have been.' Thrix paused. 'It's hard to kill a werewolf, but I couldn't say exactly how it was done.'

'What about a spell?' asked Decembrius.

185

'A spell might have done it. Though I doubt that any hunter in London would have been able to do that.'

'Who else might have used a spell?'

'Me. Except I didn't. Some anti-werewolf sorcerer we don't know about. A fire elemental, maybe.'

'Like Princess Kabachetka?'

'Possibly. She can bring a lot of sorcery to this world. But I don't know of any reason why she'd attack Gawain.'

Decembrius looked thoughtful. 'The Princess probably hates Kalix for killing Sarapen,' he mused. 'Might she have attacked Gawain for revenge?'

'It doesn't seem that likely.'

'When you went to Gawain's flat, did you sense that any other werewolves had been there?'

Thrix hesitated. 'Maybe. Kalix's scent was still there. If there were others, it was some time before I was there. I couldn't say for sure.'

'You couldn't say for sure?' Decembrius sounded sceptical. 'Is that because you don't want to?'

'Do you realise how ridiculous you're being?' said the Enchantress, her temper suddenly flaring up. 'Padding around trying to do favours for Kalix? You'll be lucky if you don't end up dead.'

'Who's going to kill me?'

'Kalix's enemies. Or Kalix herself.'

'I don't think that's likely.'

Thrix laughed. 'Look what happened to Gawain. He never really understood Kalix, and you don't either. You think she's some damaged little girl who needs rescuing. She's not. She's a killer.'

'Plenty of werewolves have been known to kill.'

'Not like Kalix. Once trouble starts she can't walk away. She goes insane. She has to kill her opponent. I'm in control when I'm a werewolf. So are you, probably. Even scum like the Douglas-MacPhees can keep themselves in check. Not Kalix. She can't control herself. Probably because she was born at the full moon.'

Decembrius frowned. He'd heard rumours that Kalix had been born in her werewolf shape, on the night of the full moon. He wasn't sure whether to believe it or not. A werewolf mother would normally give birth while she was human, producing a human baby that would not experience its first werewolf change until the next full moon. To actually be born in werewolf form was extremely rare. Kalix's enemies in the clan whispered it was this that made her insane. Perhaps it was true. Decembrius had witnessed her terrifying speed and strength, and seen her defeat far larger opponents.

'Is that why she's so strong?'

'Probably,' said Thrix. 'And so crazy. You should stay clear. One day you'll find her teeth round your throat and that will be the end of you.'

'I can defend myself.'

The Enchantress laughed. 'Plenty of werewolves thought they could defend themselves against Kalix, and they all ended up dead.' She rose to her feet, signifying that it was time for Decembrius to go. 'The most likely thing is that the Guild killed Gawain,' she said. 'Dominil thinks it's time we took the fight to them, and she might be right. Though we don't even know where their headquarters is. It's hidden, probably by sorcery.'

'Could you find it?' asked Decembrius.

'I don't know. I've never tried. Clan policy is to avoid offensive manoeuvres. Now excuse me, I have a meeting to attend.'

63

'It's strange how smooth Kalix's legs are,' said Moonglow.

'What?'

'Don't you think it's strange? She's a werewolf. You might expect she'd have a lot of extra hair. But her legs are really smooth. She never has to shave them.' Moonglow noticed a look of bewilderment on Daniel's face. 'Didn't you know that?'

'How could I know?'

'By paying attention to what's going on around you?'

'Aren't Kalix's legs her own business?'

'Maybe. But it's still interesting. You probably never even noticed she doesn't have periods, either,' sniffed Moonglow.

'How could I possibly notice that?'

'From the lack of sanitary products in the bathroom? There's only mine, even though there's three girls living here. The Hiyasta don't have periods. Different reproduction system entirely, according to Vex. Unwanted products get burned away. Well, I think they do, she wasn't very clear about it.'

Daniel felt more bewildered. 'Well, why doesn't Kalix have periods? Are werewolves different too?'

'No, they're the same. Kalix doesn't have them because she's too skinny from not eating enough and abusing her body with laudanum. It's very unhealthy. I've tried talking to her about it but she won't listen. Maybe you should try.'

'Maybe I shouldn't,' said Daniel, 'unless I want to get savaged by an angry werewolf who's fed up with me asking a lot of intimate questions.'

'I just hate it that she never eats,' said Moonglow.

Daniel, who only moments ago had been planning on retreating upstairs, immediately saw an excellent opportunity to compliment Moonglow.

'You're right. Kalix is far too skinny. Not like you.'

Moonglow's head turned, rather sharply. 'What do you mean?'

'You're not nearly as skinny as her.'

'Do you think I'm overweight?'

'Well, compared to Kalix . . .' began Daniel, then hesitated, not liking the way this was going. He tried to reformulate his sentence. 'You've got a very nice figure.'

'What, for someone who's really fat compared to Kalix?'

'Who said anything about you being fat? I never mentioned anything about being fat.' Daniel attempted to protest his innocence but was interrupted by the arrival of Kalix, who seemed to have heard part of the conversation.

'Were you talking about me?' she demanded. 'Were you calling me fat?' Kalix looked accusingly at Moonglow. 'It's your fault. You keep making me eat.'

'No, I don't.'

'Yes, you do. You probably bribed Decembrius to make me eat. And now you're talking about how fat I am.'

'No one called you fat,' cried Daniel. 'I was talking about Moonglow!'

'What? So you *do* think I'm fat!' yelled Moonglow.

In the babble of angry voices no one noticed that the Fire Queen had materialised among them. Malveria watched with interest for a few moments before Vex appeared alongside her.

'Whoa!' Vex was surprised at the commotion. 'What's going on?'

'Daniel has called everyone fat and now there is tremendous chaos,' said Malveria.

'Well, he's not going to impress her like that,' said Vex. 'Daniel, if you think Moonglow's fat you should be tactful about it.'

'Absolutely,' agreed Malveria. 'If you object to Moonglow's weight, you should be encouraging, not critical. Suggest some enjoyable exercise, for instance.'

'I don't object to Moonglow's weight! We were talking about Kalix!'

'I knew it!' cried Kalix, and ran from the room in a state of agitation.

'This is ridiculous . . .' began Daniel, but his voice tailed off as Moonglow departed angrily, with the air of a woman who might never want to talk to him again. He stood looking hopeless, not entirely understanding how his compliment had gone so badly wrong.

Malveria and Vex looked at him accusingly.

'Well, Daniel,' said Malveria. 'I came to consult with Moonglow on a matter of great importance, but it may be difficult now that you have infuriated her with a barrage of calculated insults.'

'Kalix too,' added Vex. 'He insulted her as well.'

The Fire Queen nodded. 'It shows a new side to his personality, I must say. Daniel, what moves you to torment your flatmates? Surely as the man of the house you could at least pretend to be gallant?'

'I didn't torment anyone!'

'I've got comics for Kalix,' said Vex. 'I'll try and cheer her up.'

'A wise plan, almost-adopted niece. Meanwhile I will attempt to repair the damage that Daniel has inflicted on Moonglow.'

As they left the living room Daniel kicked a CD on the floor in frustration. The plastic case splintered and he regretted his action immediately. Taking what remained of his beer collection from the fridge, he went upstairs to his room to listen to music, in a foul mood.

I hate everyone, he thought, angrily. Especially Moonglow. And Kalix. And Vex and the Fire Queen. I need new friends.

Upstairs Malveria was consoling Moonglow. 'I'm sorry that Daniel's endless stream of aggressive insults has reduced you to hysterical tears. There was no need for it.'

'Thanks,' said Moonglow.

'Perhaps it would take your mind off your misery—'

'It's OK, I'm not miserable.'

'I admire your bravery! Never let a man know he has severely wounded you with his intolerable cruelty.'

The Fire Queen rather liked being in Moonglow's room. Moonglow had decorated it darkly, and the black walls reminded Malveria of the caves she'd lived in, in her youth.

'I wanted to tell you, Moonglow, that Agrivex has completed the pre-adoption ceremony at the palace. She is now only a brief step away from becoming my lawful niece. As such, she has certain obligations.'

'What obligations?'

'Not to outrage the population. Could you possibly ensure she does not become intoxicated, miss college, insult her tutors or do anything else which may lead to disgrace?'

'I'll do my best,' said Moonglow.

'Thank you. Incidentally, is there any chance of Kalix finding a boyfriend?'

Moonglow was startled by the question. 'Why?'

'No reason.' Malveria fingered her necklace. 'I am just curious.'

'Decembrius has been hanging round. But I don't think she likes him.'

In Kalix's room Vex was showing Kalix the new werewolf comics.

'Look! In this one Bella bites a robber!'

Kalix wished that she could bite Vex. But she felt groggy from laudanum, and knew Vex would dematerialise before she could reach her.

'These are good comics,' enthused Vex. 'No wonder you like them so much!'

64

Albermarle sat on the rowing machine in the gymnasium beneath the apartment block, working his muscles methodically. There had been a time when he'd felt hopelessly out of place among the surprisingly well-toned professionals who made up the gym's clientele. Not any more. Now he was in good shape. His performance on the exercise machines wasn't much behind that of Captain Easterly.

He hummed the theme tune to *Tokyo Top Pop Boom Boom Girl* as he exercised, and was so intent on his workout that he didn't notice his much-disliked distant cousin approaching.

'Albermarle, did you submit a report criticising the entire board of the Guild for over-claiming on expenses?'

'What about it?'

'Well, did you?'

'I don't see it's any business of yours,' said Albermarle. 'Part of my duties was to check all expense claims.'

'Maybe. But did you have to report Mr Carmichael for claiming an extra night at the hotel in Brussels?'

'Why not? He did claim for an extra night. He wasn't the only one. Every member of the board padded their expenses last year.'

'They were minor infractions,' said Easterly. 'Nothing to get too worked up about.'

'When I'm asked to check expenses, I check expenses,' said Albermarle, stiffly.

'Even if it means reporting the entire board?'

'If they've all claimed too much, then yes.'

Easterly sighed. He was beginning to understand why the Board of Directors had agreed to let Albermarle go into active service as a werewolf hunter, despite his clear unsuitability for the task.

'I doubt they'll be attending your funeral,' he muttered, and walked off, shaking his head.

*

Captain Easterly had come to the gym to clear his head. For some reason he couldn't fathom, he'd woken up with his mind completely fogged. He had a vague idea that he'd been on a date the night before, but he couldn't remember anything about it. It was very strange. Had he drunk too much? Even if he had, it was very odd for his memory to be so affected.

If he had overindulged, his body felt no ill effects. His exercise went well, and the whole episode had almost disappeared from his mind by the time he returned to his apartment upstairs. He showered, shaved, cleaned his teeth, and was dressing when he opened his wardrobe to select a shirt. He was startled to see a picture of a woman staring out at him. An attractive woman, with a lot of blonde hair. Who was it? Who had put the picture there?

Easterly gazed at it, and his memory began to return. Not in a flood, but slowly. That was the woman he'd been on a date with. She was a werewolf. Her name was Thrix MacRinnalch. But she was a powerful sorceress as well as a werewolf. Her spells of bafflement were such that any hunter who got close found himself unable to retain any memories. Princess Kabachetka had given him the picture as an aid to his memory and had worked some sort of spell of her own, enabling him to penetrate the Enchantress's defences.

Easterly stared at the picture, trying to recapture images of the night before. He'd gone out to dinner with her. Apart from that, he couldn't remember much. Apparently the Princess's assistance wasn't strong enough. He'd have to ask her to boost it. He stared at the picture, and felt a great loathing well up inside him. He hated werewolves, and he hated this one more than any other. As he selected a shirt and closed the door of the wardrobe, he swore he'd kill her.

65

Sarapen's funeral was a very quiet affair. Though he'd been the Thane's eldest son and a notable werewolf, his last actions had been war and rebellion against the clan. He was due his plot in the family graveyard but there was no reason for an elaborate ceremony. The Mistress of the Werewolves wanted the affair performed with due dignity, but quickly and quietly. The only other attendees, apart from the castle chaplain, were Thane Markus, Verasa's sister Lucia, Kertal and Kurian. Those were the council members currently residing at the castle. No one else had been informed or invited.

Princess Kabachetka had delivered the body as promised but had withdrawn before the service. She waited in Verasa's private chambers, in the west wing of the castle. It was an anxious wait. If it were to be discovered that the body currently being buried wasn't that of Sarapen, it would be very awkward. The Princess was prepared to fly at a moment's notice, not relishing the prospect of fighting a gang of angry werewolves in their own castle. She had poured all her sorcerous knowledge and power into the altering of the body. It should stand up to examination. It might not have fooled Doctor Angus, the werewolves' physician, if he were to have examined it, but Angus was in Edinburgh, and Verasa had no desire for a medical examination. It probably wouldn't have fooled Thrix but she was far away in London. The Princess knew the Enchantress would never show enough interest in clan affairs to examine the body. Once it was interred, she was safe. Not only that, the Princess would then be considered a valued friend of the MacRinnalchs, if Distikka's calculations proved correct.

None of them are really sad over Sarapen, anyway, thought the Princess as she waited. His family were his enemies.

Given the Princess's own feelings towards Sarapen, which were still strong, it didn't endear them to her. The Mistress of the Werewolves was obviously a calculating woman. As for Markus, the Princess's impressions of him had been very unfavourable. Good-looking, in a feminine sort of way, but that was hardly an attribute for a leader. It's amazing that this clan could select him ahead of Sarapen, she mused, her opinion of werewolves lowering even further.

The midnight funeral did not last long. No music played. The clan bagpipes were not called for, nor was the procession of torch-bearers. Sarapen was buried quietly in the plot of land reserved for the Thane's family, and Verasa and Markus returned to the castle with the air of werewolves who had performed a necessary task satisfactorily. Sarapen had been decently buried. Clan honour was secured.

As they entered the castle Verasa was sombre, but if Markus felt the slightest sadness over the interment of his brother, he didn't show it. They were both sincere in their thanks to the Princess for the return of the body. Both had been impressed by the Princess's manners, charm and sincerity.

'Perhaps I've been too harsh in my opinion of fire elementals,' Verasa confided to her son. 'The Hainusta may not be as objectionable as the Hiyasta.'

Markus didn't regard Queen Malveria nearly as poorly as did his mother, but even so he was charmed by the Princess. Though her blonde hair falling over her dark skin was unusual, she was soberly attired, and had an air of respectability about her. She told them she was interested to find herself in Scotland for the first time, and admired the castle building.

'Its strong lines remind me of home. Tell me, what are your great cities like? I've heard much of the beauty of Edinburgh.'

'It's a fine city,' Markus assured her. 'I was there just last week, making preparations for our opera.'

'Opera?' said the Princess. 'What is this?'

'A charitable event my mother is hosting.'

'It sounds fascinating,' exclaimed the Princess. 'Please tell me more.'

66

'Is that all she told you?'

After Decembrius's encounter with Thrix, Kalix was dissatisfied. Decembrius didn't seem to have learned anything at all. 'She examined the place. She must have found out something.'

Decembrius spread his arms. 'She says not. She thought it was probably the Guild. Maybe a Begravar knife. And maybe there were werewolves there sometime, though she seemed evasive about that.' Decembrius suddenly turned west out of Soho.

'Where are we going?' asked Kalix.

'I found an interesting place. You'll like it.'

Though it was close to midnight the centre of town was still busy. Decembrius led them through the crowds and across Regent Street, where it became quieter. They walked past several small shops with men's suits in the windows. Tailors' shops, Kalix thought, though she couldn't read the signs.

'Where are we?' she asked.

'Savile Row.'

Decembrius surprised Kalix by abruptly changing into his werewolf shape and leaping up to a narrow window ledge far above them.

'Come on,' he called down. 'Before anyone sees us.'

Kalix transformed, and leapt after him. The two werewolves scrambled agilely up the side of the building, climbing several storeys before finally coming to a metal fence. Decembrius clambered over it, followed by Kalix. She found herself on a flat rooftop, three storeys above the ground.

'You like it?' asked Decembrius.

Kalix shrugged. She'd been on a lot of rooftops. There didn't seem anything to distinguish this one.

'This is the roof of the old Apple building.' Decembrius looked pleased with himself. 'This is where the Beatles played their last live gig.'

If Decembrius was expecting Kalix to be impressed, he was disappointed.

'It's a funny place to play,' she said. 'Couldn't they find anywhere better?'

'It was a famous event.'

'Oh,' said Kalix, and sounded even less impressed.

It began to rain, quite gently, and Kalix noticed the temperature had dropped. As a werewolf child Kalix had been completely impervious to the weather. She would run through the valleys around Castle MacRinnalch in deep snow and hardly notice it. These days she wasn't so immune to the climate.

'I thought you were taking me somewhere good.'

'This is good,' said Decembrius.

'I think it's stupid,' said Kalix, and decided that she didn't like Decembrius at all, which she'd known all along anyway. 'I'm going home.'

195

'Don't you want to discuss what Thrix said?'

'You didn't learn anything useful. You probably asked the wrong questions.'

'Maybe you could have done better,' said Decembrius, annoyed at Kalix for her ingratitude.

'Maybe I could.'

'Fine. Solve it yourself.'

'What do you care who killed Gawain, anyway?' demanded Kalix.

The two werewolves faced each other on the rooftop in the rain. Kalix emitted a small growl and then withdrew, climbing over the fence and making her way down the face of the building via a series of window ledges. When she reached the street below she hurried away and didn't remember to change back to her human shape till she scented some people round the corner. She pulled up the collar of her coat and hurried past a group of young people carrying guidebooks.

'This is where the Beatles played their last gig,' she heard one of them say. Kalix shook her head. She still didn't see why that was of interest to anyone.

The night bus was almost empty and the journey through the quiet, dark streets was quicker than usual. Kalix reached Kennington in twenty minutes and hurried off the bus. From habit she scanned the area and smelled the air, checking for signs of pursuit. Though her pendant masked any sign of her scent, and the sorcery provided by her sister hid her house from hunters, there had been a time when the streets of Kennington had been full of people pursuing her. It was still wise to be careful. Kalix didn't intend to let herself be ambushed while there was still vengeance to be taken for Gawain.

She was relieved that neither Moonglow nor Daniel were around when she arrived home. She wanted to think about Thrix's conversation with Decembrius. She was sure her sister was lying about something. Maybe if she wrote everything down she'd find some clue. Unfortunately, her small bedroom wasn't empty. The cat was there, a tiny bundle of dark fur.

'Go away,' said Kalix.

The car purred, pleased to see her.

'Go away, you stupid cat,' repeated Kalix, dropping her coat on the floor and kicking off her old boots. When she sat on the bed the cat leapt onto her lap and started turning this way and that, apparently quite excited to see her.

Kalix was perplexed. Dogs were always nervous of her, and she'd assumed that cats probably would be too. This cat seemed to like nothing better than trampling all over her.

I'll show this stupid cat, thought Kalix. She changed into her werewolf shape, and opened her mouth wide, displaying her alarming rows of long sharp teeth. 'You see how fierce I am? Go away before I eat you.'

But the cat apparently didn't feel in any danger of being eaten, and indeed seemed even more comfortable than before, snuggling down in Kalix's long werewolf fur. Kalix sighed, and gave up. Obviously the cat was too stubborn to leave. She sat back on the bed and took her journal from her bag. She sipped some laudanum and thought about making some notes, but now that she was home she felt tired. She could already feel the opiate dulling her senses.

'I'll make notes in the morning.' Kalix stretched out on the bed but something was wrong. She couldn't get comfortable. She looked up.

'Stop hogging the whole bed, you stupid cat! How much bed does a small cat need anyway?' Kalix pushed the cat out of the way. The cat meowed briefly in protest before moving back to settle down comfortably on Kalix's werewolf fur, and then fell asleep, purring heavily.

67

Stumbling into their house at three in the morning, Beauty and Delicious were surprised to find a large white wolf sleeping on the couch. Surprised, though not shocked; many MacRinnalch werewolves could take on the shape of a full wolf. Delicious swayed a little as she studied Dominil's sleeping form.

'I wish I could do that.'

The twins' degenerate lifestyle had robbed them of some of

their werewolf powers. Neither of them could take on the full wolf form any more. Even the simple werewolf transformation was often too difficult. Though most of their contemporaries could transform on any night, the twins generally had to wait for the full moon. It was peculiar, as Beauty had said only recently. Almost as if continually bingeing on drugs and alcohol could have affected their metabolism in some mysterious way.

'Is this reasonable behaviour?' demanded Delicious. 'What if she wakes up and attacks us?'

It wasn't such a ridiculous notion. Changing into a wolf was different from changing into a werewolf. The intellect became blurred. A MacRinnalch in full wolf form tended to become completely animal, forgetting their human identity until the morning came.

'At least she doesn't look so weird.' Beauty sat down heavily as the night's intake of alcohol caught up with her. 'I mean, the white werewolf thing is pretty strange. It's like living with a yeti.'

'She's strange enough as a human.'

The white wolf opened one eye, and growled faintly.

'Hey, are you about to get savage?' said Beauty, eying the wolf suspiciously. The wolf looked angry, then changed abruptly into werewolf form. Seconds later there was a further change, and the human Dominil sat on the couch, regarding them coldly.

'If I wanted to savage you to death I'd have done it already.'

'What's the idea of lying around on our couch being a wolf? It's dangerous.'

'The full wolf form does not diminish my intellect.'

'Well, that's a surprise,' said Beauty, and looked disgusted.

'The full wolf form is very rejuvenating.'

'It wouldn't be rejuvenating for us if you went crazy and started tearing up the place.'

'I already told you. Even as a wolf I retain my normal intellect.'

'That didn't stop you from attacking us in the castle,' said Beauty, referring to a well-remembered incident from their childhood, when the twins, aged twelve, had knocked on the door of Dominil's chamber during Halloween, looking for some sort of treat. They'd found themselves confronted by a white wolf who'd claimed to be busy working on a computer program. The young twins, insistent on receiving chocolate and unwilling to withdraw, had soon found themselves pursued down the corridor by an angry wolf. Beauty and Delicious had resented it ever since.

Delicious opened a can of lager, took a sip, and sat down on one of their deep armchairs. 'Well, while you've been lying around as a wolf – probably solving the world's problems – we've been busy. We got a gig.'

'What?'

'For Adrian's birthday. He's hired a warehouse and we're playing.'

'No you aren't.'

'Yes we are,' said Beauty, 'and it's no use turning into a white wolf and savaging us, we've agreed to do it and that's that.'

Dominil eyed the sisters with dislike. Not only did playing a warehouse gig seem like a dubious career move, it was liable to get them all killed. Dominil had been unsure as to whether or not to inform them about the hunters who now pursued them. She'd almost decided against it but the twins' unwelcome news made her change her mind.

'You can't perform in public right now. It's too dangerous.' She gave the twins a brief outline of her recent encounter with Albermarle. They sat in silence as she related the tale of her pursuit through the British Museum.

'That sounds bad,' admitted Delicious. 'But we've had hunters chasing us before, and this Albermarle sounds like an idiot.'

'He's not an idiot. He's extremely intelligent. He might not be the most competent hunter in the world but there's no telling who he might be working with. We could find ourselves up against opponents a lot more dangerous than him. Besides, he has a grudge against me. It dates back to our time at Oxford.'

'Why?'

Dominil, normally so calm, shifted uncomfortably. 'He used to . . . follow me around.'

'You mean he stalked you?'

'In a manner of speaking.'

The twins burst out laughing. Dominil was surprised. She had expected the sisters to take the news badly. By werewolf standards they weren't very fierce, and they didn't relish confrontations with hunters. 'What do you find funny?' she asked.

'You having an affair with a werewolf hunter,' cried Beauty.

'I didn't have an affair with him. I rejected his advances.'

This seemed to amuse the twins even more.

'Maybe you shouldn't have. Might have stopped him from going around trying to kill werewolves.'

'You can see why he's upset,' said Delicious. 'Poor student, probably shy, finally plucks up courage to ask Dominil out—'

'—which would take a lot of courage,' added Beauty.

'Absolutely!' agreed Delicious. 'Must have been terrifying, what with Dominil being so hostile. And what happens? She rejects him and breaks his heart. No wonder he hates you.'

Dominil did not find the conversation amusing and said so. It only made things worse.

'When you think about it, Dominil's love life has caused a lot of trouble,' observed Beauty. 'Look what happened after she rejected Sarapen. Violence, destruction – practically tore the whole clan to pieces.'

'It's like no one's safe, with Dominil going round breaking hearts everywhere.'

'What does everyone see in her?'

'Hidden passion? Dominil, do you have hidden passion?'

'You have to be more responsible,' said Delicious. 'Your chaotic love life is harming the rest of us.'

'You would be better off forgetting this nonsense and preparing yourselves for the lunar eclipse,' said Dominil, attempting to change the subject.

Beauty shrugged. 'Lunar eclipse? We're used to them. We just keep drinking till it's over.'

'We hardly noticed the last one.'

Dominil's phone vibrated in her pocket. She took it out and saw she had a message from Albermarle.

I FOUND YOUR NUMBER BECAUSE I'M SMARTER THAN YOU.

She put the phone back in her pocket. 'I think you probably shouldn't play this gig.'

'We'll be all right,' said Beauty. 'There will be a load of people there, hunters won't attack it.'

Dominil's phone vibrated again.

I'VE ALWAYS BEEN SMARTER THAN YOU.

'Who keeps sending you messages?' asked Delicious.

'No one.'

Angry at Albermarle, and frustrated by the twins' inability to take anything seriously, Dominil left the room, mounted the stairs to her office, closed the door firmly, and sat down in front of her computer.

'All that is required now,' she reflected angrily, 'is for that idiot Pete to blurt out the reason for his unhappiness, and the twins will never let me hear the end of it.'

As far as she could see, Dominil had never done anything to inflame the passions of others. It wasn't her fault if Sarapen had been moved to violence, Albermarle had become a werewolf hunter, and Pete the guitarist had turned into a love-struck idiot.

Merely a series of coincidences, she thought, and went about the business of once more trying to break through the security of the Avenaris Guild, a task which was becoming increasingly difficult, but one to which she now applied herself with even greater determination than before. Her phone vibrated for the third time.

FORGET YOUR FEEBLE ATTEMPTS AT CRACKING. YOU CAN'T GET THE BETTER OF ME.

Dominil switched off her phone.

'I'll find you, Albermarle,' she muttered, softly, 'and then I'll make you regret ruining my visit to the museum.'

68

Kalix stared blankly at the computer screen. She glanced round the class, desperately hoping that everyone else was as baffled as she was. To her dismay, all the others seemed to be working away busily. Even Vex was clicking her mouse enthusiastically. Kalix felt the palms of her hands moisten. She'd expected today's test to be difficult but wasn't quite prepared for the despair she felt as she attempted to complete Numeracy A, a beginner's test on numbers. Previously she'd scraped her way through the entry-level test, but that had been carried out with a paper and pencil, something with which she was more comfortable. And even though that test had been made up of the most basic arithmetic, her score still hadn't been anything to boast about. This test seemed a lot more difficult. It was on screen, and Kalix's computer skills were still very poor, despite Moonglow's help.

Kalix stared at the question and wondered if she was reading it correctly. It seemed to be about buying computers. Was that important? Was she meant to know about buying computers? They wanted to know how many computers had been sold by some shop in February. Kalix frowned. There was a choice of answers on screen and she was meant to click one of them. Her mind went blank. Was she meant to round something up or down? No, that had been the last question.

She looked around again. Everyone was still busy. Kalix's mouth felt dry and her hands became cold as her anxiety grew. She regretted ever agreeing to come to this place. She desperately wanted to sip some laudanum, but that only reminded her that she was almost out of opiate. To buy more she'd need to use money from her mother, and that would be withdrawn if she left college. Kalix cursed silently, and wondered how she'd ever allowed herself to be manoeuvred into this position.

Vex was still clicking away with her mouse. Kalix couldn't understand it. She was certain Vex didn't know any of the answers. She pressed the button to go on to the next question. Now it was asking about products bought in a hair salon. Kalix was baffled. She'd never been in a hair salon. Apart from the most minor trimming of split ends, her hair had never been cut. It hung down to her hips in a spectacular mane. How was she meant to know about professional hair products? Why did they want to know what sort of units they were measured in?

Kalix felt a strong urge to bite the computer. Unfortunately it was midday and she couldn't turn into a werewolf. Maybe she could just hit it? She shook her head. She couldn't hit the computer or they'd throw her out and then she'd be in disgrace. She desperately clicked forward again to look at another question, but when she saw that it concerned a graph she despaired. Kalix knew she couldn't understand graphs. They didn't make sense. Why was this test so hard? Wasn't it meant to be for beginners?

Kalix abandoned hope, and sat back in her chair, concentrating for the moment on not succumbing to an anxiety attack. Though her anxiety had never gone away, it had been less severe in recent months. Since Gawain's death she'd felt it worsening. Now Kalix felt anxious about becoming anxious. That made her more anxious. Kalix tried to divert her attention by returning her gaze to the computer screen but by now she could barely read any of the words. Abruptly, she felt her chest tighten, and she struggled to breathe. The walls of the classroom started to close in. Kalix gave way to panic.

She stood up and fled from the room, running through the corridor and down the stairs till she was outside the building where she stood gasping in the courtyard, trying to catch her breath. She glared at the old college building and swore she'd never go in there again.

Kalix noticed she was attracting attention from students coming through the front gates. Unwilling to be stared at while still trembling from panic, she slunk onto one of the old wooden benches beside the wall, out of sight of the front gate, intending to pull herself together for the journey home. That in itself would be difficult. She didn't enjoy travelling while gripped with anxiety.

Suddenly a familiar werewolf scent appeared. More than one scent. The Douglas-MacPhees were close. Kalix flattened herself against the bench and peered out through its slats. Duncan Douglas-MacPhee appeared at the college gate.

'Maybe this one?' he said.

His sister Rhona appeared beside him. 'I'm sick of checking these colleges. How are we meant to find her? She has no scent.'

'Morag hopes we might just run into her.'

'Then let Morag walk around every college in London,' growled Rhona. 'I'm tired of looking in classrooms.'

'I'm tired of arguing with doormen,' added William, appearing behind his cousins.

The trio looked at the building, blocking the gates, forcing students to detour past them.

'We've done enough for today,' said Rhona. 'We know where the likely colleges are. It's time for Decembrius to do his share. He should be able to tell us which one she's at.'

The Douglas-MacPhees turned and walked off, disappearing back through the gate towards the black transit van they'd parked outside. After they'd gone, Kalix remained hidden on the bench for some time, thinking about what she'd heard.

69

The Enchantress glared balefully at her computer screen.

'I hate this woman.'

Ann peered over her shoulder. 'Susi Surmata?'

'How did she get to be the most influential fashion writer in the country? Her writing is hopeless. No insight. And the blog has a silly name. "I Miss Susi." What sort of name is that?' Thrix had failed to elicit any response from Susi and was frustrated and annoyed at the whole affair. 'She obviously changed her mind about writing about my clothes and doesn't even have the courage to tell me.'

'How many times did you email her?'

'Once or twice. Maybe three times. Five or six times. No more than eight.'

'I make it twelve,' said Ann.

'Well, you shouldn't be counting! No wonder she hates me. How pathetic is it to keep emailing some anonymous blogger begging for a review? Now I look like a complete idiot.'

Ann studied the blog. 'She doesn't seem to update it as often as she used to.'

'Probably after seeing my designs she decided to leave the country.' Thrix drummed her fingers on the desk. 'It's not good, Ann. I was relying on selling to Eldridge's. My company is in trouble if that doesn't happen.'

'Any progress with their buyer?'

'None at all. I think they actually hate me there. I can't even get through to Kirsten Merkel any more. I know why. The woman's got a grudge against me because I've got an Abukenti handbag and she hasn't. She just can't stand it. These clothes-buyers hate designers anyway. They're jealous because we've got all the talent. Merkel's probably been brooding about the handbag and now she's taking revenge. She's lucky I don't use a spell on her.'

Ann looked alarmed at the thought of her employer carrying out a sorcerous attack on an important clothes-buyer.

Thrix banged her fist on her table, her considerable strength making the computer bounce and rattle. And with that the Enchantress changed into her golden werewolf shape, raised her snout towards the ceiling, and roared.

Ann rushed to lock the door. 'Don't do that!' she exclaimed. 'Do you want everybody in the office to know?'

Thrix snarled. She was the only werewolf in the clan who could transform during daylight, a result of the rigorous training she'd received from her sorcery teacher, Old Minerva.

The scent of jasmine suddenly appeared in the air, there was a gentle flash of light and the Fire Queen stood among them. She was smiling happily when she arrived but her expression changed to one of consternation as she saw Thrix as a werewolf.

'In daylight? What's the matter? Are you under attack?' Malveria's eyes narrowed and began to glow. Flames flickered from her fingertips, instantly transforming her from a fashionable lady of leisure into a warrior awaiting the enemy.

Thrix sighed, a deep throaty sound that rolled over her long tongue and sharp teeth. She changed back into human, and sat down heavily. 'No, no attack. But I can't find Susi Surmata and Kirsten Merkel won't talk to me.'

'Ah,' the Fire Queen said, nodding, and perched on the corner of Thrix's desk. 'Still you suspect the terrible handbag jealousy?'

'I do.'

Malveria clutched her own Abukenti handbag, an item that had brought her great pleasure. It was the season's most fashionable bag, and there were many disappointed women who still coveted one. 'So you plan to take on werewolf shape and rip her to pieces?'

'There will be no ripping to pieces!' cried Ann hastily.

Malveria looked fierce. 'The woman is an enemy and must be torn apart.'

'Would you stop acting like you're both insane?' said Ann. 'So Thrix didn't get a review she was hoping for, and now a buyer won't take her clothes. It happens. This is the fashion business.

Most people struggle. We just have to deal with it as best we can. Without ripping anyone to pieces.'

Malveria looked disappointed. 'I still feel it's a viable option.'

'If the buyer wanted the handbag so badly you could try bribing her with your own,' suggested Ann.

Thrix's eyes widened in amazement. 'I love my handbag. I'm not giving it up.'

'It's an outrageous suggestion not fitting of the esteemed personal assistant to my dearest Thrix,' chided Malveria. 'A woman does not give up her favourite bag. Particularly when it is the most fashionable item of the season. I would lead my nation to war rather than surrender mine.' She glanced at her bag. 'It's just so stylish and practical.'

Ann sighed. 'Well, you'll have to think of another plan, then. One that doesn't involve any blood. I'll ask around again about this blogger woman. Someone in London must know how to contact her. Maybe I can find out something from my friend in *Vogue*'s payroll department. They must have sent her a cheque some time.'

As Ann departed Malveria made a quick examination of her make-up and outfit in the large wall mirror, and nodded approvingly.

'Our dinner went well, yes?'

Thrix agreed that it had gone well.

The Queen looked on expectantly. 'So?'

'What do you mean?'

'You know very well what I mean. How was your subsequent date with Captain Easterly?'

'It went quite well.'

'Excellent. Was there sex and debauchery?'

'No.'

Malveria looked disappointed. 'Might there be in the near future?'

'Probably not, with my track record. But we had a nice meal and we managed not to bore each other. That's an improvement on any other date I've had recently.'

'I knew he would be suitable!' Malveria was triumphant. 'The Fire Queen does not send her esteemed friend Thrix on a date with just anyone. The moment I encountered him at the opera I knew he would make you an excellent companion. Admittedly Distikka pointed him out to me, though I still claim full credit for the match.'

'He was a good choice. But don't get your hopes up, there are still plenty of opportunities for it all to go wrong.'

'Abandon all such thoughts, Enchantress. Since your meeting he has doubtless spent every waking hour thinking of you. Really, Enchantress, I feel we may be entering a golden age.'

'I don't think I'd go that far, Malveria.'

'Why not? You have found a suitable man, your mother is pleased at you for securing the services of Mr Felicori, your hair is golden and splendid, and your clothes designing becomes better than ever. If we can just solve the minor problem of procuring a substantial sale of your clothes to Eldridge's, everything will be excellent.'

Thrix didn't feel that everything was going quite as well as the Fire Queen suggested, but Malveria brushed aside her objections.

'And as for my own life, it is equally promising. With Agrivex now frequently absent from the palace, I'm free to concentrate on dressing well and impressing the aristocracy with my operatic knowledge. It has gone down very well, you know. It's being said everywhere that Malveria, besides being best-dressed Queen in all the nations, also has excellent taste in music and culture.' She smiled very broadly, showing her perfect white teeth to good advantage.

'What about your Advisory Council?'

'Even there, there has been an improvement. Distikka protects me like a great wall of flame. At this moment she is completing the rather tedious calculations concerning the date for the Fire Festival, and that should keep the council quiet for a while.'

Distikka had indeed made the complicated calculations to ascertain the correct date for the celebration of the Vulcanalia and had presented them to the Advisory Council. The council was still unhappy that the Fire Queen hadn't done it herself, as was traditional, but was pleased to have the matter settled. Distikka grew in their esteem. As it was becoming ever more difficult to see the Fire Queen without Distikka's approval, ministers now found it necessary to seek favour with her, no matter how low-born she was.

Afterwards Distikka returned to her private chambers, awaiting the arrival of her lover, General Agripath. She'd started an affair with a Captain and, showing her usual determination, swiftly worked her way up, procuring higher-ranked suitors as her status grew. Now she was having an affair with a General who, it was said, might soon be promoted to head of the army. Distikka let him understand that, with her influence behind him, he would be, so it was a favourable alliance for both of them.

70

Around midday on Saturday, Kalix appeared in the living room. Daniel and Moonglow were eating breakfast cereal.

'You have a cat on your shoulder,' said Daniel.

Kalix sighed. 'I can't get rid of it.' She twisted her neck to study the small bundle of fur. 'Is this normal?'

'I've never seen a cat ride around on anyone's shoulder before,' admitted Moonglow, 'but it's cute.'

She leaned forward to stroke the cat's ear. The cat hissed. Moonglow looked mortified. All her life she'd got on well with cats but this one didn't seem to like her. It didn't seem to like Daniel much, either, though it tolerated Vex.

'You'd think a normal cat would be friendly to humans and maybe suspicious about werewolves, not the other way round,' said Daniel.

'Why?' asked Moonglow.

'Because of the danger of being eaten, obviously.'

'Hey!' protested Kalix. 'I don't eat cats.'

'Come on, you know it would make a tasty little mouthful,' said Daniel.

Kalix, whose fragile nature meant she was often unable to tell when Daniel was teasing her, looked mortally offended.

Moonglow tried to smooth things over. 'I think it's sweet, the way it likes you so much.'

'Maybe it thinks you're its mother,' suggested Daniel.

'Why would the cat think Kalix was its mother?'

'I've seen it happen in cartoons.'

'What? With a werewolf?'

'Well, no. But ducks and things. You know, they hatch out of their eggs and then they meet an elephant or something and they think it's their mother.'

Moonglow stared at Daniel.

'It happens all the time in cartoons,' said Daniel, defensively.

'If you say so.'

'You really need to watch more TV. Then you'd know things like that.'

Kalix was still scowling. 'I can't get rid of the stupid thing. And it takes up the whole bed.'

'You better be careful,' said Daniel, directing his words to the cat, 'in case she eats you.'

'I don't eat cats!'

'We never thought you did!' said Moonglow, looking furiously at Daniel.

'Has Kalix been eating cats again?' asked Vex brightly, appearing in the room in a gaudy yellow dressing gown.

'I never ate any cats!'

'OK. Except I thought you said you did. When you were living in that warehouse. Or was that rats? Did you eat rats?'

'No!'

'Dogs? No? I'm sure you ate something strange. Maybe the postman?'

Kalix scowled furiously, offended by the whole conversation.

Agrivex grinned at the cat. 'Don't worry, Kabby, Kalix won't eat you, she has plenty of food here.' Vex loaded up a cereal bowl with an enormous amount of cornflakes and poured sugar on top. In contrast to Kalix, Vex had a very healthy appetite.

'Why did you just call the cat Kabby?' asked Moonglow.

'Because that's its name.'

'How do you know?'

'The cat told me, of course,' said Vex.

Kalix, Daniel and Moonglow regarded Vex with some scepticism.

'The cat told you?'

'Of course.' Vex paused, noticing the odd looks that were being directed towards her. 'What's the matter?'

'Cats can't talk, you idiot,' said Kalix.

'Yes, they can.'

'No, they can't.'

'Well, I can talk to cats,' said Vex, amiably. 'She says her name is Kabby and she's pleased to be here except she wouldn't mind if you brought her a bit of fish every now and again instead of that cheap cat food. Also, a few cat toys wouldn't go amiss.'

Daniel shook his head. He'd long ago abandoned all thoughts of getting any sense out of Vex, and this just seemed to prove it.

Vex poured more cereal into her bowl. 'I've got something to cheer you up, Kalix.'

'I'm not miserable.'

'Yes, you are,' said Vex. 'You've been miserable since you fled from the classroom.'

'Did Kalix flee from the classroom?'

'Fled like Daniel confronted with a pretty girl,' chortled Vex. 'But don't worry, Kalix, it wasn't that important a test.'

'You fled from a test?' Moonglow asked.

'No. Well, yes.' Kalix looked even more unhappy.

'And there's an exam soon!' continued Vex. 'I have new coloured pencils.' She paused, and looked puzzled. 'I'm sure I was talking about something else apart from Kalix running out the class.'

'You said you had something to cheer her up.'

'Ah.' Vex broke into a broad grin. 'That's right. We have an assignment.'

Kalix looked worried. 'What's an assignment?'

'We pick a subject and write about it and then we read it to the class! I can't wait. I'm doing mine on *Tokyo Top Pop Boom Boom Girl*!' *Tokyo Top Pop Boom Boom Girl* was Vex's favourite cartoon, a piece of Japanese anime that showed every day on cable. The heroine of the cartoon was always battling evildoers, and had spiky blonde hair just like Vex's. When not visualising herself fighting imaginary supervillains, Vex could often be found singing the theme tune.

'I don't want to do an assignment.' Kalix sank in her chair.

210

'It'll be fun! We get to talk to the whole class.'

'What's the subject?' asked Moonglow.

'Anything we want. What do you think, Kalix? Maybe you could do yours on *Curse of the Wolf Girl*?'

'Definitely not!'

'Why not? You know all about it. You could give a brilliant talk on *Curse of the Wolf Girl*. There's almost no chance you'd panic and run out the classroom.'

'Could we stop talking about college?' cried Kalix, who was becoming paler and paler.

'OK,' said Vex, with her mouth full of cereal. 'So how are things going with Decembrius? Is he your boyfriend now?'

'Of course not! I don't like him.'

'Is he taking you out again?'

'He never took me out in the first place. He just took me to some stupid rooftop.' Kalix told them about their visit to the building in Savile Row. Daniel, a man with an encyclopaedic interest and knowledge of music, was quite impressed at the tale.

'I've seen a film of that Beatles rooftop gig. It must have been forty years ago. It was good.'

Vex was dismissive. 'Forty years ago? What a waste of time. Next time get him to take you somewhere better.'

'He's not taking me anywhere,' said Kalix.

'I thought he was quite nice-looking. Nice red hair. Does he dye it? Moonglow, do you think he's nice-looking?'

'Quite,' said Moonglow.

'Not as good-looking as Markus, I suppose,' said Vex. 'Now Markus, he was really good-looking.' There was a chilly silence around the breakfast table. Vex didn't notice. 'It's no wonder you fell for him. Kalix, did you think Markus was good-looking? Or do you like Decembrius better? Of course, Gawain was quite good-looking too. Hey, where's everybody going?'

Moonglow had exited the room quite abruptly, with moistened eyes. Kalix followed her immediately afterwards, pursued by the cat.

'Agrivex,' said Daniel, severely. 'Do you have to be so offensive?'

'Offensive? What do you mean?

'You know Moonglow doesn't like hearing about Markus. He

211

broke her heart. And it's hardly tactful to mention Gawain, either. Now Kalix is upset as well.'

Vex shrugged. 'Well, there's no point dwelling on it. Don't worry, Kalix will cheer up when she gets going on her assignment. And Moonglow might get happier if you got together with her.'

'I'm trying!' said Daniel.

'Really? All I see is you going around in a bad mood all the time.'

'I'm only in a bad mood because Moonglow refuses to go out with me.'

'So you think the best thing to do is shout at her and go around in a bad temper?'

'It seemed appropriate.'

Vex laughed, and poured more cereal into her bowl, again covering it with sugar. 'Well, there's your problem. You've been trying to win over a girl by being in a continual bad mood. Doomed to failure. *Cosmo Junior* says you can take the moody thing too far. Try cheering up a bit. And buy her something nice.'

'What? Like flowers?'

'Flowers? Seems like an odd choice,' said Vex. 'I was thinking more along the lines of a hedgehog. But something nice, anyway.'

Daniel sipped his tea and looked thoughtful. Though he baulked at taking romantic advice from anyone who claimed to be able to talk to cats, it was possible that he'd gone too far in the way of being ill-tempered. Being nice for a change might not be such a bad idea.

71

Decembrius's mood became bleaker. His natural tendency towards melancholy was exacerbated by the approaching eclipse of the moon. His failure to make an impression on Kalix added to his gloom. There was nothing to be done about the eclipse – werewolves just had to suffer until it passed – but he wondered if he might have approached Kalix better. He'd helped her to eat, helped her with her investigation, even helped her with maths.

None of it seemed to have made any impression. Kalix plainly didn't like him.

His small flat in Camden had begun to seem dingy and unpleasant of late. Normally comfortable on his own, Decembrius realised he was lonely. He felt around in his coat pockets until he found a scrap of paper with a number on it, and then he phoned Elizabeth, a woman he'd met last week in a bar. Decembrius had been drinking at the time but as far as he remembered she'd been pleasant enough. He hadn't planned on taking it any further, but changed his mind.

Elizabeth seemed pleased to hear from him; more than pleased, she sounded excited. Decembrius had fine cheekbones, deep blue eyes, interesting hair, a slender and powerful physique, and his werewolf nature lent something extra to his aura. Decembrius had made no particular effort to impress her but she was impressed anyway. He knew he didn't normally have to try very hard. Perhaps that was one reason he felt so depressed about Kalix. Now, when he did have to try, he'd failed.

He arranged to meet Elizabeth in the same pub and ended the call.

As soon as he arrived Decembrius knew he'd made a mistake. Though Elizabeth was pretty enough, they had nothing in common. He regretted making the arrangement. A certain gallantry on his part prevented him from allowing her to see he wasn't keen, and they left the bar together some time before it closed.

Decembrius lived in an old Victorian villa. Like many of the houses in the side streets of Camden, it had long ago been divided up into small apartments. As Decembrius approached the front door he was shocked to find Kalix there. It was difficult to get used to a werewolf who didn't have any scent. There was no light outside the door and for a moment they stared at each other in darkness. Kalix turned her head towards Elizabeth and bared her teeth.

'Go away,' she said.

'Who's she?' demanded Elizabeth. 'Your girlfriend?'

'No,' replied Decembrius. He wasn't displeased to see Kalix but he didn't like her ordering his companion around. Kalix took a step towards Elizabeth and Decembrius saw the look of utter fury on her face. She looked like a girl who was going to explode into violence any second.

'I think you'd better go,' said Decembrius to Elizabeth apologetically. 'I'll call you.'

'Don't bother,' said Elizabeth, and walked off.

Decembrius frowned at Kalix. He could smell blood when he knew he shouldn't be able to. He glanced down. There was a trickle of red coming out from under the sleeve of Kalix's coat.

'What's that?'

'Never you mind,' said Kalix. She had an open wound on her arm, the result of past cuts she'd inflicted on herself now reopened through scratching. She could smell the blood too. She liked that.

'Thanks for spoiling my date. What's the matter? Jealous?' Decembrius's attempted lightness of tone was wasted on Kalix.

'You've been working for the Douglas-MacPhees. You're helping them find me.'

Sensing that Kalix was about to transform, Decembrius hurried to put his key in the lock. 'I'm not helping them find you.' He opened the door and walked swiftly inside, followed by Kalix.

Kalix transformed. Though they were now indoors, it was still risky. The villa held eight apartments. Many of the tenants would arrive home around this time. Decembrius had no choice but to lead Kalix upstairs to his own small flat.

'Want a drink?'

Kalix dashed the glass from his hand and it shattered against the wall. Her jaws opened wide, and at that moment Decembrius remembered Thrix's warning. *Kalix will kill you.* It seemed like she might already be about to try. Decembrius transformed, taking on his dark red werewolf shape, and prepared to defend himself. 'I helped the Douglas-MacPhees sell some things to the Merchant, that's all.'

Kalix seemed certain that Decembrius intended to betray her.

'I heard them say you'd find me.'

'I never agreed to that.'

A rather maniacal light shone in Kalix's eyes. 'I'd like them to find me. At night, when I can change. Then I'll kill them all. But I'll kill you first.'

'I'll kill you if you don't stop accusing me,' said Decembrius, raising his voice. He wasn't noted for his patience, and now, in werewolf form, he wasn't quite so inclined to be kind to Kalix. 'I've been trying to protect you. The Douglas-MacPhees have been talking to Morag and Marwanis. They're all looking for you.'

'Good,' said Kalix. 'I'm looking for them too. Where can I find them?'

'They're meeting at the hotel in Church Street. Morag's got a room there. They asked me to go, but I've finished working with them.'

'Liar,' growled Kalix. 'Everyone in the clan knows you're a liar.'

Kalix stepped forward and swung her taloned paw hard and fast. Decembrius didn't see it coming. It smashed into the larger werewolf's cheekbone, sending him crashing to the floor. Decembrius rose, howling with rage, and prepared to throw himself at Kalix. At that moment there was a furious banging on the door.

'Keep the noise down! I've warned you before.'

Decembrius paused, and looked uncomfortable.

'Mrs Morrison, from upstairs. She has to get up for work early in the morning.'

Kalix growled in fury.

'And stop that growling!' shouted Mrs Morrison.

The unexpected interruption seemed to shake Kalix back towards rationality. She closed her jaws, though she still stared at Decembrius with loathing.

'I really wasn't trying to betray you, Kalix. I just needed some money. It was either work for the Douglas-MacPhees or go back to the castle. I won't meet them again. You should stay away from them too.'

'I'm going to their meeting,' snarled Kalix. 'I want to talk to Duncan. Morag and Marwanis as well.'

'Why?'

'To see what they know about Gawain.'

'They'll try to take you back to Scotland. If they don't just kill you first.'

Kalix laughed. 'That won't happen.'

215

'You can't go to that meeting, it's—'

Kalix was no longer listening. She moved towards the door, transforming on the way, and left without another word.

Decembrius followed after her and had a brief glimpse of his disapproving upstairs neighbour in the hallway before he slammed the door in frustration and sat down heavily on the one armchair in the room. He felt angry at Kalix, and himself, and the Douglas-MacPhees. How could Kalix have imagined he'd sell information about her? But perhaps it wasn't such a strange thing for her to think. He'd known all along that Kalix would take it badly if she were to learn that he'd been working with them.

Decembrius's anger faded into depression, and suddenly a shaft of worry shot through him. Kalix wouldn't really go to the meeting, would she? She surely couldn't be mad enough to walk into a roomful of her enemies on the night of the lunar eclipse?

Without warning, Decembrius found himself plunged into one of the strongest and most terrifying visions of the future he'd ever experienced. He saw the bodies of Kalix, Dominil and Thrix lying dead on the grass, with tendrils of fog trailing around their bodies. There was blood on the grass and the smell of it was all around. Such was the strength of the vision that Decembrius for a moment believed himself to be there, and looked round savagely for the assailants. When he looked back he saw his own body on top of the pile and, though this was terrifying too, it reminded him that it was some sort of vision and not reality. He backed away, shaking his head to clear it, but before he could banish the vision he was overcome by darkness as his consciousness faded and he collapsed to the floor.

72

As the afternoon turned into evening, Castle MacRinnalch was home to many unhappy werewolves. Few ventured outside to see the endless grey clouds that stretched from horizon to horizon, and the courtyard, normally alive with the raucous laughter of werewolf children, was uncommonly quiet. In her chambers, the

Mistress of the Werewolves tried to concentrate on a magazine, but dropped it with a sigh.

I'm three hundred years old, she mused. You'd think I'd be used to it by now.

A lunar eclipse never passed easily. It was a profoundly depressing experience for werewolves. As the Earth's shadow hid the moon, even the most pure-blooded were unable to transform. It brought on feelings of emptiness and despair that were almost impossible to alleviate. There was nothing to do but wait it out. The MacRinnalchs could feel the eclipse approaching, and in the hours preceding the event a great sadness descended on their homelands. From the Barons' keeps to Castle MacRinnalch, and in the farmhouses and dwellings in between, the Scottish werewolves sat indoors, some with their loved ones but many of them alone, waiting for it to pass.

Markus sat in his chamber, wrapped in the scarlet cloak that had belonged to the wife of Thane Murdo, centuries ago. The garment brought him some comfort, but not enough. All of Markus's problems rose to the surface, and he felt bored and frustrated with life. He spent most of his nights with Beatrice MacRinnalch, the assistant curator of the castle relics, who was a pleasant enough werewolf but not really sparkling company. Markus had had many girlfriends and lovers, mainly in London, away from the prying eyes of his family, and had finally fallen in love with Talixia. She'd been killed in the feud and he still missed her. Were his life different, Markus would have relieved his boredom by taking more lovers – with his extraordinary looks, women had always thrown themselves at him – but that wasn't easy in the castle. Now that he was Thane he was expected to behave in a sober fashion. Neither his mother nor the Great Council would approve of him philandering.

He faced almost the same problem with clothes. Markus had long held a liking for female attire. That hadn't been too hard to accommodate while he was free to go where he pleased. Here in the castle it was more difficult. Though he'd shared his secret with a few women in his life, he didn't think that Beatrice would take the information well, and he couldn't risk the news becoming known in the clan. The MacRinnalch werewolves might well have caught up with the modern world in some respects but Markus wasn't under any illusion that they were prepared to accept a Thane who dressed in women's clothes.

They'd probably throw me off the walls, he thought, and felt even more depressed. He sipped from a glass of wine, and wished the eclipse was over.

In London the werewolves weren't faring any better. Beauty and Delicious attempted to drink themselves through the crisis but, despite their boasting to Dominil, the eclipse affected them as much as everyone else. As it approached, their normally raucous conversation became more subdued. They found themselves sitting in front of the TV watching music stations, unable to find anything they liked, too gloomy even to hurl abuse at the screen. They eventually put on an old DVD of Joy Division playing one of their early gigs, and sat miserably in front of it, feeling that the tortured lyrics suited their mood.

'Shame he killed himself,' muttered Beauty, drinking deeply from a bottle of whisky as a close-up of Ian Curtis filled the screen.

'Doesn't seem like such a bad idea at the moment,' grunted Delicious. 'I hate these eclipses. Pass me the bottle.'

Dominil had deliberately stayed away from the twins, knowing that if she encountered them during the eclipse she'd probably be moved to attack them. She tried to ward off the malevolent effects of the disappearing moon by force of her willpower alone, telling herself that she just had to keep working and it would pass, but it was difficult. As the moon began to disappear, even her iron willpower sagged. For a moment she was overwhelmed with feelings of loss and sadness. Her mind was flooded with memories of past lovers and past disappointments. The unbreachable wall she'd erected, which had always protected her from the scorn directed at her because of her strangeness, began to crumble. For a few minutes she felt something not far from despair about being so different from everybody else. She gritted her teeth, then returned to her computer with a determined air and tried to carry on with her work.

*

At her office, Thrix was even more irritable than usual. She was forced to apologise to Ann after quite unjustifiably blaming her for losing a contract.

'I'm sorry I yelled at you,' said Thrix. 'And I shouldn't have thrown the stapler.'

'It's OK. It's only a small bruise.'

'I feel terrible. I shouldn't have come into work today. Why did I?'

'I think your exact words were: "The eclipse doesn't bother me, I'm not like other werewolves, I'm a sorceress, I can handle it easily."'

'Did I really say that? I'm a fool.' Thrix stared glumly at her computer, sighed deeply, and put it to sleep. 'What's the point in working? I'll never sell any clothes. No one will ever review my clothes. They're not worth reviewing anyway. I've never designed anything that was any good. I've got to get out of the fashion business, I'm hopeless at it.'

'Does this eclipse last long?' asked Ann, alarmed by Thrix's abrupt descent into misery.

'Only a few hours. But we can feel it coming on. I should go home.'

'You can't. You have a date.'

'How can I have a date? Werewolves don't go out on dates when there's a lunar eclipse.'

'Your exact words were: "Of course I can go out with Easterly, I'm a sorceress, the eclipse won't bother me."'

Thrix rested her head on her desk and groaned.

'I'll get you some coffee,' said Ann kindly.

73

Further west in London, Morag MacAllister, a fiery character at the best of times, was berating Marwanis MacRinnalch for organising a meeting on today of all days.

'What kind of werewolf makes an arrangement to meet on the night of the lunar eclipse? I'm liable to bite someone's head off.'

'Not when you're in human shape, I hope,' said Marwanis.

'It's the only evening I could get free when the Douglas-MacPhees could meet. They're a busy little group.'

'Busy stealing, no doubt,' said Morag. 'I hate the Douglas-MacPhees.'

'You won't hate them if they bring us Kalix.'

'Maybe not. Is Ruraich MacAndris coming too?'

'Yes.'

'I hate him as well.'

Marwanis almost smiled. Baron MacAllister's sister was hardly diplomatic. But then, Marwanis didn't care that much for Red Ruraich herself. He was always insinuating that as leader of the MacAndris Clan, he should be a Baron too, with a seat on the Great Council.

Night was falling as Red Ruraich arrived at the hotel. He strode in, slammed the door, and immediately changed into his were-wolf shape.

'Whose idea was it to meet tonight?' he growled.

'Mine,' replied Marwanis, and changed into a werewolf. They glared at each other. Morag MacAllister, not liking being the only human in the room, changed as well. The three ill-tempered werewolves stared at each other. Even in werewolf shape they could feel their powers draining away as the Earth's shadow came near to covering the moon. Finally Marwanis laughed, rather grimly, and changed back.

'Just put up with it for a few hours. It will soon be over.'

'I never get used to it,' said Ruraich harshly. 'No werewolf feels right when the moon's under attack. I feel like something's gnawing my bones.'

Morag and Marwanis both sat down. Ruraich was right. No werewolf felt right at the time of the eclipse, and they shivered at its onset.

Not far away, Kalix MacRinnalch was stepping off the Tube. She was completely oblivious to the onrushing eclipse and had no idea it was about to happen. The waves of depression and fatigue affecting her kin failed to make an impression on her. She always felt bad anyway, and didn't notice any difference.

She marched out of the station and hurried through the

darkening streets. Kalix was eager to confront Morag, Marwanis and anyone else who was there. She'd most likely be heavily outnumbered but she didn't care. As a werewolf, Kalix feared nobody, and she planned to burst into the hotel room, take on her werewolf shape, and start demanding answers about Gawain. If no answers were forthcoming, she'd savage them all until they felt like talking.

74

The Fire Queen materialised in the Enchantress's office with a flash of light that was far too bright for Thrix's liking.

'No need to stare at me in such a manner, dearest Enchantress. I am aware that it is the time of the lunar eclipse. Distikka marked it in my diary. I now carry my diary everywhere, in my splendid Abukenti bag.' Malveria paused to admire her bag once more. 'So I've come to bring you good cheer while the moon hides its face, casting you into unbearable gloom. Is it unbearable?'

'It's getting there,' growled Thrix.

'How fortunate I have arrived! I have come hither – is hither the correct word?'

'I expect so,' grunted Thrix.

'Then I have come hither from the home of Moonglow, where I was checking on the progress of my nefarious niece. Agrivex was late arriving back in our realm, thereby exposing herself to the risk of sudden death. She lacks the power to remain on Earth for more than a few days at a time.' Malveria paused, not looking too displeased at the notion of Vex meeting sudden death. 'I suspected she might be hiding from me, but it turns out Agrivex is simply resting a sore foot, after a bad bouncy-castle accident.'

'Pardon?'

'An accident sustained while playing on a bouncy castle, according to Daniel. Though I'm not certain what a bouncy castle is. I have several castles but none of them are bouncy. It's hard to see the advantage of it.'

Thrix explained that a bouncy castle was a sort of children's amusement, a large inflatable toy for children to play on.

'That would explain it. Unless Agrivex is using this bouncy-castle story merely as a way of avoiding me?'

'Why would she be avoiding you? I thought she was doing well at college?'

Malveria nodded. 'So she says. According to Agrivex she's the best student and will pass her exams with record scores, and probably cheering crowds as well. I remain suspicious, but will await events.'

'Did you heal her sore foot?'

'My dearest Thrix, the Queen of the Hiyasta doesn't waste her power healing an idiot niece who has no more sense than to bounce around on children's inflatable devices. Her sore foot will heal itself, and may the pain be a salutary lesson to her.' Malveria smiled. 'So, Enchantress, have I rescued you from the depths of misery?'

'No. I feel nauseous.'

'Oh.' Malveria was disappointed. 'I trust this will not interfere with the splendid new outfit you're designing for me?'

Thrix felt her forehead becoming moist, as if from fever. She wanted to go home and lie on the couch, and felt quite irritated by the Fire Queen's good humour.

'I've got some news that might make you feel not quite so cheerful,' Thrix said. 'About Princess Kabachetka.'

Malveria stiffened at the name. 'What about her?'

'She's been at Castle MacRinnalch.'

Malveria's smile disappeared. 'Kabachetka? What has that vile so-called princess been doing at Castle MacRinnalch? Attacking the werewolves?'

Thrix felt rather pleased to have disconcerted Malveria. That would teach her to be so cheerful during a lunar eclipse. 'No. The Princess brought Sarapen's body back.'

'What? But how could this happen?'

Thrix had been almost as surprised as Malveria at the news. The Mistress of the Werewolves had phoned to tell her that not only had Princess Kabachetka returned Sarapen's body, a private funeral had already been held. 'I thought it best to get it over with quietly,' her mother had said, probably implying that Thrix took so little notice of family affairs she didn't deserve to be invited anyway.

Malveria sat down again and looked thoughtful. 'Surprising news. Princess Kabachetka supported Sarapen against Markus. I didn't expect her to make friends with your mother. And she has returned the body? Undoubtedly there is some cunning plan here.'

'I think the cunning plan might already have been activated,' said Thrix. 'Princess Kabachetka's going to the fundraising event in Edinburgh. My mother invited her.'

'What?!' Malveria again leapt from her chair, this time levitating several inches, and staying there. 'The Princess is going to the opera?! But this cannot happen! I am not allowed to go! And she cares nothing for the opera!'

'She does now,' said Thrix. 'Mother seems to have taken quite a liking to her.'

Malveria slammed her fist on the table, which split in two. Thrix, who had been half expecting this, immediately spoke a word of sorcery, repairing the table.

'The despicable Princess has planned this all along! My fashion triumphs at the opera have been widely reported. Now she will attend this event to shame me. Enchantress, you must secure me an invitation.'

Thrix shook her head. 'I can't. Hiyastas and MacRinnalchs are still enemies, as you well know. Please don't break my table again. If I have to use sorcery again I think I'll be sick.' Thrix glanced out of the window at the faltering moon. 'And could you lower your voice? I have a terrible headache.'

Ann walked into Thrix's office. She looked round questioningly. 'Bad news?'

'The worst,' groaned Malveria. 'Defeat and disgrace at the hands of Kabachetka.' She rounded on Thrix. 'You must stop this immediately. Kabachetka cannot attend.'

'It's nothing to do with me,' protested Thrix. 'Ask my mother.'

'You know very well I cannot ask your mother! It seems to me, Enchantress, that you are not taking this seriously enough. Do you realise the shame and humiliation that confronts me in this matter?'

Thrix's nausea was increasing as the eclipse neared. 'I can't think about your shame and humiliation at the moment, I've got other things on my mind.'

The Fire Queen's eyes began to smoulder. 'What other things?'

'A business that's going rapidly downhill and a date with Easterly in the middle of the lunar eclipse. Which I wouldn't be having if you hadn't insisted on setting me up with him. Did I ask you to set me up with anybody?'

'No, but you spent endless hours talking in an irritating tone about your poor love life.'

'What irritating tone?'

'The one you use when complaining of your poor love life.'

Thrix rose to her feet, too quickly, and clutched the desk for support. 'Maybe you should concentrate on your own love life instead of interfering with mine. I'm sick of hearing about your heir. Just have one. Or don't have one. But don't keep going on about it all the time.'

Flames leapt from Malveria's fingertips and she levitated several feet off the ground. 'Now I see it all, cursed Enchantress! You have connived with your clan and Kabachetka to humiliate me! The ingratitude is startling! Felicori only sings because of me! Without me he would have no wish to associate with you or your tawdry clan of shape-shifting bumpkins.'

'No one asked you to interfere in that, either!' roared Thrix, causing Ann to take several steps backwards.

'Pah! Our association is over, Enchantress. You may be certain that I will never assist you again. Furthermore, I will laugh cruelly as your business fails. My only regret is that such a pleasant man as Captain Easterly will be forced to endure your company for the evening. Good day!'

With that the Fire Queen dematerialised so violently that the office window cracked from top to bottom.

There was a moment's silence.

'I'll call the glaziers,' said Ann, practically. 'Captain Easterly will be here to pick you up in about five minutes.'

75

In the small flat above the vacant shop in Kennington, Moonglow was conducting an inquest into the bouncy-castle incident.

'Did someone invite you onto it?'

'No,' admitted Daniel, who had a bad bruise on his forehead.

'Then what were you doing there?'

'It was Vex's fault. As soon as she saw the castle she just rushed off to join in. I could hardly keep up.'

'Why did you want to keep up?'

'To make sure everything was all right. You know, protect the children and so on.'

'Hey,' interrupted Vex. 'You were bouncing around too.'

'Only in a supervisory capacity.'

'You're lucky the parents didn't call the police,' said Moonglow. 'I don't know what you were thinking, invading a children's party and taking over the bouncy castle.'

'Do you think we could get one?' said Vex, whose injured foot hadn't diminished her enthusiasm.

'No!' said Moonglow sharply. 'Were any children injured?'

Daniel shook his head. 'The collision only involved me and Vex. Brought about by Vex's lack of bouncing skill, in my opinion.'

'I was bouncing fine till you got in the way.'

'Neither of you should have been there!' exclaimed Moonglow.

Daniel didn't see why Moonglow was making such a fuss about it. Having resolved to be nicer to Moonglow, it hurt to suffer such harsh criticism from her for what was, after all, only a minor incident.

'It's not like people were killed or anything,' he complained.

'Well, if you can't make it into college tomorrow I'm not taking notes for you,' said Moonglow.

Vex snorted. She too was finding Moonglow's unforgiving attitude difficult to understand. 'Lighten up. You're starting to sound as grumpy as Aunt Malvie.'

'Malveria hasn't been grumpy since she got rid of you from the palace,' countered Moonglow.

Daniel laughed. It was true. The Fire Queen's moods had certainly improved recently.

'Remember when she used to arrive in floods of tears?'

'She's much happier now.'

There was a dazzling flash of light in the living room as Malveria arrived, collapsing on the couch in a flood of tears.

'Maybe not all the time,' said Moonglow.

Malveria's body shook with painful emotion.

'I didn't do anything,' said Vex, defensively.

'I can't stand it,' wailed Malveria, then dissolved in tears again. Daniel shifted uncomfortably, ill at ease in the face of such powerful female misery.

'Should I make some tea?' he suggested.

Malveria raised her head from the cushion. 'Tea would be nice. Though it will not make up for the complete ruin into which my reputation has now been propelled.'

Daniel left the living room, leaving Moonglow to comfort the Fire Queen. Vex held back, still unsure if she would eventually be blamed for whatever had upset her aunt.

'What's the matter? Can we help?' asked Moonglow. The Fire Queen attempted to sit upright, failed, and buried her head in the cushion again, so it was hard to catch her words. But by the time Daniel arrived back with a tray, a teapot, three chipped mugs and one nice cup for Malveria, Moonglow had just about grasped the problem.

'Princess Kabachetka has an invitation to the MacRinnalch charity event in Edinburgh even though Malveria can't go.'

'Is that serious?' said Daniel, at which point the Fire Queen seemed to regain her strength.

She sat up abruptly, eyes blazing. 'Is it *serious*, you ask? It is a disaster of dimension-shattering proportions. When the population learns of it I will be the laughing stock of the fire nations. Even the ice nations may join in. That Princess with her head of fake blonde hair has secured an invitation to the very event that I have helped to bring about! It is intolerable!'

Malveria held her handbag to her stomach for some comfort, and accepted a cup of tea from Daniel.

'Surely Thrix can get you an invitation,' said Moonglow.

'Do not mention that treacherous creature to me! Thrix revels in my misfortune. Never again will I wear cheap, poorly designed garments from her incompetent sweatshop. Apart from possibly the new cocktail dress I am to pick up next week. After that I will have nothing to do with her.'

'Oh dear,' said Moonglow, and poured a little more tea into Malveria's cup. 'Have you been arguing again? What was it about?'

The Queen was silent for a few seconds. 'I am not quite certain, now you ask. But Thrix was most treacherous anyway, delighting in my misfortune even though I have revived her disastrous love life. As if the mild inconvenience of a lunar eclipse was in any way equivalent to the trauma I'm facing!'

Moonglow could make nothing of this, but Daniel knew about the upcoming eclipse. 'Does it affect werewolves?' he asked Malveria.

'So they claim. But I'm sure the Enchantress is making too much of it.'

'Opera's boring, anyway,' said Vex.

The Queen glared at her. 'Silence, vile girl. Concentrate on healing your foot and completing your studies. Have you been studying?'

'All the time!' enthused the young fire elemental. 'I get gold stars every day.'

'Is this true?' Malveria looked to Moonglow.

'Eh . . . yes,' said Moonglow. She was aware that Vex simply awarded herself a gold star whenever she felt like it, but didn't want to betray her.

Malveria looked mollified. 'Well, see that you keep it up, Agrivex. If you fail miserably in your exams you may find yourself in the western desert serving as cannon fodder for my army.' Malveria's tears had now dried and the fire dimmed in her eyes as she become morose. 'The Mistress of the Werewolves is an inflexible woman, and will never put aside her prejudices against the Hiyasta.' She sighed again, and clutched her handbag tighter. 'Really, without the comfort of this splendid Abukenti handbag I believe I would simply give up and expire.'

'It's a beautiful handbag,' acknowledged Moonglow, sincerely.

'Indeed it is. It has brought me great happiness. But it will not make up for the disgrace of Kabachetka appearing at the opera when I cannot do so. I simply dread to think what Beau DeMortalis will say.'

Malveria finished her tea and accepted another cup, but her mood didn't lighten. Even the annoyance of Vex trying to use the couch as a bouncy castle drew no more from her than a mild rebuke, as she contemplated her upcoming disgrace, and what to do about it.

76

Morag was annoyed. 'Did it never strike you that this isn't going to work? You want Kalix to face justice? The Mistress of the Werewolves will never allow it. You couldn't even get it on the agenda at a council meeting.'

'It will get on the agenda if I drag Kalix to the castle,' argued Marwanis. 'They'll have to do something.'

Morag was sceptical. Even if Kalix had been condemned by the council, she didn't believe they'd ever pass sentence on her.

'You underestimate how much the council hates her. Just because her mother protects her doesn't mean that no one else wants to see her punished. The Barons hate her for killing the Old Thane and half the council hate her for killing Sarapen. Even her brother Markus hates her. Verasa might be able to keep them in check while Kalix is far away but things will change once she's taken there.'

'By the Douglas-MacPhees?'

'Probably.'

Morag laughed. 'I don't see them taking her back. Kalix killed Fergus. If they get hold of her they're more likely to kill her in revenge.'

Marwanis didn't reply, causing Morag MacAllister to look curiously at her.

'Unless that's what you're hoping will happen anyway.'

'I'm not planning to kill her in cold blood,' Marwanis replied.

'Maybe you won't be too unhappy if the Douglas-MacPhees do it for you.'

Morag let it drop then, because she was now feeling too nauseous to argue, or even talk, as a shadow began to creep over the moon. From the tiny balcony outside the flat they could hear Ruraich picking out a few notes with his fingers on his violin.

'Does he never stop playing that damned thing?' Morag generally liked the sort of traditional music played by Ruraich, but now it grated. 'I wish the moon would just disappear and get it over with.'

Marwanis tried not to let herself succumb to depression. As a niece of the late Thane, she had a strong idea of how a well-bred werewolf should behave. It wasn't fitting to let the world see how bad you felt.

Morag was beyond making any pretence, and let out a low moan while sinking further into her chair. 'I should have stayed home. A werewolf can't function during the eclipse.'

'My great-great-grandfather David MacRinnalch led a raid on a castle on eclipse night,' declared Marwanis, with some pride, though the event had happened several hundred years ago.

'To hell with David MacRinnalch,' snarled Morag. She glanced at the ceiling. 'I can feel the moon going. No werewolf does anything on this night.'

The front door flew open, almost torn from its hinges by a blow that shattered the lock. There in the sagging door frame stood the slender werewolf form of Kalix.

'Apart from Kalix MacRinnalch, apparently.'

Marwanis and Morag rose to face her and the three werewolves glared at each other, each of them showing their teeth. Kalix's dark fur hung longer than the others.

'I want to know who killed Gawain!' demanded Kalix.

Marwanis looked puzzled. 'How would we know?'

77

The Enchantress suffered in the restaurant. Partly because she didn't like the food, but mainly because of the eclipse. As the moon disappeared beneath the shadow of the Earth, she deeply regretted the bravado that had made her agree to a date on this of all nights. While the rest of the MacRinnalchs were huddling in their homes, she was struggling to maintain some appearance of normality as Captain Easterly told her about his day at the magazine, where he'd been reviewing a range of men's shirts. At any other time Thrix would have been fascinated. She loved talking about clothes. Unfortunately, as the moon disappeared, she felt as if her insides were being dragged out of her, piece by piece. She'd placed several spells on herself to carry her through the evening but though her outward appearance remained flawless, inside she was suffering.

Thrix, prone to dating disasters, was keen for the evening to go well. She summoned all her energy to keep the conversation going. When that proved too much, she at least tried to listen with interest. As the waiter brought them another bottle of red wine she grabbed for it a little too enthusiastically, but if Easterly noticed, he was too tactful to show it. Buoyed by the alcohol, Thrix became a little more animated as she described her current problems.

'I was absolutely counting on selling my range to Eldridge's but their buyer let me down.'

'Kirsten Merkel?'

'That's the woman. She practically reneged on the deal. It wouldn't have happened if that talentless hack Susi Surmata hadn't let me down as well. No one can even get in touch with her these days.'

Easterly leaned forward a few inches and looked suitably concerned.

'I might be able to. Our editor knows her, I think. I'll ask him. And Merkel's not a bad woman, either; we used to work together at *Tatler*.'

'She hates me because I got the last Abukenti bag.'

'That *would* annoy her. But I can probably win Kirsten over for you.'

Thrix looked at Easterly with more affection than she'd expended on another human for a long time. Not only was he good company, he seemed to have valuable contacts as well.

It's exactly what I need, she thought. A boyfriend who's actually useful for something. Why has that never happened before?

She felt grateful to Malveria for introducing her to such an attractive man, and regretted that they'd parted on such bad terms. Then she felt the effects of the wine and the eclipse, and struggled to remain upright at the table, nodding vaguely at everything Easterly said.

78

As Kalix burst into the room, Ruraich appeared from the balcony.

'Tell me who killed Gawain or I'll kill you!' roared Kalix.

'How would we know?' repeated Marwanis.

There was a confused period of shouting. Kalix still had blood on her arm where she'd cut herself and the scent of it wasn't helping the werewolves to be calm. Though Kalix had arrived with the idea of demanding answers, she quickly began to lose any desire to talk. Faced with Marwanis, Morag and Ruraich, it seemed like a better idea to simply attack them. Morag seemed to be thinking along much the same lines, and was on the verge of attacking Kalix.

Marwanis was the calmest. She was curious as to Kalix's motivation in coming here of all places, and tried to keep the conversation going.

Kalix, however, had had enough talking. She lost her self-control and sprang forward. As she was in mid-leap, the moon finally disappeared behind the shadow of the Earth. Kalix found herself landing on the carpet in the form of a skinny girl, rather than the ferocious werewolf she'd intended.

Kalix was bemused. She couldn't understand what had just happened. Her werewolf battle-madness had just set in and having it wrenched away, along with her werewolf form, was very disorientating.

'What's wrong?' she mumbled.

Marwanis looked at Kalix with utter contempt. 'Only you could be stupid enough not to even know about the lunar eclipse.'

Kalix was perplexed, and so troubled by her unexpected loss of werewolf shape that she carelessly allowed Ruraich to creep up behind her. He picked up a table lamp and struck her across the back of the neck. Kalix fell unconscious to the floor.

'It looks like the Douglas-MacPhees won't have to search very hard to find her after all.'

Ruraich, Marwanis and Morag sat down to gather their strength, and to marvel at Kalix's ignorance. It was hard to believe that any werewolf could be completely unaware of a lunar eclipse.

'She's even more ignorant than I thought,' said Marwanis, and the others nodded in agreement.

79

Poor Wolf and Baby Wolf lived in a tiny shack in the forest. A cold wind blew through the flimsy walls and rain seeped through the ancient thatched roof. Every night Poor Wolf would go hunting for food to feed Baby Wolf, but there were few stags in the forest and hunting was bad. In the great winter there was no food to be had, and Poor Wolf and Baby Wolf were hungry all the time. Baby Wolf cried with hunger and cold, and Poor Wolf fretted and wished that he might make things better.

One night when Baby Wolf was crying with hunger there was a terrible blizzard outside. Poor Wolf looked out the window and saw the snow.

Perhaps I can pick up a stag's track in the snow, he thought. Then I can hunt it and bring it home to feed Baby Wolf. And though there had been no stag seen in the woods for months, and not even a rabbit, he ventured out into the terrible blizzard, leaving Baby Wolf wrapped in their only blanket, huddled in front of the embers of the fire made from the last of their wood.

Baby Wolf lay shivering, and waited for his father to return, and hoped he might bring a great stag, or even a rabbit, so that he could eat, and feel better. He heard a noise and thought it was his father returning but when he looked up he saw that it was Robber Wolf. Baby Wolf was terrified. He closed his eyes, and pretended to be asleep so that Robber Wolf might not kill and eat him. Robber Wolf shivered from the cold and looked around for something to steal, but there was nothing worth stealing. He bent down in front of the dying embers of the fire to warm his paws before going back out into the storm. Suddenly Poor Wolf arrived home. He opened his jaws wide, ready to attack Robber Wolf, but Robber Wolf bowed politely and excused himself.

'I sought shelter when the terrible wind and snow became too much for even my thick coat.' (Robber Wolf had a magnificent coat, much finer than Poor Wolf's.)

'Very well,' said Poor Wolf. 'You're welcome to shelter.'

Baby Wolf was very pleased to see his father home and was even more pleased when Father emptied his bag and there was a rabbit, and some dry wood.

'I caught the rabbit, lost in the storm, and then as I returned home the terrible lightning split a tree open, and dry wood fell to the ground.'

Poor Wolf stoked up the fire, and then cooked the rabbit, giving the best part to Baby Wolf and sharing the rest with Robber Wolf. After they'd eaten, Poor Wolf took a flagon of whisky from the cupboard. In it there was only half an inch of liquid, but he poured the tiny amount into two glasses and shared it with Robber Wolf, which was the polite thing to do.

That night Baby Wolf slept soundly for the first time in months, with his belly full and his paws nice and warm. Robber Wolf left as the storm died down, and thanked his host very politely for the food and shelter.

But soon Poor Wolf and Baby Wolf were cold and starving again, because the winter was long and cruel. Baby Wolf became so weak that he cried himself to sleep. Poor Wolf became increasingly anxious, and hunted for food and warmth for his child, in case he might die. Finally there came another great storm. Poor Wolf looked out the window at the rain and snow, and the wind whipping it through the trees, and prepared to go out to hunt, though he knew it was useless. There would be nothing to eat in the cold forest, and Baby Wolf would go hungry again.

There was a knock at the door. It was Robber Wolf. He had a stag round his shoulders and a great sack of dry wood in his hands. He came in with a grin, and laid the stag on the table.

'I brought this for you,' he said, 'because you were so hospitable all these cold months ago.'

In no time at all they were all warm and well fed, and Poor Wolf and Baby Wolf had enough food to last them till spring arrived and hunting was better.

Kalix woke with a jolt, and looked up to see if Robber Wolf was in the room, and wondered if it was still harsh winter outside. It had been a very long time since Kalix had dreamed about Poor Wolf and Robber Wolf, an old MacRinnalch story, told to werewolf children in the castle. Kalix had forgotten all about it until now.

She came back fully to consciousness to find herself tied to a chair. Morag MacAllister was standing over her.

The young werewolf immediately tried to transform, but couldn't. Kalix looked down at her own limbs, wondering why the change wasn't happening. Marwanis watched her struggle.

'You don't even know about the lunar eclipse, do you?'

233

Kalix glared at her and said nothing.

'How could you be so stupid?' Marwanis seemed offended by Kalix's ignorance. 'What sort of MacRinnalch are you?'

'I'll kill you,' snarled Kalix.

'You're going back to the castle. The council are going to sentence you.'

Morag MacAllister suppressed a sneer. 'Why bother dragging her back to Scotland? The Douglas-MacPhees will be here soon. That will end the problem.'

Marwanis ignored her, and spoke to Kalix. 'So what was it like, killing Sarapen?'

'It was good,' said Kalix. 'I wish I could do it again.'

Marwanis slapped Kalix hard. Kalix didn't react.

'Maybe I should just kill you now,' said Marwanis.

'I'll kill you first,' snarled Kalix, and struggled with her bonds, but they were too strong to break.

Blood still trickled down Kalix's arm, the result of her scratching her own wound. The smell was unsettling to the werewolves who, with the moon still in hiding, found it difficult to interpret their emotions. All of them were pale under the electric light, and their skins glistened with nervous perspiration.

Marwanis suddenly lost her energy and sat down heavily. 'I'll take her out to my car in a minute.'

There was a short silence, interrupted by Kalix. 'Who killed Gawain?'

Marwanis looked puzzled. She swept back a few damp strands of her long dark hair. 'Why do you keep asking that? How would I know?'

'He was your lover before he left you for me,' said Kalix. 'Then he fought Sarapen. So you hated him.'

'All true,' admitted Marwanis, 'though I'm not sure I could be bothered to hate him. But I didn't kill him.'

'Neither did I,' said Morag. 'Not that I miss him.'

Kalix struggled again with her bonds, but her strength was gone and she couldn't break free. She felt hot and nauseous, and alongside the discomfort caused by the eclipse she felt a powerful need for laudanum, which increased her misery and confusion. She bared her teeth and growled in frustration while her captors lapsed into a depressed silence. If Marwanis really planned to take Kalix back to the castle, she didn't seem to be in any hurry to do it, and the Douglas-MacPhees would be here soon.

80

'So, Captain Easterly. Tell me what you've learned about Thrix MacRinnalch.'

'She's an unusually powerful werewolf who guards herself with sorcery. Without your help I wouldn't even be able to remember she is a werewolf.'

Princess Kabachetka was unimpressed. 'I know this already. Tell me something new. How will you defeat her?'

'Well—' he began, but the Princess held up her hand. Captain Easterly had quickly learned that the Princess was a quirky and moody woman. He found her arrogant and impatient.

'One moment.' She crossed the floor of his living room to the mirror on the wall, and studied her reflection. 'Is this jacket satisfactory? I am not wholly convinced by the cut around the shoulders.'

'Yes, it's not quite right,' agreed the Captain.

Princess Kabachetka looked displeased. She hadn't expected him to agree with her. 'Instead of criticising my clothes, perhaps you could tell me something useful and justify the effort I'm expending to help you?'

'No standard attack will work against her,' said Easterly. 'She's woven a series of spells that can't be broken. Not by me or any werewolf hunter I know, anyway. Silver can't touch her. I tried sliding a silver teaspoon near her fingers while we ate, and it slid away of its own volition. Probably a silver bullet would do the same. The spells of confusion that prevent her from being tracked are very clever. If a journalist wants to write about her for a fashion magazine that's not a problem, but if I try to enter any details of her in Guild records, it just can't be done. Computer files get wiped and papers mysteriously disappear. Once I'm back at the Guild I can hardly remember anything about her. I'll need you to boost the spell you're using on me if I'm to keep pursuing her.'

'That might be dangerous.'

'I'll risk it.'

The Princess smiled. She rather liked the idea of Easterly risking his life. Perhaps he would kill Thrix and die in the process. That would be amusing.

'You told me that you'd once removed Thrix's powers,' he said. 'Can't you do that again?'

'No. She will have learned how to counteract my spell, and at this moment I'm unable to bring more sorcery into this dimension that might be suitable. I need something new, as you seem to lack the initiative to simply put a silver bullet through her heart.'

'It wouldn't work.'

The Princess eyed him suspiciously. 'Are you quite sure?'

'Yes.'

'Perhaps you wouldn't like to see the Enchantress lying in a pool of blood with a bullet through her heart. Perhaps her blonde hair has started to win you over.'

Easterly smiled. 'I'm not about to fall for a werewolf.'

'Be sure that you don't.' The Princess glared at Easterly. Though she felt no attraction towards him, she had assumed that he would naturally fall in love with her. So far he showed no signs of it. It was another mark against him.

'I did learn something useful, possibly.'

'Amaze me,' said the Princess.

'Thrix suffers the effects of the lunar eclipse, the same as other werewolves. She can guard against it to an extent, but it still weakens her.'

'How could you tell?' demanded Kabachetka.

'Just a few things I picked up on when we had dinner. She was tired, and not quite in control.'

'Perhaps you're not a very interesting date,' suggested the Princess. 'A well-cut suit does not compensate for poor conversation. But supposing you are right, and Thrix suffers under the lunar eclipse, what of it? Is there another eclipse due soon?'

'No. But you asked me to find a weakness.'

'I asked you to kill her.'

'Or find a weakness that will enable *you* to kill her. Might it not be possible for you to work some sorcery that would replicate the effect of a lunar eclipse? If you could do that, she'd be vulnerable.'

The Princess mused on this. It was worth considering. She rose to her feet, not quite as gracefully as she would have wished. She'd been several days on Earth and her strength was fading. 'I'll consider the matter.' She glanced in the mirror. 'You are quite wrong about this jacket. The cut is admirable, and suits me perfectly.'

She snapped her fingers and dematerialised, whisking herself instantly back to her own realm, where she immediately burned her jacket. The interview with Easterly had left her in a poor temper. He wasn't respectful enough, and his failure to fall in love with her was quite insulting. And as for his taste in clothes, it was obviously deficient. She pursed her lips. At least he was applying himself to his task, and had suggested a weakness in Thrix that might be exploited.

But how can I reproduce the effect of a lunar eclipse on Earth? wondered the Princess. If such moon magic exists, it is not known to the Hainusta.

Perhaps Distikka might have some ideas. The Princess sent her a message, asking Distikka to meet her and help plan the destruction of Thrix MacRinnalch.

81

As the eclipse continued, Kalix felt as though the life was being sucked from her body. Worse, she was feeling close to panic, which had never before happened in the presence of an enemy. Usually the prospect of fighting cleared her mind, leaving her calm. Now the eclipse was twisting her emotions and everything was going wrong. She could feel the attack coming on and strove to keep it at bay, unable to bear the humiliation of panicking under the scornful eyes of Morag and Marwanis.

'So are you going to take her away or not?' asked Morag.

Before Marwanis could reply, footsteps sounded outside, loud steps, with a heavy tread. The door opened and the Douglas-MacPhees trooped in.

'Well, that ends the problem,' said Morag.

'Damn you for calling us out on this night—' began Duncan, crossly, before his eyes focused on Kalix. 'But this does make up for it,' he said.

Duncan stepped towards Kalix, who writhed frantically in her bonds. As Duncan reached out, the moon finally emerged from the Earth's shadow. Kalix was first to react and jumped to her feet, snapping ropes and destroying the chair. She faced her opponents, all of whom were now transforming. Kalix felt her battle-madness enveloping her and had a brief moment of contentment. Duncan, William, Rhona, Ruraich, Marwanis and Morag might be too much for her to defeat but she could go down fighting, and she was satisfied with that. The young werewolf howled with rage and prepared to leap at Duncan when suddenly the door flew open again. Kalix had a brief glimpse of a lot of long white hair. Inexplicably, the room exploded in smoke, a thick choking gas that reduced visibility to almost zero and caused the werewolves to retch, and rub their eyes with their paws. Kalix felt herself being grabbed by the scruff of her neck and hauled away. Thoroughly confused, she was dragged from the room and found herself in a dark corridor under a flickering electric light.

'Keep going,' said Dominil.

'But—'

'*Keep going.*'

Dominil dragged Kalix along the corridor, past other doors and through a fire-escape. After a hasty flight down the emergency staircase they emerged in an alleyway with graffiti on the walls and rubbish strewn around some messy bins. Dominil pulled Kalix along until they reached the main road where she pushed Kalix into her car, illegally parked on a double yellow line. They drove off, quickly by Dominil's standards.

It was now four in the morning and the roads were quiet. When they'd put some distance between them and their enemies, Dominil halted at some traffic lights and turned to look at Kalix.

'Are you all right?'

'Yes,' mumbled Kalix.

'It wasn't the greatest idea to go bursting in on them,' said Dominil.

Kalix, who'd been expecting Dominil to start criticising her, said nothing.

'Did you really not know it was the eclipse?'

Kalix felt ashamed of her ignorance, and remained silent as they drove on through the city. 'Thanks for the rescue,' she said, eventually. 'How did you find me?'

'Decembrius called me. It's as well he did. You almost died.'

'I'd have killed them all,' said Kalix defiantly.

'No, you wouldn't. You'd have killed some of them and then they'd have killed you. Just because you're not afraid doesn't mean you're invulnerable.'

Kalix flared up in annoyance. 'Well, no one offered to help,' she said. 'You won't help me investigate, will you?'

'No, I won't. I have affairs of my own to look after.'

'Don't you care who killed Gawain?'

'Not especially.'

'Well, I do!' cried Kalix. 'And I'm not giving up.'

Dominil pulled over to the side of the quiet street and turned towards Kalix. 'Did you learn anything?'

'Not really,' admitted Kalix.

'Do you think this is the best way to spend your time?'

'What do you mean?'

'Only a few months ago your life started taking on some order. You moved in with Daniel and Moonglow. You started taking care of yourself. You were settled. You started college. All of it was a great improvement from sleeping rough. Now look at you. You've stopped eating, you're cutting yourself again and you're in a worse mental state than ever. Hunting for Gawain's killer is destroying you. Is it worth it?'

Kalix stared at Dominil, quite shocked at her frank assessment of her condition.

'I advise you to make your life normal again. Get back to your routine. You can still investigate, if you feel you have to. But there's no point letting yourself go so badly. You'll only end up dead of starvation. Or laudanum.'

'I haven't been taking that much.'

'You're lying.'

Kalix flushed angrily but didn't bother to deny it. She looked at Dominil with loathing, and refused to speak to her again.

When they reached Kennington, Kalix left the car in silence and didn't look back as she made her way to her flat.

As she lay on her bed Kalix pondered Dominil's words briefly, but found her thoughts turning towards the dream she'd had while she'd been unconscious. Poor Wolf and Robber Wolf. That was a strange thing to dream about. For some reason she felt oddly reassured to have remembered the children's tale. Normally she couldn't remember anything good about growing up at Castle MacRinnalch. But the story cast a tiny glow of warmth back in time, as it were, making some part of her childhood seem not so unpleasant. It couldn't have been entirely bad if someone was telling her stories. Who had told her the story of Poor Wolf and Robber Wolf? Her mother? It seemed unlikely. Someone must have told Kalix the traditional MacRinnalch tale, but Kalix couldn't remember who it might have been.

82

Distikka handed a sheet of parchment to the Fire Queen.

'Your itinerary, mighty Queen.'

Malveria smiled at her ever-efficient adviser.

'Almost free of tedious council meetings. Excellent work, Distikka.' Malveria now delegated Distikka to represent her whenever she could. She knew that her Council of Ministers didn't like this, but there were other, more important matters she needed to attend to. 'Distikka, can you believe that the foul Princess Kabachetka has secured an invitation to the grand charity event featuring Mr Felicori? An event to which I am forbidden to go? Is it not intolerable?'

'It's absolutely intolerable,' replied Distikka smoothly. 'Perhaps if you acquaint me with the circumstances I might be able to suggest a means of securing an invitation?'

The Fire Queen beamed. 'Of course! Well, as you know, Thrix MacRinnalch's rather barbaric family has never approved of our friendship, and nor has my First Minister Xakthan—' Malveria gave Distikka a full description of the events, personalities and problems surrounding the fundraising event. Distikka paid close attention, standing quite still in her black chain mail, listening to the Queen's every word. 'And to make matters worse, I've fallen out with Thrix.'

'A serious dispute?'

'I don't think so. Her temper was frayed by the lunar eclipse, I believe.'

'It sounds like a minor quarrel between friends that can easily be made up,' observed Distikka. 'From my knowledge of your previous friendship, I'd say that visiting the Enchantress with a bottle of wine and a cheerful greeting would probably be enough.'

'Do you think so?'

'You could compliment her hair as well.'

'An excellent idea. Thrix is susceptible to compliments about her hair. I really must not fall out with her, Distikka. Not only does she supply me with fabulous clothes, I need her to engage in some sort of romance if I'm to wrest the secret of Queen Dithean's lip colouring from her.'

Distikka nodded sagely. 'The fundraising event is a more awkward problem, certainly. But I'm sure I can find a solution. Meanwhile, be sure to encourage Thrix's relationship with Easterly. I can see that working out well.'

'Distikka, you are a marvel. Your fine advice almost makes me forgive your chain mail and sword. What is this piece of paper?'

'The promotion for General Agripath, mighty Queen. It needs your signature.'

Malveria scribbled on the parchment, authorising the general's promotion to Commander.

'If only my other problems were as easily solved,' she said, and went off to dress for her evening engagement.

83

Kalix was worn out from her adventures. It would have been comforting to change into her werewolf form, but the moon, briefly visible after the eclipse, had now disappeared. She sipped a little laudanum and thought angry thoughts about her fellow werewolves. How dare Marwanis and Morag kidnap her, and the Douglas-MacPhees try to kill her. She'd have her revenge.

Her thoughts turned to Dominil. She was grateful to the white-haired werewolf for rescuing her, but still resented Dominil's refusal to help her investigate Gawain's death. Why wouldn't she help? As for Decembrius, he'd phoned Dominil to inform her that Kalix was in trouble but he hadn't come to rescue her. Kalix hated him too. She scratched her arm without thinking about it. Blood flowed from her wound.

Her anger began to turn into anxiety. She looked at her small wooden table. On it were her bag, her journal and a few CDs. Kalix suddenly felt annoyed at the way they were strewn around. She tidied them into straight lines and felt slightly better for it. She wondered if there was anything else in her room that needed tidying, but she had very few possessions. After straightening the few clothes in her wardrobe there was nothing left.

Everyone's glad Gawain's dead, she thought. No one cares who killed him.

She stared at her feet. Her boots were old and cracked and she couldn't afford a new pair. She toyed with the ring in her nose, turning it this way and that, trying to think what to do next. An idea came to her. She examined it for a while, wondering if it was good, or stupid. After the debacle with Marwanis and the Douglas-MacPhees, Kalix no longer had much faith in her own ideas. However, this one seemed reasonable. She grabbed her coat and hurried from the room.

Upstairs, Vex was slumbering peacefully under the enormous pink duvet she'd brought from the palace. The attic, sorcerously enlarged by Queen Malveria, was now a very colourful room. Vex had brought a lot of her favourite posters and toys to brighten the place up, and wherever there was a gap in the decorations she'd hung Hello Kitty T-shirts and strings of beads bought from Camden Market so that her room now resembled a market stall itself, full of bright clothes and gaudy plastic jewellery.

'Vex, wake up!'

Vex didn't stir. Kalix shook her shoulder.

Vex opened her eyes, sat up, moaned, and lay back down again.

'Get up. I need your help.'

Vex attempted to rise again. Her spiky bleached hair pointed in all directions, concealing most of her face. She dragged some spikes a few inches to the side and peered at Kalix.

'I'm tired.'

'I need your help.'

Agrivex dragged herself out of bed, making a sorry spectacle with her crushed hair and smeared make-up. The young fire elemental didn't feel like getting up, or helping Kalix, or doing anything, but it was a sign of her good nature that she did her best.

'OK, I'm up. What are we doing? Emergency shopping?'

'No, we're investigating. Can you teleport us to Gawain's?'

Vex shook her head. Her powers of teleportation were nowhere near those of Malveria and she couldn't transport another person.

'Then we'll just have to get the bus.'

'I need breakfast,' said Vex, which frustrated Kalix. She paced around the living room while Vex ate a bowl of cereal and drank water, stopping occasionally to complain about how tired she felt.

'But it's all right. I'll feel better when we're shopping.'

'We're not going shopping!' cried Kalix. 'We're investigating.'

'Oh. All right. What are we investigating?'

'Come on,' said Kalix, and dragged her from the house.

They made an odd sight on the bus. Two thin girls, one with bleached hair in a chaotic spiky mass and yesterday's make-up still visible around her eyes, and the other with extremely long hair, rather unkempt and tangled; Kalix with her long coat and scuffed, heavy boots, Vex with a denim jacket thrown over her Hello Kitty pyjamas, and an even heavier pair of boots, black and new, bought only last week as part of Vex's apparent quest to find the largest footwear she could possibly manage.

The police had cleared away their tape from around Gawain's room. The landlord had repaired the door. The small flat was still empty but there was little sign that a crime had ever been committed there, save for the bloodstains on the floor.

'What do you want me to do?' asked Vex, for the fifth time in as many minutes.

Kalix growled in frustration. Vex seemed unable to hold a thought in her head for more than a minute.

'Read the remnants of auras. You can do that, right? I want you to tell me about everyone who visited this apartment before Gawain was killed.'

'But it was weeks ago,' complained the elemental. 'They'll all be faint now, and mixed up. I'm not that good at reading auras.'

'But you studied it,' said Kalix. 'You became better at it.'

'I forgot it all again. Can we go shopping instead?'

'Just read the auras!' yelled Kalix.

Vex started to pace round the flat, looking this way and that. Kalix took out her investigation notebook and a pencil, poised to write down names, like a detective gathering clues.

'Loads of people have been here,' said Vex. 'All the police, I suppose. And people later – repairing the door, probably.'

'What about before? What about werewolves?'

Vex complained again that it was all so faint she could hardly make anything out, but she tried. Werewolf auras were very distinctive to a Hiyasta, and there were some traces.

'I see a werewolf aura!' she shouted excitedly.

'Whose is it?' Kalix asked eagerly.

'Gawain! He was definitely here.'

Kalix almost exploded at the idiocy of this but managed to restrain herself. Vex did seem to be on the verge of discovering something.

'And some more. These horrible werewolves we met at the gig. The Douglas something?'

Kalix nodded. So the Douglas-MacPhees had been here. That was interesting.

Vex peered in a corner, then shook her head.

'There's another werewolf aura here but it's too faint, I can't make it out.'

'Try.'

'My head hurts.' Vex screwed up her face in concentration. 'Thrix,' she announced.

Kalix nodded. Thrix had been here, of course, after the death. But not before, or so she claimed.

'Did she come here more than once? Was she here before Gawain died?'

'I think so,' said Vex. The auras sort of merge here. I think they met.'

Kalix bared her teeth, and wrote something down in her slow, laborious handwriting.

'Can we go now?' asked Vex.

Kalix nodded. She felt like she'd at least made some progress. As they walked up the short corridor to the front door, Vex suddenly halted.

'There's a tiny fragment of aura left here,' she said. 'Two auras. Mixed up.'

Vex strained to make them out. Her dark features took on an orange hue with the effort, as if small flames might appear at any moment.

'Decembrius, maybe.'

'Are you sure?'

'Not sure at all. It's hardly there. It's like . . .' But Vex struggled to find the words. There was no easy way to describe the faint remnant of an aura to someone who couldn't see them. 'It might be his. But I'm probably wrong.'

Vex abruptly sat down, exhausted by her effort.

Kalix sat beside her on the bare wooden floor. She made a final note, then stared into space. Decembrius. Why would he have been here? When Vex had revived they trooped down the dark staircase. Vex halted suddenly.

'I think Dominil might have been here too.'

Kalix stared at her companion. 'Are you just making this up?'

'What do you mean?'

'You've named half the MacRinnalch Clan!'

Vex shrugged. 'I told you I wasn't sure. I'm really bad at reading auras.'

Kalix seemed on the verge of snarling at her companion but stopped herself. Vex had done her best.

'Thanks for helping,' Kalix said.

'OK. Can we go to a cafe now? I need tea. And maybe an egg sandwich.'

They walked out of the shabby old building, Vex still feeling weary and Kalix deep in thought. It had started to rain and they hurried towards the nearest small cafe. Kalix wondered if Vex's information could be relied on. If she was right, several were-wolves had been at Gawain's flat before he was murdered, and none of them had been forthcoming about it.

'Let's talk about our assignments,' said Vex, halfway through her sandwich.

'Do we have to?'

'It'll be fun. I've already got lots of pictures of *Tokyo Top Pop Boom Boom Girl*. I can't wait to stick them in a big book. What are you going to do?'

'I can't talk to the class about anything.'

'How about "My life as a werewolf"? You'd be great at that.'

'It's meant to be a secret.'

'Oh. Well, what about "I have a good friend who's a were-wolf"?'

Kalix felt like screaming. 'We're not meant to mention were-wolves at all!'

'I suppose you're right. Maybe *Sabrina the Teenage Witch*? You like that.'

Kalix wasn't keen. She did like Sabrina but felt that the rest of the class might laugh at her for doing an assignment on what was really a children's programme. Vex, a regular viewer of cartoons aimed at four-year-olds, found this difficult to understand.

'I still think you could talk about *Curse of the Wolf Girl*.'

'Only if I can tell everyone how much I hate it.'

'Why not?' said Vex. 'We can pick anything. You don't have to like it.'

Kalix was surprised. She hadn't realised that. The notion of strongly denouncing *Curse of the Wolf Girl* as a piece of anti-werewolf propaganda seemed vaguely attractive. She shook her head.

'Stop distracting me. I want to think about Gawain.'

84

Dominil stepped out of the bookshop on Charing Cross Road carrying a plastic bag containing the complete letters of Cicero. It was a weighty volume. Cicero had been a prolific letter-writer.

She intended to walk back to her flat, which was a mile or so away. Dominil had once spent a lot of time walking through the fields and glens that surrounded the castle in Scotland, and here in London she enjoyed walking the streets. Her phone rang. She took it from the pocket of her long leather coat.

'Dominil?'

'Yes.'

'What have you been doing?'

'Buying a book.'

'Anything interesting?'

'The complete letters of Cicero.'

'The last great statesman of the Roman Republic.'

'I've always admired him.' Dominil turned a corner onto a street with several small shops selling fabrics from India.

'I wouldn't have thought you'd have much time for reading these days.'

'Why not?' asked Dominil.

'Well, there's the twins' gig. That must be taking some of your time? Making them rehearse. And keeping them safe.'

'I'm quite sure they're safe.'

'I hope so. You never know what might happen to a werewolf band in London these days.'

'I wouldn't describe them strictly as a werewolf band,' said Dominil. 'Werewolf-fronted perhaps.'

The caller laughed. 'That's enough to get them into trouble. He came to a bad end, of course.'

'Who?'

'Cicero.'

'I'm aware of that.'

'Not only murdered by Mark Antony but decapitated as well, and his hand cut off and nailed up in the Roman Forum as a warning to others.'

Dominil waited at a crossing for the cars to stop, then crossed the road carefully. The day was gloomy with intermittent rain, slightly dampening her long white hair.

'Have you been to the museum recently?'

'Yes,' said Dominil, 'though my last visit was interrupted before I could fully appreciate it.'

The caller laughed again. 'I'm sorry about that.'

Dominil looked round carefully at the next corner. She didn't know how Albermarle had obtained her phone number, though she wasn't surprised that he had. He was an intelligent foe, and he had the resources of the Guild behind him. She wondered if this call was an attempt to trace her location.

'I always liked you at Oxford,' said Albermarle.

'I know. I never gave you a second thought.'

'Well, perhaps you should have,' said Albermarle angrily, losing his composure for the first time in the conversation.

'You weren't worth it,' said Dominil, with her customary lack of tact.

'Maybe if you had I wouldn't be a werewolf hunter now.'

'I suggest you look for other employment.'

A group of Japanese tourists studied Dominil curiously. Dominil walked by without paying them any attention, though she was taking a careful interest in her surroundings. Albermarle had caught her by surprise at the museum and she didn't intend to let it happen again.

'You stole my place on the quiz team.'

'You were sick. I was asked to deputise.'

'I was better by the time of the competition. I should have won that trophy!'

'And yet you didn't.'

'I'll be seeing you soon, Dominil.'

'I look forward to it.'

'Next time I'll kill you,' said Albermarle.

'On the contrary,' replied Dominil, 'next time *I'll* kill *you*.'

85

The festival in honour of the Southern Volcano was a small affair in comparison to other Hainusta festivals. Even so, Princess Kabachetka surprised the Empress by participating with a show of enthusiasm. Her brother Prince Esarax was there, being fawned over by the masses, and the Princess had decided that she'd better start improving her own profile. Much as it bored her to stand around the rim of a volcano, clapping politely while local dignitaries made speeches and threw a few sacrificed victims into the crater, she did her best to smile and wave graciously to the crowds. Though it was far from comfortable wandering around a volcano rim in high heels – a problem suffered by many of the elemental aristocracy these days – she managed to make it through the ceremony without yawning or scowling.

Afterwards, the Empress was impressed, and remarked to her minister in charge of volcanoes that the Princess had looked well.

Princess Kabachetka, meanwhile, was racing back to the capital, heading for the cavern to meet Distikka. She hurried in, her heels clicking on the black basalt floor, to find Distikka sitting on a shelf of rock, a look of disapproval on her face.

The Princess held up her hand. 'Do not start with your lectures on timekeeping. I have been pandering to the masses, as recommended by yourself. These provincial elementals are quite dreadful. I thought their speeches would never end. How is the Fire Queen?'

Distikka rose, which made her chain mail clank slightly. 'Malveria is beside herself with rage that you managed to secure an invitation. She can talk of nothing else, and plots feverishly to secure an invitation herself. The foolish woman is now so bound up in the opera, her clothes, and her status among the aristocracy that she's completely alienated her Council of Ministers. Some of them now wonder openly if she is fit to be Queen.'

Princess Kabachetka glowed with pleasure at the news. 'And General Agripath?'

'The promotion to Commander has gone through.'

'Excellent. With the council turning against her and the head of the army under your thrall – he is under your thrall, I take it?'

'Yes.'

The Princess stared at Distikka for a few moments, wondering if the small figure had what it took to bring the head of the Hiyasta army under her thrall. She hoped so. 'Then you have every chance of succeeding to the throne when we remove the Queen.' Flames of happiness radiated from the Princess's eyes at the thought of Malveria being deposed.

'Have you made any progress with a spell to attack the Enchantress?' asked Distikka.

'Very little,' admitted the Princess. 'Replicating a lunar eclipse is a difficult concept. I've asked my agents on Earth to search out a particular book, which may have some guidance on the subject.'

'We'll fail if you don't manage to negate her powers,' warned Distikka.

'I'm aware of that. And I'm also aware that while we are busy deposing Queen Malveria and destroying Thrix MacRinnalch, it will do me no good if the Empress suddenly decides to die and my brother accedes to the throne.'

'Just make sure he attends the charity event and we can take care of him at the same time.'

The Princess frowned. 'That's not so easy. How can I persuade him to attend?'

'Does he have a wife?'

'He's unmarried. He has a mistress, a quite dreadful woman who keeps forcing her way into fashionable gatherings where she doesn't belong.'

'You should cultivate her. If you can make her want to go to the opera, he'll follow along.'

The Princess shuddered at the thought of cultivating her brother's mistress, but acknowledged that it was a worthwhile idea.

Distikka rose and walked to the centre of the cavern. The Princess stood next to her and held out her arms, placing one palm on each of Distikka's shoulders. Flames flowed between them, pink in colour, travelling from Kabachetka's body into Distikka's. Distikka had been finding it difficult to completely guard her aura recently, under the eyes of so many Hiyasta elementals. Were her treachery to be glimpsed, or her ancestry to be guessed at, Queen Malveria would execute her in an instant. The extra power from Princess Kabachetka was an important means of buffering the false aura she maintained at all times.

Though the Princess and Distikka were too different ever to be friends, they'd settled quite comfortably into a working partnership. Each thought, sincerely enough, that when they took power in their respective kingdoms they would get on equably enough with each other.

86

Daniel was agog when he learned about Dominil's rescue of Kalix.

'She exploded a smoke bomb? A smoke bomb? Who has a smoke bomb?' Though Daniel had never previously displayed any liking for Dominil, news of the daring escapade seemed to completely change his opinion about her. 'She's like a werewolf secret agent! Or a ninja! Did she swarm up the wall on a rope? Did she have hidden weapons?'

'You're getting carried away,' said Moonglow.

'She's like a superhero! Do you think she has special powers?'

'Of course she has special powers. She's a werewolf.'

'I mean extra over-and-above-normal-werewolf powers.'

Moonglow smiled at Daniel's enthusiasm. He couldn't help being impressed by anything that smacked of superheroes and secret agents. Moonglow had been just as impressed by the rescue but found the whole incident very worrying. Kalix had apparently blundered into an extremely dangerous situation and would probably have been killed had it not been for Dominil's timely arrival.

'I'm looking at Dominil in a whole new light,' said Daniel. 'She probably does have some hidden weapons. Maybe ninja throwing stars.' He pretended to throw a secret ninja weapon, which drew a protest from Moonglow, who told him to concentrate on the road.

She glanced at her watch. They were driving into the centre of London and wanted to make sure they didn't arrive in the congestion-charge zone while it was still active. If they did they'd have to pay the toll, which they were anxious to avoid. Daniel slowed down a little, just in case.

They were on their way to see Yum Yum Sugary Snacks. The invitation had arrived at the last minute. Beauty had phoned to let Kalix know they were playing at a private party in a warehouse just north of Camden, near Kentish Town Tube station. Daniel would rather not have driven but they had college tomorrow and didn't feel like arriving home too late on a night bus. Moonglow had been dubious about going at all, but was swept up in Vex's uncontrollable enthusiasm. At Yum Yum Sugary

Snacks's first and only gig, Vex had been overwhelmed with excitement and immediately became their biggest fan.

Others who'd been there, mainly the MacRinnalchs, remembered the night for the vicious fight that had ensued, leading to the deaths of many werewolves. Vex just remembered what a good time she'd had.

'They're strange creatures, these werewolves,' mused Daniel, as they edged through the traffic.

Moonglow gave him a funny look, thinking that this was stating the blindingly obvious.

'I mean apart from being werewolves, which is strange enough in the first place, I admit. But that doesn't seem enough for some of them. Look at Dominil. She's the only white-haired werewolf in the clan but she wasn't satisfied with that. She went away to Oxford where she got a first-class degree and spent her time translating Latin poetry and then she learned to be some computer genius and now she's running around London, rescuing people and exploding smoke bombs.

'And what about Thrix?' he continued, warming to his theme. 'She seems to be the only blonde werewolf and you'd think that might be enough for anyone. You know, she could go around saying "I'm the only blonde werewolf, what do you think about that?" But she wasn't satisfied either. She had to go off and learn to be a sorceress as well. How difficult was that? Very difficult, I'd imagine. Must have taken years. And then she still wasn't satisfied. She went and started her own fashion business and now she's got this lust-for-success thing going on. You can tell just by looking at her. She's positively scary. Overachiever of the century, I'd say. And you know how I hate overachievers.'

'Like me, for instance?' asked Moonglow.

Daniel had to run a quick mental check to see if he was currently attempting to be kind and supportive to Moonglow, or harsh and critical. He'd changed so many times over the past few weeks that he'd started to confuse himself.

'I don't think you're an overachiever,' he said, deciding he was still in his supportive phase. 'Just a girl who likes to do well at college. A good example to us all, really.'

'We're going to see Yum Yum Sugary Snacks!' screamed Vex from the back seat, a completely unnecessary comment in

Daniel's opinion, particularly as he'd just worked himself into a good position for complimenting Moonglow.

'I wish I could study like you,' he continued. 'I've really started to work harder as a result of—'

'I can't wait to see them again!' screamed Vex. 'Last time was the best thing ever!'

Daniel abandoned his compliment and concentrated on driving.

Kalix wasn't with them. She'd chosen not to come. She had things to do, though she wouldn't specify what they were.

'Maybe she'd be better just letting it go,' said Moonglow, thinking aloud.

'What?'

'Kalix. Maybe she should just forget about trying to find out who killed Gawain. It will end badly.'

'Of course it will end badly,' said Daniel, seriously, 'but there's nothing we can do about it. No human power can prevent Kalix from doing what she wants. Unless we dosed her with more laudanum, maybe.'

Moonglow frowned. She was sure that Kalix had been taking more laudanum recently, which was another worry. And she'd stopped eating too. Probably she was cutting herself as well, though she was careful to conceal it if she was. Moonglow's worries about Kalix prevented her from looking forward to the gig, and she barely heard Daniel as he talked to her about something or other as they passed through the centre of town.

87

'Mighty Queen,' began Xakthan, 'there is some disquiet among your Advisory Council.'

'Really, Xakthan? Why is that?'

Though he was normally quite at home in the pleasant red glow of the Fire Queen's throne room, First Minister Xakthan seemed uncomfortable. As a loyal supporter of such a long-standing monarch, Xakthan was secure in his position. Even if he offended her, Malveria was not suddenly going to dismiss him. That didn't mean he was secure against her wrath. The Fire Queen in a rage could be a fearsome sight. With the full power of the Great Volcano at her fingertips, she could erupt in a quite spectacular manner. Only last month, when a careless hand-maiden had misplaced her favourite nail varnish right before a reception for the ambassador from the air elementals, the Fire Queen's temper had exploded, taking much of the southern wing of the palace with it. Builders were still making repairs. Which may be, thought Xakthan, part of the problem. While the Queen had flown into a terrible rage over nail varnish, it was a long time since he'd seen her show any passion over the state of the nation.

'There was some . . . disappointment at your failure to calculate the date for the festival, Great Queen.'

'Didn't Distikka do it?'

'Yes, but it is a task that traditionally belongs to the reigning monarch. The volcano is of such importance, and you are the only one of royal blood who can harness its power.'

Malveria waved this away. 'If Distikka is intelligent enough to calculate the date, let her get on with it.'

'The council also feels they're being shut out of your affairs. And the fighting in the western desert is not going well.'

'It's a trifling affair. A few rebels.'

'Even so, it's troubling that it's taking so long to wipe them out. I'm not certain why Commander Agripath hasn't acted more decisively—'

'Is this another of your rivalries, Xakthan?'

Her first minister protested that it wasn't, but Malveria knew Xakthan and Agripath had never got along well. Quite possibly Xakthan was simply trying to discredit his rival.

'Mighty Queen, your leadership may be questioned if—'

'Distikka!' The Fire Queen greeted her assistant's arrival far too warmly for Xakthan's liking. 'You have everything?'

Distikka nodded, and handed Malveria an elegantly woven bag. The contents clanked lightly as the Fire Queen took it in her hand.

'Xakthan, I must depart.'

'But—'

'Important matters call. Take care of affairs while I'm away.'

And with that Malveria was gone, snapping her fingers to send herself hurtling through the dimensions.

She materialised outside Thrix's apartment in Knightsbridge and knocked lightly on the door. Thrix answered right away.

'Enchantress!' The Queen greeted her friend with a kiss on both cheeks. 'I bring gifts.' Malveria swept inside.

The Enchantress, used to Malveria's volatile temper, wasn't surprised to find that their argument was now apparently forgotten.

'What gifts?'

Malveria produced several bottles with a flourish. 'Inspired by cocktail dresses you are making me. As I may have mentioned, cocktails are unknown in my world. But Distikka has secured these supplies, which she assures me are a simple introduction to something called *Martini*.'

The Queen smiled broadly. 'I believe you mix the contents of the bottles and ...' She paused. 'Enchantress, while I am not entirely clear on the cocktail instructions, I did receive the clear impression one is not meant to swig directly from the bottle of gin.'

'I'm under stress,' said Thrix, and shuddered as she swallowed the spirits.

'Problems?'

'My bank manager wants to see me. And Abukenti are bringing out a new range of shoes.'

The Fire Queen gasped. 'Shoes from Abukenti? To match their fabulous bag? But this is wonderful!'

'It's not so wonderful if we can't get them,' said Thrix. 'Look at this.'

She handed a sheet of paper to Malveria, a press release from Abukenti.

To mark the fiftieth anniversary of the Abukenti Fashion House, Abukenti has created a new and exclusive range of shoes to match this year's design classic, the Abukenti bag. Abukenti will make only one hundred pairs of these shoes, to be distributed to our most valued customers.

Underneath the writing there was a picture of a pair of shoes, silver high heels, very delicately crafted and a perfect match for the handbag.

Malveria reeled in shock as she read the press release, stunned by both the beauty of the shoes and the possibility that she might not get a pair. 'Only one hundred pairs? But this is monstrous!' She turned the paper over, as if seeking further enlightenment on the subject, but there was no more. She used the paper to fan herself briefly, then sat down, feeling faint. 'Are we among their most valued customers?' she asked, hopefully.

'I doubt it,' replied Thrix, with a pained expression. 'Not that the shoes will go to valued customers anyway. Abukenti have had such a runaway success with the bag that they're using this shoe thing as a way of grabbing more publicity. They'll hand them out to movie stars, supermodels and the editors of fashion magazines.'

'But I *must* have the shoes,' said Malveria.

'Me too,' said Thrix. 'But we're not going to get them.'

The Fire Queen was distraught.

'How could we possibly turn up for the *Vogue* fashion awards and not be wearing these shoes? We will be disgraced. Banished to the far corner for people with inferior shoes. Models will point at us and laugh.'

Thrix and the Fire Queen looked at each other in despair, contemplating the awfulness of this prospect.

'I feel faint, Enchantress. Pass me the gin.' Malveria drank, winced at the taste, then drank again. 'We must think of a plan to obtain the shoes.'

Thrix sat on the couch beside her. 'We don't have much time. They didn't even send this press release to me. I'm not important enough, apparently. I only got it because Easterly sent me a copy. The shoes will probably be on their way to their intended recipients in a few days.'

Malveria placed the bottle on the floor. Some colour had returned to her cheeks and there was a determined glint in her eye.

'Then we must cope with the crisis. I waded through a river of blood to kill the Three-headed Dragon of Despair. I won't give up these shoes without a fight.'

'We'll be facing stiff competition. I'm sure we're not the only women wondering how to get their hands on a pair.'

Malveria nodded, and looked quite fierce. 'Indeed. Already in

New York, Moscow and Milan our rivals will be plotting and scheming. We must use all our resources. Surely with the cunning of our sorcery we can obtain the shoes?'

'It hasn't brought us any closer to Susi Surmata, has it?' said Thrix, reflecting on another of her current failures. 'I still can't get in touch with her.'

'No matter, Enchantress. We must continue with that campaign while opening a new front. These people will not defeat us.'

Thrix was bolstered by the Fire Queen's spirited optimism. 'We need more information. Where the shoes are and who's getting them. When we know that, we'll know what to do. We might be able to bribe someone. Or failing that, steal a pair.'

'I will suspend all government business while we manage the crisis. We must have these shoes, and quickly.' Malveria shuddered. 'I have this continual nightmare that Princess Kabachetka may appear on *Vogue*'s "Fashionable Party People" page before me. The injustice of it chills me to the bone. Enchantress, please stop hogging the gin. I am in need of some strengthening.'

88

The days preceding the twins' warehouse gig had been full of difficulties. Beauty and Delicious were keen to play but loath to rehearse. Dominil wouldn't hear of them appearing onstage without preparing properly, no matter how small the gig. It led to arguments. Dominil got her way, at the cost of bad feeling. Once again she found herself dragging the sisters from their beds and constantly phoning the other members of the band to make sure they arrived at rehearsals on time.

As the gig approached, the twins' excitement grew, culminating, as Dominil accurately foresaw, in huge episodes of anxiety. It was something of a paradox that while the twins were keen to succeed with their band, they were also scared of going on stage. Dominil was good at bullying them into rehearsing more but not so good at reassuring them about their anxieties. The twins' standard response to their stage fright was to drink more, and as they drank rather a lot in the first place it wasn't long before neither of them was capable of picking up a guitar, or singing, or even standing upright. Dominil sighed with frustration, picked them up off the floor, dragged them home to sleep, then dragged them out next day to rehearse again.

Making everything worse, Pete was still acting foolishly. Though he'd managed to pick up his guitar again he was still calling Dominil at all hours, leaving agonised messages on her answering machine, and behaving like a depressed lover at every opportunity. Dominil felt that if she caught him looking at her with sad moody eyes one more time, she might suddenly transform and rip his head off. She was fed up with the whole thing and regretted ever having slept with him. It was a small mercy that at least he hadn't revealed the source of his unhappiness to anyone else.

As the twins' house descended into chaos with the sisters rushing round trying on clothes, discussing set-lists and occasionally throwing up from nerves Dominil remained in control. She was obliged to slightly increase her intake of laudanum – a problem she knew she'd have to deal with sometime – but she managed to organise everyone and everything for the gig, even though she had still had the distraction of Albermarle to deal with. She felt it quite likely that Albermarle would do something on the night of the gig. From the information she'd been able to gather she didn't think the Avenaris Guild would be making a large-scale attack, but she'd be surprised if Albermarle didn't make an appearance. As it was a private party it hadn't been advertised anywhere, but Albermarle seemed capable of finding out anything he needed to know.

'Do you like these shades?' yelled Beauty, rushing into Dominil's office. 'Or these ones or these ones?' Beauty tried on three pairs in quick succession.

'The first ones,' said Dominil.

Beauty looked doubtful and hurried out again. The sisters had a lot of sunglasses and a lot of clothes. Most of them were now strewn around the house as part of the three-day process of dressing for the gig. Dominil noticed she had email. She opened it. It was from Albermarle. Dominil didn't know how he'd learned her email address.

Have fun at the gig, Dominil.

Dominil closed the email. Her eyes narrowed slightly. If Albermarle thought he could unnerve her by waging psychological warfare he was going to be disappointed. Dominil could not be unnerved. She could be angered, however, and she was now. Chasing her out of the British Museum was bad enough. No one sent threatening emails to Dominil. She'd make him regret it.

89

Kalix had decided not to go to the gig but that didn't prevent her from feeling annoyed about everyone going off without her. It didn't seem that anyone had tried very hard to persuade her.

They didn't really want me to go, thought Kalix. I could tell.

The doorbell rang.

Kalix hurried downstairs. 'If that's them coming back to ask me again, I'm still not going,' she muttered. 'I hate Yum Yum Sugary Snacks and Dominil too.'

It was Decembrius.

Kalix glowered at him. 'How did you find me again?' she demanded, fingering her pendant. As far as she knew, its powers of hiding should still protect her, causing unwanted visitors to forget where she lived even if they'd visited before.

'I have powers of finding things,' said Decembrius.

'So you keep saying.'

'I found the meeting for you, didn't I?'

'Then you deserted me.'

'Lucky for you I had the presence of mind to phone Dominil.'

'Why didn't you come yourself?'

'I collapsed in a coma after I had a vision of everyone being killed.'

Kalix stared at him. 'Your visions are stupid. I don't believe you even had one.'

'I did. It was powerful.'

'You're lying,' said Kalix. 'Go away.'

Decembrius, normally proud, seemed to sag a little in the

doorway, and for a second there was something vulnerable about him.

'Could I just come in for a while anyway? I've been ... depressed.'

'Depressed? Why?'

'I don't know. It just happens.'

Kalix looked at Decembrius a little differently. She'd never known any other werewolf admit to depression before. She let him in. Tiny pieces of plaster flaked off the walls as they ascended the dark stairs. In the living room Decembrius took a seat, uninvited. The gas fire was on full and the room was warm. Kalix felt the cold more than a werewolf should, because she was permanently undernourished. They sat in silence for a while.

'Did you learn anything when they kidnapped you?'

Kalix shook her head. 'Not really. Marwanis said she didn't have anything to do with killing Gawain. So did Morag MacAllister.'

'Were they telling the truth?'

Kalix shrugged. 'I don't know. I don't know how to investigate. I'm hopeless at it.'

Though Kalix had little time for MacRinnalch traditions she went to her room and took out a bottle of the MacRinnalch malt whisky which was around a quarter full, found one glass and one old mug in the kitchen, and shared it with her guest.

'I like your nose ring,' said Decembrius.

'Thanks,' replied Kalix, surprised.

'Maybe Thrix has some investigating spells.'

'She wouldn't help. But Vex thinks she visited Gawain before he died.' Kalix looked Decembrius in the eye. 'Vex says you were there too. She saw your aura.'

There was another long silence.

'Well?' demanded Kalix.

'I did visit,' said Decembrius.

'You never told me that before. Why not?'

Decembrius shrugged. Kalix transformed, and looked threatening. Decembrius remained as human and kept his seat.

'I went there to warn him.'

'Warn him about what?' growled Kalix, stepping forward and baring her teeth. Her fangs were long and sharp and she had an urge to use them. Unexpectedly she felt something soft brush against her leg. She looked down. 'Go away, you stupid cat.'

The cat started purring and rubbed itself enthusiastically against Kalix's leg.

'Stop doing that!' cried Kalix. The cat redoubled its efforts.

'I think it wants to be fed,' said Decembrius.

Kalix shook her leg but the cat seemed to have attached itself to her fur. It began to meow. Kalix sighed with frustration and marched into the kitchen. The cat bounded along behind her, purring enthusiastically as Kalix produced a can of cat food. Kalix tried to work the can opener but found it too difficult with her werewolf claws and had to change back to human. As she emptied the food into the bowl the cat purred furiously and ran between her legs. Kalix took a carton of milk from the fridge and filled the cat's other bowl.

'Next time you interrogate someone make sure the cat isn't around,' said Decembrius, from the doorway. 'It completely spoils the effect.'

Kalix scowled at him. 'What do you mean, you went to warn Gawain? What about?'

'The Douglas-MacPhees had found out where he lived. I didn't much care about Gawain but I didn't want the Douglas-MacPhees learning your address. So I went to warn him.'

That didn't sound very likely to Kalix. She followed Decembrius back into the living room and wondered about changing back into a werewolf again and threatening him. She got as far as making the transformation when the cat wandered in from the kitchen and leapt onto her lap. It circled round a few times, then lay down comfortably.

'Every time I turn into a werewolf this cat tramples all over me.'

'At least you've made a friend,' said Decembrius.

90

In Princess Kabachetka's largest reception room, the one with the best view of the Eternal Volcano, her servant Alchet was nervous and unhappy.

'I don't want to go to Earth,' she protested. 'It's cold and damp.'

'I am not asking you to live there,' replied the Princess testily. 'I merely require you to make a brief visit.'

Alchet squirmed uncomfortably. For her, the planet Earth was a distant and frightening place, a place where, if rumours were to be believed, ugly metal machines crawled over the land and water fell from the sky. The young fire elemental couldn't bear the thought of water falling on her from the sky.

'It will extinguish me. I'll fizzle and die.'

'You won't fizzle and die!' declared the Princess. 'I visit the Earth. Do you see me fizzling and dying? Now stand still so I can work the spell. And remember, once you're there, try to come back as quickly as you can.'

'But if I'm to come back as quickly as I can why are you sending me there?'

'Did I not explain this a hundred times? I'm perfecting a new spell for prevention of travel.'

The Princess chanted a few words, waved her hand, and her young servant disappeared.

And now, she thought, for the spell of non-returning. She chanted more words, a longer spell this time. Nothing happened. The Princess was pleased.

Abruptly, Alchet materialised back in the reception room, looking shaken but relieved to be home.

The Princess glared at her furiously. 'Why have you returned?'

'You told me to.'

'But I was working a spell to prevent your return. It was meant to keep you on Earth!'

Princess Kabachetka stared angrily at Alchet as if the failure of the spell was all her fault, then dismissed her with an angry wave. The Princess slumped on a chair and felt deflated. This spell of non-returning was proving to be difficult. It seemed impossible to prevent a fire elemental from coming back to its own dimension. If the Princess couldn't even stop Alchet from returning, there was no chance of keeping the powerful Fire Queen out. It was all very well for Distikka to talk grandly about stranding Queen Malveria on Earth while she mounted a coup. Distikka wasn't the one who had to work the spell. The Princess cursed Distikka for coming up with a lot of complicated and impractical plans.

262

A liveried attendant hurried in with a message. Princess Kabachetka accepted the scroll which, when opened, disgorged fire into the air. She spoke the spell of secret decryption, and the fire formed itself into a string of burning words.

Captain Easterly has located the Abukenti shoes.

The Princess leapt in the air with excitement. The prospect of securing the most exclusive high heels in the universe was enough to make her instantly forget her previous grievance against Distikka.

When Malveria hears of this she may just die of shame, she thought, with immense pleasure. She sent back a message by the next courier: *Excellent news about shoes. Must have them. No progress with spell. Need advice.*

91

The twins were in their element at the warehouse party. Dominil hated it. The warehouse was so dark and dilapidated that she couldn't imagine why anyone would want to hold a birthday party there. It was hot, noisy, smoky, and crammed full of people, all of whom seemed to know Beauty and Delicious. Dominil, with more on her mind than just the twins' performance, had to abandon her efforts to moderate their drinking. She knew this was inviting disaster but needed to devote some attention to the possibility of Albermarle appearing.

As she squeezed through the crowd Dominil found herself confronted by Vex who, to Dominil's great displeasure, immediately hugged her. Dominil went rigid and waited for it to end.

'Hi, Dominil! Isn't this *great*! When are the band playing?'

'In about an hour.'

'I can't wait to see Yum Yum Sugary Snacks again! And I want a T-shirt like yours, can I have one?'

It was oddly loyal of Dominil to be wearing a Yum Yum Sugary Snacks T-shirt. Though she'd designed it herself it wasn't a garment she'd normally have cared to be seen in. But Dominil, as manager of the band, felt it was the right thing to do to wear their merchandise.

Daniel and Moonglow followed in Vex's wake. Dominil observed that both of them looked happy. In fact, almost everyone in the hot warehouse looked happy. Unlike Dominil, they all seemed to fit in quite naturally, feeling no discomfort at the crowd, the heat, or the noise. Dominil briefly studied Moonglow and felt some admiration for the effort she'd put into her appearance – the matching black clothes, pointed boots, heavy make-up and beads in her hair. Moonglow was in full gothic mode, and it must have taken some time to achieve the effect.

'Kalix didn't want to come,' said Moonglow. 'I think she might be with Decembrius. I'm not really sure about him . . .'

'Nor am I,' said Dominil.

Moonglow looked at the white-haired werewolf with a hint of accusation. 'Kalix said you wouldn't help her investigate.'

'That's true.'

'Why not? She probably needs your help.'

'I have too much else to do. Excuse me, I have check on the band.' With that, Dominil departed, leaving a thoughtful Moonglow behind.

Daniel led her and Vex in a wedge-shaped formation towards the bar, which had been constructed from some old crates at the side of the room.

'Cheap beer,' he muttered. 'Better than nothing, I suppose. I hoped it might be free, what with it being a birthday party.'

Daniel and Moonglow were again short of money. Only yesterday Daniel had sternly warned Vex and Kalix not to fail their exams.

'If you get dragged home in disgrace and you're not here to pay the rent, I'll be stacking shelves in the supermarket before the week is out.'

He'd followed that up with a warning to Moonglow not to transmit accurate reports of either Kalix or Vex's progress.

'Just pretend they're doing well. What harm can it do?'

Moonglow hadn't replied. Unknown to Daniel, the Mistress of the Werewolves had phoned last week. Moonglow, unable to lie, had given a reasonably truthful account of Kalix's progress at college. Her report hadn't left Verasa entirely satisfied.

*

A small storeroom at the back of the warehouse had been set aside as a dressing room for the band. There Dominil found Beauty and Delicious and the rest of their musicians, sandwiched between a crowd of friends.

'Are you ready to go onstage?'

'It's not time yet.' Delicious slurred her words.

'Yes, it is.'

'They don't have to go on yet,' said one of their friends, a young man perched on a crate with a can of lager in his hand.

'What does it have to do with you?' demanded Dominil.

'It's his party,' said Delicious, and there was some laughter at Dominil's expense for not knowing whose party it was.

'I think you should play when advertised,' said Dominil, stiffly. Dominil liked events to run on time, but everyone else seemed to have a flexible view of the programme. No one except Dominil cared if the band were late onstage. She left the storeroom and went again to the front of the building, checking for werewolf hunters. Dominil was irritated with the twins and angry with Albermarle. The noisy crowd in the warehouse wasn't helping her mood.

92

Decembrius laughed as he turned the page.

'If Arabella Wolf is so worried about eating her boyfriend, why doesn't she move somewhere else?'

'I know!' cried Kalix. 'Isn't this comic ridiculous? How can her boyfriend be such an idiot, anyway? Didn't he get suspicious when all his friends were attacked?' Kalix and Decembrius were lounging in front of the gas fire, drinking tea and reading *Curse of the Wolf Girl*. The cat was curled up comfortably on Kalix's lap.

'It's unfortunate that the wolf girl keeps being invited to these exclusive events,' mused Decembrius. 'What happens after she kills the mayor?'

'I don't know. I only have these six issues.'

'You should look for the others.'

'I don't want them.' Kalix paused. Actually, she did want them. Though she felt irritated by *Curse of the Wolf Girl*, for some reason she had an urge to collect them all. 'They only published twelve. Maybe I could look in the comic shop for more. Vex says the assistant was friendly.'

Kalix remembered Vex's suggestion that she should do her assignment on *Curse of the Wolf Girl* and felt briefly anxious again, but managed to let it go. She'd relaxed after her traumatic experience at the hands of Marwanis and Morag. Facing danger and even death wasn't such an unusual thing for her, and the unpleasant memories didn't linger, unlike certain others.

'What's it like, living with humans?' asked Decembrius. Not many MacRinnalchs had ever shared a house with anyone except fellow werewolves.

'It's really annoying.'

'Why? Do they act funny about you being a werewolf?'

'No,' admitted Kalix. 'They're OK with that. But they keep telling me to study. I hate college.'

'Then stop going.'

Kalix made a face. 'I can't. It's complicated.'

For the first time in her life Kalix seemed to have obligations to other people. It was troubling, and it made her anxious. It was tempting to just leave, but she couldn't make up her mind. She felt more comfortable with Decembrius since learning of his depression. She'd never met another werewolf with mental problems before, or at least, none that had admitted to any.

'Why is it complicated?'

'They're sort of relying on me. Dominil thinks I should go to college as well. She says I should calm down and start acting normal.' Kalix's temper rose. 'How can I do that when I'm trying to find out who killed Gawain? And live with humans, and go to college at the same time? It's too much. No wonder I get anxious. Now Moonglow's lecturing me again. Everyone should just leave me alone.'

'You should just pretend to be normal,' suggested Decembrius.

'What do you mean?'

'That's what I used to do at the castle when my mother got annoyed about me being depressed. "No self-respecting MacRinnalch werewolf ever suffered from depression before," she would say to me. It's tough when your own mother starts complaining to the Mistress of the Werewolves. So I just pretended to be normal.'

'Did it make you less depressed?'

'Not at all. But it got everyone off my back.'

Kalix considered this. She already did pretend to be normal, to an extent, trying to fit in with the household despite being a werewolf. Perhaps she could extend her pretence and hide her anxiety and depression, as Decembrius suggested. It might get everyone off her own back for a while.

93

Captain Easterly accompanied Thrix to the Young Fashion Designer awards at the Olympia Conference Centre in London. It was a reasonably prestigious event. The winners were guaranteed some good publicity in the press. Thrix had never been nominated for the award, and resented it. Now, at the ostensible age of thirty, she was too old. As they took their seats she reached over and pressed a finger lightly on Captain Easterly's cheek. 'Designer stubble?'

He smiled, and looked slightly embarrassed. 'Do you hate it?'

'It suits you. Have you been reading the papers?'

'No.' He continued to look embarrassed. 'Maybe.'

Last week a survey claiming that women found slightly unshaven men attractive had been widely reported. Thrix was amused at the thought of Easterly being influenced by a newspaper survey. He was already attractive. His charm hadn't faded, and having found a man who was not only attractive but just as interested in clothes as she was she didn't intend to let him go easily. The Enchantress was becoming very fond of Easterly.

'How did you ever survive in the army?' she'd asked him last week, breaking off suddenly from an intense hour-long discussion about the colours that would be fashionable next season.

'I didn't talk about clothes so much,' he admitted.

'Were you too busy killing people?'

Easterly didn't like to talk much about his military experiences. Thrix knew he'd been in action during his career. Thrix didn't mind. She'd been involved in violence herself when necessary, as violence sometimes was for the MacRinnalch werewolves.

The event was late starting. Both of them were used to this, and expected it. In the fashion world, events never started on time. As the lights eventually dimmed and the music changed to announce the arrival of the first models on the catwalk, Easterly's phone vibrated in his pocket. He slipped it out smoothly to see who was calling. It was Albermarle. Easterly was obliged to take the call and there was some consternation as he made his way clumsily through the fully seated audience to the corridor outside.

'What is it?' he demanded. 'I'm busy.'

'I've been arrested,' said Albermarle.

'What for?'

'Breaking and entering. Get the Guild to send me a lawyer. We'll need to smooth it over.'

'Who were you trying to burgle?'

'Dominil.'

Easterly cursed his cousin but did as he requested. Though he was furious with Albermarle, there was a code between members of the Guild. They were obliged to help each other, no matter what. It took some time for Easterly to make the required calls. When he returned to his seat he thought Thrix was a little distant.

'My cousin just got arrested for burglary,' he whispered, reasoning that coming clean was the best option.

Thrix looked surprised. 'Really?'

'He's the black sheep of the family. I sent him a lawyer.'

Thrix inched closer to Easterly, feeling that he'd provided a reasonable explanation. She knew how annoying families could be.

'I hate this collection,' he whispered, frowning in disapproval at the models who paraded by in clothes from a particularly well-regarded new designer.

It further endeared him to Thrix, who also hated the designer, and didn't see why anyone made a fuss about her uninspiring dresses.

94

Kalix read out her list of suspects to Decembrius, though she kept the paper shielded so he couldn't see how bad her hand-writing was.

'You suspect your mother?'

'She hated Gawain. She had him banished.'

Decembrius was sceptical. 'Just because she didn't like him playing around with her daughter doesn't mean she wanted him dead. I don't see why Markus would care about Gawain, either. Now he's Thane he's got other things on his mind.'

'What about Thrix?'

'Maybe Thrix,' conceded Decembrius. 'If she's as jealous as you say.'

'She is,' said Kalix fiercely.

'As for the other werewolves on your list, I suppose they're possible. Marwanis certainly hates you for killing Sarapen. So does Morag MacAllister. And the Douglas-MacPhees haven't for-given you for killing Fergus. But didn't you say that you saw Duncan Douglas-MacPhee outside the house after Gawain was dead? Why would he hang around if he'd killed him? Anyway, I can't imagine him killing Gawain. Gawain could look after him-self.'

'They might have taken him by surprise.'

Decembrius shook his head. 'You said he was wounded in the chest. He must have seen his attacker.'

'Thrix could do that,' said Kalix. 'She could have used some spell on him to make him confused and then another one to kill him.'

'You really don't like your sister, do you? What did she do to you?'

Kalix ignored the question.

'It's far more likely the Guild killed Gawain,' said Decembrius.

'Hunters couldn't kill him. He'd have killed them first.'

'Who knows what might have happened? There might have been a lot of them. They might just have got lucky. Anyone can get lucky in a fight. They might even still have one of the Begravar knives.'

Kalix ground her teeth together. She knew that Decembrius

was talking sense but, if the Guild really was responsible for Gawain's murder, she feared that she'd never be able to take revenge properly.

'I'll never find out which hunter it was. I don't even know where the Guild headquarters is.'

'It sounds to me like you should be asking for help from Thrix and Dominil,' said Decembrius and ran his fingers through his hair. 'Computing skills and sorcery. They could find the Guild if they put their minds to it.'

'But they won't help!' cried Kalix, and felt agitated.

'We should ask them again. Tactfully, maybe.'

'What do you mean, "we"?' demanded Kalix.

'Don't you want me to help?'

Kalix scowled. Now she'd opened up a little to Decembrius she was regretting it.

He surprised her by asking what else was wrong with her.

'What do you mean?'

'Apart from Gawain, what else is making you unhappy?'

'None of your business.'

'Is it college? Are you failing?'

'Of course I'm failing.'

'What's so difficult?'

'Everything. English. And maths. Can you do maths?'

'Some. I got an A level before I went to university.'

Kalix hadn't realised that Decembrius had gone to university. She regretted raising the subject. At remedial college she'd just failed her Numeracy A test, which, she suspected, was the sort of test that seven-year-olds might take at primary school. She didn't want to discuss it with anyone who'd been to university.

'Show me the problem,' he said. 'Maybe I can help.'

'It's all right,' muttered Kalix, who had no desire to let Decembrius know she'd failed such a basic test. Somehow, when she sat in class, either trying to follow the teacher's words or staring at a computer screen with headphones on, her mind just seemed to go blank. Yesterday she'd failed to add up 1,000, 469 and 21 correctly, and after that she'd despaired. As for calculating how many hours had passed from a certain point on the clock, or where anything was in a grid, Kalix was completely baffled. In class she just became too anxious to think properly. As far as she could see, everyone in the class was making more progress than she was, and it wouldn't surprise her if even Vex was better at converting simple fractions into decimals. Kalix sighed, sipped her tea, and wished that she never had to go to college again.

95

The Fire Queen settled down comfortably in the mushroom patch in Colburn Woods and waited for the Fairy Queen to arrive. Dithean, a punctual monarch, didn't keep her waiting long. She rode out from under the shadows of the trees on a fox, which she thanked graciously before fluttering onto a mushroom next to Malveria.

'You look anxious, Malveria. Was your offer rejected?'

'Word has not yet arrived.'

Malveria fretted, and pulled at the hem of her skirt. Though she adored the new range of tight-fitting skirts that Thrix had designed for her, she wasn't convinced about the length.

'I feel it should be shorter, but Thrix claims this is a more stylish length.'

'The skirt is very flattering,' said Dithean reassuringly. Dithean's own dress was so pale and diaphanous as it drifted in the breeze that at times it hardly appeared to be there. Malveria studied it enviously and wished she knew what fabric it was made from, but the fairies had many secrets and the material of the Queen's dress was probably one of them.

Along with her lip colouring, thought Malveria, and could not resist telling Dithean that Thrix was getting along splendidly with Captain Easterly.

'They make an excellent couple. I really feel they have a future.'

'We'll see,' said the Fairy Queen, and smiled.

'Distikka should have sent me a message by now,' muttered Malveria. 'But it's a hazardous mission. I wouldn't be surprised if the Mistress of the Werewolves has had her executed. And then how will I ever get to the opera?'

After considering Malveria's problem regarding the charity event, Distikka had asked the Fire Queen if she'd considered making a donation to the charity.

'Isn't that what these events are for?'

The Queen confessed she didn't know.

'I'm sure the object is to raise money for a cause,' said Distikka. 'If you offer a large sum of money for a ticket, then perhaps the Mistress of the Werewolves will forget her antipathy towards the Hiyasta and invite you.'

'Are you sure?'

'I think it's likely. After all, her prestige depends on the event raising funds.'

Though Malveria was quite used to using bribery in state affairs she had no experience of human charities. It hadn't occurred to her to offer money. There was the awkward problem of how to make contact. The Queen could hardly risk her own dignity by making the application herself like some beggar at the castle door.

'I'll undertake the mission,' Distikka had said, nobly.

'It may be very dangerous. Many of these Scottish werewolves are not civilised like the Enchantress. They might tear you apart. But now that Kabachetka is attending the event I simply must go, so we will just have to risk your life.'

So Distikka had been dispatched to offer a substantial sum to the Mistress of the Werewolves, and Malveria now awaited the outcome.

'I will regret it if Distikka is ripped to pieces. She really is the most excellent adviser. I considered sending Agrivex, whom no one would miss, but she is too stupid to carry out such a mission.'

'How is your young almost-adopted niece?' enquired the Fairy Queen.

'As foolish as ever. At this moment she's watching some band of musicians in London, and probably causing a great disturbance.'

The Fire Queen was correct. Vex was indeed causing some disturbance to those around her. The small warehouse, an old carpet showroom, was packed with guests, leaving little room for

272

dancing, but Vex was undeterred. The moment the band came on she pushed her way to the front and began leaping about enthusiastically. Vex was Yum Yum Sugary Snacks's greatest fan, and though she was a slender girl she soon cleared enough space around her by dint of her enthusiasm, her large boots, and her reckless disregard for public safety.

The rest of the audience were less enthusiastic. Most of them knew Beauty and Delicious. They were sympathetic towards the sisters but no one could pretend they were putting on a good show. From the moment Beauty fell over the drum kit it had been obvious that tonight wasn't going to be a great performance. The twins were too intoxicated to play their guitars, nor could they remember any of their lyrics. Delicious only stayed on her feet by clutching at her microphone stand. Beauty seemed to have forgotten where the audience were and stood towards the side of the tiny stage, mumbling inaudibly. The rest of the band did their best but they too had succumbed to the party spirit. Despite the strict regime of rehearsals insisted on by Dominil, the band rarely managed to start or finish a song in time with each other.

Dominil's lips were compressed in a thin disapproving line. It didn't matter to her that they were at a private party where no one really minded the terrible performance. Dominil did not like to see anything done so badly, and took the band's poor efforts as a personal insult.

'So much for the constant rehearsals,' she fumed as Beauty crashed into Hamil's keyboard and knocked it off the beer crates on which it was balanced. The music ground to a halt. There were some friendly groans, punctuated by the sound of Vex screaming her appreciation.

'Weren't they better than this last time?' said Moonglow to Daniel, somewhere in the middle of the packed room.

'Much better,' agreed Daniel.

They retreated to the makeshift bar, where Daniel bought them two pints of lager from a keg. The barman had no change and asked if they had the exact money, which led to some fumbling for coins in the darkness. Moonglow hunted in her purse while Daniel dug into his pockets and between them they came up with the exact amount. As they forced their way back through the crowd, Daniel suddenly felt an extra wave of affection for Moonglow. It seemed to him that their successful cooperation at the bar was a clear sign that he and Moonglow were destined to be together. He edged a little closer, which wasn't difficult as there was little room to move apart. Unexpectedly, Moonglow brushed a finger against Daniel's cheek.

'You haven't shaved,' she said genially.

'I forgot,' explained Daniel, who had read a report about women finding unshaven men attractive but wasn't about to admit it. He found it very significant that Moonglow had touched his cheek. Suddenly he felt quite unlike his normal self. He abruptly grabbed Moonglow and kissed her. Moonglow remained static, and didn't really kiss him back with great enthusiasm. On the other hand, Daniel noticed, neither did she fling him off or punch him in the face, both of which might have happened. He decided to press on but, without warning, he felt himself go weak. The strength vanished from his legs. He felt hot and fevered, and began to sink to the floor.

'I don't feel well . . .'

Moonglow was alarmed by the unexpected kiss and more alarmed when Daniel collapsed to the floor.

She cried out something that Daniel thought might have been to do with a curse, but it was noisy in the room and he was too ill to concentrate.

Moonglow took his arm and helped him to his feet. They tried to make their way to the back of the room, through the great crowd of revellers who were currently jeering quite amiably at the stage. Delicious had taped the set list to the floor next to her mic stand and had now managed to destroy it with a spilled pint of beer.

'Does anyone know what song we're playing next?' she asked vaguely. There were several suggestions from the crowd, but none from the band.

Dominil lost all of her remaining patience. At this rate Yum Yum Sugary Snacks would be the talk of Camden, famed for their shambling incompetence. Dominil didn't intend to let that happen, and advanced towards the stage, intent on dragging them off.

'Dominil,' came a voice, loudly, through the speakers.

Dominil froze, imagining at first that it was some ploy by

Albermarle. It was worse than that. Pete the guitarist, almost as intoxicated as the twins, had made his way towards Beauty's mic and was now pointing at Dominil. Several hundred heads turned towards her with interest.

'I love that woman!'

There were some raucous cheers.

'But since we slept together she won't speak to me again!'

The crowd erupted at the news. There was laughter, mingled with cries of 'Shame!' and 'Give him another chance!' Dominil found herself rooted to the spot, almost paralysed by Pete's unexpected announcement. In her Yum Yum Sugary Snacks T-shirt she had the uncomfortable feeling that she looked like a groupie, and she didn't know where to look as the crowd stared at her.

If the audience was hugely entertained by Pete's antics, Beauty and Delicious were equally astonished.

'You slept with Dominil?' yelled Beauty at Pete.

'The one with the white hair?' added Delicious, helpfully.

'Yes,' wailed Pete.

'Is that why you've been miserable?' shouted Beauty, her voice booming through the amplifier. 'We thought it was because of that slutty barmaid at the Rose and Crown.'

'Hey!' came a voice from the crowd. 'Who are you calling slutty?'

Dominil, who was afraid of nothing, found herself unable to cope with public ridicule. She turned on her heel, barged the people behind her out of the way and, pursued by a great deal of laughter and a few more anguished cries from Pete, left the room. At the door Dominil ran into Moonglow, who was helping a semi-conscious Daniel out of the warehouse.

'He's not very well. Can you help me get him outside?'

Without speaking, Dominil stretched out one hand, lifted Daniel into the air, brushed some onlookers aside, and carried him outside. Dominil deposited Daniel on the pavement, then looked sharply at Moonglow.

'Does everyone have to drink so much?' she demanded, then turned and walked swiftly away, her expression still dark with anger.

Moonglow called after her to tell Vex what had happened, but Dominil didn't acknowledge her.

Moonglow helped Daniel, who was sweating freely and looked very ill, into the car, took his car keys out of his pocket, got behind the wheel and started the engine. She kept sneaking anxious glances at him as she drove, wondering if this was really the result of Malveria's curse. Had Daniel triggered it by kissing her? She wasn't quite sure what form the curse might take and wouldn't have been that surprised to see Daniel turning into molten lava, or something else equally horrible. She fretted over his health and blamed herself for not making it clearer that kissing was quite out of the question.

Perhaps it's just flu, she thought as they headed south over the River Thames, which was black under the night sky. 'Or some sort of norovirus. They can make you ill really quickly.'

Hundreds of miles to the north, in Colburn Woods, Queen Malveria turned her head to gaze intently into the distance.

'What is taking Distikka so long?' she muttered. 'I really fear the werewolves have eaten her.'

'Can a fire elemental be eaten by werewolves?' wondered Dithean aloud.

'Of course. And we make for a very wholesome feast.'

'I'm not certain of that. Elementals are much like fairies, and no werewolf could devour me.'

'Please, dear Dithean, the fairy legends that the elementals are merely a branch of the fairy line are quite mistaken.'

Dithean laughed. It was the fairies' belief that the elementals were indeed merely a type of fairy, but Malveria would never allow this to be true, claiming for herself a quite different heritage.

'Distikka, while small, would be very nourishing. But I really hope she hasn't been eaten. I'm very keen to attend this opera.'

96

Albermarle's subordinates, codenamed Orion and Pictor, waited impatiently for their boss to arrive. They'd arranged to meet in the early evening, close to the warehouse in Kentish

Town, but Albermarle hadn't shown up. It was puzzling. Though Albermarle was an odd person, and not popular in the Guild, he was known to be punctual. They'd seen various revellers troop by on their way into the warehouse and had experienced a frisson of excitement when Dominil appeared: tall, white-haired, and distinctive. According to Albermarle, Dominil was a cousin of the Thane and held a seat on the Great Council of the MacRinnalchs. If they managed to kill her their status in the Avenaris Guild would rise dramatically. Fellow hunters might talk about them in the same admiring way they talked of Easterly.

'Where *is* he?' muttered Orion. 'If he doesn't get here soon we'll miss our chance.'

His companion peered out the rear window of the white van that was parked half on the road, half on the pavement, anonymous among a long line of vehicles laid up for the night.

'Probably still eating.'

They laughed.

'Is it true he really used to weigh three hundred and fifty pounds?' Albermarle had lost weight since those days but his appetite for junk food was still legendary. The hunters stopped laughing, remembering they were here on serious business. They were armed, and they'd both spent a lot of time on the shooting range beneath Guild headquarters.

Kentish Town was quiet. The North London pubs had emptied, the kebab shops had closed, and the drinkers had gone home. Though the party at the warehouse was going on through the night, not many other people were about. Minicabs drove by occasionally, and a double-decker night bus crawled up Highgate Road, but there were few pedestrians on the dark streets.

'What if she appears again and Albermarle isn't here?'

'We follow orders. Observe but don't approach.'

As a police car cruised by they flattened themselves in their seats, not wanting to be noticed and asked awkward questions. As the car disappeared from view Pictor nudged his companion.

'There she is.'

Dominil had re-emerged from the warehouse, talked briefly to a young couple, then walked off alone. Orion engaged the engine and moved the van cautiously into the road. Ahead of them Dominil took an abrupt turning and vanished down a side street. Orion turned into the same street, then halted. Dominil was nowhere in sight.

'Where is she?'

The young hunters were unsure what to do. Albermarle had instructed them to keep Dominil under observation until he arrived, but Albermarle hadn't turned up and now they were in danger of losing the werewolf. Orion, the senior of the pair, took control.

'I'm going to look.' He opened the door.

'We were told not to get out the van,' protested his companion, but Orion slipped out and stood in the poorly illuminated street, straining for a sight or sound of Dominil.

'She must have—' he began, but he didn't finish the sentence. A white werewolf appeared seemingly from nowhere, moving at tremendous speed. She clamped her jaws around Orion's shoulder, crushing the bone. Then, too quickly for Pictor to prevent it, she grabbed the door of the van and wrenched it open. Pictor found himself dragged half out the vehicle, his face only inches away from the terrifying white beast's jaws, which dripped with the blood of his companion.

'I have a message for Albermarle,' growled Dominil, quite distinctly. Pictor shook with fear, terrified to actually hear a werewolf speak.

'What message?' he gasped.

Dominil picked up Orion's unconscious body as easily as if it had been a doll and flung it into the van.

'His attempts to frighten me aren't working.'

The werewolf closed the door, without slamming it. Pictor saw her transform back into human. Still shaking with fear, he fumbled with the ignition key, finally started the van and sped off.

Dominil walked swiftly back to the warehouse. Two girls stumbled out of the entrance, clutching at each other for support.

'It's Pete's girlfriend!' they cried. Dominil gave them her fiercest scowl, but they were too inebriated to notice and were loudly wondering if Dominil's long white hair was natural as she went silently back into the warehouse.

97

Moonglow was desperately anxious when she arrived home with Daniel. She'd driven them home, though she only had a provisional licence and wasn't insured to drive Daniel's car. Normally a law-abiding woman, she'd only done it because of her concern that Daniel might be about to die. She wondered if she should take him to hospital. Daniel thought he had food poisoning, or perhaps flu, but Daniel didn't know about Malveria's curse. They struggled upstairs.

Kalix had to move sharply as Daniel slumped onto the couch.

'Good night, then?' said Decembrius, assuming that Daniel was drunk.

Moonglow glared at him, not pleased to find him here. 'He's sick.' She paused. 'Kalix, are you doing homework?!'

'No,' said Kalix, and tried to hide her book by sitting on it.

'It's good that you're doing homework!' said Moonglow, so excited by the development that she temporarily forgot Daniel.

Kalix mumbled something inaudible and looked embarrassed. 'What's wrong with Daniel?'

'I'm not sure. Help me lay him out on the couch.'

Decembrius made to assist but Kalix shooed him away. 'You should go now.'

'I thought I was helping you.'

'Daniel needs peace. Go away.'

'Fine,' growled Decembrius. 'To hell with you.'

Decembrius left swiftly, looking annoyed.

Daniel had now given up protesting that he didn't feel too bad. Sweat poured from his forehead, though he was shivering as if from the cold. Moonglow took the old grey blanket from the back of the couch and placed it over him.

'I think he's got flu,' said Moonglow uncertainly. 'I'll get some paracetamol.'

As she hunted in the kitchen cabinet for some pills, Moonglow felt close to panic. Had the brief kiss really brought on Malveria's curse? If it had, what would the result be? And what could she do about it? Should she tell Kalix? Kalix wouldn't be able to help lift a Hiyasta curse but perhaps Thrix could help. Moonglow resolved to watch Daniel closely. If he seemed to be getting worse then she'd tell Kalix everything, and apply to Thrix for assistance.

Moonglow felt furious at Malveria. Why had she placed them under such a ridiculous curse in the first place? It was unreasonable. Although, reflected Moonglow, she had agreed to it willingly enough at the time. It had saved Kalix's life.

Malveria could have just saved Kalix's life anyway, without making up ridiculous curses, she thought angrily. After all the help I've given her with make-up, not to mention comforting her after her fashion disasters.

Moonglow resolved to have some harsh words with the Fire Queen. Or would that just make everything worse? Moonglow worried some more, and didn't know what to do about anything.

98

Though Captain Easterly and Albermarle had never been friendly, the row that erupted between them after Easterly bailed his cousin out of jail was their worst ever.

'How,' raged Easterly, 'am I meant to get close to Thrix MacRinnalch if I have to leave in the middle of a fashion show to rescue my idiot cousin after he's been caught trying to rob Dominil's apartment? What were you doing there, anyway?'

'I needed to visit her flat while she was away.'

'What for?'

'It was part of my plan. But it went wrong. She moved out before I got there.'

Albermarle had been in the process of letting himself into the flat with a duplicate key when he found himself confronted by an angry family member who'd called the police. Arriving unusually rapidly, they'd apprehended Albermarle. His claim that he thought he'd been visiting a friend's apartment had failed to convince them.

On hearing the pitiful tale, Easterly came close to exploding. 'You don't need a plan to kill Dominil! You just shoot her with a silver bullet! Like you could have done tonight, except you decided to burgle her flat instead.'

Albermarle squirmed. He was already in trouble with the Guild. After he'd failed to turn up to meet his subordinates, one of them had been quite badly injured. Orion had disobeyed orders by leaving the van, but Albermarle hadn't been there to supervise him.

'I'm amazed they haven't thrown you out of the Guild already. They probably will tomorrow when the Board of Directors meets.'

They stood in one of the plushly carpeted corridors in their apartment block. The air was tinged with the scent of the many large potted plants, well tended in moist earth, that surrounded the elevator. Albermarle had the remnants of a bowl of cereal in his hand, and his huge T-shirt flopped outside his trousers.

'I was gathering intelligence,' he mumbled defensively.

'No, you weren't. You were trying to psych her out. What did you plan to do in her flat? Write a message on the wall saying "I know where you live, I'm coming to get you"?'

Albermarle's face coloured but he didn't reply.

'Do you have any idea how pathetic this is? Your job is to kill Dominil, not get revenge on her. So what if she ignored you at university? No one cares. Just get over it.'

'I *am* over it.'

'Really? I notice you've put on about twenty pounds in the last two weeks.'

Albermarle glanced at his bowl of cereal.

'Who are you to talk?' he demanded, feeling he'd had enough criticism from his cousin. 'If there's anyone wasting time it's you. You're going to fashion shows with this blonde werewolf, taking her to dinner and who knows what else. Not much sign of were-wolf-hunting going on there, is there? Maybe you should just marry her instead.'

Easterly bristled. 'All my actions have been fully approved by the Guild.'

'Only because you've spun them some story about Thrix being a sorceress. I think you like dating her.'

'She *is* a sorceress, you moron,' said Easterly. 'You can't just shoot a werewolf like Thrix. A silver bullet won't harm her.'

'There's never been a werewolf a silver bullet won't harm,' sneered his large cousin.

'She's too well protected. Thrix is the most dangerous were-wolf in London.'

'I'd say Dominil is more dangerous than that phoney sorceress. Dominil's a psychopathic killer.'

'Just because someone wouldn't date you doesn't make them a psychopathic killer. She's a werewolf. Next time, just shoot her.'

'You should take your own advice,' retorted Albermarle. 'Nice suit you're wearing, by the way. Did Thrix like it? Will she give you another date?'

Easterly glared at Albermarle, then abruptly abandoned the argument. He strode down the stairs towards his front door.

'Maybe she'll invite you to the castle!' yelled Albermarle at his retreating figure. 'You can marry into the clan! Have werewolf babies! I know you love her!'

When Easterly had disappeared, Albermarle gazed down at his empty cereal bowl. It looked very small in his hands. Still hungry, he tramped heavily upstairs to examine the contents of his fridge.

99

It wasn't far from Kentish Town to Camden but the journey was an uncomfortable one for Dominil. Having thrown the twins and their equipment into the van, she hoped she might be able to bring the evening to an end without further humiliation. Beauty and Delicious were barely conscious. Unfortunately for Dominil, as they pulled away from the warehouse, they woke up.

'Beauty, did I suffer some bizarre hallucination or did Pete just tell the whole world he was in love with Dominil?'

'I believe he did. But she discarded him.'

'It's heartless, really.'

'Cruel.'

'Dominil's like that. Just takes them off for a night of passion, breaks their hearts, then forgets them.'

Dominil drove on.

'At least the mystery is solved,' continued Delicious. 'Pete isn't miserable about any barmaids. He's miserable about Dominil.'

'I'm not surprised. Dominil's a hot werewolf. She could pose for the "hot werewolves" calendar. Dominil, do you have a bikini?'

'But seriously,' said Beauty, crawling forward in the van to place her face close behind Dominil. 'Is this wise? You know we're meant to be discreet. What's the point of me and Delicious being careful if you're going around seducing everyone? First you break that hunter's heart at Oxford and now he's trying to kill us all. And then you break Pete's heart and it practically ruins the band—'

'And don't forget Sarapen,' interjected Delicious, emerging from the mass of pink hair that covered her face. 'She drove him crazy too. That almost destroyed the clan.'

'It's like nothing's safe when she's around.'

Dominil drove on, refusing to respond to the sisters' mockery, though her face twitched slightly when they were held up by the traffic lights at Camden Tube station.

'So what was it like with Pete? Did you let yourself go?' Delicious asked mischievously.

'Did you do anything wolflike?'

There was a brief diversion while the twins discussed various lovers they'd had in the past, and occasions when they'd almost let their werewolf identities be discovered through bouts of passion.

'Because, you know, when you get that excited you can be tempted just to let the werewolf take over.'

'Of course. Any girl would.'

'Dominil more than most, probably. The way she pretends to be reserved, then just lets the passion burst out.'

The van pulled up in the side street outside the twins' house. Dominil emerged from the van, opened the back door, and lifted up an amplifier.

'Are you going to help?'

The twins shrugged.

'Have you slept with any more of the band we don't know about?' Beauty asked.

Dominil proceeded to unload the equipment herself, carrying it indoors swiftly and dumping it in the hallway. If any of the neighbours had been watching through their curtains they might have been surprised at the ease with which the tall white-haired woman carried such heavy items. They wouldn't have been surprised at the way Beauty and Delicious stumbled about, doing nothing to help.

'I think I've lost a hair extension,' said Delicious, and sat down in the front garden. 'Still, the gig went well.'

'No, it didn't,' hissed Dominil, marching past with a guitar in each hand. 'It was a terrible performance.'

'Be fair,' protested Delicious. 'Who can play a gig when half the band is pining for you? We never had a chance.'

Beauty and Delicious each felt themselves yanked to their feet by their collars.

'The equipment is inside,' said Dominil, leading them into the house. 'I'm leaving now.'

Dominil returned to the van, closed the door quietly, and drove off. She was irritated beyond measure. As soon as she arrived home she took one of her carefully measured sips of laudanum. She looked at her bottle. Though she regulated her addiction carefully, her intake had risen, very slightly. The stress caused by looking after the twins while simultaneously fighting the Avenaris Guild was considerable, even for her.

She knew that she could end the stress by moving back to the castle in Scotland. The Mistress of the Werewolves, the Great Council and her father would all welcome her back. But Dominil refused to admit defeat. She wasn't going back until events in London had run their course.

100

Princess Kabachetka threw the ancient book on the ground, picked it up, examined it with disgust, then threw it on the ground again. She considered stamping on it, but refrained for fear of damaging her elegant heels. 'This ridiculous spell cannot be done,' she yelled, though there was no one in her private cavern to hear her. 'And I'm sick of practising magic in this cave when I should be in my comfortable chambers making ready for tonight's festivities.' The Princess had spent all day trying to perfect a spell that would recreate the effects of the lunar eclipse on

Earth. 'It's all very well for Distikka to talk glibly about removing the Enchantress's powers,' she cried. 'She's not the one who has to devise the spell. I'm no good at devising spells!'

The Princess was being too critical of herself; she was a powerful user of magic, and had made spells in the past. Not as powerful as those concocted by the Empress, but effective nonetheless. But, for now, she was getting nowhere. The Earth's moon was a tremendous natural force. Replicating its effects was a task that would have challenged even the most powerful fire elemental.

No doubt the Empress could do it, thought the Princess, angrily, using the power of the Eternal Volcano. Power which she steadfastly refuses to hand over to me. A plague on her. And on the Enchantress.

The Princess was not the only one having problems with books that night. In a small Victorian backstreet in Kennington, in the little flat above the empty shop, Kalix was suffering too.

'Did I just hear a werewolf howl?' asked Moonglow in alarm.

Daniel nodded. He was lying on the couch, still sick. Moonglow had brought him a bowl of soup and a cup of tea.

'It sounds serious.'

'Relax,' said Daniel. 'She's just doing a book report.'

Another howl sounded through the house. Moonglow was troubled. She didn't like to hear Kalix howl in anguish.

'I suppose it's good that she's working,' she said, dubiously.

'It's progress. But she'll probably end up eating the book.'

'You have to stop accusing Kalix of eating everything. You know it upsets her.'

'She tried to take a bite out of your computer.'

'She was upset at the time,' reasoned Moonglow.

'She tried to eat the television.'

'Well, she was very disappointed when *Sabrina the Teenage Witch* came to an end. Anyway, I'm sure she won't eat the book.'

The bedroom door upstairs slammed, very loudly. Kalix tramped down the stairs and stormed into the living room.

'Where's your book?' asked Daniel.

'I ate it.'

'Kalix! You didn't really?'

285

'I chewed it a bit. I don't even like the stupid book! Why do I have to write a report?'

'That's what you do when you're learning,' said Moonglow, irritating the young werewolf even more.

'It's stupid. I'm not doing it.'

'You have to,' said Daniel, 'or Moonglow will report you to your mum. Then you'll be in trouble.'

Kalix immediately became agitated. 'Would you really report me?'

'Well . . .' began Moonglow, but struggled to make a satisfactory reply. 'Perhaps we could help you with the book report?' she said, to lighten the tension.

'I don't want to do it. I hate it.'

'I'm sure it's not really so bad. Vex is doing the same report and she seemed quite happy.'

Kalix clenched her fists. 'That's because she just makes everything up! She puts her own gold stars on her papers and tells everyone she's doing well! She's not doing well at all!'

'I'm sure Vex is doing her best.' Moonglow was pleased to have at least one person in the house who didn't complain all the time about education. There was the distant sound of the attic door opening followed by heavy boots descending a ladder.

Vex appeared a few seconds later, her expression very cheerful. 'I like this book!' she said. 'Look, I already got a gold star!' She opened the book to reveal a gold star that seemed to have been recently painted on the title page with nail varnish. 'Now I'm going to get started on my assignment. It's going to be great. Kalix, are you ready to start your assignment?'

Kalix growled in frustration and headed back upstairs.

Daniel groaned. 'All this talk about book reports. It's given me a relapse.'

Moonglow mopped his brow, and worried desperately. Was Daniel about to die? Should she take him to a hospital? Or would it be better to contact the Fire Queen? Perhaps Thrix might be able to help?

In her office in Soho, Thrix was looking through a very large book, a compendium of fashion contacts around the world.

'I'll find out who's getting these Abukenti shoes if it's the last thing I do,' she muttered, and applied herself to the task, very diligently.

101

Thrix and Captain Easterly's relationship had reached the stage where a minor upset in their plans no longer felt like a disaster. When he called to tell her he was running late due to a computer problem at his office the Enchantress took it in her stride.

'Just pick me up when you're ready.'

'I shouldn't be too long. But I probably won't have time to go to the warehouse.'

Thrix smiled. Easterly had a large collection of fine wines, much of which was stored in a warehouse in East London. When he couldn't find anything he wanted in his own cellar he'd visit the warehouse and pick up one of his bottles. 'Never mind. I have wine at home.'

'Fine,' he said. 'That'll do just as well.'

'You're being gallant,' Thrix told him, still smiling. 'I know you despise all my wine.'

Easterly laughed, and said he'd see her as soon as he could. Thrix allowed herself a brief pause to marvel at having a successful relationship, then reapplied herself to the list on her computer screen, a directory of Abukenti's most important clients.

'Just tell me where you're sending the shoes,' muttered Thrix, 'and I'll summon them right out of the box and into my office.'

So intent on her task was the Enchantress that she failed to notice the aroma of jasmine that suddenly pervaded her office, and was startled by the sudden appearance of the Fire Queen.

'Enchantress! I simply cannot concentrate on anything! I am so worried about the shoes! Are you making any progress?'

'I've got a list of Abukenti's most important clients. Easterly found it for me.'

'Splendid! What a fine man Captain Easterly is! I trust your relationship is moving along well?'

'We're taking it slowly,' said Thrix.

Malveria raised an eyebrow, not liking the sound of this.

'Then you must speed things up. Grab hold of him, even if it means trampling over your opponents without mercy.'

'I don't think there are any opponents.'

'At the fashion show last week, did not that make-up artist from *Cosmopolitan* magazine grapple lustfully with him?'

'I think she was just trying to get to her seat.'

'You are too trusting, Enchantress. And too hesitant. It's time to advance strongly.'

'We're thinking of going to the cinema for our next date. Is that strong enough?'

'It may be. But when he takes you home, I shall be disappointed if you once again dismiss him from your doorstep, claiming you need to rise early for work.'

Thrix glared at her friend. 'Were you spying on me?'

'A scandalous accusation, Enchantress! One is hurt and wounded. Though if I had been spying, I might have suggested that rather than send him away you should invite him upstairs for a night of passion.'

Thrix shook her head. 'Malveria, the relationship is fine. I'm just taking it slowly.'

The door opened and Thrix's assistant Ann appeared and smiled. 'I thought I heard company. Coffee?'

'Yes, please, most valued assistant. I am in need of fortifying. Thrix's chaste refusal to sleep with Captain Easterly is leading us into chaos. We will not obtain the new Abukenti shoes for my visit to the fundraising event and my life will be utterly ruined.'

Thrix turned her head sharply. 'What fundraising event?'

'Your mother's, of course.'

'But you're not going to that.'

'But I am, dearest Enchantress. Some ancient wealth from the Hiyasta Treasury smoothed the matter out.'

'You mean you bribed my mother?'

'I believe it's called a charitable donation,' said the Fire Queen. 'Distikka brokered the deal with Markus.'

Thrix shook her head. 'Mother will have a fit.'

'But is not Markus head of the clan?'

'In name he is. But Mother's the boss. I'm glad I won't be around when she finds out.'

Ann reappeared with a tray of coffee. 'Your mother and brother are on the way up.'

'What? They're not due till tomorrow.'

Ann shrugged. The Mistress of the Werewolves and Markus were currently ascending in the lift.

'It's not long till dusk. Is this one of the nights you all have to change?'

The Enchantress shook her head. 'Fortunately not.'

The Mistress of the Werewolves swept in, elegant as always. She had a warm smile on her face that faded sharply at the sight of Queen Malveria.

'Markus tells me he invited you to my event.'

'Is it not splendid?' said the Fire Queen, brightly.

Verasa didn't share her good humour. She'd been extremely displeased to learn that Markus had invited the Fire Queen, and had spent much of the plane journey to London letting him know it. Markus himself was very elegantly attired, with a beautiful long black coat draped over his suit, but he wore the expression of a werewolf who'd suffered.

Verasa faced Malveria squarely.

'Many MacRinnalchs won't be pleased to see the Queen of the Hiyasta. If you insist on coming you'll have to promise not to offend them.'

Malveria seemed to take this in good humour, to Thrix's relief.

'The Queen of the Hiyasta is famed for her civilised manner. I am quite sure I will not offend. Besides, was I not responsible for securing the services of Mr Felicori for you?'

'I understood my daughter took care of that,' said Verasa.

Malveria seemed on the point of correcting her but, determined not to start an argument, said nothing.

The door opened a few inches and Ann's face appeared. 'Thrix, can I see you for a minute, please?'

'What is it?'

Ann hurried over to Thrix, put her mouth to her ear and whispered, 'Kalix is here.'

Thrix excused herself and slipped out of the office. 'What sort of state is she in?'

'Agitated.'

'She's always agitated. How bad? Slightly moody? Insane?'

'Not too bad, I think. I put her in my office.'

Thrix frowned, very deeply. 'Ann, Easterly is on his way over. And right now there are three werewolves here.'

'Four.'

'What?'

'Four werewolves, including you.'

Thrix tapped her foot on the floor. 'Yes, I know I'm a werewolf. I meant other werewolves.'

'Oh, right.'

'Now that we've got that sorted out, could we concentrate on my problems? I've got an office full of angry werewolves and a fire elemental who's liable to burst into flames when she gets upset. Plus my crazy young sister in your room. And my boyfriend is on the way.'

'Are you calling him your boyfriend now?' asked Ann.

There was a brief pause while Thrix considered this. 'I hadn't really thought about it. Am I too old to have a boyfriend? Should I call him something else?'

'I think "boyfriend" is still all right,' said Ann.

The Enchantress felt quite pleased to have a boyfriend. She knew she wouldn't have one for long if he discovered the truth about her family. 'If he arrives before I'm finished with Kalix, try to keep him occupied. Don't let anyone turn into a werewolf. Or burst into flames. It will destroy the relationship.'

102

Thrix was scowling as she headed for Ann's office. She wasn't keen to have Easterly arrive in the middle of some violent confrontation, which, with Kalix, was always possible. As she hurried through the door she noted that Kalix wasn't looking too bad by her standards. She was at least clean, if still dressed in cast-offs. There did seem to be a mysterious smell of blood, however, though the Enchantress couldn't see where it was coming from.

'You know that Mother and Markus are here?' said Thrix, hoping that it might make Kalix leave.

Kalix made a disgusted face but wasn't put off. She didn't intend to leave till she'd questioned her sister thoroughly.

'I went to Gawain's place with Vex. She read the auras. She says you were there before he was killed.'

'Agrivex? The imbecilic fire elemental?'

'Yes.' Kalix stared at Thrix. 'So were you there?'

There was a long pause.

Kalix straightened up and glanced out the window, measuring how long it would be before night fell and she could make the change.

'I did visit him.'

'What for?'

'That's none of your business,' said Thrix, meeting her sister's eyes.

'Did you kill him?'

'Of course I didn't kill him.'

'That's what everyone says,' said Kalix. 'But I think maybe you did. He liked me better and you were jealous.'

'I've never been jealous of you in my life.'

'I think you were.'

Thrix had a brief urge to list the many reasons why she didn't feel jealous of her poor, deluded sister but simply shook her head instead. 'I didn't kill him. If Agrivex was any good at interpreting auras she'd tell you that. But she isn't. She can't interpret anything properly.'

'It was her who found out you were sleeping with Gawain,' growled Kalix.

It was true. Thrix's affair with Gawain had come to light because of Vex's correct interpretation of their auras. Thrix dismissed this as irrelevant.

'I did visit Gawain but it was weeks before he was killed.'

'Why did you visit?'

'That's none of your business.'

Kalix snarled. It was an ugly sound. She glanced out of the window again, clearly anticipating making the change.

'If you're thinking of attacking me I'll blast you out of my office with a spell. I repeat, I didn't kill Gawain. Now, I've got Mother and Markus in my office and a guest about to arrive so it's time for you to go.'

Thrix made to leave. Kalix stepped in front of her.

Before they could come into contact the door opened.

'Another visitor,' said Ann, hustling Decembrius into the office.

'Don't we have any security at all?' demanded Thrix. 'What do I pay these people for? What are you doing here?'

Decembrius seemed unwilling to explain. 'I wanted to talk to you in private.'

Thrix glared at him. 'You picked the wrong day for a were-wolf gathering. I'm busy. Talk to Kalix.'

With that, Thrix hurried back to her own office where she found Malveria in the middle of a long anecdote about the last time she'd made Princess Kabachetka look foolish. Her mother was looking bored, though Markus, who'd always rather liked Malveria, seemed interested.

'Busy?' enquired Verasa politely.

'A few unexpected callers. Fashion reps, that sort of thing.'

Verasa nodded sympathetically. Though she didn't like the way her daughter separated herself from the family, she was pleased when her business went well.

'I am so looking forward to hearing Mr Felicori sing again,' declared Malveria. Verasa looked sour. Before Thrix could smooth things over Ann appeared at the door, gesturing frantically.

Thrix went over to her so she could whisper in her ear again.

'Your boyfriend phoned. He'll be here soon. And Kalix and Decembrius have started to fight.'

Thrix excused herself and rushed from the room, passing several of her employees before arriving in Ann's office to find Kalix and Decembrius struggling with each other. At that moment, night fell. They turned into werewolves, and kept struggling.

'Are you trying to ruin me?' yelled Thrix. 'I've got fifteen human employees out there who don't know I'm a werewolf. What's the idea of transforming here? What are you fighting about, anyway?'

'She started it,' said Decembrius.

'He keeps following me around,' said Kalix.

'I wasn't following you around. I came here to see Thrix.'

'I was here first. Go away.'

'*You* go away.'

They started pushing each other again, and growling.

'Stop this immediately!' cried Thrix, and dragged them apart.

The door opened and Ann appeared. 'It's a while since we've seen Dominil,' she said.

'What? Is she here as well?'

'Waiting downstairs at the desk.'

Thrix clutched her brow and swept back a few strands of golden hair. 'Send her up.' She glared at Kalix and Decembrius. 'Stop fighting. Change back into human. And then leave.'

She hurried back towards her office, just in time to see Dominil stride from the lift rather regally, her long white hair hanging down in sharp contrast to her black leather coat. Several designers observed her with admiration, assuming she must be a new model hired by their employer.

'Dominil. What do you want? Malveria's here and so are my mother and Markus. And Easterly is on his way.'

'Easterly?'

'My, eh . . . new boyfriend.'

'I have some serious problems with hunters that I wished to discuss in private,' explained Dominil.

'Can't it wait?'

The door to Thrix's office opened. Verasa looked out.

'Dominil! How nice to see you.' The Mistress of the Werewolves held Dominil in high regard these days.

Dominil greeted her and Markus politely in return as she entered the office. Queen Malveria, always rather interested in Dominil's unusual nature, looked intently at the newcomer with interest.

Her coat hangs on her so well, she mused. Is it just because she is rather tall?

'Could we talk before Easterly arrives?' asked Dominil.

'Easterly?' said Markus.

'The new man in her life,' explained Malveria helpfully.

'A human?' said Verasa with disapproval.

Malveria looked surprised. 'Were you not aware of this? But you must know that Thrix has had great trouble in finding a suitable werewolf. One cannot expect her to remain loveless and disappointed for ever. She has done that for long enough.'

'Thank you, Malveria,' said Thrix. 'Perhaps you could discuss my failures another time.'

'What does this Easterly do?' asked Verasa.

'He's the fashion editor for a men's lifestyle magazine,' said Thrix, which didn't seem to meet with her mother's approval.

'It's not like there aren't plenty of werewolves in Scotland,' Verasa pointed out. 'Only last month I offered to introduce you to that nice George MacRinnalch. He has his own law firm in Edinburgh now.'

'George MacRinnalch is the most boring werewolf in the whole clan!' exclaimed Thrix, now very irritated.

'Well, he doesn't dye his hair, wear strange piercings, or desert his clan. In that way, he may be boring. But he's very respectable and he works hard.'

'But would he suit a werewolf of Thrix's creative temperament?' said Malveria.

'Could you stop discussing me like I'm not here? I'm doing just fine with Easterly.'

'You certainly are,' agreed Malveria, supportively. 'He is a splendid man. And there is no need to concern yourself that he's late.'

'Why would I concern myself? He was held up at the office.'

'Not by the make-up artist from *Cosmopolitan*, we hope,' murmured Malveria.

'What?' said Markus, immediately interested.

'Some magazine floozy who's been flinging herself all over him. I have been urging Thrix to take action but of course she holds back. A great mistake, in my opinion. At this very moment Mr Easterly may be engaged in lustful encounters with this trollop.'

'There are no lustful encounters going on!' yelled Thrix, mortified to be having this conversation while her mother was in the room.

The intercom buzzed.

'That'll be Easterly now,' muttered Thrix, flicking the switch.

'There's a girl called Moonglow here to see you,' came Ann's voice.

'Moonglow!' cried Malveria. 'Now that *is* entertaining!' She looked towards Markus. 'Have you seen young Moonglow since you broke her heart with great cruelty?'

'What?' demanded Verasa.

'Moonglow, who lives with Kalix, as you know,' explained Malveria cheerfully. 'But perhaps you did not know about the breaking of her heart by Markus? I'm sorry if I have inadvertently raised a delicate subject.'

Malveria didn't look at all sorry as Markus shifted uncomfortably under his mother's gaze.

'Send Moonglow up,' said Thrix with some relish, thinking that there was no reason for her to be the only one suffering embarrassment.

'What's that terrible crashing noise next door?' asked Verasa.

'My designers,' said Thrix. 'Energetic meeting.'

She hurried back to Ann's office where she found Decembrius and Kalix still pushing each other. Ann's desk had been overturned and papers were spilled on the floor.

'What's the meaning of this?'

'He keeps stalking me.'

'Your sister is insane,' said Decembrius.

'I've had enough of this,' growled Thrix. 'Change back into human right this minute.'

Boosting her strength by use of a discreet little spell, the Enchantress grabbed hold of the pair of them and hauled them through into her office to deposit them in front of her mother. 'Perhaps *you* can control them. Maybe ask Decembrius why he hasn't attended any council meetings.'

It was Decembrius's turn to squirm uncomfortably under the stony gaze of the Mistress of the Werewolves.

'I've been busy,' he muttered.

'Busy stalking me,' said Kalix.

'Are you stalking my daughter?'

'Of course not! Who'd stalk that scrawny little wretch?'

'Hey!' roared Kalix, and immediately transformed into a werewolf again, baring her teeth. Decembrius did likewise and they began pushing each other. Several others changed as well. It was difficult for any werewolf to remain as human while in the presence of other werewolves, particularly ones who were brawling. Making everything worse, there was a smell of blood in the room from the cut in Kalix's arm. Though concealed from sight by her coat, the odour was obvious to all the werewolves.

'Will you all change back to human!' yelled Thrix. 'My boy-friend is due here any moment!' She spun round in alarm as the door opened again and was relieved when Moonglow appeared. Not that Moonglow was a welcome visitor, but at least she already knew about werewolves.

'Moonglow!' cried Malveria, enthusiastically. 'How splendid to see you.'

Moonglow rocked in surprise at the sight that greeted her.

'Eh ... hello, Kalix, Decembrius, Dominil, Mistress of the Werewolves, Queen Malveria, Thrix ... and Markus. Is this some sort of meeting?'

'Kalix wouldn't be here if it was,' said Decembrius smugly. 'She's still banished.'

'You never attend anyway,' said the Mistress of the Werewolves.

'I'm too busy.'

'Too busy to support the new Thane?' Verasa looked to Markus for support but on Moonglow's arrival Markus had edged away and now seemed to be concentrating on the carpet.

Malveria regarded him with great interest and was entertained by his discomfort, which he surely deserved for breaking Moon-glow's heart. But she also noticed how perfect his complexion was, and felt slightly jealous.

'What do you want?' demanded Thrix.

'I need to speak to you about something,' said Moonglow.

'Obviously. What is it?'

'It's private,' said Moonglow, and refused to look cowed, even in the face of so many werewolves. Meeting Markus was a blow but she tried not to show it.

'Then it will have to wait,' said Thrix, 'as will everyone else. What's the matter with you all? Have I failed to make it clear that I'm trying to get on with my own life? Did someone mistake that for "Thrix would like to see as many werewolves as possible, all the time"? I want you all out of here before Easterly arrives.'

'Who's Easterly?' asked Moonglow.

'Her new boyfriend,' answered Decembrius.

'He doesn't seem to be making her very happy,' said Markus.

'You'd do well not to be offensive to me,' roared Thrix. She

296

took a deep breath. 'Now. Am I expecting any more unwanted visitors?'

Everyone shook their heads.

Just then something crashed against the outside door.

'Apart from Agrivex, possibly,' said the Fire Queen apologetically. 'I asked her to meet me here.'

Thrix sighed, opened the door, and hauled Vex inside. The young fire elemental's teleportation had gone wrong, as it often did.

'Hi, everyone,' she said, brightly. 'Is this a party? Can I come?' She looked ruefully at her arm. 'I bumped my elbow.'

She waved her arm in the direction of Malveria, who turned her nose up, then towards Moonglow, who stepped forward to rub it better.

Vex beamed at everyone. 'I got another gold star at college.'

'Stop making things up!' yelled Kalix.

'It's my fourth gold star this week.'

'She just makes it up,' muttered Kalix to Decembrius.

'Maybe if you studied harder you'd get a gold star too,' said the Mistress of the Werewolves.

'We have an exam soon!' cried Vex.

Kalix's heart sank. She felt her mother's gaze on her.

'An exam? Kalix, I was not informed you had an exam. Shouldn't you be home studying?'

'I've been studying,' mumbled the young werewolf, and stared at her feet, appalled at this turn of events. Her academic life was stressful enough without it becoming a subject for discussion among her family. The Mistress of the Werewolves, showing no tact whatsoever, rounded on Moonglow.

'Has my daughter been studying for her exam?'

Moonglow hesitated.

'Of course Kalix has been studying,' said Decembrius. 'All the time. Only yesterday I saw her learning maths.'

Kalix was surprised at Decembrius coming to her defence, and grateful. Decembrius's opinion might not count for much with her mother these days, but it was good to have someone on her side.

Thrix banged her fist on her desk. 'Everyone. Change back into human now. Easterly can't find my office full of werewolves.'

There was a general flickering of transformation. Thrix extended her gaze to Malveria and Vex. 'And please don't burst into flames.'

'We would not dream of it. You can rely on the Hiyasta not to cause social embarrassment.' The Fire Queen fingered her necklace. 'I'm very keen for you to succeed with Easterly, I assure you.'

103

Distikka left her lover, Commander Agripath, in the early morning and made her way in silence over the red fields that served as a military training ground for the Commander's regiment. She wore a dark cloak with a hood that shielded her face, though the two soldiers who escorted her were aware of her identity. They were part of Agripath's personal staff and could be trusted not to talk. Distikka and Agripath were keen to keep their affair a secret for now.

'Not that it would be a disaster if the Queen were to learn of it,' reflected the small fire elemental, treading lightly past the burning trenches that formed part of the training ground. 'The Queen's adviser having an affair with the head of the army is not taboo. She'd be relieved I wasn't making eyes at any of the aristocracy.'

Distikka tightened her lips in a tiny sneer. She had a very low opinion of the Hiyasta aristocracy. Interested only in gossip, clothes and scandal, as far as she could see. Some of them were even worse than the Queen. Distikka glanced up briefly, peering through the small slit in her hood at the Great Volcano which rose up majestically behind the Queen's Imperial Palace.

'When I take control of the volcano I'll get rid of them all.'

Only a person of royal blood could control the Great Volcano. No one else could tap into its power.

'But she is not aware that one family member survives,' mused Distikka as she passed from the military area into the walled gardens around the palace. Her black chain mail clinked slightly as she walked, muffled by her enveloping cloak. 'If Princess

Kabachetka can just manage to strand the Queen on Earth for even the briefest of times, I'll seize the volcano while Agripath secures the realm with the army.'

If it all went smoothly, Distikka would be ruler of the Hiyasta in the space of a few hours. She didn't anticipate too much opposition. Malveria's popularity was on the wane. Her council actively disliked her because she ignored them. The population didn't like the way the Queen no longer turned up for sacrifices. The rumour that she hadn't even bothered to calculate the time of the Vulcanalia had been extremely damaging.

Distikka watched a faint curl of smoke rise from the volcano. She glanced back towards the now distant military camp. Commander Agripath was a fine soldier. He came from the famous line of dragon warriors and his reputation was deservedly high. It was necessary to have him on her side while she mounted a coup. But she didn't much like him as a person, and didn't enjoy his rather burning touch. She'd get rid of him too, when things had quietened down, and she'd secured the throne.

As she arrived in the privacy of her own rooms in the official buildings close to the palace, Distikka felt a faint pulse of heat in her hand. It was a signal that Princess Kabachetka needed to speak to her. The signal was rarely used, for though the Princess's sorcerous message was well disguised there was always the risk of discovery.

Distikka spent most of the day dealing with official business. In the evening she travelled in secret to the Princess's cavern. There she found Princess Kabachetka downcast.

'Our plans won't work. No spell can replicate an eclipse of the moon. I can't attack Thrix. Nor can I prevent Malveria from returning to her realm.'

Distikka considered the Princess's words. In a way, she regretted that she had to be involved with Kabachetka. She was prone to giving up too easily. Thrix meant nothing to Distikka, whose only real aim was to topple Malveria. But Distikka knew that without the Princess's sorcery she'd never succeed in stranding the Queen on Earth for the time necessary to take control of the volcano.

'If your Hainusta sorcery won't work, how about some other sort?'

'What would you suggest? It's not so easy to just find new pieces of sorcery. If it was, everyone would do it.'

'How about the Werewolf Enchantress? Perhaps, being a werewolf, she may know something about controlling the moon that we don't?'

'She might. But I can hardly ask her for a spell, can I?'

'Where did the Werewolf Enchantress learn her sorcery?'

'From some dreadful old hag named Minerva MacRinnalch, I believe. But she has retired to seclusion.'

'Perhaps, before she retired, she left some records,' suggested Distikka. 'Few people like to pass from the world without leaving some testament to their achievements.'

The Princess pondered this. Finding any record of Minerva's sorcery seemed like a difficult endeavour. She resented that in her relationship with Distikka she seemed to be doing most of the work. However, she knew she'd never defeat Malveria without Distikka's help. As a pair, they appeared to need each other.

'Possibly we could find something of Minerva's. Where would we need to look?'

104

Captain Easterly was taken by surprise by the gathering. He looked round, taking in the expense and elegance of Malveria and Verasa's outfits, the frozen splendour of Dominil, the scruffy youthful beauty of Kalix and Vex, and the surly bohemian appearance of Decembrius.

'Should I have dressed better? I wasn't expecting a party.'

'Just a few family visitors,' said the Enchantress, with a note of desperation in her voice. She hurried forward, partly to embrace him and partly to place herself between Easterly and the large group of werewolves who were studying him with interest.

Markus strode forward to greet the newcomer. He cut an elegant figure, one that wouldn't have been out of place on the cover of Easterly's magazine. 'I'm Markus, Thrix's brother. Pleased to meet you.'

Thrix looked around, waiting for some sort of greeting from

the rest of her family. None was forthcoming. Vex looked bored. Kalix looked angry and bored. Decembrius was slyly studying his reflection in the wall-size mirror and Dominil was absorbing the scene without any show of interest or emotion. Verasa looked rather sternly at the human who was dating her eldest daughter.

'My mother. And my cousins,' said Thrix to Easterly, weakly. 'It's been lovely to see you all, really. We must do it again soon. But now I—'

'I *have* to talk to you,' interrupted Moonglow, firmly.

Easterly looked at the black-clad girl, with her dark make-up and her odd feather earrings. She didn't seem to quite fit in with the rest.

'Another cousin?' he asked Thrix.

'Business acquaintance. But really, our business can wait till tomorrow.'

'No, it can't,' declared Moonglow, who didn't intend to back down. Daniel was sick and she wasn't about to be expelled from the office before she'd even had the chance to talk about it.

'I really could do with a few words too,' said Malveria. 'The shoe crisis is far from over.'

'I had hoped to talk more about the charity event,' said Verasa.

'I also—' began Dominil.

Thrix held up her hand. 'Fine. Everyone has to talk to me. My personal life is obviously of no importance.' Thrix glared at them all, but if she was hoping she might make them go away she was disappointed.

'Would you like me to wait outside?' said Easterly, pleasantly. 'I can get some coffee from Ann.'

Thrix nodded, unable to think of a better alternative. As Easterly departed she rounded on her family angrily.

'This had all better be important. What's the idea of ruining my date, anyway?'

'Is your date really that important?' asked her mother.

'It is of great importance,' said Malveria sympathetically. 'The Enchantress has not had sex for some time.'

'Really?' said Markus. 'How long?'

'That's none of your business!' yelled Thrix.

'Do not despair, dearest Enchantress,' continued Malveria. 'It is merely bad luck. Though perhaps you are not as encouraging as

301

you might be. Is that outfit entirely suitable? Given the desperate circumstances, perhaps you should attack more with the breasts?'

'What?'

'A little more cleavage is surely acceptable?'

Decembrius burst out laughing. 'You should definitely attack more with the breasts.'

Moonglow squashed all further discussion of Thrix's cleavage by loudly announcing that Daniel was ill and she wanted something done about it. The Enchantress was baffled.

'Why are you telling me? I'm not a doctor.'

'Daniel's ill because he kissed me.'

This gained everyone's interest, even Kalix and Vex's.

'Did you give him some disease?'

'No. The kiss activated the curse.'

'What are you talking about?' demanded Thrix, completely mystified. 'What curse?'

'Malveria's curse. I'm sure you know about it. The curse that says we can never be together. The one that saved Kalix's life. Now it's taking effect but Daniel doesn't deserve to die just because he kissed me.'

The Enchantress, apparently bewildered, looked towards the Fire Queen who, for her part, now seemed intent on studying her reflection in the mirror.

'Malveria. Is this true?'

'It may be.'

'So Daniel's going to die if he gets together with Miss Black Eyeliner here?'

'I forget the exact details . . .'

'I assume this is the Daniel who looked after Kalix?' said the Mistress of the Werewolves, with the air of a woman who knew you couldn't trust a Hiyasta. 'Kalix, did you know about this?'

Kalix shook her head. 'I like Daniel. Don't kill him.'

'Who said he will die?' protested Malveria. 'It may only be a serious and uncomfortable illness. One can never be sure. It's all very well everyone looking at me in this monstrously accusing manner, but the bargain was entered into with the full agreement of Moonglow, as payment for the tremendous power I was obliged to use to save Kalix's life. I had to travel almost to the Forests of the Werewolf Dead. That's a difficult and dangerous journey for a Hiyasta. Afterwards I felt very unwell, and showed little interest in shoes for several days.'

'So that's why you saved Kalix's life?' said Thrix. 'I thought it was a favour for me.'

Vex was worried. 'If Daniel dies can I still go to college?'

'Daniel's not going to die!' cried Moonglow.

'I don't want to leave college,' said Vex, appealing to her aunt. 'We're going to be cheerleaders.'

'There aren't any cheerleaders!' screamed Kalix. 'Stop making things up!'

'No MacRinnalch werewolf will be a cheerleader,' declared the Mistress of the Werewolves, stiffly. 'Kalix, it is quite inappropriate. I forbid it.'

Kalix sighed, and shook her head.

'You shouldn't have kissed Daniel,' said Markus, unwisely.

Moonglow rounded on him and told him not to interfere in her business. She glared at her former lover with hurt and loathing, but when Decembrius asked her if she'd really entered into the agreement knowing what it meant she was forced to acknowledge that she had.

'Then you should take the consequences.'

'I agree,' announced Malveria.

'It's stupid,' said Kalix, and hit Decembrius on the arm. They began pushing each other again.

Malveria ignored them. 'One cannot just withdraw from such a bargain at will. Think what my court would say were they to learn that I had allowed a curse to lapse, out of sympathy for a human.'

'I don't care what your court says,' said Moonglow. 'Lift the curse.'

The Enchantress groaned, muttered a spell to securely lock her office door, then spoke into the intercom. 'Ann, make Easterly more coffee. This is going to take a while.'

105

It took the Enchantress almost two hours to clear her office of unwelcome visitors.

The Fire Queen left unwillingly. 'My intelligence services report strong activity among Princess Kabachetka's fashion advisers. They believe she may be trying to secure the Abukenti footwear.'

'Malveria, I'll get to work on the shoes as soon as I can.'

The Queen departed with her head bowed.

Verasa watched her go with some puzzlement. 'Didn't you once tell me that Queen Malveria waded through a river of blood to kill a dragon?'

'She did.'

'It seems unlikely.'

'There aren't any dragons left,' said Thrix, defensively. 'These days she's more interested in fashion.'

'You seem to have been an excellent influence on her,' said Verasa, at which Thrix bristled but made no reply.

Verasa and Markus left with their dignity intact after receiving a promise from Thrix to meet them the next day to discuss the fundraising event. Verasa's farewell to Decembrius was notably frosty. Not only had he failed to attend council meetings, he had too many earrings, and she suspected he might even be wearing eyeliner. Undoubtedly the twins had been a bad influence on him. She took some comfort from the fact that her daughter didn't seem to welcome his advances. He wasn't a suitable partner for her. Verasa thought there was something untrustworthy about him.

As Malveria had at least agreed to examine Daniel, Moonglow was satisfied, though suspicious, and left with the Fire Queen and Vex.

Hardest to get rid of was Kalix. She refused to leave until she received some answers about Gawain. Why had Thrix visited him?

This was the last thing Thrix wanted to talk about and it seemed for a moment that she'd be forced to use a spell to send her young sister howling from the office.

Finally Decembrius suggested that he and Kalix should come back the next day. Surprisingly, Kalix agreed. Kalix's dislike of Decembrius seemed to have lessened since he'd stood up to the Mistress of the Werewolves and the Thane, refusing to back down when they'd criticised him for not attending council meetings.

'I'm busy in London. I'll come to the castle when I'm ready and not before.'

Verasa was offended, Markus was annoyed, but Kalix was pleased. For the first time, she regarded Decembrius as an ally against her family.

They left together, which finally allowed Thrix to give Captain Easterly some attention.

'I've drunk a lot of coffee,' Easterly said on the journey home.

The Enchantress was apologetic about his long wait. 'My family does sometimes get in the way.'

Captain Easterly made light of it in his good-mannered way. He seemed quite interested in Thrix's family and listened politely as Thrix berated them all. Though it was some time past rush hour, traffic was still dense, and they made slow progress amongst the endless stream of cars and buses.

'It's lucky I didn't cook anything,' muttered Thrix. 'It would have been ruined.'

Easterly looked at her questioningly. As far as he remembered, Thrix had invited him to dinner.

'The food's being brought in,' Thrix explained. 'I let the caterer know we'd be late.'

They drove on slowly.

'I'm not a very good cook,' admitted Thrix. 'Actually, I can't cook at all.'

Easterly shrugged. 'Who has time to cook these days? I never do.'

That was untrue. Easterly was a good cook. Thrix appreciated him lying about it.

'Your mother must be quite an important figure in Scotland.'

'Important in fundraising for charity, anyway, which is what she seems to like doing best these days.'

'I didn't know you were born in a castle.'

Thrix was embarrassed and pretended she hadn't heard. Here in London it always seemed a little strange to have been born in a castle. She tended not to mention it. Perhaps, she reflected, as she pulled her Mercedes slowly into the underground car park beneath her apartment, it wasn't such a bad thing that Easterly had met her relations. At least it was over with. She'd wondered about inviting him to Scotland, to the charity event, but had hesitated, not wishing to inflict her family on him. Now he'd met them and didn't seem too shaken by the experience. Perhaps she should invite him. It would teach her mother not to lecture her about who she went out with.

When they entered the apartment there was a bank statement lying on the carpet. Thrix opened it, winced, and threw it on the table. If she didn't start earning more money quickly, Thrix Fashions would be going out of business.

106

Daniel, lying on the couch feeling very poorly, woke up to find an angry-looking Elemental Queen staring down at him. He struggled to rouse himself into a sitting position, having been lectured previously by Moonglow about being disrespectful to visitors. The Fire Queen showed little interest in whether he sat up or not, and spoke sharply to Moonglow.

'This is what you dragged me over here for? This is not the curse. This is one of your many foul human diseases, the minor sort which produces a slight temperature and a runny nose.'

'And vomiting,' added Moonglow.

Malveria wrinkled her nose. 'Made worse, no doubt, by the ingestion of cheap beer.' The Queen levitated a few inches and looked down at Moonglow. 'Kindly do not bother me about matters like these in future. The Queen of the Hiyasta does not concern herself with runny noses, nor with vomiting.'

'I'm sorry,' said Moonglow. 'I thought he was really ill.'

'Pah!' Malveria seemed in an excessively bad mood. 'He will be if he keeps kissing you. The bargain remains in place. Now I have important affairs to deal with. When the detestable Agrivex arrives, inform her that I will allow no delay in her returning to the palace.'

With that, the Fire Queen dematerialised in the violent flash of light that inevitably followed her when she was in a bad mood.

Daniel blinked, sat up, and looked wonderingly at Moonglow. 'What was that about?'

'I asked Malveria to . . . take a look at you. I was a bit worried.'

'OK. Thanks.' Daniel was puzzled about the Queen's ill temper. 'I suppose she only deals with serious cases.'

'How are you feeling?'

'A bit better.'

Kalix arrived home, moving briskly. The young werewolf was hungry. Her appetite, always small, had all but vanished under the weight of her concerns. She'd rarely made the change into her werewolf shape, existing mainly on laudanum, tea, and whatever alcohol she could find around the house. But tonight she'd changed back and forth several times at Thrix's office during her struggles with Decembrius. Not even Kalix could do that without the werewolf form demanding to be fed. As soon as she reached the top of the stairs she transformed once more and headed straight for the kitchen.

'Need meat,' she muttered to Moonglow, in passing.

Moonglow always made sure that the fridge was well stocked with meat around the time of the full moon, and at other times she'd still put meat there, hoping to tempt Kalix.

The young werewolf appeared back from the kitchen. 'More meat,' she said, and looked eager.

'There's another joint of beef in the fridge. On the lower shelf.'

Kalix hurried off.

At that moment the doorbell rang and Moonglow moved swiftly, scurrying down the dark stairwell to take delivery of the large pizza she'd ordered. Now that she knew Daniel wasn't dying, she thought it was a good idea to make sure he ate too. She paid for it with a large handful of loose change, and by the time she'd reached the top of the stairs Kalix was emerging from the kitchen again.

'More meat?' she said, hopefully.

'Sorry, vegetarian pizza.'

Kalix looked disappointed, and muttered something that might have been 'stupid vegetarians'. She followed Moonglow back into the living room anyway, and hung around eagerly as she opened the box.

'Still hungry?' asked Moonglow, with a smile. She tore off a large piece of the pizza and handed it to Kalix. It disappeared between her great jaws. For a few moments there was a happy domestic scene as Moonglow, Daniel and Kalix ate together.

'Good pizza,' said Daniel.

'I need more meat,' said Kalix.

'I think you've eaten it all.'

Kalix looked disappointed and headed back to the kitchen.

The cat appeared, attracted by the genial atmosphere. Seeing food on offer, and none of it for the cat, it began meowing.

'I'll make tea,' said Moonglow, rising from the couch, 'and feed the cat.'

Moonglow headed for the kitchen where Kalix was busy examining the contents of the fridge.

'Aha!' she cried triumphantly. 'Meat soup!' Kalix dragged a carton from the fridge and began using her werewolf talons to rip it open.

'There's no meat in that,' said Moonglow.

'There is,' said Kalix, holding up the carton. 'Look! Elk and potato!'

'It's *leek* and potato.'

Kalix's face fell. 'Leek?'

'Yes.'

'No elk at all?'

'I'm afraid not,' said Moonglow, and felt rather sorry for the young werewolf, who seemed quite crestfallen.

'I wanted elk,' mumbled Kalix, sounding very disappointed.

'Perhaps I could find one at the butcher's tomorrow,' said Moonglow to cheer her up, though in reality Moonglow hated the thought of anyone eating an elk, even Kalix. She quickly fed the cat, then went about the business of making tea, returning to the living room shortly afterwards carrying a neatly arranged tray. Moonglow was fastidious about her tea making and the tea in the pot needed to brew for a few minutes before she deemed it ready.

The downstairs door opened and closed with a bang. There was the sound of heavy footsteps, interrupted by the sound of boots slipping on the stairs and a slight cry of pain.

'Vex is home,' muttered Daniel.

The young fire elemental appeared, rubbing her arm. 'I bumped my elbow a little bit,' she said. 'Don't worry, I'll be OK. Is there tea for me? Good. Was Aunty Malvie here? Is Daniel going to die?'

'Daniel's not dying. And your aunt wants you back at the palace immediately.'

Vex made a face. 'I'm meant to go to this stupid Fire Festival, the Vulcanalia. I can't stand it. It's the most tedious thing ever.'

'What happens?'

'Everyone ties fire ribbons in their hair and goes off in a big parade to the Great Volcano. Then we all chant some stuff around the volcano, swoop through the flaming fields beside it, watch some re-enactments of great moments in Hiyasta history, the Queen blesses the crowd, everyone extends their aura till the whole place is full of flames, there's some singing and dancing and a bit more swooping through the flaming fields. And maybe there's some hymns to the sun, I forget exactly.' Vex sighed. 'It's the most boring thing ever. I hate it.'

'It doesn't *sound* boring.'

'It is if your aunt makes you go every year. I keep telling her I'd rather just stay in bed but she won't let me out of it. Not that Aunt Malvie's shown much interest herself, really. She let Distikka work out the correct date, which is some big scandal, I don't know why.' Vex frowned. 'I hate Distikka. You wouldn't believe the way Aunt Malvie goes on about her. At the palace it's all "Distikka can do this, Distikka can do that. Distikka doesn't need help with her shoelaces." I really hate her. Do we have any wine?'

Vex rushed off to the kitchen. Seconds later she reappeared, carrying a half-full bottle of wine.

'Did you know there's a wolf in the kitchen eating cat food?'

'What?'

'There's a wolf in the kitchen eating cat food.'

Daniel and Moonglow sprang from the couch.

'Has she eaten the cat as well?'

'I didn't notice.'

There was a rush for the kitchen. There they were confronted by an unexpected sight. Kalix, still lusting for meat, had trans-formed into her full wolf shape – something she very rarely did –

and was now munching her way through the food in the cat bowl. Rather surprisingly, the cat didn't seem to mind that much and was eating from the other side of the bowl, grabbing what scraps it could before Kalix got there.

'We'll need more cat food,' said Daniel.

Kalix licked the bowl clean and still didn't seem satisfied. Nor was the cat, which was understandable, as it hadn't got much of its promised meal.

'You better open another tin,' Daniel said.

'I'm not sure about this,' said Moonglow.

The cat began meowing. Kalix started padding round the kitchen, panting.

'I don't think Verasa would be very pleased about her daughter eating cat food.'

Kalix began growling, either at the mention of her mother's name or because she was still hungry. The cat redoubled its meowing. Daniel opened the kitchen cupboard and took out a tin.

'The public demands more cat food,' he said. 'We better serve it up before there's a riot.'

He emptied the cat food into the bowl from which Kalix and the cat again began eating.

Moonglow, Daniel and Vex left them to it, and returned to the living room.

'That was unexpected,' said Moonglow.

'She's certainly got a powerful appetite.' Daniel was a little impressed.

'I'm not really sure about her eating cat food, though.'

Daniel shrugged. 'It looks healthy in the adverts. It'll keep her coat shiny.'

Not long afterwards Vex nodded off to sleep on the couch. She smelled strongly of wine. Moonglow was troubled.

'We're supposed to be looking after them.'

'We *are* looking after them.'

'Vex is drunk and Kalix is eating cat food!'

'Well, we're doing our best,' said Daniel.

'I'd better pay the rent before Malveria and Verasa start asking for their money back.'

107

Mr Carmichael had never stood out as a well-dressed man. He owned three suits, which he rotated throughout the month. Today's choice, a very conservative grey, looked particularly dated as he visited the offices of Captain Easterly's magazine. The young receptionist regarded him unsympathetically. She seemed suspicious when he claimed to have an appointment with their men's fashion editor. After checking her calendar she reluctantly directed him to Easterly's office, which, in keeping with the eclectic nature of the magazine, was cluttered with an odd assortment of formal and informal clothes, electronic gadgets, toys, snacks and artwork.

It was unusual for Mr Carmichael to visit any of his operatives in the field but Easterly was now unwilling to visit the Guild's headquarters. He feared that Thrix's sorcery might detect any close involvement with other werewolf hunters. So he said, anyway. But Easterly had always exhibited a somewhat cavalier attitude towards the rules. Mr Carmichael suspected he might just not feel like visiting their headquarters these days.

'Albermarle thinks you might be going over to the other side.'

'Albermarle's an idiot.'

Mr Carmichael sipped coffee which, despite coming from the most modern coffee-making machine on the market, sent to the magazine for review, had been given to him in a plastic cup.

'He thinks you've become too close to this werewolf ... this ... what was her name?'

'Thrix MacRinnalch.'

'It's odd that none of our other operatives seem to have heard of her.'

'She's a sorceress,' explained Easterly for what seemed like the hundredth time. 'Her defences make it almost impossible to get close to her. Even when a hunter does come across her, he soon forgets.'

'Very unusual for a werewolf to be a sorceress.'

'I've reported all this before. Her sorcery makes us forget about her. I've spent weeks gaining her trust.'

'But you can't kill her?'

'Not yet.'

'Why not?'

'I've explained that a hundred times too. No attack would work. Her body repels silver. You could fire a bullet at her from point-blank range and it still wouldn't penetrate.'

'So what do you plan to do?'

'Wait for the right moment. Meanwhile I'm tracking her all the time.'

'You mean you've bugged her?'

'Not exactly,' said Easterly. 'Her defences would detect any sort of listening device, but her sorcery hasn't quite moved with the times. Albermarle gave me a code to enter into her mobile phone. There's no mechanism involved so she hasn't detected it.'

'You said you weren't getting on well with Albermarle. But he's helped you track your target?'

'I never said he wasn't good with technology. He's excellent. He'd be worth more to the Guild if he just stayed in the background. He's only helping track the Enchantress because he thinks it will bring him closer to Dominil.'

'You think Albermarle is too personally involved with Dominil?'

'I do.'

'He says exactly the same about you and Thrix.'

'He's wrong.'

Mr Carmichael was reassured, to an extent. He didn't think Easterly was falling in love with Thrix MacRinnalch, as Albermarle claimed. There might be more of a connection than Easterly was prepared to admit, but he didn't doubt that when the opportunity arose, Easterly would kill her.

Carmichael fumbled in his wallet. 'Where's my receipt for lunch gone? Since Albermarle reformed our expense claims I have to keep track of every damned thing.'

108

The Enchantress was surprised by the security chain that prevented the door from opening fully. It seemed an unusual precaution for a strong werewolf like Dominil.

'Worried about burglars?' she asked.

'I'm worried about Albermarle.' Dominil slipped the chain loose and let her cousin in. 'I've been as careful as I could be to keep this address secret. Did you make sure no one followed you?'

'No one can follow me anywhere.'

'I hope you're right. You're the only one I'm telling about my movements these days.'

Thrix looked curiously at her cousin.

'Why is this Albermarle such a problem? We've dealt with hunters before.'

'Albermarle is more intelligent. When I locate him, he's gone, and when I hide, he finds me.'

Dominil's temporary apartment was small, clean and extremely austere. The landlord had painted the walls white for his new tenant and Dominil hadn't done anything to change it. Her computer was on the table and her coat hung by the door. Apart from that, the flat could almost have been uninhabited.

'Where did you find this place?'

'I walked into a letting agency and took it at random. It's best if I stay away from clan properties. Albermarle would find me. He's in command of a group of hunters these days and that's too many silver bullets to dodge.' Dominil shook her head. 'It's hard to imagine the Albermarle I knew at university being in charge of anyone. Though it's not hard to imagine him working every minute of the day to track me down. He always was obsessive.'

'Breaking his heart probably made it worse.'

Dominil pursed her lips. 'I've heard enough about that from the twins. I didn't think it was funny coming from them, either.'

'Sorry,' said Thrix. 'If he's really this dangerous, let me help you kill him.'

Dominil shook her head. 'If you can hide me from him for a little while that'll be enough. I want to kill him myself.'

'Are you letting this get personal, Dominil?'

'He chased me out of the British Museum. No one can do that.'

Thrix nodded. She noticed that Dominil was dressed a little more casually than usual. The black trousers she wore were plain and not particularly well cut. Her black sweatshirt was old, well

313

worn. Practical, Thrix supposed, but not smart. Despite this, Dominil's hair was still well cared for. Long, thick and lustrous, as was Thrix's, but straight rather than curling.

'I'll find my bottle of whisky.'

Thrix waved this away. 'Don't worry, I don't need it.'

Dominil ignored her and went into the kitchen, returning with a bottle of the MacRinnalch malt and two clean glasses.

'To us,' said Thrix, raising her glass, 'and clan traditions. And to the departed spirit of Gawain MacRinnalch, may he wander happily in the Forests of the Werewolf Dead.'

Dominil looked sharply at her visitor. 'What?'

Thrix put down her glass on the bare wooden table. 'I'm remembering Gawain.'

'Gawain has been dead for a while.'

'I know,' said Thrix. 'But he didn't get much of a send-off. I doubt many werewolves raised a glass to his departure. Maybe his sister, wherever she is. And Kalix, of course. She took it badly.'

'I understood your affection for Gawain faded away some time ago.'

'It did. Which doesn't mean I wanted him dead. He was a fellow MacRinnalch, after all.'

Thrix looked pointedly at her empty glass. Dominil refilled it for her but remained silent.

'I was surprised you refused to help Kalix look for his killer,' said Thrix.

'As is quite obvious, I have other things on my mind.'

'True. Albermarle and the twins. That's a lot to take care of.' Thrix sat back in her seat and seemed to relax. 'Whoever killed Gawain probably expected it would end there. After all, who would care that he was dead? But if they'd thought it through, they'd have realised that my crazy sister wouldn't let it go. Kalix loved him with all her youthful passion and that doesn't fade so easily. You know I'm on her list of suspects?'

'I believe I am too,' said Dominil.

'It's unfortunate for the killer that Kalix is friendly with a Hiyasta who can detect people's auras after they've gone. Fire elementals are good at that. Of course, Agrivex isn't the brightest Hiyasta around. If a really powerful elemental – Queen

Malveria, for instance – were to apply herself, there's no telling what she might learn, even now.'

'Perhaps you should suggest it to Kalix,' said Dominil, coolly.

There was a very long silence, interrupted only by a faint humming from the elderly fridge in the kitchen.

'Why did you kill Gawain?' said Thrix abruptly.

If Thrix was hoping for a reaction, she was disappointed.

Dominil's expression remained completely calm. 'That's a peculiar question.'

'Peculiar? Maybe. But I'm sure you did kill him. I went back to Gawain's flat to take another look around. Because I'm fed up with Kalix annoying me. Which is another of her talents. She's dogged, if not that bright. She might even find out the truth in the end.' Thrix paused for a reaction, which again was not forthcoming.

'Mostly I use my sorcery for fashion work, and personal protection. I wouldn't claim to have any great skills at investigating. But Old Minerva taught me a lot, up on that mountain. The Personal Fragment Collection Spell, for instance.'

Thrix took a small plastic bag from the pocket of her elegant coat. 'Tiny dust particles, flakes of skin and so on. They came from you.'

'I already acknowledged I was there,' countered Dominil. 'I visited Gawain on Kalix's behalf.'

Thrix drew out another small plastic bag. 'These came from the wound in Gawain's chest. Tiny pieces of you, transferred when you stabbed him. Which raises another interesting point. What did you stab him with? The only thing I know that could kill a werewolf like that is the Begravar knife, and that's safely back at the castle.'

'It's possible for a werewolf to be killed by a silver-coated knife.'

'Possible, but rare. Generally it would need another strong werewolf to be holding the knife. Is that what you used?'

'You seem to be making a lot of assumptions,' said Dominil. 'I'm sure there could be other explanations for dust fragments from me being on Gawain's wound.'

'We're not in a courtroom. Nor are we giving evidence to the Great Council. I don't know if I could prove whether or not you

315

killed Gawain. But I'm quite sure you did.' Throughout the conversation Dominil had remained calm, which the Enchantress found irritating. The least a werewolf could do, on being accused of murdering a fellow MacRinnalch, was look guilty about it.

'Perhaps you should report your suspicions to the Thane,' suggested Dominil.

'I have a feeling he knows already.'

There was another long silence. The fridge went quiet for a few moments before spluttering into life again. Outside there was a constant low rumbling as traffic edged round a nearby corner.

'I might not have gone to Oxford but I'm not stupid, Dominil. I don't imagine you killed Gawain on a whim. That would be very unlike you. I believe you went there for a reason. Markus probably knew what it was. I'll get the truth out of him if I can't get it out of you. So why not just tell me what happened?'

Dominil weighed Thrix's words for a few moments. 'Very well. Markus sent me there to retrieve the Begravar knife.'

'But it went back to the castle after the fight in London.'

'One of them did, the one that belonged to the clan. There was another, brought there by the hunter Mikulanec. I don't know how Gawain ended up with it but he did. He took it home with him. Later he attempted to sell it to the clan. For a lot of money.'

'I can understand that. Gawain probably needed money.'

'He had no great liking for the clan, either,' said Dominil, 'after they banished him.'

'So Markus sent you there to steal the knife?'

'He sent me to negotiate. And he paid me for the mission, in case you're wondering why I went. I've never had any of the family wealth turned over to me. I've taken pay from both the Mistress of the Werewolves and the Thane at various times. Unfortunately, in this instance there were complications. Markus baulked at the price Gawain was asking. Gawain suggested that if the MacRinnalchs didn't want to buy the knife someone else might.'

Thrix's eyes widened. She hadn't expected to hear that. 'You mean the Avenaris Guild? Gawain would never do that.'

Dominil gave the faintest of shrugs. 'I don't know how serious he was. Probably it was just a bargaining ploy. Or perhaps he'd really come to hate the MacRinnalchs. I can't say they treated him that well. And when Kalix rejected him again he took it very badly.'

Thrix poured more whisky for herself.

'When this happened I still had access to the Guild's computers. I read a report that suggested that certain hunters might have been contacted about buying a valuable item. That gave some credence to Markus's suspicion that Gawain might sell them the knife.'

'So he dispatched you.'

'He hired me. I found Gawain in an agitated state. At first he said he wasn't going to sell the knife at all. When I pointed out that it was no use to anyone who didn't know how to activate it, he said that perhaps there were other people than the MacRinnalchs who knew how to activate it. We started to argue.' Dominil sipped from her glass. 'Gawain was a strong werewolf. When the moon came up he transformed. I reasoned that he might well be a more capable fighter than myself.'

'So you stabbed him?'

'I picked up the knife and told him the deal was concluded.'

'You mean it was just lying there?'

'I'd asked to see it,' said Dominil. 'Gawain probably thought he could defeat me if I tried to take it. He didn't know that I could activate the knife. I learned that when I was trying to kill Sarapen. Gawain lunged at me and I spoke the words to bring the knife to life. I hoped that Gawain would become confused and I could leave. You know the confusion the Begravar knife causes in werewolves. Unfortunately, he was too strong to be put off completely. He still managed to rush at me. I too was confused.'

'But not too confused to stab him?'

'That's right.'

The Enchantress gazed at Dominil, amazed at her lack of emotion as she described Gawain's death. 'What happened then?'

'I took the knife to Scotland and handed it over to Markus, who paid me as agreed.'

'I can see why you didn't want to help Kalix investigate.'

'Exactly.'

'I don't like this at all,' muttered Thrix. 'Gawain might have hated the clan but there was no reason to kill him.'

'He attacked me,' said Dominil. 'With my mind affected by the knife's power, I wasn't in a position to do anything clever.' Dominil sipped the last of her whisky and refilled her glass. 'I believe it's possible he did intend to sell the knife to the Guild. When Kalix visited the flat she encountered hunters. Possibly they'd simply tracked down a werewolf and moved in for the kill. But it's possible that they might have been there to do business.'

'How did you even know where he lived?'

'The address was on the letter Kalix showed me.'

Thrix didn't need to say how Kalix would feel if she ever learned that Dominil had killed Gawain after taking his address from the love letter he'd written to her. She looked at Dominil, wondering about her story. Dominil wasn't known for telling lies. But she wasn't known for her patience, either. Thrix wondered if Dominil might simply have attacked Gawain when she became tired of negotiating. 'You know that Kalix won't let the matter drop?'

'I was acting within the parameters of clan law.'

Thrix laughed. 'That won't save you if she finds out. Kalix doesn't pay a lot of attention to clan law.'

'I doubt she'll learn what happened.'

'How do you know I won't tell her?'

'Why would you? I protected the clan. I was working for the Thane.'

Thrix shook her head. 'I'm not pleased at any of this. I won't tell Kalix. But I wouldn't bet against her finding out, somehow or other.'

'If she does, I'll explain things to her,' said Dominil, evenly.

'A lot of good that will do. Kalix is a psychopath.'

'You exaggerate.'

'Haven't you noticed how many people she's killed? And werewolves?'

'That doesn't make her a psychopath,' objected Dominil. 'She's been forced into violence. There was the clan feud, and hunters pursuing her. Every werewolf will kill to protect itself, in the right circumstances.'

'True. But not as eagerly as Kalix. Her so-called battle madness is no more than an excuse for her bloodthirsty nature, if you ask me. Kalix can't hold back once she gets started. She has to kill.'

'Perhaps no one ever taught her to hold back,' suggested Dominil. 'She spent much of her childhood alone. She was neglected in the castle.'

Thrix looked momentarily uncomfortable. 'I'd left the castle long before she was born.'

'Your parents were both there. So were Sarapen and Markus. I don't believe Kalix was on the receiving end of much affection. Quite the opposite, in fact.'

'Since when do you care about affection? You appear to have no emotions.'

'I have emotions. I just keep them to myself. And my father, while not warm, did care for me as a child.'

'Well, maybe you should have taken Kalix into your family,' said Thrix sarcastically.

'I did care for her occasionally. Small things, when she was lonely.'

Thrix was sceptical. 'If you were a surrogate mother to Kalix it's the first I've heard about it.'

'I don't claim I was a surrogate mother. But I looked after her a few times, when she was very young, and the rest of your family was busy elsewhere.'

'That's not going to prevent her attacking you if she learns you killed Gawain,' said Thrix.

109

Markus was busy at Andamair House. He'd hired contractors to prepare the galleries for the audience, and the stage for Felicori, who would be singing a selection of well-known arias from Verdi and Puccini, along with some lesser-known songs selected from his own favourites. Markus intended that he should perform in front of a suitable backdrop and had hired a set designer from Edinburgh who'd had great success last year with his designs for *Othello*. Lorries carrying equipment rolled into the grounds of the mansion followed by teams of theatre workers, all supervised by Markus. He was happier than he'd been at any time since being elected Thane. The Mistress of the Werewolves left him mostly alone, trusting his taste, and even those MacRinnalchs who didn't regard him as a particularly suitable head of the clan acknowledged that if anyone was to make a success of the affair, it would be Markus.

There was still some unhappiness at the prospect of so many humans invading MacRinnalch territory. The great mansion of Andamair House was located on the outskirts of Edinburgh, a long way from Castle MacRinnalch, but, even so, it had never hosted a human gathering. There were mutterings of discontent, and some dark jokes about what might happen to the Mayor of Edinburgh if he stayed too long on their grounds. On the other hand, the refurbishment provided work, much of which Markus gave to werewolves from the clan, and the income was appreciated. The complaints of those werewolves who didn't like the thought of humans visiting their mansion were mitigated by the money that flowed into their pockets. Flora MacRinnalch, who ran a business selling timber not far from the castle, had been badly hit by a downturn in the construction industry, but as Markus sent in another order for wood and her trucks headed south, fully laden, she found herself warming to the whole project. Business was business, after all. As a clan, the MacRinnalchs had never felt shy about making money.

Markus stayed in Edinburgh during the week, returning to the castle only at weekends. He was still spending his nights there with Beatrice, the assistant curator of the castle relics. While not an exciting relationship, it was comfortable. Comfortable enough for Markus to now tell her about his fondness for cross-dressing, which had gone smoothly enough. Markus was relieved, though he hadn't really expected it to go that badly. Markus had had many lovers and it was rarely that any of them, human or werewolf, had objected to his liking for female clothes. It still wasn't something he'd have liked to be known throughout the clan – the Barons certainly wouldn't have approved – but he was comfortable with Beatrice knowing. She was sympathetic, and though she was too small for most of her clothes to fit Markus, she did let him try on a few blouses that he liked in the privacy of her rooms at the castle.

110

Merchant MacDoig was fatigued after his day's work.

'I'm not as young as I was, son.' He sank into his favourite leather armchair in the rooms above his shop. 'It takes a powerful amount of concentration to send papers through the dimensions.'

His son looked at him with some concern as he placed a teapot on the huge mantle above the old-fashioned fireplace that warmed the Merchant's feet. It was illegal to burn coal in London these days, but the Merchant liked his fireplace. The furnishings in the shop were as antiquated as his frock coat and embroidered waistcoat. The Merchant had lived an unnaturally long life and had no wish to change. The teacup that the Young MacDoig handed to his father was an exquisite piece of antique Staffordshire china, part of a set from the display cabinet that was itself a valuable piece of furniture. Merchant MacDoig had never consciously surrounded himself with luxuries but it pleased him that the ancient furnishings he'd taken good care of were now priceless artefacts. It showed that it wasn't always a good idea to modernise.

'So what does the Princess want with copies of pages from a book of moon-spells?'

'Something bad, no doubt, probably concerning Thrix MacRinnalch. She still hates her.'

The Merchant sipped his tea, holding the small cup quite gracefully in his large hand. He looked thoughtful.

'I remember when the old clippers sailed into London carrying tea in chests, all the way from China. I saw the *Cutty Sark* coming in on her maiden voyage. Must have been 1872 or thereabouts.' The *Cutty Sark* was still preserved, a floating museum-piece in Greenwich. The Merchant had a notion to visit it some time. He'd always liked the sight of a ship in full sail, bringing goods from distant lands. Now they arrived by air. It wasn't the same. 'I don't know what the Princess hopes to achieve but if it concerns the moon, it's bound to be bad for werewolves.'

The Merchant had done a lot of business with the MacRinnalchs. They were good customers. Verasa MacRinnalch, for instance, was a fine woman; no one could deny it. But business was business, and if Princess Kabachetka had been prepared to offer him such a substantial sum of money to obtain photocopies from a book in Castle MacRinnalch, and transport the material to her dimension, he wasn't going turn it down.

'It's lucky for us that Kertal still has gambling debts.' Kertal, a cousin of the Thane, still lived in the castle. He was always in need of money. 'I doubt he's given that much consideration to what the Princess might do with the information.'

The Merchant drank his tea, relaxing into his armchair, and wondered if it was too early for a dram. He liked his drop of whisky in the evenings but never let it interfere with work.

'We've an order for silver bullets,' said Young MacDoig.

The Merchant nodded. 'Aye, I saw that. The Guild's made a quicker recovery than I thought they would. Best check the warehouse, son, you never know how many silver bullets we'll be selling in the next few weeks. If Princess Kabachetka's got some plot afoot against the MacRinnalchs, the Avenaris Guild will probably try and get in on it somehow.'

111

Vex managed to persuade a not-too-reluctant household that the best way to celebrate Daniel's recovery from his illness would be a shopping expedition. Moonglow liked the idea. Though she was still worried about money, Daniel's sickness had been stressful, and she'd been working hard at college recently. Daniel was keen to leave the house after several days on the couch. They were all surprised when Kalix agreed to accompany them.

'She needs more comics for her assignment,' explained Vex. '*Curse of the Wolf Girl.*'

'How many more do you need? Six?'

'Seven.'

'I thought you had six issues already?'

'I chewed up number four because it was so annoying.' Kalix scowled. 'I'm going to denounce them to the whole class. I'm going to let them know you can't write rubbish like that about werewolves.'

They took the Northern Line from Kennington to Tottenham

Court Road. Unlike some other underground routes, the Northern Line hadn't been renovated recently and the carriages were still old, rickety, and not very clean.

'So,' announced Vex in her loudest voice, 'you never really talked about this curse thing.'

'What curse thing?'

'You know. You and Daniel not being able to get together.'

'This probably isn't the time—'

'It's quite difficult really,' said Vex, 'what with Daniel practically risking his life for passion. What are you going to do about it? Why's everyone gone quiet?'

Daniel and Moonglow were staring at their feet, and even Kalix looked uncomfortable.

'What's the matter? It's no use just ignoring it. We should be thinking of a plan to get the curse lifted. I'm good with plans. Daniel, if you're ever going to succeed with Moonglow we have to think of a plan.'

Moonglow went bright red, and studied her shoes with even more interest.

'Would you just be quiet?' urged Daniel.

As soon as the train rolled into Tottenham Court Road Tube station, Daniel and Moonglow hurried to the doors, eager to escape from Vex's terrible lack of tact.

She pursued them relentlessly along the platform. 'How about if Daniel pretends to be dead for a while? That might get the curse lifted. No good? OK, what about if Moonglow pretends to go mad?'

Outside the station they passed a busker who was performing a spirited medley of early Elvis Costello hits. Daniel, always sympathetic to musicians, dropped some coins into his hat.

'I know,' cried Vex. 'How about if – oww! Kalix just punched me in the arm. Why did you do that?'

'Because you're being tactless and stupid.'

'How?'

'Moonglow and Daniel don't want to discuss the curse. You're embarrassing them.'

Vex was puzzled. 'I'm sure you're wrong. Daniel, is Kalix right? Am I embarrassing you?'

'Yes.'

'But don't you want to—'

'Here's the comic shop,' interrupted a relieved Moonglow.

'Thank God,' sighed Daniel, and hurried inside.

'This way!' shouted Vex, leading them downstairs. 'Hey look, it's the friendly assistant who likes manga.'

Agrivex approached a large man in a baggy T-shirt at the counter and then, to general surprise, burst into the theme song for *Tokyo Top Pop Boom Boom Girl*. Customers looked round in amusement while the assistant greeted Vex cheerfully.

'She really has a talent for making friends,' observed Daniel.

As Vex introduced Kalix to her friend at the counter – 'She's a really big *Curse of the Wolf Girl* fan' – Daniel adroitly drew Moonglow aside, into a section of the shop that sold toys.

'Why are we hiding behind a giant model robot?' asked Moonglow.

'We're not hiding. I just wanted a quiet place to talk.'

'What about?'

Daniel hesitated, then plunged in. 'Malveria's curse. What if it wasn't there? Would we be going out?'

'I don't know.'

Daniel sensed Moonglow's reluctance but persisted anyway. 'I think we would be. I mean, why not?'

'I've been living with this curse for months. I don't know what would have happened without it. Maybe we should just not talk about it.'

Daniel felt his spirit drain. 'Fine. We'll not talk about it. I almost die of some deadly disease after kissing you but you don't want to talk about it. '

'You didn't have a deadly disease. It was a cold, or one of these sudden viruses.'

'A severe one. Probably made worse by Malveria's sorcery. If I keel over and die because I'm overcome with passion, the least you can do is talk about it.'

'Will you stop saying you were overcome with passion? You just drank too much.'

'It's the same thing. So how about it? Without the curse, would we be going out?' Daniel hadn't intended to pursue the subject so relentlessly but Moonglow's failure to address it was irritating him.

'I keep telling you, I don't know!' protested Moonglow. 'Have you noticed how annoying you've been recently? Always angry about something?'

'That's only because you were being unreasonable. Which I now forgive you for. Obviously you were concerned about my health.'

'Well, it was annoying anyway. It's been stressful enough in the house without you being angry and playing loud music all the time. If I hear We Slaughtered Them and Laughed one more time I'm going to grind their CD under a spiky heel.'

Daniel was wounded. 'I thought you liked them!'

'No one likes them apart from you. A world without the grim sound of We Slaughtered Them and Laughed would be an improvement.'

'You're making it sound like I'm obsessed.'

'You are.'

Daniel pondered this. 'So what you're really saying is if I didn't spend so much time listening to We Slaughtered Them and Laughed, then you'd go out with me?'

'That's not what I said at all! What's the point of discussing it, anyway? Malveria's curse won't go away. We're stuck with it.'

'Maybe we could get the curse lifted? Malveria's not so intractable really.'

Moonglow went silent again, and whether she was thinking that it would be a good idea to get the curse lifted or not, Daniel couldn't tell.

At that moment Vex appeared. 'Are you hiding behind the giant robot? Can I hide too? Kalix got three more comics. Now she's got eight.'

Kalix was deep in conversation with the large assistant, who was pointing out something in one of her new comics. Kalix looked interested, and actually laughed at something he said.

The atmosphere was strained between Moonglow and Daniel as they left the shop. Fortunately Vex was preoccupied with a *Tokyo Top Pop Boom Boom Girl* action figure she'd bought, and ceased tormenting them about their relationship.

'You were a long time talking to the assistant, Kalix.'

'He liked my hair.'

Daniel looked concerned. 'Your hair? What's he talking about your hair for? Did he try to pick you up? Was it creepy?'

Kalix shook her head. 'He wasn't creepy. He just said my hair was so long it reminded him of some woman he knew. She's Scottish, too. He was OK.'

'He's called Albermarle,' said Vex. 'He's really interesting. He knows loads about comics and games and manga.'

Moonglow turned towards Daniel. 'Is "manga" those comics you have with the Japanese schoolgirls in really short skirts?'

'I told you before, they were secret agents. The short skirts were just a disguise.'

'And the tiny little halter tops?'

'Also a disguise.'

'Wouldn't a really short skirt and a tiny little top be a really bad disguise? Everyone would look at you.'

'You just don't understand comics,' said Daniel.

'Why not just admit you were leering at pictures of girls in short skirts?'

'Who's been leering?' said Vex, brightly.

'Daniel.'

'Ignore everything Moonglow says. She knows nothing about comics.'

112

The Fire Queen rode out in her silver carriage, a light and wondrously elegant vehicle she used for social engagements.

'I do much prefer this to the official state carriage. One never feels entirely comfortable in that huge golden edifice.'

'The population loves to see you in your golden carriage, Your Highness.'

'Very true, Gruselvere. And I do appreciate the cheering.'

The silver carriage made its way through the outskirts of the fashionable area that surrounded the palace, part of a small procession that included palace dignitaries and Malveria's retinue of guards and servants. Distikka was riding in the carriage in front.

'I thought the Vulcanalia went well.'

Gruselvere nodded. 'I have never heard such a roar as when you led them through the Great Volcano. The ceremony was magnificent.'

Malveria smiled. It had indeed been magnificent. The new alterations to her state robes, as recently tailored by Thrix MacRinnalch, had been widely admired. Admittedly, several members of her council had chafed at the alterations, remarking that they were the most traditional of Hiyasta garments and had remained unchanged for hundreds of years. But as Malveria pointed out, she was far more slender than previous occupants of the throne, and having state robes that hid her figure made no sense.

The two other occupants of the carriage, young handmaidens, suddenly giggled and hid their faces behind their fans.

'Will you stop this interminable giggling?' the Queen demanded with mock severity. She turned to Gruselvere. 'They think I'm unaware of their obsession with the handsome young valet currently employed by Duke DeMortalis. I am well aware of it, ladies. Nothing in the palace escapes my attention.'

The handmaidens giggled again. Beau DeMortalis's new valet had been creating quite a stir among the servants; almost as much as the Duke himself. As one of the nation's richest and most eligible bachelors, the Duke stirred hearts wherever he went. The Fire Queen had never regretted sparing his life, valuing both his wit and his dress sense.

Gruselvere shushed the handmaidens. 'I packed another full outfit in an extra carriage.'

The Queen nodded. The upcoming soirée at the town house of the Countess Rechen-Gaval was a relatively informal affair. Three outfits should be sufficient. Malveria, however, never liked to take risks, and travelled with several spare outfits. Though her clothes were designed by Thrix, and could be relied on to outshine her rivals, it was wise to have something in reserve. The finest dress could be ruined by a careless hand at the punch bowl.

'One really cannot trust the young Countess's servants. Not that I trust the Countess, either. I regret the death of her mother.'

'You despised her mother.'

'True,' admitted Malveria, 'but at least you knew where you

stood with her. Thanks to her unfortunate passing, I am now obliged to be civil to her daughter, at least till she proves herself unworthy. There is bad blood in the family. Fortunately the appalling Agrivex is not here to shame us.'

Gruselvere nodded. Though the wardrobe mistress could not really picture what Vex's life on Earth was like, she understood that the Fire Queen was moderately pleased with her niece's progress.

Malveria sighed. 'But the tedium of greeting the new Countess – have you noticed how sturdy her ankles are? – is nothing compared to the misery of enduring Kabachetka's company. I so regret having to invite these barbaric neighbours to our festival.'

'There's no need to worry,' said Gruselvere. 'These days she's hardly even a rival.'

'True. I have laid waste to her on the battleground of style. Even so, I do hate to meet the Princess. One is grateful that her appalling mother is indisposed.'

'What's the matter with her?'

Malveria shrugged. 'Who knows? Some minor complaint, no doubt. The Empress has always been a dreadful hypochondriac.' The Queen frowned, very deeply. 'And there is always the matter of the card table.' A few flames flickered around her fingertips. She doused them quickly, knowing it was unbecoming to exhibit such emotion in front of young handmaidens, but she couldn't keep the anger out of her voice. 'It's intolerable that I'm doomed to defeat because of the Duchess's appalling play. Might not the Queen be expected to have a competent partner at the card table? If Gargamond makes another foolish bid I will certainly say something very harsh to her.'

'The Duchess is an important ally,' ventured the Queen's dresser, who was not unaware of palace politics.

'I know. But does this give her the right to humiliate me in front of the assembled Hiyasta aristocracy? I think not.' Malveria snapped her fingers. 'Handmaidens. Stop giggling and attend to my make-up. The terrible prospect of partnering Gargamond has caused me to glow and may have affected my eyeliner. Initiate repairs, and be quick about it. I'm also experiencing doubts about my lip colouring. Really, this is all very stressful.'

113

The Douglas-MacPhees were angry about Decembrius failing to meet them as arranged, particularly as he owed them money.

'Maybe we should pay him a visit,' suggested Rhona.

'Maybe we should,' agreed Duncan, and led his companions towards their dusty old black van.

If the Douglas-MacPhees weren't pleased with Decembrius, Kalix MacRinnalch was feeling a little more kindly towards him. He'd stood up to her mother. He hadn't seemed intimidated by Thrix, either. Kalix had long felt the need for an ally against her family. She still didn't much like it that he was obviously attracted to her. She didn't feel much attraction towards him. Now that Gawain was dead, Kalix didn't feel like she'd ever be attracted to anyone again.

The young werewolf travelled north, sitting upstairs on a double-decker bus, doing her best to ignore a group of noisy schoolchildren who'd been screaming at each other from the moment they swarmed on board. She tried calling Decembrius but he didn't answer, which irritated her. He hadn't answered his phone all day. She wondered if she might have got the arrangement wrong, though she was sure she hadn't.

The schoolchildren reminded Kalix of her upcoming exam, which brought on a larger jolt of anxiety than she was expecting. The thought of sitting an exam was enough to make her palms sweat. She tried to put it to the back of her mind, but it was difficult. For some reason her life seemed to be revolving around an exam. Daniel and Moonglow kept talking about it. Vex wouldn't shut up about it. Even her mother knew about it. If Kalix failed, then Moonglow would treacherously tell her mother and then the whole family would know. Probably the whole clan. Kalix could imagine them talking far and wide in the Scottish werewolf community about how the old Thane's wayward daughter had once more shown herself to be a failure.

I don't even want to do the exam, fumed Kalix as the bus trundled north past Mornington Crescent. I'm not going to do it. I'm not doing my assignment either. Why should I?

As she thought this she couldn't help but feel the bottle of laudanum, which was very light, in her pocket. She was running out, and needed more. Her only source of income was the allowance from her mother which would be withdrawn if she left college.

I can't pass the exam, thought Kalix, quite miserably. It's just a huge humiliation waiting to happen. I can't even do the test.

According to Vex, the class had to sit a small test to prepare them for the exam. Moonglow said this was a good idea, but to Kalix it just meant more worry. The thought of tests and exams was extremely stressful for her and had been causing her almost continual anxiety. Acting on Decembrius's advice that she should pretend to be normal – though perhaps not in a way Decembrius would have anticipated – she'd given herself a permanent reminder. On her own in her room, Kalix had cut a small letter N into her upper arm. Sitting in the bus, she brushed her hand against the wound. It hurt, but the memory of what she'd done reassured her a little.

Kalix got off the bus in Camden. As she walked through the streets, heading for Decembrius's small apartment, she unexpectedly caught his scent, coming on the light breeze from the west. Scents were difficult to pick up in the polluted city but this was quite clear. Decembrius wasn't far away. She turned left down Gloucester Avenue to investigate, and immediately caught the scent of other werewolves she recognised. The Douglas-MacPhees. Kalix came to an abrupt halt. What were they doing here, close to Decembrius? Decembrius had sworn he had nothing more to do with them. She glanced up at the sky. Though winter was coming to an end, the nights were still long and there was only half an hour or so till dusk. Kalix didn't mind meeting the Douglas-MacPhees again. She owed them something. But she'd rather be in her werewolf shape when she paid them back. Anxiety now forgotten, Kalix advanced slowly through the side streets, following the now mingled scents of Decembrius and the Douglas-MacPhees.

114

Though Captain Easterly's apartment block wasn't quite as opulent as some in the neighbourhood, it did offer its residents valet and maid services, personal shopping and an in-house florist. Easterly didn't use their cleaning services, not trusting strangers in his apartment, though he had used the florist to send flowers to Thrix. As for Albermarle, he used the personal shopping service to bring him pizza and Chinese food. As Easterly rang his bell, Albermarle opened the door in an oversized T-shirt with food stains on the front. He looked at Easterly suspiciously. 'Well?'

'The code worked. I can listen to Thrix's calls.'

Albermarle nodded, and let his cousin in.

'Good work,' said Easterly. He almost added, 'If only you'd stick to intelligence gathering and stop trying to be a hunter.' But he refrained. They'd had that argument many times, and Albermarle wasn't going to change his mind now.

Though Easterly was accustomed to his cousin's habits, he couldn't help noticing the clutter everywhere. He moved a model star-fighter on the table to make space for the folder he was carrying.

'Don't touch that!' cried Albermarle, and fussily put it back. He lined it up exactly with the models beside it.

Captain Easterly pursed his lips. His cousin was becoming more obsessive-compulsive, something he remembered from previous occasions when he'd been under stress. No one could touch his models. Moving a model spaceship was liable to lead to a temper tantrum.

Albermarle tore off another huge slice of pizza and busied himself with eating.

Easterly looked on impatiently. 'Does the tracking work at long range?'

'It should. Where is she going?'

'Scotland. I'm thinking of going with her.'

'To Scotland?' Albermarle was interested. 'To the castle? That's dangerous.'

'Not the castle. Some other MacRinnalch property, near Edinburgh. They're holding a charity event.'

'A charity event?' Albermarle was surprised. 'Werewolves?'

'I know. It's ridiculous.'

Albermarle lowered his pizza. 'Is Dominil going to this event?'

'Can't you stop obsessing over her?'

'I'm not obsessing over her. Or the quiz team.'

Easterly sighed in frustration. He'd heard the story of the university quiz team many times. Somewhere, hidden away in Albermarle's belongings, there was a copy of the university magazine chronicling the event. On one well-thumbed page was a report of a competition between Albermarle's college and another of the Oxford colleges. Dominil had been the star of the occasion, demonstrating such powers of intellect and memory as to virtually win the contest single-handed. Her score on the evening had been more than that of her three team-mates put together. Thanks to her, Albermarle's college had won the competition. This brought Albermarle no pleasure.

'She shouldn't have been in the team. I was captain.'

'You got sick. They had to pick a substitute.'

'She never even tried out for the team! When they needed someone to replace me they just went right to Dominil like she was something special. She wasn't anything special.'

'I thought she scored a record number of points?'

'I'd have done the same,' sniffed Albermarle. 'She got a lot of easy questions.'

'Maybe if you hadn't eaten so much the day before you wouldn't have got sick.'

'I was nervous,' protested Albermarle. 'Food calms me down. Do you think if I wrote to the college and told them Dominil was a werewolf they might retrospectively disqualify her?'

'I think if you don't stop obsessing about a silly little university quiz that happened years ago then Dominil will kill you even quicker than she's probably going to anyway.'

'I wasn't even that sick,' said Albermarle. 'I could still have competed if she hadn't barged in ahead of me. And you know what happened after that?'

'She refused to go out with you?'

'No! Well, yes. Like she was too good for me just because she won some infantile quiz. And people thought she was attractive. I never thought she was attractive.'

'Then why did you ask her out?'

'I was just sorry for her. With that weird white hair. It's not natural. I always knew there was something strange about her.'

'Albermarle, let it go.'

'Let it go? Whose side are you on? Humanity or the were-wolves? So is she going to be at this event in Edinburgh or not?'

Easterly wasn't sure, but thought she probably would be.

'If the Mistress of the Werewolves is organising it, most of the important MacRinnalchs are bound to be there. If I see her I'll bring you a report.'

'I won't need a report,' replied Albermarle. 'I'll go myself.'

'I don't think that's a good idea.'

'Why not?'

Easterly's expression hardened. 'You're not exactly an experienced hunter, are you? You can't go mingling with werewolves in their own territory. You'll get killed.'

'I've managed so far, haven't I? And I'm fed up with you criticising me. Just leave me alone to hunt Dominil.'

'Fine. Go to Edinburgh. Don't blame me when you get your head ripped off. Now, could we get on with things? I'm in a hurry.'

'Why? Is your werewolf girlfriend waiting for you?'

'I don't have a werewolf girlfriend and I'm getting fed up with you saying I do.'

'You love Thrix!' mocked Albermarle.

'You love Dominil!' retorted Easterly, and immediately regretted allowing himself to be dragged down to Albermarle's level.

'At least I don't send her flowers.'

'How do you know I've been sending flowers?' demanded Easterly.

'Because, unlike you, I can gather intelligence. I'm telling you, Easterly, your kind of hunting is on the way out. Running around like an action hero isn't good enough these days. Today's werewolf hunter needs technology skills and you don't have them. It's not me who's unsuitable, it's you. You're out of date. Now excuse me, I have a pizza to finish. And then I'm going to track some werewolves.'

115

Decembrius caught the scent of the Douglas-MacPhees before he came out of Regent's Park. He didn't bother turning back.

Decembrius would rather not have encountered them but had no intention of fleeing. Even so, he noted that the moon wasn't far from rising. He walked slowly over the small bridge that led from the park over the railway line into the side streets of Camden. There on the pavement stood Duncan, Rhona and the huge William. In their leather jackets, bandannas and tattoos they didn't look out of place in the heart of Camden, but here in the quieter side streets their appearance stood out. Decembrius wouldn't have been surprised to find that a few net curtains were twitching as nervous homeowners wondered why the rough-looking trio were loitering here.

'Decembrius. You were meant to be meeting us.'

The two siblings and their cousin studied Decembrius, their hostility quite evident on their faces. Duncan stepped in front of him while Rhona and William moved to either side.

'So?' said Duncan.

'So what?'

'Do you have our money?'

'Not yet.'

'Really? Yet you've been to see the Merchant. And he gave our money to you.'

There was a brief and very tense silence.

'So where is it?' snarled Rhona, and moved closer.

'You'll get your money.'

'We'd better get it right now.'

'You'll have to wait,' said Decembrius, who was wondering how to extricate himself from this uncomfortable situation. He cursed himself for ever getting involved with the Douglas-MacPhees. He'd tried to distance himself from them but he'd failed because he needed money. Now he'd unwisely taken goods to the Merchant and kept the money. Decembrius wasn't under any illusions that he was more honest than the Douglas-MacPhees.

'We can just do it here,' muttered Rhona, and slipped a knife from inside her pocket.

'Or we can wait till the moon rises, then take him into the park,' said William.

'Either way it's the money or your hide,' added Duncan.

The sky was growing overcast and already the clouds were shutting out the last rays of the sun. A faint breeze ruffled

Decembrius's hair. He wondered if it would be better to try to fight his way out now or wait till they all transformed. Neither option was appealing. It was unfortunate that the Douglas-MacPhees, while not MacRinnalchs, were pure-blooded enough to change on any night. It made them formidable, powerful among their clan, and explained why Baron MacPhee had been forced to expel them from his lands.

'What's going on?' came a voice, and everyone jumped, for the approach had been so silent that none of them had heard it. Nor had anyone scented the presence of a werewolf. They turned to find the slender figure of Kalix MacRinnalch looking at them.

'Damn you and that pendant,' muttered Duncan, casting his eyes on the jewel that hung around Kalix's neck, protecting her from detection. 'Maybe it's time we took that for ourselves.'

Kalix didn't seem troubled by the threat. She looked at Decembrius. 'Why were you talking to the Douglas-MacPhees? Were you trying to sell me out?'

'Of course I wasn't.'

Duncan was sharp-witted enough to realise what this implied. 'Sell her out? You mean you've known where she was all along? While we've been looking for her?'

'I never said I'd help you find Kalix.'

Rhona laughed. 'He's been protecting her. Isn't that sweet?'

'I don't need his protection,' said Kalix, and looked at them with contempt. 'I'm going now. If any of you try to stop me I'll kill you.' Kalix turned to leave.

'I could do with your help,' said Decembrius, trying to sound casual.

'I don't care,' said Kalix. 'Sort it out yourself.' She started to walk away.

The Douglas-MacPhees laughed.

'Looks like you've made your girlfriend angry.'

'We'll see you soon,' called Duncan after Kalix, and then turned again to Decembrius. 'Now, about the money you owe us.'

At that moment everyone's attention was caught by the approach of another werewolf, this time one that they could all scent. A small silver car drew up, parked in a no-parking spot, and Red Ruraich MacAndris emerged. With his large frame and straggling ginger hair, he never appeared quite at home in the city. He took in the scene before him and nodded briskly to the Douglas-MacPhees.

'I'm surprised,' he said dryly, in an accent even more densely Scottish than that of the Douglas-MacPhees. 'You've actually managed to find Kalix.'

Kalix, surrounded in daylight by the three Douglas-MacPhees and Red Ruraich MacAndris, showed no anxiety. Faced with the prospect of fighting, the young werewolf found her mind clearing. She was moved to smile and tell Ruraich she was glad she'd killed Sarapen, which infuriated him. He sprinted towards her.

Abruptly there came the sound of what seemed like a silenced gun, not loud but distinctive. A patch of red erupted in Ruraich's chest and he pitched forward onto the pavement, shot from behind. There was a brief second of incredulity as the werewolves looked for the source of the gunfire. Unable to locate it, they scattered wildly as another shot sounded. At one time it had been unheard of for werewolf hunters to fire in daylight, for fear of killing a human instead of a werewolf. That didn't seem to be the case any more.

Kalix sprinted through the corner of a garden. Finding herself confronted by a tall wire fence, she hauled herself over it in an instant and tumbled down a steep bank towards the railway which ran past the park. The line was broad, with eight tracks, and cut deeply into the earth. Kalix made to hurry across but was suddenly dragged backwards.

'What—'

It was Decembrius. At that moment a train hurtled past on the nearest track.

'No need to throw yourself in front of a train,' said Decembrius.

Kalix wrenched her arm free and scowled, not wanting to be saved by Decembrius. They hurried across the line but were halted by another train, coming from the opposite direction. They were on a long bend and visibility was limited in both directions. Crossing eight tracks was a hazardous business. Just then another shot rang out and a bullet ricocheted away off the metal rails.

'Damn this,' roared Decembrius, scanning the bank above for their assailants, without success.

Both werewolves fled across the tracks as the train disappeared. As they reached the opposite side they could feel night arriving. The moon was close and they'd be able to change, if they survived that long.

'Get down,' yelled Decembrius. Kalix felt herself once again dragged by her companion, this time to the ground.

'There's one of them on the opposite bank,' he said. 'We're trapped.'

The two werewolves flattened themselves down, trying to stay out of the firing arc of the hunters above them. Another train roared past, deafeningly loud at such close range.

'We need the moon,' gasped Decembrius. 'And thanks for helping me with the Douglas-MacPhees.'

'You didn't deserve help,' growled Kalix.

'I'd have helped you.'

More shots sounded, though whether they were directed at them or other werewolves still at the scene they didn't know. Neither Kalix nor Decembrius had had time to notice where the Douglas-MacPhees had gone after Ruraich was hit.

Kalix began to edge up the bank.

'Don't! You'll get shot!'

Kalix only growled in return. To find herself under attack, to actually see a fellow werewolf shot, was too much for her rational self.

'Wait till you change!' hissed Decembrius. 'We'll attack as werewolves!'

Kalix couldn't wait. She lost all reason as her battle madness descended. Making no effort to conceal herself she sprinted up the bank. Her skinny frame flew up the grassy slope, her long hair flying out behind her, a look of murderous rage in her eyes. Halfway up, the moon rose, and she transformed. She accelerated up the steep incline. Catching sight of a figure at the top of the bank, she hurtled over the fence, moving with incredible speed, jaws open, teeth bared, aching to kill and to taste the blood of her opponents. She neither heard the next shot that was fired nor felt it as it whistled through the fur on her shoulder, but somersaulted off the top of the fence to arrive, howling with

337

rage, at the side of a large hunter who turned and ran. He made it only a few steps before Kalix descended on him and sank her teeth into the back of his neck, picking him up like a doll, shaking him wildly and flinging his body to the ground. Though he was already dead from the terrible bite she smashed her taloned foot into his body before raising her snout, eager for another victim. She scented more humans nearby and began crashing through the bushes beside the railway fence, oblivious to any thought of danger from the hunters' guns.

As she burst into a clearing she found herself confronted by two more members of the Guild. One of them began to run, but his companion raised his pistol and pointed it directly at the werewolf. Kalix flew through the air and took his arm in her jaws in the brief second before he squeezed the trigger. He yelled in pain as she dragged him to the ground and almost decapitated him with a swipe from her talons. Again, though he was killed instantly, Kalix bit his lifeless corpse and stamped on it cruelly before setting off in pursuit of the other hunter.

Decembrius had by this time reached the top of the bank and clambered over the fence. He couldn't keep up with Kalix and ran desperately in her wake, convinced that he was going to find her bullet-riddled body lying dead in the bushes. He passed her first victim and then her second, and sprinted through the clearing into a small clump of trees where he almost collided with Kalix who was savaging the dead body of a third hunter. Decembrius, who never lost his rationality, looked on in shock as Kalix tore the body to pieces, sending blood splattering over the nearby trees and over her own fur, which was now heavily stained.

At that moment a huge Rottweiler erupted onto the scene. It could have been with the Guild; they did use trained dogs to hunt werewolves. It could have been a stray. Or even a family pet, out in the park to run around. Kalix didn't wait to find out. As the dog advanced she grabbed its foreleg, sank the talons of her other hand into its neck and lifted it into the air. She bit its neck and there was a sickening crunching noise as the bones splintered. Kalix tossed the heavy carcass away without another glance, then looked around eagerly for more victims.

'Enough,' said Decembrius, and reached out to touch her.

Kalix snarled. Her eyes were still dark, burning, and full of madness. She began sniffing around, still growling, looking for another victim.

'This way.' Decembrius tried to lead her deeper into the trees. He was acutely aware that there could still be other hunters around. Even if there were no more members of the Guild, there were sure to be plenty of innocent people in Regent's Park. With Kalix in her present state, Decembrius didn't trust her not to kill anyone she came across. Even though he'd once accompanied the terrifying Sarapen MacRinnalch into battle, Decembrius had never experienced anyone as frighteningly berserk as Kalix. She snarled and growled as he led her on, turning her head this way and that, looking for hunters.

Kalix's tongue was lolling from her mouth, and she opened and closed her great werewolf fangs.

'I think we're safe now,' said Decembrius. 'We should change back and get out of here.' He could see a path nearby; they were almost at the spot where the trees gave way to open parkland. Two joggers went past and Decembrius found himself holding tightly onto Kalix lest she leap out and attack them.

Kalix licked blood from her lips. 'I want more hunters.'

'We should go.' Decembrius tried to pull Kalix along but she lashed out at him. He avoided the blow but, being himself in an agitated state, was unable to control himself completely. He struck out in retaliation, though not fiercely. Kalix swiped his paw out the way and then hit him again. This time the blow connected and Decembrius crashed backwards into a tree. Enraged, he leapt at Kalix and they tumbled to the ground. Decembrius landed on top and his weight pinned her down but he arched himself backwards to avoid having her sink her teeth into his neck. He looked into her maddened eyes. 'We should get out of here,' he repeated.

Abruptly the madness seemed to fade from Kalix's eyes and she transformed back into human. Decembrius did the same, still on top of her. Then, without thinking what he was doing, he kissed her. Kalix immediately kissed him back, quite fiercely.

After a few seconds she thrust him away. 'Don't do that!' she said and lashed out again.

'Stop trying to hit me,' growled Decembrius.

Kalix looked at him with disgust, then leapt to her feet. 'Go and play with the Douglas-MacPhees. You're a traitor. Don't come near me ever again.' With that, she turned and left.

'Hey, I didn't make you kiss me!' called Decembrius, then winced in pain from Kalix's final blow. He couldn't recall having been hit so hard by anyone he'd kissed before. Decembrius grinned. He couldn't smell any other werewolves in the area, and the sounds of battle had long since faded. Apart from the joggers in the distance he seemed to be alone. He composed himself, then set off, heading along the bank, looking for a safe place to cross the railway line. Emerging from the trees he ran straight into a young couple with two children in tow.

'Have you seen our dog?' asked one of the children.

'Your dog?'

'Rexy. He's a Rottweiler. He ran off.'

The family looked at him expectantly.

Decembrius shook his head. 'I didn't pass a dog. Probably best looking in the other direction.'

Decembrius hurried off, not wanting to be in the vicinity if the family found what little remained of their pet after Kalix had torn it to pieces. He scrambled quickly over the fence, down onto the railway line, up the opposite slope and over a wall into the back gardens of a row of terraced houses, then hurried back into the evening streets of Camden.

116

Dithean NicRinnalch, Fairy Queen of Colburn Woods, was waiting for Minerva MacRinnalch when she arrived, though Minerva hadn't warned her she was coming, and hadn't been seen in these parts for many years. The Fairy Queen sat on a branch of a silver birch tree, her dark green apparel standing out in contrast to the pale bark. The ancient werewolf smiled when she saw her.

'I never could catch you unawares.'

Minerva MacRinnalch was very old; she'd known the Fairy Queen's mother, and Dithean's mother had passed on two hundred years ago. Despite her years she showed no signs of frailty. She was still a strong werewolf, though she led a very peaceful life in her retirement.

Minerva remained at her normal size, politely declining the Fairy Queen's offer to make her smaller for the duration of her visit. She looked around at the forest. She'd chosen this spot because she remembered the silver birch trees. Minerva liked the contrast of their pale bark with the darker alders and rowans. Colburn Woods was one of the few untouched remnants of the ancient Caledonian forest that had once covered the whole of Scotland. Dithean fluttered from her branch, perching on the tip of a blaeberry shrub. A bee droned lazily past, but it was used to the fairies and ignored her.

'I can't quite see what my old pupil is doing,' said Minerva.

'Thrix? She rarely visits me these days. Though Queen Malveria does.'

'Really? What for?'

'Some respite from the troubles of being a ruler. And also to learn the secret of my lip colouring.'

'Are you going to tell her?'

'We've made a bet.'

Minerva smiled. 'The fairies always were fond of gambling.'

'As is Malveria. It lends weight to our contention that the Hiyasta are a branch of the fairy line, though Malveria will never admit it.'

'Your legend of the origins of the fire elementals is hardly flattering,' pointed out Minerva. 'A group of fairies who became obsessed with fire, eventually having their wings burned off, then growing large and clumsy.'

'It sounds bad when you put it like that,' agreed Dithean.

'What's your wager?'

'My lip colouring against Malveria's Santorini necklace, depending on whether Thrix MacRinnalch can find a happy relationship.'

'You think she can't?'

Queen Dithean smiled, and curled her wings. 'Do you think she can?'

'I'm not really in touch with such things these days. I won't pass an opinion.'

Dithean laughed. 'You know as well as I do that the Thane's offspring will never be happy.'

Minerva gazed towards the south. 'What has Malveria told you about Thrix?'

'Her business enterprise has money problems.'

Minerva, graceful in her werewolf form under the moonlight, nodded. She had long hair all over her body, as was common for a MacRinnalch werewolf.

'Very odd for a werewolf to be so obsessed by clothes.'

'It's odd for a werewolf to learn sorcery,' pointed out Queen Dithean, 'but you did it hundreds of years ago. And outraged your family, as I remember.'

Minerva laughed. 'I did. As did Thrix. I'm worried about her. Do you know why that might be?'

'I don't think I do. Nothing Queen Malveria said was too worrying.' Queen Dithean's golden hair shone in the moonlight. A badger poked its head out from its set, and stared, fascinated by the sight.

'Malveria did mention that Thrix had a new man in her life.'

'A husband?' asked Minerva, surprised.

'A lover.'

Minerva turned her old, wise eyes towards the south again, and looked down through the valleys and glens of Scotland, past the towns and cities of the lowlands, right into the depths of England, all the way into the heart of London. She nodded. 'I could never understand why Thrix was so keen on living in the city.'

There was a long silence. A family of hedgehogs walked past, three spiky young cubs following their mother.

'I can see trouble coming.'

'Of course,' agreed the Fairy Queen. 'Thrix's relationship will falter, winning me the necklace.'

Minerva frowned. 'Something worse than that, I think.'

117

'I had a terrible time at university today!' exclaimed Daniel. 'Translating Chaucer! In front of other people! I'm still bridling at the memory.'

'You look like you're bridling,' said Moonglow.

'I'm completely bridling. What happened to the modern education system? Haven't we advanced beyond making people translate Chaucer in front of their whole tutorial group? Is this really helping anyone?'

'I assume it went badly?' said Moonglow.

'A disaster. Middle English may not survive the experience. I'm sure my tutor was laughing at me. Is he allowed to do that? Is this pizza ever going to arrive? Am I meant to spend the whole day translating Chaucer and then just starve to death?'

The doorbell rang. Daniel's face brightened, but before he could make it downstairs Kalix appeared, carrying the pizza box.

'I met the delivery boy,' she mumbled.

'OK,' said Daniel. 'Let's have the pizza.'

'Sorry,' said Kalix, and dropped the empty box on the table. 'I was hungry.'

Daniel was staggered by Kalix's treachery. 'You ate the whole thing on the way up the stairs?' Daniel looked to Moonglow for support. 'Kalix ate my pizza!'

'Hungry evening as a werewolf, Kalix?' asked Moonglow.

Kalix nodded.

'I could tell. You always need to eat after you've been a werewolf.'

'What about my pizza?' demanded Daniel. 'I had a hungry day too.'

'Phone for another one.'

Daniel picked up the phone, complaining that it had been cheaper when Kalix just stuck to having an eating disorder, rather than devouring everything in sight.

Kalix said nothing. She didn't intend telling her flatmates anything about the evening's events. She'd learned that it wasn't a good idea to tell them about werewolf battles unless it was really necessary.

Vex appeared in the room, smiling at the world, pleased with her new clothes. She wore a substantial pair of boots that reached her knees, and a short skirt, making her look rather elflike.

'Hi, everyone! Do you like my new boots? Aunt Malvie bought them for me because I got another gold star!'

343

Moonglow smiled, not entirely sincerely. She had an idea that some day there might be a reckoning concerning Malveria, and Vex's alleged gold stars.

'Isn't college great? Hi, Kalix, you're looking cheerful, is it because you kissed Decembrius?'

There was a brief moment of shock.

'I didn't kiss Decembrius.'

'Yes, you did. I can see it in your aura.'

'Didn't I tell you never to read my aura again?'

'I forgot. Do you like my new boots?'

'Did you kiss Decembrius?' asked Moonglow.

'Do I need to order extra pizza?' said Daniel. 'Because I really need a whole one myself. If you're going to start eating more because you've been kissing or something, then let me know now and I'll order extra.'

'I didn't kiss anyone.'

'Apart from Decembrius,' said Vex.

Kalix sighed. Vex was renowned as the worst reader of auras in the Hiyasta nation yet somehow she still managed to come up with the occasional deadly accurate interpretation, usually at the most inappropriate moment.

'All right, I kissed Decembrius. But it's none of your business.'

If Kalix thought she could get away with this in a house shared with three other young students, she was mistaken. Vex wanted details, Daniel wanted details, and even Moonglow wasn't about to ignore such an interesting piece of gossip. Kalix found herself confronted by three eager faces, all wanting to hear more.

'It just sort of happened.'

'Did he grab you?'

'Did you grab him?'

'He fell on top of me.'

'Ah,' said Daniel sagely. 'The old accidental-falling-on-top-of-you technique.'

'So how long did you kiss him for?'

'Only a second. He took me by surprise. I didn't mean to do it. I was confused.'

'What happened after that?'

'I punched him, and told him to go away.'

'It sounds romantic.'

'I don't know if I approve of all this kissing,' declared Vex, to general astonishment. 'We've got exams to think about, and an assignment. We're meant to be studying.'

'You never study at all!'

'I've been doing well in class. But face it, you're not doing so well. I'm just saying this for your own good.'

Kalix threw up her hands in annoyance. If it had come to Agrivex lecturing her about studying her life must have gone severely wrong.

'I'm going to my room,' she said.

'Are you going to study?' Vex looked towards Moonglow. 'Make her study.'

'What happened after Decembrius kissed you and you hit him?' asked Daniel. 'Did he hit you back? Is that a werewolf thing?'

But Kalix had departed, brushing roughly against the cat on the way. The cat, thinking this was a good game, raced after her.

In her room, Kalix had to push it out of the way as she attempted to write in her journal. For some reason the cat liked nothing better than lying on any page that Kalix attempted to write on.

'Decembrius kissed me,' she wrote, slowly, 'and there was a fight with hunters.' She shuddered. Following on from Decembrius's suggestion that she should pretend to be normal in front of other people she'd been bottling up her emotions. When stressed or anxious she took care to hide it from Daniel and Moonglow. It did make her life easier, in some ways. She no longer had to answer questions about her state of mind or listen to well-meaning advice which usually just made her more stressed. But pretending to be normal had disadvantages too. She could feel her emotions pent up inside her, waiting to break out. She'd felt like screaming at Daniel over the pizza, though she knew there was no reason to, and now that feeling had faded it left her anxious again. Kalix absent-mindedly ran her fingernails over the letter N she'd cut in her arm, making it bleed. She watched the blood trickle down, and felt a little better.

*

Downstairs, Moonglow was troubled. She knew Kalix didn't tell them everything that went on in her life as a werewolf.

'I don't think Kalix would have kissed Decembrius without some powerful outside stimulation. Like a fight or something.'

'Who would she be fighting?'

'I'm sure there are still werewolves who are out to get her.'

'Can I kiss you?' said Daniel.

'How did that follow on from what I just said?'

'We were talking about kissing.'

'No, we weren't. Anyway, you'd get sick.'

'What if I wouldn't?'

'But you would.'

'You're avoiding giving me a proper answer,' complained Daniel. He slumped into the couch. 'How did we get cursed anyway? It's uncalled for, in this day and age. I'm going to listen to music.'

'Don't play it too loud.'

'And you keep complaining about my music. Life is hell.' Daniel went upstairs to sulk, and listen to music through headphones.

118

Decembrius hurried to the twins' house in Camden, looking for Dominil. He told her about events in the park, including the notable piece of news that Red Ruraich had been shot. Decembrius didn't know if he'd been killed or not. It was grave news, anyway. Ruraich was head of the MacAndrises, and though they were small in numbers they were an ancient werewolf clan. Ruraich was known to everybody.

'We seem to be losing to the Guild,' said Dominil.

'I wouldn't say that.' Decembrius grinned. 'They don't have as many hunters as they used to. Thanks mainly to Kalix.'

'She killed a hunter?'

'Three, I think. She's quite a savage when she gets going.'

From Decembrius's tone, Dominil sensed that he rather admired Kalix's display of savagery. That wasn't unusual for a

MacRinnalch. No werewolf would ever be unpopular among the clan for killing the hated hunters.

Dominil called Thrix, who called the castle, spreading the news. The Mistress of the Werewolves was deeply shocked. Once more she wished that the werewolves in London would return to the castle. At least they'd all be in Scotland in a fortnight, for her fundraising event, or the Yum Yum Sugary Snacks gig.

Markus was in Edinburgh, attending to the preparations at Andamair House. When he received a call from his mother, he immediately arranged to return to the castle. As Thane, he needed to be at Castle MacRinnalch to reassure the clan once news of Red Ruraich became known.

He felt sorry to be leaving Heather MacAllister. She was a designer, not long out of Edinburgh University, a member of the MacAllister werewolf clan, currently employed on the renovations. She was a pretty werewolf, dark-haired, quite petite. Markus had begun an affair with her a week or so ago. He hadn't really intended to, but had fallen into it after they'd both been working late. They'd planned to drive back to Edinburgh separately but had been delayed by a thick fog rolling in from the sea. The fog, called haar by the local inhabitants and not uncommon in the area, blanketed the region, making driving impossible. Finding themselves stranded in Andamair House for the night, it hadn't taken much for Markus and Heather to get together.

Possibly it hadn't been the wisest thing to do. The Mistress of the Werewolves would not be pleased to find her son dating two werewolves at the same time. Baron MacAllister might be offended too, if he learned of it. Heather was his grand-niece, and he took an interest in her career.

Before returning to the castle, Markus posted money to Dominil for the hunters she'd killed, as arranged. While his mother and the Barons' natural reaction was to withdraw from the south altogether, Markus rather wished that he could go there himself. Markus wasn't the strongest werewolf in the clan, but he was a spirited fighter and hated the hunters as much as anyone. He'd welcome the opportunity to fight them. But the Thane couldn't just abandon his duties to fight on the streets of London.

He wondered why more werewolves around the castle didn't do just that. Those without family or work responsibilities could go to London and help fight the Guild. Few did so. The clan had grown used to keeping its true nature quiet. Most MacRinnalchs wanted nothing more than to grow up and live near their place of birth, and to be left alone. Perhaps that was a failing, mused Markus. No MacRinnalch believed that the Avenaris Guild could ever trouble them in their Scottish stronghold, but what if they were wrong? If the Guild were to grow in strength, and gain confidence through victories in London, who knew what might happen? Perhaps one day the MacRinnalchs would find the Guild on their doorstep.

In London, at the twins' house, Decembrius felt suddenly weary as his exertions caught up with him. Dominil offered him the use of one of the spare rooms. Before retiring he asked her about Kalix.

'What about her?'

'She isn't getting anywhere with Gawain. Finding his killer, I mean.'

'So?'

'I thought you might have a suggestion.'

'I suggest you help her to pass her exam,' said Dominil. 'That would be a more worthwhile way of spending your time.'

'I don't think Kalix would see it like that.'

'Probably not.' Dominil stared at Decembrius with her deep black eyes. It was unsettling. 'Do you care who killed Gawain? Or are you just trying to impress Kalix?'

Decembrius didn't reply.

'I take it your powers of perception haven't returned?'

'How did you know they'd gone?'

'It was obvious.'

Decembrius felt deflated, and abandoned the conversation. He didn't like Dominil and couldn't imagine why he'd thought it worthwhile to ask her anything about Kalix.

Dominil left him to sleep, feeling slightly relieved that Decembrius's powers of seeing showed no sign of returning. If he learned about Gawain's death, and told Kalix, there would be trouble.

119

'Isn't this fun?' enthused Vex.

Kalix didn't reply. They were on their way to college to take a test in preparation for the upcoming exam. The young werewolf couldn't imagine anything less fun. Moonglow kept insisting there was nothing to worry about. Kalix gritted her teeth, and swore that if Moonglow tried to reassure her one more time she'd leap out of the car and walk there herself. When Daniel pulled up at the kerb she fled the vehicle as quickly as she could. Behind her, Vex was assuring Daniel and Moonglow that everything was going to go well.

'I have new pencils and everything!' she said cheerfully, 'and a new yellow marker and a *Tokyo Top Pop Boom Boom Girl* mouse mat!'

'Good luck,' said Daniel and Moonglow.

Vex hurried after Kalix, but as she rounded the old stone gate at the front of the college she almost ran into two girls who were finishing off their cigarettes before going inside. Vex tried to duck past them unnoticed. She was unsuccessful. The larger of the two grabbed her arm.

'Look. It's Spiky Hair.'

Vex's spiky bleached hair had already elicited disparaging comments from the pair. Vex didn't know what they did at the college, but for some reason they didn't seem to take to her.

'What's this?' demanded the smaller of the two, who wore a tracksuit and some pieces of gold jewellery. She grabbed the music player that dangled from Vex's neck. It was a cheap player, very out of date. The girls laughed.

'Let go of it,' said Vex.

'Didn't we tell you not to bother us again?'

'I wasn't bothering you.'

'Yes, you were.'

Vex tried to pull away but she lacked the strength, and the two girls held her tight while removing her music player. Vex, having no idea why she was being bullied, didn't know what to do. She asked the girls to let go of her again but they just laughed again.

'I don't like your hair.'

Vex started to choke as the larger girl increased the pressure of her grip. They were interrupted by a menacing growl, a sound that didn't seem like it should have come from the lips of the skinny girl who appeared beside them.

'Let her go,' said Kalix.

The girls laughed some more. The larger one swung a lazy slap at her, which Kalix nimbly avoided. She looked at Vex.

'Has this happened before?'

Vex looked uncomfortable. 'A few times. It's OK.'

Kalix grabbed the larger girl's wrist and twisted it. She yelped in pain. Kalix let go and then slapped the girl hard across the face. The force of the blow sent her crashing to the ground.

Her friend looked on in alarm and took a step back. 'Don't hit me.'

Kalix hit her, as hard as she'd hit her friend. She tumbled to the ground, with blood coming from her lip. Kalix reached down and retrieved Vex's music player. Not yet satisfied, she tore the large girl's own music player from her neck. She dropped it on the ground and stamped on it. The player shattered into small pieces under her boot. Kalix seemed to enjoy the destruction, and aimed a kick into the smaller girl's ribs. This time she screamed in pain. Kalix raised her foot again.

'OK, let's go,' said Vex, and grabbed hold of Kalix to drag her away before she did anything worse. Kalix looked back as she was being led away, and shouted at the girls on the ground.

'If you bother Vex again I'll kill you.'

Vex hurried them into the building.

'Why didn't you tell me you were being bullied?'

'I didn't want to worry anyone.'

'It's not a worry. If anyone picks on you again, tell me. I'll sort it out.'

They walked into their exam. The physical confrontation, though minor by Kalix's standards, had a beneficial effect on her mental state, calming her down. When the papers arrived on her desk she wasn't quite as agitated as she might have been.

I'm not going to fail this test, thought Kalix, logging on to her personal page on the computer. I'm going to think positively like Moonglow suggested, and I'm going to pass.

She clicked the mouse, bringing up the first question.

To be answered in ten seconds – *Add £1.20 to £2.78.*

Kalix's palms began to sweat. I was wrong, she thought. I'm not going to answer a single question and I'm going to fail. She reached nervously beneath her sleeve to scratch her arm, irritating the wound and making a little blood flow.

120

The Fire Queen had not anticipated enjoying her evening's entertainment and her judgement proved to be sound. Young Countess Rechen-Gaval, who had only just inherited her title, was far too full of herself for the Queen's liking, and dangerously well dressed. Her cocktail dress was a vibrant red, sculpted quite simply, and reminded Malveria of something she'd admired in this month's issue of *Elle*. The Countess had accessorised it with a pair of shoes by Missoni and a silk belt. The whole outfit was extremely stylish. Malveria recalled with regret that Thrix had advised her that belts were being worn with cocktail dresses this season. Malveria had rejected Thrix's advice. Gazing at the Countess, she realised she'd made a mistake.

It quite put Malveria off the refreshments. Her mood brightened a little when Beau DeMortalis arrived and complimented her clothes and beauty, but before the Queen could fully appreciate it, the Countess appeared. She somehow managed to drape herself over the Duke and lead him away on the pretence of needing advice at the card table.

'As I suspected,' said Malveria to her friend Duchess Gargamond. 'The new Countess is a shameless trollop, much as her mother was.'

Gargamond was eager to play whist at the card tables in the next room.

'Must we?' sighed the Queen. 'Kabachetka will be there. I can feel a headache coming on already.'

'Come on, Malveria,' said the Duchess, and actually clapped Malveria on the shoulder, something that very few elementals would have been allowed to do. 'We'll show these youngsters what we're made of.'

Malveria winced, not liking the implication that she herself might be anything but young. She followed the Duchess into the card room, fearing the worst. Her spies had told her that Kabachetka had been studying assiduously with a new card-master and, while the Princess was undoubtedly a stupid woman, there was no telling how her game might have improved.

The Queen settled down reasonably comfortably with her partner for a game of whist with the Sorceress Livia and Lady Esuvius, neither of whom were likely to do anything to upset her. She noticed Distikka sitting with Princess Kabachetka at the far end of the room, and was pleased. She'd asked Distikka to keep Kabachetka away from her for as long as possible and her Personal Adviser, efficient as always, was doing just that.

121

Kalix stood outside her front door in the rain, reflecting gloomily on her latest failure at college. The drain at the side of the road was blocked, as it often was, causing a pool of water to lap onto the pavement. The pavement itself was cracked and broken, with some of the old paving stones starting to sink, producing uneven ridges which could trip an unwary pedestrian. Along with the boarded-up shopfront, it all made for a depressing sight. Kalix sighed as the rain flattened her hair, allowing her odd wolflike ears to show through. After a long delay, she slid her key into the lock, desperately hoping there was no one home. She didn't want to talk about her test. She crept quietly upstairs and sneaked into the living room.

'Kalix! How did the test go?'

'Daniel!' cried Moonglow. 'I told you not to ask Kalix about it.'

'Sorry.'

'You're so tactless. Kalix won't want to talk about it in case it went badly. Though I'm sure it went well. How did it go?'

'Badly,' said Kalix.

'Oh.'

'I failed.'

'You got the results already?'

'No. But I know I failed anyway.'

Moonglow tried to be reassuring. 'You probably did better than you imagine.'

'I failed.'

'How can you be sure?'

'Because I panicked and ran out the room again.'

There was a silence, broken only by the dull hissing of the old gas fire.

'Did you answer many questions before fleeing?'

'I didn't even write my name.'

'It sounds like a quick exit.'

'It might be a new record,' muttered Kalix. 'I'll have to check later.' She dropped her bag of books on the floor and slumped onto the couch, looking so small and pathetic that Moonglow was almost moved to tears.

'It started well. Vex was being bullied.'

'What?'

Kalix told them about the two girls who'd harassed Vex. When she described how she'd battered them to the ground, Moonglow looked shocked. Knocking people down wasn't Moonglow's idea of the right thing to do. Daniel, however, was enthusiastic. Knocking down bullies was exactly the right thing to do in his eyes.

'I wish you'd been around at my school,' he said. 'There's a few people I'd like to have seen beaten senseless.'

'Well, that was a bad start to the day,' said Moonglow.

'No, it wasn't. It was a good start for me. Fighting usually makes me feel better. I felt fine till I opened up the test. Then I panicked. The room started spinning and I couldn't breathe and I just ran out.' Kalix slumped even lower on the couch. 'Now I'll have to leave college and everything's ruined.'

Moonglow wasn't about to let this level of negativity pass unchecked. 'Nonsense. Everything will be fine. Daniel, make tea while I talk to Kalix.'

Daniel departed to make tea.

'It was just a test to get you ready for your exam. You can still pass that. If you're having such problems with anxiety, the college will understand. We'll talk to them. Maybe they'll let you retake the test.'

Kalix was resolute in her misery and wouldn't be comforted. A few minutes later, as she sipped the tea supplied by Daniel, she admitted that it wasn't just her failure at the exam that was making her unhappy.

'I feel bad about Vex too, being bullied. She said it had happened before. It must have been going on and I didn't even notice it.'

'But you helped her today.'

'I should have helped her before. You know what Vex is like. She can't protect herself.' The young werewolf sighed. 'I shouldn't have let her be bullied.' At this, Kalix seemed to shrivel into a small ball of misery and self-loathing, leaving even the determinedly positive Moonglow lost for words. 'I thought I could find out who killed Gawain and I've no idea how to do it. I ask questions and everyone just ignores me. I thought I could go to college like a normal person and I can't do that either. I can't pass a simple test and I couldn't even look after Vex against two stupid bullies.'

Kalix rose to her feet and walked slowly towards her bedroom, leaving Daniel and Moonglow baffled about what they might say or do to make things better. Even the certain knowledge that Kalix would now be taking laudanum couldn't induce Moonglow into action, because she really didn't know what to say.

122

Despite the deficiencies of her partner, the Fire Queen fared moderately well at the card table for most of the evening, but it all went wrong when she was finally matched against Princess Kabachetka. Distikka had done an excellent job of keeping them apart, engaging Kabachetka in a lengthy conversation for most of the evening, but finally the blow struck. After the standard rotation at the tables, Malveria found herself sitting opposite the hated Princess. They smiled at each other politely.

'I so enjoyed your Fire Festival,' said the Princess.

'You are my most honoured guest.'

'My mother deeply regrets she was unable to attend.'

'Her presence has been sorely missed.'

The Fire Queen and the Princess gazed at each other with loathing, each taking care not to let it show in either their expression or their aura. The Princess's partner, a Lady Tecton, was unknown to the Fire Queen. Malveria regarded her with suspicion. It was unusual for Kabachetka to appear with an unknown partner. Usually she would associate with only the most fashionable Hainusta.

'I do admire your cocktail dress,' said Kabachetka to Malveria, 'though we are mostly wearing them with belts this season. You were perhaps wise to resist the change. The current fashion would not necessarily suit you.'

Malveria bridled, but said nothing. Play began, with the Duchess Gargamond immediately plunging her team into trouble by an over-ambitious attempt to win a trick. Kabachetka's partner, Lady Tecton, scooped up the hand.

'I am very much looking forward to the operatic event at Andamair House,' said Princess Kabachetka.

'As am I,' responded Malveria.

'I'm delighted that you eventually managed to secure an invitation. When I myself was invited in the first rank of guests, I was quite worried that you had not been thought of. Is that another round to us? Well played, Lady Tecton.'

Malveria tapped her foot in irritation as their opponents' points mounted up. Gargamond was playing worse than ever, and Malveria was put off her game by the dreadful error she'd made in wearing a beltless cocktail dress. Kabachetka had out-styled her, and it was her own fault for rejecting Thrix's advice. She pulled herself together, and concentrated on her cards.

'Your Abukenti bag has proved a great hit this season,' said the Princess, as her partner dealt.

'Really,' said the Queen nonchalantly.

'It was a great coup for you to secure such a fabulous item so early.'

'Thank you.'

'I suppose Abukenti's anniversary shoes will be the next item to really attract attention.'

Malveria felt herself going cold, not liking the way the conversation was going. Why had Kabachetka mentioned the Abukenti shoes?'

'It will be a while before they're attainable,' Malveria said cautiously.

'To some people, no doubt,' said the Princess, and smiled at the Queen. 'But for others, they may arrive early.'

Malveria gritted her teeth. 'Really?'

'So I understand. Is that another hand to us? My goodness, Lady Tecton, you *are* playing well. We seem to be well ahead on points.'

Malveria's playing went steadily downhill, beset as she was with worries over her dress and the dreadful prospect of Princess Kabachetka securing a pair of Abukenti shoes before her. The Princess had clearly been hinting at just that and it put Malveria completely off her game. With the Duchess Gargamond making her customary series of errors, and Lady Tecton apparently being the finest card player ever to emerge from the Hainusta nation, the outcome was inevitable. Malveria plummeted to a heavy defeat, losing by a margin rarely seen. The Queen was sure that people at neighbouring tables had stopped their own games to watch hers, and she felt the room go silent as the game ended. She rose to her feet and smiled at the Princess.

'Such an entertaining match, Princess Kabachetka and Lady Tecton. You quite had the better of us.'

'We do appear to have won,' agreed the Princess. 'No doubt you'll have better fortune next time. I look forward to seeing you at the operatic event.'

'I look forward to seeing you, too. Duchess Gargamond, shall we take a walk in the garden for a little air?'

123

'Is it possible we're not as smart as we think we are?'

The Enchantress's question caught Dominil by surprise. Dominil was not prone to announcing her intelligence to the world, but nor was she about to admit to any lack of it.

'Why do you ask that?'

'Well, let's see,' said Thrix. 'Using my sorcery and your computer skills, we've spent the entire day searching for Albermarle, the Guild, Susi Surmata and a pair of exclusive shoes. And what have we discovered? Nothing. Not a trace. Hunters and bloggers are nowhere to be found.'

Thrix passed her hand across her forehead and for a moment looked seriously concerned. She'd taken Dominil into her confidence regarding the poor state of her financial affairs and the importance of finding Susi Surmata. Dominil had found it difficult to accept that a single review from a fashion writer, no matter how popular, would make such a difference, but Thrix assured her that it would. Consequently, she was attempting to help Thrix locate the mysterious Susi. In return, Thrix was trying to find Albermarle.

'The Guild's much better hidden than it used to be. Electronically speaking, I mean,' explained Dominil. 'Albermarle's work, I presume.'

'They've got some sorcerous way of hiding their location, too. Unless it's just that my powers have waned. Which is possible.' Thrix closed the book she was holding, an elderly tome printed in a very old typeface, hardly legible in places. 'Maybe I can find something useful at the castle. Minerva donated some of her work to the library there. I haven't looked at it for a long time.' Thrix looked troubled. 'Maybe I've neglected my sorcery in pursuit of fashion.'

'This is no time for maudlin introspection,' said Dominil, sternly. 'Everywhere werewolves go in London, Albermarle seems to know about it. I need to know how he's doing it.'

'Beauty and Delicious talking out of turn, perhaps? Or Kalix? None of them are exactly security conscious.'

'Albermarle has found out things they couldn't know. My latest phone number, for instance, which I took care to obtain under a false name. I gave it to no one but you and the Mistress of the Werewolves. Within twelve hours Albermarle was sending me messages.'

Thrix's spacious living room was a little messier than usual, with Dominil's two laptop computers on the table and a batch of papers strewn around them. Here at least, under the sorcerously protected roof of the Enchantress, they were safe from prying eyes.

'I wish I could find out who's getting these Abukenti shoes,' sighed Thrix. 'A pair of those would really cheer me up.'

'I hardly think they're of the same importance as our other concerns.'

'Don't you ever go weak at the thought of a great pair of heels, Dominil? Sorry, foolish question. OK, let's get back to the serious stuff.'

The Fire Queen exploded into existence in the middle of the room. 'Enchantress! My cocktail dress is very inferior!'

Thrix pursed her lips. 'The serious stuff may have to wait . . .'

Malveria's dramatic appearance flooded the room with yellow light and the powerful aroma of jasmine. She confronted the Enchantress, standing inches away from her with her hands on her hips. Tiny flames shot from her fingertips. 'Your poor fashion advice has caused me to lose concentration at the card table, leading to shame and mortification at the hands of the appalling Kabachetka!'

'Malveria, what are you talking about?'

'Did I not explain it all most clearly? The beltless cocktail dress you supplied me with has brought me to the brink of ruin!'

'I told you belts were fashionable with cocktail dresses this season.'

'That is not how I recall the matter,' sniffed Malveria, and folded her arms. 'I believe you've been so busy with Easterly you've been neglecting me.'

'That's not true.'

'It is. Dominil! How pleasant to see you. Would you pass that wine in my direction? All the most fashionable ladies were wearing belted cocktail dresses.'

'I told you that you needed a belt. You rejected it.'

'A proper fashion adviser would not have let me reject it.' Malveria sat down heavily in an armchair. 'The whole thing quite befuddled my mind, leading to disastrous play at the card table, made worse by the dreadful Duchess Gargamond. Kabachetka utterly vanquished us.' She shuddered at the memory. 'Afterwards I was so enraged I spoke very harshly to the Duchess. As a result she has withdrawn from the season at the palace and gone home to her castle to sulk, taking her regiment with her.'

'Her regiment? Isn't that the imperial volcano guard?'

'Pah! I would not trust the Duchess's regiment to guard a small fire. The volcano will be fine till I appoint a replacement. But Enchantress, I have not even told you the worst of the news. Kabachetka hinted strongly that she may be about to procure the Abukenti shoes!'

'What? That's impossible.'

'You underestimate the loathsome cunning of the woman. There's every danger that we'll walk into the operatic charity event and find ourselves completely out-shoed.'

Thrix screwed up her face. 'Mother's managed to persuade a lot of fashion-magazine people to attend. If Kabachetka turns up wearing the only Abukenti shoes in the place . . .'

Malveria wailed. 'We shall be eclipsed. Really, Enchantress, if Kabachetka is photographed for the "Fashionable Party People" page, I shall simply *die*.' She took a large gulp from her wine glass. 'There is no end to the woman's crimes. She maliciously recruited a card partner whose play put ours to shame. Already it will be the talk of the palace. Even now, Beau DeMortalis is probably regaling all and sundry with humorous anecdotes about my discomfort.'

'In case everyone has forgotten,' interrupted Dominil, 'we were looking for information about the Guild. We've just had an extremely serious incident. Ruraich MacAndris was shot, and Kalix killed three hunters.'

'Kalix is always killing hunters,' said Malveria. 'It keeps her happy. Incidentally, did you know she kissed Decembrius?'

Dominil's face muscles twitched at the total irrelevance of this.

Thrix, however, was interested. 'Are you sure?'

'So I am reliably informed. One is not wholly surprised. They were last seen fighting, but such strife may often lead to passion. I have experienced such a thing myself. Enchantress, do you think there is any chance of Kalix and Decembrius forming some sort of happy relationship?'

'I've no idea. Why?'

'Idle curiosity,' replied Malveria. 'Do *you* have a boyfriend, Dominil?'

'I have a stalker. Does that count?'

'Might he become a boyfriend?'

'It's not very likely.'

'I understood a young guitarist had expressed an interest?'

Dominil looked pained to learn that the Fire Queen somehow knew about that.

'His interest is unwelcome.'

Malveria looked disappointed. 'Well, Thrix, I trust at least that your affair with Easterly is progressing well?'

'Quite well.' Thrix was puzzled. 'Why are you suddenly interested in the love lives of the MacRinnalch werewolves?'

'No reason. It's not like anyone suspects you of being too self-obsessed to ever be happy. And if they did, I would certainly not agree.'

'Could we get back to thinking about Albermarle?' asked Dominil.

'Of course,' said Thrix. 'Right after Malveria has told me everything she knows about Kabachetka and the shoes.'

Dominil regretted, as she had before, that such a senior and powerful werewolf as Thrix appeared to be interested only in clothes, while all around them were werewolf hunters who, as far as Dominil could see, were currently in the ascendant.

124

Of all the dramatic and emotional scenes that had played out at Daniel and Moonglow's flat since they first encountered Kalix, none was so loud, vociferous and full of outrage as Vex's reaction to Queen Malveria's refusal to let her travel to Edinburgh to see Yum Yum Sugary Snacks. Vex was staggered by her aunt's intransigence, an act of treachery so overwhelming that she could barely come to terms with it.

'What do you mean, I can't go and see them play? I *have* to.'

'You are not going, dismal niece. You need to remain here and study for your exam.'

'But I *have* to see them play! Yum Yum Sugary Snacks are the best thing ever!'

'It's out of the question.' The Fire Queen, still smarting after her humiliation at the card table and disastrous choice of cocktail dress, was in no mood to placate her not-quite-adopted niece. 'The whole idea is preposterous. I sent you to this dimension to improve your notoriously feeble mind. You will not miss classes in order to gallivant off to some concert by a werewolf band in Edinburgh.'

'But it's only one night! I can still study.'

'Edinburgh is many hundreds of miles from here. The journey would take some time, and you need that time for study.'

'Couldn't she teleport?' suggested Daniel, who, while not wishing to find himself on the wrong side of Malveria's wrath, nonetheless sympathised with Vex. For Daniel, not being able to see a favourite band would also have been a severe blow.

'Teleport? My niece? Agrivex cannot teleport more than half a mile without becoming lost, and bruising herself in the process. She only makes it to this dimension because I have illuminated a path for her. Were she to attempt to transport herself to Edinburgh we would never see her again.'

Vex pushed out her lips, knowing this was true but not willing to admit defeat. '*You* could take me. You're going to Edinburgh for the opera at the same time.'

'Out of the question, dreadful niece. I will be engaged in important matters of fashion and do not want to be dragging along the scruffiest Hiyasta ever to plague the land of the elementals.'

'I won't cause any trouble,' pleaded Vex. 'Once we're there you won't even see me! I'll just go to the gig!'

'Impossible. I will be there for several days and could not transport you back.'

'It's not fair!' roared Vex. 'I want to go!'

'You cannot. And that is the end of the matter.'

'But I've been studying hard! Look at all my gold stars!'

Vex held up one of her exercise books, which was, as she claimed, covered in gold stars.

Malveria frowned, and wondered, not for the first time, if Agrivex's progress at college was quite as spectacular as she claimed. She noticed that both Moonglow and Daniel looked rather uncomfortable as Vex brandished the book.

'You may be the finest student at the institute of learning,' said Malveria, 'though I admit to some doubts. However, it matters not. Missing several days' study, when your exam is imminent, is out of the question. That is my final word on the matter.'

'I hate you!' roared the young fire elemental, and as she did so a small flame flickered from her eye. 'Ow! I burned myself.'

Malveria shook her head in frustration and snapped her fingers, extinguishing the flame. 'Did I not instruct you not to do that?' The Queen looked at Moonglow. 'My niece is the only fire elemental yet known who is prone to burning herself.'

'I didn't even know she could ignite,' said Moonglow.

'Her dramatic lack of power and control makes it unsafe for her to do so in this dimension.'

'Changing the topic slightly . . . About this curse . . .' ventured Daniel.

'Curse? What curse?'

'The curse on Moonglow and me. Isn't it time to let it go?'

Daniel had picked a poor time to make his appeal. Already angry, Malveria stared at him frostily and dismissed his application with a curt shake of her head.

'But it's completely unfair! I wasn't even consulted!'

Malveria adopted an imperious expression, the sort she might use on the throne when displeased with her council.

'Had the bargain not been struck, young human, Kalix would be dead. Would you have preferred that?'

Daniel attempted to look defiant. 'You had no right to curse me when I didn't know anything about it.'

Malveria swivelled towards Moonglow. Moonglow was dressed in black as always, something the Queen, who loved colour, could never quite fathom. 'What about you, Moonglow? Would you wish that our bargain had never been struck?'

Moonglow sagged. She didn't want to answer. She lifted her palms a few inches, looked hopeless, and told them no, she wouldn't have wished that. 'I couldn't just let Kalix die.'

'And that,' declared Malveria triumphantly, 'is the end of the affair. As I have already explained, I could not extend such power in helping a werewolf without exacting a price. My peers would

362

have mocked me otherwise. The bargain was fair, and the curse will not be removed. Now, Agrivex, attend to your studies and do not dare to go to Edinburgh. If you disobey me, the consequences will be dire.'

With that, Malveria dematerialised, leaving behind a depressed Daniel and a furious Vex.

'I'm going to the gig anyway,' she declared. 'See if she can stop me.'

'How could you get there?' asked Daniel.

It was a reasonable question. Vex lacked the necessary power and skill to teleport 330 miles north to Edinburgh, and she had no money to pay the train fare. Every spare penny in the house, belonging to either Vex, Kalix, Moonglow or Daniel, was currently tucked away in a series of envelopes in Moonglow's room, ready to pay off the crippling household debts.

'I'll get a lift in the band's van! I can be a roadie.' Vex was advancing towards the phone, ready to call Dominil, when another flash of light brought Malveria back into the room.

'One more thing, most dismal of nieces. Do not attempt to travel with the band. I've informed Dominil that you are not to go, as you are busy studying. Dominil approves of my decision. Now farewell.' Malveria vanished.

Vex scowled, and sat down heavily on the old sofa. 'This really sucks,' she said. 'I hate everything.'

125

At the headquarters of the Avenaris Guild, Mr Carmichael was fending off complaints from irate werewolf hunters.

'Why has my expense claim been rejected?'

'Since when do we have to fill out Form 226a in triplicate?'

'They're asking me to pay back £2,000!'

'How am I meant to keep track of every penny when I'm out hunting werewolves?'

Mr Carmichael, who believed that a calm centre of operations was important for a successful operation, did his best to mollify his senior hunters.

'There have been some problems with our new financial structure. I've taken steps to improve matters.'

'You mean you've sacked Albermarle?' Everyone knew that Albermarle had been responsible for the rigorous policing of expense claims.

'We've moved him to another position,' said Mr Carmichael, smoothly. 'He's engaged in field operations now.'

This caused some consternation among the assembled hunters.

'Couldn't you have just moved him into another office post? The man's an idiot but there's no need to kill him.'

'Albermarle passed our tests and asked for the transfer,' said Mr Carmichael. 'I'm sure he'll perform satisfactorily. Easterly is there to take care of things.'

'Poor Easterly, having to take care of that fool.'

Albermarle hadn't turned up to his strategy meeting with Captain Easterly this evening. Easterly didn't really care. There was no talking to Albermarle. He'd all but abandoned trying to look after him. He was far more concerned with his date tonight with Thrix MacRinnalch. Yesterday he'd talked with Princess Kabachetka and had once more asked her to boost the sorcery that enabled him to see Thrix for what she was. The Princess had warned him again that he was endangering his life.

'Too much fire may burn you out, Easterly.'

Easterly deemed it to be worth the risk. The destruction of Thrix would surely be the greatest achievement in the history of the Guild.

'Are you still planning to travel to Edinburgh?'

Easterly wasn't certain. Last time they'd talked, Thrix seemed to have gone off the idea. 'She says she's not so keen for me to meet her family again.'

The Princess laughed. 'No doubt. You must increase your efforts at wooing her, Captain Easterly. My spell will be ready by then, and I'll need you close at hand to kill her.'

Easterly nodded.

The Princess studied his aura. She frowned. There was something about it she didn't like. 'Do I sense a lack of enthusiasm for killing her?'

'I'll do it. You don't need to worry about that.'

The Princess's eyes narrowed. 'Be sure that you do.' She examined his aura suspiciously. To her annoyance, Easterly still showed no sign of falling in love with her, which she took as a great insult.

Captain Easterly was pleased to hear Thrix's voice when she called, but was disappointed to hear her cancelling their date.

'I'm sorry, I've had too bad a day. I'm late and I'm tired and I'm going home. Would you mind cancelling the table?'

The Enchantress was worn out after her abortive attempts to locate either Albermarle or Susi Surmata. She was also depressed after reading the latest financial figures for her company. Shops just weren't buying her clothes and she barely had enough money left to keep paying her employees. If things went on like this, her fashion house would go bankrupt. She drove back to her apartment trying to come up with a solution, but couldn't see a way out of the situation.

At his office, Easterly mused for a while. Thrix had said she wanted to be alone. That might mean it was a good time to leave her alone. Or it might mean it was a time for a lover to make a bold move. He decided on the bold move. He threw on a suit, put a bottle of wine in a bag, hurried downstairs to the garage and drove towards Thrix's apartment. They'd booked a table at an expensive restaurant and while he couldn't entirely make up for missing that, he intended to arrive with something.

When Thrix got home she was astonished to find Easterly waiting on the doorstep with several plastic bags.

'Chinese takeaway,' he explained. 'It's the best I could find in a hurry.' He produced a small, rather crumpled flower. 'I took this off a jar on the table.'

Finding Easterly on her doorstep with food and a flower, even though she'd quite rudely cancelled their date, had a powerful effect on Thrix. Her eyes welled up with tears, something that very rarely happened. She embraced him quite tenderly, on the pavement, before leading him upstairs to her apartment. She suddenly thought she might be falling in love.

126

Kalix emerged from the bath and studied her naked figure in the mirror. Though her exertions as a werewolf had recently caused her to eat more, it didn't seem to have affected her. She was still as skinny as ever. Her ribs were clearly visible. Her eyes were a little more sunken, the flesh around them a little greyer, probably from her increased intake of laudanum after another visit to Merchant MacDoig's shop. Her skin had a slightly unhealthy yellowish tone. Her neck and shoulders were badly scratched, remnants of her fight in the park. There were fresh cuts, high up on her arms, self-inflicted, and more on her thighs. Surrounding these cuts were the thin white marks of older scars.

Kalix was not yet eighteen. From a distance she looked younger: close up, she looked more worn than a seventeen-year-old should.

'I'm a mess,' she muttered, but she didn't care. She shivered. There was a small electric heater mounted high up on the bathroom wall but it had never worked. Kalix wrapped herself in the old dressing gown that hung behind the door and trailed water between the bathroom and her bedroom where she began the long process of drying her hair. She fiddled with her nose ring, and felt some anxiety about Decembrius, who was due to arrive soon to help her study.

On the small table lay a piece of paper, printed very clearly in Moonglow's hand. It was a list of the money that Kalix owed for household bills. Moonglow had given an identical piece of paper to each of them. Kalix, Vex and Daniel had accepted them gloomily, and wondered how they were going to pay. According to Moonglow they were only a few days from having their phone and heating cut off.

When Decembrius arrived Moonglow let him in and directed him to Kalix's room.

'It's a werewolf study party,' she said to Daniel. 'Isn't that cute?' She stopped, and looked concerned. 'Do you think he's going to try and fall on her again?'

'Why would he do that?'

'Maybe it's his way of making advances.'

Daniel doubted it. Decembrius gave the impression of being a confident werewolf, one who was unlikely to resort to such subterfuge. 'I don't think he'd pretend to fall on Kalix twice. Think how suspicious it would look.'

Moonglow continued to worry. 'Should I check on them?'

'You're making the mistake of thinking Kalix is twelve years old, and you're her parent. You're not. Leave them alone.'

Upstairs, Kalix greeted Decembrius without any show of pleasure.

'Don't try kissing me again.'

'Why would I want to? You think I'm short of girlfriends?'

'Then go visit them.'

'You asked me to come and help you.'

'No, I didn't. You wanted to come.'

'No, I didn't. I just came because Dominil suggested it.'

They eyed each other with dislike. Kalix thrust a few papers at Decembrius. 'This is what I'm meant to be learning.'

Decembrius looked at the papers. None of it seemed too difficult. He couldn't see why Kalix was having such trouble.

'Let's make a start,' he suggested.

'Is Ruraich dead?'

'Yes.'

'I wonder how the hunters found us?'

'Who knows? Let's study. None of this arithmetic is very hard, you can do it.'

Kalix didn't seem keen to start. 'It's strange the way the hunters seem to find us more easily these days. Why is that?'

'Are you going to study or not?'

'We should kill them all. And their dogs.'

'Right. Maybe after you've passed your exam. And that dog you killed wasn't a hunting dog, it was a family pet.'

'How do you know?'

'I met the family.'

Kalix shrugged. 'I hate dogs. And sharks.'

'Sharks? What do sharks have to do with anything?'

'I saw them on TV. I don't like them.'

Decembrius felt exasperated. 'Well, if we meet any sharks I'll

367

bear it in mind. Meanwhile, are you going to look at this test paper?'

'I could beat a shark,' said Kalix.

'Let's look at some fractions.'

'If you try and kiss me again there's going to be trouble.'

'I wouldn't kiss you if you were the last werewolf on the planet.'

'Good. I wouldn't let you, anyway.'

'Fine. As long as we're clear.'

'And you should shave,' said Kalix, looking at the stubble on Decembrius's chin. 'You look stupid like that.'

Decembrius scowled. 'Do you want to do these fractions or not?'

'No.'

'Well, we're going to, anyway.' Decembrius opened the book and sat down.

Kalix leaned over and closed the book. 'I need you to help me. Not with studying. With Gawain.'

'Gawain?'

'I need to know who killed him. But I don't know how to investigate properly. Everyone just denies everything.'

'You want me to visit some people with you?'

'No. It won't get me anywhere. I need you to see something. You've got powers, right? You can see things that are hidden? That's what people say.'

'It's not easy . . . I don't really have much control over it.'

'You could try.' Kalix looked into Decembrius's eyes, and seemed very earnest.

Decembrius was about to lie but abandoned it abruptly. 'I can't. My powers disappeared months ago. They don't work any more.'

'But you had a vision . . . you said you saw everyone dead.'

'That was a one-off. I've no control over it.' He stared at the carpet. 'I haven't been keen for anyone to find out.'

'Oh.'

They sat in silence for a while.

Decembrius sighed, very heavily. 'Sometimes I wake up so depressed about it I can't get out of bed.'

127

Princess Kabachetka could hardly remember when she'd been in such a fine mood. Not since being mistaken for a model at the Milan fashion show, certainly. The head of her intelligence services had managed to infiltrate the Abukenti organisation and locate the anniversary shoes. Any day now, a pair should be illicitly on their way to her. It was the best news she could have hoped for. Let Thrix and Malveria strut around with their Abukenti bags. She would outshine them at the charity event.

Not only that, the Princess's comprehensive victory at the card table was the talk of her court. How angry the Fire Queen had been! Of course, Malveria had tried to conceal her dismay, but news had quickly spread.

'Afterwards she raged at Duchess Gargamond for her poor play! Duchess Gargamond has gone back to her own castle, taking her regiment with her.' The Princess laughed. 'Malveria is storming round the palace shouting at kitchen maids.'

Alchet, Kabachetka's handmaiden, laughed at the image, but only briefly. The unfortunate girl knew that the Princess had called her here for another of her dreadful experiments. 'Please don't strand me on Earth,' she pleaded. 'Water will fall from the sky and I'll be extinguished.'

'Will you stop complaining? You will not be extinguished. Wet, maybe, but not extinguished. And I'll only strand you there for a moment or two.'

'I don't want to die on that wet planet!'

'If you die you will have the satisfaction of knowing you were of great assistance to me. Now kindly stand still while I transport you to the human dimension. Once there, attempt to bring yourself back.'

The young handmaiden gloomily did as she was told, standing with her arms wrapped around her for protection, already glancing anxiously above her as if expecting water to start cascading onto her at any moment. The Princess spoke a few words and Alchet dematerialised.

Princess Kabachetka drew some papers from her bag. Not a roll of the parchment on which spells were customarily written, but a few sheets of photocopied paper, sent by Merchant MacDoig.

'Well, Minerva,' muttered the Princess. 'Let us see if your sorcery is as good as people have claimed.'

The Princess intoned a few long sentences, then waited. Nothing happened, which was good. She took out a small mirror and checked her make-up. It was satisfactory, though she was not entirely convinced by her lipstick. The Princess tucked the mirror away then muttered another word. Immediately Alchet crashed back into the room, wailing in terror and falling to the ground.

'I was trapped between worlds! Oh, it was terrible.' The handmaiden broke down in tears.

'Excellent,' muttered the Princess. 'I can now strand a fire elemental between the dimensions.'

'How long for?' wondered Distikka, later in the day, in the privacy of Kabachetka's underground chamber.

'With Alchet, as long as I like. For such a powerful elemental as Queen Malveria, I'm not sure. Probably no longer than a few minutes.'

'That should be enough. She'll be stranded long enough for you to work the moon spell, creating the eclipse. I take it you can now do that?'

The Princess believed she could. 'Minerva could shift the effects of the moon. I am forced to admit that she was a powerful and ingenious werewolf. I think I can use her writings to produce the equivalent of an eclipse of the moon.'

'Very good. Malveria will be stranded. Thrix will lose power and can then be killed. I'll take control of the volcano and dispose of Malveria when she returns. Prince Esarax too can be disposed of, if you succeed in making him travel. In less than two weeks I'll be Queen of the Hiyasta and you will be heir to the throne of the Hainusta.'

After Distikka had departed, Kabachetka walked through to the chamber where the dimensions met and time stood still. She laid her hand on Sarapen's cold body.

'Kalix will die too,' she said, as if he could hear her. 'I'll have vengeance for you as well.'

128

As was customary, most of the werewolves on the Great Council took on their werewolf shape for the council meeting. They gathered around the circular table, a huge old piece of oak in the great stone chamber at the heart of Castle MacRinnalch. Though electricity had long flowed into the castle, the meetings of the council were illuminated by torchlight as they always had been, and a great log fire blazed at one end of the room.

Present at the meeting were Markus, Verasa, Dulupina, Tupan, Dominil, Baron MacAllister, Baron MacPhee, Baron MacGregor, Thrix, Decembrius, Lucia, Kertal and Kurian.

'Council members missing are Marwanis, Butix and Delix,' announced Clan Secretary Rainal. 'And Kalix,' he added, to general discomfort. It was an awkward matter that the youngest daughter of Verasa and the Old Thane was still technically a member of the council, though unable to travel to the castle without being arrested. She had been condemned for her assault on the Old Thane, and had escaped before sentencing. The council had so far been unable to resolve the anomaly, either by expelling Kalix from the council or quashing the judgement against her. So many council members loathed Kalix that dropping the condemnation seemed impossible. Nor could she be easily expelled, with the Mistress of the Werewolves unwilling to give up on her daughter.

'I take it that everyone is aware of the bad news from London?' said Markus.

Word of Red Ruraich's death had quickly spread throughout the MacRinnalch lands. The death of such a prominent werewolf was a grim piece of news, though perhaps not a shock. Ruraich had been in London, after all. The Avenaris Guild had their headquarters there. It wasn't just the Mistress of the Werewolves who thought it far safer for the clan to stay close to their ancestral homelands. The Barons regarded the modern trend of young werewolves travelling south as a dangerous practice that should be discouraged. Red Ruraich hadn't been young, but he'd chosen to travel and now he was dead.

Though no one was impolite enough to castigate Ruraich so soon after his death, Baron MacPhee expressed the commonly held opinion that it had been almost bound to happen. 'I don't see why Ruraich was in London, anyway. Was there not enough music for him to play here?'

There was some agreement round the table, but Dominil protested. 'Ruraich wasn't the only werewolf in London. There are others, including council members, whose business has taken them there – myself, the twins, Thrix and Kalix.'

'Kalix is not a member of this council.'

'Yes, she is. She hasn't been removed.'

There was another moment of awkward silence.

'Decembrius has also been in London recently,' continued Dominil.

'But he doesn't live there!' exclaimed Lucia sharply, annoyed at the suggestion that her son had deserted them. Eyes turned towards Decembrius, curious as to where the red-haired werewolf would claim to live. This was his first visit to a council meeting. Decembrius remained silent.

'Perhaps,' said Dominil, 'instead of retreating every time we suffer some blow from the Guild, we should seek to advance.'

'What do you mean?'

'I mean take the fight to them. Go where they're strongest, and destroy them.'

'You want to send werewolves flooding down to London to take on the Guild?' asked Baron MacPhee. The Baron was a very large werewolf, particularly in girth, who spent most of his time at council meetings wishing they were over so he could get round to eating the stags that were roasting in the kitchens. 'That's a sure way to get us killed, and probably discovered by the rest of the world. We've depended on our discretion for centuries and I don't see any reason to change it just because that idiot Ruraich got himself killed.' Ruraich hadn't been that popular with the Barons. The MacPhees, MacGregors and MacAllisters had never liked the way the head of the MacAndrises had continually pushed for more influence.

'I'm damned if I'll risk my clan in London for the sake of Ruraich MacAndris,' agreed Baron MacAllister.

'If the Guild keeps growing in strength, who's to say they won't attack us here?' said Dominil.

'Do you expect them to grow in strength?' asked Markus.

Dominil did. Everything she'd seen of the Guild's files and records led her to believe that they were still recruiting.

'There are a lot of werewolf hunters in Europe who are looking for employment. The Guild will pay them well and give them the opportunity to fight against the MacRinnalchs. That's a powerful incentive. If we don't take care we'll find ourselves faced with a strong opponent right on our doorstep. We should stop them now.'

Dominil found little support. Though Markus seemed interested – to the annoyance of his mother – few others were prepared to countenance such a plan of action.

'The hunters will never come here,' said Lucia. 'They'd die if they did, and they know it.'

There was general agreement round the table. Dominil looked in vain to her fellow London-dweller Thrix for support. Thrix had her mind on other things, mostly Captain Easterly, who'd succeeded in sweeping her off her feet with his cartons of takeaway food and single battered flower. Thrix felt a glow of happiness that even a visit to Castle MacRinnalch couldn't extinguish.

129

'I'm fed up chasing Kalix all over London,' complained William, lowering his vast bulk onto the old couch. 'It's impossible. She's got no scent and when you get near the place she lives, you get lost. Face it, unless we just happen to run into her in the street, we'll never catch her.' William seemed almost willing to give up the chase. Rhona was also wavering.

Duncan, the eldest, railed at them. 'What sort of werewolves are you? We're not giving up. She killed Fergus. When your brother is killed you don't ignore it, you take revenge. And if that's not enough for you, Marwanis is still offering her reward.' Duncan cursed his siblings, and Decembrius for betraying them. 'He should have led us to her. Now he's trailing round after her like a puppy.'

'Maybe Marwanis will find out something,' said Rhona.

Marwanis had hired an investigator to check the entry rolls of London colleges, thinking that Kalix might be found that way.

'We tried looking at colleges. We couldn't find her,' protested William.

'We got bored halfway through. Maybe Marwanis will do better,' said Duncan.

There was a heavy knocking at the door. The Douglas-MacPhees paused, and looked at each other. They received few visitors and were suspicious of callers. William tramped through the hallway to see who it was, while Duncan and Rhona prepared for trouble. Recently they'd become more involved in the criminal underworld in London, and that inevitably brought enemies.

William arrived back with a parcel in his hand.

'What is it?'

'Our Deep Purple boxed set from Amazon.'

'Great,' said Duncan. 'Put it on.'

The Douglas-MacPhees had never stopped liking the 70s heavy rock they'd grown up with. Duncan studied the box while William put on the music. 'I remember stealing their first album.' He smiled fondly at the memory. 'Must have been back in 1970. Saw them in Glasgow, too, great gig.'

Rhona scowled. 'I wanted you to take me but you wouldn't.'

'You were an annoying brat when you were young.'

'You should have taken me along.'

Duncan looked pained. 'How could I? Who goes to a gig with his baby sister? The other werewolves would have laughed at me.'

'So? You could still have taken me. I wanted to see them.'

Duncan raised his arms hopelessly. His younger sister had an annoying habit of bringing up events from their childhood that always cast him in a bad light. He hated it when she made him feel guilty.

'All right, I'm sorry. I made up for it afterwards, didn't I? I've looked after you since then.'

'I suppose so.'

It was true. Duncan had looked after her. Rhona was pacified. The Douglas-MacPhees turned Deep Purple up loud, nodded their heads in time to the music, and wondered if Marwanis might find out which college Kalix was attending.

130

Kalix withdrew to her favourite clump of bushes in Kennington Park, where she could be alone. Studying last night had been both stressful and tiring, and she was fed up with all company.

I'm going to lie here all day, she thought, and not speak to anyone.

'Ow!' came a cry from nearby, quite unexpectedly. 'I'm stuck on a thorn!'

It was Vex.

Kalix gritted her teeth.

'Hey, Kalix, I'm stuck in the bushes! I need help!'

The young werewolf sighed, and made her way reluctantly through the bushes to find Vex struggling vainly with the thorns that were tangled up in her extremely baggy jersey.

Kalix looked at her with disdain. 'Can't fire elementals do anything? How about burning your way out?'

Vex grinned. 'Aunt Malvie doesn't like me using fire on Earth. She thinks I'll have an accident.'

Kalix helped Vex to free herself, then demanded to know what she was doing here.

'I came to find you.'

'But I came here to be alone.'

'I know. I thought you might like some company.'

'Why would I want company if I want to be alone?' Kalix was exasperated. Vex looked at her with interest. Kalix had enough experience of the elementals to be suspicious. 'Are you reading my aura?'

'No. I know you don't like it. I wouldn't study your aura just for instance to see if you slept with Decembrius.'

'Of course I didn't sleep with Decembrius! He slept on the floor.'

'I know. I saw it in your aura. So, what are we doing now?

Staying in this clump of bushes? It's a bit cold. Should we go to the cafe?'

'I'm not doing the exam,' announced Kalix.

Agrivex reeled in shock, a mannerism reminiscent of Malveria. 'What do you mean? You have to do it. Otherwise you'll be thrown out and then Aunt Malvie might not let me go to college any more.'

'I don't care. I'm not doing it.'

'But your mother won't pay your rent. We'll all go broke. Everything will be in chaos.'

Kalix was resolute. She'd decided to abandon college. 'My mind is made up,' she said, rather grandly. 'I'm not going back.'

'What about your assignment?'

'I'm not doing it, either.'

'You have to!' declared Vex. 'I won't let you give up.'

'There's nothing you can do.' Kalix noticed that Vex had begun to glow, very faintly, as if the fire that comprised her being was heating up. It was unusual for Vex.

'Why do you want to leave?'

'I never wanted to go in the first place. Anyway, I can't pass the exam so there's no point. What's the matter with you? Is that a flame coming out your finger?'

A tiny spout of flame was indeed flickering from one of Vex's fingers, which was quickly joined by another. 'You can't just leave,' insisted Vex. 'You'll ruin everything. I'm depending on you. How can you be so selfish?'

'I'm not being selfish!'

'Yes, you are,' cried Vex. 'Aunt Malvie will make me leave too and I'll have to go back to that stupid boring palace. You're ruin-ing *everything*. You never think about anyone else! You just do exactly what you want all the time!'

Kalix was taken aback by Vex's vehemence. 'Well, what about you? You do exactly what you want as well. Did you ever think about anyone else?'

'I do things for other people all the time! I got you the were-wolf comics, didn't I?'

'I hate those stupid comics.'

Vex looked hurt. 'You should have said before that you didn't like them.'

'I *did* say before! You just never listened.'

'Well, at least I did something to try and cheer you up! Have you any idea how miserable you are?'

'College isn't going to make me any happier!' roared Kalix. 'And while we're on the subject, could you stop going on about gold stars, cheerleading teams, and all your other delusions? Can't you get it into your head it's just some pathetic little institute for stupid people? It's not the nation's number one university!'

'I know that!' shouted Vex.

'You do?'

'Of course I know. I'm just trying to make the best of it. I was trying to make it fun. Did you ever think I might be trying to encourage you by pretending it was a great place to be?'

Kalix hadn't. The strange idea that Vex was actually aware of the true nature of their college came as a surprise. They looked at each other in the bushes for a few moments. The flames that flickered around Vex's fingers spluttered and died. She looked ruefully at her hand. 'My fingers are sore.'

'You shouldn't catch fire,' said Kalix. 'You're not used to it. You'll hurt yourself.'

There were a few more moments of silence.

'OK, I'll do the exam. But you know I'm going to fail.'

'No, you won't!' cried Vex. 'We're both going to pass!'

They walked out of the bushes and through the park, heading for the small cafe on the outskirts.

'Did you really hate the werewolf comics?'

Kalix suppressed a sigh. 'No, I think they're great. Thanks for buying them.'

Vex was pleased. 'I knew you liked them really! We have to look for more. You only need four to complete the set. It'll be like a treat for passing the exam.'

'I can't wait,' said Kalix. 'It'll really make it all worthwhile.'

131

While the Barons and the rest of the council members gorged themselves on venison after the council meeting, the Enchantress ate almost nothing and attempted to leave as soon as she politely could. Though she tried to slip out unobtrusively she failed to make it past her mother.

'Thrix, you've hardly touched your food,' said the Mistress of the Werewolves.

'I'm not really hungry.'

'Couldn't you at least try some of the venison?'

'I'm fine, really.'

Her mother looked at her with disapproval. Werewolves were hearty eaters, particularly in the security of their own castle. The Mistress of the Werewolves had always felt disgraced by Kalix's refusal to eat as a young teenager, knowing that it would be gossiped about. The common feeling among the clan was that if a werewolf wasn't eating properly, there was something badly wrong, possibly with the parents. Having endured this with Kalix, Verasa didn't want anyone to start whispering about her other daughter.

'I had a large meal last night. I'm really not hungry,' insisted Thrix. 'Stop looking at me like you're trying to judge my weight. I'm fine.'

'Are you depressed?'

'Not at all.' Thrix was far from depressed. She was happy after last night's encounter with Easterly, though she didn't intend explaining this to her mother. The argument they'd have about that would come soon enough anyway, when Thrix brought Easterly to the fundraising event.

Thrix excused herself and walked swiftly through the dark stone corridors. Her pleasure over the success of her relationship hadn't banished her other problems from her mind. She was heading for the combined library and museum, where Beatrice took care of the archives, both books and historical artefacts. Thrix didn't know Beatrice that well and was surprised at how eagerly the young werewolf greeted her.

'Thrix! It's so good to see you!'

'It's good to see you too, Beatrice.'

Thrix didn't entirely approve of Beatrice's outfit, and her hair, while an attractive dark brown, could have been styled better. She was pretty, though – pretty enough to keep Markus interested, apparently. Thrix guessed that Beatrice's pleasure at seeing her might be connected with Markus. Please don't ask me about Markus, she thought.

'I need to talk about Markus,' said Beatrice.

'Oh . . . well, I'm quite busy just now. I'm looking for a book written by Minerva MacRinnalch, I need to check on some—'

'I've been seeing Markus for months now,' said Beatrice, showing no interest in searching for a book by Minerva MacRinnalch.

'And?'

'Is he seeing someone else?'

'Why do you think that?'

'He doesn't pay me as much attention as he used to.'

Of course, thought Thrix. Markus flits from one lover to another and always will. Not wishing to upset Beatrice, she kept the thought to herself. 'I really need to see Minerva's book; it contains information I can't find anywhere else.'

'So Markus *is* seeing someone?' said Beatrice.

'I never said that.'

'You didn't deny it!'

'How would I know? I live in London.'

'You're his sister,' insisted Beatrice. 'You talk.'

'No, we don't. I'm really not that close to Markus.'

'I think he's going to leave me,' said Beatrice, and her voice broke. She began to sob behind her book counter.

Well, that's great, thought Thrix. This is just what I needed.

Thrix was saved by the unexpected arrival of Dominil.

'Looking for a book?' asked Thrix.

'I had read the entire contents of this library by the time I was ten. Why is Beatrice crying?'

'Markus.'

'I wouldn't waste your tears,' said Dominil. 'Thrix, I need to talk to you about this Surmata woman, right away.'

Thrix felt a little guilty at abandoning the tearful Beatrice, and rather wished she could emulate Dominil's total lack of empathy.

'I believe you may be in danger.'

'We always seem to be in danger these days.'

'True. However, there's something very suspicious about this fashion blogger. Her name, principally. Do you know any Finnish?'

Thrix was bewildered at the idea she might know any Finnish, and shook her head.

'I picked up a little at Oxford during a comparative study of mythology. So, about Susi Surmata. *Susi* is the Finnish word for wolf.'

'I suppose that's just a coincidence . . .'

'It might be. But I felt there was something familiar about the word *Surmata*, too. I've just checked. It translates as kill, or slay. If you turned Susi Surmata round, and read it as Surmata Susi, it might be translated as "slay the wolf".'

The Enchantress pondered Dominil's words. 'Is this really significant?'

'That a fashion blogger you're involved with has a name that could mean "slay the wolf"? I'd say so.'

Thrix wasn't sure, and still felt it might be a coincidence. 'She might not have anything to do with Finland.'

'Her blog is called "I Miss Susi".'

Thrix nodded. She'd thought it was an odd name.

'*Imisusi* is Finnish for werewolf. Which, apparently, she wants to slay.'

'Are you suggesting she's a werewolf hunter?'

'It seems quite likely,' said Dominil. 'You've managed to hide yourself well with your sorcery. But fragments of information still filter through to the Guild. I've seen snippets that suggest they know there's a werewolf involved somehow with the fashion world. What if this is a way to draw you out?'

'But the damned woman keeps avoiding me.'

'Maybe that's just a clever way to force you to confront her.'

Thrix puckered her lips in anger. 'If the blogger I'm relying on to review my clothes turns out to be a werewolf hunter I'm really not going to be pleased.'

'Now I've warned you, you can take steps to make sure you don't encounter her.'

'Are you crazy?' said Thrix. 'I really need that review.'

'If you try to meet her you just might find yourself walking into a trap.'

'I'll deal with that when the time comes. One way or another Susi Surmata is going to review my clothes.'

132

Moonglow elbowed her way awkwardly into Kalix's bedroom with a tray in her hands.

'I've brought you some tea and biscuits.' Moonglow beamed. 'It's so exciting having a study group in our house!'

Daniel and Kalix were far less enthusiastic than Moonglow, though they were grateful for the tea and biscuits. Daniel had offered to help Kalix prepare her assignment and they'd been joined by Vex, who did seem to be enjoying the proceedings. Moonglow, to her regret, had been banished. According to Daniel, normal people couldn't study in the presence of such an educational enthusiast. It would put Kalix off. Moonglow felt some resentment, but acknowledged that her presence might distract Kalix. The young werewolf hated displaying her lack of education.

'How is it going?' Moonglow asked.

'Great!' cried Vex, bouncing to her feet. 'My report on *Tokyo Top Pop Boom Boom Girl* is fantastic! Look, I've stuck pictures in this book and I've listed all her secret powers and everything! And I'm going to start off by singing the theme tune! Daniel recorded the music for me.' Vex, still quite ignorant about technology on Earth, had been thrilled when Daniel presented her with a recording of the theme music and had been singing along with it ever since.

Moonglow smiled. She appreciated Vex's enthusiasm, even if she was slightly doubtful about doing a report on a cartoon. Moonglow instinctively felt that a book would be a more proper subject. However, she understood that the remedial college probably needed to broaden their remit to encourage their students. Kalix and Vex could do their assignment on anything they chose.

Like Vex, Moonglow had also suggested that *Sabrina the Teenage Witch* might be a suitable subject for Kalix, as it was her favourite programme, but the young werewolf had rejected this. She feared she'd look stupid in class if she turned up with a report on a children's TV show. So she'd decided to write about *Curse of the Wolf Girl*, and was now struggling to complete the project. With her limited vocabulary, bad handwriting and poor computer skills it was an arduous task.

'Kalix has a lot of great ideas,' said Daniel encouragingly. 'I've been helping her get them in order. Do you want to hear them?'

'Yes!' said Moonglow, much too enthusiastically. Kalix shrank into her seat, immediately embarrassed.

'Kalix has a few trenchant criticisms.' Daniel read from his notes. 'The author knows nothing about werewolves and should be arrested for writing such rubbish. The comic is highly prejudicial against werewolves and portrays them as mindless beasts who just kill people all the time. Werewolves really don't kill people all that often, unless there's a good reason, and you can't blame them for that. It's not werewolves' fault if hunters keep on chasing them. It's the hunters' fault so why don't you pick on them instead? The artist has no idea what a werewolf looks like and should be forbidden to draw anything ever again, and also sent to prison. The editor of this comic is obviously mentally defective for letting such rubbish go into print. The story is the most stupid story ever written and the heroine, Arabella Wolf, is the most annoying person ever. She should be punched in the face. Also, it's not true that werewolves eat children. Very few children have ever been eaten by werewolves. Maybe one or two, but it's not a big werewolf problem. The comic should be withdrawn from sale before it poisons people's minds.'

'So Kalix doesn't like it?'

'She hates it.'

'It's really stupid,' said Kalix, quite vehemently, 'and all the characters are ridiculous and unbelievable. Apart from Arabella Wolf's boyfriend. He's an astronomer who does kung fu. I quite like him.'

'I thought she killed her boyfriend in issue three?' said Daniel.

'She got another one in issue four. But then she killed him as well in five. She got another one in issue seven.'

'What happened in issue six?'

'She was quite lonely.'

'I can see why.'

Vex burst into song again, while Daniel studied the comics and Kalix continued to complain about the general anti-werewolf tone of the work.

'I'll leave you to it,' sad Moonglow. 'Just shout if you want more tea.'

133

Dominil called the twins from the castle.

'I'll be back in London the day after tomorrow, after I've checked the venue in Edinburgh. I hope you've been practising – you're playing in one week.'

Beauty and Delicious had been rehearsing with the band, or claimed they had, though Dominil wouldn't have been surprised to learn that they'd spent their time in an alcoholic stupor.

'Don't worry, we'll be fine when we get on stage.'

'You weren't fine at the warehouse.'

'Not our fault,' protested Beauty. 'We were put off by Pete obsessing about you.'

'You were put off long before that happened.'

'He's still depressed. Why don't you give him a chance?'

'Absolutely not,' said Dominil.

'Delicious!' called Beauty, over her shoulder. 'Dominil's ruining our career again.'

Dominil said a curt goodbye and ended the call. Her phone rang again immediately.

'Hello, Dominil. Are you having a nice time at the castle?'

'Aren't you getting sick of calling me, Albermarle?' said Dominil, and regretted it immediately, in case it sounded like Albermarle's psychological campaign was succeeding.

'You didn't deserve to be in that university quiz team.'

'Get over it,' said Dominil, and closed her phone. She felt an unexpected urge to sip some laudanum, though it was some hours till her regular scheduled dose. Albermarle was getting to her, a little.

In the heart of the castle, the Enchantress was making another attempt to find Minerva's book, but the library was shut. Thrix placed her hand over the lock and spoke a few words. The door sprang open. Thrix walked in to find a partially clothed Markus and Beatrice embracing on a chair.

'What are you doing here?' cried Markus, leaping to his feet.

'Looking for a book. This is the library.'

'I found the book you were looking for.' Beatrice hurriedly

buttoned her blouse. 'Someone had left it in the photocopying room. It was tucked away under some files.'

This struck Thrix as odd.

'The photocopying room? Has someone been taking copies?'

Beatrice didn't know.

'This book contains a lot of powerful sorcery. No one should be taking copies. It shouldn't be on display, it should be locked away.'

'It is, normally,' said Beatrice. 'I don't know who could have taken it from the secure bookcase.'

Thrix took the book and departed, leaving a discomfited Markus and Beatrice behind. She studied the index as she ascended the long stone staircase to her rooms. The book was written in Minerva's own hand. As far as Thrix knew, there were no other copies apart from this one and Minerva's. It was troubling that someone might have been photocopying parts of it. Minerva's sorcery was far too powerful to be used by anyone except a very experienced practitioner.

'OK, Minerva,' muttered Thrix, opening the book in her room. 'What do you have to say about finding someone who really doesn't want to be found?'

If Thrix did succeed in finding anything useful, she hoped it wouldn't involve too many obscure herbs. She was well versed in herb lore, thanks to her training with Minerva, but these days she preferred to work her magic without resorting to trips to the countryside. It was a long time since Thrix had tramped around looking for herbs, and she didn't relish the prospect.

'I suppose I could visit Colburn Woods and say hello to Queen Dithean. I owe her a visit. And the fairies will probably point me in the right direction for the herbs.'

134

On the day she was due to present her assignment, Kalix left the house early. Encouraged by Vex and Daniel, she'd prepared well. But she was so anxious about talking in front of the class that she'd started to feel the troubling sense of unreality that came on in times of particularly high stress. She felt disassociated from her own body. Almost as if she was watching herself from outside. Kalix hated the feeling and found it impossible to cope with anyone while it lasted. Knowing that she wouldn't be able to keep up her pretence of being normal in front of her flatmates, she slipped out early, arriving at college before the gates were even open. The young werewolf walked a long way round the back of the building and then sat down to wait.

She sat, unwashed and miserable, till she heard the sounds of students entering the building. Head bowed, she made her way inside. Kalix knew that her tutor would hate her assignment and just wanted to get it over with as quickly as possible. She was surprised to find a note taped to her locker.

Help me. I'm in the boiler room – Vex.

'What now?' mumbled Kalix. 'What trouble has that idiot got herself into?'

Kalix trudged off towards the stairs that led down to the boiler room, a place she'd never visited before. What Vex was doing here she couldn't imagine. As she walked in, the room was dark. The light came on quite suddenly and she found herself confronted by the Douglas-MacPhees. Duncan inclined his head towards his sister. 'You were right.' He turned towards Kalix. 'I thought we'd need some half-decent plan to kidnap you. But Rhona said you were so stupid all we had to do was leave you a note. And here you are.'

'And here we are,' said Rhona.

William moved his huge bulk in front of the door. 'You know what we're going to do with the reward on your head? Pay for a nice memorial for Fergus. He deserves something.'

Duncan took out his long machete from beneath his leather jacket. 'I once said I'd cut out your heart. I meant it.'

Kalix was trapped with the Douglas-MacPhees. Trapped in daylight, when she couldn't transform. She dropped into her fighting crouch, raising her arms and fists in front of her. She wasn't scared but she was expecting to die. She felt annoyed that she was going to die before she'd avenged Gawain, but other than that, she just hoped she could take one of the Douglas-MacPhees with her. She waited for her attackers to spring.

'This time there's no one to rescue you.' Rhona sprang

towards Kalix. Abruptly, and inexplicably, she was flung back, rebounding as if off an invisible wall.

'Except me,' said Thrix.

Kalix turned sharply, her fists still raised and her teeth bared. Her battle madness didn't come on quite as strongly when she wasn't a werewolf, but she didn't think that clearly either. She couldn't understand why her older sister had suddenly appeared.

'You and your filthy sorcery!' screamed Duncan, and leapt for the Enchantress. Thrix repelled Duncan as easily as she had Rhona, and he went sprawling across the room, leaving a long trail on the dusty floor. Thrix stepped towards Kalix, her high heels clicking on the wooden floorboards. 'That's a really good teleportation spell Minerva made,' she murmured. 'Much better than my old one.' She looked with disgust at the Douglas-MacPhees. 'You really are a vile collection of bullies. Do you never get fed up chasing my sister around?'

Rhona's dark eyes blazed from underneath her black headband. 'You won't always be here to rescue her.'

'Rescue her? I'm not exactly here to rescue her.' Thrix took Minerva's book from her handbag. 'And really, I am very busy.'

'What do you mean, you're not here to rescue her?'

'I don't think my sister would thank me for rescuing her. She'd probably resent it if I took her away. Wouldn't you, Kalix? You always like fighting, don't you?'

'Then let us fight,' said William, in his deep, earthy voice, 'and stop interrupting.'

'I'm going to let you fight,' replied Thrix, 'but I'm going to even things up.'

The Enchantress flicked open the book, and smiled. 'That Minerva. No one ever made spells like her. The clan had no idea how powerful she was.' Thrix brushed a speck of dust from her dress. She was perfectly attired, and her stylish frock stood out in sharp contrast to the leather jackets of the Douglas-MacPhees and the shabbiness of Kalix's old coat. 'She recorded a few spells before she retired. Spells she never taught anyone, as far as I know. Certainly not me, and I was her best pupil. I particularly like this one – Spell for Producing Moonlight in Daytime.' Thrix looked up from her book. 'I don't think anyone except Minerva ever used it. But there's always a first time.'

With that, Thrix began to intone the spell. It was short, and the language was both unfamiliar and ugly. The light dimmed and took on an unexpected yellow tone. A feeling that was familiar to all werewolves filled the room.

'What have you done?' demanded Duncan.

'I've brought moonlight into the day,' said Thrix, 'and between Kalix and the three of you, that should even things up.'

The last words of the Enchantress were lost in the great roar that erupted from Kalix as the young werewolf realised what had happened, and transformed instantly into her werewolf shape. Her battle madness descended immediately and she flew at her attackers. Duncan, Rhona and William changed quickly, and the werewolf Kalix descended among their werewolf shapes in a frightening whirlwind of teeth and talons. As a werewolf, Kalix was virtually oblivious to danger; tackling three werewolves, even wolves as large and vicious as the Douglas-MacPhees, meant absolutely nothing to her. She smashed Rhona out of the way and sank her talons into Duncan's shoulders. William managed to land a powerful blow on her face but Kalix didn't feel it. She raked her talons across Duncan's chest, causing blood to spurt out in a great arc, threw him down, then brought her foot into Rhona's midriff so that the female werewolf collapsed, howling in pain. With Duncan and Rhona down, Kalix was free to take on the huge William. He was far too slow to trouble Kalix. She sank her teeth into his throat and they fell to the ground, William screaming in pain and desperately trying to shake his opponent off before she severed his artery or snapped his neck.

As Kalix dragged William down, Duncan made an effort to rise. He was a spirited werewolf himself and, though dazed from Kalix's attack, he wasn't about to give up. Kalix was far too quick for him. She was always too quick for her ponderous relatives. Unlike any other werewolf in the clan, Kalix had been born at the time of the full moon. It had given her brutal strength and terrifying speed. She batted Douglas with her claw and he crashed to the floor. Something like a grin appeared on Kalix's werewolf features. Blood dripped from her jaws and a mad light shone in her eyes. She paused for a fraction of a second at the satisfying sight of her three enemies lying broken in front of her. Then she moved forward to kill them all.

Kalix raised her talon and brought it down hard on Rhona's face but by the time the talon landed it had transformed back into a human fist. Rhona groaned, but didn't die. Kalix looked at her pink skin, and her fingers, and felt confused. She looked down at herself. She'd become human again. The moonlight had faded.

'Put it back,' she said, thinking that Thrix had nullified the moon spell to prevent Kalix from killing her opponents. But when she looked round she saw that Thrix was sitting on the floor with her mouth open and perspiration glistening on her forehead. Something was wrong. Kalix struggled to control her thoughts. It was confusing to be snatched from her battle-maddened werewolf state before she'd killed her opponents. She didn't know what to do. Thrix coughed, and moaned, distracting Kalix further. She took a step away from the Douglas-MacPhees.

'What's wrong?'

'That was a difficult spell,' said Thrix, so quietly that Kalix strained to hear. 'I think there may be a problem.'

Kalix crossed over to her sister. Abruptly the book in Thrix's hand glowed with a fierce yellow light that expanded around them, sucking Kalix into some sort of vortex in which she was tossed around before landing with a bump beside Thrix on the floor. The floor seemed to have been changed to grass. They'd been transported to a dark patch of countryside, with a few trees around them and a forest in the distance.

'What is this? Where are we?'

'We're near the Forests of the Werewolf Dead,' said Thrix.

'What? Why?'

'The spell was too powerful. I couldn't control it properly.'

Kalix glanced around her anxiously. 'Get us out of here,' she said.

'I can't,' whispered Thrix. 'No escape from the Forests. But it's a pleasant place. We'll walk to the Forests together when I get my strength back.'

With that Thrix smiled, closed her eyes, and lay on the grass. In the distance Kalix heard the call of a werewolf, waiting in the Forests to welcome them.

Well, this is stupid and annoying, thought the young werewolf. She shook her sister but there was no response. 'Great rescue!' she cried. 'You've killed us both!'

'Welcome to the outskirts of the Forests,' said a huge grey wolf, emerging from the shadows. 'Shall I accompany you inside?'

'I'm not coming inside. I'm not ready to die yet.'

The wolf smiled. 'But you're here. Let me accompany you.'

Kalix held up her hand. 'Not interested. I'm leaving.'

The grey wolf smiled. 'You can't leave.'

'That's what you think,' said Kalix, and batted him out of the way. She picked up Thrix, tossed her over her shoulder and set off in the opposite direction to the Forests.

'This is quite irregular!' called the wolf from behind her, but didn't attempt to follow.

Kalix marched through long swampy grass with her sister over her shoulder. Above her the sky was an ominous grey and the air was damp around her werewolf snout. Thrix opened her eyes a fraction and asked Kalix what was happening.

'Your stupid spell took us to the Forests of the Werewolf Dead and now I'm taking us out.'

'You can't leave the Forests,' whispered Thrix.

'Would everyone stop saying that?' said Kalix. 'I'm leaving. I'm not dying yet.' Kalix marched on. As a werewolf she felt strong enough to carry her sister over the rough terrain. In the distance she fancied she saw a patch of blue sky and made towards it. The dampness turned into rain and a wind sprang up, cold enough to penetrate Kalix's thick fur. She shivered, and kept on going. As she rounded a clump of bushes she found herself confronted by a werewolf she recognised. She looked at him suspiciously.

'Ian MacAndris,' he said, politely.

'Do I know you?'

'You killed me. After the gig, in the fight with Sarapen.'

'Sorry about that,' said Kalix, and marched past him.

'You can't leave the Forests,' he called after her. 'You'll like it here.'

'I'll be back soon enough,' muttered Kalix. She tramped on towards the patch of blue sky. The Enchantress had now lapsed into unconsciousness and her weight was pulling Kalix down. She paused for a second to catch her breath.

'I refuse to give up,' she said, to no one. 'I'm not being killed by some stupid spell. I still have to avenge Gawain.'

A sudden distressing thought struck her: I have to hand in my assignment!

There was a chuckle from in front of her. Another werewolf had appeared.

'No need to worry about assignments in the Forests. Stay here where you belong.'

Kalix eyed the stranger. 'Did I kill you too?'

'No. The Enchantress did.'

'Then I expect you deserved it,' muttered Kalix, and attempted to walk on by.

The werewolf stepped in front of her. 'Why do you want to leave?'

Kalix scowled. She was rapidly becoming fed up with all this.

'I'm going to hand in my assignment. Now get out of my way before I bite you.'

The werewolf moved to one side.

At least, thought Kalix, they don't seem violent. Am I really in the Forests of the Werewolf Dead or is this just some delusion brought on by Thrix's spell? Kalix couldn't tell. But she thought that if she really was in the Forests of the Werewolf Dead she might feel more at peace.

Kalix moved Thrix onto her other shoulder and started walking. Now she was confronted by more werewolves who looked balefully at her as she passed by. Kalix recognised some of them as werewolves she'd killed. She knew they hated her.

It's not my fault, she thought. You'd have killed me if you could.

The ground seemed heavier and the rain came down in torrents. The wind picked up so that Kalix had to struggle with her burden, pushing her way against the elements. Suddenly Gawain stepped out of a shadow. Gawain her great love, now dead.

'Don't leave, Kalix. Stay here with me.'

'I'm not ready,' said Kalix, and started to cry. 'I'm going to avenge you.'

'I don't need vengeance. Forget your troubles. Stay here with me.'

'No!' Kalix's tears mixed with the rain. She lost her grip on

Thrix and her sister tumbled to the ground, sending muddy water splashing over them. Gawain moved forward to help but Kalix screamed at him to get back.

'You're not really here! This isn't real!'

'It is.'

'No, it isn't.'

Kalix steeled herself to ask Gawain a question she really didn't want to ask. 'If you're really here, who killed you?'

Gawain smiled. Kalix used to love his smile, but it didn't seem appropriate now. 'I can't tell you that.'

'Why not?'

A strong gust of wind rocked Kalix back on her heels. Gawain seemed to be going backwards, fading away from her.

'Who killed you?' she yelled.

Gawain waved. 'Ask your sister.'

'Thrix? Why? Does she know?'

But Gawain was gone, lost in the torrential rain that now poured down from above. Kalix grabbed Thrix, threw her over her shoulder again, and marched on, slower as the wind and the rain and the distant forest sapped her will and energy.

'You can't go back,' came a distant voice.

'Just watch me,' muttered Kalix, and struggled on. For the first time she was gripped with fear, and she knew there was something unpleasant in front of her. She tried to wake her sister.

'Wake up, Thrix,' said Kalix, miserably. 'Father is round the next corner and I can't face him.'

Thrix wouldn't wake. Kalix sighed, and tramped past some bushes, eyes downcast. She knew her father was waiting for her. All her life Kalix had hated and feared him. She'd never regretted her final burst of madness that had driven her to attack him, nor had she regretted his death. Now she had to confront him again. As she turned a corner in the path, the rain intensified, the distant patch of blue sky disappeared from view, and her father stepped out from the trees. Unlike the other werewolves she'd met here, her father still had the wounds that had sent him to his death. There was blood on his face and neck. Kalix shuddered at the smell of it.

The Old Thane had been a huge werewolf. Even late in life his strength had been immense. Not even Sarapen had surpassed him. No one had harmed him in battle, until the thin, scrawny, and insane Kalix took it upon herself to hurl herself at him at the top of the main staircase in Castle MacRinnalch, fixing her jaws around his throat and dragging him down. He'd never recovered from the wounds she'd inflicted.

Kalix looked up at the tall figure of her father, and remembered that while she'd lived at the castle she could never recall a single kind word from him, but she could remember many, many bad things.

'You are a piece of filth,' said her father.

'I know,' said Kalix.

'You weren't fit to live, and you're not fit for the Forests. The clan was cursed the day you were born.'

'Let me past.'

'Never. You died and I'll kill you again, right here.'

'I didn't die and you won't kill me.' Kalix laid Thrix down on the wet grass and prepared to defend herself but, as she did so, lightning flashed overhead and her father seemed to flicker as if he was an apparition rather than solid. Kalix waited, but no attack came. 'I don't think you're even really here.'

Kalix hauled Thrix over her shoulder again and pushed past her father, though in the growing storm, with the wind now buffeting her, she couldn't tell if he was real or not. But she could feel his hatred quite distinctly, and the hatred of the other werewolves she'd met, the ones she'd killed, and those slain by the Enchantress, their malice reaching out and clutching out at them, trying to drag them back.

If this is really the Forests of the Werewolf Dead, thought Kalix, I hope there are some nicer parts.

She struggled on, now up to her ankles in mud, with the dead weight of her sister dragging her down, the wind and rain pulling at her ragged coat, and the dreadful malevolence of her enemies threatening to crush her completely. Her ever-present feeling of self-loathing became so intense that it seemed to solidify and hover around her head in an ugly black cloud, thick and cloying.

'I refuse to give up,' she said, out loud, then felt foolish for saying it but struggled on anyway. She lifted her head. In front of her, the patch of blue sky was visible again. If she could just reach it she could leave this place, which she had to, because she had things to do, though at this moment Kalix couldn't remember what they were.

135

Kalix struggled towards the sliver of blue sky, half dragging and half carrying Thrix. She could still hear the voices of the were-wolves behind her, some threatening, some imploring her to stay, but she ignored them all. When she finally reached the slender rays of sunlight that penetrated the gloom she felt a tinge of warmth enter her body. Kalix and Thrix immediately tumbled back into the real world, sprawling heavily on the floor of the boiler room where Kalix lay gasping from her exertions. She'd hauled herself and her sister back from the netherworld.

There was no sign of the Douglas-MacPhees. Thrix coughed heavily and woke up. 'What happened?'

'Your stupid spell took us to the Forests of the Werewolf Dead, that's what happened. And you were no help when we got there.' Kalix rose to her feet, and winced with pain. She ached everywhere, and struggled to control her nausea. She was wet and filthy. She attempted to dust herself off but gave it up as hopeless.

Thrix rose to her feet, quite lithely. Having been unconscious throughout most of the ordeal, she didn't seem as badly affected as Kalix.

'Was that really the Forests? I'm not certain.'

'Wherever it was I don't want to go back. Next time you're going to rescue me, don't bother.'

'Don't bother? If I hadn't bothered, the Douglas-MacPhees would have killed you by now. You weren't going to beat those three in human shape.'

'You took me somewhere I had to meet my father and Gawain!' screamed Kalix. 'You hear that? Our father! And Gawain! And I still want to know who killed him.'

Kalix put her face as close as she could to her sister's, though she was several inches shorter than Thrix. 'Who killed Gawain?'

'I don't know.'

'You're lying. Gawain said you knew.'

'Gawain?'

'He was in the forests.'

Thrix shook her head. 'I think that was an illusion.'

'You're lying, anyway. You know who killed him.'

They regarded each other with stony dislike. Thrix wondered if she was going to have to defend herself. 'Don't you have an assignment?'

Kalix growled. She'd almost forgotten about her assignment. She picked up her bag and hurried from the boiler room, up the stairs into the corridor and along to her tutor's room. She was still shivering as she passed a few other students in the corridor.

It's not fair, she thought. They only had to get on a bus to hand in their assignments. I had to fight my way out of the Forests of the Werewolf Dead.

136

The Fire Queen prepared herself with the greatest of care, calling on her full complement of dressers, make-up artists and hairstylists. This evening she was due to attend the reception organised by the Mistress of the Werewolves to welcome Felicori to Edinburgh, and she intended to dazzle from the outset.

'I owe it to Mr Felicori to look my best,' she explained to her assembled staff. 'He's about to visit Scotland for the first time and I do not want him to suffer from shock. The kindest critic could not call it a civilised nation. When one considers that as well as local dignitaries, there will be several werewolves in attendance, one can see the need to take precautions. One does not expect the MacRinnalchs to turn up in kilts and start eating people, but you can never be sure.'

'Does Mr Felicori know that Verasa MacRinnalch is a werewolf?' asked Iskiline, the Fire Queen's chief dresser. Like all of the Queen's attendants, Iskiline had only the vaguest notion of life on Earth.

'No, Verasa will never be discovered as a werewolf. She is too controlled a woman. But as for some of her clan . . .' Malveria glanced at the attendant who was adjusting the hem of her evening dress, and raised a cautionary finger. 'Careful,' she said. 'It may not be safe to expose too much flesh. The Scots are a pale-skinned people as a rule, with a sickly hue. Too much exposure to the warm and resplendent coffee tones of Queen Malveria may drive them into a frenzy.'

Malveria's evening dress, in pale grey, had been designed by the Enchantress and had succeeded in satisfying the Queen's desire for something both conservative and alluring. She put on her shoes, adopted a suitable expression, and looked at herself in the mirror. She smiled. 'I do look splendid as the refined woman of culture. Thoughtful and intelligent, yet with hidden fire? Do I have hidden fire?'

'You are full of hidden fire,' Iskiline assured her.

'Like a Queen who, after listening to the opera in a refined manner, may yet privately indulge in the broad pleasure of the boudoir?'

'Definitely.'

'Good. One does not like to be thought of as incapable of enjoyment. Bring me my wrap. Not the dragon scale – dragons are extinct on Earth, and it may cause comment.'

Distikka arrived as Malveria was about to depart. Though the Fire Queen was pleased to see her, her attendants were not. The Queen's dressers always had the impression that Distikka regarded them as frivolous.

'Distikka! Are you ready to assume the reins of command while I attend this important function? Splendid. Now stand back, my journey to Edinburgh will take concentration. I do not want to materialise in the wrong place. If I miss my destination I may end up in some wretched fishing village, with rain pouring from the sky.'

Her attendants murmured in alarm at the thought of the Fire Queen being rained on, but Malveria reassured them. 'There is no need to worry. I have the power to withstand falling water. But my evening dress may suffer. Farewell, Distikka, and make sure you look after things properly. Don't let the council bully you into any unwise decisions.'

Malveria floated down through the dimensions. She located the hotel in which Felicori's reception was taking place and was just about to materialise when, to her great displeasure, she almost collided with Princess Kabachetka.

'Kabachetka! What are you doing here?'

'Welcoming Mr Felicori to Edinburgh, of course.'

'Preposterous. He does not want to be welcomed by you. You will more likely frighten him away.'

'It's fortunate that I'm here,' countered the Princess. 'One look at your ill-fitting gown may divert him so badly that he can no longer sing.'

'You dare call my gown ill-fitting?' roared Malveria. 'This gown was designed by the peerless Thrix MacRinnalch. A shame you have not yet found a designer to match.'

'I believe she's overrated,' sniffed the Princess.

Malveria laughed lightly. She knew Kabachetka was jealous of Thrix's designs. 'Felicori will not welcome your presence,' she scoffed. 'He's a man of culture.'

'I have an abundance of culture.'

'Please. The Hainusta don't appreciate the opera: they're too busy throwing sacrifices into that little volcano of theirs, to try and keep it alight.'

'What?' The Princess was outraged. 'You dare insult our volcano? Our volcano is better than yours.'

'Pah. Your puny pile of ash is no match for the Great Volcano of the Hiyasta.'

'There is nothing great about that little candle. I hear it goes out at night and has to be relit with matches.'

It was Malveria's turn to be outraged. 'The Great Volcano never goes out. That's why it's called *great*.'

'Well, ours is called the Eternal Volcano. Eternal is better than great.'

'No, it isn't.'

'Yes, it is.'

'Just because the Hainusta call it the Eternal Volcano doesn't mean it's anything special. A slightly warm hill might be a more accurate description. With gentle slopes where children play. Compared to the raging inferno of the Great Volcano, the so-called Eternal Volcano is a mere pimple.'

'The Fire Queen would have more experience of pimples than I,' sniffed the Princess. 'One understands her skin care requirements grow more extensive as she ages.'

'Skin care? There is no skin care in Malveria's palace. The Fire Queen is renowned for her natural beauty. Something you might reflect on next time you ladle bleach onto your vulgar brassy tresses.'

'I am a natural blonde!' exploded Kabachetka.

'Pah. Your dark roots say otherwise.'

'Our volcano is better than yours.'

Princess Kabachetka and the Fire Queen suddenly found themselves materialising in a corner of the hotel foyer, and rapidly adjusted their manner to suit the surroundings.

'I am here to attend the reception for Mr Felicori.'

'I am also here to attend the reception for Mr Felicori.'

'Are you together?' asked the receptionist.

'Certainly not,' they replied in unison.

The Queen and the Princess took a step away from each other and did their best to pretend they'd never met before. The receptionist was unperturbed. He'd already welcomed a host of people from the opera world into the hotel and had grown used to their eccentricities. He led Queen Malveria and Princess Kabachetka into the reception room, where both made ready to spring on Mr Felicori at the earliest opportunity.

137

Moonglow was on the phone to her friend Alicia. 'Well, Daniel isn't really exciting. But I like him. He's nice. You know, he came in last night with the shopping done exactly right, even the correct brands, and I gave him a big list, including shampoo and tampons.'

'I wouldn't really have expected Daniel to be so organised.'

'Me neither. But he has expertise in shopping for women. He once looked after both his sisters and his mother while they were ill, when he was still at school.' Moonglow had always felt rather kindly towards Daniel for that.

The conversation was suddenly interrupted by the appearance of Kalix and Vex, back from college.

'We gave our talks for our assignments,' said Vex loudly.

Moonglow ended her phone call. 'How did it go?'

'Fantastic! I sang the theme song and then showed pictures on the computer screen and told everybody about *Tokyo Top Pop Boom Boom Girl* and everyone was really interested! The teacher thought it was great too!'

For once, Moonglow had no trouble believing Vex. The amount of work she'd put into her assignment had been impressive. Daniel's computer expertise had been marshalled into producing words, music and pictures, one of which Vex had even had transferred onto a T-shirt, something that Moonglow wouldn't have thought she was capable of doing. Moonglow had no doubt that Vex's overwhelming enthusiasm for the subject would have carried her through successfully.

'They said it was one of the best assignments ever!'

Moonglow looked towards Kalix, afraid to ask how her presentation had gone.

'Kalix was a big success too!' said Vex, saving Moonglow the trouble.

Daniel appeared in room.

'Vex was telling me about her presentation,' Moonglow told him.

'It was fantastic! And so was Kalix! You should have heard her talk about the comics. The class was amazed.' Vex paused. 'After they got over all the mud and stuff. Why were you covered in mud when you arrived?'

'No reason,' muttered Kalix.

'Did your presentation really go well?'

Kalix nodded. It had. While not quite as comprehensive a treatment as Vex's, she'd still put a lot of work into it. She'd held the class's interest with her impassioned denouncement of *Curse of the Wolf Girl*. When the class applauded at the end, Kalix, for the first time ever, felt it wasn't so bad being at college.

She looked down at the bundle of comics she carried in a plastic bag. 'Now I never have to read these comics again.' She paused. 'Except I've got eleven out of twelve. I'd like to know what happened in the last one. Something stupid, no doubt.'

Kalix looked towards Daniel. Daniel had signed up at the comic shop's website, requesting an alert if the missing issue of *Curse of the Wolf Girl* arrived in stock.

'I'll let you know if they get it in,' promised Daniel.

'Do you want to hear my *Tokyo Top Pop Boom Boom Girl* poem?' cried Vex.

'We've already—'

'If I was friends with Tokyo Top Pop Boom Boom Girl
I'd ask her for help against my aunt, the Evil Fire Queen.
We'd storm the palace
Then we'd go to see Yum Yum Sugary Snacks
The werewolf band
Who are the best thing ever.'

'You know, seriously,' whispered Moonglow to Daniel, 'I'm starting to like her poetry.' Moonglow headed for the kitchen to make tea.

Vex beamed at Daniel. 'It's been a good day all round. Me and Kalix have a big triumph at college and Moonglow likes you.'

'What?'

'She said she likes you. We heard her on the phone when we were coming upstairs.'

'Tell me her exact words,' said Daniel, eagerly.

'She said you were nice.'

Daniel's face fell. 'She said I was nice?'

'Isn't that good?'

'No one wants a boyfriend who's nice. You need to be exciting.'

Vex looked confused. She'd expected Daniel to be pleased. 'I think she said you were competent as well.'

Daniel groaned. 'That's even worse. I've no chance of ever going out with her.' He slumped onto the couch. 'I should be exciting. Now Moonglow is laughing at me for being nice and competent.'

Neither Kalix nor Vex were convinced that Moonglow was doing anything of the sort. But the conversation came to an abrupt end when Moonglow arrived back in the room with her tea tray.

*

Later that night, in bed with the cat lying next to her, Kalix's sharp wolfish ears picked up the sound of Daniel in his room, playing We Slaughtered Them and Laughed quietly to himself. It was a sign that he was depressed, and she felt quite sad about his hopeless passion for Moonglow.

138

'Is there any point asking you again not to go to Edinburgh?' asked Captain Easterly.

'No,' replied Albermarle.

'Dominil will kill you.'

'Dominil's on the run. I've got her baffled and confused.'

'So you keep saying.'

'Because it's true.' Satisfaction showed on Albermarle's face. 'She can't make a phone call without me listening in. I know every move she makes. What are you complaining about, anyway? Thanks to me we've been tracking Thrix as well.'

It was true. Albermarle's technical skills had enabled both himself and Easterly to track their targets. Listening to private phone calls, they'd gathered a host of information about the werewolves' movements.

'I never said you weren't good at intelligence work. That doesn't mean you should chase after Dominil in Edinburgh. Leave it to me; I'll take care of her after I've dealt with Thrix.'

'Stop butting in, Easterly. Isn't it enough that people are always going on about what a great hunter you are? You're not stealing the credit for hunting Dominil.'

Easterly was exasperated. His cousin's jealousy of his position in the Guild seemed to be getting worse.

'I'm not interested in stealing anyone's credit. I'm interested in hunting werewolves.'

'Hunting? Is that what you call it?'

Easterly tensed. 'What do you mean?'

'I mean for a man who's hunting a werewolf you've certainly bought Thrix a lot of nice presents.'

'That's part of the plan.'

'Right. Spending three hours in a warehouse searching through your precious wine collection for the perfect bottle. Very necessary.' Albermarle turned his podgy face on Easterly with supreme contempt. 'Face it, Easterly, you've fallen in love with Thrix. Everyone knows. It's the talk of the Guild.'

Easterly was indignant.

Albermarle grinned. 'I don't suppose you're the first hunter to fall in love with a werewolf. She's an attractive woman, if your picture of her can be believed.'

Albermarle swept up Easterly's notebook, which contained the notes he needed to keep his affair with Thrix moving smoothly. Though her defensive spells still caused him to lose track of things at times, Easterly's continued proximity to her had now made him more sure of his ground. Thrix had accepted him as a partner and her spells no longer erased his memories.

'I'm not in love with Thrix and no one at the Guild thinks I am.'

'Yes, they do.'

'Who does?'

'Everyone. We were all talking about it at Smith's leaving party last week. You weren't there, of course. You took Thrix to a fashion show instead.'

'Might I remind you that you're the one currently making a complete fool of himself due to his passion for a werewolf?'

'I'm not passionate about Dominil.'

'Yes, you are.'

'I'm not. I used to be. I'm over it now.'

'Is that why you've put on twenty pounds in the past few weeks?'

Albermarle glowered at Easterly, and put his hands over his belly. 'I'm just building up my strength.'

'Of course. And that's why you've been sending her text messages every day?'

'It's all part of my psychological warfare.'

Easterly was about to let Albermarle know what he thought of his psychological warfare but was halted in his tracks by an exclamation of surprise from his companion.

'Who's this?' Albermarle pointed to a picture in Easterly's notebook.

'That's Kalix MacRinnalch, Thrix's sister.'

Albermarle studied the blurred photo, taken in the street some months ago by a Guild agent.

'I met her,' said Albermarle. 'She came into the comic shop. I gave her some advice.'

'What about?'

'Comics, of course.'

Easterly stared at his cousin.

'She's a werewolf! You're supposed to hunt them down, not give them advice about comics.'

'Hey!' protested Albermarle. 'I didn't know she was a werewolf!'

'You're meant to be able to sense that sort of thing. Didn't you suspect at all?'

'I had no reason to.'

'What sort of comics was she buying?'

'Werewolf comics,' admitted Albermarle, and looked embarrassed.

Easterly spluttered. 'Werewolf comics? You met Kalix MacRinnalch, werewolf princess, buying werewolf comics, and you didn't suspect for a moment that she might actually *be* a werewolf?'

'Hey, I don't go around looking for werewolves every minute of the day. I like to switch off when I'm working at the shop. How was I meant to suspect anything?'

'Maybe the family resemblance to Dominil? Or the MacRinnalch accent? Or the fact that I showed you a picture of her the first day you joined the organisation?'

'I did think she looked a little familiar,' admitted Albermarle.

'Dammit, Albermarle, if Carmichael finds out you've been swapping comics with Kalix MacRinnalch he'll kick you out of the Guild. Probably from the top-floor window.'

'Who says I was swapping comics? I just gave her some advice. Well, I did swap her one comic. But only to be helpful.' Albermarle flared up in his own defence. 'I'm a friendly, helpful guy. You probably wouldn't understand. Hey, at least I'm not obsessed with her like you are with Thrix.'

'That's because you're already obsessed with Dominil!'

The doorbell rang.

'Excuse me,' said Albermarle, pointedly. 'I have a food delivery. I'll see you in Edinburgh.'

139

Dominil had predicted that the journey from London to Edinburgh would be a severe trial. Four hundred miles in a car with the twins would have tested anyone's patience. Dominil did most of the driving, partly because she didn't trust either of the sisters and partly in an attempt to distance herself from their constant inane conversation. As she proceeded steadily up the motorway she managed to ignore most of what they said but not, unfortunately, the soundtrack the twins had brought along for the journey. Beauty and Delicious had programmed what they thought was suitable music, and played it loudly through one of the speakers in the back of the van. Dominil, never a great fan of glam rock, winced as 'Mama Weer All Crazee Now' thundered out for what seemed like the tenth time.

'Woohoo, it's Slade!' cried Beauty, clambering over onto the front seat from the back of the van, a manoeuvre that caused her mass of pink hair to temporaily blind Dominil.

Dominil angrily brushed it from her face. 'Do you have to keep playing that?' she said with irritation. Her words were mostly lost beneath the music and the noise of the van, which was quite elderly and didn't run smoothly.

'What's that?' yelled Beauty. 'You want to hear it again?'

Dominil gritted her teeth and kept on driving. She was determined to complete the journey as quickly as possible. So far she'd resisted the frequent requests from the twins to pull over into a service station where they could fill themselves up with whatever food and sweets were on offer. Dominil had other things on her mind. Albermarle had sent her many text messages over the past few days. He'd phoned her and he'd emailed her. His infantile campaign of psychological harassment did not in itself worry Dominil, but it made her wary of what might happen next. Presumably at some stage he was planning to take action. Dominil thought it unlikely that he'd

403

dare to stage an attack on Edinburgh, but she was on her guard.

Something else troubled her: Thrix's report that someone might have been copying Minerva's spells in the castle library. Why would that be? Apart from Thrix, there were no other sorcerers in the clan. There seemed no reason for anyone to copy Minerva's spells. Unless, as Dominil suggested, they were to be transmitted to someone outside the clan.

It's unlikely, but not impossible, she thought. We've had clan members sell information before.

Dominil's thoughts were interrupted by an outbreak of laughter so loud as to almost drown out The Sweet, another of the twins' glam rock favourites.

'Dominil,' cried Beauty, turning down the music to let herself be heard. 'Did you really dress up as Wonder Woman for a party at university?'

Dominil's lips compressed to the thinnest of lines. She drove on without replying. Delicious's head appeared over the back of the seat.

'Someone just sent us a text saying you dressed up as Wonder Woman. Is that true?'

Dominil pretended not to hear, and kept on driving. She hoped that Albermarle did show up in Edinburgh. If he did, she would certainly kill him.

140

Albermarle's assistants, Orion and Pictor, were doubtful about his plan. It seemed rash to travel to Scotland to confront a strong werewolf like Dominil in her own territory. Orion hadn't fully recovered from the mauling that Dominil had given him and still wore bandages over his damaged shoulder.

'There's nothing to worry about,' Albermarle told them, rather condescendingly. 'For one thing, she won't be in her own territory. She'll be in Edinburgh. Dominil comes from some place in the Highlands, a long way north. She'll be just as out of place in the city as us. Besides, when we confront her she'll be powerless.'

'Why?'

'She won't be able to turn into a werewolf. It's part of a plan I've worked out with Easterly. Don't worry, it's all in hand.'

Albermarle was distorting the truth. He knew about Captain Easterly's scheme for removing werewolf powers by way of Princess Kabachetka's sorcery, but he hadn't learned of it through any shared planning. Albermarle had been listening in to Easterly's phone calls. Had Easterly known, he'd have been livid. Nonetheless, Albermarle's assistants were reassured by the mention of Easterly. He was a very respected hunter. If Albermarle was collaborating with him, it must be part of a well-organised enterprise.

'We'll soon see who's the smartest,' said Albermarle.

'What?'

Albermarle faltered. He hadn't really meant to say that out loud. 'Just be ready to leave tonight. And bring plenty of bullets.' With that he left his companions to make final preparations for their journey, and headed back to the comic shop.

Albermarle was standing behind the counter downstairs when Kalix came in. He smiled at her.

'I've been expecting you.'

Kalix nodded. Daniel had received an alert from the comic shop that the missing isue of *Curse of the Wolf Girl* had come in, and told Kalix immediately.

Albermarle noted that Kalix seemed to have deteriorated. Her hair, once shiny, was lank again and there were dark circles around her eyes. Her cheeks had sunk a fraction and her frame, always slight, was completely swamped by her old coat. There was a hint of a stain on her hand that might have been blood, as if it had dripped there from her arm and been carelessly wiped off.

Albermarle reached below the counter and produced a comic. 'Last issue of *Curse of the Wolf Girl*.'

Kalix stared at it with dull eyes. 'I don't really like these comics. But . . .'

'But you had to complete the set.' Albermarle finished the sentence for her, sympathetically. He understood perfectly. Having eleven issues out of twelve would have made him uncomfortable too. He handed over the comic while Kalix fumbled for money in her pocket.

'It's my lunch break,' said Albermarle. 'I'm going to the cafe down the road. Do you want to come?'

Kalix was surprised to be asked. She wasn't looking for company. But she quite liked Albermarle, and she appreciated him hunting out the last comic for her, so she agreed.

They walked out of the shop onto Oxford Street, and Albermarle led them down several back streets to Lucia's.

'This is the last traditional working man's cafe in the centre of town,' he told Kalix.

Lucia's had never been modernised. It still had tables covered in yellow formica, hard wooden chairs, and a steamy, friendly atmosphere. It was frequented by delivery drivers and students. A large woman behind the counter took orders on a tiny notepad, and shouted through to the cook in the back. The cafe had made no concessions to modern ideas of healthy eating and proudly advertised its all-day English breakfast of bacon, fried eggs, beans, sausages, fried tomatoes, mushrooms, toast and chips, with a few additional options. Albermarle was a frequent visitor and the woman behind the counter greeted him cheerfully.

'Full English breakfast.'

Kalix felt slightly nauseous, surrounded by the aroma of so much food. She struggled to read the menu but wasn't hungry anyway. 'Just a cup of tea, please.'

The waitress gave Kalix her tea at the counter, pouring it into a large blue mug from a huge urn that simmered constantly on the counter, meanwhile shouting through Albermarle's order.

'I come here a lot,' said Albermarle as they sat down. 'It's one of my favourite cafes. There were a few like this in Oxford when I was there.'

There were two bottles of sauce on the table, a bottle of vinegar, a salt cellar, and some packets of sugar in a bowl. Albermarle absent-mindedly arranged them in neat order.

'I do that too,' said Kalix.

'What?'

'Arrange things.'

A different waitress appeared and placed cutlery in front of each of them. Kalix straightened them out, as did Albermarle.

'So you don't like the comics?' asked Albermarle.

'No. Every issue is stupid. Whoever wrote them doesn't know anything about werewolves. I mean, what werewolves would probably be like.'

Kalix sipped tea from her mug and glanced at her comic. Albermarle's food arrived, a huge plate crammed to the edges, overhanging where the toast lay at the side. He ate a sausage, and an egg, then patted his lips with a paper napkin. 'I know who killed Gawain,' he said.

141

Distikka materialised in Princess Kabachetka's hotel room in Edinburgh. She took in her surroundings quickly – suspicious, as always, of this dimension. Distikka didn't see what the Fire Queen found attractive about Earth, and she didn't intend to visit again once she'd taken power. The luxury of Kabachetka's hotel suite meant nothing to her. Distikka had grown up in a monastery dedicated to poverty, and had no inclination to wealth.

'Distikka. Some wine? Would you care to visit the balcony? The view of Edinburgh Castle is rather attractive.'

Distikka waved away both offers. 'I can only visit for a very short time. Is everything in order?'

'It is. Malveria attended the reception and was as ludicrous as ever in her attentions to Mr Felicori. I let her have her way. It's helpful that she's distracted.'

'We should go through our plan one more time.'

'Please, Distikka.' The Princess was irritated. 'We've been through it a hundred times.'

'Then once more will do no harm.'

'Fine,' sighed the Princess. 'When the Queen and the Enchantress attend the opera tomorrow, we will tell the Queen of an emergency at home, causing her to leave. Our spell will strand her between the dimensions. Once she's out the way, my spell to bring on a lunar eclipse will remove the Enchantress's powers. Boosted by the strength I've given him, Easterly will kill her. By the time the Queen finally breaks through and returns to her palace you will have taken control of the Great Volcano and you will kill her. Nothing should go wrong. Unless you lack the power to defeat the Queen.'

'Gargamond's regiment no longer defends the palace. Nothing can prevent me from taking control of the volcano, and the army.'

'Malveria has overcome great odds before.'

Distikka was unperturbed. 'Malveria has grown soft. Even without the balance of forces in my favour, I'd still defeat her. Is Prince Esarax attending?'

The Princess nodded. She had succeeded in luring her brother to the event, thanks to her wooing of his consort, Lady Krimsich.

'I persuaded the foolish woman that her status at court would be greatly increased were she to attend. She is dragging my brother with her, much to his displeasure. Your agents will intercept him on his journey back, and dispose of him?'

'That's correct.'

'Are you sure that will happen?' demanded the Princess. 'If Esarax survives and I'm implicated, I'll be executed.'

'It will happen. By this time tomorrow I'll be ruler of the Hiyasta and you will be heir to the Hainusta throne.'

The Princess smiled. How pleased she would be to be rid of Thrix and Malveria. With them out of the way, taking revenge on Kalix shouldn't be too difficult. Her smile faded quickly.

'I'm still worried about Malveria. If she senses anything amiss she might warn Thrix.'

'I don't think Malveria will sense anything,' said Distikka confidently. She opened the rough military bag she carried and produced something which made the Princess's eyes glitter with desire.

'*The Abukenti shoes*,' the Princess whispered in awe.

'Our intelligence services tracked them down. I imagine that when you turn up to the opera wearing these shoes, Malveria's outrage will prevent her from sensing anything else.' Distikka looked on dispassionately as the Princess flung off her shoes to put on the Abukenti high heels.

'They are the most fabulous shoes ever made!' cried the Princess. 'Are they not the most fabulous shoes ever made?'

'They look flimsy and impractical.'

The Princess bit back a retort. It was wearying sometimes, being in partnership with a woman who wore chain mail, and seemed to disapprove of anything else. No matter what Distikka thought of them, the shoes would certainly distract Queen Malveria. Once Malveria saw the Princess wearing them she'd most probably be roused to such a fury that she'd be unable to think rationally.

The Fire Queen had had a splendid time at the reception, using her friendship with Mr Felicori to good advantage. Even though the MacRinnalchs who were there clearly disapproved of her, her firm friendship with the singer meant that she couldn't be ignored. Indeed, she managed to dominate the event from start to finish, eclipsing Kabachetka, Verasa MacRinnalch, and every other rival for Mr Felicori's attention.

Verasa was obliged to answer questions about her as friends and supporters of the charity wondered about the glamorous woman at Mr Felicori's side.

'I don't know much about her,' said Verasa, maintaining her charm though inside she was seething. 'Yes, she is quite a beauty. And she made a very large donation to the charity.'

On the way back from the reception Captain Easterly told Thrix he loved her. Thrix was taken by surprise, not expecting such a declaration at this stage, particularly as Easterly had been obliged to endure an evening of hostile suspicion from her relatives. But she wasn't taken aback for long, and found herself telling him that she loved him too, as the elderly black cab took them from the reception to their hotel. Afterwards, in the hotel room with Easterly, she didn't regret saying it.

142

Kalix's low growl was barely audible over the noise in the cafe.

'How do you know about Gawain? Do you know—'

'Yes,' said Albermarle. 'I know what you are.'

'Are you a hunter?'

'Certainly not,' said Albermarle smoothly. 'But I did do some computer work for them.'

409

'Then maybe I should just kill you now.'

'In daylight?'

'You think I haven't killed hunters in daylight?'

It hadn't occurred to Albermarle that she might have. He attempted to pacify her. 'I'm not a hunter. My cousin is. I happened to learn a few things, that's all. My cousin's been listening in on some phone calls. A woman called Thrix? Is that right?'

Kalix stared at him. She hadn't abandoned the idea of killing him right now, but she needed to learn what he knew.

'What about Gawain?'

'Well, I don't know much about him really, but when my cousin—'

'Get to the point,' growled Kalix. 'Who killed him?'

Albermarle hesitated. He'd planned to lead up to this more gradually, building a convincing picture of himself as an innocent party, but he hadn't bargained on Kalix's instant ferocity. The muscles in her face were already twitching and her body came an inch off the chair, as if she was ready to spring.

'Dominil,' said Albermarle. 'Dominil killed him.'

'Dominil?! How do you know?'

'My cousin bugged her phone. She talked to Thrix about it. She stabbed him with some sort of special knife. One that kills werewolves.'

Kalix's face was now contorting in an alarming manner and Albermarle could hear her breath quickening. He slipped his hand inside his coat, ready to use his gun if necessary. Terrible trouble would ensue were he to actually shoot someone in this cafe, where he was known, but he was starting to think it might come to that. The young werewolf with the abnormally long hair seemed to be descending into madness before his eyes. Too late, Albermarle realised that Kalix was nothing like Dominil. She couldn't be reasoned with.

'Dominil killed Gawain,' she muttered. Her black eyes bore into Albermarle. 'And you're a hunter.'

'Computer help only.'

'If you keep sliding your hand towards your gun I'll kill you right now. What else do you know?'

'Not much. Except someone called Markus paid her to do it.'

For a second Kalix's vision dimmed, as if the weight of

information was crushing her skull. She shook her head and snarled, partly at Albermarle, and partly at the world. Could Dominil really have killed Gawain? It might explain why Dominil wouldn't help look for his killer. And why Thrix hadn't been much help either. Kalix didn't think to ask Albermarle why he was telling her this. She wasn't interested in his motivation. Nor was she interested in continuing the conversation. She leapt to her feet, picked up her chair, then brought the heavy piece of furniture crashing down on Albermarle's head. There was a stunned silence as the large man crumbled to the ground. Kalix kicked him, then ran out the cafe, coat trailing behind her and the hint of a tear in her crazed eyes.

143

The Enchantress's heels clicked noisily on the old stone staircase. She'd promised to visit Dominil when she arrived in Edinburgh, but didn't have much time. She had to make an excuse to leave Captain Easterly, something she'd been loath to do. The thought of Easterly back in her hotel room brought a warm smile to her face, and she was still smiling when Dominil answered the door. It pulled open heavily; the tenement, an old stone building, was a very solid edifice, more so than any modern apartment.

'I've done my best to check for hunters, Dominil. I can't trace any. I think we'll be all right.'

Dominil thanked Thrix. She appreciated her help.

'But when the twins are playing their gig,' continued Thrix, 'I'll be quite a long way away, over on the other side of the city, at Mother's event. Do you really think Albermarle might show?'

'It's hard to say. From the Guild's point of view, I don't see it as a sensible move. But Albermarle's not sensible. He's intelligent, but not sensible.'

'It doesn't sound like he'd be able to persuade the Guild to mount any sort of large-scale attack. How many werewolves will be at the gig, apart from you and the twins?'

'Four or five. There's Cameron, the organiser, and a few other young MacRinnalchs who generally go to his events. It should be enough to keep us safe.' Dominil almost smiled. 'I'm not entirely against the idea of Albermarle showing up.'

'I know. But it will be best if you can confront him in London instead. Once we get back, I'll find him for you, I promise.'

'How are arrangements for your opera?'

'Good, I think. Markus has taken care of most of it. As far as I can gather he's got all of Scotland's most fashionable people, and the richest donors, all heading our way.'

'That's a large crowd to be on werewolf property at night.'

Thrix nodded, and almost laughed at the thought. 'It could be tricky. But there won't be that many werewolves there. Markus didn't offer any wide-scale invitation to the clan. A few senior members, but not many others.'

Thrix's phone rang. It was Easterly. She answered it and spoke briefly, before giggling. 'I can't talk about that! I'm not alone.' Thrix giggled again.

Dominil looked on impassively.

Thrix shut off her phone. 'Sorry about that. It was Easterly.'

'So I surmised.'

'He told me he loved me,' said the Enchantress. Dominil didn't reply, but picked up a bottle of MacRinnalch whisky and poured a glass for Thrix.

'Is this to congratulate me for being in love?' asked Thrix.

'Do you need to be congratulated for being in love?'

'I wouldn't mind.'

Dominil remained silent.

The Enchantress felt a twinge of annoyance. 'You might say something nice.'

'I might.'

'But you're not planning to.'

There was another silence.

'What's the matter? Don't you approve? Is it because he's human? What about you? Have you ever been in love?'

'No,' replied Dominil, without hesitating.

'Maybe you should try it.'

'I understand it requires a suitable partner.'

'I'm sure there's a werewolf for you somewhere, Dominil,' said Thrix, who was gripped by the feeling that, really, everyone should be in love.

'Love's hardly been a positive force among the clan recently, has it? More like an excuse for violence and revenge. The MacRinnalchs have a habit of confusing love, violence and revenge.'

'You're exaggerating,' protested Thrix. 'Plenty of werewolves fell happily in love and didn't kill anyone afterwards.'

'If so, none of them made it into our legends,' said Dominil. 'Can you think of any MacRinnalch love story that doesn't involve some sort of bloody revenge?'

'What about Jamie MacRinnalch and the Baroness? They lived happily ever after.'

'Only after slaughtering the Baron and his entourage.'

'Did they? Then how about young Flora MacRinnalch and the handsome werewolf bandit? I remember hearing that story when I was young.'

'Flora killed the bandit after he kidnapped her sister.'

'Are you sure?'

'Yes. For some reason every MacRinnalch love story ends in mayhem and slaughter,' said Dominil.

'Well, maybe so,' conceded Thrix. 'But that's probably just because we like exciting stories. In the real world, a MacRinnalch can have just as happy an affair as anyone else.'

'Let us hope that's true,' said Dominil. 'Though it's hard to see much innocent romance blossoming around us. Revenge, on the other hand, is always popular. Did you know that Marwanis is still offering a reward for Kalix?'

'Well, Kalix is annoying,' said Thrix.

'I wouldn't be so flippant about it. If Marwanis did succeed in getting rid of Kalix, your own family would no doubt look for revenge themselves.'

Thrix looked resigned. 'Probably.'

'Even apart from that, Kalix is looking for revenge herself, for Gawain. Which would involve—'

'You.'

'Yes. Me.'

'I don't think Kalix will find out you killed Gawain. She's not that intelligent.'

Dominil wasn't so sure. 'Kalix is intelligent. And she's persistent.'

'So how do you feel about the prospect of her finding out?'

'I don't feel anything. If it happens I'll deal with it.'

The twins clattered noisily through the front door.

'Hi, Thrix! Edinburgh's awful, what a place, I swear I'm never coming back. Hey, did you know Dominil once dressed up as Wonder Woman?'

The twins carried on unsteadily to the rooms at the back of the apartment to begin the long process of readying themselves for the gig. Hair, clothes and make-up could take a long time.

Thrix looked at Dominil. 'Wonder Woman?'

'An ill-judged attempt to fit in with my fellow students at a party, during my first term.'

'Where did you get the costume?'

'I rented it.'

'Didn't Wonder Woman have an invisible plane?'

'Could we drop the subject, please?' said Dominil testily.

'Or was it an invisible lasso? I'm surprised you told the twins.'

'I didn't tell them – it was Albermarle. He's trying to humiliate me.'

'You really screwed him up, didn't you?'

'Apparently,' said Dominil. She wasn't the sort of werewolf to snarl wolfishly while in human form, something both Thrix and Kalix had been known to do, but her lips parted slightly, giving a glimpse of her very white teeth. 'I'll do worse to him next time we meet.'

The Enchantress had had enough of Dominil's talk of revenge and violence. Though Thrix and Dominil were not close, they'd been getting on better in recent weeks. But now Thrix resented Dominil's refusal to congratulate her on her love affair, or even acknowledge it, and felt that she really didn't care much for her white-haired cousin.

The twins trooped back into the living room, looking sheepish.

'Dominil, you know that new digital recorder we bought that *Musician Magazine* described as the best portable recording device on the market?'

'What about it?'

'We spilled beer over it.'

Delicious brought out a shiny silver box from behind her

back. Dark liquid dripped from every surface. It was a surprise to see that a metallic device could look so soggy.

'Do you think you could get it fixed for us before the gig tomorrow?'

Beauty and Delicious took in the look on Dominil's face and hurried out of the room before she could explode.

'I may have to kill them as well,' she muttered. 'It's not like anyone would miss them.'

144

Decembrius was bored with being depressed but that didn't stop him from being depressed. He wished it would go away but knew from experience that it wouldn't. His depression had settled down to stay and would take some time to depart. Decembrius made some effort to just accept it, but that was never all that successful. He sat on his couch drinking whisky, felt dissatisfied with that, and slid down to sit on the floor with his back to the couch. He didn't feel any more comfortable there.

The doorbell rang. He decided not to answer it. It rang again, and kept ringing. Then the door started shaking as someone threatened to break it down.

The Douglas-MacPhees, thought Decembrius morosely. Fine. I'll fight them. I've nothing better to do.

He transformed into his werewolf shape and opened the door. It wasn't the Douglas-MacPhees, it was Kalix.

'You're looking worse than usual,' said Decembrius.

It was true. Kalix's eyes managed to be both sunken from stress and puffy from tears. Her cheeks were hollow and her hair was a tangled mess. She barged in without being invited.

Decembrius didn't feel that pleased to see her. He was still full of desire for Kalix but thought now that it would never go well.

'Did Dominil kill Gawain?'

Decembrius was surprised. 'I don't know. Why do you think that?'

'A hunter just told me.' Kalix gave Decembrius a brief description

415

of her encounter with Albermarle. 'I've been to see Dominil but she's not there. Neither are the twins.'

'They've gone to Edinburgh. They have a gig.'

'Oh.' Kalix had forgotten about that, even though Vex had been going on about it for weeks. 'I called her but her phone's dead.'

'She keeps changing the number,' explained Decembrius. 'She's having problems with hunters, too.'

'Did Dominil kill Gawain?'

'How would I know?'

'You have powers of seeing,' said Kalix, intensely. 'Use them. I want to know.'

'I told you already, my powers don't work any more.'

'Then make them start working again,' said Kalix, flaring up.

'I can't just switch it on and off.'

'Try it.'

Decembrius felt himself becoming angry. 'It's OK for you to demand I try it. It doesn't feel good when it doesn't work. I'm depressed already. If I try using my powers and it fails again, it will be enough to send me over the edge. I'll be depressed for months and I might never come out of it.' Decembrius was resolute. He feared the effect it would have on him if he tried and failed.

Kalix let the matter drop. She poured a small amount of Decembrius's whisky into her glass, and a larger amount into his, and they talked for a while about the castle in Scotland, and places they liked in London.

'I like your T-shirt,' said Kalix.

Decembrius looked pleased. It was an unusual T-shirt, with a face on it. He'd bought it only the day before.

'Who is it?'

'Soo Catwoman.'

'Who's that?'

'One of the earliest punks in London. A lot of people copied her style. I bought it from her website.'

Kalix leaned closer, as if to study the T-shirt. Then she took hold of Decembrius and kissed him. He kissed her back. After a few minutes, Kalix suggested they should go into the bedroom.

Decembrius's bedroom was tiny, hardly larger than the bed. It smelled quite pleasantly of incense. Kalix half undressed and lay next to him on the bed. Decembrius wanted Kalix very much, and kissed her quite passionately. His breathing deepened.

Kalix felt his fingers digging into her back. Abruptly, she sat up. 'I want to know who killed Gawain,' she said. 'Use your powers or I'm leaving.'

Decembrius, a little muddled from a combination of whisky and passion, looked puzzled. 'What?'

'Use your powers or I'm leaving.'

'Did you just half seduce me so that you could get information?'

'Yes.'

'I ought to kick you out.'

'Then you'll be sorry, won't you? So what's it going to be? You using your powers and me staying, or not using them and me leaving?'

Decembrius glared at Kalix. 'This isn't cunning, you know. Cold and calculating, maybe.'

'I'm getting fed up waiting,' said Kalix.

Decembrius grunted in annoyance, and sat up on the bed. 'Try and keep quiet. I'll do my best.'

They sat in silence for a long time, Decembrius completely still, Kalix occasionally sipping from the glass she'd brought into the bedroom.

Abruptly Decembrius opened his eyes, and after a brief moment of disorientation nodded his head. 'I think she did it.'

'You *think*?'

'It wasn't all that clear. But I saw something. I think Dominil stabbed him.'

Kalix growled. 'I'll kill her.'

145

The day of Verasa MacRinnalch's charitable function brought less anxiety than she'd anticipated. It had been a complicated operation, bringing Felicori and an orchestra to Andamair

House, meanwhile pulling in every wealthy donor and anyone else who could help, but the Mistress of the Werewolves and Markus had worked hard in the preceding months. As the day arrived, there seemed to be nothing in the way of success.

'I was expecting a last-minute hitch,' Verasa told Markus, 'but it all seems to be going smoothly.'

Markus agreed. Everything had been taken care of. Catering was readied, cameras were in place, the stage was satisfactory; every detail appeared to be in order, right down to Felicori's favourite brand of mineral water. In around twelve hours' time Andamair House should be full and Felicori would step on stage in front of a packed audience of guests who'd paid extremely handsomely for the privilege. Verasa would be well on the way to hosting one of the most prestigious fundraising events ever seen in Scotland.

'Thank you for working so hard, Markus,' she said, and put her arms round him in an affectionate embrace.

There was one cloud on the horizon for Markus. Beatrice hadn't been due to attend, not being a senior enough member of the clan to be automatically invited. She'd told Markus that she'd be away on the night, visiting her family who lived in a small village east of the castle. Unexpectedly, on learning of this Verasa had chided Markus, telling him that he really should take Beatrice to Andamair House. Verasa liked Beatrice, and regarded her as a suitable companion for Markus on the night. Markus had duly invited her and Beatrice was thrilled.

Unfortunately, reflected Markus, things might become complicated. Heather MacAllister would be there too. As the set designer, she was one of the small crew of working werewolves who'd be on site all night. That could be awkward. Markus had been juggling his relationships. Neither Beatrice nor Heather knew about each other. They weren't going to be very pleased to find out. Nor would his mother. Nor would Baron MacAllister, if he chose to attend.

Markus chafed, and thought to himself that the Thane of the MacRinnalchs really shouldn't have to worry about offending the family because of a minor complication like having two girlfriends at the same event. It seemed, however, that he did.

Markus wasn't even sure which of them he liked best. Heather

MacAllister was definitely a more suitable companion intellectually; a brighter sort of werewolf. But Beatrice was pleasant as well, in her own way. And, on the plus side, she was now quite enthusiastic about Markus's liking for female clothes, something of which Heather was not yet aware.

Markus didn't know what to do, and decided he'd just hope for the best. It was possible that Heather would be so busy and Beatrice so distracted by the power of Felicori's voice that they wouldn't encounter each other. He'd survived such tricky situations before, once or twice, by dint of luck and his charm, and perhaps that would carry him through again.

146

Kalix woke up in the middle of the night with a dull headache. She hadn't meant to fall asleep but her increased intake of laudanum had rendered her drowsy. The room was dark but Kalix's wolflike eyes could see perfectly. Decembrius was asleep beside her. She looked at him for a few seconds, without expression. She rose silently and, without making the slightest sound, dressed quickly, then slipped from the bedroom into the only other room in the small flat. Decembrius's wallet was on the table. Kalix emptied it, taking the few pounds it contained and shoving them deep into the pocket of her old jeans. She checked that her keys, bus pass and laudanum were in her coat pockets, then left in silence. Kalix had no feelings about sleeping with Decembrius: her thoughts were directed solely towards the treacherous Dominil.

Kalix found a night-bus stop and waited, eager to get home, though anxious lest she was at the wrong stop. Kalix could make out bus numbers but still struggled to read the destinations on the bus stops. She sometimes worried about taking the wrong bus on an unfamiliar route, or boarding the bus on the wrong side of the road and travelling in the opposite direction. A bus arrived before long and she stepped on. Even on the night bus, where people's gazes were directed mainly to the floor, her unkempt appearance drew some attention. Kalix didn't notice.

She stared at her boots, her eyes narrowed in rage. A small twitch made the corner of her mouth vibrate.

It was three in the morning when Kalix arrived home.

Vex was sitting on the couch, watching cartoons. 'Hi, Kalix! Been having a good time?'

'I need to get to Edinburgh right away. Can you take me there?'

'How?'

'You can teleport.'

'Afraid not,' said Vex. 'I can hardly take myself anywhere and I can't carry anyone else.'

Kalix was disappointed. She knew that Vex wasn't powerful like Queen Malveria but had been hoping her powers might have increased. 'I'll have to get a train. Do you have any money?'

Vex shook her head. Every penny she had had gone towards the emergency house fund for paying bills, as had everyone else's.

'Why are you going to Edinburgh? Are you going to see Yum Yum Sugary Snacks? If you're going I'm going too.'

'I'm not going to the gig.'

'Are you going to the opera?'

Kalix made a rude remark about the opera. 'I'm going to see Dominil. She killed Gawain.'

'Dominil? Are you sure?'

'Sure enough. I need money. Where's Moonglow?'

Vex shrugged. 'She went out with Daniel and some friends to the pictures. They didn't come back. Do you think they might be—'

'I don't care what they're doing. Where did Moonglow put the money for the bills?'

'Upstairs in her room. But you can't take that. Moonglow will go crazy.'

It was Kalix's turn to shrug. 'I need it.'

Vex followed Kalix upstairs to Moonglow's room. Moonglow had put money for various bills in a series of envelopes on the desk beside her computer. Kalix emptied each one of them, stuffing the notes into her pockets.

'I don't think this is the best idea,' said Vex. 'Moonglow said if we didn't pay these bills disaster would follow.'

'She'll think of something. Moonglow's smart.'

'Daniel said he couldn't raise another penny.'

'I don't care,' snarled Kalix. 'I'm taking it anyway.'

Watching Kalix take the money, Vex became agitated. Though the young fire elemental also struggled with the idea of acting responsibly, Moonglow had managed to impress on her the importance of paying the bills. Vague thoughts of having their phone, gas and electricity cut off floated into her mind, along with the ever-present terror of her aunt taking her out of college. 'You know Aunt Malvie will blame me for this?'

'Sorry,' said Kalix. 'But I'm doing it anyway.'

'You'll miss our exam. All your work will be wasted.'

'I don't care.'

'Aren't you banned from going to Scotland? Your clan will kill you.'

'My clan can do what they like,' said Kalix, 'after I've seen Dominil.'

'Are you going to kill her?'

Kalix didn't answer. 'I have to go now.'

Vex moved in front of her. 'Kalix, I know you get cranky when I read your aura, but . . .'

'What?'

Vex saw that Kalix had slept with Decembrius. She decided not to mention it.

'Eh . . . nothing. But something really bad is going to happen if you take this money and go to Edinburgh.'

'Is that in my aura?'

'No.' Vex shook her head. 'But it's obvious anyway. Can't you just stay here and keep on pretending to be normal?'

Kalix was surprised. Vex's reading of emotions was more acute than she'd realised. 'You knew about that? Well, I'm giving up pretending to be normal. I was never very good at it. I need to leave now.'

She reached out to push Vex roughly out the way, then pulled back. 'Please move out the way. I don't want to push you.'

Vex very glumly stepped aside.

Kalix left the room without looking back, and her boots clattered on the wooden stairs as she left the flat and walked out into the dark night.

147

There was an unusual amount of traffic between the dimension of the fire elementals and the Earth. Not only had the Fire Queen and Princess Kabachetka made the journey but the Princess's brother had too, brought there very unwillingly by his consort, Lady Krimsich. Prince Esarax's indignation at being dragged away from his regiment was heightened by the Princess's insistence that he dress formally so he spent the early part of the evening looking stiff, uncomfortable, and out of place. Lady Krimsich, however, was thrilled to be there, and talked endlessly to the Princess in an excited whisper.

'This is a wonderful occasion. Such splendid fashion everywhere. I am so looking forward to the music, Princess. Really, we must make this a regular engagement, and come to the opera together often.'

'We must indeed,' replied the Princess, meanwhile thinking that if things went according to plan, Krimsich would be disposed of quickly, and good riddance to her.

Malveria brought Iskiline with her as a companion, knowing that the Enchantress would be there with Captain Easterly and not wishing to risk being left on her own. Not that that was likely to happen, given Malveria's social skills, but one never knew. As she said to Thrix, 'One does not want to be left standing alone like a grape.'

'You mean lemon.'

'Are lemons lonelier than grapes?'

'I'd say so.'

'I suppose grapes do tend to come in bunches. Like MacRinnalchs. Did you have a pleasant talk with your mother and Markus?'

Thrix made a face. Shortly after arriving she'd been shepherded to a corner of the room by her mother and lectured, along with Markus, on the importance of them getting along better. Thrix, feeling very uncomfortable, had gazed into the middle distance, as had Markus. It was a long time since Thrix and Markus had got on well; almost never in their adult lives.

'You've never told me the cause of your argument. Whatever

the reason, I won't have it any longer. I had four children and the eldest is dead. As for my youngest . . . who knows how Kalix will end up? But I won't have this constant unpleasantness. Your father has gone now and we're the family. That means something to me, do you understand?'

Markus and Thrix mumbled that, yes, they did understand. Thrix had found the whole experience intolerable. She'd never enjoyed being lectured by her mother, and despite her own power and achievements had never managed to take it lightly. Verasa could be very intimidating.

'That's all I have to say. Whatever you argued about in the past it's time to forget it, and start getting on. Now I'll leave you two to talk.' Verasa walked off, leaving her two offspring wondering how long they had to remain in each other's company before they could decently leave. The source of their original argument was too painful to broach. It was all very well their mother telling them to make it up, but even the mention of it was bound to infuriate Markus. Long ago, Thrix had discovered Markus's liking for female clothes, and had mocked him for it, quite cruelly. Markus had hated her ever since.

Thrix regretted it. If she'd discovered it now, after a long career in the fashion world, she would have taken it in her stride. But she'd been young at the time, and unprepared for such a discovery about her older brother. When she'd tried to apologise, years later, Markus had refused to accept it, and simply became angrier that she'd dared to bring up the subject. It seemed like a wound that couldn't be healed.

'Mother's gone off with some sponsors,' grunted Markus. With that he left, not looking back. Thrix returned to Malveria and gulped down a glass of wine.

Malveria took a tiny mirror from her bag, and examined her lips.

'They are never perfect. It is a trial. Dearest Enchantress, may I presume that things are going famously with Easterly?'

'Yes,' replied Thrix immediately.

The Fire Queen looked relieved. 'But do I detect some distraction?'

'I was thinking about Susi Surmata.'

'It is vexing. She *must* write about you.'

423

'Now Dominil has me thinking she's a werewolf hunter which is another worry.'

'Well,' said Malveria, 'if she is a werewolf hunter, I have no doubt you will dispatch her, as you have dispatched many others. And we will find someone else to write about your beautiful clothes.'

'You're more confident than me. I don't like it, Malveria. There seems to be a lot of hunter activity going on at the moment. I'm wondering if this event might attract some unwelcome visitors.'

'Here in Scotland? Unlikely, surely. Who could attack you? You are far too strong.'

'I suppose so,' said Thrix. 'Although it would put a bit of a dampener on Mother's event if it ends up with werewolves and hunters running all over the place. And I don't like it that Kabachetka is here. Remember what she did before? She removed our sorcery and left us vulnerable to Sarapen.'

'True. A vile act for which I have not forgiven her. But we cannot be caught like that again, Enchantress. We are forewarned. I have protected us against any conceivable attack that Kabachetka could mount. There is nothing to worry about, I assure you.' Malveria accepted a glass of champagne from a passing waiter. 'Andamair House looks splendid. Markus has done a wonderful job of preparation. I really feel, Enchantress, that the fates are turning in our favour. Mark my words, by this time next week you will have received an enormous order for clothes, and I will be the leading photograph in *Vogue*'s "Fashionable Party People" page. Nothing can go wrong.'

Malveria turned round, emitted a cry of anguish, and abruptly fainted.

Thrix looked down at her, puzzled and alarmed. 'Malveria? What's the matter?' Thrix bent down to cradle her friend's head. 'Malveria?'

'I just saw Kabachetka,' gasped the Queen, struggling to get her words out. 'She is wearing the new Abukenti shoes!'

'What?' Thrix let go of Malveria's head and whirled round. There was Kabachetka, swanning her way towards them.

'Malveria, get up. Don't let her see you fainted.'

The Fire Queen struggled to her feet. 'It is a great effort, Enchantress. Support me in case I lose consciousness again.'

Princess Kabachetka passed gracefully through the gathering crowds, drawing admiring looks for her brilliant blonde hair and elegant evening dress. It wasn't just her appearance. There was something about her, an air of complete self-assurance; the air of a woman who knew she was wearing the best shoes in the building.

Malveria, only moments before an equally confident figure, wilted as the Princess approached.

'Malveria,' drawled the Princess, sounding, to Thrix's ears, unnecessarily exotic. 'How lovely to see you.'

Kabachetka glanced briefly in the direction of her ankles. Malveria's eyes followed. She bit her lip. The Abukenti shoes were undeniably fabulous.

The Princess smiled and, deciding that no more words were necessary, moved serenely on, followed by several admirers and a crowd of photographers.

'How did she manage to get hold of the shoes?' Malveria moaned.

Thrix glanced at her own high heels. She'd loved them when she put them on a few hours ago but now they looked dull and clumsy. 'I hate these shoes,' she muttered.

'Mine are far worse,' sighed Malveria, eyeing her own stilettos with loathing. 'What was I thinking when I selected them?'

Thrix and Malveria slouched to the side of the room, dispirited by the appearance of Princess Kabachetka in her priceless Abukenti shoes. They took a seat on one of the antique couches placed there by Markus and his interior decorators.

'How terrible this is,' sighed Malveria. 'When Beau DeMortalis learns of it he will be very cutting, I know it.' A stray flame flickered from her index finger.

'Control your flames, Malveria! This is a human event, remember. Apart from a few werewolves.'

Thrix waved to a waiter, who ignored her. She twitched her lips, muttering a discreet spell, and the waiter felt a violent tug on his sleeve, propelling him towards her. He arrived in confusion, not quite knowing how he'd got there. Thrix took two glasses of champagne from the tray and, after a moment's reflection, two more. She kept two for herself and handed the others to Malveria. 'We'll just have to drink our way through the evening.'

Malveria nodded, and started on the champagne with the air of a defeated woman.

At that moment Captain Easterly arrived, handsome in his formal attire.

'I brought you some champagne. I see you have some already . . . two glasses each . . . should I get rid of this?'

'Just hand it over,' said Thrix sharply, and grabbed for the glass. Malveria did likewise.

Easterly looked baffled. 'Five minutes ago you were both cheerful. What happened?'

Thrix explained about the shoes. Easterly was sympathetic, which was fortunate. An unsympathetic response would have caused the Enchantress to end the relationship there and then.

'Don't worry,' said Easterly, comfortingly. 'So she got the shoes first. She doesn't look that good in them.'

'She will undoubtedly be photographed as a "Party Person" for *Vogue*,' said Malveria, who was particularly crushed by the thought.

Her companion Iskiline, looking flustered, arrived from the bar in the next room. She was unused to her surroundings and had found it difficult to place her order. She looked in some confusion at Malveria and Thrix, each of whom held three glasses of champagne.

'Should I take these back?'

'Don't be ridiculous,' said Malveria sharply, and reached for the glass.

148

The Advisory Council of the Hiyasta were pleased to learn that Commander Agripath had moved additional troops to the outskirts of the Great Volcano. It was slightly irregular, as they had received no formal order from the Fire Queen, but Malveria had failed to take measures to replace the defences left short by the withdrawal of Duchess Gargamond's regiment. It was somewhat galling for the council to receive this information from Distikka. The Queen's adviser seemed to be doing everything these days but at least it was done.

'I don't know what Queen Malveria was thinking of by allowing Gargamond to withdraw her troops,' complained the Minister for Lava. 'The Great Volcano has been vulnerable in the past weeks; it's high time the gaps were plugged.'

There was general agreement around the council table. The volcano had been left poorly defended.

Only First Minister Xakthan seemed to disapprove. 'No troops should be moved in that area without express orders from the Queen,' he pointed out. 'It's very irregular, and possibly illegal.'

'The Queen left me with full responsibility for the defence of the realm,' said Distikka.

First Minister Xakthan remained uncomfortable. He didn't like it that troops were being moved while the Queen was away, and he had a suspicion that there was more to the relationship between Distikka and the Commander than they acknowledged. He returned to his office and sent for the head of his intelligence services.

The head of the intelligence services, by now on Distikka's payroll, assured the First Minister that there was nothing to be concerned about. Distikka's relationship with the Commander was strictly professional.

First Minister Xakthan was not completely reassured. He couldn't say why, but many years in the world of Hiyasta politics had given him a nose for trouble. He discreetly arranged for Queen Malveria's personal guard to be moved closer to the slopes of the volcano. They were a small force, but completely loyal, and they were all experienced warriors.

149

Kalix bought a one-way ticket to Edinburgh. As the train left King's Cross station she was sitting on her own, and though it was crowded no one took the seat next to her. Kalix looked too mad, dirty and altogether strange for anyone to want to spend five hours next to her. Her eyes were both sunken and wild. Her beauty had faded under the weight of her anxiety. Her cheap, slightly ragged clothes, not so noticeable on the streets of London, stood out painfully in comparison with those of her fellow travellers. The guard who strolled up and down the aisle took a long look at her. He checked again on her several times, waiting to see if she did anything odd that might require him to take action, but Kalix just sat there, staring down at the small table in front of her, hardly moving, rarely blinking, lost in some world of her own. Occasionally her lips moved, and an expression of anger floated across her features. Other passengers stared at her, but Kalix was oblivious to them. She was focused entirely on confronting Dominil. The more she anticipated it, the more violent her rage became. Dominil had killed Gawain and then lied about it. Kalix was determined to kill her in revenge.

Blood trickled down the inside of her arm where Kalix had put a cut through the letter she'd inscribed there. Though the people around her couldn't smell the blood the way a werewolf would have, they could sense that something was deeply wrong.

Halfway through the journey, the child in the facing seat abruptly started crying, unnerved by Kalix. The child's mother shot a hostile glance at Kalix, then took her child, her luggage and herself off to another carriage, so that in the crowded train Kalix now sat completely alone. People no longer stared at her but shrank from even acknowledging the presence of the crazed young girl who'd sat for hours, unmoving, grim-faced, dirty, occasionally muttering to herself under her breath. On one occasion Kalix bared her teeth, and that was disturbing too. When she twisted her face in an expression of rage, people wondered if it was time to call the guard, or perhaps leave the carriage altogether, to get away from her unsettling presence.

150

Vex felt dissatisfied. More than dissatisfied, she felt agitated. She took a can of beer from the fridge, opened it, and sat down to watch an episode of *Doctor Who*. But even that didn't soothe her mind, though she was a fan of the show.

Kalix shouldn't have gone off to Edinburgh. Something bad will happen. And she'll miss her exam, she thought.

Vex wondered if she should be doing something. What that might be, she had no idea. Daniel and Moonglow weren't around. They'd gone to the cinema last night and still hadn't returned. Vex sipped her beer and puzzled over what she might do. She couldn't ask her aunt for help; Malveria was in Edinburgh. Besides, she'd forbidden Agrivex to go anywhere till she'd sat her exam, on pain of being thrown into the Great Volcano.

I can't follow Kalix to Edinburgh, thought the young fire elemental. I'll miss my exam and then I'll be dragged back to the palace in disgrace.

Vex looked round at her surroundings. The small living room, like the rest of the flat, was cheaply furnished and showing its age. But it was comfy too, and hospitable. It felt like home. Vex didn't want to be dragged back to the palace. She liked living with Daniel and Moonglow and Kalix. But Kalix will probably be killed by her clan or a hunter or something, she thought.

The programme started again, and Vex managed not to think about anything till the next advert break.

Even if I did want to follow Kalix, I can't, she told herself. I don't know where Edinburgh is, and I couldn't get there if I did. Kalix took every penny from the house so I can't get a train ticket. It's too far for me to travel through space. Aunt Malvie's right; I am the worse teleporter in the Hiyasta nation.

Vex felt slightly depressed, and wished she'd worked a bit harder on improving her travelling skills. She sank back in the couch, rather gloomily, and felt hopeless in the face of adversity. It was a new feeling for her, and one that she didn't like. She picked up the control and flicked through the channels, hoping for a new episode of *Tokyo Top Pop Boom Boom Girl* to divert her attention. There weren't any new episodes, only repeats. However, as the theme music started to play, a strange feeling stirred her spirit.

Tokyo Top Pop Boom Boom Girl wouldn't just give up like this, she thought. She'd do something heroic.

Vex finished her beer and hurried upstairs to her room where she put on her favourite *Boom Boom Girl* T-shirt, a trusty pair of boots and her mittens.

429

What else would I need for a journey? she wondered. I've never packed for a journey before.

Vex filled up a carrier bag with some underwear, another pair of boots, and two more T-shirts. 'That should do it. Now, where is Edinburgh?'

Vex hurried from her attic, downstairs to Daniel's room. She had a vague idea she'd seen Daniel looking at a map when he'd been about to drive home to his parents' house. It was hard to find anything in Daniel's room, it being almost as chaotic as Vex's. Fortunately Daniel had left his road map of the British Isles on the table next to his computer. Vex tucked it in her bag, went back to the living room and wrote a note.

Kalix has gone to Edinburgh to kill Dominil. I've gone to Edinburgh to save Kalix. Vex

After some consideration, she drew a gold star underneath, reasoning that it was a well-presented note. With that, she concentrated as hard as she could and dematerialised, off on her journey to Scotland.

151

Decembrius woke up feeling less depressed than he had for a long time. His desire for Kalix had been so strong that it had been affecting his moods and behaviour. In the first dim seconds of consciousness he turned over in bed to put his arm round her but as he came awake he realised she'd gone. Decembrius was disappointed. He'd wanted to wake up and find Kalix beside him. He rose, and walked naked into the small living room. The first thing he saw was his wallet lying open on the table. He checked it and found that it was empty. Kalix had stolen his money. Beside the empty wallet was his bottle of MacRinnalch whisky, which Kalix appeared to have finished. Decembrius stared at the empty wallet and bottle for a few moments, then burst out laughing.

'She sleeps with me, probably only to get information, then leaves in the middle of the night, robbing me in the process. You have to admire her for being single-minded.'

Decembrius laughed again, and felt that he liked Kalix more

than ever. There was no one else like her in the clan. No one so spirited, or so beautiful. Would she have reached her home yet? Probably. Decembrius wanted to talk to her and wondered if he should phone. Kalix had never actually given him her phone number but Decembrius had craftily taken a note of it when he'd visited to help her study.

He hesitated. If he phoned now he might seem needy. Cloying, even. Suddenly his head was filled with a vision of blood flowing down an old staircase. Decembrius slumped onto the couch, holding his head till the vision departed. Though he'd been having this sort of experience most of his life, it was always draining.

What did that mean? he wondered. Blood flowing down an old staircase?

The phone rang.

'Is Kalix there?' a girl asked.

'No – who's this?'

'Moonglow. Who lives with Kalix. I'm worried.' Moonglow told Decembrius about Vex's note.

'You just let her go off to Edinburgh? I thought you were meant to be looking after her.'

'We weren't here,' protested Moonglow, though she did feel guilty about letting Kalix leave. It had been a mistake to visit friends and stay over at their house. They shouldn't have left Kalix on her own.

'Can you help?'

'I'll try,' replied Decembrius, and put the phone down.

Decembrius cursed. He should have realised that this was going to happen and taken care to prevent Kalix from leaving, but their lovemaking had sent him into a deep sleep. He grinned at the memory of their time together. Kalix was keen enough, even if she didn't want to admit it, he told himself. He stopped grinning. Now she's going to Scotland and the clan will most probably kill her.

He hurried to get ready. Decembrius was too vain to rush out of the house entirely unprepared, so he brushed his hair in front of a mirror, and cleaned his teeth. He put on the radio, rejected the first pre-set station, and the second, found the Sex Pistols on a third, and let it play while he dressed.

'"Pretty Vacant",' he mused. 'Would that be me or Kalix?'

Inspecting himself in the mirror, he was satisfied with his

431

appearance. There was a tiny smear of eyeliner at the corner of his eye. He could fix it on the way to Edinburgh. He threw a few clothes in a bag and then hurried out of the flat, ready to drive.

As soon as he got through his front door he was grabbed roughly by the throat. William Douglas-MacPhee held him in an iron grip. Duncan sneered at him.

'Careless, Decembrius. Did you not smell us?'

'He looks like he's in a hurry,' said Rhona. She sniffed the air. 'Have a nice time with Kalix?'

'Kalix isn't here any more,' said Decembrius.

'We weren't looking for her. We were looking for you.' William rammed Decembrius's head against the wall.

Decembrius tried to stay on his feet but Rhona kicked the back of his legs and he tumbled to the floor. The three Douglas-MacPhees began kicking him savagely. Decembrius was a strong wolf, but no match for the combined ferocity of the Douglas-MacPhees. He attempted to rise but made it only onto one knee before a tremendous blow from William sent him crashing to the ground again. Rhona kicked him in the face and Duncan stamped on his ribs before leaning down to drag his head roughly off the floor.

'Don't annoy us again or we'll kill you,' he snarled, then slammed his head down. William kicked him again. The Douglas-MacPhees took a step back, looking at their work. Decembrius had been very badly beaten and was bleeding both from his mouth and his nose.

'Tell Kalix we'll be seeing her soon.'

The Douglas-MacPhees turned and clattered their way heavily down the stairs. Decembrius tried to rise but failed, and had to crawl back into his flat where he lay on the floor, his face contorted with pain from the savage beating.

152

'Are you sober?' asked Dominil.

'No,' admitted the twins.

'Are you ready to play?'

'No.'

'Can you remember your songs?'

'No.'

'Can you at least remember the name of your band?'

Beauty and Delicious looked downcast. A few hours before they were due to play, stage fright had once again overwhelmed them. They were sitting in the largest room of the tenement in Leith Walk, staring blankly at the television.

'We thought we wouldn't bother doing the gig,' said Beauty, and her sister grunted in agreement.

Dominil breathed heavily. 'It's time for us to leave.'

'We're not going.'

'You see a pattern of behaviour here?' demanded Dominil. 'A gig is proposed. You are excited and keen. I organise everything. Then at the last minute you get stage fright and won't go on.'

'Pattern? No, I don't think there's a pattern. Delicious, do you see any pattern?'

'I don't think so.'

'Stand up,' said Dominil.

'We're not going.'

Dominil picked up one sister in each hand, lifting them off their feet.

'If we weren't so fashionably skinny, you wouldn't be able to do that,' protested Beauty.

'It's time to play. The rest of the band is waiting. Let's go.' Dominil hustled the unwilling twins downstairs and into the band's van.

Pete, Adam and Hamil greeted them all enthusiastically. They were in a strange city, playing a small gig, and they were looking forward to it. They knew that they might be playing in front of a small audience, who might not like them. They knew that they'd have to set up their equipment themselves and afterwards carry it all back into their van, probably receiving only a token payment. It didn't trouble them. They'd enjoy the gig anyway. So might the twins, eventually, though at this moment they were slumped motionless in the back of the van, looking anything but enthusiastic.

'Stage fright again?' asked Pete. 'Or just drunk?'

'Both,' replied Dominil. 'They'll be fine when they get there.'

As they drove through the Georgian streets towards the venue, the fog started to become thicker.

'I never knew Edinburgh was so foggy,' observed Pete.

'They call the fog haar,' said Dominil. 'A cold mist from the North Sea. It's quite common on the east coast of Scotland. The word comes either from Middle Dutch *hare*, a biting wind, or Frisian *harig*, meaning damp.'

'Someone make her stop talking,' groaned Beauty from the back of the van.

They arrived at the venue and began to unload their equipment. Dominil hefted a large amplifier cabinet onto her shoulder.

'Let me help you with that,' said Pete.

'I'm fine.'

'But it's heavy.'

Dominil was irritated. 'I don't need your help.'

'I'm sorry I got drunk and told everyone we slept together.'

'Fine.'

'I didn't mean to announce it to the whole warehouse.'

'Could we concentrate on getting our equipment inside?'

'I've never met anyone like you, Dominil. How about we give it a try?'

'I don't think that would be a good idea.'

'I do.' Pete smiled at her, and started to look besotted again.

Dominil tried to ignore him. Her phone vibrated in her pocket. She read the message.

hope the preparations for the gig are going well. albermarle

Dominil was tempted to text back, telling Albermarle she was going to kill him the first chance she got. Tormenting her with unwanted text messages while she was already being tormented by a love-sick guitarist was surely the last straw. She restrained her urge.

'Who was that from?' asked Pete.

'No one.'

'Oh. Do you have a boyfriend?'

'No.'

They carried some more equipment inside.

'So who was the text from?'

'It's really not your business.'

'Could we go out together sometime?'

434

Dominil turned to shout at the rest of the band. 'Are you going to hang around out there all day? Get that equipment indoors and be quick about it!'

153

Decembrius regained consciousness, crawled back into his flat, washed the blood off his face, then set out for Edinburgh. He had no money for a train or plane ticket but he had petrol in his tank so he drove. The journey through North London was frustratingly slow but when he reached the motorway the traffic was less and he made reasonably good time up the M1. He knew he could cover the distance in eight or nine hours if there were no serious delays. His inner werewolf strength and his desire to save Kalix carried him through the start of his journey but by the time he'd reached Northampton he was starting to flag. The Douglas-MacPhees had beaten him badly and he ached all over. He had a raging thirst and his head pounded unpleasantly. He tried to keep a steady pace, ignoring his discomfort, but by the time he neared Leeds he knew he couldn't carry on. No matter how urgently Decembrius wanted to reach the capital of Scotland, he wasn't going to get there like this. He was more likely to lose control of his car and crash.

As the sun went down, Decembrius pulled into a service station. He used the change in his pockets to put a small amount of petrol into the engine and bought a bottle of water from the store. The clerk looked at the livid bruises on his face, but didn't comment.

Decembrius returned to his parked car, drank the water, and then decided that he had to take something of a risk. It was ingrained into all MacRinnalch werewolves from the earliest age that they were never to transform while there was a chance that they might be seen, but this was an emergency. He moved his car to the furthest part of the compound, locked the doors, took off his coat, draped it over his head, curled up in the seat, and changed into his werewolf form. As the familiar shape descended on him he immediately felt his strength returning. He closed his eyes to sleep for a little while as a werewolf and regain his strength.

*

Decembrius was not the only one having a difficult time reaching Edinburgh. Vex, with a bag of T-shirts in one hand and a map in the other, was attempting to negotiate the British Isles, despite her poor teleporting skills and her complete lack of any sense of direction.

'Is this Edinburgh?' she asked a stranger, hopefully, after materialising in an alleyway and wandering out onto the main street.

'Edinburgh? This is Southampton.'

'Is that near Edinburgh?'

'It's about as far away as you can get.'

'Oh.'

Vex realised she'd travelled in the wrong direction. It was very confusing. Her aunt had made a path for her from the palace, through the dimensions, to Moonglow's flat, but everywhere else all looked the same. Vex attempted to point herself in the right direction, slipped back into the space between dimensions, and teleported again. She popped back into existence several hundred feet in the air and began plummeting towards the ground.

This is troubling, she thought, and dived back into nether space. Some minutes later she managed to land by the roadside in an unknown town. She approached an elderly lady at a bus stop.

'Is this Edinburgh?'

'This is Cardiff,' replied the elderly lady. 'You're in Wales.'

Agrivex walked off glumly.

This is difficult, she thought. Maybe I should give up.

She remembered Kalix rescuing her from the bullies at college, and how much she didn't want Kalix to be arrested and thrown into a dungeon at the castle, and then probably killed and eaten by her savage clan. Vex resolved to keep on going. Not bothering to check if anyone could see her, she popped out of existence again, clutching her map and hoping for the best.

154

The Enchantress was despondent.

'Don't worry about the shoes,' said Captain Easterly. 'So what if that woman Kabachetka gets her picture in *Vogue*? Soon you'll be dominating the magazine when your collection hits the high streets.'

'My collection is never going to hit the high streets.'

'People are going to buy your clothes if I have to bully the entire staff at my magazine to write about you in every issue for the next six months.'

Thrix almost laughed. 'You write for a men's magazine.'

'Doesn't matter. My family owns the magazine. I'll get it done. Don't worry; I'll sort it out for you. I know that buyer at Eldridge's, she doesn't scare me. I'll work something out with her.'

Easterly and Thrix had taken a seat in the reception hall, waiting, along with many others, for the performance to begin.

Easterly curled a strand of her hair round his finger. 'You're so beautiful.'

Thrix's eyes became misty. 'I love you,' she said.

'I love you too,' said Easterly.

Thrix kissed Captain Easterly quite passionately, though they were in a room full of people, most of them on their best behaviour before the opera started.

In the private area behind the stage the Fire Queen was not faring so well. Everywhere she went, the dreadful Princess Kabachetka seemed to follow her, tormenting her with her new Abukenti shoes. Malveria could hardly bear it. Making matters worse, the Princess was accompanied by some dreadful Hainusta woman with a screeching voice and another elemental who, Malveria thought, might have been her brother. She bridled. What was Kabachetka doing, inflicting her dreadful Hainusta family on this civilised gathering? Humans would not wish their gatherings to be infected with Hainusta. And nor would werewolves, she was sure. Yet Kabachetka was swanning around from one group to another, batting her ridiculous eyelashes in all directions and generally being a menace. Malveria could not imagine why anyone would be taking pictures of her, though it seemed to be happening constantly.

Malveria made up her mind to confront her and put her in her place, but quickly realised it was hopeless. Kabachetka was armed with the best shoes in the room, and there was nothing Malveria could do about it. No matter how barbed a comment the Queen might make, it would not puncture the Princess. Malveria knew she would lose the encounter. She took a glass of champagne from a waiter, downed it swiftly, took another, and walked away from Kabachetka and her admirers. Finding herself in front of a door marked PRIVATE – PERFORMERS ONLY, Malveria whispered a word, causing the door to open, and went through unobserved.

Mr Felicori, in conversation with his vocal coach, was surprised to find Malveria appearing as if from nowhere by his side.

'Eh . . . delightful to see you. Wasn't that door locked?'

'A wise precaution,' said Malveria. 'Strong measures are needed to keep Kabachetka at bay.'

'Yes . . . I am just making some final preparations—'

'Of course, don't let me interrupt.'

'I need to concentrate—'

'Absolutely. A superb singer such as yourself cannot be continually disturbed by fake-blonde princesses tramping through your dressing room every minute, boasting about their footwear. A little wine?'

Malveria settled down comfortably on one of the couches in Mr Felicori's nicely appointed dressing room, and sighed. 'Life seems like a terrible trial, I must confess. I did not expect to be outflanked by Kabachetka yet here she is, her feet clad in a superior fashion, being photographed at this very minute for a piece in the *Vogue* "Fashionable Party People" page. When DeMortalis learns of it he will be very cutting.'

Malveria took out a tiny lace handkerchief and dabbed her eyes, while Mr Felicori and his vocal coach looked on, completely bewildered.

155

Alone at her small table in the crowded train, Kalix drifted off into a very uncomfortable sleep, full of bad dreams and intrusions from the outside world. Laudanum coursed through her veins, as well as the last of the whisky she'd taken from Decembrius. Her mind went back to the night she'd spent with him. She woke briefly to think that she didn't like him any better now. Or perhaps she did. She didn't want to think about it now. Kalix was too fixated on revenge. She drifted off to sleep again, this time leaning forward and sprawling over the table so that her hair splayed everywhere. While this still seemed like strange behaviour, it was a relief to those on the opposite side of the aisle who no longer had to look nervously at the young girl's maddened features which had been upsetting them for the past two hundred and fifty miles.

Kalix half dreamed and half imagined that she was Baby Wolf in the forest, and Robber Wolf rescued her from the huntsmen who'd captured her. She woke up startled, looking around for hunters, then realised it was a dream. The thought of Baby Wolf being rescued by Robber Wolf brought a brief ray of sunshine into her troubled soul. A moment later a buffet cart was pushed noisily through the carriage, with a caterer offering tea and coffee, and Kalix snarled angrily at the woman, confusing her for a second with Moonglow, who was always trying to force her to eat. The travellers around Kalix tried to ignore this further piece of anti-social behaviour and checked their watches, longing to arrive in Edinburgh and be free of their uncongenial travelling companion.

When the train finally pulled into Waverley Station in Edinburgh, Kalix rose swiftly from her seat. As she headed towards the door, people stepped out of the way as if she might be contagious. Kalix walked through the turnstile, handing her crumpled ticket to a bored-looking attendant, then walked swiftly through the concourse. She had to push her way through a crowd who'd gathered round a stall offering free cupcakes, advertising a local bakery. Someone actually thrust a small cake into her hand. Kalix mangled it in her palm and dropped it on the concourse. Several pigeons, wheeling about in the space below the great transparent panels of the station roof, descended swiftly to squabble over the crumbs. Kalix ignored them and picked up her pace, barging through the crowd. Two transport policemen looked at her curiously, but didn't interfere.

As she emerged from the station night was falling and the fog was thickening. She pulled a scrap of paper from the deep pockets of her coat. The flier gave the location of the gig where she'd find Dominil. Kalix had been in Edinburgh several times as a girl and knew where she was going. She marched swiftly through the city, looking neither left nor right, snarling occasionally at pedestrians who blocked her way on the pavement. Blood now dripped from inside the sleeve of her coat onto her hand, the result of the wounds she'd self-inflicted, and scratched again on the journey. The letter N on her arm was now completely obliterated. Kalix had given up pretending to be normal.

156

Decembrius made a strong recovery. His sleep had cost him an hour in journey time but the bold move of taking on his werewolf form completely revived him. He felt well. Promising himself that he'd be revenged on the Douglas-MacPhees sometime, he put his car into gear and rejoined the motorway.

'Time to rescue that idiot Kalix,' he muttered, and grinned. He liked the idea of rescuing Kalix.

He presumed that she'd be heading for the Yum Yum Sugary Snacks gig. That was where Dominil would be. There might be a few younger werewolves at the gig, Decembrius supposed, but no one who was senior in the clan. Any of the older werewolves who'd chosen to leave their homelands for Edinburgh this weekend would most probably have gone to Andamair House to support the Mistress of the Werewolves. That was fortunate for Kalix. If she did run into any senior members of the clan they'd certainly attempt to detain her and take her back to the castle. Kalix might be allowed, through the influence of her mother, to exist quietly in London, but they wouldn't put up with her impudence in appearing back in Scotland.

As a member of the Great Council, Decembrius himself might be criticised for going to the gig rather than the opera, but he didn't care. What could they do? Expel him from the council? Decembrius knew he was unsuitable to be on the council anyway. Let them expel him. His bravado was temporarily reduced by the thought of what his mother would say. Decembrius didn't exactly fear Lucia but he hated it when she lectured him, as she undoubtedly would were he banished from the council. She'd never let him hear the end of it. Decembrius dismissed thoughts of his mother and drove on as fast as he dared without attracting unwanted attention from the occasional police car that sat on the hard shoulder or in lay-bys. Being pulled over for speeding was the last thing he needed. He wasn't sure what time Kalix had caught the train, but he'd be lucky if he reached the gig in time.

'Don't kill Dominil, Kalix,' he muttered. 'The MacRinnalchs will never forgive you. You'll have to flee the country.'

Musing that fleeing the country with Kalix didn't seem like that bad an idea, he pulled out into the right-hand lane, sped past several articulated lorries, and found himself now only eighty miles from Edinburgh, and making good time.

157

As the doors to the auditorium opened and the crowd in the outside rooms began to file in to hear the performance, Princess Kabachetka managed to isolate Captain Easterly for a few moments of snatched conversation.

'Easterly, is everything in order?'

'Yes.'

'You must be sure to strike quickly. At the start of the performance I will cause Queen Malveria to be stranded between dimensions. Soon afterwards the Enchantress will lose her powers. You must kill her quickly, in case the Queen returns.'

'I know the plan.'

The Princess smiled, and looked happier than Easterly had ever seen her.

'Do you require more of my power?'

Easterly shook his head. 'I have enough.'

The Princess touched his arm anyway, and he felt some heat flow into his body.

'Just in case. It would not do for the Enchantress to discover you at the last minute. It is fortunate that you encountered me, Easterly. Without my powers you could not have concealed yourself from her sorcery. You would have been discovered as a hunter, and killed.'

'I suppose so.'

'You know the Enchantress would kill you instantly were she to discover the truth?'

Easterly made no reply.

Princess Kabachetka's eyes narrowed. She still had her doubts about Easterly. 'When I am heir to the Hainusta throne, and Distikka is ruler of the Hiyasta, you will have many powerful friends. Or many powerful enemies, if you get things wrong.'

'I won't get things wrong. And who do you think you're threatening, anyway? You think you scare me, Princess?'

The Princess laughed. 'Not as much as I should. But that's because you don't fully appreciate my power. Kill the Enchantress when the chance arrives, Easterly, and we shall all be happy. Now excuse me, my ridiculous brother and his appalling consort are approaching and I must take them into the auditorium. I trust that my appearance in these splendid shoes had the desired effect on the Enchantress and the Fire Queen?'

'They were upset.'

The Princess laughed once more. She'd known that securing the Abukenti shoes and scoring such a fashion triumph would wound Thrix and Malveria deeply. She'd accurately predicted that both would resort to wine to bolster their crushed spirits, and consequently let down their guards even further. Which, she observed, they had. Neither Thrix nor Malveria could be said to be at their brightest at the moment.

The Princess disappeared in the crush, and Easterly found himself beside the Mistress of the Werewolves as he entered the auditorium. She greeted him stiffly.

'My daughter's companion,' she said to a woman Easterly didn't recognise. Probably a MacRinnalch, from the cast of her features. Easterly felt a sudden thrill, knowing that he was in the presence of many werewolves and was here under the unwitting protection of one of their number. How many MacRinnalchs might be in the audience tonight? In amongst the crowd of wealthy patrons of the arts, Easterly was sure he'd spotted at least five or six probable werewolves. He'd have to be very careful to dispose of Thrix in some private way, to allow himself a

442

chance of escape. It was a task only the most expert of werewolf hunters could manage. He wondered where that most inexpert of werewolf hunters, Albermarle, was. In London, he hoped. If Albermarle followed up on his plan to attack Dominil tonight, he would surely die.

Albermarle and his junior associates just didn't have the strength to cope with Dominil, particularly as there was every likelihood of other werewolves being around her at the gig. These werewolves would be unaffected by the Princess's spell. When she brought on the eclipse of the moon to steal the Enchantress's powers, it would only work in a small area. Anyone outside of Andamair House would be unaffected. If Albermarle chose that moment to attack Dominil, he'd undoubtedly be defeated.

158

The Thane was not at his best. He greeted guests and charmed benefactors while sharing hosting duties with his mother but seemed, for some reason, distracted.

'Are you all right?' asked Beatrice, not for the first time.

'Of course. Why wouldn't I be?'

'You keep looking over your shoulder.'

Markus brushed the question aside, claiming to be merely concerned that their guests were all being properly looked after. But Markus was indeed distracted. He was here with Beatrice at his side, while Heather was, as far as he knew, currently working backstage. If Heather appeared in the reception hall while he was with Beatrice, there was going to be an embarrassing scene.

I really should have organised things better, he told himself. I am Thane, after all.

Just before the assembled crowd was due to filter into the auditorium the Mistress of the Werewolves approached him, embraced him, and thanked him warmly for his support.

'I really couldn't have organised this without you.'

Markus embraced his mother in return, unselfconsciously. Verasa smiled at Beatrice. She'd come to like the young castle-archivist more and more and now regarded her as a reasonably suitable partner for her son. While Beatrice was not from the most glorious of werewolf heritages – which would have been better, given that Markus was Thane – she was at least respectable. As far as Verasa had been able to find out, there were no skeletons in the young werewolf's closet. Nothing that might bring disgrace on the clan. If only, thought Verasa, she could encourage Markus to settle down, the clan might finally begin to enjoy some sort of peace and sobriety. Though the scars of the recent feud had faded, they hadn't disappeared. Nothing would unite the MacRinnalchs like a good wedding, particularly one that involved the Thane.

Verasa's attention was claimed by a party of executives from a banking corporation who were very large sponsors of the event. She led them into the hall, leaving Markus and Beatrice behind.

Beatrice, who always felt a little tense in the presence of the Mistress of the Werewolves, relaxed. 'I think she's starting to like me.'

Markus smiled. 'She always did like you. She just wasn't sure if you were a suitable partner.'

'It's a pity my family didn't fight at Bannockburn.' The MacRinnalchs had a proud history. They had often marched to war in support of the Kings of Scotland. 'Unfortunately, my family doesn't seem to include any illustrious ancestors.'

'But no humans, either.' Markus smiled. 'That would really be the end.'

They kissed. A photographer took their picture, because Markus was so handsome, and they made an excellent couple.

'Hello, Markus.'

They stopped kissing and looked round. Heather MacAllister was smiling at them.

'Hello,' said Heather brightly, speaking to Beatrice. 'I'm Markus's girlfriend. Or I thought I was. And you would be?'

159

Cameron MacRinnalch's previous gigs had been moderately successful, without attracting a huge amount of interest. Cameron would have been surprised to learn of the efforts that were now being made by various people to get to his latest one. Kalix, fresh off the train from London, was marching through the foggy city, paying scant regard to traffic or pedestrians, eyes fixed on some point a few feet ahead of her on the pavement, her mouth hanging open. Decembrius was some way behind but not far from the city. He wondered if he should look for a parking space in the middle of town, which might be difficult, or abandon his car further out and hurry onwards on foot. Meanwhile Vex had popped up on a small island off the north coast of Scotland, and was wondering why there was so much sea everywhere. Fierce breakers rumbled towards her on the shore.

'Hmm. This doesn't look right.'

She attempted to ask a seal, rolling lazily on the beach, if she was anywhere near Edinburgh, but the seal didn't seem in the mood for talking. Vex looked quizzically at her map, glanced at the sun, trying to gauge which direction she might be going in, then set off again, disappearing from view and leaving the seal in peace.

Inside the small venue, Dominil wasn't impressed.

'Having driven four hundred miles, I expected something better.'

Dominil regarded her surroundings with distaste. The club was little more than a cellar underneath a tattoo parlour, with a tiny stage, a small bar, and not much room for an audience. It was dark, smelled of damp, and the dressing room was the size of a cupboard.

'The warehouse was better than this.'

'Relax,' said Pete. 'It's rock and roll.'

'I hate it,' mumbled Beauty. Neither she nor her sister had yet embraced the spirit of rock and roll. Both were still suffering from nerves. Dominil suggested that they retire to the small dressing room and attend to their make-up which, she knew, would occupy their attention. The twins did so, closing the door behind them, leaving Dominil and the others to set up their equipment.

'They'll be fine once the gig starts,' said Dominil.

'Have you had a boyfriend recently?' asked Pete, trying, and failing, to sound casual.

445

'No, but I've had some stalkers,' muttered Dominil, and busied herself preparing for the soundcheck. It didn't take long to set up. The stage was barely large enough for their amplifiers and speakers.

'Are the twins ready to soundcheck?'

Dominil went to check on them, hoping that the process of doing their make-up would have calmed them down. The other alternative was that they'd be lying on the floor in an advanced state of intoxication. She slipped into the tiny dressing room.

'What on Earth?'

Beauty, perched on a chair in front of a cracked mirror, was in her werewolf shape. That was a surprise, because neither of the twins could transform at will.

'What happened?'

'I don't know.'

'Why did you change? And how?'

'I don't know. It just happened.'

At that moment Delicious involuntarily transformed as well.

'Stop doing that. Change back.'

The twins laughed.

'This is funny!' Beauty exclaimed.

'No, it isn't. You've got a gig to play. Change back.'

But the sisters claimed not to be able to. They hadn't meant to change in the first place, and now they seemed to be stuck.

'Trust you to be the first werewolves ever to get stuck,' said Dominil, angrily. 'Are you sure you can't change back?'

The twins strained to make the transformation, without success. They were so unused to making the change at all, apart from around the full moon, that the whole experience was quite strange. They stopped laughing, realising the seriousness of the situation.

'We can't go on stage like this. Can we?'

'No.'

'Could we pretend we were in costume?'

'That's the most ludicrous idea I've ever heard.' Dominil clenched her fists in frustration. Trust the twins to come up with some new way of ruining everything. 'Just change back – it's not difficult. I'll show you.' She changed into her werewolf shape and stood in front of the sisters. 'Now, concentrate—'

At that moment Pete walked into the dressing room. Finding himself confronted by three werewolves, he moved faster than anyone had ever seen him move before, leaping backwards in shock and crashing against the wall so violently that he knocked himself out. He slid down the wall to lie unconscious on the floor.

'Well, that's fantastic,' said Dominil. 'Now the guitarist knows we're werewolves.'

'And he's unconscious.'

Dominil pushed a chair against the door to keep it closed, then bent down over Pete.

'Don't kill him!' Delicious looked worried. 'It's not his fault he found out we're werewolves.'

'I wasn't planning on killing him. Though it might make our lives easier.'

160

'I'm defeated.' Moonglow was hunched on the couch, her hands thrust deep in the pockets of her shiny latex jacket.

Daniel couldn't remember ever seeing her quite so dejected. It would have been an excellent opportunity for stepping in and cheering Moonglow up. Unfortunately, Daniel was too dejected to make the attempt. The loss of their money was a shattering blow, one which made it impossible to feel any emotion except depression and defeat.

'I'll get a job,' said Daniel.

Moonglow nodded. She would have to find work as well, to pay their debts. 'But it won't help us right away. If we don't pay the electricity today we're going to be disconnected. And the phone bill needs to be paid by tomorrow.'

'What about the council tax?'

'Also tomorrow.' Moonglow sighed, loudly. 'I thought we could help Kalix. I was mistaken. Every time we do, she just lets us down. I can't believe she took that money.'

Daniel didn't argue. If Moonglow had come to the end of her patience with Kalix it was understandable.

'I hope she's safe in Scotland.' Moonglow's expression darkened. 'But if she comes back, she'll have to move out. I'm not living with someone who steals from us.'

'What about Vex?'

'I don't know. Right now I don't care.' Moonglow put her hand on the phone, then withdrew it. 'I really can't bear asking my parents for money.'

Daniel nodded. He knew how embarrassing that was going to be. If he could have asked his own family for money he would have, but Daniel's mother didn't have any money to spare. He shifted uncomfortably, wincing a little. His back was sore. After going out with friends the previous night they'd stayed over. Moonglow had slept in the spare bed. Daniel, gallantly, had volunteered to sleep on the couch. Now he had a stiff neck.

'I expect Malveria will take Vex home anyway,' said Moonglow, 'when she learns that she's missed the exam.' Kalix and Vex's final exam was tomorrow. In addition to her fury over the missing money, Moonglow was outraged that they'd simply disappeared when they were due to sit their exam. 'Looking after them was a complete waste of time.'

Daniel stared at the sheet of paper in his hands. 'Can you help me with this?'

'What is it?'

'My application for work at the supermarket, stacking shelves. Every time I try to write my name, my eyes go blurry.' Filling in his application form, Daniel felt quite bitter about everything. 'I should have known the minute we met a werewolf that no good would come of it.'

161

Though the gigs Cameron MacRinnalch had previously organised had not been spectacularly successful, the venue he used was small enough not to require a huge audience to generate a good atmosphere. Tonight the usual crowd of students was augmented by a few of the younger MacRinnalchs, students themselves mainly, sent to university in Edinburgh by werewolf parents keen for their children to better themselves. There was a great feeling in the room as they waited for the band to appear. Yum Yum Sugary Snacks, being even more obscure than the rest of the bill, were on first.

In the privacy of the dressing room it seemed like they might never go on at all.

'What are we going to do?' Dominil desperately tried to think of some sort of story they could tell Pete to get them out of this mess, but she knew it was hopeless. Pete had seen Beauty and Delicious as werewolves, and it couldn't be undone. 'Unless he thought he was hallucinating. Does Pete take drugs?'

'Of course not,' said Beauty. 'He is a guitarist in a rock band, after all.'

The twins burst out laughing.

'This is not funny,' growled Dominil. 'And will you please change back before anyone else sees you?'

'I kind of felt like I almost changed when I laughed,' said Beauty. 'Dominil, could you say something funny? Sorry, foolish question.'

It was a mystery why the twins had suddenly transformed. Dominil's immediate thought was that the return to Scotland, possibly in conjunction with the twins' intake of alcohol, might have affected their metabolisms somehow.

'I wonder if Pete might have amnesia after banging his head? We might get away with it if you change back right now.'

Beauty and Delicious strained to transform. They couldn't.

Pete's eyes flickered open. 'What's going on?' He rubbed his head, and hauled himself to his feet, looking annoyed. 'You should have told me you were going to wear costumes. It gave me a fright.'

'I told you we could say that!' cried Beauty. 'Dominil said it was ridiculous.'

'Where did you get the masks?' Pete marched over to Delicious and pulled her ear.

'Ouch.'

Pete looked troubled. Delicious's ear seemed very realistic. It didn't look like part of a mask. As his eyes adjusted to the poor

449

light he noticed that her entire body seemed to be a different shape.

'What's going on?'

There was a long silence, punctuated by the sound of people outside shouting orders at the bar.

'Well, this is awkward,' said Beauty.

Dominil, always resourceful, found herself out of ideas.

'We really are werewolves. *That*'s what's going on,' said Beauty. 'Normally we keep it secret.'

Suddenly realising that it was true, Pete looked terrified, and opened his mouth to yell. Abruptly, he closed his mouth and stopped looking so terrified. He turned to Dominil. 'You're a werewolf too, aren't you?'

'No.'

'Yes, you are! You're just like them! Can I see you as a werewolf?'

'I'm not a werewolf.'

'I know you are. I bet you make a really nice werewolf!'

The twins sniggered.

Pete looked excited. 'This explains a lot.'

He stepped closer to Dominil, which, in the tiny dressing room, brought him almost into contact with her.

'I'll never tell anyone you're a werewolf. I'd never give you away.'

'Thank you,' said Dominil, dryly.

Adam, the drummer, knocked on the door. 'What's going on in there? It's almost time to play.'

'We're not ready yet,' replied Beauty.

'We need to use the dressing room too,' shouted Adam.

'What for?'

'Simon needs to do his make-up.' It was a reasonable point. Simon the bass player always wore some make-up on stage.

'I've got a new shirt to try on,' called Hamil, the keyboard player.

'Finally they all decide to make an effort,' muttered Dominil inside the dressing room. 'Well, Butix, Delix. This is it. Either you change back to human now or we call off the gig and smuggle you out with blankets over your heads. What's it to be? Pete, if you're opening your mouth to say something personal about me, close it immediately or you'll regret it.'

450

Pete closed his mouth.

Beauty and Delicious once more strained to change back. Again, there was no result. The twins looked hopelessly at each other.

'I can't change,' Beauty whined.

'What if we're stuck for ever?' Delicious looked distraught. 'We'll never be able to go out again!'

Suddenly, and very unexpectedly, Pete threw his arms round Dominil and attempted to kiss her. Dominil, outraged, pushed him away, very roughly. He bounced off the wall and slid to the floor again. The twins roared with laughter. Pete making a desperate grab for Dominil was one of the funniest things they'd ever seen.

'What do you think you're doing?' demanded Dominil.

'I thought a sudden shock might make them change.'

'This is not a bad case of hiccups. It's the fundamental core of our being.'

Pete looked abashed, and sore. Beauty and Delicious roared with mirth. Delicious actually slid off her chair, and as she hit the ground she changed back to human. Moments later, her sister did likewise.

'Hey, we changed back.'

Dominil looked at them gravely.

'Apparently, uncontrollable laughter has shaken your metabolisms back into some sort of order.' She swivelled to glare at Pete. 'Don't ever do that again.'

'Could I see you as a werewolf?'

'If you do it'll probably be the last thing you ever see. Now, is everyone ready to play?'

'I can't just go onstage and play guitar right after finding out about werewolves,' protested Pete. 'I'll need time to think about things.'

'You don't *have* any time,' snapped Dominil. 'I've driven this pair of idiots four hundred miles up the motorway, not to mention doing whatever is necessary to place your limited talents before the public. If you don't get up there and make it sound good, then you're going to discover how mean a werewolf can be.'

'She can be a really mean werewolf,' said Delicious.

'She's notorious for it,' agreed Beauty. 'You should stay away from her.'

'I think I'd be OK about going out with a werewolf.' Pete was philosophical. 'I'd make allowances.'

'The MacRinnalch werewolves do not seek allowances from their boyfriends,' said Dominil icily. 'Not that you will ever be my boyfriend. Now *play*.'

Shortly afterwards, Yum Yum Sugary Snacks trooped onstage. The unexpected transformation problem had at least cleared the anxiety from the sisters' minds, and they appeared onstage looking excited. The crowd cheered. Though it was dark in the venue, the gloom couldn't entirely obscure the incredible candy-floss pink and brilliant electric blue of the twins' hair. They ambled into position, greeted the audience cheerfully, and announced their first song.

After the string of humiliations I've suffered, thought Dominil, this had better be good.

Pete started up their first number, launching into it with gusto.

'You're playing the wrong song,' yelled Beauty.

There was a period of confusion while the band argued about which song they were meant to be opening with. The crowd laughed and jeered. Dominil hung her head.

Why did I involve myself with these people? she wondered. Was my life really so full of ennui?

Her phone vibrated in her pocket. She took it out, reading the message on the illuminated screen.

dominil you're a fool. i tricked you. we weren't after you at all. we've removed the enchantress's powers and now we're going to kill her. love from albermarle, your more intelligent friend

Dominil looked at the message, then looked at the stage. Delicious had now fallen over, while Pete had started up another song. Beauty shouted at him again, telling him it was the wrong one. No one seemed sure. Their set was rapidly degenerating into chaos. Dominil put her phone back in her pocket and marched out of the cellar. Cameron MacRinnalch called to her as she walked past him at the desk.

'Leaving the gig?'

'I have to go to the opera.'

452

162

'Do you really, honestly like opera?' asked the Enchantress.

'Not much,' admitted Captain Easterly.

Thrix was relieved. 'Me neither. Thanks for coming anyway.'

'Thanks for inviting me.'

They pressed closer to each other in their seats. The lights had dimmed and the audience awaited the entrance of the renowned Felicori. The great ballroom at Andamair House, restored and refurbished by Markus, with its candelabras in place and seating installed for the occasion, looked like a very suitable venue for the famous singer. Not as illustrious as the great opera houses of Europe, but intimate and refined nonetheless.

The Mistress of the Werewolves was pleased with Markus's work. But as the lights went down, Verasa was troubled. For one thing, there was no sign of Markus. For another, Felicori was late appearing onstage. Verasa could hear some important sponsors whispering to each other as they waited in the semi-darkness.

'What's the delay?'

The crowd, while too polite to jeer, became tangibly unsettled as the opera singer failed to appear. Verasa waited a few moments before rising gracefully from her seat and heading backstage. People had donated a lot of money to be here. She didn't intend to let her event be ruined.

In the backstage area she grasped hold of the first stagehand she encountered. 'Have you seen Mr Felicori?'

'I think he's still in his dressing room.'

'He should be onstage.'

'They're temperamental, opera singers.'

'They can be temperamental on their own time,' muttered Verasa, heading for Felicori's dressing room. 'Not on mine.'

Unexpectedly, she bumped into Princess Kabachetka. Verasa regarded her suspiciously. She was a fire elemental, after all. Not as dreadful as Malveria, certainly, but still not to be entirely trusted. 'What are you doing here?' she asked the Princess.

'I slipped away to rescue Mr Felicori.'

'Rescue him? From who?'

'Queen Malveria, of course. It is she who detains him, undoubtedly.'

'How do you know that?'

'I can sense her aura from here. Who knows what she may be doing in his dressing room?'

Now quite alarmed, Verasa picked up the pace. She burst into the dressing room without knocking, fearing the worst. The sight that met her wasn't quite as bad as she'd imagined. Malveria was seated on a small couch, weeping freely, while Felicori and his vocal coach were apparently trying to console her.

'Mr Felicori! You're due onstage.'

The singer looked apologetically towards Verasa. 'I'm sorry. But my friend is quite distressed. We have been attempting to comfort her . . .'

163

As Kalix approached the dark doorway that led down to the cellar she could sense the presence of several werewolves. The MacRinnalch scent was unmistakable. Beauty and Delicious were here, and a few others. But not, as far as she could tell, Dominil. She hurried down the stairs into a tiny corridor lined with posters advertising obscure local bands. She knew immediately that the young man sitting at the table, taking money, was a werewolf. She grabbed him by the throat and bared her teeth.

'Where's Dominil?'

Cameron MacRinnalch shrank from Kalix's grasp. He'd never met Kalix before but he recognised her immediately from her reputation. Stories of her madness circulated in the clan, stories that grew bloodier in the telling. She'd killed three huge MacAndris werewolves, Sarapen's bodyguards, cutting them down in an instant. She'd massacred any amount of werewolf enemies at the great battle in London. Kalix had killed werewolves and men from one end of the country to the other and now she was here, with madness in her eyes and the stench of blood seeping from her hidden wounds. Cameron wilted under the terrible strength that flowed from her skinny frame. 'She left!'

'Where did she go?'

'The opera!' Cameron felt desperate. He was strong like any MacRinnalch, but young, and unused to fighting. He knew that Kalix could kill him. 'The opera at Andamair House.'

'The charity event?'

Cameron nodded, and looked terrified.

Kalix let go of his throat. She growled. So Dominil had gone to Andamair House. Kalix had been there as a child. It was some distance away. She didn't know the bus routes. Perhaps she could take a taxi.

From inside the cellar came the raucous sound of Yum Yum Sugary Snacks, pounding out a disjointed version of 'Vile Werewolf Whore', one of the songs they'd written about Dominil. The smell of Kalix's blood and the strength of his own fear gave Cameron MacRinnalch a desperate yearning to take on his own werewolf shape. He struggled against it, fearing that Kalix would kill him if he did.

'I need money for a taxi.'

'Take this,' said Cameron, desperate for Kalix to leave. He thrust the metal box containing his takings towards her. Kalix scooped up some notes, stuffed them into her pockets, and ran back up the stairs, her hair and coat flying in her wake. Behind her Cameron MacRinnalch shuddered. He regretted putting on the gig. Yum Yum Sugary Snacks were terrible, and Kalix was worse. The encounter left him shaken. He'd never met a werewolf like Kalix before. She wasn't civilised. She was violent and insane. Yum Yum Sugary Snacks came to a grinding halt midway through a song. There was a terrible cacophony of jeers, screams and feedback. Cameron shuddered again. Perhaps he should forget about promoting music, and just concentrate on his studies.

164

'Please leave this dressing room,' demanded the Mistress of the Werewolves. 'Mr Felicori is late on stage.'

The Fire Queen regarded Verasa with dislike. She resented anyone ordering her about. Nonetheless, realising that this was not the best place for an argument, she withdrew as gracefully as she could.

'I knew it was a mistake to attend this event,' she muttered as she left. 'I shouldn't have let the Mistress of the Werewolves talk me into it. The MacRinnalchs cannot be trusted to behave in a civilised manner. And what are you doing in my presence, Kabachetka?'

'Assisting you to walk straight. How much champagne did you consume?'

Malveria eyed her with loathing. 'You may have defeated me in the matter of shoes, but that does not disguise your—' She halted. She couldn't think of a suitable insult. The shoe upset, and the champagne, seemed to have erased her imagination. She scowled, and made to depart.

Behind her the Princess steeled herself, and almost lost her nerve. If she didn't get this part right the whole plan would fail, and disaster would follow. Princess Kabachetka sent all her power into her aura, rendering it impossible to read, or so she hoped. The Queen of the Hiyasta had great powers when it came to interpreting auras. On the other hand, thought the Princess, she is full of champagne and disappointment. It's now or never. She reached forward, lightly tapping the Fire Queen on the shoulder.

Malveria spun around. 'What do you want, vile Princess?'

'To say goodbye.'

Malveria's expression brightened. 'Are you leaving?'

'No. But you are. Leaving your throne, that is.'

'Pardon?'

'Distikka is at this moment taking over your realm. She belongs to the royal blood, being the granddaughter of your forgotten brother Gravan. She can control the volcano, and will be in charge by the time you arrive back.'

If the Princess expected the Fire Queen to leap in alarm, she was disappointed. Malveria merely narrowed her eyes and studied the Princess very closely. 'What is this nonsense?'

'It's not nonsense. No doubt you can tell from my aura that I'm telling the truth.'

'I can tell from your aura that you're using all your power to prevent it from being read.'

'I'm also telling the truth. Distikka is your relative. She claims power over the volcano, and the throne. By the time you get home, she'll be Queen.'

Malveria put her face close to her rival's, scanning it. 'Why would you tell me this?'

'To laugh at you before you die.'

Malveria stepped back, snapped her fingers, and dematerialised. The Princess smiled, and walked back into the main hall where Felicori was now in full song, the glory of his opening aria making the audience forget that they'd had to wait.

'Goodbye, Malveria,' muttered the Princess. 'By the time you make it through the barrier I've set up, Distikka really will be in control. And now, Enchantress, while the Queen is away, it's time to deal with you.'

It bothered the Princess that in this realm, the Enchantress was probably her equal in power. Thrix was undoubtedly prepared for any piece of Hainusta sorcery, at least any piece that could be brought to Earth.

'But you are not prepared for the sorcery of your old teacher, are you?' she muttered beneath her breath as she slipped back into the main auditorium. Minerva MacRinnalch's work was fascinating. Particularly her spell for producing a false eclipse of the moon.

At the far end of the hall, the Princess saw Markus MacRinnalch leaving the building, apparently in pursuit of some woman.

You will suffer too, thought the Princess maliciously, though she didn't really care about Markus. Thrix and Kalix were her main targets.

The Princess muttered a short sentence, speaking Minerva's spell.

'The werewolves may find it much more painful than a normal eclipse, being unnatural, and wrenched through the fabric of time, as it were. Now I really must sit down. Mr Felicori seems to be in excellent form.'

The Princess made her way to her seat, apologising sweetly to the people she disturbed on the way.

*

The Enchantress was relieved when Felicori finally appeared on the stage. After the effort her mother had put into the event she deserved success.

'If it goes well she might not notice when I don't turn up to the next council meeting.'

Captain Easterly slid his hand into hers and they sat contentedly together, a couple who, while not exactly fans of the opera, were happy to be there together. Suddenly Thrix's senses felt a tiny prickle of apprehension, followed immediately by a great wave of nausea. She struggled to remain upright in her seat. The nausea was overwhelming and she fought to avoid throwing up over her evening dress. Thrix's head swam. The pleasant haze brought on by Easterly's company, the warmth in the room, and champagne, turned into a thick, dense fog that clouded her senses and made it difficult even to think. Thrix suddenly put her hand to her mouth and lurched forward.

'What's the matter?' whispered Easterly.

'I'm going to be sick.'

Easterly didn't hesitate. Showing no self-consciousness about making a fuss in front of the audience, he rose, took Thrix's arm, helped her to her feet, then unapologetically pushed past the rows of seated people, taking Thrix with him.

'Take me outside, I need air.'

Easterly guided Thrix out.

Oh God, she thought blearily. Everyone will think I'm drunk.

As Thrix and Easterly reached the door, Felicori soared to the conclusion of an aria from *Aida*. The audience burst into applause and he bowed in the spotlight. Easterly supported Thrix as they made their way through the door that led to the gardens of Andamair House. Outside, a heavy fog was swirling around the grounds.

'Take me where no one can see. There's a maze on the other side of the lawn.'

Easterly hadn't asked what was the matter. Thrix thought that was gallant of him, given that the only credible explanation was that she'd drunk too much.

'No one can see us here,' said Easterly, leading her to the edge of the maze, and then a few yards inside. 'Do you want to sit down?'

165

Decembrius hurried down the stairs into the cellar. From within the room below came an odd noise, a mixture of guitars, screams and breaking furniture. At the foot of the stairs he met Cameron MacRinnalch, who he didn't know but sensed immediately was a werewolf.

Cameron was aghast as Decembrius approached. Normally he'd have been pleased to welcome any fellow werewolf into the venue, particularly one with red hair, a leather coat and multiple earrings. But Decembrius had a livid bruise on his cheek and several deep scratches on his face. He had regained his vitality but his injuries would take longer to heal.

'Is Dominil MacRinnalch here?'

'She left. Went to the opera.'

'Has Kalix been here?'

Cameron nodded. 'She left, too.'

Decembrius glanced towards the door. 'What's that racket?'

'I think the twins might be fighting with the audience.'

Decembrius grunted, and hurried back up the stairs. His car was double-parked and as he arrived several drivers were gathering round in the narrow street, wondering who was responsible for the obstruction. Decembrius brushed them out the way without a word and set off towards Andamair House.

Seconds after he'd gone, Vex popped into sight on the pavement. She looked around her, smiled with satisfaction, and trotted down the stairs.

'I finally got here. You're a werewolf, right?'

Cameron regarded her suspiciously. As this latest visitor wasn't a werewolf, there seemed no reason why she should have recognised him as one.

'Who are you?'

'Vex. I'm a fire elemental.'

'I've never heard of fire elementals.'

'Oh . . . Well, here I am. Is Kalix here?'

Cameron shook his head wearily. He longed to be back in his Halls of Residence, studying quietly. There was the sound of breaking glass, then a guitar started up and Yum Yum Sugary Snacks lurched into a frantic version of 'Yum Yum Cute Boys', another crowd-pleaser. Judging by the accompanying noise from the audience it appeared that half of them were enjoying the performance and the other half were rioting.

'I want to see the band!' cried Vex, and clenched her fists in frustration. 'Can't see the band. Have to find Kalix. Where is she?'

'She went to the opera. With everyone else.'

Vex held out her map. 'Could you show me where it is?'

Cameron looked at Vex's map, which had a section showing Edinburgh City Centre. Unfortunately, it didn't extend quite far enough outside the city to show the precise location of Andamair House.

'It's just a bit further than the last page. By the time you get there you'll probably be able to see it.'

'OK.'

Vex leaned forward and kissed Cameron on the forehead.

He looked surprised. 'Why did you do that?'

'I thought you were looking depressed,' said Vex brightly. 'Next time you put on Yum Yum Sugary Snacks, I'll be here for sure. Bye!'

Vex dematerialised.

Cameron MacRinnalch shrank back in his chair. 'And I thought it was strange being a werewolf,' he muttered. 'Tonight is really terrible. I wish that awful band would stop playing.'

166

The maze at Andamair House had hedges that were taller than a man. Once inside, a person was completely hidden from view. Captain Easterly led the Enchantress in, as she'd asked him to.

Thrix had a fear of showing weakness in public and didn't want anyone to see her so ill. She regretted at first that Easterly was with her, and would rather have suffered alone. But as the freezing tendrils of the cloying fog brushed her skin and she felt the reassuring warmth of his body beside hers, she changed her mind and was glad he was with her. Easterly knew her well. If he assumed she'd simply over-indulged in alcohol, that wouldn't be so bad. He wouldn't be outraged. She felt a moment of extra warmth towards him before almost doubling over with nausea.

'What *is* this?' wondered Thrix, desperately. 'Illness? Sorcery? It feels like an eclipse, but worse.' She felt too bad to think clearly and struggled to remain conscious. 'I need to sit down.'

Easterly led Thrix to a solid wooden bench, set back in one of the arbours that were scattered throughout the maze. Since Markus had taken on responsibility for Andamair House, the grounds had been well cared for and the maze was tall and neatly trimmed. Easterly helped her to sit down. She slumped against him.

'I feel terrible,' she mumbled. 'I'm sorry.'

Easterly put his arm round her. 'You don't need to apologise.'

'I think I drank too much.'

'I don't think so. It could have been something you ate. I'm not sure all the food in there was well prepared.'

Thrix appreciated his tact. Again she felt the warmth of his body and it comforted her. 'Thanks for looking after me.'

She felt Easterly kiss her lightly on the side of her head. A sudden spasm of pain in her abdomen made her wince, and she clung onto her lover more tightly, waiting till it passed. Her forehead was damp with perspiration and she felt Easterly dab it with a handkerchief. Thrix let her head drop into Easterly's lap. She felt as helpless as a kitten, defeated by whatever malevolent force was attacking her.

And I did drink too much anyway, she thought, and regretted it. She shivered. Her evening dress wasn't suitable for outdoor wear, not with the cold fog rolling off the sea.

'Let me put my jacket round you.' Easterly gently eased himself off the bench.

Thrix closed her eyes and felt him place his jacket on her shoulders. 'Thank you.'

The night was still and the sound of Felicori's voice carried far, his perfect baritone penetrating the walls of Andamair House and spreading over the grounds. The orchestral music floated over the trees and hedges, seeming almost to merge with the haar as it blanketed the area.

'Thrix,' said Easterly.

Thrix, prone on the bench, turned her head. 'What?'

461

'There's something I should tell you.'

Thrix managed a weak smile, expecting to hear Easterly tell her again that he loved her.

'I'm a werewolf hunter.'

The Enchantress blinked. She tried to move, but another wave of pain racked her body. 'You can't be.'

There was a click as Easterly took a silver gun from his pocket and flicked off the safety catch. When she saw the gun, a tear rolled down the Enchantress's cheek and she tried to speak, but couldn't.

167

'What's this?' Duncan glanced round at his sister, surprised at the music that suddenly filled their transit van.

'"Celeste Aida". Sung by Felicori. I thought we might get a taste of what we're in for.'

Duncan laughed. 'I don't think we'll be hearing much of the opera.'

The Douglas-MacPhees were some way behind their fellow werewolves in their journey to Edinburgh. They hadn't intended to go, being generally unwelcome in Scotland, but Marwanis had suggested it and she was still paying them well.

'If Decembrius is on his way, he must be chasing Kalix,' she'd said when they'd called her. 'You'd better get up here as soon as you can.'

'We're not all that welcome in Scotland.'

'You're only banished from the MacPhee's estates. The MacRinnalchs can't stop you from going to Edinburgh. If you can catch Kalix here it will be perfect. We'll drag her back to the castle.'

The Douglas-MacPhees had set off in their old van.

'Maybe we shouldn't have beaten up Decembrius,' mused Duncan. 'Before he told us what he was doing, I mean.'

'He deserved it, anyway,' said William. Neither Duncan nor Rhona disagreed.

'*Celeste Aida, forma divina.*'

'I don't much care for Felicori's singing,' stated Duncan.

'I don't mind it,' said Rhona. She let the aria finish, then clicked the music player to bring on Motörhead. The Douglas-MacPhees all liked Motörhead. 'We're making good time,' she observed. 'The van's holding up well.' Despite the dilapidated appearance of their vehicle, it ran smoothly. Duncan had it serviced regularly, knowing that it never paid to have your transport out of commission. 'So are we still meant to kill Kalix or not?'

'Kill her, capture her, whatever,' Duncan answered. 'Marwanis will still pay us.'

In the back of the van, William nodded his huge head to the beat of the music. 'We've been chasing her a long while. It's time we cashed in on the deal.'

168

Dominil, taking a logical decision that it would be best to abandon her normal careful driving, made good time from Edinburgh to Andamair House. She'd tried calling both the Enchantress and the Mistress of the Werewolves but had been unable to contact either of them. She was, by her standards, very concerned about Albermarle's message. Thrix was the most powerful werewolf in the clan but if, as Albermarle claimed, the Guild had found some way to remove her powers, she might be vulnerable.

But there are other werewolves there, reasoned Dominil. How could they attack her? Albermarle was cunning. Perhaps he'd found some way to isolate Thrix. Dominil fretted, and wished she could go faster, but the fog was now lying thickly, slowing all traffic.

The great gate that led into the Andamair estate was manned by attendants. Several of them had worked for the MacRinnalchs before, and recognised Dominil. She was waved through without delay and continued on towards the country house. It lay some way down the drive and was blocked from view by trees, though above the treetops some light from the mansion could be seen, even through the fog.

Dominil screeched round the final corner of the long driveway and headed for the large temporary car park some way to the side of the house. She parked by the side of a huge lorry, one of the vehicles that had brought the stage equipment. She was still some way from the front entrance but as she emerged from her car she could already hear the voice of Felicori floating over the grounds, amplified and projected through the still night air.

'*Onor, Virtude, Amore, Mi preparano il premio?*'

Dominil recognised the line. *Does honour, virtue and love, prepare me a reward?* 'I doubt it,' she muttered. She swiftly scanned the area, looking for any sign of werewolf hunters. Finding none, and reassured by the lack of any sort of outcry, she started towards the house. At that moment two things happened simultaneously, neither of them good. Firstly, she was hit by a wave of nausea that caused her to gasp, and sink against her car for support. Secondly, Albermarle walked out from behind the huge truck and grinned at her.

'Hello, Dominil. Nice to see you again. Not feeling well?'

Dominil immediately attempted to transform into her were-wolf shape but, to her horror, nothing happened. She screwed up her face with the effort and tried again.

'Trying to become werewolf?' asked Albermarle in the light, bantering tone he might have used in the comic shop. 'Not going to work, I'm afraid.' He looked triumphantly at Dominil, waiting for her to speak.

Dominil glared at him, but remained silent.

Albermarle made an impatient sound. 'Stop trying to spoil it. Ask me why you can't become a werewolf.'

Dominil eyed him without expression, and remained silent. She tried to move but failed, and remained on one knee beside her car, at the back of the car park, hidden from view by the other cars and the fog.

Albermarle quickly lost patience. 'Fine. Don't ask. That's just like you. Well, I'll tell you why you can't become a werewolf. Because there's a spell in place that's emulating the effect of the lunar eclipse. Making you weak, nauseous and generally power-less.' He drew a black gun from his pocket, slipping off the safety catch and pointing the weapon at Dominil. 'You think you're so superior, don't you? Best degree at Oxford and students falling over themselves to ask you out.' He frowned, as if again reliving some old bad memory, and raised his voice. '*I* should have been in that quiz team.'

Dominil remained silent.

'Who's the clever one now? Me, that's who. I've outsmarted you every step of the way. I've bugged your phone, listened to all your conversations, read your email and followed you around the country. You couldn't move without me knowing about it. And now I've brought you here. You've fallen right into my trap.' Albermarle smiled. 'I'm smarter than you.'

A gentle breeze blew over Dominil's face, again bringing with it the sound of Felicori, now singing an aria that she knew well. Somewhere in the distance there was a muffled bang, a noise that might have been a gun being fired. Albermarle glanced over his shoulder. 'I sent my two companions off to see what they might find. You might not be the only werewolf getting a silver bullet tonight.' He inched closer to Dominil. 'Admit I'm smarter before I put a bullet through your heart.'

Dominil tried to gather her strength. Her intellect told her that it was hopeless, that she had no strength, that she wasn't going to reach Albermarle before he pulled the trigger, but she didn't intend to go down without a fight.

'Admit it!' roared Albermarle.

Dominil could see the gun vibrate slightly as Albermarle's fury made him tremble. She sneered, though even moving her mouth seemed like an effort. 'I'd never go out with you,' she said.

Albermarle's eyes widened with fury. 'That's not what I was talking about!' he screamed. He kicked Dominil hard in the face and she toppled to the ground. 'I never wanted to go out with you! And I'm still more intelligent than you. That's why I'm up here with the gun and you're down there!' He walked forward till he stood right over Dominil. He pointed the black automatic pistol at her heart. 'I'm smarter than you and that's all there is to it. Admit it or I'll kill you.'

169

Beau DeMortalis, Duke of the Black Castle, left the Duchess Gargamond's town house later than he'd intended. Dawn was already breaking, and in a short while the fiery daylight of the

Hiyasta sun would illuminate the land. The Duke frowned. It really wouldn't be done for him to be seen here. For one thing, he had no business being at the Duchess's town house as she had withdrawn to her castle, and hadn't asked him to visit. For another, it would do his standing at court no good were it to be discovered that he was carrying on a liaison with the Duchess's junior kitchen maid.

'But who could have believed the Duchess had such a beautiful junior kitchen maid?' reasoned the Duke. 'It was simply beyond my power to resist.'

He pulled up his collar, lowered his head, and walked swiftly past the military training ground and barracks that until recently had housed the Duchess's regiment. If he could make it back into the rows of elegant villas that adjoined the palace he could claim he was simply out for an early morning stroll. Anyone who knew him well might wonder why the famously well-dressed Duke was taking a morning stroll in an evening coat, but even so, that was better than the Queen learning of his liaison with a junior kitchen maid. Malveria had been irked by his comments about her recent losses at the card table and would welcome the chance to spread gossip about his rather shameful relationship. He paused, as the hot morning wind brought the distant sound of marching feet to his ears.

'That's odd. Why is Commander Agripath marshalling troops at this unearthly hour?'

As he watched, the Commander led out battalion after battalion of troops, making their way the short distance to the volcano, which dominated the landscape, rising high above the palace in the foreground. He was startled by the sudden appearance of First Minister Xakthan, running towards him in a manner quite unsuited to the dignity of the government's most senior member.

'First Minister! What is going on?'

'Distikka is mounting a coup! Commander Agripath is supporting her with his troops and they're heading for the volcano! Distikka believes she can take control of the Great Volcano.'

'Preposterous. Only the Queen can do that.'

'Or a member of the Royal Family. Which Distikka now claims to be. She's proclaiming herself ruler at this moment.'

'But this is simply ridiculous,' said the Duke. 'Where is the Queen? She'll swiftly put an end to this nonsense.'

First Minister Xakthan looked anguished. 'The Queen is missing. She has not returned from the Earth! No one knows where she is!'

'Then who's defending the volcano?'

'Fifty troops from her personal guard. That's all there is. Every other soldier in the capital is under the command of Agripath and Distikka.'

The Duke took off his coat, laying it on the ground with regret. It was an exceptionally fine coat, and he was fanatically fond of his elegant clothes, but it would hinder him in running. He loosened his sword in its scabbard and set off at a sprint towards the volcano. As he ran, he tried to sense where Queen Malveria might be. Her powerful aura could usually be perceived this close to the palace, but the Duke searched in vain. In this hour of great crisis there was no sign of Malveria.

The Fire Queen was stranded, somewhere in limbo between the dimension of the Earth and her own. Immediately after she'd received the warning from Princess Kabachetka, Malveria had flown with all haste back to her realm, but instead of arriving back in an instant in the hot environs of her palace, as she would normally have done, she found herself trapped in a cold region of endless grey. Somehow the pathway between the worlds had been filled with some soft ethereal substance that she couldn't penetrate.

Malveria raised her hands to fire bolts of the most powerful energy, seeking to clear the obstruction out the way, but it was useless. Her fire was enveloped by the grey mist and it hardly receded at all.

'This is no use,' she raged aloud. 'I'm making no progress. Eventually my power will run out and I still won't have reached the palace. Damn Kabachetka and damn Distikka!'

Malveria turned round and headed back to Earth to seek assistance from the Enchantress but neither was this easy. The way back was also full of the grey mist, hiding the path and obstructing her movements. But it was less dense, and through sheer force of will, the Queen edged her way slowly back towards the Earth.

467

When Beatrice MacRinnalch and Heather MacAllister stormed out of the building, Markus wasn't sure what to do. Should he go after them? He didn't like the way they'd left together and he had the uncomfortable feeling that they might now be in the grounds together, criticising him. Whichever way you looked at it, he did seem to be at fault for ending up at one event with two girlfriends. Markus vacillated. If he went after them he'd probably miss the start of Felicori's performance. But if he went into the auditorium alone the disappearance of his date would probably cause comment. What if he located them, anyway? There didn't seem much chance of smoothing things over. They'd probably just unite against him. Markus knew, from a few previous painful episodes, that that was likely to happen.

Finally, some sort of sense of duty made him leave the building in pursuit. It was dark and foggy outside, and though Beatrice and Heather were both werewolves, quite capable of looking after themselves, he didn't like the thought of them wandering around, probably upset.

I'd better go and find them. And apologise, for all the good that will do, he thought.

In the extensive grounds outside, Orion and Pictor were making their way through a small wooded area, hunting for werewolves.

'But if we meet any, how will we know they're werewolves?' wondered Orion. 'We can't just go shooting people and hope for the best.'

'If they're sick, they'll be werewolves,' Pictor reminded him. 'Anyone stumbling along looking ill must be being affected by the spell.'

Orion wasn't fully convinced. 'Do you believe that? I think Albermarle is just making it up.'

'Well, if he is we're probably all going to die.'

They crept as silently as they could through the trees, not knowing where they were going or who they might meet. Both of them regretted ever coming here with Albermarle to this strange, hostile, foggy place, full of werewolves who might or might not be suffering from some sort of sorcerously produced illness. When Albermarle had explained his plan it hadn't sounded so bad. Now they were here, they didn't like it much.

The Enchantress looked at Captain Easterly, barely able to comprehend what was happening.

'You're a hunter?'

'I am. From the Guild.'

'But I'd have known.'

'Princess Kabachetka helped me. She hid me from you. And she made this spell from Minerva's notes.'

Thrix's eyes filled with tears. 'But I was in love with you.'

She tried to stand up but her strength was gone. She couldn't become a werewolf and she couldn't summon a spell. She could hardly raise herself on one elbow. The nausea from Kabachetka's sorcery merged with a great wave of despair as she realised that the man she'd fallen in love with was about to kill her. A tear escaped from her eye. She wiped it away, and attempted again to change into her werewolf shape. Nothing happened. For the first time in her long life, Thrix was unable to transform. The false eclipse had robbed her of all her werewolf powers. It flickered through her mind that Minerva really knew how to construct a spell. Unfortunately she'd never get the chance to congratulate her old teacher. Thrix composed her face, gathered her MacRinnalch spirit, and spoke to Easterly. 'So what are you waiting for?'

There was a long moment of silence. Easterly could feel his heart beating wildly as he stood with the gun pointed at Thrix's chest. The sound of it drowned out the strains of the opera, still floating over from Andamair House. He lowered his gun. 'I love you too,' he said.

Thrix and Easterly looked at each other, not knowing what to do or say. Thrix felt herself crying and now she didn't attempt to wipe away the tears. She shivered and convulsed as another wave of pain racked her body.

'I didn't know it would hurt you this badly,' said Easterly. He put his gun back into its holster. His jacket had slid from Thrix's shoulders and he placed it over her again to warm her. 'I'm sorry.'

Their faces were close together. Easterly brushed a tear from Thrix's face, then leaned closer to her. At that moment there was a crashing noise from the top of the hedge and a fierce growling. A slender brown shape dropped to the ground. It was Kalix. Kalix as a werewolf, apparently unaffected by Kabachetka's spell. Her jaws hung open and her eyes were insane.

'Bad hunter,' she snarled.

'Kalix, wait—' began Thrix.

Kalix didn't hear her. Before Easterly could react, Kalix sank her talons into his shoulders, dragged him towards her, and bit his neck. There was a terrible cracking sound as bones broke. Blood spurted over Kalix, Thrix and the hedges around them. Kalix let go of Easterly and growled as his lifeless body fell to the ground. She glared down at the corpse.

'Bad hunter,' she said again. Then, with hardly a glance at Thrix, she was off, scrambling and leaping over the tall hedges, leaving Thrix on the bench, with the body of her former lover a few feet away and his blood splattered over her golden hair.

172

Dominil looked up and laughed.

'You're not smart, Albermarle. You're an idiot.'

'An idiot? I'm the one who trapped you here! Maybe I should just pull this trigger!'

'If you weren't an idiot you'd have done something better with your life than hunt werewolves.'

'Werewolves deserve to be hunted!'

Dominil almost smiled. 'You didn't seem to think that when you kept asking me out.'

'I didn't know you were a werewolf then.'

'Maybe if you put your efforts into finding a girlfriend instead of hunting werewolves you wouldn't still be obsessed with me.'

'That's it,' cried Albermarle. 'Now I'm really going to kill you.' He pointed the gun, but lowered it again. 'You know I'm more intelligent than you. You just won't admit it.'

Dominil tried again to become werewolf but failed. She wondered if she could possibly keep Albermarle talking till the spell wore off. If it ever wore off, something about which she had no evidence.

'I've never counted an encyclopaedic knowledge of comics as a sign of intelligence,' she said.

'I know a lot more than that!'

'Really?' The music floated over the car park. 'What's this aria?'

Albermarle looked uncomfortable.

'Opera was never my strong point.'

Dominil laughed, though the effort hurt her.

'You just think you're so superior, don't you!' yelled Albermarle. 'Well, you're not. And no amount of changing the subject to opera or comics alters the fact that I won. I trapped you here. I'm smarter than you.' Albermarle drew himself up to his full height. 'And you know what? I'm over you, Dominil MacRinnalch. I don't care how intelligent or attractive you think you are. You're *nothing*. You've got no emotions. You're going to live your whole life and never love anything. At least I know what loving something means.' Albermarle put his gun back in his concealed holster. 'Not only am I smarter than you, I'm superior. You see, I'm capable of changing. I'm not a robot like you. I can change my mind. And now I don't care enough about you to even kill you. Go on, be a werewolf. I don't care. I outsmarted you and now I'm leaving. You can spend the rest of your life being miserable and caring about nothing. You'd have been lucky to get a date with me. You don't deserve it.'

Dominil dragged herself to her feet. 'Leaving would be a good idea. If you stay here I'll kill you.'

'You'll kill me? Not very likely. I've got a gun and you can barely move.'

'Maybe so. But I'm Dominil MacRinnalch and I'll tear your arm off before you can pull the trigger.'

Albermarle hesitated. 'Rubbish. You can't turn into a werewolf.'

'I'll do it anyway.' Dominil bared her teeth.

Albermarle took a step backwards. 'You're nothing. I'm over you. I'm leaving.'

He turned to go. A dark shape dropped from the sky, coming from the top of the truck. It landed on Albermarle. He screamed as Kalix bit into his neck. They crashed to the ground together, but such was Albermarle's strength that he managed to drag himself to his feet and stand for a moment with Kalix hanging on to his neck, her feet right off the ground. Then he succumbed to the terrible pressure of her jaws. His arteries ruptured and he collapsed to the ground, dying in seconds. Kalix disentangled herself, rose to her feet and growled.

'Bad hunter.' Kalix turned her blood-soaked snout towards Dominil and snarled. 'Transform.'

'I can't.'

'Yes, you can. It's night. Make the change.'

Dominil struggled to rise. 'I can't change. Some sort of spell. I don't know why it's not affecting you.'

'You have to change!' yelled Kalix.

'Why?'

'So I can kill you.'

173

The Fire Queen limped back to Earth, arriving in the gardens of Andamair House to witness the unexpected sight of the Enchantress cradling the dead body of her lover.

Malveria gasped at the sight. 'Thrix! What happened? Did you find him cheating on you? Did you have to take such brutal revenge?'

Thrix raised her eyes, which, Malveria noted, were brimming with tears, to the detriment of her make-up.

'Captain Easterly was a werewolf hunter.'

'Preposterous! I introduced him to you.'

'Thanks for that.'

Malveria stared at Easterly's body, very offended that he'd turned out to be a werewolf hunter. 'What a mournful occurrence. It's a sad day when one is forced to slaughter a lover. I myself—'

'I didn't kill him.'

'You didn't?'

'No. I broke down in tears and sobbed like a baby.'

'Oh.' Malveria looked disbelieving. Easterly had clearly died from a werewolf bite.

'I was still crying when Kalix arrived. She killed him.'

'Ah. Was he about to kill you?'

Thrix shook her head. 'I don't think so. He loved me too. Or so he said. We never got the chance to discuss it fully.'

'Kalix is not one to let romance stand in the way of a good massacre.'

Thrix started to cry.

'Dearest Enchantress, I sympathise greatly with your pain. But I cannot console you at this moment, nor let you weep. I need your help, most urgently, or my Kingdom will fall.'

'What?' sniffed Thrix.

Malveria appraised her of the situation. 'So you see, Kabachetka and Distikka have outsmarted us completely. Distikka will soon take control of the Great Volcano and the Realm.'

'Can she really do that?'

'If she is a blood relative, as she claims, then yes.'

Thrix let go of Easterly's body.

Malveria helped her to her feet. She glanced at the blood on her hands and clothes, and shuddered.

Applause thundered inside Andamair House as Felicori completed another aria, and the sound rolled over the grounds outside.

'Felicori is singing beautifully tonight.' The Fire Queen looked wistfully towards the great mansion. 'Now help me break through Kabachetka's barrier and return home.'

'I don't have any power. Kabachetka's eclipse spell has robbed me of my werewolf power and it seems to have weakened my sorcery as well.' Another tear rolled down Thrix's cheek. She stared forlornly down at Easterly's corpse. 'He was going to take me to Milan in the summer – he had a house there.'

Malveria wasn't listening. She was wondering what she could possibly do to save her throne. She'd counted on Thrix lending her strength to the attempt to break through Kabachetka's barrier. It seemed that that wouldn't happen now. She'd have to fight her way through herself. Malveria knew she wouldn't make it in time. By the time she burned her way through the blocking spell created by Kabachetka, Distikka would have overrun the Great Volcano and taken control. When Malveria finally returned all she could expect would be to be blasted out of existence with the full force of the volcano.

'But I will take her with me if I can,' she muttered, 'and as many of her traitorous supporters as possible. The Fire Queen does not admit defeat, and will go down fighting.'

174

The fundraising event had gone splendidly. Felicori was in excellent form, and the audience thrilled to his rendition of favourite arias mixed in with operatic obscurities of his own choosing. There had been a brief interruption when several members of the audience appeared to sicken simultaneously. A stout gentleman in a box, Baron MacPhee, was taken ill quite suddenly and had to be helped outside. Several other distinguished-looking members of the audience also left, but the interruptions were minor and didn't spoil the occasion.

In the front row, Verasa MacRinnalch felt extremely ill, and remained upright through force of will alone. Along with the other werewolves present, the Mistress of the Werewolves had suffered the baleful effects of Princess Kabachetka's spell but had refused to show any sign of suffering. She'd heard some noise behind her, as if other members of the audience might have left, but was unable to turn round to check for fear of collapsing. Verasa's first thought was that some major outbreak of food poisoning had occurred, which would be bad for her event. But as the concert proceeded without further interruption, she realised that this was not the case. It was a relief, though at present she felt too ill to fully appreciate it. The seat beside her was empty – Markus had not come into the auditorium and the annoyance she felt about that still remained, even in her sickened state.

*

Markus was prowling through the undergrowth, on the trail of Beatrice and Heather, when the sickness struck. He gasped, sank to his knees, and wondered how it was possible that there should be an eclipse of the moon at this moment, for Markus recognised the symptoms. But an eclipse was impossible, of course, no matter how bad he felt. He might have remained where he was had he not at that moment caught the sound of another person being sick.

Beatrice, he thought immediately, recognising the sound. He'd heard Beatrice being sick before after she'd over-indulged at a clan celebration. He crawled forward. Though his senses were dulled, he knew she was behind the next bush, with Heather beside her.

This is going to be a strange reunion, he thought, and attempted to drag himself forward. At that moment there came another sound, the sound of two men approaching through the trees. Two men who were trying to move quietly and failing, by werewolf standards.

Orion and Pictor came out of the fog in front of Heather and Beatrice.

'They look sick,' said Orion.

'They must be werewolves.'

'Are you werewolves?' demanded Orion, a little doubtfully.

Neither of the distressed young females answered. The two hunters both drew weapons.

'Albermarle wasn't so stupid after all,' said Pictor.

Markus attempted to transform, despite his illness. He was startled to find that he couldn't. For a second he quailed. To be suddenly unable to transform was a terrible experience for a MacRinnalch. The hunters raised their guns. Then Markus succeeded in doing what other werewolves that night had failed to do. Telling himself that he was the Thane and could not just let two clan members die without doing anything about it, he raised himself to his feet and jumped through the bushes, directly at the two hunters whose guns were pointing at Beatrice and Heather. Markus crashed into them. All three tumbled to the ground and a gun went off, but as the hunters scrambled to their feet, Markus realised he couldn't rise. The leap had used up all his energy and he couldn't move. He, Beatrice and Heather were now easy prey for their foes.

175

Vex came out of the sky like a shooting star and crashed to Earth right on top of Captain Easterly's body.

'Ew!' She dragged herself to her feet. 'What's all this blood? Why is Thrix crying?'

'Probably because you landed on her recently deceased boyfriend, imbecilic niece,' replied the Fire Queen.

'Oh. Sorry about that.' Vex's eternal good humour had finally been worn out by the rigours of the journey. It was cold and hostile in the teleporting space, especially to someone as unused to it as she was. Her shoulders drooped. 'I bumped my elbow,' she said, sadly. 'And I think I lost my mittens.'

Malveria loomed threateningly. 'Explain yourself. Didn't I instruct you not to come to Scotland? Did you go to see the werewolf band?'

'Definitely not! I'm looking for Kalix.'

Malveria glanced at Easterly's body. 'You're in the right place. Why are you looking for her?'

'Because she's going to kill Dominil.'

'Ah.' Malveria nodded. 'So she found out.'

'Have you seen her?'

'She has been here. But forget Kalix for the moment.'

'I can't.'

'You will. I need your assistance.'

Vex looked surprised. It wasn't often that Malveria needed her. 'What for?'

'To save my kingdom.'

'Oh. Do I have to do stuff?'

'Yes.'

'Will it be hard?'

'Stop babbling and attend to me. What is this?'

There was another flash of light, gentler this time, as First Minister Xakthan appeared in their midst. He was bleeding

476

from a wound in his chest, and flames flickered around his hands.

'Great Queen, I have found you at last! You must return immediately. The traitor Distikka is taking control of the volcano!' He shuddered. It was many hundreds of years since he'd made the journey to Earth and he hadn't liked it then. 'I broke free to look for you. There is very little time left. Distikka is on the lower slopes, advancing with Commander Agripath's regiments.'

'Who defends the volcano?'

'Only your personal guards, fifty or so, many of whom have fallen. And Duke DeMortalis, who fights with great courage.'

Malveria raised an eyebrow. 'Beau DeMortalis?'

'He was in the area.'

'Ah. The junior kitchen maid?'

'I believe so.'

'He never could resist a pretty face. Unfortunately I cannot return, First Minister. Kabachetka has somehow used MacRinnalch sorcery to block my path. Don't look at the Enchantress in that manner, it's not her fault.'

'What's that noise?'

'The opera. Mr Felicori is in good form. How long till Distikka takes control of the whole volcano?'

'Minutes. Without you to lead us and use the volcano's power we can't hold out.'

'I will make as much speed as possible, First Minister. Thrix will assist me. But her power also has been affected by Kabachetka, and I doubt we can arrive soon enough.'

The First Minister drew himself up, nodded, and saluted. 'I will return to give my life in the defence of the volcano. It has always been an honour to serve you.'

'Thank you, First Minister. But I hope you don't have to give your life just yet. We must send a blood relative to defend the volcano until I can return.'

'But you don't have any other relatives,' objected First Minister Xakthan. 'You got rid of them all.'

'And I still don't regret it. But, for the meantime, I must have one. Agrivex, prepare to become my niece.'

'What?'

'You've been through the pre-adoption ceremony already. I

can make you my full niece now, with power of inheritance. You must return with the First Minister, channel the power of the volcano, and hold out till I return.'

Vex looked bewildered. 'Will this involve fighting?'

'It will. The enemy is at the gates.'

'What gates?'

The Queen rolled her eyes. 'I spoke metaphorically. Once Distikka reaches the top of the volcano, she will use her royal blood to control it. If that happens, we're finished. You must take control of the volcano yourself, and add your power to its defence.'

Vex quailed. 'I don't know how to do that. I'll be killed.'

Malveria looked her not-yet-adopted niece in the eye. 'Yes, very likely you will be. And I shall soon follow you into death. But we must try. Only you can buy me the time I need.'

Vex sighed. 'This really sucks. Just when I was doing so well at college and everything. I was so going to pass that exam.' She gazed sadly at her hands. 'I wish I hadn't lost my mittens. OK, make me your niece or whatever and I'll do my best.'

Malveria wasted no time on ceremony. She placed her thumb-nail on her forearm and ripped the flesh. A mixture of blood and fire flowed from the wound. She pulled Vex's face onto her arm and made her taste the substance.

'Ew!' protested Vex. 'This is really gross.'

'You now share my blood. I pronounce you my official niece and heir.'

'Do you have to drink my blood too?'

'Mercifully not.'

Vex and Malveria stared at each other, not really knowing how to say goodbye for what was probably the last time.

'We should go,' said the First Minister. 'Agrivex, stay at my side. I can guide us to the volcano quickly.'

Vex shrugged, and stood next to him. Both he and Malveria snapped their fingers at the same time, and Xakthan and Vex disappeared from view, leaving Malveria and Thrix alone in the maze.

'It's odd how Kabachetka has outsmarted us again. Aren't we more intelligent than her?' asked Thrix. 'Is it possible we allow ourselves to be distracted by other things?'

'I really can't think of any.' Malveria touched Thrix on the arm. 'Let me lend you some strength, till the eclipse passes.'

Thrix straightened up as a little of Malveria's fire flowed into her body. Her nausea disappeared.

'Now let us see if we can clear away the spell which prevents my return,' Malveria announced.

176

Dominil supported herself by leaning against her car. At her feet, Albermarle's body lay broken and bleeding, and in front of her, Kalix's werewolf jaws quivered with anger.

'You travelled here to kill me?'

'Yes.'

'Why?'

'Gawain.'

Dominil nodded slowly.

'You admit you killed him?'

'I do.'

Kalix's eyes were burning. Dominil's were cold and black. The evening breeze threw a few strands of her long white hair across her face.

'Change,' said Kalix.

'There's no point repeating that. I can't, till the spell wears off.'

'Then I'll wait.'

The tense silence was too much for Kalix in her enraged state. She wanted more than anything to attack Dominil. Ever since she'd learned that Dominil was responsible for Gawain's death her rage had been growing, and the unexpected circumstance of Dominil being unable to change into her werewolf shape was infuriating her. And though she wasn't thinking very rationally, it was even more annoying that her cousin wasn't offering any explanation for her actions.

'Why did you kill him?' screamed Kalix.

'He attacked me.'

'You're lying!'

'He attacked me,' repeated Dominil. 'It was him or me. I chose not to let it be me.'

Kalix abruptly lost control and struck Dominil across the face.

Dominil fell to the ground. With the baleful spell still affecting her, she struggled to stay conscious. Kalix howled in anger and frustration. She couldn't kill Dominil like this. No werewolf could take on their werewolf shape and kill another werewolf who was human. It would be dishonourable beyond measure. Dominil struggled to rise, Kalix struggled to control herself. Now there was the smell of blood from Dominil's wound, further adding to Kalix's madness. She smashed her paw into the bonnet of the car, denting it. 'Change!'

Dominil hauled herself to her feet and looked Kalix in the eye. 'I'll change as soon as I'm able to,' Dominil growled.

Kalix growled back, and inched towards her. She stank of her victims' blood and her jaws hung open. Everything about her surroundings was adding to her madness: Dominil; the dead hunter; the proximity of other werewolves who hated her; the cloying fog; and the music that still drifted over from Andamair House. 'I hate this music.' Kalix shook her head, as if to banish the sound. At that moment Felicori began to sing again.

Si combattè, si vinse.

Kalix's werewolf ears twitched. There was something about the tune that seemed familiar. She didn't know why. She inched towards Dominil again but halted. Her ears were still twitching. 'What is this tune? I know it.'

Dominil regarded her quite calmly, it seemed, though she was facing death. 'This? It's from *Numitore*, by Giovanni Porta. An opera about Romulus and Remus who were raised by a wolf. Quite an obscure song. I haven't heard it for a long time.'

Kalix felt uncomfortable and didn't know why. Something was nagging at the back of her mind. She tried to ignore the music and focus on Dominil. Maybe she didn't have to wait till Dominil was a werewolf. Perhaps she could do it now. Her jaws opened wider. She closed them abruptly. Why did she recognise this tune from an opera she'd never heard of?

'You sang it, didn't you? When I was a child at the castle?'

'I believe so,' said Dominil.

Kalix looked troubled, and stared at the ground for a moment. She looked up at the night sky, and then at Dominil. 'Did you tell me stories about Robber Wolf and Baby Wolf?'

Dominil nodded. 'I'd forgotten that.'

Kalix closed her jaws. For the first time the fire in her eyes dimmed a little. 'I couldn't remember who told me those stories. It was you.'

Kalix screwed up her face. The stories were her only pleasant memory from her whole childhood. In the whole hateful time at the castle, suffering from her father and the rest of the family, she could only remember one pleasant thing. The tales about Robber Wolf and Baby Wolf. Now it turned out that it was Dominil who'd told them to her. 'Why did you tell me stories?'

Dominil shrugged her shoulders a fraction of an inch. 'You seemed like a lonely little child. I knew what that was like.'

'Did I sit on your knee?'

'Not quite. You sat next to me on the bed.'

Kalix suddenly had a vivid memory of sitting next to the teenage Dominil, listening raptly while Dominil told her stories about Robber Wolf, Poor Wolf and Baby Wolf. She had a brief urge to sit there again.

To Dominil's surprise, Kalix changed back into human.

'I liked those stories.' Kalix suddenly felt overwhelmingly tired, and sat on the ground. 'Why did you kill Gawain?'

'I had to. He attacked me. He'd been brooding for a long time and he wasn't thinking very clearly. The whole affair with you and your sister affected his mind. He ended up hating the clan. It was a mistake to visit him, but once I'd done it I couldn't get away without fighting.'

Kalix felt her eyes go moist, and blinked to prevent them filling with tears. She thought about her childhood at the castle. It hadn't been happy. Since she'd left she didn't seem to have managed to make things much better. The clan hated her, her family hated her, she was stupid and illiterate, she couldn't eat properly, she suffered from anxiety and depression and never got anything right. Now she'd stolen money from Daniel and Moonglow to come here and kill Dominil, but she didn't want to kill Dominil any more. She didn't want to do anything. Kalix felt herself sinking beneath a huge wave of depression, and hung her head.

Dominil could not quite bring herself to embrace the unhappy young werewolf but managed to put her hand on her shoulder.

'Now there's a charming sight,' came a man's voice.

'Dominil comforts crazy young Kalix,' added a woman.

The Douglas-MacPhees stepped from the shadows.

'You felt that spell, Dominil?' Duncan asked. 'Powerful, wasn't it? Where'd that come from? No matter, it's gone now.'

'So it has,' said Dominil, and transformed immediately.

Duncan turned to Kalix. 'Well, here you are in Scotland. Half the Great Council's over there in Andamair House and they'll all be keen to see you. Would you like to walk over quietly with us, or should we drag you? Either way's fine with us.'

The Douglas-MacPhees advanced. Dominil stood in their way, but for once Kalix wasn't keen to enter into her battle madness and remained on the ground, not even taking on her werewolf shape.

177

'That was quite a gig,' said Beauty.

'Are the fire crews still here?'

'I think they've left. The police are still asking questions, though.'

The Yum Yum Sugary Snacks gig had turned into a riot; quite an achievement given the size of the venue.

'You wouldn't have thought there were enough people there to cause that much damage.' Delicious drank from a bottle of beer, part of the small rider provided by the venue for the band. Neither sister could honestly say they regretted that their gig had ended in a riot.

'It's a shame Hamil and Adam got arrested.'

Beauty shrugged. 'Dominil will sort it out when she gets back.'

'Where'd she go to?' No one was able to tell them. It was unusual for Dominil to disappear while they were playing.

'It will spare us a lecture, anyway.'

Dominil had odd ideas about music. Possibly she wouldn't agree that it was a good thing for the gig to end in a riot.

Pete slipped into the tiny dressing room. He looked pale and shaken.

'Our guitarist,' said Beauty. 'The main culprit.'

'Did you consciously decide to play the set list backwards at the wrong speed?'

Pete looked guilty, but made an attempt to justify his poor performance. 'How was I meant to play properly when I'd just learned you were werewolves?'

'I suppose it was a shock.'

'No need to throw your guitar at the audience, though. That really sparked things off.'

The twins laughed. Events had degenerated so quickly it was hard to apportion blame. At the end of the show, with the fire alarm ringing and people fighting all over the stage, it had taken the arrival of the police to put a stop to the ugly affair. In the process two of the band had been arrested. The twins hadn't been. Somehow, when the police arrived, they'd managed to look frail: a pair of skinny girls with bright hair caught up in a brawl started by everyone else.

Pete sat down on a beer crate and took one of the remaining cans of lager. 'I'd like to see Dominil as a werewolf again.'

'Ask her when she comes back. She'll be happy to show you.'

'How come she can change? Don't werewolves need a full moon?'

'The MacRinnalch werewolves can do it any night. Well, apart from us. We've been having a bit of trouble recently.'

'So when do *you* change?'

'With us it's unpredictable.'

'Is it good being a werewolf?'

'It's great. We wouldn't have it any other way.'

'Do you think Dominil will go out with me now?'

'Definitely,' said Beauty.

'She told us she likes you,' agreed Delicious.

'Hey, look, I've changed again.' Beauty was pleased. 'Do you think it's because we're in Scotland? Maybe it encourages it or something.'

'I can do it too,' said Delicious, joining in. 'This is loads better. You see, Pete—'

But Pete wasn't listening. He'd fainted.

'Too much beer, I expect. Pete's always been a bit of a lightweight.'

'Hey, Pete, wake up. If you want to win Dominil over it's no good fainting every time someone turns into a werewolf.'

'She'll be insulted.'

'Of course. No werewolf would like it.'

'But other than that, you're really in with a good chance.'

The twins weren't sure whether to wait where they were or go off to look for Dominil. They didn't really want to risk visiting Andamair House, where there would be a lot of boring were-wolves from the Great Council.

'And the opera too. I don't want to hear any opera.'

'Maybe it's ended now?'

The recital had not quite ended, though Felicori was now on his final number. Princess Kabachetka, enjoying the performance, was surprised to find a stranger suddenly appearing next to her. For one thing, she didn't think the seat next to her had been empty, and for another, she didn't see the stranger arrive. Apparently she had materialised from nowhere, unseen by anyone.

'Who are you?' she asked.

'Minerva MacRinnalch. I'm displeased. Thanks to you, I've had to leave my mountain top for the first time in twenty years.'

'No, you haven't,' said the Princess. 'You left there quite recently, to visit the Fairy Queen.'

'True. But I'm still not pleased. You've used my sorcery, thereby violating the secrets of the MacRinnalchs.'

'Well, you shouldn't have left them lying round in the castle library,' said the Princess. 'A child could have picked that lock.'

'The spells are mine and I'm taking them back. As of now, they will no longer work for you. And I believe you will fail in your endeavours, Princess Kabachetka.'

178

Dominil grabbed Kalix's wrist and hauled her to her feet. 'We're being attacked,' she said. 'It's time to change.'

Kalix sniffed, wiped her nose, and then sat down again.

Dominil growled angrily and tossed the white hair that hung around her werewolf shoulders. 'Do you have to have an emotional crisis right this minute? Full-on battle madness would be more appropriate.'

The Douglas-MacPhees came closer, and behind them appeared two more werewolves.

MacAndrises, Dominil thought. Enemies of Kalix, of course. Dominil swore, which she rarely did.

'I can't tell you how fed up I am with being pursued by every werewolf and werewolf hunter in the country.' She stepped forward and stood waiting for her opponents, an utterly savage expression on her face.

'Just move out the way, Dominil,' said Duncan. 'We're not after you.'

'Don't you ever get tired of chasing Kalix?'

Duncan shrugged. 'We get paid for it.'

Tyres squealed not far away. A door slammed and a figure appeared through the fog. It was Decembrius.

'What's happening?' he asked, moving to Kalix's side as he spoke. Dominil nodded at him, though something in her expression suggested he'd arrived here rather late. She turned back to Duncan.

'Decembrius and I are both members of the Great Council. I wouldn't advise you to attack us.'

'Why not?' Marwanis MacRinnalch stepped out of the cloying fog, with Morag MacAllister at her side. 'I'm on the council too. I'll tell them it was justified.'

'How would it be justified?'

'Kalix is an outlaw. We're arresting her.'

'No, you're not,' said Decembrius.

Duncan Douglas-MacPhee laughed. 'Wasn't one beating enough? Do you want more?'

Dominil and Decembrius were faced with seven werewolves. The odds wouldn't have been so bad were Kalix to have helped, but that didn't seem likely. She was still sitting on the ground. The Douglas-MacPhees, the MacAndrises, Marwanis and Morag spread out, ready to advance.

Another figure suddenly strode out of the fog that was still blanketing the car park. It was Tupan MacRinnalch, Dominil's father, brother to the late Thane. Tupan was also a member of the Great Council.

Rhona Douglas-MacPhee laughed. 'Soon you'll be able to hold a meeting right here.'

'Did everyone else feel that sickness?' asked Tupan. He looked at the scene before him. 'Dominil, what's going on here?'

'These werewolves want to arrest Kalix.'

'And?'

'I'm not inclined to let her be arrested.'

Tupan frowned deeply. He was quite a tall werewolf, older than the others but still lean and strong.

'She should be arrested.'

Dominil didn't reply to her father, but nor did she move away from Kalix.

'There are eight of us and two of you,' said Marwanis. 'Three if you count that piece of dirt snivelling at your feet. Clan law is on our side, and so are the numbers.'

'I don't like to hear you calling Kalix a piece of dirt,' said Decembrius, raising his voice.

'I'd say it was appropriate. Now, are you going to hand her over or do we have to take her?' Marwanis stepped forward and growled, and her growling made the other werewolves agitated. They moved to follow her.

'Stop it. There isn't going to be any fighting.'

It was Markus. With a little blood on his forehead and two werewolves behind him, Heather and Beatrice. Markus, however, remained as human, and looked furious.

'How dare you cause trouble here! How dare you even turn werewolf. There's a hall full of humans right next door, listening to the opera. What do you think it would do to the clan if you were discovered?'

'We were after Kalix,' growled Duncan.

'Leave her alone,' said Markus.

'Why would we do that?'

'Because I'm telling you to, and I'm the Thane.'

'We're not that impressed with you as Thane.'

'Are you not? I'm not impressed with you as werewolves. Now leave. Kalix is my responsibility.'

The two MacAndrises, not so uncaring of clan etiquette, took a few steps backwards, but the Douglas-MacPhees were slow to retreat.

Marwanis refused to back down at all. 'Kalix has to be arrested. She attacked the old Thane. And she killed Sarapen.'

'Killing Sarapen wasn't a crime,' said Dominil. Marwanis looked at her with almost as much loathing as she directed at Kalix.

The sounds of Felicori's encore drifted over from the hall, followed by tumultuous applause.

'Everyone change back,' commanded Markus. 'People will be in this car park soon. You MacAndrises – there are hunters' bodies strewn around the grounds. Pick them up and get rid of them. Everyone else, start acting human and get back into the house and look like you're supporting the event. Apart from you – Duncan, Rhona and William. You're not welcome here. Leave the grounds.'

The Douglas-MacPhees remained as werewolves, and looked towards Marwanis.

'I'm not letting Kalix walk out of here,' Marwanis stated.

'She's in my custody now,' said Markus. 'I'm the Thane.'

'Then why don't we take her before the Great Council? Most of them are inside.'

'I'll do what's necessary.'

'You're going to let her go!' yelled Marwanis, enraged.

'I'm going to confer with the Mistress of the Werewolves.'

Marwanis spat on the ground. 'You and your mother.' She directed a look of loathing at Kalix, then marched off, disappearing instantly into the fog.

'Kalix and Dominil,' said Markus. 'We're going to see the Mistress of the Werewolves.'

179

'This is insulting,' raged the Fire Queen, halfway between dimensions. 'Other elementals are free to come and go, yet I am trapped here. Someone will pay.'

The Enchantress had added her power to Malveria's and together they chipped away at the spell that prevented Malveria from returning home. Both knew there was little chance of arriving in time. The combined forces of Distikka and Commander Agripath must surely have swept the Fire Queen's guard away by now, even with Vex channelling the power of the volcano.

'She might turn out to have a talent for it,' muttered Thrix.

'She probably just fell in.'

The pair intensified their efforts as the mist that hid Malveria's realm began to dissipate.

'We're almost there, Enchantress. Once the pathway opens I won't have time to bid farewell or thank you, so I do so now.'

'What?'

'For all your assistance, and the beautiful clothes. I am deeply grateful.'

'That's good to know,' said Thrix. 'But we're not saying goodbye just yet. I'm coming with you.'

'You are unused to fighting in my realm and will die quickly on the volcano.'

'We'll see about that.'

Malveria paused, though she had no time to spare. 'Really, Thrix, you should go home.'

'What for? To look at my dead boyfriend?' Thrix gritted her teeth, and fired another bolt of energy at the grey mass ahead of them. It split apart, and an orange light shone through.

'We are here,' said the Queen. 'Prepare for battle.'

Malveria and Thrix materialised on the higher slopes of the Great Volcano just in time to see Vex's foot blown off. She tumbled to the ground, blood and fire leaking from her body. The young fire elemental had performed quite heroically, sending the power of the volcano to First Minister Xakthan and his supporters, but she'd finally been overwhelmed by the strength of the opposition. Huge bolts of fire fell all around, turning the sky red, as Distikka advanced up the mountain.

Malveria took it all calmly. 'How many of my Guard remain, First Minister?'

'Around thirty, Your Highness.'

'And Distikka?'

'An army of several thousand. They control two-thirds of the volcano.'

'How did Agrivex manage?'

'Very well, and bravely. She saved the day. Till now.'

Malveria turned to her friend. 'Enchantress, could you stabilise Agrivex's body? I have no time to heal her now but will see what I can do when this affair is over.'

Thrix, who'd already slipped off her high heels, nodded and rushed to try to prevent more blood and fire from leaking out of the now-unconscious Vex. There wasn't much left of her foot, but what there was the Enchantress gathered up and placed beside her.

A huge explosion rocked the ground, sending burning shrapnel over their heads, as Commander Agripath's advance guard sent a great arc of fire towards the Queen.

'DeMortalis?' said Malveria. 'I did not expect to see you here.'

The Duke's handsome face was scarred from the battle, and his elegant clothes were ragged and charred. 'It seemed like a good day for a fight,' he replied. 'Though I did have an appointment with my tailor which I've regrettably had to miss.'

Malveria smiled. She took a step forward to address the fire elementals who remained at her side. All around were the bodies of fallen comrades. 'Gentlemen.' She raised her voice over the sound of the thunderous fire. 'We are fortunate. It is rare that the opportunity presents itself to perform great deeds of valour that will be talked about in ages to come. We will advance, dispatch the enemy, and return in triumph to let the bards sing songs about us. If any of you would rather not participate in this glorious victory, please feel free to withdraw.'

No one withdrew. Malveria stretched out her hand and a sword belonging to one of her dead guards sprang from the ground into her grasp. As she took hold of it, a great tongue of fire rolled out along the blade. Her eyes blazed and her long dark hair turned red with flames. 'First Minister, is that a dragon?'

'I'm afraid so. Commander Agripath's family trait has awakened and he has made the transformation.'

'Indeed. It is some time since I fought a dragon. Well, First Minister, as there seems no opportunity for a tactical approach, I suggest we simply charge the enemy. Let us see if Malveria, Xakthan and thirty warriors are a match for Distikka, the dragon Agripath, and his regiment.'

With that, the Fire Queen roared out the traditional battle cry of her family and charged downhill, followed by her ragged band.

180

Markus led Kalix and Dominil into Andamair House by one of the service doors at the back of the house. They found themselves in a small warren of corridors once used by servants. Unlike the rest of the great mansion, these corridors were unadorned, and quite cramped. They followed Markus up a tiny stone staircase, worn smooth from hundreds of years of use by maids, cooks and cleaners. As they emerged into a deserted corridor, Kalix was lagging behind. She came to a halt and leaned against the wall.

'What's wrong?' asked Markus. 'Are you hurt?'

Kalix stared at the floor and didn't answer.

'We have to hurry,' urged Markus impatiently. 'I don't want the Barons sniffing you out; it will lead to more trouble.'

Kalix refused to move.

'Kalix has suffered some sort of mental collapse,' announced Dominil.

Kalix felt quite offended. 'No, I haven't. I'm just sick of everything.'

'Well, it's time to get over it.'

Kalix stared at her angrily. 'You just don't understand how other people work, do you?'

'Possibly not. Anyway, you have things to do.'

Kalix felt uncomfortably like a child being bullied. 'What things?'

'You have to talk to your mother. And your exam starts in fourteen hours.'

'My exam? I'm not doing my exam.'

'Why not?'

'I've got other things to think about.'

'You can think about them later. You've been studying for months and it would be foolish to let it all go to waste.'

'I'm not doing it.'

'Yes, you are.'

Kalix glared at her cousin. 'I remember now. When you told me those stories about Robber Wolf, you were mean afterwards. You threw me out of your room.'

'You were probably hanging round being annoying. I could only be comforting for a limited amount of time.'

'Hurry up,' said Markus. 'Our mother will only be up here for a little while.'

Kalix quailed. 'I don't want to see her.'

The door at the end of the corridor opened, and there stood the Mistress of the Werewolves.

'Wait here,' said Markus, and he disappeared into the room to talk to Verasa, leaving Kalix outside.

Kalix sighed deeply. She wasn't looking forward to her interview with the Mistress of the Werewolves. It was a long time since she'd talked to her mother in private.

181

The Fire Queen and her small band of warriors hurtled down the slope of the Great Volcano. As Malveria charged into battle she used the power of the volcano to cast a spell, protecting her followers from the spears and arrows of their enemies, and sheltering them from the rain of fire-bolts that arched through the sky.

The Fire Queen headed straight towards Commander Agripath, who now led his troops in the shape of a great dragon. When she arrived in front of him there was a brief pause in the tumult of battle. Malveria looked into the dragon's eyes.

'Congratulations on your transformation, Commander. Your family have always made excellent dragons.'

Agripath hadn't been expecting to encounter the Queen and was not inclined to talk. He spread his crimson wings and rose into the air, intending to plummet onto Malveria and rip her apart with his terrifying claws. Malveria didn't wait for his assault. As soon as he left the ground, she flew towards him. With the power of the volcano coursing through her, Malveria was now at her strongest. She swung her fiery sword at the dragon's head. Agripath evaded the blow and thrust a talon at the Queen. She deflected the blow with her sword, and in doing so cut the dragon's scaly skin.

Agripath roared furiously and shook his great tail. A plume of flames shot from his mouth, engulfing the Queen. Malveria dispersed them with a wave of her hand. As the flames cleared she was frowning angrily.

'You have ruined my beautiful clothes.'

Beneath them the slopes of the volcano were covered with smoke and flames. Agripath's troops were hindered by the Queen's protective spell but still tried to press forward with their superior numbers. Duke DeMortalis yelled out the traditional battle cry of his family as he urged his men to hold firm.

The dragon beat its wings, rising further in the air before once more plunging through the smoke-filled sky. This time the flames which came from his mouth were greater than before. Malveria disappeared in a ball of smoke and flame. It took some time for the blaze to dissipate. When the sky finally cleared, Malveria was still hovering motionless in the air.

'I killed the Three-headed Dragon of Despair,' she called, contemptuously, 'and he was a mighty opponent. But you are newly formed, and not the dragon he was.' Malveria raised her sword and struck the dragon full on the face, causing it to rear backwards and roar in pain.

'Distikka has been a very bad influence on you. And I notice, Agripath, that she seems to have fled the scene, leaving you to take the consequences.'

With that Malveria struck again. Her flaming blade sliced through Agripath's neck, and as the dragon's head tumbled through the blackened air to land crashing in the midst of his troops below, they lost heart, and turned to flee.

182

When the Mistress of the Werewolves found herself facing Kalix, even thinner and more ragged than she'd expected, she found herself lost for words. Kalix was almost beyond her help. The family schism had robbed them of any intimacy they might once have had as mother and daughter. Kalix would probably have said they'd never had any to begin with.

'Markus told me why you came here. What are you planning to do now?'

'I'm leaving. Decembrius is giving me a lift back to London.'

Verasa nodded. 'That's probably best.'

'I need to get back for my exam.'

Verasa was surprised. 'You're going to do it? Are you well enough?'

'Dominil says I should do it. She's probably right. Anyway, if I don't, then Vex might not do it either. I don't want her to give up.'

Verasa nodded. At least her daughter was making some sort of effort. 'I'm sorry you can't stay. The council, they're still angry about . . .'

Kalix looked at the ground. The attack on her father was one of the many subjects that they couldn't talk about. Like her laudanum addiction, and her eating problems, and her life in London. Nothing could be talked about without it leading to a lecture from her mother, and a furious argument. They both knew that, so they left everything unsaid.

'I'm glad to see you safe,' said Verasa, with an effort.

'I have to ask you something,' said Kalix.

'What?'

Kalix felt every muscle tensing up, and squirmed with humiliation at what she was about to say. 'I need money.'

'Of course. For the journey.'

'More than that. I need quite a lot. I took money from Daniel and Moonglow to pay my fare to Edinburgh.'

'You *took*? You mean you stole it?'

Kalix nodded. She was unable to look her mother in the face and felt that she'd rather have confronted a room full of enemies than admitted to her mother that she'd stolen money from her flatmates.

'Why did you—' began Verasa angrily, but checked herself. There was, she supposed, no point in starting another argument. But she couldn't keep the annoyance and disapproval out of her voice. 'Do you steal other things?'

'Sometimes,' muttered Kalix. 'Not much these days.'

Verasa looked at her ragged daughter, and thought of the grand event happening all around them, and the family wealth, and the great castle in the Highlands, and wondered again how Kalix could possibly have ended up like this. Her boots and coat were so ragged, her face so sunken. It was shameful, for her and the clan. Verasa, prepared for emergencies, carried a large handbag with her. Not as fashionable as that carried by her daughter, but a good item, given her as a present by Thrix. She fished around inside it and drew out an elegantly embroidered wallet.

'Here you are.' She handed over a bundle of notes to Kalix, who took them wordlessly and stuffed them in her pocket.

'I should go now. Before anyone catches me.'

'I'll keep everyone busy for a while,' said her mother. 'You can slip out with Decembrius. No one will see you.'

They stood in silence.

'Do you need anything else?'

Kalix shook her head. She still writhed with the humiliation, though she'd expected her mother to lecture her more.

'Thanks for the money.' Kalix hurried from the room, and ran off to where Decembrius was waiting for her in the car park.

183

The Fire Queen plucked an arrowhead from her arm, refusing to wince at the pain even though it had embedded itself deeply in the flesh. 'We seem to have achieved victory, First Minister.'

First Minister Xakthan nodded, very wearily. It had been a ferocious battle, the effects of which had caused a landslide on the northern face of the Great Volcano. Fires raged over the face of the mountain and tall plumes of choking smoke spiralled into the sky. The crisis was over, for the moment. Malveria, fuelled by the Great Volcano, had transformed into a warrior queen, driven back her enemies, dispatched Commander Agripath and reasserted her control. Troops from her palace guard, stationed some way away at the edge of the capital, were now arriving to finish the operation. As Malveria watched, they marched up the volcano in ordered battalions.

'Rather late in the day,' she observed. 'But I understand Distikka had taken control of my lines of communication and orders could not be got to them in time. It's fortunate we have not lost our fighting skills, First Minister.'

First Minister Xakthan nodded, but remained expressionless.

'Well fought, Duke DeMortalis,' called Malveria. The Duke was sitting on a rock some distance away, receiving medical attention. 'Did not the Duke fight well, First Minister?'

'Yes.'

Malveria looked at him sharply, not liking the tone of his reply. 'First Minister, we have just won a famous victory. Yet you seem downcast. Why is this?'

'No reason, Mighty Queen.'

Malveria brushed her fingers over the wound on her arm, closing up the skin. 'You never were great at concealing your aura. You can't hide your displeasure from me.'

'I'm not feeling any displeasure.'

The Queen raised an eyebrow.

'Very well,' said Xakthan. 'We've narrowly escaped a crisis that should never have happened. It *wouldn't* have happened if you hadn't ruled in such an incompetent manner. Thanks to your reckless abandonment of affairs of state you very nearly brought the Hiyasta nation to ruin! If you hadn't been away at fashion shows every day, ignoring your duties as Queen, Distikka would never have been able to stage her rebellion. The blame for this dreadful affair is entirely your own.'

The Fire Queen paled slightly. Xakthan was her most loyal supporter. He'd never delivered a speech remotely resembling this. She felt her aura flicker, the merest fraction. She controlled it.

'As you say, First Minister, I may possibly have erred slightly. I will take more care in future. And we will not mention it again.'

'Very well.'

'Now, let us attend to Agrivex.'

Vex still lay near the top of the volcano. Her eyes were open, but she stared into the distance and her aura was fading.

'Am I going to die?'

'That has not yet been determined. Stay still while I attempt to heal you.'

There was a long silence as the Fire Queen struggled to save her niece's life. The orange glow that surrounded Malveria flowed from her into her niece, but Vex's own aura continued to fade.

'Aunt Malvie,' whispered Vex weakly.

'Yes?'

'I didn't really get any gold stars at college.'

'I know, dismal niece. But you did your best. Now lie still and be quiet while I attempt to grow you a new foot.'

Malveria remained calm on the outside but strained mightily inside, and was obliged to summon up a great portion of the power of the Great Volcano because even a fire elemental could not grow a new foot with ease. And even though there were other pressing matters she should be attending to, Malveria expended more power in her attempt to heal Vex than she could ever remember using before.

184

Kalix kept her head down as she left Andamair House by the servants' entrance. The haar was lifting and there were a few guests milling around the main entrance, saying their farewells. She hurried past the trucks that had carried equipment into the mansion, making her way towards Decembrius's car, keen to leave this place as quickly as possible.

I'm sick of everything, was all she could think.

As she passed by one of the trucks a hand grabbed her collar and yanked her back.

'Hello, Kalix.' Marwanis put her face close to Kalix's. 'You killed Sarapen. If no one else will take revenge for that, I will.'

'I don't want to fight any more,' said Kalix.

'I do,' replied Marwanis, and struck Kalix in the face. Even in her human shape, Marwanis was strong. Kalix reeled from the blow. Marwanis hit her again. Kalix sagged.

'You're really not going to fight back? That's fine with me.'
Marwanis punched Kalix a third time, this time causing blood to
erupt from her nose. Kalix fell on one knee from the force of the
blow. Marwanis changed into her werewolf form and then
kicked out. Her taloned foot caught Kalix in her ribs, sending her
flying backwards. She slammed against the side of a car and lay
on the ground. Marwanis advanced.

Kalix, who was sick of everything and didn't want to fight,
knew that Marwanis would kill her if she did nothing. She also
knew that if she transformed, she'd kill Marwanis. She wouldn't
be able to stop herself. Then she'd be in more trouble for killing
a member of the Great Council; trouble that would never end.
Kalix wondered if she should just lie on the ground and do nothing, but as Marwanis bent over her she transformed as her
werewolf nature took over. She sprang at Marwanis and was
about to fasten her jaws round her neck when she was again
grabbed from behind and hauled backwards.

'Well, well. Fighting werewolves. Isn't that just what the
Thane lectured us about?'

It was Decembrius.

Kalix growled and yelped, struggling to close with her opponent. Her battle madness had not quite descended fully but it was
only seconds away. Marwanis, finding herself outnumbered,
halted her attack but growled at them, a terrible sound, full of
hate.

'It's time for us to go,' said Decembrius.

Kalix stopped struggling and, quite suddenly, changed back
into human.

Marwanis looked at her and was pleased she'd managed to
bloody her face at least. 'I despise you, Kalix MacRinnalch,' she
spat. 'You're a disgrace to the clan. You'll never get anything out
of life except loneliness and unhappiness.'

'That's all right,' muttered Kalix. 'I never expected anything
anyway.'

Decembrius opened the back door of his car, propelled Kalix
inside, started the engine and drove off as quickly as he could,
causing a few others in the car park to step back swiftly to avoid
being run over.

'So much for not fighting,' said Kalix, sighing.

Decembrius looked at her bloody face and laughed, which Kalix didn't think was very appropriate.

'Why did you pick that moment not to fight?'

'Because I'm stupid.'

'You've got that right.'

Decembrius drove steadily on through the early hours of the morning, covering the miles between Edinburgh and London. The motorway was quiet and they made good time. They travelled south mostly in silence, but about two-thirds of the way through the journey Decembrius suggested they stop for a while.

'I've been driving a long time. We could get a room in one of the travel hotels.'

'Forget it. I'm not getting a room with you.'

Decembrius laughed.

Kalix had the feeling that sleeping together had been a bad idea, and as such should never be mentioned again, but Decembrius was annoyingly unrepentant. As far as he was concerned it had been an excellent idea and he'd be happy to do it again.

'I don't see why we shouldn't stop off somewhere.'

'I do,' said Kalix. 'I need to get home.'

'What for?'

'I'm doing my exam.'

'Who cares about your exam?'

Kalix did, apparently, though she wasn't sure why. She yawned, then winced in pain. She'd been feeling bad enough before Marwanis had pummelled her, and now she felt a lot worse. The young werewolf lay down in the back seat, and went to sleep.

185

The Enchantress could not stay long in the Fire Queen's realm. It required sorcery for a human to visit, even for a short time. Thrix had not only visited but had lent her power to Malveria during the great battle. Knowing the Fire Queen to be busy both with her niece and the huge political ramifications of the rebellion, she slipped away quietly.

Thrix never enjoyed the journey through the cold space between dimensions, and on this occasion she felt as if her spirit were being sucked from her body.

She arrived home with the elation of battle now drained from her body and the memory of Captain Easterly painfully on her mind.

She opened a bottle of wine, sat on the couch, and wondered who she hated most – Easterly, herself or Kalix. All three seemed like worthy targets for her anger. She loathed Easterly for deceiving her, herself for being stupid enough to fall in love with him, and Kalix for killing him.

No one else would blame Kalix, she knew. Kalix was guilty of many things but killing a werewolf hunter wasn't one of them. Any other MacRinnalch, learning of the affair, would agree that Kalix had done the right thing. A hunter chasing a werewolf had to be killed. There were no exceptions. It was in the werewolves' nature and would never change. There was no point in protesting. That was the way it was. It didn't prevent Thrix from hating her sister bitterly.

Did he actually fall in love with me at the end? she wondered. Was he giving up being a hunter?

Thrix wasn't sure. She thought he was. She finished the whole bottle of wine and opened another, drinking till she managed to pass out unconscious on the couch.

186

Dominil accepted money from Markus as payment for the death of Albermarle, though she did point out that it had been Kalix who killed him.

'You can give it to her if you like. As Thane, I can't pass money on to Kalix. There's going to be enough trouble as it is after I let her go.'

'You once voted that Kalix should remain an outlaw. What changed your mind?'

Markus wasn't sure. Unless it had been the lecture from his mother that the family had to get on better. That wasn't going to convince the Barons when they learned of the affair. Each of them still wanted Kalix punished for her attack on the old Thane.

'The next Great Council meeting should be interesting,' he mused.

'I'll be here to support you and the Mistress of the Werewolves,' said Dominil.

'Mother's furious about werewolves running around outside when her guests were inside.'

'Was the event a success?'

'A great success. Mother now ranks as one of Scotland's most profitable fundraisers.'

Markus accompanied Dominil to her car in silence. When they got there he asked, 'Do you want to know what happened with Beatrice and Heather?'

'No.'

'I saved them both from the hunters. It was lucky, of course. If the spell hadn't ended right then, we'd all have been killed. But Beatrice and Heather were impressed. Now they—'

'Goodbye, Markus,' said Dominil, getting into the car and shutting the door.

Markus watched her drive off, and felt disappointed. He'd wanted to tell someone the story of Beatrice and Heather. Fortunate or not, it had been quite heroic to save them. And now he seemed to have two girlfriends who both liked each other, which seemed an interesting occurrence.

Some time later, on the journey back to London, Dominil was thoughtful, though the twins were boisterous.

'That gig was a lot better than I expected.'

'You wouldn't have thought a small crowd could create so much destruction.'

'It was one of the all-time great gigs.'

Dominil looked over her shoulder. 'It was a terrible gig. You played dreadfully when I was there, and from the sound-desk recording, it got worse after I left.'

The twins scowled. Though Dominil had been engaged in bailing out those members of the band who'd been arrested, and rounding up the twins for the journey home, somehow she'd also managed to listen to a recording of the gig and was already criticising them for it.

'Hey, that wasn't our fault,' protested Beauty. 'The band played badly because Pete was in shock after discovering you were a werewolf.'

'Which was careless of you,' added Delicious.

'Though it hasn't put him off you. Are you going to go out with him now?'

'No,' said Dominil.

'I think you should give him a chance. Now you've killed Albermarle there's a space in your calendar.'

'I'm not going out with some idiotic musician.'

The twins were dissatisfied.

'Have a heart, Dominil.'

'If you have one . . .'

'Presumably some sort of pumping mechanism for circulating the blood . . .'

'Why not give him a chance?' Beauty was suddenly worried. 'You weren't thinking of killing Pete, were you?'

Dominil didn't reply.

'You can't kill him just because he's found out we're werewolves. He's our guitarist.'

'Then he'd better be discreet,' muttered Dominil.

187

Vex was taken to her bed in her old room at the palace, where she lay underneath her enormous pink quilt, with her fluffy dragon, and continued to recover. Outside in the Hiyasta Nation there was a whirlwind of military and political activity as the Fire Queen reasserted her control, but inside Vex's bedroom there was peace, by order of Malveria. The room had been tidied since Vex had left to go to college, and while this did not quite suit Vex's temperament the Queen no longer shuddered at the mess as she entered.

'Aunt Malvie, when I was Queen I passed a decree.'

'Stop babbling, idiot niece. You did not pass any decrees.'

'I did so,' insisted Vex.

'You were engaged in brutal warfare, in a spirited if incompetent fashion. And you were never Queen.'

'I was so. I was in charge of the Great Volcano.'

'You may have been Queen for a moment, technically. But you did not pass any decrees.'

'I did. When I arrived at the volcano there was a sort of pause. Everyone was surprised to see me there. Especially when I announced that I was now your official niece and temporary ruler. And while I was plugging myself into the volcano, I passed a new decree. I had a right to do it.'

Malveria was displeased, and didn't hide it. 'I didn't send you back as my adopted niece so that you could pass foolish decrees. If you've awarded yourself a gigantic clothes allowance I will have it nullified immediately.'

'I lifted the curse.'

'What curse?'

'The curse on Daniel and Moonglow. I made a decree saying you had to remove it. It's only fair.'

Malveria appeared to struggle for breath as she digested the audacity of her niece's actions. 'You dared to issue a decree nullifying an Imperial curse? A curse put in place by the Queen of the Hiyasta?'

Vex brought her fluffy dragon closer for protection, but still managed to look her aunt defiantly in the eye. 'I did. And it was legal. I was Queen at the time.'

'You were *not* Queen!'

'I was *so!*'

'In a technical sense, possibly. That did not give you the right to issue decrees!'

'Yes, it did,' insisted Vex, stubbornly. She groaned. 'Ooohhh, my foot hurts. It's so painful. Ever since it was blown off when I was defending the kingdom. While you couldn't return. Ooohhh, it's so painful.'

The Queen rolled her eyes. 'It is not that painful, most dismal of nieces. I can tell from your aura.'

'It's really painful. I think I'm going to faint with pain.'

Malveria tapped her fingers on the duvet. 'Very well, I will allow your decree. The curse is lifted. Possibly I should be grateful you did not sell the palace furniture to buy boots and T-shirts. But be warned. No amount of moaning and pretending to be in pain will gain you any more of your ridiculous wishes. Are you clear on that?'

'Yes, Aunt Malvie.'

'And will you stop calling me Aunt Malvie? It's an affront to my dignity. Now lie there quietly while your foot heals.'

Later the Fire Queen spoke to her First Minister, telling him of Vex's decree.

'Perhaps we can work it to our advantage,' she told him. 'Let it be known that while performing heroically on the Great Volcano, Agrivex also lent assistance to two friends on Earth. If we are to persuade the population that my imbecilic niece is actually fit to be a member of the Royal Family it will do no harm to let them know she's loyal to her friends.'

First Minister Xakthan nodded, and enquired about Agrivex's health.

'She's recovering. She will be well, but needs to rest. Even a fire elemental does not grow a new foot easily.'

An attendant hurried into the throne room.

'Mighty Queen, Agrivex has been spotted leaving her room.'

'What?!' Malveria snapped her fingers, transporting herself to the corridor outside Vex's room. There she found her niece limping along on crutches.

'Where are you going, abominable niece?'

'Kitchens. I thought I'd pick up a sandwich before doing my exam.'

'What?'

'My exam. It's today.'

Malveria strode in front of her niece to stop her progress. 'Return to bed immediately. You are not in any condition to do an exam.'

'But I have to.'

'No, you don't.'

'I'll fail at college.'

Malveria prepared to yell at her niece, then, remembering she was still grateful to Vex, softened her tone. 'You can do the exam another time. We will explain about your injuries and I'm certain it can be rearranged.'

'I want to do it now.'

'You can't.'

'I can.'

The Queen's temper began to fray. 'Why are you suddenly insistent about doing an exam? It is the last thing you would normally be eager to do.'

'Kalix might not go if I don't.'

'What?'

'Kalix. She's not as keen on college as I am. If I'm not there to encourage her she might not do the exam. Then she'll get thrown out and she'll be in trouble with her family and everything. I have to make sure she does it.'

Malveria was temporarily stuck for a reply. She wasn't expecting altruism on this scale from Vex. 'It's not really your responsibility to look after Kalix,' she began. 'Stop setting your face in a determined manner. I don't like it.'

'I'm going.'

'No, you are not.'

'I am.'

'I absolutely forbid it.'

'I'd like a sandwich first.'

'You are going straight back to bed.'

'Very well,' said Vex, with dignity. 'I'll go without the sandwich.'

And with that, she snapped her fingers, dematerialising with an efficiency the Queen would have once admired, but now deplored.

188

Vex materialised in the living room of Moonglow and Daniel's flat, took one step, groaned, and lay down on the floor.

Perhaps this wasn't such a good idea, she thought, screwing up her face. Who'd have thought having your foot blown off and then stuck back on again would be so painful?

She heard the downstairs door open, and soft footsteps coming up the stairs.

Kalix entered stealthily. She looked at Vex in surprise. 'Why are you lying on the floor? What's that on your leg?'

'A Hiyasta fire-sorcery leg-healing device. I had my foot blown off. Aunt Malvie fixed it. It's really sore.'

Kalix looked baffled. 'You had your foot blown off? When?'

'Yesterday, on the volcano. But it got healed.'

'Shouldn't you be resting?'

'I wanted to make sure you did the exam.'

'You idiot,' said Kalix. 'I only came back to make sure *you* did it.'

Kalix lay down on the couch and moaned.

'You look terrible,' said Vex.

'I feel terrible. I've been fighting and getting into trouble and everything's a disaster.'

They lay in the darkness in silence.

'I got money to pay Daniel and Moonglow back,' said Kalix.

'Good.'

'But I expect they'll throw me out of the house now for stealing.'

'Maybe. Me too, I expect.'

The pair drifted off into uncomfortable slumber in the living room. Early next morning Kalix called a taxi as neither of them felt able to face public transport, and they slipped quietly out of the house.

Vex groaned as she tried to put weight on her injured leg. 'College isn't as much fun as I thought it would be.'

'It's exactly as much fun as I thought it would be. You know I'm going to fail this exam?'

'So am I. Why are we doing it?'

Neither of them could say for sure. But they got into the taxi and headed for the old stone building just south of the river, each clutching a bag with their notebooks inside.

189

Dominil found the Enchantress in a poor state. After answering the intercom and buzzing her cousin in, Thrix had staggered back to the couch where she lay with her eyes closed. The TV was on, there were papers strewn around the floor and two empty bottles of wine were resting on the small table.

'What are you doing?' asked Dominil.

'Drinking to forget I'm a werewolf. You're not helping.'

'Why would you want to forget you're a werewolf?'

'You fall in love and then your lover turns out to be a werewolf hunter. Then he gets his throat ripped out. It's not pleasant for anyone.'

Dominil nodded, in her serious way. 'I'm sorry the affair ended in an unsatisfactory manner.'

'Unsatisfactory? That's not the word I'd use.' Thrix hauled herself upright and groped for a half-full glass of wine.

'Perhaps coffee might be more appropriate?'

Thrix laughed; a slurred, unhappy laugh. 'I've reached the last refuge of the MacRinnalchs. When there's nothing else to do, drink yourself into oblivion.'

'I don't think that's the best way of dealing with things.'

'Why not? It works for the rest of the family.'

'Life will carry on, Thrix. The MacRinnalchs are fortunate to have a very long lifespan. There will be other men.'

'Other werewolf hunters, you mean. For Kalix to kill.' Thrix's eyes narrowed. 'I hate Kalix.'

'She acted according to the principles of the clan.'

'I know. I still hate her.' Thrix looked up. 'So how do you feel about her after she tried to kill you?'

'We came to an understanding. And I was reasonably grateful to her for killing Albermarle, though I'd rather have done it myself. Perhaps, Enchantress, if the notion of romance is too troubling you could immerse yourself in your work?'

Thrix drank some wine, then scooped up some papers.

'I don't have any work. I'm going bankrupt. Take a look at my bank statements.'

Dominil glanced at the papers. The Enchantress did seem to owe a lot of money. But by this time Dominil's sympathy was running out. She never had much to spare, and she hadn't come here to discuss Thrix's problems.

'I have news. I've located Susi Surmata. I finally tracked down the computer she's been using.'

This got her cousin's attention. A small light appeared in Thrix's previously dull eyes. 'Where is she?'

'Epping. A little way north-east of central London. The last stop on the Central Line.'

'That's very suspicious,' said Thrix. 'No genuine fashion blogger would live there. There are no decent shops for miles.' She hauled herself upright again. 'Are you coming with me?'

'I still advise caution,' said Dominil. 'She's been trying to lure you to her. Simply ignoring her would be safest.'

'But are you coming with me?'

'Yes. I get paid for killing werewolf hunters.'

'Really? Who by?'

'Markus.'

Thrix looked at her reflection in the wall mirror and shuddered. 'I'll just fix myself up first.' She hurried off to the bathroom to wash and attend to her hair.

Dominil herself had not had time to take care of her hair as she would have liked and was wearing a fine woollen hat, borrowed from Delicious. Along with her leather coat, it gave her something of the appearance of a commando. While waiting for Thrix, she took the empty bottles of wine to the kitchen. It was messy, and looked as if Thrix had attempted to prepare food, given up, and turned to alcohol instead.

Thrix arrived back having put her golden hair in order in a surprisingly short time. She wore a jacket which, while resembling something military, was obviously an expensive fashion item.

'It's the best I can do in terms of hunting apparel.'

'I've made you a flask of coffee for the journey,' said Dominil.

'I'm not that drunk.'

'Yes, you are.'

They set off in Dominil's car.

'Kabachetka's moon-eclipse spell was powerful, and unexpected.'

'It was.' Thrix frowned. 'I was completely debilitated.'

'We all were. Apart from Kalix. It's strange the way she remains unaffected by events that affect other werewolves. Something to do with her unusual birth at the full moon, perhaps.'

'And being crazy?'

507

'So the family would believe.'

'I hate Kalix.'

They drove on for a long way in silence.

'What outcome are you hoping for with Susi Surmata?' asked Dominil, as they reached the outskirts of London. 'Reluctant fashion blogger, or secret werewolf hunter?'

'Good question.' Thrix sipped from the flask. 'If she's really a fashion writer I might still be able to persuade her to write about me. It could save my career. On the other hand, I *would* like to kill someone.'

190

There was a startled buzz from the assembled students as Kalix and Vex hobbled into the exam room. Kalix was so disfigured with cuts, bruises and abrasions that she might have walked straight out of a car crash. Vex had signs of recent burns all over her neck, and parts of her hair had been singed off. Her leg was held rigidly by some sort of otherworldly-looking cast.

'Are you—?' began the tutor who was overseeing the exam.

'We're fine,' muttered Kalix. 'Bring on the exam.' Kalix helped Vex into her seat, then eased herself painfully into her own. Her ribs ached where Marwanis had kicked her.

'You could apply for an extension,' the tutor suggested.

'We're fine,' insisted Kalix. 'Let's just get this over with.'

The tutor looked at the pair very dubiously, perhaps wondering if they might expire while doing the exam, which could reflect badly on the college.

'Well, if you're sure . . .'

'I have new colour markers,' called Vex, and managed to grin, though weakly.

Papers were laid on every desk, face down, and the students logged on to their computers.

'Turn over your papers now, and begin the exam.'

Kalix turned over the paper. One good thing about the violence and fighting, she thought, picking up her pencil. It seems to have got rid of my anxiety.

Kalix could hardly feel any emotions at all. The events of the last few days had left her numb. However, that was an improvement on the way she'd felt last time in class, so she got down to work, just wanting the exam to be over so that she could fail and never have to come here again. Even the disgrace she'd feel in front of her clan didn't seem to matter much any more. Let them mock her. She didn't care, about them or anything else.

191

Princess Kabachetka was in a state of terror and despair as she made the long cold journey back to her own realm. Her plans had failed. Everything had gone wrong.

I'm finished, thought the Princess miserably. Curse that Minerva MacRinnalch. My mother will have learned of my failure to defeat Thrix and Malveria, and my attempt to usurp Esarax. She will now throw me in the volcano, unless Esarax beats her to it.

Shivering, she materialised in the corridor outside her private chambers to find herself confronted by a battalion of grim-faced palace dignitaries and hard-eyed soldiers. The Princess quailed, but gathered herself, intending to meet her end as bravely as she could. Councillor Tarentia, one of the Empress's senior advisers, stepped forward and spoke gravely.

'Princess Kabachetka. We have been awaiting your return.'

'I was led astray by others—' began the Princess.

'I have bad news about the Empress.'

'I demand a personal hearing! Close perusal of events will establish my innocence.'

'She is dead.'

The Princess blinked. 'Pardon?'

'Great Empress Asaratanti is dead.'

The Princess was bewildered. What was Councillor Tarentia talking about?

'The Empress is not dead. I saw her only this morning.'

'I am afraid that she expired during her afternoon sleep.'

'How?'

'From natural causes, Princess. The Empress was, of course, very old.'

The Princess considered this. It was true, of course. Though the Empress had concealed her age by means of cunning sorcery and some cosmetic surgical enhancement, she was almost 2,000 years old. That was a considerable age, even for the most powerful of the Hainusta. It just hadn't occurred to the Princess, or anyone else, that she might die today.

Princess Kabachetka had a brief second of joy, realising that her mother was not about to throw her in the Great Volcano, but her spirits sank as she surveyed the soldiers who cluttered up her corridor. Now that the Empress was gone, there was only one possible outcome. Esarax would be the new ruler. Undoubtedly he had already seized power and was now about to rid himself of his much-disliked sister.

What a dreadful mistake to choose this moment to try and strand him on Earth, thought the Princess. My plans have gone tragically wrong and now I must suffer for it.

'Where is Esarax?' she asked. 'I expected him to at least do the deed in person, not send his troops.'

'He is dead,' said Councillor Tarentia.

'What do you mean, he's dead? You said the Empress was dead.'

'The Prince has gone, too,' said Tarentia, in his gravest voice. 'He was apparently killed in the process of transporting himself through the dimensions. The Prince, I believe, was not skilled in this area. It's a dreadful blow for our nation. The population is in such a state of turmoil that we hardly know what to do. We have been awaiting your return most eagerly, Princess.'

The Princess looked at him suspiciously. 'Why?'

'To declare you Empress, of course. You are the natural heir.' Councillor Tarentia got down on one knee. From behind him another dignitary handed him a tiara, then knelt swiftly, along with everyone else in the corridor. Princess Kabachetka, dumbstruck, accepted the tiara, placing it lightly in her bright blonde hair.

'So I'm the new Empress?' she asked at last.

'Yes, Mighty Empress.'

'Are you absolutely sure?'

'Quite sure.'

Kabachetka looked around at the sea of kneeling bodies. She frowned. This was a lot to take in. Her expression brightened after a second or two. She was the new Empress after all, and she wasn't about to complain.

'There is much work to be done,' declared Empress Kabachetka. 'The nation must be revived and healed. I will need – eh – to be made harmonious with the Eternal Volcano.'

'It has already been done, Empress. You are now in full control of the power of the volcano.'

Empress Kabachetka smiled. After a poor start, the day had really turned out well.

192

The Enchantress and Dominil arrived in Epping. Susi Surmata lived in a house on the edge of the forest. A quiet location, the sort of place where hunters might gather. They slid out of the car quietly and confidently; a pair of hunting werewolves. The moon was up and each was prepared to transform in an instant.

'If there's trouble just kill,' said Dominil.

'Don't worry.'

They walked towards the front door of the picturesque though run-down detached house. The front garden was overgrown with moss and weeds and was surrounded by a hedge that hadn't been trimmed for a long time. Both Dominil and Thrix noted that, once in the garden, they couldn't be seen by anyone outside.

'OK, Miss "Slay the Wolf",' muttered Thrix, 'time to meet a real werewolf.'

She knocked on the door. Their keen senses immediately heard noises from inside. The lock turned, and by the time the door opened Thrix had transformed into her werewolf shape. She barged her way inside, followed by the werewolf Dominil.

Standing in front of them was a young woman with terror in her eyes, and an unusual blue jacket. She opened her mouth, perhaps to scream, but fainted instead. The werewolves paused, and sniffed the air.

'No one else at home,' Thrix said.

They looked down at the young woman.

'She doesn't look much like a hunter.'

'Maybe I should bite her anyway,' suggested Thrix, who was still unusually eager to engage in violence.

'Does she look like a fashion writer?'

'Possibly. That's quite a stylish jacket.'

'She's coming round.'

The young woman opened her eyes, looked up at them, but seemed unable to speak.

Thrix bent down, grasped her and hauled her upright quite roughly, slamming her against the wall, the violence of the movement sending the long blonde hair that hung from Thrix's arms and shoulders whipping around her frame. 'OK, Susi, or whatever your name really is. I know your secret. You're a werewolf hunter and you've been trying to trap me. Bad mistake.' Thrix opened her jaws.

'Oh, God!' cried Susi. 'I'm a werewolf too!'

Thrix paused. 'No, you're not.'

'I am.'

'You don't smell like any werewolf I've ever met.'

'I am! Really! I thought I was the only one! Don't kill me!'

Dominil put her snout close to the young woman. 'Could be a werewolf. Not Scottish, though.'

Thrix relaxed her grip, though she still held Susi fast. 'Explain yourself.'

'I'm a werewolf.'

'Yes, you said that already,' growled Thrix. 'But what's the idea of refusing to write about my clothes and then disappearing and not writing your blog any more?'

The young woman looked anguished, and also confused. 'Who are you?'

'Thrix MacRinnalch.'

The light of partial understanding dawned in Susi's eyes. 'Oh. I liked your clothes.'

'But you didn't write about them, did you? Do you know how embarrassing that was for me after I told the buyer at Eldridge's you were going to? It cost me the contract.'

'I'm sorry.'

'What's the idea of calling your website "Slay the Wolf"?' said Dominil. 'In Finnish?'

'Because I wanted to die,' wailed Susi and burst into tears. 'You don't know how I've suffered. I thought I was the only werewolf. It's been so terrible. I couldn't take it any longer.'

'That doesn't explain the Finnish language.'

'I come from Finland.'

'Oh.'

Thrix let go of Susi.

'How did you find me?'

'We tracked you over the internet. We're smart werewolves. Are you about to cry again?'

'Perhaps we should give her a moment to compose herself,' suggested Dominil. 'Discovering you're not the only werewolf in the world may perhaps be a shock.'

193

'It was just terrible on that volcano. There was fire everywhere and soldiers and I had to merge my own essence with lava and feed it to Xakthan and then there was more fire and everything and then I got my foot blown off.' Agrivex sighed, and peered at her foot. 'They stuck it back on. It hurts.'

Vex was lying on the couch. After returning from the exam her strength had given out completely. Kalix had helped her upstairs into the living room and onto the couch. Kalix herself lay on the floor in front of the fire, unable to move. Her hair splayed out around her in a huge semicircle. The cat was sleeping contentedly at her side.

'So what was it like in Scotland?' Vex asked.

'Fighting. Hunters. Killing. That sort of thing.' Kalix ached from her exertions. She'd filled herself up with laudanum but it hadn't taken away her pain. It seemed to her that she ached more than she should, even with the injuries she had, and had done since returning from Scotland. 'I hurt.'

'So do I.'

'At least we did the exam.'

'I thought I'd feel better afterwards.'

For some reason, neither of them felt much elation at finishing their college work.

'I expect I failed,' admitted Kalix.

'Me too.'

They lay in silence for a while.

'Do you think Moonglow will be very angry about the money?' asked Kalix.

'Yes.'

'We paid it back.'

'She'll still be angry.'

The downstairs door opened and closed, rather noisily. Two pairs of footsteps sounded on the stairs. Moonglow came in, followed by a sheepish-looking Daniel. She halted, glared at Kalix and Vex, then slammed her bag onto the table. Not satisfied with the noise, she took some papers from her pocket and slammed them on the table too.

'There you are! Do you know the trouble I've had because we didn't have money to pay these bills? I had an arrangement with my bank which would have started clearing all the debts. Except I was supposed to pay money into the bank. Which I couldn't. Because you took it.'

Kalix felt herself shrivelling up on the floor. She hadn't been looking forward to this, and had no idea how to defend herself.

'We paid it back,' volunteered Vex. 'Kalix put it in your room.'

'It's too late! My bank cancelled the payments and now all my debt schedules are messed up. We'll need to pay even more to get it straightened out! I've had to borrow money from my mum! Do you have any idea how humiliating that was? I've never been in debt before! You knew how important that money was! We spent enough time collecting it. And what happened? You just decided to steal it!' Moonglow stood with her hands on her hips, transferring her hostile glare from Kalix to Vex and back again.

'I had my foot blown off,' said Vex.

'You probably deserved it,' raged Moonglow, displaying a lack of sympathy that the young fire elemental found quite upsetting. 'And it doesn't excuse you stealing money!' She looked at Kalix. 'What's your excuse?'

514

'I needed to get to Scotland.'

'Really? More than we needed electricity? More than we didn't need bailiffs from the council coming round and taking away our stuff? Have you ever met bailiffs? They're not pleasant.'

'Well,' began Daniel, 'if we have the money back now, we can work out some new schedules for paying the debts and—'

'Don't you talk to me about new schedules!' roared Moonglow. 'You're just as bad as them. If you hadn't spent all your money on CDs and comics we wouldn't have got into such a mess in the first place.'

'That's harsh!'

'No, it isn't! Why am I the only one that can be sensible about money? Why are you three all so stupid and irresponsible that we get into this mess every time there's a bill? I'm not your mother, you know. You have absolutely no idea how to behave. Daniel, you think it's fine to spend everything on whatever you like and look what happens. You can't pay the bills. And you know what else? I'm *really* sick of your music. If I hear We Slaughtered Them and Laughed one more time I'm going to throw the CD out the window and then I'll wipe it off your computer too. As for you—' Moonglow whirled towards Vex. 'You're as bad. Worse, in fact. When you moved in here you were meant to be acting like a responsible person and you've just been a complete disaster from the first day. You buy clothes, make-up, boots, and you never save money even though I've told you time and again you need to. So we end up in a mess. And when I finally get it all sorted out, what happens? You help Kalix steal the money anyway. Probably because you were drunk at the time. You drink too much as well. I'm sick of you.'

Vex shrank back on the couch. 'My foot hurts,' she said, but Moonglow showed no signs of sympathy.

'As for you, Kalix,' Moonglow continued, 'I'm more than sick of you. I'm just completely fed up with your behaviour. You can't join in normal society. No matter how much we try to encourage you, you just spoil everything. You don't save money for bills, probably because you're spending it on alcohol and laudanum. You won't eat so you get ill, you cut yourself so you get even more ill. You're hostile, unfriendly, you won't let anyone help you and

515

you spend most of your time sulking in your room anyway. Have you any idea what a terrible flatmate you are? Why should I have to put up with that? We've helped you enough times; we've been understanding about everything and what happens? You end up stealing from us. I'm sick of you. I'm sick of you all.'

Moonglow paused for breath, with every sign of launching into a fresh tirade. But she was halted by the sudden arrival of the Fire Queen.

'Forgive me for interrupting,' said Malveria. 'I hovered nearby for a while, enjoying your verbal assault, which is no doubt entirely justified.'

'I think it was unsympathetic,' said Vex.

'Silence, dismal niece. Every word of Moonglow's was quite fair. It is a miracle she lasted so long before losing her temper with you. Moonglow, I do apologise for my niece's appalling spend-thrift ways and general idiocy. Agrivex, it's time to return to the palace. I must attend to your healing. You should not have left, though I accept that it was spirited to insist on sitting your exam.'

'Exam?' said Moonglow. 'You did your exam?'

Vex nodded.

'Did you do it too?'

'Yes,' muttered Kalix.

'Oh. I didn't realise that. I thought you'd missed it.'

'So does that make everything all right?' asked Kalix hopefully.

'No, it doesn't. It makes it a bit better.' Moonglow's anger faded slightly. She'd assumed that Kalix and Vex had missed their exam. She was slightly mollified, though not enough to forgive them for embarrassing her in front of her mother and her bank manager.

'I have just endured the most stressful meeting of my Advisory Council,' announced Malveria. 'For some reason, there is a terrifying backlog of official business. Would a cup of tea perhaps be possible?'

Moonglow nodded, and her natural good manners pushed her bad temper temporarily aside. She went off to the kitchen to put the kettle on.

'Moonglow's really mad at us,' sighed Vex.

'No wonder,' said her aunt. 'You humiliated her in front of her

516

mother. No one likes that. And her bank manager also. I am not sure what that entails, but I know Thrix hates it too.' Malveria studied Kalix for a moment. 'Your aura is unusual. But it always has been. Not quite the same as other werewolves.'

Kalix didn't reply. She knew she wasn't quite the same as other werewolves.

'The eclipse spell didn't affect your power to transform. Truly, you are very resistant to sorcery. I expect you ache now, most painfully?'

Kalix nodded.

'The effects of running around fighting while all other werewolves were suffering, I imagine. Though you resisted the spell, it still had its effects on you. You will hurt for some days to come, I'm sure.' The Queen turned to Daniel. 'The curse on yourself and Moonglow is lifted. Through Agrivex's intervention it's now removed. So that is some good cheer for your household. Although—' She paused, and gazed out the window at the terraced houses opposite. 'It is one thing to pine in a romantic fashion for someone you are not allowed to have. It's quite another when there is no barrier preventing the union. The prospect of romance, once unhindered, may not be quite as pleasant as you imagined.'

'Thanks for that,' said Daniel, not looking as happy as might have been expected.

194

Susi Surmata's rustic little home was packed with clothes. Frocks, hats, shoes, and coats hung from the walls and over every available chair and table. The Enchantress was briefly diverted from her mission.

'This is a fantastic collection.'

'I've been collecting since I was a child,' sniffed Susi. 'These days I get free samples as well.'

'Of course,' said Thrix. 'Since you've transformed yourself into the nation's most influential fashion blogger, you must get a lot of free clothes.'

Susi burst into tears again.

'I'd have thought that was a good thing.' Thrix looked at Dominil. 'Isn't that a good thing?'

'I believe she's still crying about being a werewolf.'

'Yes, I suppose you're right. Do you think that's what made her blogs so effective? A love of clothes mixed in with angst about being a werewolf?'

'I thought I was alone . . . Oh, my life has been so terrible. My adopted parents kept it all secret when I grew up in Finland – I was an orphan and they took me in when I was a baby. Since they died I've hardly been able to stand it—'

Dominil felt herself losing patience. Tears annoyed her, and she found it offensive that anyone should be so upset about being a werewolf. 'The MacRinnalchs like being werewolves,' she told Susi.

'Really?'

'Of course. We're very civilised.'

'What do you do?'

'I kill people for money.'

Susi burst into tears again.

'Dominil! Try and be tactful. It must have come as a great shock to her, learning that there are other werewolves. Susi, I suggest the best thing for you is to get straight back to work. A well-written review of my latest fashion collection would probably do wonders for your self-confidence.'

Susi didn't seem to hear the Enchantress.

'Eventually I couldn't stand it any more. I hid my loneliness with my love of clothes—'

'I can understand that,' said Thrix.

'—But all those night-time fashion shows became too much for me. I was always frightened I was going to lose control, change into a werewolf and eat someone.'

'We don't eat people.'

'Kalix might,' said Thrix, darkly. 'But really, Susi, there's no need to despair. There are plenty of werewolves at the castle in Scotland. Once you meet them you'll feel better. After you've written your article you can go straight there.'

'It means so much to me to know there are other werewolves around. I thought I was a freak!' wailed Susi.

Thrix pursed her lips. 'I really could do with that article being written.'

'I don't want to write any more! I want to go to Scotland and meet my fellow werewolves!'

Thrix moved a little closer to Susi. 'Write the article,' she said, 'or you won't make it out of this room, never mind go to Scotland.'

'You told me werewolves were civilised creatures,' protested Susi. 'Now you're threatening me!'

'We *did* go to all the trouble of finding you,' said Dominil. 'So why don't you just get it done, and then we'll send you off to Scotland.'

'Is the article really that important?'

'If Eldridge's don't buy my stock I'm going to go out of business.'

Susi dried her eyes and looked thoughtful. 'I did like your clothes. I suppose I could write it. Eldridge's usually do what I tell them. I don't think much of their chief buyer, really.'

'She's an idiot,' agreed Thrix, 'but she generally follows your advice.'

Dominil and Thrix retired to the kitchen to give Susi a moment to compose herself. Thrix looked with interest at the vintage clothes stacked on top of the washing machine.

'I hope she toughens up in Scotland,' said Dominil. 'No one likes a werewolf who sobs all the time.'

195

Kalix sat with Decembrius in his car, not far from her home. It was late into the night. The pavements were deserted, and the nearest street lamp wasn't working, casting Decembrius's car into a deep shadow.

'So where were we?' asked Decembrius.

'We weren't anywhere.'

'I'm sure we were somewhere. That's right. We slept together, then you robbed me.'

'I paid you back.'

Decembrius didn't care at all that Kalix had taken his money, and had been surprised when she'd repaid him.

'It was a good night together, anyway.'

'If you say so,' grunted Kalix.

Decembrius grinned. 'I didn't think it was so bad.'

'I did.'

'Didn't sound like it at the time. I think you enjoyed it well enough.'

Kalix made a face. Decembrius never seemed abashed in any way. His confidence was intriguing, even if she still didn't like him much.

Decembrius fiddled with the radio, trying to find music he liked.

'I'm not sleeping with you again,' said Kalix.

'OK. It wasn't that great, anyway.'

Kalix was offended. 'What do you mean, it wasn't that great?'

'Have you seen yourself recently? There's hardly enough to get hold of.'

'Good. I wouldn't want you to get hold of me. You know how much I don't like your stupid red hair? It looks ridiculous.'

'It looks fine. At least it sees a brush every now and then. Unlike yours.'

'There's nothing wrong with my hair,' said Kalix.

'Nothing that shampoo wouldn't fix.'

'I hate you.'

'What are you doing in my car if you hate me?'

'Hiding from Moonglow. She keeps lecturing me.'

'I expect you deserve it,' said Decembrius, and laughed.

'You're stupid.'

'You're stupid too.'

They lapsed into silence.

'So. You want to come back to my place?'

'No,' said Kalix, though she didn't get out of the car.

196

'What are these unpleasant black garments?'

'Your mourning clothes, Empress Kabachetka. For the deaths of your mother and brother.'

'Ah! Of course, my mourning clothes. Yes, there is certainly much mourning to be done. No one is sadder than I about their untimely deaths. One is utterly grief-stricken.'

The new Empress attempted to look sad while examining the clothes. Her expression swiftly changed to one of strong distaste. She was sure these garments would not be flattering.

'How long is this mourning for?'

'Three months, Your Majesty.'

'That seems a very long time. Life continues, you know. One must struggle on.'

'Three months is traditional.'

'Very well. But remind me to send to my designer for some better mourning clothes. I can't disappoint the population by starting my reign in these inferior outfits.'

Empress Kabachetka was cheered by the thought of the stylish black frocks she could buy. And a new hat, of course, she thought, with a demi veil. It would be a very chic affair. After all, she reasoned, now she had control of the treasury there was no one to stop her spending whatever she wanted. Not only that, she had full control of the Eternal Volcano, the greatest power in the land, and she was already a skilful user of sorcery. With the volcano's power at her command an Empress could do a lot.

'Send for my hairstylist. We will need a lighter shade of blonde to offset all this dark clothing.'

197

'Thanks for getting the curse lifted,' said Daniel. 'It was nice of you.'

'Don't mention it,' grinned Vex. Her foot was feeling better and she was returning to normal. 'Now you're free to scoop up Moonglow.'

Daniel looked pensive. 'I thought I'd start off slowly.'

'Probably a good idea. Because you've been acting pretty weird towards her, really, what with being nice, then being horrible, and trying to make her jealous, and shouting at her and everything.'

'Thanks.'

'And starting all these arguments, and generally acting like you were an idiot.'

'I get the picture. Did I really act that badly?'

'Totally. All these arguments, and you storming out the room and stuff. Moonglow probably hates you.'

Daniel looked forlorn. 'Life is useless,' he muttered.

'I wouldn't say that. Moonglow's quite forgiving. Yes, she did say only last week that she wouldn't go out with you in any circumstances whatsoever. That doesn't mean the situation is hopeless.'

'It doesn't?'

'No.'

'Well, what can I do to make things better?'

'I've no idea,' admitted Vex. 'It's beyond me. You really messed things up. But something might turn up. Do you want to watch *Tokyo Top Pop Boom Boom Girl*?'

But Daniel was by this time on his way to his room to play music, and lie on his bed staring at the ceiling, somehow not at all encouraged by Vex's youthful optimism.

198

'My dear friend the Enchantress is most grateful for your help with the fashion writer. Instead of closing her business she is hiring new staff, ready to deliver orders of great magnitude to the nation's high streets.'

The Fire Queen noted that Dominil showed no ill effects from her recent experiences. Her hair was again in beautiful condition and her skin was clear. 'You are looking well, Dominil. Might you be a werewolf in love?'

'No.'

Malveria sighed, though she hadn't really expected any other answer. 'The MacRinnalchs do seem notably bad at romance. One wonders how any new werewolves ever appear. Still, I did not come here to talk about that. I came to talk about Agrivex.' She paused, and lowered her voice. 'It pains me to admit it, but I owe Agrivex a favour for her bravery in my defence.'

'And?'

'There is very little chance she will actually have passed the exam—'

'Are you asking me to cheat for her?'

Malveria was startled by Dominil's perception. 'How quickly you grasp the important heart of the matter. The Enchantress refuses to assist me, citing pressure of work. In reality, she is unwilling to engage in anything that might involve helping Kalix. So I now apply to you. Help me change Agrivex's score so she may pass the exam.'

'No.'

'Why not?'

'It's unethical. I'm not falsifying exam results.'

'Show some sympathy, Dominil. If not for Agrivex's sake, then for mine. If she fails her exam I will be obliged to recall the wretched girl and she will once more infest the palace.'

'Isn't she your heir now? Shouldn't she be at the palace?'

'Agrivex's presence can only hinder the process of making the population accept her as a member of the Royal Family. Were she to blunder around the palace in her preposterous clothes and terrible hair, the citizens will remember what a fool she is, and rebel in protest. Really, Dominil, it would be of immense help to me if you would do this.'

'I don't want to do it. It's unethical.'

Malveria nodded. She opened her Abukenti bag and took out a large purse, from which she withdrew a bundle of banknotes.

Dominil looked at the money. 'It's more unethical than that.'

Malveria drew out another bundle of notes.

'I may be able to help,' said the white-haired werewolf.

The Fire Queen travelled through space, taking Dominil with her. To anyone not used to the journey, the void was a cold, troubling place with a freezing wind that plucked at the soul. As they emerged, Malveria looked at Dominil for any sign of a reaction. Dominil didn't appear to be affected in any way. The Queen felt disappointed.

'The offices of the college examining board.'

Dominil nodded, and sat in front of a computer. 'You want me to give Agrivex a pass mark. What about Kalix? If she's failed, do you want me to improve her score?'

'I don't know. Perhaps the choice should be yours? As a were-wolf, you may empathise more with her?'

'I'm all out of empathy,' muttered Dominil. She called up the relevant files. Malveria looked over her shoulder, though she had difficulty making sense of anything on a computer screen unless it concerned fashion. 'Kalix passed her exam. Fifty-eight per cent.'

'Is that good?' Malveria found percentages hard to under-stand.

'Not great. But she passed.'

'What about my niece?'

Dominil tapped the keyboard. 'She didn't make it. Forty-two per cent. That's forty-two points out of a hundred.'

'Oh well, that's not as bad as I feared. Perhaps not so bad at all, given the trauma she suffered on the volcano. Can you fix matters?'

Dominil nodded, and added ten points to Vex's score. 'She'll pass, with fifty-two per cent.'

'Excellent,' said the Fire Queen. 'I quite dreaded having her at the palace all the time. The days she spends on Earth are a relief for everyone.' Malveria caught sight of her reflection in a mirror, and paused. 'My lips are simply not satisfactory. Dominil, is there really no chance of you forming a happy relationship in the next few days?'

'No.'

'Could you not give the guitarist another chance?'

'If he's lucky I'll let him live.'

Malveria sighed, but brightened as she examined her shoes. 'How splendid my new Abukenti shoes are. Do you like them?'

'No.'

The Queen shook her head. 'I do not think we shall ever be great friends, Dominil. But thank you for helping Agrivex.'

199

Markus woke up early, with Beatrice on one side of him and Heather on the other. All things considered, life hadn't gone too badly in the past few weeks. The fundraising event had been a great success, despite the difficulties surrounding it, and his romantic entanglements had resolved themselves quite satisfactorily. Markus planned to relax and enjoy himself for a few days. In his opinion, he deserved a holiday. He was lucky to be alive. If the moon-eclipse spell hadn't ended when it did, the hunters would have killed him. It had been spirited to throw himself at them, even though his werewolf powers were missing. Beatrice and Heather had certainly appreciated the rescue.

Markus's intention of spending the day in his chambers was spoiled by a summons from the Mistress of the Werewolves. She was already worrying about the next council meeting.

'What exactly are we going to tell the Barons?'

Markus shrugged. 'Do we have to tell them anything?'

'Of course. Marwanis will already have informed anyone who'll listen that Kalix was here and we let her go. I don't see any way of smoothing that over. They'll be furious. Particularly MacPhee. He's never got over the death of the late Thane. As for Great Mother Dulupina, she's already furious. I've been avoiding her for the past two days.'

Markus couldn't suggest anything that might pacify the Barons. 'But we can probably outvote them when the time comes. It's going to be a stormy meeting, even so.'

Verasa shook her head. 'The clan needs some peace. Trust Kalix to put in an appearance and spoil everything. My family. What's the matter with them?' She looked at her favourite son. 'I still want you all to get along better. Did you talk to Thrix?'

'I tried. I don't think we'll ever be friends.'

Verasa looked south over the rolling green fields that led away from the castle. 'Maybe we're not destined for peace just yet, anyway. I think I've been mistaken about the Avenaris Guild.'

'In what way?'

'I thought we could keep them at arm's length. I thought we were safe here in Scotland. Apparently I was wrong.'

Verasa wasn't the only werewolf who'd been shaken by the appearance of hunters at the charity event. In the lands of the MacRinnalchs there was widespread alarm that the Guild had come so far north to attack them.

'Perhaps we need to change our policy,' said Verasa. 'Perhaps we should take the fight to them.'

Markus nodded. In this, he was in full agreement with his mother.

200

Kalix sat in the sunshine on a small patch of grass. It was the first warm day of spring. On one side of her was Tower Hill Tube station, on the other, a remnant of the ancient Roman wall, built to protect London almost two thousand years ago.

The young werewolf had arrived early. She took a comic from her bag, still in its plastic cover and protected by a sheet of cardboard.

'Last issue of *Curse of the Wolf Girl*,' she murmured.

Kalix was pleased to have completed her collection, but she wasn't expecting this comic to be any better than the others. It would be just as annoying. It wouldn't even reach any conclusion. There wouldn't be a neat ending. Although issue number 12 was the last episode published, *Curse of the Wolf Girl* hadn't been conceived as a twelve-part series. It had been meant to be an ongoing publication but had been cancelled after the twelfth episode because of poor sales. As in life, there would be loose ends.

As the sun picked out the bright, bold colours on the cover, Kalix felt a little less hostile towards the comics. The story might be ridiculous but at least, thanks to *Curse of the Wolf Girl*, she'd made a good presentation at college. She'd stood up and talked to the whole class, something she wouldn't have thought she could ever have done. If that had not gone so well she probably wouldn't have sat her exam. Kalix was surprised to have passed her exam, and pleased. She was much more pleased than she admitted to anyone.

Kalix sat and read in the sun. Her reading came a little easier now, though not much. Halfway through, she found herself struggling with some words and took a break. She looked round at the Roman wall. Dominil had asked her to meet here. Whether because Dominil now lived nearby, or just because she liked the ancient wall, Kalix didn't know.

Kalix had thought a lot about Dominil in the past few days. She'd decided, on reflection, that it probably wasn't fair to blame her for killing Gawain. She realised she was in no position to criticise a fellow werewolf for being too violent. Kalix had certainly done worse. If Dominil's story of Gawain attacking her were true, Dominil had a right to defend herself.

Kalix pursed her lips. If Dominil's story were true. With Dominil, it was impossible not to suspect that she might just have become bored talking. But Kalix thought she probably believed her story. Gawain had been alienated from the clan, and had had cause for resentment. Kalix's last words to Gawain, spoken after learning of his betrayal of her with Thrix, had been 'I'll kill you.' Then he'd disappeared. He couldn't have felt very warmly towards the MacRinnalchs after his banishment from the clan and his rejection by Kalix. Perhaps it had all become too much.

Kalix felt ashamed. She couldn't really blame Dominil for becoming involved in a violent werewolf confrontation. Kalix had done enough of that herself. She'd killed the Thane, and Sarapen.

Unexpectedly, Dominil had phoned to say she had money for Kalix. Money for killing hunters, from Markus. That was the reason they were meeting. Kalix badly needed money. At home, Moonglow was still struggling to ward off the chaos caused by the non-payment of bills.

The young werewolf reapplied herself to the comic. The ending wasn't too unsatisfactory, all things considered. There were numerous loose ends left hanging, but at the end of the comic Arabella Wolf said goodbye to New York and went off to Los Angeles, seeking a new life.

Kalix nodded. It's probably best for you to start a new life, she thought. I did that too, moving to London. Sometimes you need to make a new start.

She put the comic carefully back in its wrapping. She looked up. Dominil would be here soon. On the phone Dominil had sounded quite normal. Apparently she'd already forgotten about Kalix trying to attack her.

She probably didn't even care, thought Kalix.

Kalix wondered about the morality of accepting money for killing. She didn't feel entirely comfortable about it. Kalix knew there was too much violence in her life. She knew she couldn't control herself when she became violent. For the first time, she wondered if she should make more of an effort.

Kalix glanced again at the ancient Roman wall. She liked it. There was something comforting about such an old structure.

'But I don't want to take the money,' she said, out loud, to no one.

Kalix got up and walked off. She decided she didn't want to be paid for killing. She'd get money some other way.

201

Empress Kabachetka entered her private underground cavern. They had served her well, but she'd be leaving them soon. As Empress of the Hainusta, she had access to much nicer underground cavern. However, there was something she needed to do here first. She walked through the dim caves to the place at the end where space and time ran oddly together, the place where Sarapen was still suspended between life and death, still pierced by the wound that would kill him if he woke.

'Or would have killed him if he woke,' she muttered, 'were I not now able to command the full power of the Eternal Volcano, and the secret spells of my late mother, may she walk contentedly wherever she now happens to be walking.'

She gazed down at Sarapen's face, which, while in repose, had never looked entirely peaceful.

'Time to get up,' she said, and laid a very powerful hand on his shoulder.

202

Three months after she'd made the bet with the Fairy Queen, Malveria made her way unwillingly to Colburn Woods. She was loath to give up her precious necklace, but a wager with the Fairy Queen couldn't be reneged on. Doing so would undoubtedly have terrible consequences.

'Recent experience, Queen Dithean, may tend towards

supporting your view that the MacRinnalch women are too self-obsessed to form lasting relationships. But is this really fair? They do suffer peculiar circumstances, living as werewolves in the world of humans.'

'True,' admitted Queen Dithean. 'And we could make allowances. Even a moderately happy love affair might win you the bet. How did Thrix's relationship with Easterly end?'

'He's dead. But that's hardly a fair test. He was a werewolf hunter, after all.' Malveria pursed her lips. 'It wasn't the most successful introduction I've ever made.'

'Who else did you have hope for? Dominil, I believe? What happened to the man who pursued her?'

'Also dead.'

'Oh dear.'

'Though there was another suitor for Dominil,' said Malveria.

'Any hope of success?'

'He may escape with his life, if he's fortunate.' Malveria put her hand to her necklace. 'Of course, there is young Kalix. Should we entirely give up hope regarding her? She's been in the company of Decembrius, an . . . eh . . . entertaining rogue, who may just be the werewolf for her.'

Queen Dithean raised one hand. 'Let's see how they're getting on, shall we?' She opened up a small portal in space, managing somehow to produce a picture of Kalix and Decembrius. They were sitting in Decembrius's car, arguing. As Malveria watched, Kalix violently punched Decembrius on the shoulder, and they started shoving each other.

'Forget Kalix,' said Malveria.

'Marwanis?'

'Threatening to kill the rest of the clan. No lover in prospect.' Queen Malveria sighed. 'Stupid werewolves.' Sadly, she unclasped the necklace and handed it over.

Queen Dithean Wallace Cloud-of-Heather NicRinnalch smiled graciously, adjusted the necklace's size with a twitch of her fingers, and placed it round her neck. A warm glow lit up her features. 'Thank you, Malveria. It's a beautiful necklace.'

'I hope you get several thousand years' pleasure from it,' said Malveria, wistfully. 'As my family had before I gambled it away.'

*

529

Later, the Fire Queen paid a visit to the Enchantress, her first for some time.

'I regretted missing last week's Japanese fashion show. Affairs of state detained me.'

Thrix welcomed her in, pleased to see Malveria apparently back to normal.

The Queen slipped off her shoes, settled down on the couch, and held out her hand gratefully for the proffered glass of wine. 'You're dressmaking? At home? I haven't seen you do that for a while.'

Though Thrix was an expert seamstress, she did little actual dressmaking these days. Thrix delegated the making to others.

'I do love to see a dress being made.' The Queen strolled through to the next room, where the dress, almost finished, was draped over a mannequin. 'What a lovely item! Formal in its way, but playful too. I love the collar.' She looked at her friend with an arch expression. 'Who is this for? Are you hiding an important client from me?'

'It's nothing,' said Thrix.

'Nothing? Such a beautiful dress? Tell me who it's for. Is it for me?'

'I'm afraid not. It's a sort of private commission. No one you know.'

Malveria pouted, not liking Thrix to keep anything secret. 'I can't help noticing, dearest Enchantress, that you are taking great care to disguise your aura. What is it you don't wish me to know?'

'Do I have to be investigated every time you call round?'

'How very unfair! Malveria has the greatest regard for her friend's privacy. I will say no more about the matter.' She sipped her wine. 'So who is the dress for?'

'Malveria!'

'Why is it such a great secret? Here you are, carefully constructing a beautiful dress in your own apartment, not even trusting the esteemed dressmakers you employ. Obviously it must be for someone of great importance.' Malveria looked worried. 'Not the Ice Queen's daughter, I hope? Her hips will never fit into this garment.'

'No, not the Ice Queen's daughter. The Japanese fashion programme is about to start.'

Malveria seemed to have lost interest in the programme. She circled the almost-finished dress, examining it in detail.

'Made for rather a tall woman. Unusually broad shoulders . . . small hips . . . but something is wrong. Has the client no bust at all?' The Queen's face suddenly lit up. 'This dress is for a man! I'm right! I can see it in your aura.'

'Didn't we have an agreement that you wouldn't interpret my aura when I didn't want you to?'

'I believe the agreement had a clause excluding all mysterious dresses.'

'No, it didn't.'

'Who is the man? Someone at your fashion house?'

'I'm not telling you.'

'Fine,' sniffed the Queen. 'Keep your secrets. I am not concerned. I shall take my wine and watch the Japanese fashion programme in perfect tranquillity.'

They returned to the previous room and sat down on Thrix's huge couch.

'Tell me who the dress is for,' Malveria said after a few minutes.

'No.'

'One might say you owe me a favour. I lost my necklace because of you.'

'Don't blame me if the Fairy Queen outsmarted you.'

'I might have succeeded if the MacRinnalch women hadn't all decided to slaughter their boyfriends. You really must stop doing that. It's so off-putting for potential suitors.'

'Malveria, my boyfriend was a werewolf hunter.'

'But did you really try to work things out? You still might have had a future.'

Thrix sighed. 'When Kalix gets involved in your relationships, there is no future.'

Malveria wisely decided to drop the subject, and they watched as a young Japanese model strode along a catwalk in a short silk wrap, which Malveria rather liked.

'Has the transaction with Eldridge's been completed?' she asked.

'My clothes are on the way to their stores at this moment. I'm solvent again, thanks to Susi's review.'

'Ah. The writer who turned out to be a werewolf. That was fortunate.'

The review of Thrix's latest collection on the newly updated I Miss Susi blog was as glowing a piece of journalism as had ever appeared on the website. As well as the order from Eldridge's, other fashion buyers had been in contact, expressing strong interest. Various members of the fashion industry had since called Thrix to congratulate her.

'Hypocrites,' muttered Thrix. 'They're eaten up with jealousy.'

'Does that annoy you, Enchantress?'

'Not at all. I love it. And I'm guaranteed a few more good write-ups before she gives up the business to roam around the castle.'

'Perhaps she may encounter Markus there. I hope he likes the dress you're making for him.'

'What? How did you guess that?'

Malveria smiled. 'One does not become Queen of the Hiyasta without a certain level of intelligence. A survey of all the men you know reveals only one who might conceivably wear it. I take it the matter is secret?'

'It's very secret. Even Mother doesn't know and she knows everything.'

'Has he often worn dresses?'

'Yes. It's his thing, you might say. And it's private.'

'I am the soul of discretion. Really, it should not be such a surprise. He *is* a rather pretty man. But I have seen him with women, no?'

'Markus has never had any problems finding girlfriends. You'd be surprised how many women are attracted to a good-looking werewolf in a dress.'

The Queen nodded. She could imagine it, just about. 'Are you making him matching accessories? A hat? A nice handbag?'

'Malveria, please drop the subject. I don't even know if the dress is a good idea. I wouldn't be surprised if he just wraps it round my throat. But he might like it. I don't think he's ever had anything specially made for him before.'

Thrix studied the pictures she had as reference material – several pages from magazine articles featuring male models in female attire, and an original copy of David Bowie's *The Man Who Sold the World*, showing the singer in a dress.

'I'm certain he will like it,' said Malveria. 'Do you think you could make me something similar?'

'I will.'

'But with ample room in the chest, of course. The Fire Queen has always been famously well endowed.'

'Of course.'

Malveria and Thrix sat next to each other on the couch, drinking wine and watching the Japanese fashion show.

Thrix really didn't know if Markus would accept the dress as a peace offering, but she hoped he would. Their mother was right. It was time that they stopped arguing. Her mother might be right about the Guild, too. Perhaps it was time to take the fight to them.

203

'This sucks so badly,' said Vex, struggling through from the storeroom with a large box of tinned tomatoes. 'I hate stacking shelves.'

'Is our shift nearly finished?' asked Kalix, wearily dragging a huge cage of assorted cereals on a trolley that rattled on worn-out metal wheels.

'Another three hours,' said Daniel, grimly, trying to balance two boxes of tinned pears.

'Stacking shelves is the worst thing ever,' said Vex.

Moonglow appeared. In contrast to Kalix, Vex and Daniel, all dressed in blue overalls, she looked rather crisp in a clean white coat. Her hair was tied back quite severely, lending her an efficient appearance.

'Everything on the checklist complete?' she asked, brandishing her clipboard.

Daniel glared at her. 'Not yet. We've still half a truck to unload before we finish the shelves.'

Moonglow tut-tutted. 'You're a little behind schedule. Try and pick up the pace.'

Moonglow walked out. The three looked at each other in disgust.

'How come she gets the cushy job with the clipboard while we have to stack shelves?'

'She is the smartest,' sighed Daniel. 'It's the way of the world.'

'It's really unfair,' said Vex.

'I hate stacking shelves,' said Kalix wearily.

'Then next time don't steal all the money for paying the bills.'

'I wish I'd never learned how to write,' moaned the young werewolf. 'Then I wouldn't have been able to fill in the application form for this place.'

The three flatmates carried on unloading the truck and transferring the seemingly endless flow of goods into the storerooms, and from there onto the shelves of the supermarket.

'How are things with Decembrius?' asked Daniel.

'Terrible. I slept with him one time and now everything is awkward and difficult. We keep fighting.'

'Welcome to the world of normal relationships.'

From Kalix's expression, it was obvious she didn't like the world of normal relationships very much. They seemed to be a lot more complicated than her previous youthful passion.

'Are you going to ask Moonglow out, now the curse has been lifted?' Vex asked Daniel.

Daniel shook his head. 'She says senior staff can't go out with juniors. It's against company policy.'

'Maybe when we've stopped working here you can try again.'

'Maybe. At least she's stopped shouting at us, now we're earning money.'

Vex struggled to lift an enormous crate of tinned soup. Kalix helped her, and together they loaded it into a giant metal cage on wheels, ready to take it into the supermarket and fill the shelves.

Vex sighed. 'I thought if you passed an exam you got a better job?'

'Not your first one. You have to pass more exams than that.'

'Oh. Well, I suppose we'll have to do more. Hey, Kalix, do you want to be cheerleaders at college next year? I can really see us in some nice little outfits.'